THE ROAR OF THE CRITICS FOR
THE LION'S GAME

"AN INCREDIBLY FAST-PACED THRILLER...A testament to not only DeMille's great storytelling skills but also to his superb attention to detail."
—*Philadelphia Inquirer*

"THOROUGHLY ENJOYABLE...a first-person protagonist whose laugh-out-loud witticisms blend handily with the violence at hand... Corey as a character is simply irresistible."
—*Dallas Morning News*

"ON TOP OF HIS GAME...Nelson DeMille, as always, entertains in *THE LION'S GAME*...A compelling contest of a cop vs. master terrorist...His opening gambit is a gotcha."
—*New York Daily News*

"PAIRS TERRIFIC SUSPENSE WITH NONSTOP WISE-CRACKING...DeMille sweeps you along with his masterful cross-cutting between the good guys and the bad, slaying both the extremist Middle Eastern mind-set and our own lowbrow American culture."
—*Entertainment Weekly*

"HIS BEST THRILLER YET...THE ACTION UNFOLDS AT AN ADRENALINE-DRAINING PACE...[the] true master of testosterone thrillers."
—*New York Post*

"COREY'S BACK. THIS TIME, HE'S EVEN BETTER THAN EVER...DeMille maintains the suspense."
—*St. Louis Post-Dispatch*

"BREEZILY NARRATED, HIGH-OCTANE...A COMPUL-SIVELY READABLE THRILLER."
—*Publishers Weekly* (starred review)

"A THRILLER FROM A STORYTELLER AT THE TOP OF HIS GAME."
—*Sunday Oklahoman*

NOVELS BY NELSON DeMILLE

Available from Grand Central Publishing

By the Rivers of Babylon

Cathedral

The Talbot Odyssey

Word of Honor

The Charm School

The Gold Coast

The General's Daughter

Spencerville

Plum Island

The Lion's Game

Up Country

Night Fall

Wild Fire

The Gate House

The Lion

The Panther

The Quest

WITH THOMAS BLOCK

Mayday

Nelson DeMille

The Lion's Game

GRAND CENTRAL
PUBLISHING

NEW YORK   BOSTON

Copyright © 2000 by Nelson DeMille
Introduction copyright © 2010 by Nelson DeMille
Preview of *Radiant Angel* copyright © 2015 by Nelson DeMille

Grand Central Publishing
Hachette Book Group
1290 Avenue of the Americas
New York, NY 10104

www.HachetteBookGroup.com

Printed in the United States of America

LSC-C

Originally published in hardcover by Grand Central Publishing.

First trade edition: January 2002
Reissued: May 2010; February 2015

10 9 8 7 6 5 4 3 2

Grand Central Publishing is a division of Hachette Book Group, Inc.

The Grand Central Publishing name and logo is a trademark of Hachette Book Group, Inc.

The Hachette Speakers Bureau provides a wide range of authors for speaking events. To find out more, go to www.hachettespeakersbureau.com or call (866) 376-6591.

The publisher is not responsible for websites (or their content) that are not owned by the publisher.

The Library of Congress has cataloged the hardcover edition as follows:

DeMille, Nelson.
    The lion's game / Nelson DeMille.
      p. cm.
    ISBN 978-0-446-52065-2
    I. Libya—History—Bombardment, 1986—Fiction. 2. Terrorism—
Prevention—Fiction 3. Serial murders—Fiction. I. Title.
    PS3554.E472 L56 2000
    813'.54—dc21
                                                          99-052476

ISBN 978-1-4555-8182-5 (reissue pbk.)

In loving memory of Mom—
A member of the Greatest Generation

Author's Note

The fictional Anti-Terrorist Task Force (ATTF) represented in this novel is based on the actual Joint Terrorist Task Force (JTTF), though I have taken some dramatic liberties and literary license where necessary.

The Joint Terrorist Task Force is a group of hard-working, dedicated, and knowledgeable men and women who are in the front line in the war against terrorism in America.

The characters in this story are entirely fictitious, though some of the workings of the law enforcement agencies portrayed are based on fact, as is the American air raid on Libya in 1986.

Introduction

It's often easier to write an introduction to a book that's been around a while; the introduction becomes, in a sense, more of a thoughtful retrospective on the book, written with the advantages of hindsight and history.

The Lion's Game was written in 1999 and published in January 2000. I make this point because of the events of September 11, 2001. Many readers of this book believe that there are references in *The Lion's Game* that predict that horrific day, and many people have called *The Lion's Game* prescient and even prophetic. And while this is flattering to any writer, I don't claim to be a bestselling Nostradamus. Bestselling, yes, Nostradamus, no.

How then did I apparently predict some of the events of September 11, 2001, without a crystal ball? The answer is simple: The handwriting was on the wall for all to see. The facts of the first attack on the North Tower of the World Trade Center, which occurred on February 26, 1993, were obviously well known when I wrote *The Lion's Game*, and are even mentioned in the book. That attack by Islamic extremists, using a truck bomb parked in the underground parking garage of the North Tower, should have been a wake-up call to America. But we, the American public and the media, did not see this attack as a warning of what was to come.

The men and women who work in the field of anti-terrorism, however, *did* understand the implications of what happened. When I began researching *The Lion's Game*, I was fortunate to have an entrée into the workings of the Joint Terrorism Task Force in New York City, which is made up mostly of FBI agents and NYPD detectives, as well as retired detectives, such as my character of John Corey. You'll meet some of these men and women in this work of fiction, though names, titles, and procedures have been changed for obvious reasons of confidentiality and national security.

But back to 9/11. While conducting interviews with JTTF personnel for *The Lion's Game*, I kept hearing about "the next attack," and here is what I heard almost two years *before* the actual events of September 11, 2001: The World Trade Center would again be targeted, and the attack would be carried out by suicide pilots, flying small private jets loaded with fuel and explosives, which would be flown into the North and South Towers of the Trade Center.

This was eerily close to what actually happened, so when the events of the morning of September 11, 2001, unfolded, I was not taken completely unaware. And neither were the people who had spent years investigating terrorist threats to this country.

By the evening of 9/11, I'd gotten dozens of phone calls and e-mails, many from the media, asking me how I "knew" this was going to happen. Well, I didn't know, but things that I learned while researching *The Lion's Game* had obviously worked their way into my mind and into this story.

If *The Lion's Game* is at all prescient, it is so because of the job I gave to my main character, John Corey.

We first met John Corey in *Plum Island*, where the book opens on the North Fork of Long Island and Corey is recuperating from bullet wounds, which will ultimately force him into early retirement from his job as an NYPD homicide detective.

Plum Island was meant to be a stand-alone book—not the beginning of a series—but reader reaction to John Corey was so positive that I decided to bring him back, which I did here in *The Lion's Game*. The problem I'd created, however, was that at the end of *Plum Island*, Corey is no longer with the NYPD.

My first thought was to somehow get him back on the job as a homicide detective and use that as the basis for a series. But a chance encounter with a guy I knew who was a former NYPD detective gave me another idea—something more original. This man had taken a job as a contract agent with the Federal Joint Terrorism Task Force and had begun a new career in counter-terrorism—and that sounded like a good way to bring John Corey back.

At first, however, I wasn't sure about having my former NYPD character working with the Feds in a job that he had no experience in nor apparent aptitude for. But as it turned out, the Joint Terrorism Task Force (which I fictionalized as the Anti-Terrorist Task Force) worked out well for John Corey and for a continuing series—and thus the follow-up book to *Plum Island* was *The Lion's Game*, in which we see John Corey reincarnated as a contract agent working for the FBI in counterterrorism.

When I made this decision about Corey working for the Task Force, this was a relatively unknown organization, but post-9/11 the Task Force was very much in the news, and Corey's new job, as well as the plots of the John Corey books, had become the stuff of headlines. So, maybe *that* was prescient—or just fortuitous.

The Lion's Game is based on an historical event—the American air attack on Libya of April 15, 1986. This attack was in retaliation for a Libyan terrorist bombing of a German nightclub frequented by American military personnel. And our retaliation bombing of Libya by the U.S. Air Force in 1986 led to the Libyans planting a bomb on Pam Am Flight 103, which exploded over Lockerbie, Scotland, on December 21, 1988, killing 270 people.

The Lion's Game is basically about a further Libyan retaliation for the 1986 air raid on that country. What I try to show in *The Lion's Game*, and also in *The Lion* (the sequel to *The Lion's Game*), is the circle of worldwide violence that has been set in motion by attacks and retaliations that have taken place for nearly thirty years. This has become, as I say in my John Corey books, a war without a clear beginning and a war without an end in sight.

For action/adventure novelists, the war on terrorism is the new Cold War, providing what seems to be a reliable supply of plots, villains, heroes, and, unfortunately, victims. Like most Americans, I was very happy when the Cold War ended, and I will be just as happy if the war on terrorism ends someday; I will find other things to write about.

But until then, global terrorism will remain in the news, and as with every war, novelists will attempt to give some insights and try to make some sense of the violence and mayhem that journalists report.

As I said earlier, a new introduction to an old book is less of an introduction and more of a historical perspective, and hopefully interesting to my readers who've followed the career of John Corey in five of my novels, including the newest, *The Lion*.

The Lion's Game has survived in print for over a decade and hopefully will survive many more decades because it is as timely today as when it was written. Or if you think this book is prescient or prophetic, then it may be more timely now than when I wrote it.

But I leave that judgment to you, the reader. Enjoy!

Nelson DeMille
New York, 2010

BOOK ONE

America, April 15, The Present

Death is afraid of him
because he has the heart of a lion.

—Arab proverb

Chapter I

You'd think that anyone who'd been shot three times and almost become an organ donor would try to avoid dangerous situations in the future. But, no, I must have this unconscious wish to take myself out of the gene pool or something.

Anyway, I'm John Corey, formerly of the NYPD, Homicide, now working as a Special Contract Agent for the Federal Anti-Terrorist Task Force. I was sitting in the back of a yellow cab on my way from 26 Federal Plaza in lower Manhattan to John F. Kennedy International Airport with a Pakistani suicide driver behind the wheel.

It was a nice spring day, a Saturday, moderate traffic on the Shore Parkway, sometimes known as the Belt Parkway, and recently renamed POW/MIA Parkway to avoid confusion. It was late afternoon, and seagulls from a nearby landfill—formerly known as a garbage dump— were crapping on the taxi's windshield. I love spring.

I wasn't headed off on vacation or anything like that—I was reporting for work with the aforementioned Anti-Terrorist Task Force. This is an organization that not too many people know about, which is just as well. The ATTF is divided into sections which focus on specific bunches of troublemakers and bomb chuckers, like the Irish Republican Army, Puerto Rican Independence Movement, black radicals, and other groups that will go unnamed. I'm in the Mideastern section, which is the biggest group and maybe the most important, though to be honest, I don't know much about Mideastern terrorists. But I was supposed to be learning on the job.

So, to practice my skills, I started up a conversation with the Pakistani guy whose name was Fasid, and who for all I know is a terrorist, though he looked and talked like an okay guy. I asked him, "What was that place you came from?"

"Islamabad. The capital."

"Really? How long have you been here?"

"Ten years."

"You like it here?"

"Sure. Who doesn't?"

"Well, my ex-brother-in-law, Gary, for one. He's always bad-mouthing America. Wants to move to New Zealand."

"I have an uncle in New Zealand."

"No kidding? Anybody left in Islamabad?"

He laughed, then asked me, "You meeting somebody at the airport?"

"Why do you ask?"

"No luggage."

"Hey, you're good."

"So, you're meeting somebody? I could hang around and take you back to the city."

Fasid's English was pretty good—slang, idioms, and all that. I replied, "I have a ride back."

"You sure? I could hang around."

Actually, I was meeting an alleged terrorist who'd surrendered himself to the U.S. Embassy in Paris, but I didn't think that was information I needed to share with Fasid. I said, "You a Yankee fan?"

"Not anymore." Whereupon he launched into a tirade against Steinbrenner, Yankee Stadium, the price of tickets, the salaries of the players, and so forth. These terrorists are clever, sounding just like loyal citizens.

Anyway, I tuned the guy out and thought about how I'd wound up here. As I indicated, I was a homicide detective, one of New York's Finest, if I do say so. A year ago this month, I was playing dodge-the-bullets with two Hispanic gentlemen up on West 102nd Street in what was probably a case of mistaken identity, or sport shooting, since there seemed to be no reason for the attempted whack. Life is funny sometimes. Anyway, the perps were still at large, though I had my eye out for them, as you might imagine.

After my near-death experience and upon release from the hospital,

I accepted my Uncle Harry's offer to stay at his summer house on Long Island to convalesce. The house is located about a hundred road miles from West 102nd Street, which was fine. Anyway, while I was out there, I got involved with this double murder of a husband and wife, fell in love twice, almost got killed. Also, one of the women I fell in love with, Beth Penrose by name, is still sort of in my life.

While all this was going on out on eastern Long Island, my divorce became final. And as if I wasn't already having a bad R&R at the beach, I wound up making the professional acquaintance of a schmuck on the double homicide case named Ted Nash of the Central Intelligence Agency who I took a big dislike to, and who hated my guts in return, and who, lo and behold, was now part of my ATTF team. It's a small world, but not that small, and I don't believe in coincidence.

There was also another guy involved with that case, George Foster, an FBI agent, who was okay, but not my cup of tea either.

In any case, it turns out that this double homicide was not a Federal case, and Nash and Foster disappeared, only to reappear in my life about four weeks ago when I got assigned to this ATTF Mideastern team. But no sweat, I've put in for a transfer to the ATTF's Irish Republican Army section, which I will probably get. I don't have any real feelings about the IRA either way, but at least the IRA babes are easy to look at, the guys are more fun than your average Arab terrorist, and the Irish pubs are primo. I could do some real good in the anti-IRA section. Really.

Anyway, after all this mess out on Long Island, I get offered this great choice of being hauled in front of the NYPD disciplinary board for moonlighting or whatever, or taking a three-quarter medical disability and going away. So I took the medical, but also negotiated a job at John Jay College of Criminal Justice in Manhattan where I live. Before I got shot, I'd taught a class at John Jay as an Adjunct Professor, so I wasn't asking for much and I got it.

Starting in January, I was teaching two night classes at JJ and one day class, and I was getting bored out of my mind, so my ex-partner, Dom Fanelli, knows about this Special Contract Agent program with the Feds where they hire former law enforcement types to work with ATTF. I apply, I'm accepted, probably for all the wrong reasons, and here I am. The pay's good, the perks are okay, and the Federal types are mostly schmucks. I have this problem with Feds, like most cops do, and not even sensitivity training would help.

But the work seems interesting. The ATTF is a unique and, I may say, elite group (despite the schmucks) that only exists in New York City and environs. It's made up mostly of NYPD detectives who are great guys, FBI, and some quasi-civilian guys like me hired to round out the team, so to speak. Also, on some teams, when needed, are CIA prima donnas, and also some DEA—Drug Enforcement Agency people who know their business, and know about connections between the drug trade and the terrorist world.

Other team players include people from the Bureau of Alcohol, Tobacco and Firearms of Waco, Texas, fame, plus cops from surrounding suburban counties, and New York State Police. There are other Federal types from agencies I can't mention, and last but not least, we have a few Port Authority detectives assigned to some teams. These PA guys are helpful at airports, bus terminals, train stations, docks, some bridges and tunnels under their control, and other places, like the World Trade Center, where their little empire extends. We have it all pretty much covered, but even if we didn't, it sounds really impressive.

The ATTF was one of the main investigating groups in the World Trade Center bombing and the TWA 800 explosion off Long Island. But sometimes we take the show on the road. For instance, we also sent a team to help out with the African embassy bombings, though the name ATTF was hardly mentioned in the news, which is how they like it. All of this was before my time, and things have been quiet since I've been here, which is how *I* like it.

The reason the almighty Feds decided to team up with the NYPD and form the ATTF, by the way, is that most FBI people are not from New York and don't know a pastrami sandwich from the Lexington Avenue subway. The CIA guys are a little slicker and talk about cafés in Prague and the night train to Istanbul and all that crap, but New York is not their favorite place to be. The NYPD has street smarts, and that's what you need to keep track of Abdul Salami-Salami and Paddy O'Bad and Pedro Viva Puerto Rico and so on.

Your average Fed is Wendell Wasp from West Wheatfield, Iowa, whereas the NYPD has mucho Hispanics, lots of blacks, a million Irish, and even a few Muslims now, so you get this cultural diversity on the force that is not only politically cool and correct, but actually useful and effective. And when the ATTF can't steal active-duty NYPD people, they hire ex-NYPD like me. Despite my so-called disability, I'm armed, dangerous, and nasty. So there it is.

We were approaching JFK, and I said to Fasid, "So, what did you do for Easter?"

"Easter? I don't celebrate Easter. I'm Muslim."

See how clever I am? The Feds would've sweated this guy for an hour to make him admit he was a Muslim. I got it out of him in two seconds. Just kidding. But, you know, I really have to get out of the Mideast section and into the IRA bunch. I'm part Irish and part English, and I could work both sides of that street.

Fasid exited the Shore-Belt-POW/MIA Parkway and got on the Van Wyck Expressway heading south into JFK. These huge planes were sort of floating overhead making whining noises, and Fasid called out to me, "Where you going?"

"International Arrivals."

"Which airline?"

"There's more than one?"

"Yeah. There's twenty, thirty, forty—"

"No kidding? Just drive."

Fasid shrugged, just like an Israeli cabbie. I was starting to think that maybe he was a Mossad agent posing as a Pakistani. Or maybe this job was getting to me.

There's all these colored and numbered signs along the expressway, and I let the guy go to the International Arrivals, a huge structure with all the airline logos, one after the other out front, and he asked again, "Which airline?"

"I don't like any of these. Keep going."

Again, he shrugged.

I directed him onto another road, and we were now going to the other side of the big airport. This is good trade craft, to see if anybody's following you. I learned this in some spy novel or maybe a James Bond movie. I was trying to get into this anti-terrorist thing.

I got Fasid pointed in the right direction and told him to stop in front of a big office-type building on the west side of JFK that was used for this and that. This whole area is full of nondescript airport services buildings and warehouses, and no one notices anybody's comings and goings, plus the parking is easy. I paid the guy, tipped him, and asked for a receipt in the exact amount. Honesty is one of my few faults.

Fasid gave me a bunch of blank receipts and asked again, "You want me to hang around?"

"I wouldn't if I were you."

I went into the lobby of the building, a 1960s sort of crap modern architecture, and instead of an armed guard with an Uzi like they have all over the world, there's just a sign that says RESTRICTED AREA—AUTHORIZED PERSONNEL ONLY. So, assuming you read English, you know if you're welcome or not.

I went up a staircase and down a long corridor of gray steel doors, some marked, some numbered, some neither. At the end of the corridor was a door with a nice blue-and-white sign that said CONQUISTADOR CLUB—PRIVATE—MEMBERS ONLY.

There was this electronic keycard scanner alongside the door, but like everything else about the Conquistador Club, it was a phony. What I had to do was to press my right thumb on the translucent face of the scanner, which I did. About two seconds later, the metrobiotic genie said to itself, "Hey, that's John Corey's thumb—let's open the door for John."

And did the door *swing* open? No, it *slid* into the wall as far as its dummy doorknob. Do I need this nonsense?

Also there's a video scanner overhead, in case your thumbprint got screwed up with a chocolate bar or something, and if they recognize your face, they also open the door, though in my case they might make an exception.

So I went in, and the door slid closed automatically behind me. I was now in what appeared to be the reception area of an airline travelers' club. Why there'd be such a club in a building that's not near a passenger terminal is, you can be sure, a question I'd asked, and I'm still waiting for an answer. But I know the answer, which is that when the CIA culture is present, you get this kind of smoke-and-mirrors silliness. These clowns waste time and money on stagecraft, just like in the old days when they were trying to impress the KGB. What the door needed was a simple sign that said KEEP OUT.

Anyway, behind the counter was Nancy Tate, the receptionist, a sort of Miss Moneypenny, the model of efficiency and repressed sexuality, and all that. She liked me for some reason and greeted me cheerily, "Good afternoon, Mr. Corey."

"Good afternoon, Ms. Tate."

"Everyone has arrived."

"I was delayed by traffic."

"Actually, you're ten minutes early."

"Oh…"

"I like your tie."

"I took it off a dead Bulgarian on the night train to Istanbul."

She giggled.

Anyway, the reception area was all leather and burled wood, plush blue carpet, and so forth, and on the wall directly behind Nancy was another logo of the fictitious Conquistador Club. And for all I knew, Ms. Tate was a hologram.

To the left of Ms. Tate was an entranceway marked CONFERENCE AND BUSINESS AREA that actually led to the interrogation rooms and holding cells, which I guess could be called the Conference and Business Area. To the right, a sign announced LOUNGE AND BAR. I should be so lucky. That was in fact the way to the communications and operations center.

Ms. Tate said to me, "Ops Center. There are five people including yourself."

"Thanks." I walked through the doorway, down a short hallway, and into a dim, cavernous, and windowless room that held desks, computer consoles, cubicles, and such. On the big rear wall was a huge, computer-generated color map of the world that could be programmed to a detailed map of whatever you needed, like downtown Islamabad. Typical of most Federal facilities, this place had all the bells and whistles. Money is no problem in Fedland.

In any case, this facility wasn't my actual workplace, which is in the aforementioned 26 Federal Plaza in lower Manhattan. But this was where I had to be on this Saturday afternoon to meet and greet some Arab guy who was switching sides and needed to be taken safely downtown for a few years of debriefing.

I kind of ignored my teammates and made for the coffee bar, which, unlike the one in my old detective squad room, is neat, clean, and well stocked, compliments of the Federal taxpayers.

I fooled around with the coffee awhile, which was my way of avoiding my colleagues for a few more minutes.

I got the coffee the right color and noticed a tray of donuts that said NYPD and a tray of croissants and brioche that said CIA and a tray of oatmeal cookies that said FBI. Someone had a sense of humor.

Anyway, the coffee bar was on the operations side of the big room and the commo side was sort of elevated on a low platform. A lady duty agent was up there monitoring all the gidgets and gadgets.

My team, on the operations side, was sitting around somebody's empty desk, engaged in conversation. The team consisted of the aforementioned Ted Nash of the CIA and George Foster of the FBI, plus Nick Monti of the NYPD, and Kate Mayfield of the FBI. WASP, WASP, Wop, WASP.

Kate Mayfield came to the coffee bar and began making herself tea. She is supposed to be my mentor, whatever that means. As long as it doesn't mean partner.

She said to me, "I like that tie."

"I once strangled a Ninja warrior to death with it. It's my favorite."

"Really? Hey, how are you getting along here?"

"You tell me."

"Well, it's too soon for me to tell you. You tell me why you put in for the IRA section."

"Well, the Muslims don't drink, I can't spell their f-ing names on my reports, and the women can't be seduced."

"That's the most racist, sexist remark I've heard in years."

"You don't get around much."

"This is not the NYPD, Mr. Corey."

"No, but *I'm* NYPD. Get used to it."

"Are we through attempting to shock and appall?"

"Yeah. Look, Kate, I thank you for your meddling—I mean mentoring—but in about a week, I'll be in the IRA section or off the job."

She didn't reply.

I looked at her as she messed around with a lemon. She was about thirty, I guess, blond, blue eyes, fair skin, athletic kind of build, perfect pearly whites, no jewelry, light makeup, and so on. Wendy Wasp from Wichita. She had not one flaw that I could see, not even a zit on her face or a fleck of dandruff on her dark blue blazer. In fact, she looked like she'd been airbrushed. She probably played three sports in high school, took cold showers, belonged to 4-H, and organized pep rallies in college. I hated her. Well, not really, but about the only thing we had in common was some internal organs, and not even all of those.

Also, her accent was hard to identify, and I remembered that Nick Monti said her father was an FBI guy, and they'd lived in different places around the country.

She turned and looked at me, and I looked at her. She had these piercing eyes, the color of blue dye No. 2, like they use in ice pops.

She said to me, "You came to us highly recommended."

"By who? Whom?"

"Whom. By some of your old colleagues in Homicide."

I didn't reply.

"Also," she said, "by Ted and George." She nodded toward Schmuck and Putz.

I almost choked on my coffee. Why these two guys would say anything nice about me was a total mystery.

"They aren't fond of you, but you impressed them on that Plum Island case."

"Yeah, I even impressed myself on that one."

"Why don't you give the Mideast section a try?" She added, "If Ted and George are the problem, we can switch you to another team within the section."

"I love Ted and George, but I really have my heart set on the anti-IRA section."

"Too bad. This is where the real action is. This is a career builder."
She added, "The IRA are pretty quiet and well behaved in this country."

"Good. I don't need a new career anyway."

"The Palestinians and the Islamic groups, on the other hand, are potentially dangerous to national security."

"No 'potentially' about it," I replied. "World Trade Center."

She didn't reply.

I'd come to discover that these three words in the ATTF were like, "Remember Pearl Harbor." The intelligence community got caught with their pants down on that one, but came back and solved the case, so it was a draw.

She continued, "The whole country is paranoid about a Mideast terrorist biological attack or a nuclear or chemical attack. You saw that on the Plum Island case. Right?"

"Right."

"So? Everything else in the ATTF is a backwater. The real action is in the Mideast section, and you look like a man of action." She smiled.

I smiled in return. I asked her, "What's it to you?"

"I like you."

I raised my eyebrows.

"I like New York Neanderthals."

"I'm speechless."

"Think about it."

"Will do." I glanced at a TV monitor close by and saw that the flight we were waiting for, Trans-Continental 175 from Paris, was inbound and on time. I asked Ms. Mayfield, "How long do you think this will take?"

"Maybe two or three hours. An hour of paperwork here, then back to Federal Plaza, with our alleged defector, then we'll see."

"See what?"

"Are you in a rush to get somewhere?"

"Sort of."

"I feel badly that national security is interfering with your social life."

I didn't have a good reply to that, so I said, "I'm a big fan of national security. I'm yours until six P.M."

"You can leave whenever you want." She took her tea and rejoined our colleagues.

So, I stood there with my coffee, and considered the offer to take a hike. In retrospect, I was like the guy standing in quicksand, watching it cover my shoes, curious to see how long it would take to reach my socks, knowing I could leave anytime soon. Unfortunately, the next time I glanced down, it was up to my knees.

Chapter 2

Sam Walters leaned forward in his chair, adjusted his headset-microphone, and stared at the green three-foot radar screen in front of him. It was a nice April afternoon outside, but you'd never know that here in the dimly lit, windowless room of the New York Air Traffic Control Center in Islip, Long Island, fifty miles east of Kennedy Airport.

Bob Esching, Walters' shift supervisor, stood beside him and asked, "Problem?"

Walters replied, "We've got a NO-RAD here, Bob. Trans-Continental Flight One-Seven-Five from Paris."

Bob Esching nodded. "How long has he been NO-RAD?"

"No one's been able to raise him since he came off the North Atlantic track near Gander." Walters glanced at his clock. "About two hours."

Esching asked, "Any other indication of a problem?"

"Nope. In fact…" He regarded the radar screen and said, "He turned southwest at the Sardi intersection, then down Jet Thirty-Seven, as per flight plan."

Esching replied, "He'll call in a few minutes, wondering why we haven't been talking to him."

Walters nodded. A No-Radio status was not that unusual—it often happened between air traffic control and the aircraft they worked with. Walters had had days when it happened two or three times. Invariably, after a couple of minutes of repeated transmissions, some pilot would respond, "Oops, sorry…" then explain that they had the volume down or the wrong frequency dialed in—or something less innocuous, like the whole flight crew was asleep, though they wouldn't tell you that.

Esching said, "Maybe the pilot and co-pilot have stewardesses on their laps."

Walters smiled. He said, "The best explanation I ever got in a NO-RAD situation was from a pilot who admitted that when he laid his lunch tray down on the pedestal between the pilots' seats, the tray had pressed into a selector switch and taken them off-frequency."

Esching laughed. "Low-tech explanation for a high-tech problem."

"Right." Walters looked at the screen again. "Tracking fine."

"Yeah."

It was when the blip disappeared, Walters thought, that you had a major problem. He was on duty the night in March 1998 when *Air Force One*, carrying the President, disappeared from the radar screen for twenty-four long seconds, and the entire room full of controllers sat frozen. The aircraft reappeared from computer-glitch limbo and everyone started to breathe again. But then there was the night of July 17, 1996, when TWA Flight 800 disappeared from the screen forever...Walters would never forget that night as long as he lived. *But here*, he thought, *we have a simple NO-RAD*...and yet something bothered him. For one thing, this was a very long time to be in a NO-RAD status.

Sam Walters punched a few buttons, then spoke into his headset microphone on the intercom channel. "Sector Nineteen, this is Twenty-three. That NO-RAD, TC One-Seven-Five, is coming your way, and you'll get the handoff from me in about four minutes. I just wanted to give you a heads-up on this in case you need to do some adjusting."

Walters listened to the reply on his headset, then said, "Yeah...the guy's a real screwup. Everyone up and down the Atlantic Coast has been calling him for over two hours on VHF, HF, and for all I know, CB and smoke signals." Walters chuckled and added, "When this flight is over, this guy's going to be doing so much writing, he'll think he's Shakespeare. Right. Talk to you later." He turned his head and made eye contact with Esching. "Okay?"

"Yeah...tell you what...call everyone down the line and tell them that the first sector that makes contact will inform the captain that when he lands, he's to call me on the telephone at the Center. I want to talk to this clown myself so I can tell him how much agro he's caused along the coast."

"Canada, too."

"Right." Esching listened to Walters pass on the message to the next controllers who would be getting jurisdiction of Trans-Continental Flight 175.

A few other controllers and journeymen on break had wandered over to the Section 23 console. Walters knew that everyone wanted to see why Supervisor Bob Esching was so far from his desk and out on the floor. Esching was—in the unkind words of his subordinates—standing dangerously close to an actual work situation.

Sam Walters didn't like all these people around him, but if Esching didn't shoo them off, he couldn't say anything. And he didn't think Esching was going to tell everyone to clear out. The Trans-Continental No-Radio situation was now the focus event in the control center, and this mini-drama was, after all, good training for these young controllers who had pulled Saturday duty.

No one said much, but Walters sensed a mixture of curiosity, puzzlement, and maybe a bit of anxiety.

Walters got on the radio and tried again. "Trans-Continental Flight One-Seven-Five, this is New York Center. Do you read me?"

No reply.

Walters broadcast again.

No reply.

The room was silent except for the hum of electronics. No one standing around had any comment. It was unwise to say anything in these kinds of situations that could come back to haunt you.

Finally, one of the controllers said to Esching, "Paper this guy big-time on this one, boss. I got off to a late coffee break because of him."

A few controllers laughed, but the laughter died away quickly.

Esching cleared his throat and said, "Okay, everybody go find something useful to do. Scram."

The controllers all wandered off, leaving Walters and Esching alone. Esching said softly, "I don't like this."

"Me neither."

Esching grabbed a rolling chair and wheeled it beside Walters. Esching studied the big screen and focused on the problem aircraft. The identity tag on the screen showed that it was a Boeing 747, and it was the new 700 Series aircraft, the largest and most modern of Boeing's 747s. The aircraft was continuing precisely along its flight plan, routing toward JFK International Airport. Esching said, "How the hell could all the radios be non-functioning?"

Sam Walters considered for a minute, then replied, "They can't be, so—I think it has to be either that the volume control is down, the frequency selectors are broken, or the antennas have fallen off."

"Yeah?"

"Yeah…"

"But…if it was the volume control or the frequency selectors, the crew would have realized that a long time ago."

Walters nodded and replied, "Yeah…so, maybe it's total antenna failure…or, you know, this is a new model so maybe there's some kind of electronic bug in this thing and it caused total radio failure. Possible."

Esching nodded, "Possible." *But not probable.* Flight 175 had been totally without voice contact since leaving the Oceanic Tracks and reaching North America. The Abnormal Procedures Handbook addressed this remote possibility, but he recalled that the handbook wasn't very clear about what to do. Basically, there was nothing that could be done.

Walters said, "If his radios are okay, then when he has to start down, he'll realize he's on the wrong frequency or that his volume control is down."

"Right. Hey…do you think they're all asleep?"

Walters hesitated, then replied, "Well…it happens, but, you know, a flight attendant would have come into the cockpit by now."

"Yeah. This is too long for a NO-RAD, isn't it?"

"It's getting to be a little long…but like I said, when he has to start down…you know, even if he had total radio failure, he could use the data link to type a message to his company operations, and they'd have called us by now."

Esching had thought about that and replied, "That's why I'm

starting to think it's antenna failure, like you said." He thought a moment and asked Walters, "How many antennas does this plane have?"

"I'm not sure. Lots."

"Could they all fail?"

"Maybe."

Esching considered, then said, "Okay, say he's aware of a total radio failure...he could actually use one of the air-to-land phones in the dome cabin and call someone who would have called us by now. I mean, it's been done in the past—you could use an airphone."

Walters nodded.

Both men watched the white radar blip with its white alpha-numeric identification tag trailing beneath it as the blip continued to crawl slowly from right to left.

Finally, Bob Esching said what he didn't want to say. "It could be a hijacking."

Sam Walters didn't reply.

"Sam?"

"Well...look, the airliner is following the flight plan, the course and altitude are right, and they're still using the transponder code for the transatlantic crossing. If they were being hijacked, he's supposed to send a hijacking transponder code to tip us off."

"Yeah..." Esching realized that this situation didn't fit any of the profiles for a hijacking. All they had was an eerie silence from an aircraft that otherwise behaved normally. Yet, it was possible that a sophisticated hijacker would know about the transponder code and tell the pilots not to touch the transponder selector.

Esching knew he was the man on the spot. He cursed himself for volunteering for this Saturday shift. His wife was in Florida visiting her parents, his kids were in college, and he'd thought that going to work would be better than sitting around the house alone. Wrong. He needed a hobby.

Walters said, "What else can we do?"

"You just keep doing what you're doing. I'm going to call the Kennedy Tower supervisor, then I'll call the Trans-Continental Operations Center."

"Good idea."

Esching stood and said, for the record, "Sam, I don't believe we have a serious problem here, but we would be lax if we didn't make some notifications."

"Right," Walters replied as he mentally translated Esching's words to, *We don't want to sound inexperienced, panicky, or too incompetent to handle the situation, but we do want to cover our asses.*

Esching said, "Go ahead and call Sector Nineteen for the handoff."

"Right."

"And call me if anything changes."

"Will do."

Esching turned and walked toward his glassed-in cubicle at the rear of the big room.

He sat at his desk and let a few minutes pass, hoping that Sam Walters would call him to announce they'd established contact. He thought about the problem, then thought about what he was going to say to the Kennedy Tower supervisor. His call to Kennedy, he decided, would be strictly FYI, with no hint of annoyance or concern, no opinions, no speculation—nothing but the facts. His call to Trans-Continental Operations, he knew, had to be just the right balance of annoyance and concern.

He picked up the phone and speed-dialed Kennedy Tower first. As the phone rang, he wondered if he shouldn't just tell them what he really felt in the deepest part of his guts—*something is very wrong here.*

Chapter 3

I was sitting now with my colleagues: Ted Nash, CIA Super Spook; George Foster, FBI Boy Scout; Nick Monti, NYPD good guy; and Kate Mayfield, Golden Girl of the Federal Bureau of Investigation. We'd all found swivel chairs from unoccupied desks, and everyone had a ceramic coffee mug in his or her hand. I really wanted a donut—a sugar donut—but there's this thing with cops and donuts that people find funny for some reason, and I wasn't going to have a donut.

We all had our jackets off, so we could see one another's holsters. Even after twenty years in law enforcement, I find that this makes everyone's voice a couple of octaves lower, even the women.

Anyway, we were all leafing through our folders on this alleged defector, whose name was Asad Khalil. What cops call the folder, by the way, my new friends call the dossier. Cops sit on their asses and flip through their folders. Feds sit on their derrières and peruse their dossiers.

The information in the folder is called the book on the guy, the information in the dossier is called, I think, the information. Same thing, but I have to learn the language.

Anyway, there wasn't much in my folder, or their dossier, except a color photo transmitted by the Paris Embassy, plus a real short bio, and a brief sort of This-is-what-we-think-the-prick-is-up-to kind of report compiled by the CIA, Interpol, British MI-6, the French Sûreté and a bunch of other cop and spook outfits around Europe. The bio said that the alleged defector was a Libyan, age about thirty, no known family, no other vitals, except that he spoke English, French, a little Italian, less German, and, of course, Arabic.

I glanced at my watch, stretched, yawned, and looked around. The Conquistador Club, in addition to being an ATTF facility, doubled as an FBI field office and CIA hangout and who knew what else, but on this Saturday afternoon, the only people there were us five of the ATTF team, the duty officer whose name was Meg, and Nancy Tate out front. The walls, incidentally, are lead-lined so that nobody outside can eavesdrop with microwaves, and even Superman can't see us.

Ted Nash said to me, "I understand you might be leaving us."

I didn't reply, but I looked at Nash. He was a sharp dresser, and you knew that everything was custom-made, including his shoes and holster. He wasn't bad-looking, nice tan, salt-and-pepper hair, and I recalled quite distinctly that Beth Penrose got a little sweaty over him. I had convinced myself that this was not why I didn't like him, of course, but it certainly added fat to the fires of my smoldering resentment, or something like that.

George Foster said to me, "If you give this assignment ninety days, then whatever decision you make will be given serious consideration."

"Really?"

Foster, as the senior FBI guy, was sort of like the team leader, which was okay with Nash, who was not actually *on* the team, but drifted in and out if the situation called for CIA, like it did today.

Foster, dressed in his awful blue-serge-I'm-a-Fed suit, added, rather bluntly, "Ted's leaving on overseas assignment in a few weeks, then it will only be us four."

"Why can't he leave *now?*" I suggested subtly.

Nash laughed.

By the way, Mr. Ted Nash, aside from hitting on Beth Penrose, had actually added to his list of sins by threatening me during the Plum Island thing—and I'm not the forgiving type.

George Foster said to me, "We have an interesting and important case that we're working on that involves the murder of a moderate Palestinian by an extremist group here in New York. We need you for that."

"Really?" My street instincts were telling me that I was getting smoke blown up my ass. Ergo, Foster, and Nash needed a guy to take the fall for something, and whatever it was, I was getting set up to go down. I felt like hanging around just to see what they were up to, but to be honest, I was out of my element here, and even bozos could bring you down if you weren't careful.

I mean, what a coincidence that I wound up on this team. The ATTF is not huge, but it's big enough so that this arrangement looked just a little suspicious. Clue Number Two was that Schmuck and Putz *requested* me on this team for my homicide expertise. I was meaning to ask Dom Fanelli how he'd heard about this Special Contract Agent thing. I'd trust Dom with my life and I have, so he was okay on this, and I had to assume that Nick Monti was clean. Cops don't screw other cops, not even for the Federal government—*especially* not for the Federal government.

I looked at Kate Mayfield. It would really break my cold, hard heart if she was hooked up with Foster and Nash to do me.

She smiled at me.

I smiled back. If I was Foster or Nash and I was fishing for John Corey, I would use Kate Mayfield as bait.

Nick Monti said to me, "This stuff takes some getting used to. And you know, about half the cops and ex-cops who sign on here leave. It's like we're all one big happy family, but the cops are like the kids who didn't go to college, live at home, do odd jobs, and always want to borrow the car."

Kate said, "That's not true, Nick."

Monti laughed. "Yeah, right." He looked at me and said, "We can talk about it over some brews."

I said to all assembled, "I'll keep an open mind," which means, Fuck you. But you don't want to say that because you want them to keep dangling the bait. It's kind of interesting. Another reason for my bad manners was that I was missing the NYPD—The Job, as we called it—and I guess I was feeling a little sorry for myself and a little nostalgic for the old days.

I looked at Nick Monti and caught his eye. I didn't know him from The Job, but I knew he had been a detective in the Intelligence Unit, which was perfect for this kind of work. They supposedly needed me for this Palestinian homicide case and I guess other terrorist-related homicide cases, which was why I was given a contract. Actually, I think they have a contract out on me. I said to Nick, "Do you know why Italians don't like Jehovah's Witnesses?"

"No...why?"

"Italians don't like *any* witnesses."

This got a big laugh out of Nick, but the other three looked like I'd just had a brain fart. The Feds, you have to understand, are so very politically correct and anal retentive, so very fucking frightened of the Washington Thought Police. They're totally cowed by the stupid directives that come out of Washington like a steady stream of diarrhea. I mean, we've all gotten a little more sensitive and aware of our words over the years, and that's good, but the Federal types are positively paranoid about offending anybody or any group, so you get stuff like, "Hello, Mr. Terrorist, my name is George Foster, and I'll be your arresting officer today."

Anyway, Nick Monti said to me, "Three demerits, Detective Corey. Ethnic slur."

Clearly Nash, Foster, and Mayfield were somewhere between annoyed and embarrassed that they were indirectly being made fun of. It occurred to me, in a sensitive moment, that the Feds had their own issues with the NYPD, but you'd never hear a word of it from them.

Regarding Nick Monti, he was about mid-fifties, married with kids, balding, a bit of a paunch, and sort of fatherly and innocuous-looking, the kind of guy who looked like anything but an Intell man. He must have been good or the Feds wouldn't have stolen him from his NYPD job.

I perused the dossier on Mr. Asad Khalil. It appeared that the Arab gentleman moved around Western Europe a lot, and wherever he had been, some American or British person or thing had met with a misadventure— a bomb in the British Embassy in Rome, bomb in the American Cathedral in Paris, bomb in the American Lutheran Church in Frankfurt, the ax murder of an American Air Force officer outside of Lakenheath Airbase in England, and the shooting death in Brussels of three American schoolkids whose fathers were NATO officers. This last thing struck me as particularly nasty, and I wondered what this guy's problem was.

In any case, none of the aforementioned stuff could be directly linked to this Khalil guy, so he had been put under the eye to see who he associated with, or to see if he could be caught in the act. But the alleged asshole seemed to have no known accomplices, no ties to or affiliations with anybody or anything, and no known terrorist connections, except Kiwanis and Rotary. Just kidding.

I scanned a paragraph in the dossier, written by a code-named agent in an unnamed intelligence agency. The paragraph said, "Asad Khalil enters a country openly and legally, using his Libyan passport and posing as a tourist. The authorities are alerted, and he is watched to see who he makes contact with. Invariably, he manages to disappear and apparently leave the country undetected, as there is never any record of his departure. I highly recommend detention and interrogation the next time he arrives at a point of entry."

I nodded. Good idea, Sherlock. That's exactly what we were going to do.

The thing that bothered me about this was that Asad Khalil didn't sound like the kind of perp who would show up at the American Embassy in Paris and give himself up when he was way ahead on points.

I read the last page of the dossier. Basically what we had here was a loner with a bad attitude toward Western Civilization, such as it is. Well, okay, we'll see what the guy is up to real soon.

I studied the color photostat from Paris. Mr. Khalil looked mean, but not ugly mean. He was the swarthily handsome type, hooked nose, slicked-back hair, and deep, dark eyes. He'd had his share of girls or boys or whatever floated his boat.

My colleagues chatted about the case at hand for a moment, and it seemed like all we were supposed to do today was take Mr. Khalil into protective custody and bring him here for a quick preliminary interrogation, a few photos, fingerprints, and all that. An asylum officer from the Immigration and Naturalization Service would do some questioning and paperwork, too. There are a lot of redundancies built into the Federal system so that if something goes wrong, there are no fewer than five hundred people passing the buck around.

After an hour or two here, we'd escort him to Federal Plaza, where, I suppose, he would be met by the appropriate people, who, along with my team, would determine the sincerity of his defection to Christendom and so forth. At some point, a day, a week, or months from now, Mr. Khalil would wind up in some CIA place outside of Washington where he'd spill his guts for a year and then get some bucks and a new identity, which, knowing the CIA, would make the poor guy look like Pat Boone. Anyway, I said to my colleagues, "Who has blond hair, blue eyes, big tits, and lives in the south of France?"

No one seemed to know, so I told them, "Salman Rushdie."

Nick got a good laugh out of that and slapped his knee. "Two more demerits."

The other two guys smiled tightly. Kate rolled her eyes.

Yeah, I was being a little over the top, but I didn't ask for this gig. Anyway, I only had one more bad joke and two more obnoxious comments left.

Kate Mayfield said, "As you may have read in our assignment memo from Zach Weber, Asad Khalil is being escorted by Phil Hundry of the FBI, and Peter Gorman of the CIA. They took charge of Khalil in Paris, and they are flying Business Class in the dome section of the 747. Mr. Khalil may or may not be a government witness and until that's established, he's in handcuffs."

I inquired, "Who gets the frequent flyer miles?"

Ms. Mayfield ignored me and continued, "The two agents and Mr. Khalil will deplane first, and we will be in the jetway, at the door of the aircraft, to meet them." She glanced at her watch, then stood and looked at the TV monitor and said, "Still inbound, still on time. In about ten minutes we should get moving toward the gate."

Ted Nash said, "We certainly don't expect any trouble, but we should be alert. If anyone wanted to kill this guy, they have only a few opportunities—in the jetway, on the way back here in the van, or in transit to Manhattan. After that, Khalil disappears into the bowels of the system, and no one will see or hear from him again."

Nick said, "I've arranged for some Port Authority police officers and NYPD uniformed guys on the tarmac near the van, and we have a police escort to Fed Plaza." He added, "So if anyone tries to whack this guy, it'll be a kamikaze mission."

"Which," said Mr. Foster, "is not out of the question."

Kate said, "We slapped a bulletproof vest on him in Paris. We've taken every precaution. Shouldn't be a problem."

Shouldn't be. Not right here on American soil. In fact, I couldn't recall either the Feds or the NYPD ever losing a prisoner or a witness in transit, so it looked like a walk in the park. Yet, all my kidding aside, you had to handle each one of these routine assignments as though it could blow up in your face. I mean, we're talking terrorists, people with a cause, who have shown they don't give a rat's ass about getting a day older.

We verbally rehearsed the walk through the terminal, to the gate, down the jetway service stairs, to the aircraft parking ramp. We'd put Khalil, Gorman, and Hundry into an unmarked van with Kevlar armor inside, then, with one Port Authority police car in the lead, and one as a trail vehicle, we would head back to our private club here. The Port Authority police cars had ground control radios, which, according to the rules, we needed in the ramp area and in all aeronautical areas.

Back at the Conquistador Club, we'd call an Immigration guy to get Khalil processed. The only organization that seemed to be missing today was the Parking Violations Bureau. But rules are rules, and everyone has their turf to protect.

At some point, we'd get back in the van, and with our escorts, we'd take a circuitous route to Manhattan, cleverly avoiding Muslim neighborhoods in Brooklyn. Meanwhile, a paddy wagon with a marked car would act as decoy. With luck, I'd be done for the day by six and in my car, heading out to Long Island for a rendezvous with Beth Penrose.

Meanwhile, back at the Conquistador Club, Nancy stuck her head in the room and said, "The van is here."

Foster stood and announced, "Time to roll."

At the last minute, Foster said to Nick and me, "Why don't one of you stay here, in case we get an official call?"

Nick said, "I'll stay."

Foster jotted down his cell phone number and gave it to Nick. "We'll keep in touch. Call me if anyone calls here."

"Right."

I glanced at the TV monitor on my way out. Twenty minutes until scheduled landing.

I've often wondered what the outcome would have been if I'd stayed behind instead of Nick.

Chapter 4

Ed Stavros, the Kennedy International Airport Control Tower Supervisor, held the phone to his ear and listened to Bob Esching, the New York Center Air Traffic Control Shift Supervisor. Stavros wasn't sure if Esching was concerned or not concerned, but just the fact that Esching was calling was a little out of the ordinary.

Stavros' eyes unconsciously moved toward the huge tinted windows of the control tower, and he watched a big Lufthansa A-340 coming in. He realized that Esching's voice had stopped. Stavros tried to think of something to say that would sound right when and if the tape was ever played back to a roomful of grim-looking Monday morning quarterbacks. Stavros cleared his throat and asked, "Have you called Trans-Continental?"

Esching replied, "That's my next call."

"Okay...good...I'll alert the Port Authority Police Emergency Service unit...was that a 700 series?"

"Right," said Esching.

Stavros nodded to himself. The Emergency Service guys theoretically had every known type of aircraft committed to memory in regard to doorways, escape hatches, general seating plans, and so forth. "Good...okay..."

Esching added, "I'm not declaring an emergency. I'm just——"

"Yeah, I understand. But we'll go by the book here, and I'll call it in as a three-two condition. You know? That's *potential* trouble. Okay?"

"Yeah...I mean, it could be..."

"What?"

"Well, I'm not going to speculate, Mr. Stavros."

"I'm not asking you to speculate, Mr. Esching. Should I make it a three-three?"

"That's your call. Not mine." He added, "We have a NO-RAD for over two hours and no other indication of a problem. You should have this guy on your screen in a minute or two. Watch him closely."

"Okay. Anything else?"

"That's it," said Bob Esching.

"Thanks," said Ed Stavros and hung up.

Stavros picked up his black direct-line phone to Port Authority Communications Center, and after three rings, a voice said, "Guns and Hoses at your service."

Stavros did not appreciate the humor of the Port Authority police officers who doubled as firemen and Emergency Service personnel. Stavros said, "I have an incoming NO-RAD. Trans-Continental Flight One-Seven-Five, Boeing 747, 700 series."

"Roger, Tower. Which runway?"

"We're still using Four-Right, but how do I know what he'll use if we can't talk to him?"

"Good point. What's his ETA?"

"Scheduled arrival time is sixteen-twenty-three."

"Roger. Do you want a three-two or a three-three?"

"Well…let's start with a standard three-two, and we can upgrade or downgrade as the situation develops."

"Or we can stay the same."

Stavros definitely did not like the cocky attitude of these guys—and they were mostly all guys, even the women. Whoever had the bright idea of taking three macho occupations—Emergency Service, firemen, and cops—and rolling them all into one, must have been crazy. Stavros said, "Who is this? Bruce Willis?"

"Sergeant Tintle, at your service. To whom am I speaking?"

"Mr. Stavros."

"Well, Mr. Stavros, come on down to the firehouse, and we'll put you in a nice fireproof suit and give you a crash ax, and if the plane blows, you can be among the first to get on board."

Stavros replied, "The subject aircraft is a NO-RAD, not a mechanical, Sergeant. Don't get overly excited."

"I love it when you get angry."

Stavros said to Tintle, "Okay, let's get this on the record. I'm going to the Red Phone." Stavros hung up and picked up the Red Phone and hit a button, which again connected him to Sergeant Tintle, who this time answered, "Port Authority—Emergency Service." This call was official and every word was recorded, so Stavros stuck to procedure and said, "This is Tower Control. I'm calling in a three-two on a Trans-Continental 747-700, landing Runway Four-Right, ETA approximately twenty minutes. Winds are zero-three-zero at ten knots. Three hundred ten souls on board." Stavros always wondered why the passengers and crew were called souls. It sounded as though they were dead.

Sergeant Tintle repeated the call and added, "I'll dispatch the units."

"Thank you, Sergeant."

"Thank you for calling, sir. We appreciate the business."

Stavros hung up and rubbed his temples. "Idiots."

He stood and looked around the huge Tower Control room. A few intense men and women sat staring at their screens, or talking into their headsets, or now and then glancing out the windows. Tower Control was not as stressful a job as that of the actual air traffic controllers sitting in a windowless radar room below him, but this was a close second. He remembered the time two of his men had caused the collision of two airliners on the runway. It had been his day off, which was why he was still employed.

Stavros walked toward the big window. From his height of over three hundred feet—the equivalent of a thirty-story building—the panoramic view of the entire airport, bay, and Atlantic Ocean was spectacular, especially with clear skies and the late afternoon sun behind him. He looked at his watch and saw it was almost 4:00 P.M. He would have been out of here in a few minutes, but that was not to be.

He was supposed to be home for dinner with his wife at seven, with another couple. He felt fairly confident that he could make it, or at least be no more than fashionably late. Even later would be okay when he arrived armed with a good story about what had delayed him. People thought he had a glamorous job, and he played it up when he'd had a few cocktails.

He made a mental note to call home after the Trans-Continental landed. Then he'd have to speak to the aircraft's captain on the phone, then write a preliminary report of the incident. Assuming this was nothing more than a communications failure, he should be on the road by six, with two hours of overtime pay. *Right.*

He replayed the conversation with Esching in his mind. He wished he had a way to access the tape that recorded his every word, but the FAA wasn't stupid enough to allow that.

Again, he thought about Esching's phone call—not the words, but the tone. Esching was clearly concerned and he couldn't hide it. Yet, a two-hour NO-RAD was not inherently dangerous, just unusual. Stavros speculated for a moment that Trans-Continental Flight 175 could have experienced a fire on board. That was more than enough reason to change the alert from a standard 3-2 status to a 3-3. A 3-4 was an imminent or actual crash, and that was an easy call. This unknown situation was a tough call.

And, of course, there was the remote chance that a hijacking was in progress. But Esching had said that there was no hijacking transponder code being sent.

Stavros played with his two options—3-2 or 3-3? A 3-3 would definitely call for more creative writing in his report if it turned out to be nothing. He decided to leave it a 3-2 and headed toward the coffee bar.

"Chief."

Stavros looked over at one of his tower controllers, Roberto Hernandez. "What?"

Hernandez put down his headset and said to his boss, "Chief, I just got a call from the radar controller about a Trans-Continental NO-RAD."

Stavros put down his coffee. "And?"

"Well, the NO-RAD began his descent earlier than he was supposed to, and he nearly ran into a US Airways flight bound for Philly."

"Jeez..." Stavros' eyes went to the window again. He couldn't understand how the Trans-Continental pilot could have missed seeing another aircraft on a bright, cloudless day. If nothing else, the collision warning equipment would have sounded even before visual contact was made. This was the first indication that something could be really wrong. *What the hell is going on here?*

Hernandez looked at his radar screen and said, "I've got him, Chief."

Stavros made his way to Hernandez's console. He stared at the radar blip. The problem aircraft was tracking unmistakably down the instrument landing course for one of Kennedy's northeast runways.

Stavros remembered the days when being inside an airport Control Tower meant you'd usually be looking out the window; now, the Control Tower people mostly looked at the same electronic displays that the air traffic controllers saw in the dark radar room below them. But at least up here they had the option of glancing outside if they wanted to.

Stavros took Hernandez's high-powered binoculars and moved to the south-facing plate glass window. There were four stand-up communications consoles mounted ninety degrees apart in front of the wraparound glass so that tower personnel could have multiple communications available while standing and visually seeing what was happening on the runways, taxiways, gates, and flight approaches. This was not usually necessary, but Stavros felt a need to be at the helm, so to speak, when the airliner came into view. He called out to Hernandez, "Speed?"

"Two hundred knots," Hernandez answered. "Descending through fifty-eight hundred feet."

"Okay."

Stavros picked up the Red Phone again. He also hit the Control Tower emergency speaker, then transmitted, "Emergency Service, this is Tower, over."

A voice came over the speaker into the silent Tower Control room, "Tower, Emergency Service."

Stavros recognized Tintle's voice.

Tintle asked, "What's up?"

"What's up is the status. It's now a three-three."

There was a silence, then Tintle asked, "Based on what?"

Stavros thought that Tintle sounded less cocky. Stavros replied, "Based on a near-miss with another aircraft."

"Damn." Silence, then, "What do you think the problem is?"

"No idea."

"Hijacking?"

"A hijacking doesn't make the pilot fly with his head up his ass."

"Yeah…well—"

"We have no time to speculate. The subject aircraft is on a fifteen-mile final for Runway Four-Right. Copy?"

"Fifteen-mile final for Runway Four-Right."

"Affirmed," Stavros said.

"I'll call out the rest of the unit for a three-three."

"Right."

"Confirm aircraft type," Tintle said.

"Still a 747, 700 series, as far as I know. I'll call you when we have visual."

"Roger that."

Stavros signed off and raised his binoculars. He began to scan from the end of the runway and methodically out from there, but his thoughts were on the radio exchange he just had. He recalled meeting Tintle a few times at the Emergency Committee liaison meetings. He didn't particularly like Tintle's style, but he had the feeling that the guy was competent. As for the cowboys who called themselves Guns and Hoses, they mostly sat around the firehouse playing cards, watching TV, or talking about women. They also cleaned their trucks a lot—they loved shiny trucks.

But Stavros had seen them in action a few times, and he was fairly sure they could handle anything from a crash to an onboard fire and even a hijacking. In any case, he wasn't responsible for them or the situation after the aircraft came to a halt. He took a little pleasure out of the knowledge that this 3-3 scramble would come out of the Port Authority budget and not the FAA budget.

Stavros lowered the binoculars, rubbed his eyes, then raised the binoculars and focused on Runway Four-Right.

Both rescue units had rolled, and Stavros saw an impressive assortment of Emergency Service vehicles along the perimeter of the runway, their red beacons rotating and flashing. They were spaced far apart, a procedure designed to avoid having a monster aircraft like a 747 wiping them all out in a crash landing.

Stavros counted two RIVs—Rapid Intercept Vehicles—and four big T2900 fire trucks. There was also one Heavy Rescue ESU truck, two ambulances, and six Port Authority police cars, plus the Mobile Command Post, which had every radio frequency of every affiliated agency in New York as well as a complete phone center. He also spotted the Hazmat—the Hazardous Material Truck—whose crew had been trained by the United States Army. Parked in the far distance was the mobile staircase truck, and the mobile hospital. The only thing missing was the mobile morgue. That wouldn't roll unless it was needed, and there was no rush if it was.

Ed Stavros contemplated the scene—a scene he had created simply by picking up his red telephone. One part of him didn't want there to be a problem with the approaching aircraft. Another part of him...he hadn't called a 3-3 in two years, and he became concerned that he'd overreacted. But overreacting was better than underreacting.

"Seven miles," Hernandez called out.

"Okay." Stavros began another patterned search of the horizon where the Atlantic Ocean met the New York haze.

"Six miles."

"I got him." Even with the powerful binoculars, the 747 was hardly more than a glint against the blue sky. But with every passing second, the airliner was growing in size.

"Five miles."

Stavros continued to stare at the incoming aircraft. He'd watched thousands of jumbo jets make this approach, and there was absolutely nothing about this particular approach that troubled him, except for the fact that even now the aircraft's radios were eerily silent.

"Four."

Stavros decided to talk directly to the person in charge of the rescue teams. He picked up a radiophone that was pre-set to the Ground Control frequency and transmitted, "Rescue One, this is Tower."

A voice came back on the speaker. "Tower, this is Rescue One. How may I help you today?"

Oh, God, Stavros said to himself, *another wise-ass.* It must be the qualification for the job. Stavros said, "This is Mr. Stavros, Tower Supervisor. Who is this?"

"This is Sergeant Andy McGill, first guitar, Guns and Hoses. What can I play for you?"

Stavros decided that what he didn't want to play was this idiot's game. Stavros said, "I want to establish direct contact with you."

"Established."

"Okay...subject aircraft is in sight, McGill."

"Right. We see him, too."

Stavros added, "He's on track."

"Good. I hate it when they land on top of us."

"But be prepared."

"Still NO-RAD?"

"That's right."

"Two miles," said Hernandez and added, "Still on track. Altitude eight hundred feet."

Stavros relayed this to McGill, who acknowledged.

"One mile," said Hernandez, "on track, five hundred feet."

Stavros could clearly make out the huge jetliner now. He transmitted to McGill, "Confirm a 747-700. Gear down, flaps seem normal."

"Roger that. I got a fix on him," McGill replied.

"Good. You're on your own." Stavros ended his transmission and put the radiophone down.

Hernandez left his console and stood beside Stavros. A few other men and women with no immediate duties also lined up at the windows.

Stavros watched the 747, mesmerized by the huge aircraft that had just passed over the threshold of the runway and was floating down toward the concrete. There was nothing about this aircraft that looked or acted any differently from any other 747 touching down. But suddenly, Ed Stavros was certain that he wouldn't be home in time for dinner.

Chapter 5

The van dropped us off at the International Arrivals terminal in front of the Air India logo, and we walked to the Trans-Continental area. Ted Nash and George Foster walked together, and Kate Mayfield and I walked behind them. The idea was to not look like four Feds on a mission, in case someone was watching. I mean, you have to practice good trade craft, even if you're not real impressed with your opponents.

I checked out the big Arrival Board, and it said that Trans-Continental Flight 175 was on time, which meant it was supposed to land in about ten minutes, arriving at Gate 23.

As we walked toward the arrival area, we scoped out the folks around us. You don't normally see bad guys loading their pistols or anything like that, but it's surprising how, after twenty years in law enforcement, you can spot trouble.

Anyway, the terminal was not crowded on this Saturday afternoon in April, and everyone looked more or less normal, except the native New Yorkers who always look on the verge of going postal.

Kate said to me, "I want you to be civil to Ted."

"Okay."

"I mean it."

"Yes, ma'am."

She said, with some insight, "The more you bug him, the more he enjoys it."

Actually, she was right. But there's something about Ted Nash that I don't like. Partly, it's his smugness and his superiority complex. But mostly, I don't trust him.

Anyone waiting for an international flight is outside the Customs area on the ground floor, so we walked over there and worked the crowd a little, looking for anyone who was acting in a suspicious manner, whatever that means.

I assume that the average terrorist hit man knows that if his target is protected, then the target is not going to come out through Customs. But the quality of terrorists we get in this country is generally low, for some reason, and the stupid things that they've done is legendary. According to Nick Monti, the ATTF guys tell dumb terrorist stories in the bars—then bullshit the press with a different story about how dangerous these bad guys are. They *are* dangerous, but mostly to themselves. But then again, remember the World Trade Center. Not to mention the two embassy bombings in Africa.

Kate said to me, "We'll spend about two minutes here, then go to the gate."

"Should I hold up my 'Welcome Asad Khalil' sign yet?"

"Later. At the gate." She added, "This seems to be the season for defections."

"What do you mean?"

"We had another one in February."

"Tell me."

"Same kind of thing. Libyan guy, looking for asylum."

"Where did he turn himself in?"

"Same. Paris," she said.

"What happened to him?"

"We held him here for a few days, then we took him down to D.C."

"Where is he now?"

"Why do you ask?"

"Why? Because it smells."

"It does, doesn't it? What do you think?"

"Sounds like a dry run to see what happens when you go to the American Embassy in Paris and turn yourself in."

"You're smarter than you look. Did you ever have anti-terrorist training?"

"Sort of. I was married." I added, "I used to read a lot of Cold War novels."

"I knew we made the right move in hiring you."

"Right. Is this other defector under wraps or is he able to call his pals in Libya?"

"He was under loose custody. He bolted."

"Why loose custody?"

"Well, he was a friendly witness," she replied.

"Not anymore," I pointed out.

She didn't reply and I didn't ask any further questions. In my opinion, the Feds treat so-called defecting spies and defecting terrorists a lot nicer than cops treat cooperating criminals. But that's only my opinion.

We went to a pre-arranged spot near the Customs door and met the Port Authority detective there, whose name was Frank.

Frank said, "Do you know the way, or do you want company?"

Foster replied, "I know the way."

"Okay," Frank said. "I'll get you started." We walked through the Customs door, and Frank announced to a few Customs types, "Federal agents here. Passing through."

No one seemed to care, and Frank wished us good luck, happy we didn't want him to make the long walk with us to Gate 23.

Kate, Foster, Nash, and I walked through the big Customs and baggage carousel area and down a corridor to the Passport Control booths where no one even asked us our business.

I mean, you could show some of these idiots a Roy Rogers badge and walk through with a rocket launcher over your shoulder.

In short, JFK is a security nightmare, a teaming cauldron of the good, the bad, the ugly, and the stupid, where thirty million travelers pass in and out every year.

We were all walking together now, down one of those long surreal corridors that connect the Passport and Immigration area to the arrival gates. In effect, we were doing the reverse of what arriving passengers do, and I suggested we walk backwards so as not to attract attention, but nobody thought that was necessary or even funny.

Kate Mayfield and I were ahead of Nash and Foster, and she asked me, "Did you study Asad Khalil's psychological profile?"

I didn't recall seeing any psychological profile in the dossier and I said so.

She replied, "Well, there was one in there. It indicates that a man like Asad Khalil—Asad means 'lion' in Arabic, by the way—that a man like that suffers from low self-esteem and has unresolved issues of child-hood inadequacy that he needs to work through."

"Excuse me?"

"This is the type of man who needs an affirmation of his self-worth."

"You mean I can't break his nose?"

"No, you may not. You have to validate his sense of personhood."

I glanced at her and saw she was smiling. Quick-witted fellow that I am, I realized she was jerking me around. I laughed, and she punched my arm playfully, which I sort of liked.

There was a woman at the gate in a sky blue uniform holding a clip-board and a two-way radio. I guess we looked dangerous or something because she started jabbering into the radio as she watched us approaching.

Kate went on ahead and held up her FBI creds and spoke to the woman, who calmed down. You know, everybody's paranoid these days, especially at international airports. When I was a kid, we used to go right to the gate to meet people, a metal detector was what you took to the beach to find loose change, and a hijacking was what happened to trucks. But international terrorism has changed all that. Unfortunately, paranoia doesn't necessarily translate to good security.

Anyway, Nash, Foster, and I went up and schmoozed with the lady, who it turned out was a gate agent who worked for Trans-Continental. Her name was Debra Del Vecchio, which had a nice ring to it. She told us that as far as she knew, the flight was on time, and that's why she was standing there. So far, so good.

There is a standard procedure for the boarding, transporting, and deplaning of prisoners and their escorts; prisoners and escorts board last and deplane first. Even VIPs, such as politicians, have to wait for prisoners to deplane, but many politicians eventually wind up in cuffs and then they can deplane first.

Kate said to Ms. Del Vecchio, "When you move the jetway to the aircraft, we will walk to the aircraft door and wait there. The people we're meeting will deplane first, and we'll escort them down the service stairs of the jetway onto the tarmac where a vehicle is waiting for us. You won't see us again. There will be no inconvenience to your passengers."

Ms. Del Vecchio asked, "Who are you meeting?"

I replied, "Elvis Presley."

Kate clarified, "A VIP."

Foster asked her, "Has anyone else asked you about this flight?"

She shook her head.

Nash studied the photo ID pinned to her blouse.

I thought I should do or say something clever to justify the fifty-dollar cab ride from Manhattan, but short of asking her if she had an Arab boyfriend, I couldn't think of anything.

So, the five of us stood around, trying to look like we were having fun, checking our watches and staring at the stupid tourist posters on the wall of the corridor.

Foster seemed suddenly to remember that he had a cell phone, and he whipped it out, delighted that he had something to do. He speed-dialed, waited, then said, "Nick, this is George. We're at the gate. Anything new there?"

Foster listened to Nick Monti, then said, "Okay...yes...right... okay...good..."

Unable to entertain himself any further with this routine phone call, he signed off and announced, "The van is in place on the tarmac near this gate. The Port Authority and NYPD have also arrived—five cars, ten guys, plus the paddy wagon decoy."

I asked, "Did Nick say how the Yankees are doing?"

"No."

"They're playing Detroit at the Stadium. Should be fifth inning by now."

Debra Del Vecchio volunteered, "They were behind, three to one, in the bottom of the fourth."

"This is going to be a tough season," I said.

Anyway, we made dumb talk for a while, and I asked Kate, "Got your income tax done yet?"

"Sure. I'm an accountant."

"I figured as much." I asked Foster, "You an accountant, too?"

"No, I'm a lawyer."

I said, "Why am I not surprised?"

Debra said, "I thought you were FBI."

Kate explained, "Most agents are accountants or lawyers."

Ms. Del Vecchio said, "Weird."

Ted Nash just stood there against the wall, his hands jammed into his jacket pockets, staring off into space, his mind probably returning to the good old days of the CIA-KGB World Series. He never imagined that his winning team would be reduced to playing farm teams. I said to Kate, "I thought you were a lawyer."

"That, too."

"I'm impressed. Can you cook?"

"Sure can. And I have a black belt in karate."

"Can you type?"

"Seventy words a minute. And I'm qualified as a marksman on five different pistols and three kinds of rifles."

"Nine millimeter Browning?"

"No problem," she said.

"Shooting match?"

"Sure. Anytime."

"Five bucks a point."

"Ten and you're on."

We shook hands.

I wasn't falling in love or anything, but I had to admit I was intrigued.

The minutes ticked by. I said, "So, this guy walks into the bar and says to the bartender, 'You know, all lawyers are assholes.' And a guy at the end of the bar says, 'Hey, I heard that. I resent that.' And the first guy says, 'Why? Are you a lawyer?' And the other guy says, 'No, I'm an asshole.'"

Ms. Del Vecchio laughed. Then she looked at her watch, then glanced at her radio.

We waited.

Sometimes you get a feeling that something is not right. I had that feeling.

Chapter 6

Crew Chief Sergeant Andy McGill of the Emergency Service unit, aka Guns and Hoses, stood on the running board of his RIV emergency fire and rescue truck. He had pulled on his silver-colored bunker suit, and he was starting to sweat inside the fireproof material. He adjusted his binoculars and watched the Boeing 747 make its approach. As far as he could determine, the aircraft looked fine and was on a normal approach path.

He poked his head into the open window and said to his firefighter Tony Sorentino, "No visual indication of a problem. Broadcast."

Sorentino, also in his fire suit, picked up the microphone that connected to the other Emergency Service vehicles and repeated McGill's status report to all the other ESV trucks. Each responded with a Roger, followed by their call signs.

McGill said to Sorentino, "Tell them to follow a standard deployment pattern and follow the subject aircraft until it clears the runway."

Sorentino broadcasted McGill's orders, and everyone again acknowledged.

The other crew chief, Ron Ramos, transmitted to McGill, "You need us, Andy?"

McGill replied, "No, but stay suited up. This is still a three-three."

"It looks like a three-nothing."

"Yeah, but we can't talk to the pilot, so stand by."

McGill focused his binoculars on the FAA Control Tower in the far distance. Even with the reflection on the glass, he could tell that a number of people were lined up at the big window. Obviously the Control Tower people had gotten themselves worked up about this.

McGill opened the right side door and slid in beside Sorentino, who sat in the center of the big cab behind the steering wheel. "What do you think?"

Sorentino replied, "I think I'm not paid to think."

"But what if you *had* to think?"

"I want to think there's no problem, except for the radios. I don't want to fight an aircraft fire today, or have a shoot-out with hijackers."

McGill didn't reply.

They sat in silence a few seconds. It *was* hot in their fire suits, and McGill clicked up the cab's ventilating fan.

Sorentino studied the lights and gauges on his display panel. The RIV held nine hundred pounds of purple K powder, used to put out electrical fires, seven hundred fifty gallons of water, and one hundred gallons of lite water. Sorentino said to McGill, "All systems are go."

McGill reflected that this was the sixth run he'd made this week and only one had been necessary—a brake fire on a Delta 737. In fact, it had been five years since he'd fought a real fire on an aircraft—an Airbus 300 with an engine ablaze that almost got out of control. McGill himself had never had a hijack situation, and there was only one man still working Guns and Hoses who had, and he wasn't on duty today.

McGill said to Sorentino, "After the subject aircraft clears the runway, we'll follow him to the gate."

"Right. You want anyone to tag with us?"

"Yeah...we'll take two of the patrol cars...just in case they have a situation on board."

"Right."

McGill knew that he had a good team. Everyone on the Guns and Hoses unit loved the duty, and they'd all come up the hard way, from crap places like the Port Authority bus terminal, bridge and tunnel duty, or airport patrol duty. They'd put in their time busting prostitutes, pimps, drug dealers, and drug users, rousting bums from various places in the far-flung Port Authority empire, chasing toll beaters and drunks on the bridges and tunnels, taking runaway kids from the Midwest into custody at the bus station, and so forth.

Being a Port Authority cop was a strange mix of this and that, but

Guns and Hoses was the plum assignment. Everyone in the unit was a highly trained volunteer, and theoretically they were ready to fight a blazing jet fuel fire, trade lead with crazed terrorists, or administer CPR to a heart attack victim. They were all potential heroes, but the last decade or so had been pretty quiet, and McGill wondered if the guys hadn't gotten a little soft.

Sorentino was studying a floor plan of the 747-700 on his lap. He said, "This is one big mother."

"Yup." McGill hoped that if it was a mechanical problem, the pilot was bright enough to have jettisoned the remaining fuel. It was McGill's belief that jetliners were little more than flying bombs—sloshing fuel, superheated engines, and electrical wires, and who-knew-what in the cargo holds, sailing through space with the potential to take out a few city blocks. Andy McGill never mentioned to anyone the fact that he was afraid of flying and in fact never flew and never would. Meeting the beast on the ground was one thing—being up there in its belly was another.

Andy McGill and Tony Sorentino stared out the windshield into the beautiful April sky. The 747 had grown larger and now had depth and color. Every few seconds it seemed to get twice as big.

Sorentino said, "Looks okay."

"Yeah." McGill picked up his field glasses and focused on the approaching aircraft. The big bird had sprouted four separate bogies—gangs of wheels—two from beneath its wings and two from mid-fuselage, plus the nose gear. Twenty-four tires in all. He said, "The tires seem intact."

"Good."

McGill continued to stare at the aircraft that now seemed to hover a few hundred feet above and beyond the far end of Kennedy's two-mile-long northeast runway. McGill, despite his fear of flying, was mesmerized by these magnificent monsters. It seemed to him that the act of taking off and landing was something near to magic. He had, a few times in his career, come up to one of these mystical beasts when their magic had disappeared in smoke and fire. At those times, the aircraft had become just another conflagration, no different than a truck or

building that was intent on consuming itself. Then, it was McGill's job
to prevent that from happening. But until then, it seemed that these flying behemoths had arrived from another dimension, making unearthly
noises and defying all the laws of earth's gravity.

Sorentino said, "Almost down…"

McGill barely heard him and continued to stare through his field
glasses. The landing gear hung down with a defiant gesture that seemed
to be ordering the runway to come up to them. The aircraft held its
nose up high, with the two nose-mounted tires centered above the level
of the main landing gear. The flaps were down, the speed, altitude, and
angle were all fine. Shimmering heat waves trailed behind the four giant
engines. The aircraft seemed alive and well, McGill thought, possessing
both intent and intensity.

Sorentino asked, "See anything wrong?"

"No."

The 747 crossed the threshold of the runway and dropped toward
its customary touchdown point of several hundred yards beyond the
threshold. The nose pitched up slightly just before the first of the main
tires touched and leveled themselves from their angled-down initial
position. A puff of silver-gray smoke popped up from behind each
group of tires as they hit the concrete and went from zero to two hundred miles an hour in one second. From the touch of the first main tires
until the pair of tires on the nose strut dropped to make contact with
the runway had taken four or five seconds, but the grace of the act made
it seem longer, like a perfectly executed football pass into the end zone.
Touchdown.

A voice came over the emergency vehicle's speaker and announced,
"Rescue Four is moving."

Another voice said, "Rescue Three, I'm at your left."

All fourteen vehicles were moving and transmitting now. One by
one, they drove onto the runway as the huge airliner passed them.

The 747 was now abreast of McGill's vehicle, and he had the
impression that the rollout speed was too fast.

Sorentino hit the gas pedal, and the RIV V8 diesel roared as the
vehicle sped onto the runway in pursuit of the decelerating jet.

Sorentino said, "Hey, Andy—no reverse thrust."

"What...?"

As the RIV gained on the aircraft, McGill could now see that the cascading scoops behind each of the four engines were still streamlined in their cruise position. These hinged metal panels—the size of barn doors—were not deployed in the position to divert the jet blast to a more forward angle during rollout, which was why the aircraft was going too fast.

Sorentino checked his speedometer and announced, "One hundred ten."

"Too fast. He's going too fast." McGill knew that the Boeing 747 was designed and certified to stop with just its wheel brakes and this runway was long enough, so it wasn't a huge problem, but it was his first visual indication that something was wrong.

The 747 continued its rollout, decelerating more slowly than usual, but definitely slowing. McGill was in the lead pursuit vehicle, followed by the five other trucks, who were followed by the six patrol cars, who were followed by the two ambulances.

McGill picked up his microphone and gave each of the vehicles an order. They closed on the big, lumbering aircraft and took up their positions, one RIV to the rear, two T2900 trucks on each side, the patrol cars and ambulances fanned out to the rear. Sorentino and McGill passed under the mammoth wing of the aircraft and held a position near the nose as the jet continued to slow. McGill stared at the huge airliner out the side window. He called out to Sorentino over the roar of the jet engines, "I don't see any problem."

Sorentino concentrated on his speed and spacing, but said, "Why doesn't he use his reverse thrust?"

"I don't know. Ask him."

The Boeing 747 slowed and finally came to a stop, a quarter mile short of the end of the runway, its nose bobbing up and down twice from the last of its momentum.

Each of the four T2900 vehicles had positioned themselves forty yards from the aircraft, two on each side, with the RIVs at front and rear. The ambulances stopped behind the aircraft, while the six patrol cars paired up with an Emergency Service vehicle, though each patrol car was further from the aircraft than the fire trucks. The six men in the patrol cars got out of their vehicles, as per standard operating procedures, and were taking precautionary cover on the sides of their cars away from the aircraft. Each man was armed with a shotgun or an AR-15 automatic rifle.

The men in the trucks stayed in their vehicles. McGill picked up his microphone and broadcast to the other five trucks, "Anyone see anything?"

No one responded, which was good, since procedurally the other rescue vehicles would maintain radio silence unless they had something pertinent to say.

McGill considered his next move. The pilot hadn't used reverse thrust, so he'd had to apply a lot of wheel brakes. McGill said to Sorentino, "Move toward the tires."

Sorentino edged their vehicle closer to the main tires on the aircraft's starboard side. Putting out brake fires was the meat and potatoes of what they did for a living. It wasn't hero stuff, but if you didn't get some water on super-heated brakes pretty soon, it wasn't unusual to see the entire landing gear suddenly erupt into flames. Not only was this not good for the tires, but with the fuel tanks right above the brakes, it also wasn't good for anyone or anything within a hundred-yard radius of the aircraft.

Sorentino stopped the vehicle forty feet from the tires.

McGill raised his field glasses and stared hard at the exposed brake disks. If they were glowing red, it was time to start spraying, but they looked dull black like they were supposed to.

He picked up the microphone and ordered the T2900 vehicles to check the remaining three gangs of wheels.

The other vehicles reported negative on the hot brakes.

McGill transmitted, "Okay...move back."

The four T2900 vehicles moved away from the 747. McGill knew that the flight had come in NO-RAD, which was why they were all there, but he thought he should try to call the pilot. He transmitted on the ground frequency, "Trans-Continental One-Seven-Five, this is Rescue One. Do you read me? Over."

No reply.

McGill waited, then transmitted again. He looked at Sorentino, who shrugged.

The emergency vehicles, the police cars, the ambulances, and the 747 all sat motionless. The Boeing's four engines continued to run, but the aircraft remained still. McGill said to Sorentino, "Drive around where the pilot can see us."

Sorentino put the RIV in gear and drove around to the front right side of the towering aircraft. McGill got out and waved up at the windshield, then, using ground controller hand and arm signals, he motioned for the pilot to continue toward the taxiway.

The 747 didn't move.

McGill tried to see into the cockpit, but there was too much glare on the windshield, and the cockpit was high off the ground. Two things occurred to him almost simultaneously. The first thing was that he didn't know what to do next. The next thing was that something was wrong. Not obviously wrong, but quietly wrong. This was the worst kind of wrong.

Chapter 7

So we waited there at the International Arrivals gate—me, Kate Mayfield, George Foster, Ted Nash, and Debra Del Vecchio, the Trans-Continental gate agent. Being a man of action, I don't like waiting, but cops learn to wait. I once spent three days on a stakeout posing as a hot dog vendor, and I ate so many hot dogs that I needed a pound of Metamucil to get me regular again.

Anyway, I said to Ms. Del Vecchio, "Is there a problem?"

She looked at her little walkie-talkie, which also has this readout screen, and she held it up to me again. It still read ON THE GROUND.

Kate said to her, "Please call someone."

She shrugged and spoke into the hand radio. "This is Debbie, Gate Twenty-three. Status of Flight One-Seven-Five, please."

She listened, signed off, and said to us, "They're checking."

"Why don't they know?" I asked.

She replied patiently, "The aircraft is under Tower Control—the FAA—the Feds—not Trans-Continental. The company is called only if there's a problem. No call, no problem."

"The aircraft is late getting to the gate," I pointed out.

"That's not a problem," she informed me. "It's on time. We have a very good on-time record."

"What if it sat on the runway for a week? Is it still on time?"

"Yes."

I glanced at Ted Nash, who was still standing against the wall, looking inscrutable. As with most CIA types, he liked to give the impression that he knew more than he was saying. In most cases, what appeared to be quiet assurance and wisdom was actually clueless stupidity. Why do I hate this man?

But to give the devil his due, Nash whipped out his cell phone and punched in a bunch of numbers, announcing to us, "I have the direct dial to the Control Tower."

It occurred to me that Mr. Nash actually did know more than he was saying, and that he knew, long before the flight landed, that there might be a problem.

Supervisor Ed Stavros in the FAA Control Tower continued to watch the scene being played out on Runway Four-Right through his binoculars. He said to the controllers around him, "They're not foaming. They're moving away from the aircraft...one of the Emergency Service guys is hand-signaling to the pilot..."

Controller Roberto Hernandez was talking on a telephone and said to Stavros, "Boss, the radar room wants to know how long before they can use Four-Left and when we can have Four-Right available to them again." Hernandez added, "They have some inbounds that don't have much holding fuel."

Stavros felt his stomach knotting. He took a deep breath and replied, "I don't know. Tell radar...I'll get back to them."

Hernandez didn't reply, nor did he pass on his supervisor's non-answer.

Stavros finally grabbed the phone from Hernandez and said, "This is Stavros. We have...a NO-RAD—yeah, I know you know that, but that's all I know—look, if it was a fire, you'd have to divert anyway and you wouldn't be bugging me—" He listened, then replied tersely, "So tell them the President's getting a haircut on Four-Right and they have to divert to Philly." He hung up and was immediately sorry he'd said that, though he was aware that the guys around him were laughing approvingly. He felt better for half a second, then his stomach knotted again. He said to Hernandez, "Give the flight another call. Use the Tower and Ground Control frequencies. If they don't answer, we can assume they haven't had any luck with their radio problems."

Hernandez picked up a console microphone and tried to raise the aircraft on both frequencies.

Stavros focused the binoculars and scanned the scene again. Nothing had changed. The giant Boeing sat stoically, and he could see the exhaust heat and fumes behind each of the power plants. The various Emergency Service vehicles and the police cars held their positions. In the far distance, a similarly composed team sat well away from the runway, burning fuel and doing what everyone else was doing—nothing. Whoever it was that had been trying to get the pilot's attention—probably McGill—had given up and was standing there with his hands on his hips looking very stupid, Stavros thought, as though he were pissed off at the 747.

What didn't make sense to Stavros was the pilot's inaction. No matter what the problem was, a pilot's first inclination would be to clear an active runway at the earliest opportunity. Yet, the Boeing 747 just sat there.

Hernandez gave up on the radio and said to Stavros, "Should I call someone?"

"There's no one left to call, Roberto. Who are we supposed to call? The people who are supposed to get the fucking aircraft out of there are standing around with their fingers up their nose. Who should I call next? My mother? She wanted me to be a lawyer—" Stavros realized he was losing it and calmed himself down. He took another long breath and said to Hernandez, "Call those clowns down there." He pointed toward the situation at the end of Four-Right. "Call Guns and Hoses. McGill."

"Yes, sir."

Hernandez got on the radiophone and called Unit One, the lead Emergency Service vehicle. Sorentino answered and Hernandez asked, "Situation report." He hit the speaker phone button, and Sorentino's voice came up into the silent room. Sorentino said, "I don't know what's happening."

Stavros grabbed the radiophone and, trying to control his anxiety and annoyance, said, "If you don't know, how am I supposed to know? You're there. I'm here. What is going on? Talk to me."

There was a few seconds of silence, then Sorentino said, "There's no sign of a mechanical problem...except—"

"Except *what?*"

"The pilot came in without reverse thrust. You understand?"

"Yes, I fucking well understand what reverse thrust is."

"Yeah, so...McGill is trying to get the flight crew's attention—"

"The flight crew has everyone else's attention. Why can't we get *their* attention?"

"I don't know." Sorentino asked, "Should we board the aircraft?"

Stavros considered this question and wondered if he was the person to answer it. Normally, Emergency Service made that determination, but in the absence of a visible problem, the hotshots down there didn't know if they should board. Stavros knew that boarding an aircraft on the runway with its engines running was potentially dangerous to the aircraft and to the Emergency Service people, especially if no one knew the intentions of the pilot. What if the aircraft suddenly moved? On the other hand, there *could* be a problem on board. Stavros had no intention of answering the question and said to Sorentino, "That's your call."

Sorentino replied, "Okay, thanks for the tip."

Stavros didn't care for this guy's sarcasm and said, "Look, it's not my job to—Hold on." Stavros was aware of Hernandez holding a telephone out to him. "Who is it?"

"A guy who asked for you by name. He says he's with the Justice Department. Says there's a fugitive on board Flight One-Seven-Five who's in custody, and he wants to know what's happening."

"Shit..." Stavros took the phone and said, "This is Mr. Stavros." He listened and his eyes widened. Finally, Stavros said, "I understand. Yes, sir. The aircraft came in without radio contact and is still sitting at the end of Runway Four-Right. It's surrounded by Port Authority police and Emergency Service personnel. The situation is static."

He listened, then replied, "No, there's no indication of a real problem. There was no hijacking transponder call sent out, but the aircraft did experience a near miss—" He listened again, wondering if he should even mention the reverse thrust thing to someone who might overreact to a relatively minor mechanical problem, or maybe an oversight on the pilot's part. Stavros wasn't sure exactly who this guy was, but he sounded like he had power. Stavros waited until the man finished, then said, "Okay, I understand. I'll get on it—" He looked at the dead phone, then handed it back to Hernandez. The decision had just been made for him and he felt better.

Stavros put the radiophone to his mouth and transmitted to Sorentino, "Okay, Sorentino, you are to enter the aircraft. There's a fugitive on board. Business Class in the dome. He's cuffed and escorted so don't be pulling guns and scaring the passengers. But take the guy and his two escorts off the aircraft and have one of the patrol cars take them to Gate Twenty-three where they'll be met. Okay?"

"Roger. But I have to call my Tour Commander—"

"I don't give a shit who you call—just do what I asked. And when you get on board, find out what the problem is, and if there is no problem, tell that pilot to get off the damned runway and proceed to Gate Twenty-three. Lead him in."

"Roger."

"Call me after you board."

"Roger."

Stavros turned to Hernandez and said, "To make matters worse, this Justice Department guy tells me not to reassign Gate Twenty-three to any other aircraft until he gives me the go-ahead. I don't assign gates. The Port Authority assigns gates. Roberto, call the Port Authority and tell them not to reassign Gate Twenty-three. Now we're short a gate."

Hernandez pointed out, "With Four-Right and -Left closed, we don't need many gates."

Stavros uttered an obscenity and stormed off to his office for an aspirin.

Ted Nash slipped his cell phone in his pocket and said to us, "The aircraft came in without radio contact and is sitting at the end of the runway. There was no distress signal sent out, but the Control Tower doesn't know what the problem is. The Emergency Service people are there. As you heard, I told the Tower to have them enter the aircraft, bring our guys here, and keep the gate free."

I said to my colleagues, "Let's get out to the aircraft."

George Foster, our fearless team leader, replied, "The aircraft is surrounded by Emergency Service. Plus, we have two people on board. They don't need us there. The less that changes, the better."

Ted Nash, as usual, stayed aloof, resisting the temptation to disagree with me.

Kate concurred with George, so I was the odd man out, as usual. I mean, if a situation is going down at Point A, why stand around at Point B?

Foster took out his cell phone and dialed one of the FBI guys on the tarmac. He said, "Jim, this is George. Small change in plans. The aircraft has a problem on the runway, so a Port Authority car will bring Phil, Peter, and the subject to this gate. Call me when they get there, and we'll come down. Okay. Right."

I said to George, "Call Nancy and see if she's heard from Phil or Peter."

"I was just going to do that, John. Thank you." Foster dialed the Conquistador Club and got Nancy Tate on the phone. "Have you heard from Phil or Peter?" He listened and said, "No, the aircraft is still on the runway. Give me Phil's and Peter's phone numbers." He listened and signed off, then dialed. He held the phone out to us, and we could hear the recorded message telling us our party was unavailable or out of the calling area. George then dialed the other number and again got the same message. He said to us, "They probably have their phones off."

That didn't get any salutes, so George added, "You have to shut off the cell phones in flight. Even on the ground. But maybe one of them will break the rules and call the Conquistador Club. Nancy will call us."

I thought about this. If I got worried every time I couldn't complete a cell phone call, I'd have ulcers by now. Cell phones and beepers suck anyway.

I considered the situation as an academic problem thrown at me by an instructor. At the Police Academy, they teach you to stick to your post or stick to the plan until ordered to do otherwise by a superior. But they also tell you to use good judgment and personal initiative if the situation changes. The trick is to know when to stick and when to move.

By all objective standards, this was a time to stay put. But my instincts said to move. I used to trust my instincts more, but I was out of my element here, new to the job, and I had to assume these people knew what they were doing, which was nothing. Sometimes, nothing is the right thing.

Debra Del Vecchio's walkie-talkie squawked, and she held it to her ear, then said, "Okay, thanks." She said to us, "Now they tell me that Air Traffic Control called Trans-Continental operations a while ago and reported that Flight One-Seven-Five was NO-RAD."

"No rat?"

"NO-*RAD*. No radio."

"We already know that," I said. "Does this happen often? NO-RAD?"

"I don't know..."

"Why is the plane sitting on the end of the runway?"

She shrugged. "Maybe the pilot needs someone to give him instructions. You know—what taxiways to use." She added, "I thought you said it was a VIP on board. Not a fugitive."

"It's a fugitive VIP."

So, we stood there, waiting for the Port Authority cops to collect Hundry, Gorman, and Khalil and bring them to the NYPD and Port Authority escort vehicles outside this gate, whereupon Agent Jim Somebody would call us, and we'd go down to the tarmac, get in the vehicles, and drive to the Conquistador Club. I looked at my watch. I was going to give this fifteen minutes. Maybe ten.

Chapter 8

Andy McGill heard the blast of his truck's horn and moved quickly back to his vehicle and jumped on the running board. Sorentino said to him, "Stavros called. He said to enter the aircraft. Some Federal types called him, and there's a fugitive on board, in the dome. The perp is cuffed and escorted. Take him and his two escorts out and turn him over to one of the patrol cars. They all have to go to Gate Twenty-three where some NYPD and PA vehicles will be waiting." Sorentino asked, "Are we taking orders from this guy?"

For a brief second, McGill considered a connection between the fugitive and the problem, but there seemed to be no connection, not even a coincidence, really. There were a lot of flights that came in with escorted bad guys, VIPs, witnesses, and whatever—a lot more than people knew. In any case, there was something else in the back of his mind that kept nagging at him and he couldn't recall what it was, but it had something to do with this situation. He made a mental shrug and said to Sorentino, "No, we're not taking orders from Stavros or the Feds ... but maybe it's time to board. Notify the Tour Commander."

"Will do." Sorentino got on the radio.

McGill considered calling the mobile staircase vehicle, but it was some distance away, and he really didn't need it to get into the aircraft. He said to Sorentino, "Okay, right front door. Move it."

Sorentino maneuvered the big truck toward the right front door of the towering aircraft. The radio crackled and a voice came over the speaker saying, "Hey, Andy. I just remembered the Saudi Scenario. Be careful."

Sorentino said, "Holy shit ..."

Andy McGill stood frozen on the running board. It all came back to him now. A training film. About twenty years ago, a Saudi Arabian Lockheed L-IOII Tristar had taken off from Riyadh Airport, reported smoke in the cabin and cockpit, then returned to the airport and landed safely. There was apparently a fire in the cabin. The aircraft was surrounded by fire trucks, and the Saudi Emergency Service people just sat around and waited for the doors to pop open and the chutes to deploy. But as luck and stupidity would have it, the pilots had not depressurized the aircraft, and the doors were held closed by the inside air pressure. The flight attendants couldn't get them open, and no one thought to use a fire ax to smash a window. The end of the story was that all three hundred people on board died on the runway from smoke and fumes.

The infamous Saudi Scenario. They'd been trained to recognize it, this looked like it, and they'd blown it big-time. "Oh, shit..."

Sorentino steered with one hand and handed McGill his Scott pack, which consisted of a portable compressed air bottle and full face mask, then his crash ax.

As the RIV got under the door of the aircraft, McGill scrambled up the hand and foot rungs of his fire truck to the flat roof where the foaming cannon was mounted.

Rescue Four had joined his truck and one of the men stood on the second truck's roof behind that truck's foaming cannon. McGill also noticed that one of the men from a patrol car had suited up and was deploying a charged high-pressure water hose. The other four fire trucks and the ambulances had moved farther away in case of an explosion. McGill noted with some satisfaction that as soon as someone said Saudi Scenario, everyone knew what to do. Unfortunately, they'd all sat around too long, like the Saudi firefighters they had laughed at in the training film.

Mounted on the roof was a small collapsible ladder, and McGill extended it out to its six-foot length and swiveled it toward the door. It was just long enough to reach the door handle of the 747. McGill put on his mask, took a deep breath, and climbed the ladder.

Ed Stavros watched through his binoculars. He wondered why the Emergency Service team had gone into a fire-fighting mode. He had never heard of the Saudi Scenario, but he knew a fire-fighting scenario when he saw one. He picked up his radiophone and called McGill's vehicle. "This is Stavros. What's going on?"

Sorentino didn't respond.

Stavros called again.

Sorentino had no intention of broadcasting the fact that they'd belatedly figured out what the problem might be. There was still a 50-50 chance that it wasn't the Saudi Scenario, and they'd know in a few seconds.

Stavros called again, more insistent this time.

Sorentino knew he had to reply. He transmitted, "We're just taking necessary precautions."

Stavros considered this reply, then said, "No indication of a fire on board?"

"No...no smoke."

Stavros took a deep breath and said, "Okay...keep me posted. Answer my calls."

Sorentino snapped back, "We're in a possible rescue situation. Stay off the frequency. Out!"

Stavros looked at Hernandez to see if his subordinate had heard the Guns and Hoses idiot get nasty with him. Hernandez pretended he did not, and Stavros made a mental note to give Roberto a high efficiency report.

Stavros next considered if he should call anyone concerning this fire-fighting deployment. He said to Hernandez, "Tell Air Traffic Control that Runways Four-Left and -Right will be down for at least fifteen more minutes."

Stavros focused his binoculars and stared at the scene at the end of the runway. He couldn't actually see the right front door, which was facing away from him, but he could see the deployment of the vehicles. If the aircraft blew and there was still a lot of fuel on board, the vehicles that had moved off a hundred yards would need new paint jobs. The two fire trucks near the aircraft would be scrap metal.

He had to admit that there were times when the Emergency Service people earned their pay. But still, his job was stressful every minute of his seven-hour shift. Those guys got stressed maybe once a month.

Stavros remembered what the nasty Emergency Service guy had

said—*We're in a possible rescue situation*. This in turn reminded him that his part in this drama had officially ended as soon as the 747 had come to a halt. All he had to do was keep advising Air Traffic Control of the status of the runways. Later, he'd have to write a report consistent with his taped radio transmissions, and consistent with the fate of the aircraft. He knew that his telephone conversation with the Justice Department guy was also taped, and this, too, made him feel a little better.

Stavros turned away from the big window and went to the coffee bar. If the aircraft blew, he knew he'd hear it and feel it, even up here in his tower. But he didn't want to see it.

Andy McGill shouldered his fire ax in his left hand and put the back of his gloved right hand against the aircraft's door. The back of the fire glove was thin and theoretically you could feel heat through it. He waited a few seconds, but felt nothing.

He moved his hand to the emergency external door handle and yanked on it. The handle moved out away from its recess, and McGill pushed up on the handle to disarm the automatic escape chute.

He glanced behind and below and saw the fire-suited guy from the patrol car on the ground to his right. He had the charged hand-line aimed directly at the airliner's closed door. The other fire truck, Rescue Four, was fifty feet behind his own, and the guy on the roof was aiming the foaming cannon at him. Everyone had full bunker gear and Scott packs on and he couldn't tell who was who, but he trusted all of them, so it didn't matter. The guy at the foaming cannon gave him a thumbs-up. McGill acknowledged the gesture.

Andy McGill held the handle tight and pushed. If the aircraft was still pressurized, the door wouldn't budge, and he'd have to smash through the small door window with his crash ax to depressurize the aircraft and vent any fumes that might be inside.

He kept pushing and all of a sudden the door began to open inward. He let go of the handle and the door automatically continued to pull itself in, then retracted up into the ceiling.

McGill ducked below the threshold of the door to escape any out-pouring of smoke, heat, or fumes. But there was nothing.

Without losing another second, McGill pulled himself up into the airliner. He looked around quickly and saw he was in the forward galley area, which was where he belonged according to the floor plans on file. He checked his face mask and air flow, checked his gauge to make sure his tank was full, then propped his fire ax against the bulkhead.

He stood there in the galley and peered across the wide-bodied fuselage to the other exit door. There was definitely no smoke, but he couldn't be sure about fumes. He turned back to the open door and sig-naled to the men with the fire hose and cannon that he was okay.

McGill turned back into the aircraft and proceeded out of the galley into an open area. To his right was the First Class cabin in the nose, to his left was the huge Coach section. In front of him was the spiral staircase that led into the dome where the cockpit and Business Class section were.

He stood there a moment and felt the vibrations of the engines through the airframe. Everything seemed normal except for two things: it was too quiet, and the curtains across the Coach and First Class areas were drawn closed. FAA regulations called for them to be open during takeoff and landing. And if he thought further about this situation, he would have wondered why none of the flight attendants had appeared. But that was the least of his problems, and he put it out of his mind.

His instinct was to check out one or both of the curtained compart-ments, but his training said to proceed to the cockpit. He retrieved his crash ax and moved toward the spiral stairs. He could hear his breathing through the oxygen mask.

He took the steps slowly, but two at a time. He stopped when he was chest-level to the upper deck and peered into the big dome of the 747. There were sets of seats paired along both sides of the dome, eight rows in all, for a total of thirty-two seats. He couldn't see any heads above the big, plush seats, but he could see arms draped over the rests of the aisle seats. Motionless arms. "What the hell...?"

He continued up the staircase and stood at the rear bulkhead of the dome. In the center of the dome was a console on which lay magazines, newspapers, and baskets of snacks. Late afternoon sunlight filled the dome through the portholes, and dust motes floated in the sunbeams. It was a pleasant scene, he thought, but instinctively he knew he was in the presence of death.

He moved up the center aisle and glanced left and right at the passengers in their seats. Only about half the seats were occupied, and they were mostly middle-aged men and women, the type you'd find in Business Class. Some were reclined backwards with reading material on their laps, some had their service trays open and drinks sat on the trays, although McGill noticed that a few glasses had tipped and spilled during the landing.

A few passengers had headphones on and appeared to be watching the small individual television screens that came out of the armrests. The TVs were still on, and the one closest to him showed a promo film of happy people in Manhattan.

McGill moved forward and turned to face the passengers. There was no doubt in his mind that all of them were dead. He took a deep breath and tried to clear his mind, tried to be professional. He pulled the fire glove off his right hand and reached out to touch the face of a woman in the closest aisle seat. Her skin was not stone cold, but neither was it body temperature. He guessed she had been dead for a few hours, and the state of the cabin confirmed that whatever had happened, had happened long before preparations to land.

McGill bent over and examined the face of a man in the next row. The face was peaceful—no saliva, no mucus, no vomit, no tears, no tortured expressions...McGill had never seen anything quite like this. Toxic fumes and smoke caused panic, horrible suffocation, a very unpleasant death that could be seen on the faces and in the body contortions of the victims. What he was seeing here, he concluded, was a peaceful, sleep-like unconsciousness, followed by death.

He looked for the cuffed fugitive and the two escorts and found the handcuffed man in the second from last row of the starboard side seats, sitting in the window seat. The man was dressed in a dark gray suit and though his face was partly hidden by a sleeping mask, he looked to McGill to be Hispanic or maybe Mideastern or Indian. McGill never could tell ethnic types apart. But the guy sitting next to the cuffed man was most probably a cop. McGill could usually pick out one of his own. He patted down the man and felt his holster on his left hip. He then looked at the man sitting by himself in the last row behind these two and concluded that this was the other escort. In any case, it didn't matter any longer, except that he didn't have to lead them off the aircraft and put them in a car; they were not going to Gate 23. In fact, no one was going anywhere except to the mobile morgue.

McGill considered the situation. Everyone up here in the dome was dead, and since the entire aircraft shared the same internal atmosphere and air pressure, then he knew that everyone in First Class and Coach was also dead. This explained what he'd seen and not seen below. It explained the silence. He considered using his radio to call for medical assistance, but he was fairly certain no one needed assistance. Still, he took the radio off its hook and was going to transmit, but he realized he didn't know quite what to say, and he didn't know how he would sound yelling through his oxygen mask. Instead, he keyed the radio button in a series of long and short squelch breaks to signal that he was okay.

Sorentino's voice came over the radio and said, "Roger, Andy."

McGill walked to the rear lavatory behind the spiral staircase. The door sign said VACANT, and McGill opened the door, assuring himself that no one was in there.

Across from the lavatory was the galley, and as he turned away from the lavatory, he saw someone lying on the floor in the galley. He moved toward the body and knelt. It was a female flight attendant, lying on her side as though she were taking a nap. He felt her ankle for a pulse, but there was none.

Now that he was certain that no passengers needed aid, McGill went quickly to the cockpit door and pulled on it, but it was locked, as per regulations. He banged on the door with his hand, and shouted through his oxygen mask, "Open up! Emergency Service! Open up!" There was no response. Nor did he expect any.

McGill took his crash ax and swung at the cockpit door where the lock was. The door sprang in and hung half open on its hinges. McGill hesitated, then stepped into the cockpit.

The pilot and co-pilot sat in their seats, and he could see their heads tilted forward as if they'd nodded off.

McGill stood there a few seconds, not wanting to touch the pilots. Then he said, "Hey. *Hey*. Can you hear me?" He felt slightly stupid talking to dead men.

Andy McGill was sweating now, and he felt his knees trembling. He was not a queasy man, and over the years he had carried his share of burned and dead bodies out of various places, but he had never been alone in the presence of so much silent death.

He touched the pilot's face with his bare hand. Dead a few hours. So, who had landed the aircraft?

His eyes went to the instrument panels. He'd sat through a one-hour class on Boeing cockpits, and he focused on a small display window that read AUTOLAND3. He had been told that a computer-programmed autopilot could land these new-generation jets without the input of a human hand and brain. He didn't believe it when he'd heard it, but he believed it now.

There was no other explanation for how this airship of death had gotten here. An autopilot landing would also explain the near-miss with the US Airways jet, and would probably explain the lack of reverse thrust. For sure, McGill thought, it explained the hours of NO-RAD, not to mention the fact that this aircraft was sitting at the end of the runway, engines still running, with two long-dead pilots. *Mary, mother of God . . .* He felt sick and wanted to scream or vomit or run, but he stood his ground and took another deep breath. *Calm down, McGill.*

What next?

Ventilate.

He reached above his head for the escape hatch, activated the lever, and the hatch popped open, exposing a square of blue sky.

He stood a moment, listening to the now louder sound of the jet engines. He knew he should shut them down, but there seemed to be no risk of explosion, so he let them run so that the air exchange system on board could completely purge itself of whatever invisible toxin had caused this nightmare. The only thing he felt good about was the knowledge that even if he'd acted sooner, it wouldn't have changed anything. This was sort of like the Saudi Scenario, but it had happened while the aircraft was still aloft, far from here. There had been no fire, so the 747 hadn't crashed like the Swissair jet near the coast of Nova Scotia. In fact, whatever the problem was had affected only human life, not mechanical systems or electronics. The autopilot did what it was programmed to do, though McGill found himself wishing it hadn't.

McGill looked out the windshields into the sunlight. He wanted to be out there with the living, not in here. But he waited for the air conditioning systems to do their job and tried to remember how long it took to completely vent a 747. He was supposed to know these things, but he had trouble keeping his mind focused.

Calm down.

After what seemed like a long time, but was probably less than two minutes, McGill reached down to the pedestal between the flight seats and shut off the four fuel switches. Nearly all the lights on the console went off, except those powered by the aircraft's batteries, and the whine of the jet engines stopped immediately, replaced by an eerie silence.

McGill knew that outside the aircraft, everyone was breathing easier now that the engines had shut down. They also knew that Andy McGill was okay, but they didn't know that it was he, not the pilots, who had shut down the engines.

McGill heard a noise in the dome cabin, and he turned toward the cockpit door and listened again. He called out through his oxygen mask, "Anybody there?" Silence. Spooky silence. Dead silence. But he *had* heard something. Maybe the ticking of the cooling engines. Or a piece of hand luggage had shifted in the overhead compartment.

He took a deep breath and steadied his nerves. He recalled what a medical examiner once told him in a morgue. "The dead can't hurt you. No one's ever been killed by a dead man."

He looked into the dome cabin and saw the dead staring back at him. The coroner was wrong. The dead can hurt you and kill your soul. Andy McGill said a Hail Mary and crossed himself.

Chapter 9

I was getting antsy, but George Foster had established a commo link through Agent Jim Lindley down on the tarmac, who in turn was talking directly to one of the Port Authority cops nearby, and the PA cop had radio contact with his Command Center, who in turn had contact with the Tower, and with their Emergency Service units down on the runway.

I asked George, "What did Lindley say?"

"He said that an Emergency Service person has boarded the aircraft and the engines are shut down."

"Did the Emergency Service guy radio a situation report?"

"Not yet, but he broke squelch to signal that everything was okay."

"He broke squelch and they could hear that outside the plane? What did that guy have for lunch?"

Ted and Debbie laughed. Kate did not.

George drew an exasperated breath and informed me, *"Radio* squelch. The guy has an oxygen mask on, and it's easier to signal with squelch breaks than to try to talk—"

"I know," I interrupted. "Just kidding." You don't often get a great straight man like George Foster. Certainly not on the NYPD where everyone was a comedian, and every comedian wanted to be top banana.

Anyway, my act was wearing thin here at the steel door of Gate 23. I suggested to George, "Let me go outside and establish personal liaison with Lindley."

"Why?"

"Why not?"

George was torn between having me in his sight and getting me out of his sight, out of his face, and out of his life. I have that effect on superiors.

He said to everyone, "As soon as the Emergency Service guy gets our people off the aircraft and into a Port Authority car, Lindley will call me, and then we'll go down the stairs and onto the tarmac. It's about a thirty-second walk, so hold your horses. Okay?"

I wasn't going to argue with this guy. For the record, I said, "You're in charge."

Debra Del Vecchio's radio crackled. She listened, and informed us, "The Yankees tied it in the fifth."

So, we waited at the gate while circumstances beyond our control caused a minor delay in our plans. On the wall was a tourist poster showing a night view of the illuminated Statue of Liberty. Beneath the photo in about a dozen languages was Emma Lazarus' words, "Give me your tired, your poor, your huddled masses yearning to breathe free, the wretched refuse of your teeming shore. Send these, the homeless, tempest-tost to me, I lift my lamp beside the golden door!"

I learned that by heart in grade school. It still gave me goose bumps.

I looked at Kate, and we made eye contact. She smiled, and I smiled back. All things considered, this was better than lying in Columbia Presbyterian Hospital on life support systems. One of the docs told me later that if it weren't for a great ambulance driver and a great paramedic, I'd be wearing a toe tag instead of an ID bracelet. It was that close.

It does change your life. Not outwardly, but deep inside. Like friends of mine who saw combat in Vietnam, I sometimes feel like my lease ran out, and I'm on a month-to-month contract with God.

I realized that this was about the time of day I'd taken three bullets on West 102nd Street, and the first-year anniversary was three days ago. The day would have passed unmarked by me, but my ex-partner, Dom Fanelli, insisted on taking me out for drinks. To get into the spirit of the occasion, he'd taken me to a bar on West 102nd Street, a block from the happy incident. There were a dozen of my old buds there, and they had this big pistol range target of an outlined man labeled JOHN COREY, with three bullet holes in it. Cops are weird.

*   *   *

Andy McGill knew that everything he did or failed to do would come under microscopic scrutiny in the weeks and months ahead. He'd probably spend the next month or two testifying in front of a dozen state and Federal agencies, not to mention his own bosses. This disaster would become firehouse legend, and he wanted to be certain that he was the hero of that legend.

His mind went from the unknown future to the problematic present. What next?

He knew that with the engines shut down, they could be started again only by using the onboard auxiliary power unit, which was beyond his training, or by using an external auxiliary power unit that would have to be trucked out to the aircraft. But with no pilots to start the engines and taxi the airliner, what they actually needed was a Trans-Continental tug vehicle to get this aircraft off the runway and into the security area, out of sight of the public and the media. McGill put his radio to his face mask and called Sorentino. "Rescue One, this is Rescue Eight-One."

McGill could barely hear Sorentino's "Roger" through his head gear. McGill said, "Get a company tug here, ASAP. Copy?"

"Copy Trans-Continental tug. What's up?"

"Do it. Out."

McGill exited the cockpit, walked quickly through the dome and down the spiral staircase to the lower deck, then opened the second exit door across the fuselage from the one he'd entered.

He then pulled back the curtain to the Coach section and stared down the long, wide body of the 747. Facing him were hundreds of people, sitting up or reclining, perfectly still, as though it were a photograph. He kept staring, waiting for someone to move or to make a sound. But there was no movement, no response to his presence, no reaction to this alien in a silver space suit and mask.

He turned away, crossed the open area, and tore open the curtain to the First Class compartment and walked quickly through, touching a few faces, even slapping a few people to see if he could get a response.

There were absolutely no signs of life among these people, and a totally irrelevant thought popped into his head, which was that First Class round-trip tickets, Paris to New York, cost about ten thousand dollars. What difference did it make? They all breathed the same air, and now they were just as dead as the people in Economy Class.

McGill walked quickly out of the First Class compartment and back into the open space, which held the galley, the spiral staircase, and the two open doors. He went to the starboard side door and pulled his mask and headgear off.

Sorentino was standing on the running board of their RIV, and he called out to McGill, "What's up?"

McGill took a deep breath and called down, "Bad. Real bad."

Sorentino never saw his boss look like that, and he assumed that real bad meant the worst.

McGill said, "Call the Command Center...tell them everyone on board Flight One-Seven-Five is dead. Suspect toxic fumes—"

"Jesus Christ."

"Yeah. Have a Tour Commander respond to your call. Also, get a company rep over to the security area." He added, "In fact, get everyone over to the security area. Customs, Baggage, the whole nine yards."

"Will do." Sorentino disappeared inside the cab of the RIV.

McGill turned toward the Coach section. He was fairly certain he didn't need his Scott pack, but he carried it with him, though he left his crash ax against a bulkhead. He didn't smell anything that seemed caustic or dangerous, but he did smell a faint odor—it smelled familiar, then he placed it—almonds.

He parted the curtain, and trying not to look at the people facing him, he moved down the right aisle and popped open the two exit doors, then crossed the aircraft and opened the two left doors. He could feel a cross-breeze on his sweat-dampened face.

His radio crackled, and he heard a voice say, "Unit One, this is Lieutenant Pierce. Situation report."

McGill unhooked his handheld radio and responded to his Tour Commander, "Unit One. I'm aboard the subject aircraft. All souls aboard are dead."

There was a long silence, then Pierce replied, "Are you sure?"

"Yes."

Again, a long silence, then, "Fumes? Smoke? What?"

"Negative smoke. Toxic fumes. I don't know the source. Aircraft is vented, and I'm not using oxygen."

"Roger."

Again, a long silence.

McGill felt queasy, but he thought it was more the result of shock than of any lingering fumes. He had no intention of volunteering anything and he waited. He could picture a bunch of people in the Command Center all speaking at once in hushed tones.

Finally, Lieutenant Pierce came on and said, "Okay...you've called for a company tug."

"Affirmative."

"Do we need...the mobile hospital?"

"Negative. And the mobile morgue won't handle this."

"Roger. Okay...let's move this whole operation to the security area. Let's clear that runway and get that aircraft out of sight."

"Roger. I'm waiting for the tug."

"Yeah...okay...uh...stay on board."

"I'm not going anywhere."

"Do you want anyone else on board? Medical?"

McGill let out an exasperated breath. These idiots in the Command Center couldn't seem to comprehend that everyone was dead. McGill said, "Negative."

"Okay...so I...I guess the autopilot landed it."

"I guess. The autopilot or God. It wasn't me, and it wasn't the pilot or the co-pilot."

"Roger. I guess...I mean, the autopilot was probably programmed—"

"No 'probably' about it, Lieutenant. The pilots are cold."

"Roger...no evidence of fire?"

"Again, negative."

"Decompression?"

"Negative, no oxygen masks hanging. *Fumes.* Toxic fucking fumes."

"Okay, take it easy."

"Yeah."

"I'll meet you at the security area."

"Roger." McGill put his radio back on his hook.

With nothing left to do, he examined a few of the passengers, and again assured himself that there were no signs of life aboard. "Nightmare."

He felt claustrophobic in the crowded Coach compartment, creepy with all the dead. He realized he'd rather be in the relatively light and open space in the dome where he could better see what was happening around the aircraft.

He made his way out of Coach, up the spiral staircase, and into the dome. Through the port windows he saw a tug vehicle approaching. Through the starboard windows, he saw a line of Emergency Service vehicles heading back to the firehouse, and some heading toward the security area.

He tried to ignore the bodies around him. At least there were fewer of them up here, and none of them were children or babies. But no matter where he was on this aircraft, he thought, he was the only living, breathing soul aboard.

This wasn't precisely true, but Andy McGill didn't know he had company.

Tony Sorentino watched the Trans-Continental tug vehicle drive up to the nose wheels. The vehicle was a sort of big platform with a driver's cab at each end so that the driver could pull up to the nose wheel and not have to back up and chance causing damage. When the hookup was made, the driver would change cabs and drive off.

Sorentino thought this was clever, and he was fascinated by the vehicle. He wondered why Guns and Hoses didn't have one of these, then remembered that someone told him it had to do with insurance. Each airline had its own tugs and if they snapped off the nose wheel of a hundred-fifty-million-dollar aircraft, it was their problem. Made sense. Still, Guns and Hoses should have at least one tug. The more toys the better.

He watched as the Trans-Continental driver hooked a fork-like towbar to each side of the nose wheel assembly. Sorentino walked over to him and said, "Need a hand?"

"Nope. Don't touch nothing."

"Hey, I'm insured."

"Not for this you're not."

The hitch was complete, and the driver said, "Where we headed?"

"The hijack area," Sorentino said, using the more dramatic but still correct name for the security area.

The driver's eyes darted to Sorentino, as Sorentino knew they would. The driver glanced up at the huge aircraft towering above them, then back to Sorentino. "What's up?"

"Well, what's up is your insurance rates, pal."

"Whadda ya mean?"

"You got a big, expensive hearse here, buddy. They're all dead. Toxic fumes."

"Jesus Christ Almighty."

"Right. Let's get rolling. As fast as you can. I lead, you follow. I have a vehicle in trail. Don't stop until you're in the security pen."

The driver moved to the front cab as if he were in a daze. He climbed in, engaged the huge diesel, and began moving off.

Sorentino got into the cab of his RIV and moved off ahead of the tug vehicle, leading it to a taxiway that in turn led to the security area, not far from Runway Four-Right.

Sorentino could hear all kinds of chatter on his radio frequencies. No one sounded very happy. He broadcast, "Unit One moving, tug and aircraft in tow, Unit Four in trail."

Sorentino maintained a fifteen-mile-per-hour speed, which was all that the tug could do pulling a 750,000-pound aircraft behind it. He checked his sideview mirrors to make sure he wasn't too close or too far from the aircraft. The view in his mirrors was very strange, he thought. He was being followed by a weird vehicle that didn't know its ass from its dick, and behind the vehicle was this monster silver aircraft, being pulled along like a string toy. *Jesus, what a day this turned out to be.*

* * *

Inaction is not John Corey's middle name, and I said to George Foster, "I'm again requesting permission to go out to the tarmac."

Foster seemed indecisive as usual, so Kate said to me, "Okay, John, you have permission to go down to the tarmac. No further."

"I promise," I said.

Ms. Del Vecchio turned and punched in a code on the door's key-pad. The door opened, and I walked through it, down the long jetway, and descended the service stairs of the jetway to the tarmac.

The convoy that was to take us to Federal Plaza was grouped close to the terminal building. I moved quickly to one of the Port Authority police cars, flashed my tin, and said to the uniformed officer, "The subject aircraft is stalled at the end of the runway. I need to get to it now." I got into the passenger side, deeply regretting my lie to Kate.

The young PA cop said, "I thought the Emergency Service guys were bringing your passenger here."

"Change of plans."

"Okay…" He started driving slowly, and at the same time called Tower Control to get permission to cross the runways.

I was aware of someone running alongside the car and by the looks of him, he had to be FBI agent Jim Lindley. He called out, "Stop."

The Port Authority cop stopped the car.

Lindley identified himself and said to me, "Who are you?"

"Corey."

"Oh…where you going?"

"Out to the aircraft."

"Why?"

"Why not?"

"Who authorized—"

All of a sudden, Kate came up to the car and said, "It's okay, Jim. We're just going to check it out." She jumped in the back seat.

I said to the driver, "Let's go."

The driver said, "I'm waiting for permission to cross—"

A guy's voice came over the speaker and said, "Who's asking for permission to cross the runways and why?"

I grabbed the microphone and said, "This is..." Who was I? "This is the FBI. We need to get out to the aircraft. Who is this?"

"This is Mr. Stavros, Tower Control Supervisor. Look, you can't cross—"

"It's an emergency."

"I *know* there's an emergency. But why do you have to cross—"

I said, "Thank you." I told the Port Authority cop, "Cleared for take-off."

The PA cop protested, "He didn't—"

"Lights and siren. I really need you to do this for me."

The cop shrugged, and the car moved off the tarmac toward the taxiway, its flashers and siren going.

The Tower Control guy, Stavros, came on the speaker again, and I turned down the volume.

Kate spoke for the first time and said to me, "You lied to me."

"Sorry."

The PA cop cocked his thumb over his shoulder and asked me, "Who's that?"

"That's Kate. I'm John. Who are you?"

"Al. Al Simpson." He turned onto the grass and followed the taxiway east. The car bumped badly. He said, "Best to stay off the taxiways and runways."

"You're the boss," I informed him.

"What kind of emergency?"

"Sorry, I can't say." Actually, I had no idea.

Within a minute, we could see a big 747 silhouetted on the horizon.

Simpson turned and crossed over a taxiway, then headed across more grass, avoiding all kinds of signs and lights, and headed toward a big runway. He said to me, "I really need to call Tower Control."

"No, you don't."

"FAA regulations. You can't cross—"

"Don't worry about it. I'll keep an eye out for airplanes."

Simpson crossed the wide runway.

Kate said to me again, "If you're trying to get fired, you're doing a good job."

The 747 didn't look as though it were too far away, but it was an optical illusion and the silhouette didn't get much bigger as we traveled cross-country toward it. "Step on it," I said.

The patrol car bounced badly over a patch of rough terrain.

Kate asked me, "Do you have a theory you'd like to share with me?"

"No."

"No, you don't have a theory, or no, you don't want to share?"

"Both."

"Why are we doing this?"

"I got tired of Foster and Nash."

"I think you're showing off."

"We'll see when we get to the plane."

"You like to throw the dice, don't you?"

"No, I don't *like* to throw the dice. I *have* to throw the dice."

Officer Simpson was listening to Kate and me, but offered no insights and took no sides.

We drove on in silence, and the 747 still seemed out of reach, like a desert mirage.

Finally, Kate said, "Maybe I'll try to back you up."

"Thanks, partner." This, I guess, is what passes as unconditional loyalty amongst the Feds.

I looked at the 747 again, and this time it definitely hadn't gotten any bigger. I said, "I think it's moving."

Simpson peered out the window. "Yeah...but...I think they're towing it."

"Why would they tow it?"

"Well...I know they shut down the engines, so sometimes it's easier to get a tow instead of restarting them."

"You mean you don't just turn a key?"

Simpson laughed.

We were making better time than the 747 and the distance started to close. I said to Simpson, "Why aren't they towing it this way? Toward the terminal?"

"Well...it would seem to me that they're heading toward the hijack area."

"What?"

"I mean, the security area. Same difference."

I glanced back at Kate, and I could see she was concerned.

Simpson turned his radio volume up, and we listened to the radio traffic. What we heard was mostly orders, reports on the movement of vehicles, a lot of Port Authority mumbo jumbo that I couldn't make out, but no situation report. I guess everyone else knew the situation but us. I asked Simpson, "Can you tell what's going on?"

"Not really...but I can tell it's not a hijacking. Don't think it's mechanical either. I hear a lot of Emergency Service trucks going back to the house."

"How about medical?"

"Don't think so—I can tell by the call signs that they're not calling for backup medical—" He stopped short and said, "Uh-oh."

"Uh-oh, what?"

Kate leaned forward between us.

"Simpson? Uh-oh, what?"

"They're calling for the MM and the ME."

Which means Mobile Morgue and Medical Examiner, which means corpses.

I said to Simpson, "Step on it."

Chapter 10

Andy McGill peeled off his hot bunker suit and threw it on an empty seat beside a dead woman. He wiped the sweat from his neck and pulled the fabric of his dark blue police shirt away from his wet body.

His radio crackled, and he heard his call sign. He spoke into the mouthpiece, "Unit Eight-One. Go ahead."

It was Lieutenant Pierce again, and McGill winced. Pierce said in a patronizing voice, "Andy, we don't want to bug you, but we have to be sure, for the record, that we're not missing an opportunity to deliver medical aid to the passengers."

McGill glanced through the open cockpit door and out the windshield. He could see the opening of the enclosed security pen only about a hundred feet ahead. In fact, Sorentino was nearly at the gates now.

"Andy?"

"Look, I personally checked out about a hundred passengers in each of the three cabins—sort of like a survey. They are all cool and getting colder. In fact, I'm in the dome now, and it's starting to stink."

"Okay...just checking." Lieutenant Pierce continued, "I'm in the security area now, and I see you're almost here."

"Roger. Anything further?"

"Negative. Out."

McGill put the radio on his belt hook.

His eyes went to the three men he was supposed to escort out of the aircraft. He walked over to the two sitting together—the Federal agent and his cuffed prisoner.

McGill, because he was a cop first and a fireman second, thought he should retrieve the pistols so there would be no problem later if they disappeared. He opened the suit jacket of the agent and found the belt holster, but there was no piece in it. "What the hell...?"

He moved to the agent in the row behind and checked for a pistol, again finding the holster but no gun. Strange. Something else to worry about.

McGill realized he was very thirsty and moved to the rear galley. He knew he shouldn't be taking anything, but he was parched. He tried to ignore the stewardess on the floor as he looked around. He found a small can of club soda in the bar cabinet, fought with his conscience for half a second, then popped open the can and took a long swig. He decided he needed something stronger and unscrewed the top of a min- iature bottle of Scotch. He downed the Scotch in one gulp, chased it with club soda, and threw the can and bottle into the trash bin. He let out a little burp, and it felt good.

The aircraft was slowing, and he knew that when it stopped, the cabins would be swarming with people. Before that happened and before he had to talk to the bosses, he had to pee.

He stepped out of the galley, went to the door of the lavatory and pulled on it, but it was locked. The little red sign said OCCUPIED.

He stood there a second, confused. He'd checked the lav when he came into the dome. This made no sense. He tugged on the door again, and this time it opened.

Standing in the lavatory facing him was a tall, dark man wearing a blue jumpsuit with a Trans-Continental logo on the breast pocket.

McGill was speechless for a second, then managed to say, "How did you..."

He looked at the man's face and saw two deep black eyes boring into him.

The man raised his right hand, and McGill saw that the man had a lap blanket wrapped around his hand and arm, which seemed odd. "Who the hell are you?"

"I am Asad Khalil."

McGill barely heard the muffled sound of the shot and never felt the .40 caliber bullet piercing his forehead.

"And you are dead," said Asad Khalil.

*   *   *

Tony Sorentino passed through the opening of the security pen, aka the hijack area.

He looked around. This was a huge horseshoe-shaped enclosure with sodium vapor lights mounted on tall stanchions, and he was reminded of a baseball stadium, except that the whole area was paved with concrete.

He hadn't been in the security pen for a few years, and he looked around. The blast fence rose about twelve feet high, and every thirty feet or so was a shooter's platform behind the fence. Every platform had an armored shield with a gun slit, though no one was manning any of the positions as far as he could tell.

He looked in his sideview mirrors to be certain the tug guy hadn't panicked at the opening and stopped his vehicle. The fence on each side of the opening was low enough so that the wings of just about any commercial jetliner would clear, but the tug guys didn't always get it.

The tug was still behind Sorentino and the wings of the 747 sailed over the fence. "Keep moving, bozo. Follow Tony."

He glanced around at the scene spread out over the concrete. Nearly everyone had gotten here before him. He spotted the Mobile Incident Command Center, a huge van inside of which were radios, telephones, and bosses. They had direct communication with half the world, and by now they'd called the NYPD, the FBI, the FAA, maybe even the Coast Guard, who sometimes helped out with helicopters. For sure they'd called the Customs people and the Passport Control people. Even if the passengers were all dead, Sorentino thought, no one got into the USA without going through Customs and Passport Control. There were only two differences in today's procedures—one, everything would be done here and not at the terminal, and two, the passengers didn't have to answer any questions.

Sorentino slowed his RIV and checked his position and the position of the 747. A few more feet and they'd be centered.

Sorentino also spotted the mobile morgue and a bigger refrigerator truck near it, surrounded by a lot of people in white—the crew who would tag and bag the passengers.

On each side of the enclosure were mobile staircase trucks, six in all.

Standing near each mobile staircase were his own guys, Port Authority cops and EMS people, positioned to get on board and begin the shitty job of unloading the corpses.

He also saw a lot of Trans-Continental vehicles—trucks, conveyor belts, rollers, baggage carts, and a scissor truck to unload the baggage containers in the hold. There were about twenty Trans-Continental baggage handlers standing around in their blue jumpsuits, holding their leather gloves. These guys usually had to hustle or a supervisor was up their ass. But the unloading of Flight 175 was not going to be timed.

Sorentino also spotted a Port Authority mobile X-ray truck to check out the baggage. He also noticed four catering trucks, which weren't there to put food on board, he knew. The catering trucks, which could raise their cabins hydraulically to the level of the 747 doors, were actually the best way to unload bodies.

Everybody was here, he thought, everybody and everything that normally took place at the terminal was here. Everybody except the people waiting for Flight 175 to get to the gate. Those poor bastards, Sorentino thought, they'd be in a private room soon with Trans-Continental officials.

Sorentino tried to imagine Trans-Continental making all those notifications, keeping track of what morgue the bodies were in, getting the baggage and personal effects back to the families. *Jesus.*

And then, in a few days or weeks, when this 747 was all checked out and the problem was fixed, it would be back on the line, earning money for the company. Sorentino wondered if the passengers' families would get rebates on the tickets.

A Port Authority cop was standing in front of Sorentino's RIV now and motioning him forward a little, then the guy held up his hands and Sorentino stopped. He checked his sideview mirrors to make sure the idiot in the tug stopped, too, which he did. Sorentino reached up and turned off his rotating beam. He took a deep breath, then put his face into his hands and felt tears running down his cheeks, which surprised him because he didn't know he was crying.

Chapter II

Kate, Officer Simpson, and I didn't say much, we just listened to the patrol car radio. Simpson switched frequencies and made a call directly to one of the Emergency Service vehicles. He identified himself and said, "What's the problem with Trans-Continental One-Seven-Five?"

A voice came over the speaker and said, "Seems to be toxic fumes. No fire. All souls lost."

There was complete silence in the patrol car.

The speaker said, "Copy?"

Simpson cleared his throat and replied, "Copy, all souls lost. Out."

Kate said, "My God...can that be?"

Well, what more was there to say? Nothing. And that's what I said. Nothing.

Officer Simpson found the taxiway that led to the security area. There was no urgency any longer, and, in fact, Simpson slowed down to the fifteen-miles-per-hour speed limit, and I didn't say anything.

The sight in front of us was almost surreal—this huge aircraft lumbering along the taxiway toward this strange-looking wall of steel that had a wide opening in it.

The 747 passed through the opening in the wall, and the wings passed over the top of the wall.

Within a minute, we were up to the opening, but there were other trucks and cars ahead of us who'd waited until the 747 cleared. The other vehicles—an assortment of everything I'd ever seen on wheels—started to follow the 747, causing a small traffic jam.

I said to Simpson, "Meet us inside." I jumped out of the patrol car and started running. I heard a door slam behind me and heard Kate's footsteps gaining on me.

I didn't know why I was running, but something in my head said, "Run!" So I ran, feeling that little pencil-shaped scar area in my lung giving me a problem.

Kate and I did some broken-field running around the vehicles and within a minute we were inside this huge enclosure, filled with vehicles, people, and one 747. It looked like something out of *Close Encounters of the Third Kind*. Maybe the *X-Files*.

People who run attract attention, and we were stopped by a uniformed Port Authority cop, who was joined quickly by his sergeant. The sergeant said, "Where's the fire, folks?"

I tried to catch my breath and say, "FBI," but only managed a sort of whistle that came out of my bad lung.

Kate held up her Fed creds and said, without any huffing or puffing, "FBI. We have a fugitive and escorts aboard that aircraft."

I got my creds out and stuck the case in my outside breast pocket, still trying to catch my breath.

The Port Authority sergeant said, "Well, there's no rush." He added, "All dead."

Kate said, "We have to board the aircraft to take charge of... the bodies."

"We have people to do that, miss."

"Sergeant, our escorts are carrying guns as well as sensitive documents. This is a matter of national security."

"Hold on." He put his hand out, and the police officer beside him laid a radio in his palm. The sergeant transmitted and waited. He said to us, "Lots of radio traffic."

I was tempted to get uppity, but I waited.

The sergeant said, while we waited, "This bird came in total NO-RAD—"

"We know that," I said, happy that I'd picked up this jargon recently.

I looked at the 747, which had stopped in the center of the enclosure. Mobile staircases were being driven up to the doors, and soon there would be people on board.

The sergeant wasn't getting a reply to his call, so he said to us, "You see that Mobile Incident Command vehicle over there? Go talk to somebody in there. They're in direct contact with the FBI and my bosses."

Before he changed his mind, we hurried off toward the Mobile Command vehicle.

I was still breathing hard, and Kate asked me, "Are you okay?"

"I'm fine."

We both glanced over our shoulders and saw that the Port Authority sergeant was busy with something else. We changed course and headed toward the aircraft.

One mobile staircase was now in place at the rear of the aircraft, and a few Emergency Service guys were heading up the stairs followed by men and women in white, plus some guys in blue jumpsuits, and a guy in a business suit.

A gentleman never climbs a staircase behind a lady with a short skirt, but I gave it a try and motioned for Kate to go first. She said, "After you."

So we got on the stairs and went through the door of the aircraft and into the huge cabin. The only lights were emergency floor lights, probably powered by batteries. There was some illumination from the late afternoon sunlight through the port side windows. But you didn't need a lot of light to see that the cabin was about three-quarters full and that no one in the seats was moving.

The people who had entered with us stood motionless and quiet, and the only sounds came through the open doors.

The guy with the suit looked at Kate and me, and I saw he had a photo ID on his breast pocket. It was actually a Trans-Continental ID, and the guy looked awful. In fact, he said to us, "This is awful...oh, my God..."

I thought he was going to cry, but he got himself under control and said, "I'm Joe Hurley...Trans-Continental baggage supervisor..."

I said to him, "FBI. Look, Joe, keep your people out of the aircraft. This may be a crime scene."

His eyes opened wide.

I really didn't think at that point that this was a crime scene, but I wasn't totally buying the toxic fumes accident thing either. The best way to get control of a situation is to say, "Crime Scene," then everyone has to do what you say.

One of the Port Authority Emergency Service guys came over and said, "Crime scene?"

"Yeah. Why don't you all go to a door and hold up the traffic awhile until we look around. Okay? There's no rush collecting the carry-on baggage or the bodies."

The EMS guy nodded, and Kate and I moved quickly up the left aisle.

People were starting to come on board through the other open doors, and Kate and I held up our creds and called out, "FBI. Please stop where you are. Do not enter the aircraft. Please move back onto the staircases." And so forth.

This got the traffic slowed down, and people started to congregate at the doors. A Port Authority cop was on board, and he helped stop traffic as we made our way to the front of the aircraft.

Every now and then, I glanced over my shoulder and saw these faces staring into nowhere. Some had their eyes shut, some had their eyes open. *Toxic fumes*. But what *kind* of toxic fumes?

We got to this open area where there were two exit doors, a galley, two lavatories, and a spiral staircase. A bunch of people were jamming into the area, and we did our routine again, but it's hard to stop a tide of people at a disaster site, especially if they think they have business there. I said, "Folks, this is a possible crime scene. Get off the aircraft. You can wait on the stairs outside."

A guy in a blue jumpsuit was on the spiral staircase, and I called up to him, "Hey, pal. Get down from there."

People were moving back toward the exit doors, and the guy on the spiral staircase was able to get down to the last step. Kate and I squeezed our way past him, and we went up the staircase, me first.

I took the spiral stairs two at a time, and stopped as soon as I was able to see into the dome cabin. I didn't think I needed a gun, but when in doubt, pull it out. I drew my Glock and stuck it in my belt.

I stood in the dome cabin, which was brighter than downstairs. I wondered if the Emergency Service guy who had gone on board and discovered this was still on board. I called out, "Hey! Anybody home?"

I moved to the side to let Kate up. She came up and moved a few feet away from me, and I saw she hadn't drawn her piece. In fact, there seemed to be no reason to suspect that there was any danger on board. The Port Authority Emergency Service guy had reported that everyone was dead. But where was the guy?

We stood there and scoped the scene out. First things first, and the first thing was to make sure there wasn't any danger to us, and you have to check out closed doors first. A lot of bright detectives have had their clever deductions blown out of their brains while they were poking around a crime scene with their heads in a cloud.

In the rear of the dome was the lavatory to the left, and the galley to the right. I motioned to Kate, and she drew her piece from under her blazer as I moved toward the lav. The little sign said VACANT, and I pushed on the folding door and stood aside.

She said, "Clear."

In the galley, a stewardess lay on the floor on her side, and out of habit, I knelt down and felt her ankle for a pulse. Not only was there no pulse, she was cold.

Between the galley and the lav was a closet, so I covered while Kate opened the door. Inside were passengers' coats, jackets, hanging garment bags, and odds and ends on the floor. It's nice to travel Business Class. Kate poked around a few seconds, and we almost missed it but there it was. On the floor, under a trench coat, were two green oxygen bottles strapped to a wheeled cart. I checked both valves, and they were open. It took about three seconds for me to suspect that one bottle had held oxygen, and the other had held something not so good for you. Things were starting to come together.

Kate said, "These are medical oxygen bottles."

"Right." I could see she was also putting things together, but neither of us said anything.

Kate and I moved quickly up the aisle and stood at the cockpit door, which I could see had its lock smashed. I pulled on the door and it swung open. I stepped inside and saw that both pilots were slumped forward in their seats. I felt for a pulse in both their necks, but all I got was cold, clammy skin.

I noticed that the overhead hatch was open, and I guessed that the EMS guy who'd come on board had opened it to vent the cockpit. I stepped back into the dome cabin.

Kate was standing near the seats in the back of the cabin. I walked over to her and she said, "This is Phil Hundry..."

I looked at the guy sitting next to Hundry. He was wearing a black suit, his hands were cuffed, and he had a black sleeping mask over his face. I reached over and pulled the mask up. Kate and I both looked at the man, then finally she said, "Is that...? That doesn't look like Khalil."

I didn't think so either, but I didn't have a clear image of Khalil in my mind. Also, people's faces really transform in some weird way when they're dead. I said, "Well...he looks Arab...I'm not sure."

Kate reached out and ripped the man's shirt open. "No vest."

"No vest," I agreed. Something was very strange here, to say the least.

Kate was now leaning over the guy in the seat behind Phil Hundry, and she said to me, "This is Peter Gorman."

That at least was reassuring, two out of three wasn't bad. But where was Asad Khalil? And who was the stiff posing as Khalil?

Kate was now staring at the Arab guy and said to me, "This guy is...who? An accomplice? A victim?"

"Maybe both."

My mind was trying to sort all this out, but all I knew for sure was that everyone was dead, except maybe one guy who was playing dead. I looked around the cabin and said to Kate, "Keep an eye on these people. One of them may not be as dead as he looks."

She nodded and raised her pistol in a ready position.

"Let me have your phone," I said.

She took her flip phone from her blazer and handed it to me. "What's George's number?"

She gave it to me and I dialed. Foster answered and I said, "George, this is Corey—just listen, please. We're in the aircraft. The dome. Everyone is dead. Hundry and Gorman are dead—okay, I'm glad Lindley is keeping you informed. Yeah, we're in the dome, and the dome is on the plane, and the plane is in the security area. Listen up—the guy with Phil and Peter does not look like Khalil—that's what I said. The guy is cuffed, but he has no vest. No, I'm not certain it isn't Khalil. I don't have a photo with me. Kate isn't sure, either, and the photo we saw sucks. Listen…" My mind tried to come up with a plan of action, but I wasn't even sure what the problem was. I said, "If this guy next to Phil isn't Khalil, then Khalil may still be on board. Yeah. But he may have slipped off the plane already. Tell Lindley to tell the Port Authority guys to call their bosses ASAP and have the security area sealed off. Don't let anybody out of this enclosure."

Foster wasn't interrupting, but I could hear him mumbling things like, "Good Lord…my God…how did this happen…awful, awful…" and other genteel mush.

I said, "Khalil has apparently killed two of our people, George, and the score is Lion, a few hundred, Feds, zero. Put out an alert around the airport. Do what you can with that. What can I tell you? An Arab guy. See if you can get this whole airport sealed up, too. If this guy gets out of here, we've got a problem. Yeah. Call Federal Plaza. We'll set up a command post at the Conquistador Club. Get all of this rolling as soon as possible. And tell Ms. Del Vecchio the aircraft will not be proceeding to the gate." I hung up and said to Kate, "Go down and tell the PA cops we need the enclosure sealed tight. People can come in, but nobody gets out. Roach motel."

She hurried down the staircase, and I stood where I was, looking at the faces around me. If that wasn't Khalil next to Hundry—and I was about ninety percent certain it wasn't—then Khalil could still be on board. But if he'd acted quickly, he was already out in the security enclosure with about two hundred other people—people who had on every kind of clothing imaginable, including business suits like the Trans-Continental supervisor. And if Khalil acted very quickly, and very decisively, he was already on some kind of vehicle headed out of here. The airport barrier fence was close by, and the terminals weren't more than two miles from here. "Damn it!"

Kate came back up the stairs and said, "Done. They understand."

"Good." I said to her, "Let's check these people out."

We both moved up the aisle and examined the dozen or so male bodies in the dome cabin. One of the passengers had a Stephen King novel on his lap, which turned out to be appropriate. I got to a guy whose body was completely covered with two lap blankets. He had a black sleeping mask on his forehead, and I pulled it off and saw that the guy had sprouted a third eye in the middle of his forehead. "Over here."

Kate came over to me as I pulled the lap blankets off the body. The guy was wearing a navy blue police shirt and BDU pants. On the shirt was a Port Authority police emblem. I let the blankets fall to the floor and said to Kate, "That's got to be the EMS guy who boarded the aircraft."

She nodded and said, "What has happened here?"

"Nothing good."

You're not supposed to touch things at a crime scene unless you're trying to save a life, or if you think the perp is around, and you're supposed to use latex gloves, but I didn't even have a condom on me— nevertheless, we checked out the other bodies, but they were all dead, and they were all not Asad Khalil. We looked for, but didn't find a shell casing. We also popped open all the overhead compartments, and in one of them, Kate found a silver fire suit, fire ax, and an oxygen pack with a fire mask, all of which obviously belonged to the dead EMS guy.

Kate went back to Phil Hundry. She pulled Hundry's jacket open to reveal his belt holster, which was empty. There was an FBI badge case pinned inside Hundry's jacket, and she pulled it off, then took his breast pocket wallet and passport.

I went over to Peter Gorman, opened his jacket, and said to Kate, "Gorman's gun is also missing." I recovered Gorman's CIA credentials, passport, wallet, and also the keys to the handcuffs, which were obviously returned to Gorman's pocket after they'd been used to uncuff Khalil. What I didn't find was any extra Glock magazines.

I checked the overhead rack, and there was an attaché case there. It was unlocked, and I opened it and saw it belonged to Peter Gorman.

Kate retrieved Hundry's attaché case and also opened it.

We rummaged around the attaché cases, which held their cell

phones, papers, and some personal items, such as toothbrushes, combs, tissues, and such, but again, no extra magazines. There were no overnight bags because agents are supposed to travel hands-free, except for the attaché case. As for the real Khalil, the only thing they'd let him have was the clothes on his back and, therefore, his dead double was clean, too.

Kate said to me, "Khalil didn't take any personal items from Phil or Peter. Not their passports, not the creds, not even their wallets."

I opened Gorman's wallet and saw about two hundred dollars in cash and some French francs. I said, "He didn't take Gorman's money either. He's telling us he has lots of resources in America, and we can keep the money." I added, "He's got all the ID and cash he needs, plus his hair is blond by now, and he's a woman."

"But you'd think he'd take all this as a screw-you gesture. They usually do. They show it to their buddies. Or bosses."

"The guy's a pro, Kate. He doesn't want to get caught with hard evidence."

"He took the guns," she pointed out.

"He needed the guns," I said.

Kate nodded and put all the items in the attaché cases and said, "These were good guys."

I could see she was upset, and her upper lip was trembling.

I got on the phone again and called Foster. I said, "Phil's and Peter's guns and magazines are missing—yeah. But their creds are intact. Also, the EMS guy on board is dead—shot through the head. That's right. The murder weapon was probably one of the missing Glocks." I gave him a quick update and said, "Consider the perp armed and real dangerous." I signed off.

The cabin was getting warm now, and a faint, unpleasant odor was starting to fill the air. I could hear gases escaping from some of the bodies.

Kate had moved back to the cuffed man and was feeling his face and neck. She said, "He's definitely warmer. He died only about an hour ago, if that."

I was trying to piece this together, and I had a few pieces in my hands, but some pieces were scattered around the aircraft, and some were back in Libya.

Kate said, "If he didn't die with everyone else, how did he die?" She pulled open his jacket, but there were no signs of blood. She pushed his head and shoulders forward to check for wounds. The head, which had been resting comfortably against the back of the seat, rolled to the side in a very unnatural way. She rotated the man's head and said, "His neck is broken."

Two Port Authority Emergency Service cops came up the spiral stairs into the dome. They looked around, then they looked at Kate and me. One of them asked, "Who are you?"

"FBI," Kate replied.

I motioned the guy toward me and said, "This man here and that guy behind him are Federal agents, and the guy in cuffs is their...was their prisoner. Okay?"

He nodded.

I continued, "The FBI crime lab people will want photos and the whole nine yards, so let's leave this whole section as it is."

One of the guys was looking over my shoulder. "Where's McGill?" He looked at me. "We lost radio contact. You see an Emergency Service guy up here?"

"No," I lied. "Only dead people. Maybe he went downstairs. All right, let's get out of here."

Kate and I took both attaché cases, and we all moved toward the staircase. I asked one of the Emergency Service cops, "Can this aircraft land itself? Like on autopilot?"

"Yeah...the autopilot would bring it in...but...jeez, you think they were all dead?...yeah...the NO-RAD..."

The two Emergency Service cops started talking a mile a minute. I heard the words NO-RAD, reverse thrusters, toxic fumes, something called the Saudi Scenario, and the name Andy, who I guessed was McGill.

We were all in the open area below, and I said to one of the PA cops, "Please stand on these stairs and don't let anyone up to the dome until the FBI crime lab comes."

"I know the drill."

The curtains to the Coach and First Class section had been tied back, and I could see that the cabin was clear, but people still congregated at the doors on the mobile staircase.

I could feel and hear thumping below my feet, and I knew that the baggage handlers were clearing out the hold. I said to one of the Port Authority police officers, "Stop the unloading of the baggage, and please get everyone away from the aircraft."

We entered the First Class compartment, which held only twenty seats, half of which were empty. We did a quick search of the area. Although I wanted to get moving and off this aircraft, we were the only two Feds on the scene—the only two live Feds—and we needed to gather what information we could. As we poked around, Kate said, "I think Khalil gassed this whole aircraft."

"It would appear so."

"He must have had an accomplice who had those two oxygen bottles that we found in the closet."

"One oxygen, one not."

"Yes, I understand that." She looked at me and said, "I can't believe Phil and Peter are dead...and Khalil...we lost our prisoner."

"Defector," I corrected.

She gave me an annoyed look, but said nothing.

It occurred to me that there were a hundred easier ways for a bad guy to slip into the country. But this guy—Asad Khalil—had picked about the most in-your-face-fuck-you way I could imagine. This was one bad dude. And he was loose in America. A lion in the streets. I didn't even want to think what he was going to do next to top this act.

Kate was thinking along similar lines and said, "Right under our noses. He killed over three hundred people before he even landed."

We moved out of the First Class compartment into the open area near the spiral staircase. I said to the Port Authority cop I had asked to guard the staircase, "By the way, what's the Saudi Scenario?"

The guy explained it to Kate and me, and added, "This is something different. This is a new one."

Kate and I moved away from the PA cop, and I said to her, "How about the Dracula Scenario?"

"What do you mean?"

"You know—Count Dracula is in a coffin on a ship from Transylvania to England. His accomplice opens the coffin, and Dracula gets out and sucks the blood of every man on board. The ship comes in by itself, like magic, with all the crew and passengers dead, and Dracula slips off into the peaceful country of England to commit more unholy horrors." If I were a good Catholic, I would have crossed myself right there and then.

Kate stared at me, wondering, I guess, if I was nuts or in shock. I'm definitely nuts, and I admit to being a little in shock. I mean, I thought I'd seen it all by now, but there are few people on earth who'd seen anything like this, except maybe in war. Actually, this *was* war.

I looked into the big Coach cabin and saw that the paramedics had talked themselves on board. They were going through the aisles, making pronouncements of death, and neatly tagging each body with a seat and aisle number. Later, each body would be bagged. Tag and bag. What a mess.

I stood near the starboard side door and breathed some fresh air. I had the feeling we were missing something—something of great importance. I asked Kate, "Should we look through the dome again?"

She contemplated the question and replied, "I think we gave it a good once-over. Galley, lav, cockpit, closet, cabin, overheads...Forensics will be happy we didn't pollute the scene too much."

"Yeah..." There was still something I'd forgotten, or maybe overlooked...I thought about the Fed creds and wallets and passports that Khalil didn't take, and although I'd explained that to Kate and to myself, I was beginning to wonder why Khalil didn't take that stuff. Assuming everything he did had a purpose, what was the purpose of doing the opposite of what we'd expect?

I racked my brains, but nothing was clicking.

Kate was looking through one of the attaché cases and said to me, "There doesn't seem to be anything missing here either, not even Khalil's dossier or the crypto sheets, or even our instruction memo from Zach Weber—"

"Wait a minute."

"What's the matter?"

It was starting to come together. "He's trying to make us think he's done with us. Mission complete. He wants us to think he's headed into the International Departures building, and he's clean going in there. He wants us to think he's headed out on a flight somewhere, and he doesn't want this stuff on him in case he's spot-checked."

"I'm not following. He is or he isn't trying to catch an outbound flight?"

"He wants us to think he is, but he isn't."

"Okay...so he's staying here. He's probably out of the airport by now."

I was still trying to put this together. I said, "If he didn't take the creds because he wanted to be clean, why did he take the guns? He wouldn't take the guns into the terminal, and if he escaped from the airport, there would be an accomplice with a gun for him. So...why does he need two guns inside the airport...?"

"He's prepared to shoot his way out," Kate said. "He kept the bulletproof vest on him. What are you thinking?"

"I'm thinking..." All of a sudden, I thought of the February defector, and this totally unbelievable thought popped into my head. "Oh, shit...!" I ran to the spiral staircase and barreled past the guy I'd posted there, took the steps three at a time, and charged into the dome, moving quickly to Phil Hundry. I grabbed his right arm, which I now noticed had been sort of tucked close to his body with his hand wedged between his thigh and the center armrest. I pulled his arm up and took a look at his hand. The thumb was missing, cleanly severed by a sharp instrument. "Damn!"

I grabbed Peter Gorman's right arm, pulled it away from his body, and saw the same mutilation.

Kate was beside me now, and I held up Gorman's lifeless arm and hand.

She seemed shocked and confused for about one half second, then said, "Oh, no!"

We both charged down the spiral stairs, out the door, and tore down the mobile stairs, knocking a few people aside. We found the

Port Authority police car we'd come in, and I jumped in the front while Kate jumped in the back. I said to Simpson, "Lights and siren. Let's get moving."

I pulled Kate's cell phone out of my pocket and called the Conquistador Club. I waited for Nancy Tate to answer, but there was no answer. I said to Kate, "Conquistador is not answering."

"Oh, God…"

Simpson headed toward the opening in the security enclosure, weaving through a dozen parked vehicles, but when we got to the opening in the wall, we were stopped by Port Authority cops, who informed us that the area was sealed. "I know," I said, "I'm the guy who had it sealed." The cops didn't give a shit.

Kate handled it properly, holding up her FBI credentials, using a little logic, a little pleading, a little threatening, and some common sense. Officer Simpson helped, too. I kept my mouth shut. Finally, the PA cops waved us through.

I said quickly to Simpson, "Okay, listen. We have to get to the west end of the airport where all those service buildings are. The most direct and fastest route."

"Well, the perimeter road—"

"No. Direct and fast. Runways and taxiways. Move."

Officer Simpson hesitated and said, "I can't go on the runway unless I call the Tower. Stavros is pissed—"

"This is a ten-thirteen," I informed him, which means Cop in Trouble.

Simpson hit the gas, as any cop would do with a 10-13.

Kate asked me, "What's a ten-thirteen?"

"Coffee break."

After we'd cleared a bunch of vehicles, I said to Simpson, "Now pretend you're an airplane and get up to take-off speed. Hit it."

He put the pedal to the metal and the big Chevy Caprice accelerated down the smooth concrete runway like it had afterburners. Simpson got on his radio and told the Tower what he was doing. The Tower guy sounded like he was going to have a coronary.

Meanwhile, I whipped out the cell phone and dialed the

Conquistador Club again, but there was no answer. "Shit!" I dialed Foster's cell phone and he answered. I said, "George, I'm trying to call Nick—Yeah…Okay, I'm on my way there. Whoever gets there first, use caution. I think Khalil is headed that way. That's what I said. Khalil took Phil's and Peter's thumbs—Yeah. You heard me right."

I put the phone in my pocket and said to Kate, "George couldn't get through either."

She said, softly, "God, I hope we're not too late."

The car was doing a hundred now, eating up the runway.

In the distance I saw the old building in which the Conquistador Club was housed. I wanted to tell Simpson there was no need to hurry any longer, but I couldn't bring myself to do that, and we were up to a hundred and ten. The car began to shimmy, but Simpson didn't seem to notice or care. He glanced at me, and I said, "Eyes on the road."

"Runway."

"Whatever. See that long glass building? At some point, start to decelerate, find a service road or taxiway, and go toward that building."

"Right."

As we got closer, I saw an upside-down 3IR painted on the runway, and further on I could see that the runway ended, and I realized there was a high chain-link fence separating us from the building. We shot past a service road that looked like it headed toward a gate in the fence, but the gate was a hundred yards to the right of where I needed to be. Simpson suddenly veered off the runway, and the car two-wheeled for a few seconds, then came down with a big thump and bounce.

Simpson took his foot off the gas but didn't brake. We literally sailed and skimmed across the grass, pointed directly at the building beyond the fence. The Caprice hit the chain link and went through it like it wasn't there.

The car settled down onto the blacktop, Simpson hit the brakes, and I could feel the anti-lock mechanism pumping and pulsating as Simpson fought the wheel for control. The car skidded and fishtailed, then came to a screeching halt about ten feet from the building's entrance. I was half out of the car and said to Simpson, "Stop anyone coming out of the building. The perp is armed."

I drew my piece and as I ran toward the entrance, I noticed our escort vehicles from Gate 23 approaching across the far side of the parking lot. I also noticed a Trans-Continental baggage cart vehicle near the building. This did not belong there, but I thought I knew how it got there.

Kate passed me and ran into the building, gun drawn. I followed and said, "Cover the elevators." I ran up the staircase.

I stopped short of the hallway, stuck my head out and looked both ways, then ran down the corridor and stopped beside the door of the Conquistador Club, my back to the wall, out of sight of the scanning video camera whose monitors were all over the offices inside.

I reached out and pressed my right thumb to the translucent scanner, and the door slid open. I knew it would close again in three seconds, and as a security feature, it would not open again for three long minutes, unless someone inside opened it. So, I spun into the doorway just as it began closing, then crouched with my automatic extended, sweeping the reception area.

Nancy Tate was not at her desk, but her chair was against the back wall, and her phone was ringing insistently. Keeping my back to the wall, I came around the long, counter-type desk and saw Nancy Tate on the floor, a bullet hole in her forehead and a puddle of blood on the plastic mat, wet and gleaming around her face and hair. This did not surprise me, but it made me angry. I prayed that Asad Khalil was still here.

I knew I had to stay put to cover both doors that led from the reception room, and it was only a few seconds before I saw Kate on the monitor mounted on Nancy's desk. Behind her were George Foster and Ted Nash. I reached out and hit the door button, shouting, "Clear!"

The three of them barreled into the reception room, guns drawn. I spoke quickly, "Nancy is on the floor here. Gunshot wound to the head. Kate and I will go into the Ops Center, you two check out the other side."

They did what I said and disappeared through the doorway leading to the cells and interrogation rooms.

Kate and I moved quickly into the big operations and control center, taking minimum precautions. I think we both knew that Asad Khalil was long gone.

I walked over to the desk where we'd all sat not so long ago. All the chairs were empty, all the coffee mugs were empty, and Nick Monti lay on the floor, facing up at the high ceiling, his eyes wide open, and a big pool of blood around his body. His white shirt showed at least two entry wounds in the chest, and he hadn't had time to go for his gun, which was still in his holster. I bent over him and checked for a pulse, but there wasn't any.

Kate walked quickly up the three steps to the communications platform, and I followed. The duty officer had obviously had a few seconds to react because she was out of her chair and crumpled against the far wall beneath the huge electronic maps of the world. There was blood splattered on the wall and all over her white blouse. Her holster hung over the back of a chair along with her blue blazer and her pocketbook. Again, I checked for signs of life, but she was dead.

The room murmured and crackled with electronics and a few voices came faintly through the speakers. A Teletype was clattering, and a fax machine went off. On the console was a tray of sushi and two chopsticks. I looked again at the dead duty officer against the wall. The last thing she expected today was trouble in the very heart of one of the most secure and secret facilities in the country.

Foster and Nash were in the room now, looking at Nick Monti. Two Port Authority uniformed cops were also in the room, also looking at Monti and sort of gawking at the facility. I yelled out, "Get an ambulance!" We didn't really need one, but this is what you have to say.

Kate and I came down from the commo platform, and all four of us moved off to a corner. George Foster looked white, as if he'd seen his efficiency report. Ted Nash looked, as always, inscrutable, but I saw a look of worry cross his face.

No one spoke. What was there to say? We'd all been made to look like the fools we probably were. Beyond our little career problems, hundreds of people were dead, and the guy who caused this massacre was about to disappear into a metropolitan area of sixteen million people, which might be half that number this time tomorrow if the guy had access to something nuclear, chemical, or biological.

Clearly, we had a major problem. Clearly, too, neither Ted Nash,

George Foster, Kate Mayfield, nor John Corey needed to trouble themselves about it. If the ATTF operated the way the NYPD did, we'd all be transferred to school crossing guard duty.

But at least Nick Monti would be given an Inspector's Funeral, and a posthumous medal of honor. As I said, I wondered what the outcome of this would have been if I'd stayed behind instead of Nick. Probably I'd be lying where he was, about to get my body outlined in chalk.

I stared at the desk where we all had sat, and I tried to imagine Khalil running into the room, looking left and right, seeing Monti, Monti seeing him…The offensive guy always has the edge. And Nick didn't even know he was in the game. He thought he was on the sidelines.

Everyone saw me looking at the desk and at Nick, and they were not as stupid or insensitive as they seemed, so they figured what was going through my head, and George took me by the shoulder and turned me away. Kate said, "Let's get out of here."

No one argued with that. Nash gathered the dossiers from the desk, and where there had been five—one for each of us—there were now four. Obviously, Mr. Khalil had helped himself to one of them, and now he knew what we knew about him. Incredible.

We walked back to the reception area that was becoming filled with NYPD and Port Authority cops. Someone had found the security disarming switch, and the door was in the open position.

I took Khalil's photo out of one of the dossiers and went over to a uniformed Port Authority lieutenant and gave him the photo. I said, "This is the suspect. Get this out to every cop on duty. Tell them to stop and search every vehicle leaving this airport. Check the parking lots, taxis, trucks, even official vehicles."

"That's already in the works. Also, I've put out a citywide alert."

Kate added, "Also, check the departure terminals for this guy."

"Will do."

I said to the lieutenant, "There's a Trans-Continental vehicle outside. One of those baggage cart trucks. I think that's what the perp arrived in, so have it towed into a processing area. Let us know if you find a Trans-Continental uniform or jumpsuit anyplace."

The PA lieutenant got on his radio and called his command center.

The wheels were starting to move, but Asad Khalil had moved faster, and the chances of bottling him up inside this airport had passed about ten or fifteen minutes ago.

Foster was getting upset with all these NYPD and Port Authority people milling around, so he said, "Okay, everyone please clear out. This is a crime scene, and we want to preserve it for the lab. Keep someone at the door. Thank you."

Everyone left except for a Port Authority sergeant, who motioned us over to Nancy's desk. He pointed to an empty teacup and we looked at it. Sitting in the cup, in about a half inch of tea, were two thumbs.

The sergeant asked, "What the hell is that?"

George Foster replied, "I have no idea," although he knew where the thumbs came from, and why they were no longer attached to their owners' hands. But it's best to get into the cover-up mode very quickly and to stay in that mode right up until the moment you're under oath. And even then, a few memory lapses are okay. National security and all that.

So, what started out as a routine assignment ended up as the crime of the century. Shit happens, even on a nice spring day.

Chapter 12

We all walked out of the Conquistador Club into the sunlight and saw more vehicles pulling up. Our team leader, Mr. George Foster, said to us, "I'll call headquarters and have all our stakeouts alerted and increased."

The ATTF, by the way, stakes out houses of known and suspected terrorists, bomb chuckers, their friends, families, and sympathizers. The NYPD guys who work for the ATTF supply the shoe leather for this. The Feds give the city of New York more money than the job is worth, and everyone is happy.

Foster went on, "We'll increase phone taps, pull in some informants, and put Khalil's photo out to every law enforcement agency in the country."

George Foster went on a bit, making sure we knew he was on top of things, and building up everyone's confidence and morale, not to mention creating some credibility for himself for the moment when he had to kiss major ass.

And speaking of that, eventually someone who we couldn't totally bullshit was going to show up here, so I suggested, "Maybe we should go back to Federal Plaza and on our way there get our facts straight."

Everyone thought that was a fine idea. Troubled minds think alike.

We needed a scapegoat to stay behind, however, and Foster knew that he was it. He said, "You three go ahead. I have to stay here and... brief whoever shows up. Also, I have to put out the alert, and get the crime lab here." He added, to convince himself, I think, "I can't leave. This is a secure FBI facility, and..."

I added helpfully, "And there's no one left to secure it."

He looked annoyed for the first time since I'd met him. He said to me, "It's a restricted area with classified data and..." He wiped some sweat off his lip and looked at the ground.

George Foster was realizing, of course, that Mr. Asad Khalil had known about this sanctum sanctorum, had penetrated into the heart of it, and taken a crap on the floor. Foster also knew how this had happened vis-à-vis February's bogus defector. There were six tons of shit about to fall on George Foster, and he knew it. To his credit, he said, "This is my responsibility and my...my..." He turned and walked away.

Mr. Ted Nash, of course, belonged to an organization that specialized in sidestepping tons of falling shit, and I knew that nothing was going to splatter his bespoken suit. He turned and walked toward Simpson's patrol car.

As for me, having been recently assigned to this sterling team, I was pretty clean and would probably stay that way, unless Nash figured out a way to push me under the shit storm. Maybe that's why he wanted me around. Kate Mayfield, like George Foster, had no umbrella, but she'd covered herself a little by joining me in my ride to the aircraft. I said to her, "I've got nothing to lose here, and I *will* try to cover for you."

She forced a smile and replied, "Thanks, but we'll just tell it like it happened and let Washington decide if any of us is at fault."

I rolled my eyes, but she pretended not to notice. She added, "I intend to stay on this case."

"You'll be lucky if they don't put you back into Accounting."

She informed me coolly, "We don't operate like that. It is policy to keep an agent on a case that he or she has bungled, as long as you're straight with them and don't lie to them."

"Really? I think the Boy Scouts have a similar policy."

She didn't reply.

A horn was honking, and it was Ted Nash waiting impatiently in the passenger seat of Officer Simpson's car. We walked over to the car and got in the back where the two attaché cases sat. Nash said to us, "Officer Simpson has gotten permission to take us to lower Manhattan."

Simpson informed us, "I'm so deep in shit because of you guys, it doesn't matter what I do anymore."

Kate said, "I'll take care of it. You did a fine job."

"Whoopie," said Officer Simpson.

We rode in silence a few minutes, out toward one of the exits near the warehouses.

Finally, Nash said to me, "You did a good job, Detective."

This sort of caught me by surprise, including the use of my former exalted title. I was speechless, and I began thinking that maybe I'd gotten old Ted all wrong. Maybe we could bond, maybe I should reach out and tousle his hair and say, "You big galoot—I love you!"

Anyway, we got to an exit gate, and a Port Authority cop waved us on with barely a look. Obviously, the word hadn't gotten out to everyone. I told Simpson to stop.

I got out of the car and flashed my Fed creds and said to the guy, "Officer, have you gotten the word to stop and search all vehicles?"

"Yeah...but not police cars."

This was frustrating, and it pissed me off. I reached into the car and retrieved a dossier. I took out the photo and showed it to him. "Have you seen this guy?"

"No...I think I'd remember that face."

"How many vehicles have come through here since you got the alert?"

"Not many. It's Saturday. Maybe a dozen."

"Did you stop and search them?"

"Yeah...but they were all big trucks filled with crates and boxes. I can't open every box, unless it looks like the Customs seal has been tampered with. All the drivers had their Customs stuff in order."

"So you didn't open any crates?"

The guy was getting a little pissed at me and said, "I need some backup for that. That could take all day."

"How many vehicles passed through here right before you got the alert?"

"Maybe...two or three."

"What kind of vehicles?"

"Couple of trucks. A taxi."

"Passenger in the taxi?"

"I didn't notice." He added, "It was before the alert."

"Okay…" I gave him the photo and said, "This guy is armed and dangerous, and he's already killed too many cops today."

"Jesus."

I got back in the car and we proceeded. I noted that the PA cop didn't start with us and make us open the trunk, which is what I would have done if some wise-ass just busted my balls. But America wasn't ready for any of this. Not at all ready.

We got on the parkway and headed back toward Manhattan.

We drove in silence awhile. The Belt Parkway traffic was what the helicopter traffic idiot would call moderate to heavy. Actually, it was heavy to horrible, but I didn't care. I watched Brooklyn pass by out the right window, and I said to my Federal friends, "There are sixteen million people in the metropolitan area, eight million in New York City. Among them are about two hundred thousand newly arrived immigrants from Islamic countries, about half of them here in Brooklyn."

Neither Kate nor Nash commented.

Regarding Khalil, if he had indeed disappeared into these teeming millions, could the ATTF root him out? Maybe. The Mideastern community was pretty closed, but there were informants, not to mention loyal Americans amongst them. The underground terrorist network was badly compromised, and to give the Feds credit, they had a good handle on who was who.

So, for that reason, Asad Khalil was not going to make contact with the usual suspects. No one who was bright enough to pull off what he'd just pulled off was going to be stupid enough to join up with anyone less intelligent than he was.

I considered Mr. Khalil's audacity, which his sympathizers would call bravery. This man was going to be a challenge, to say the least.

Finally, Nash said to no one in particular, "About a million people slip into this country illegally every year. It's not that difficult. So, what I think is that our guy's mission was not to get into the country to commit an act of terrorism. His mission was to do what he did on the aircraft and at the Conquistador Club, then get out. He never left the airport and unless the Port Authority police have caught him, he's on an outbound plane right now. Mission accomplished."

I said to Ted Nash, "I've already discarded that theory. Catch up."

He replied tersely, "I've discarded the other possibilities. I say he's airborne."

I recalled the Plum Island case, and Mr. Nash's illogical reasoning and far-out conspiracy theories. Obviously the man had been trained beyond his intelligence and had forgotten how to even spell common sense. I said to him, "Ten bucks says we hear from our boy very soon and very close by."

Nash replied, "You're on." He turned in his seat and said to me, "You have no experience in these things, Corey. A trained terrorist is not like a stupid criminal. They hit and run, then hit and run again, sometimes years later. They don't revisit the scene of their crimes, and they don't go hide out at their girlfriend's house with a hot gun and a bag of loot, and they don't go to a bar and brag about their crimes. He's airborne."

"Thank you, Mr. Nash." I wondered if I should strangle him or smash his skull in with my gun butt.

Kate said, "That's an interesting theory, Ted. But until we know for sure, we're alerting the entire ATTF Mideast section to stake out all houses of known terrorist sympathizers and suspects."

Nash replied, "I have no problem with standard operating procedure. But I'll tell you this—if this guy is still in the country, the last place you're going to find him is where you think he'll show up. The February guy never showed up after he bolted, and he never will. If these two guys are connected, they represent something new and unknown. Some group we know nothing about."

I'd already figured that out. Also, on one level, I hoped he was right about Khalil being airborne. I wouldn't mind losing the ten bucks, even to this schmuck, and much as I'd like to get my hands on Asad Khalil and lump him up until his mother couldn't recognize him, I really wanted him someplace else, where he couldn't do any further damage to the good old US of A. I mean, a guy who would kill a planeload of innocent people undoubtedly had an atomic bomb up his sleeve, or anthrax in his hat, or poison gas up his ass.

Simpson asked, "Are we talking, like, Arab terrorist?"

I replied bluntly, "We're talking the mother of all terrorists."

Nash said to Simpson, "Forget everything you heard."

"I heard nothing," replied Simpson.

As we approached the Brooklyn Bridge, Kate said to me, "I think you may be late for your date on Long Island."

"How late?"

"About a month."

I didn't reply.

She added, "We'll probably fly to Washington first thing tomorrow."

This was the Fed equivalent, I guess, of going to One Police Plaza to face the music and dance. I wondered if there was an escape clause in my hiring contract. I had it in my desk at Federal Plaza. I'd have to give it a quick read.

We went over the bridge and exited into the canyons of lower Manhattan. No one said much, but you could smell the brain cells burning.

Police cars don't have regular AM/FM radios, but Officer Simpson had a portable radio, and he tuned to 1010 WINS News. A reporter was saying, "The aircraft is still in the fenced-off security area out by one of the runways, and we can't see what's going on, though we've seen vehicles arriving and leaving the area. What appeared to be a large refrigerated truck left the area a few minutes ago, and there is speculation that this truck was transporting bodies."

The reporter paused for effect, then continued, "Authorities haven't released an official statement, but a spokesperson from the National Transportation Safety Board told reporters that toxic fumes had overcome the passengers and crew, and there *are* some fatalities. The aircraft, though, has landed safely, and all we can do is hope and pray that there are few fatalities."

The anchorwoman asked, "Larry, we're hearing rumors that the aircraft was out of radio contact for several hours before it landed. Have you heard anything about that?"

Larry, the on-the-scene guy, said, "The FAA has not confirmed that, but an FAA spokesperson did say that the pilot radioed in that he was experiencing some fumes and smoke on board, and he thought it was something chemical, or maybe an electrical fire."

This was news to me, but not to Ted Nash, who commented cryptically, "I'm glad they're getting their facts straight."

Facts? It seemed to me that lacking any smoke in the aircraft, someone was manufacturing it and blowing it up everyone's ass.

The radio reporter and the anchorlady were going on about the Swissair tragedy, and someone recalled the Saudi air tragedy. Nash turned off the radio.

I realized Kate was looking at me. She said softly, "We don't know what happened, John, so we won't speculate. We'll avoid talking to the news media."

"Right. Just what I was thinking." I realized I had to watch what I said.

What I was also thinking was that the Federal law enforcement and intelligence agencies were sort of like a cross between the Gestapo and the Boy Scouts—the iron fist in the velvet glove and all that. We won't speculate meant, Shut up. Not wanting to wind up in protective custody for a year, or maybe worse, I said, with real sincerity, "I'll do whatever I have to do to bring this guy to justice. Just keep me on the case."

Neither of my teammates replied, though they could have reminded me that I wanted out not too long ago.

Ted Nash, Super-Spy, gave Officer Simpson an address a block away from Federal Plaza. I mean, jeez, the guy's a cop, and even if he was stupid, he could figure out that we were going either to 26 Federal Plaza, or 290 Broadway, the new Fed building across the street from Fed Plaza. In fact, Simpson said, "You want to walk to Federal Plaza?"

I laughed.

Nash said, "Just pull over here."

Officer Simpson pulled over on Chambers Street near the infamous Tweed Courthouse, and we all got out. I thanked him for driving us, and he reminded me, "I have damage to the front of the patrol car."

"Charge it to the Feds," I said. "They're collecting a trillion dollars today."

We began walking up lower Broadway. It was dusk now, but it's always dusk down here in the skyscraper caverns of lower Manhattan. This was not a residential or shopping district, it was a government district, so there weren't many people around on a Saturday, and the streets were relatively quiet.

As we walked, I said to Mr. Nash, "I have this sort of impression that maybe you guys knew we'd have a problem today."

He didn't reply right away, then said, "Today is April fifteenth."

"Right. I got my tax return in yesterday. I'm clean."

"Muslim extremists attach a lot of significance to anniversary dates. We have a lot of watch dates on our calendar."

"Yeah? What's today?"

"Today," said Ted Nash, "is the anniversary date of when we bombed Libya in nineteen eighty-six."

"No kidding?" I asked Kate, "Did you know that?"

"Yes, but I attached little significance to it, to be honest with you."

Nash added, "We've never had an incident on this date before, but Moammar Gadhafi makes an anti-American speech every year on this date. In fact, he made one earlier today."

I mulled this over awhile, trying to decide if I'd have acted any differently if I'd known this. I mean, this kind of stuff was not in my clue bag, but if it was, I might have at least put it into my paranoia pocket. I love being a mushroom, as you can imagine—kept in the dark and fed a lot of shit—and I asked my teammates, "Did you forget to tell me?"

Nash replied, "It didn't seem terribly important. I mean, important that you know."

"I see," which means, "Fuck you," of course. But I was learning to talk the talk. I asked, "How did Khalil know he'd be transported today?"

Nash replied, "Well, he didn't know for sure. But our Paris Embassy can't or won't hold a man like this for more than twenty-four hours. That much he probably knew. And if we *had* held him in Paris longer, nothing would have been much different, except for the missed symbolic date."

"Okay, but you played his game and transported him on the fifteenth of April."

"That's right," answered Mr. Nash. "We played his game, wanting to arrest him here on the fifteenth."

"I think you're going to miss the date."

He didn't reply to this, but informed me, "We took extraordinary security precautions in Paris, at the airport, and on the aircraft. In fact, there were also two Federal Air Marshals on board, undercover."

"Good. Then nothing could go wrong."

He ignored my sarcasm, and said, "There is a Hebrew expression, shared by the Arabs, that says, 'Man plans, God laughs.'"

"Good one."

We reached the twenty-eight-story skyscraper, called 26 Federal Plaza, and Nash said to me, "Kate and I will do the talking. Speak only if spoken to."

"Can I contradict you?"

"You'll have no reason to," he said. "This is the one place where only the truth is spoken."

So, with that bit of Orwellian information in my head, we entered the great Ministry of Truth and Justice.

April 15, I reflected, now sucked for two reasons.

BOOK TWO

Libya, April 15, 1986

*The air strike will not only diminish Colonel Gadhafi's
capacity to export terror, it will provide him with incentives and
reasons to alter his criminal behavior.*

—President Ronald Reagan

It is a time for confrontation—for war.

—Colonel Moammar Gadhafi

Chapter 13

Lieutenant Chip Wiggins, Weapons Systems Officer, United States Air Force, sat silent and motionless in the right seat of the F-111F attack jet, code named Karma 57. The aircraft was cruising along at a fuel-saving 350 knots. Wiggins glanced at his pilot, Lieutenant Bill Satherwaite, to his left.

Ever since they'd taken off from the Royal Air Force Station Lakenheath in Suffolk, England, some two hours before, neither man had said much. Satherwaite was the silent type anyway, Wiggins thought, and not given to useless chatter. But Wiggins wanted to hear a human voice, any voice, so he said, "We're coming abeam of Portugal."

Satherwaite replied, "I know that."

"Right." Their voices had a slight metallic ring to them as the words filtered through the open cockpit interphone that was the actual verbal connection between the two men. Wiggins took a deep breath, sort of a yawn, beneath his flight helmet, and the increased flow of oxygen caused the open interphone connection to reverberate for a second. Wiggins did it again.

Satherwaite said, "Would you mind not breathing?"

"Whatever makes you happy, Skipper."

Wiggins squirmed a little in his seat. He was getting cramped after so many hours of sitting restrained in the F-111's notoriously uncomfortable seat. The black sky was becoming oppressive, but he could see lights on the distant shore of Portugal and that made him feel better for some reason.

They were on their way to Libya, Wiggins reflected—on their way to rain death and destruction down on Moammar Gadhafi's pissant country in retaliation for a Libyan terrorist attack a couple weeks ago on a West Berlin disco frequented by American military. Wiggins recalled that the briefing officer made sure they knew *why* they were risking their lives in this difficult mission. Without too much spin, the briefing officer told them that the Libyan bomb attack on La Belle disco, which killed one American serviceman and injured dozens of others, was just the latest in a series of acts of open aggression that had to be answered with a display of resolve and force. "Therefore," said the briefing officer, "you're going to blow the shit out of the Libyans."

Sounded good in the briefing room, but not all of America's allies thought this was a good idea. The attack aircraft from England had been compelled to take the long way to Libya because the French and the Spanish had refused them permission to cross over their airspace. This had angered Wiggins, but Satherwaite didn't seem to care. Wiggins knew that Satherwaite's knowledge of geopolitics was minus zero; Bill Satherwaite's life was flying and flying was his life. Wiggins thought that if Satherwaite had been told to bomb and strafe Paris, Satherwaite would do it without a single thought about why he was attacking a NATO ally. The scary thing, Wiggins thought, was that Satherwaite would do the same thing to Washington, D.C., or Walla Walla, Washington, with no questions asked.

Wiggins pursued this thought by asking Satherwaite, "Bill, did you hear that rumor that one of our aircraft is going to drop a fuck-you bomb in the backyard of the French Embassy in Tripoli?"

Satherwaite did not reply.

Wiggins pressed on. "I also heard that one of us is going to drop a load on Gadhafi's Al Azziziyah residence. He's supposed to be there tonight."

Again, Satherwaite did not answer.

Finally, Wiggins, annoyed and frustrated, said, "Hey, Bill, are you awake?"

Satherwaite replied, "Chip, the less you know and the less I know, the happier we will be."

Chip Wiggins retreated into a moody silence. He liked Bill Satherwaite and liked the fact that his pilot was of the same rank as he, and couldn't order him to shut up. But Satherwaite could be a cold, taciturn son-of-a-bitch in the air. He was better on the ground. In fact, when Bill had a few drinks in him, he seemed almost human.

Wiggins considered that maybe Satherwaite was nervous, which was understandable. This was, after all, according to the Ops briefing, the longest jet attack mission ever attempted. Operation El Dorado Canyon was about to make some kind of history, though Wiggins didn't know what kind yet. There were sixty other aircraft somewhere around them, and their unit, the 48th Tactical Fighter Wing, had contributed twenty-four F-111F swing-wing jets to the mission. The tanker fleet that was flying down and back with them was a mix of the huge KC-10s and the smaller KC-135s—the 10s to refuel the fighters, and the 135s to refuel the KC-10s. There would be three midair refuelings on the three-thousand-mile route to Libya. Flying time from England to the Libyan coast was six hours, flying time toward Tripoli in the pre-attack phase was half an hour, and time over target would be a long, long ten minutes. And then they'd fly home. Not all of them, but most of them. "History," Wiggins said. "We are flying into history."

Satherwaite did not reply.

Chip Wiggins informed Bill Satherwaite, "Today is Income Tax Day. Did you file on time?"

"Nope. Filed for an extension."

"The IRS focuses on late filers."

Satherwaite grunted a reply.

Wiggins said, "If you get audited, drop napalm on the IRS headquarters. They'll think twice before they audit Bill Satherwaite again." Wiggins chuckled.

Satherwaite stared at his instruments.

Unable to draw his pilot into conversation, Wiggins went back to his thoughts. He contemplated the fact that this was a test of endurance for crew and equipment, and they'd never trained for a mission like this. But so far, so good. The F-111 was performing admirably. He glanced out the side of his canopy. The variable wing was extended at thirty-five degrees so as to give the airplane its best cruise characteristics for the long formation flight. Later, they'd hydraulically sweep the wings back to a streamlined aft position for the attack, and that would mark the moment of the actual combat phase of the mission. *Combat.* Wiggins really couldn't believe he was going into actual Jesus H. Christ combat.

This was the culmination of all they'd been trained for. Both he and Satherwaite had missed Vietnam, and now they were flying into unknown and hostile territory against an enemy whose anti-aircraft capabilities were not well known. The briefing officer had told them that the Libyan air defenses routinely shut down after midnight, but Wiggins couldn't believe that the Libyans were quite that stupid. He was convinced that their aircraft would be picked up on Libyan radar, that the Libyan Air Force would scramble to intercept them, that surface-to-air missiles would rise to blow them out of the sky, and that they would be greeted by Triple-A, which did not mean the American Automobile Association. "Marcus Aurelius."

"What?"

"The only Roman monument still standing in Tripoli. The Arch of Marcus Aurelius. Second century A.D."

Satherwaite stifled a yawn.

"If anybody hits it by mistake, they're in big trouble. It's a UN designated world heritage site. Were you paying attention at the briefing?"

"Chip, why don't you chew gum or something?"

"We begin our attack just west of the Arch. I hope I get a glimpse of it. That kind of stuff interests me."

Satherwaite closed his eyes and exhaled in an exaggerated expression of impatience.

Chip Wiggins returned to his combat thoughts. He knew that there were a few Vietnam vets on this mission, but most of the guys were untested in combat. Also, everyone from the President on down was watching, waiting, and holding their breath. After Vietnam, and after the *Pueblo* fiasco, and Carter's screwed-up rescue mission in Iran, and a whole decade of military failures since Vietnam, the home team needed a big win.

The lights were on in the Pentagon and the White House. They were pacing and praying. *Win this one for the Gipper, boys.* Chip Wiggins wasn't going to let them down. He hoped they wouldn't let him down. He'd been told that the mission could be aborted at any time, and he feared the crackle of the radio with the code words for abort—Green Grass. As in the green, green grass of home.

But a little piece of his mind would have welcomed those words. He wondered what they'd do to him in Libya if he had to bail out. *Where did that thought come from?* He was starting to think bad things again. He glanced at Satherwaite, who was making an entry in his log. Satherwaite yawned again.

Wiggins asked, "Tired?"

"No."

"Scared?"

"Not yet."

"Hungry?"

"Chip, shut up."

"Thirsty?"

Satherwaite said, "Why don't you go back to sleep? Or better yet, I'll sleep and you fly."

Wiggins knew this was Satherwaite's not-too-subtle way of reminding him that the Weapons Systems Officer was not a pilot.

They sat again in silence. Wiggins actually considered catching a nap, but he didn't want to give Satherwaite the opportunity to tell everyone back at Lakenheath that Wiggins slept the whole way to Libya. After about half an hour, Chip Wiggins looked at his navigation chart and instruments. In addition to his job as Weapons Systems Officer, he was also the navigator. He said to Satherwaite, "At nine o'clock is Cabo de São Vicente—Cape Saint Vincent."

"Good. That's where it belongs."

"That's where Prince Henry the Navigator set up the world's first school for sea navigation. That's how he got his name."

"Henry?"

"No, Navigator."

"Right."

"The Portuguese were incredible mariners."

"Is this something I need to know?"

"Sure. You play Trivial Pursuit?"

"No. Just tell me when we're going to change heading."

"In seven minutes we'll turn to zero-nine-four."

"Okay. Keep the clock."

They flew on in silence.

Their F-111 was in an assigned position in their cruise flight formation, but because of radio silence, each aircraft maintained position by use of their air-to-air radar. They couldn't always visually see the other three aircraft in their flight formation—code named Elton 38, Remit 22, and Remit 61—but they could see them on radar and could key off the flight leader, Terry Waycliff in Remit 22. Still, Wiggins had to anticipate the flight plan to some extent and know when to stare at the radar screen to see what the lead aircraft was doing. "I enjoy the challenge of a difficult mission, Bill, and I hope you do, too."

"You're making it more difficult, Chip."

Wiggins chuckled.

The flight of four F-111s all began their turn to port in unison. They rounded Cabo de São Vicente and headed southeast, aiming right for the Strait of Gibraltar.

An hour later they were approaching the Rock of Gibraltar on the port side and Mount Hacho on the African Coast to starboard. Wiggins informed his pilot, "Gibraltar was one of the ancient Pillars of Hercules. Mount Hacho is the other. These landmarks defined the western limits of navigation for the Mediterranean civilizations. Did you know that?"

"Give me a fuel state."

"Right." Wiggins read the numbers off the fuel gauges, commenting, "Remaining flight time about two hours."

Satherwaite looked at his instrument clock and said, "The KC-10 should be rendezvousing in about forty-five minutes."

"I hope," Wiggins replied, thinking, *If we somehow miss the refueling, we'll have just enough fuel to get us to Sicily and we'll be out of the action.* They had never been out of range of land and if they'd had to, they could jettison their bombs in the drink and put down at some airport in France or Spain and casually explain that they'd been on a little training mission and had run short of fuel. As the briefing officer had said, "Do not use the word 'Libya' in your conversation," which had gotten a big laugh.

Thirty minutes later, there was still no sign of the tankers. Wiggins asked, "Where the hell is our flying gas station?"

Satherwaite was reading from the mission orders and didn't reply.

Wiggins kept listening for the code signal over the radio that would announce the approach of the tankers. After all this time in the air and all this preparation, he didn't want to wind up in Sicily.

They flew on without speaking. The cockpit hummed with electronics, and the airframe pulsed with the power of the twin Pratt and Whitney turbofans that propelled the F-111F into the black night.

Finally, a series of clicks on the radio told them that the KC-10 was approaching. After another ten minutes, Wiggins saw the contact on his radar screen and announced the approach to Satherwaite, who acknowledged.

Satherwaite pulled off power and began to slide out of the formation. This, Wiggins thought, was where Satherwaite earned his pay.

In a few minutes, the giant KC-10 tanker filled the sky above them. Satherwaite was able to speak to the tanker on the KY-28 secured and scrambled voice channel, which could be used for short-range transmissions. "Kilo Ten, this is Karma Five-Seven. You're in sight."

"Roger, Karma Five-Seven. Here comes Dickey."

"Roger."

The KC-10 boom operator carefully guided the refueling nozzle into the F-111's receptacle, just aft of the fighter's cockpit. Within a few minutes the hookup was completed, and the fuel began to flow from the tanker to the fighter.

Wiggins watched as Satherwaite finessed the control stick in his right hand and the engine throttles in his left to maintain the jet fighter in exact position so that the refueling boom would stay connected. Wiggins knew this was an occasion for him to stay silent.

After what seemed like a long time, the green light near the top of the tanker's boom flicked off and an adjacent amber light came on, indicating an auto disconnect. Satherwaite transmitted to the tanker, "Karma Five-Seven clearing," and eased his aircraft away from the KC-10 and back toward his assigned spot in the formation.

The tanker pilot, in acknowledgment that this was the last refueling before the attack, transmitted, "Hey, good luck. Kick ass. God bless. See you later."

Satherwaite responded, "Roger," then said to Wiggins, "Luck and God have nothing to do with it."

Wiggins was a little annoyed at Satherwaite's too cool jet-jockey crap and said to him, "Don't you believe in God?"

"I sure do, Chip. You pray. I'll fly."

Satherwaite tucked them back into the formation as another jet peeled off for its refueling.

Wiggins had to admit that Bill Satherwaite was a hell of a pilot, but he wasn't a hell of a guy.

Satherwaite, aware that he'd ticked off Wiggins, said, "Hey, wizo," using the affectionate slang term for a weapons officer, "I'm going to buy you the best dinner in London."

Wiggins smiled. "I pick."

"No, I pick. We'll keep it under ten pounds."

"Figures."

Satherwaite let a few minutes go by, then said to Wiggins, "It's going to be okay. You're going to drop them right on target, and if you do a good job, I'll fly right over that Arch of Augustus for you."

"Aurelius."

"Right."

Wiggins settled back and closed his eyes. He knew he'd gotten more than Satherwaite's quota of non-mission words, and he considered that a small triumph.

He thought ahead a bit. Despite the small knot in his empty stomach, he was really looking forward to flying his first combat mission. If he had any qualms about dropping his bombs, he reminded himself that all their mission targets, his own included, were strictly military. In fact, the briefing officer at Lakenheath had called the Al Azziziyah compound "Jihad University," meaning, it was a training camp for terrorists. The briefing officer had added, however, "There *is* a possibility of some civilians within the military compound of Al Azziziyah."

Wiggins thought about that, then put it out of his mind.

Chapter 14

Asad Khalil struggled with two primitive instincts—sex and self-preservation.

Khalil paced impatiently across the flat roof. His father had named him Asad—the lion—and it seemed that he had consciously or unconsciously taken on the traits of the great beast, including this habit of pacing in circles. He suddenly stopped and looked out into the night.

The Ghabli—the hot, strong southerly wind from the vast Sahara—was blowing across northern Libya toward the Mediterranean Sea. The night sky appeared misty, but in fact the distortion of the moon and stars was caused by airborne grains of sand.

Khalil looked at the luminous face of his watch and noted that it was 1:46 A.M. Bahira, the daughter of Captain Habib Nadir, was to arrive at precisely 2:00 A.M. He wondered if she would come. He wondered if she had been caught. And if she'd been caught, would she confess to where she was going and with whom she was going to meet? This last possibility troubled Asad Khalil greatly. At sixteen years old, he was perhaps thirty minutes away from his first sexual experience—or he was several hours away from being beheaded. He saw an uninvited mental image of himself on his knees, head bowed as the massively built official executioner, known only as Sulaman, swung the giant scimitar toward the back of Khalil's neck. Khalil felt his body tense, and a line of sweat formed on his forehead and cooled in the night air.

Khalil walked to the small tin shed on the flat rooftop. There was no door on the shed, and he peered down the staircase, expecting to see either Bahira, or her father with armed guards coming for him. This was lunacy, he thought, pure madness.

Khalil moved to the north edge of the roof. The concrete rooftop was surrounded by a shoulder-high, crenellated parapet of block
and stucco. The building itself was a two-story-high structure built
by the Italians when they controlled Libya. The building was then,
as it was now, a storage facility for munitions, which was why it was
safely removed from the center of the military compound known as Al
Azziziyah. The former Italian compound was now the military headquarters and sometimes residence of the Great Leader, Colonel Moammar Gadhafi, who this very night had arrived at Al Azziziyah. Khalil
and everyone else in Libya knew that the Great Leader made a habit of
changing locations often, and that Gadhafi's erratic movements were a
safeguard from either assassination or an American military action. But
it was not a good idea to comment on either possibility.

In any case, Gadhafi's unexpected presence had caused his elite
guards to be unusually alert this night, and Khalil was worried because
it seemed that Allah himself was making this assignation difficult and
dangerous.

Khalil knew beyond a doubt that it was Satan that had filled him
with this sinful lust for Bahira, that Satan had made him dream of her
walking naked across moonlit desert sands. Asad Khalil had never seen
a naked woman before, but he had seen a magazine from Germany, and
he knew what Bahira would look like unveiled and undressed. He pictured each curve of her body as he imagined it would be, he saw her long
hair touching her bare shoulders, he recalled her nose and mouth as he'd
seen them when he and she had been children, before she was veiled. He
knew she looked different now, but strangely the child's face still sat on a
wonderfully imagined woman's body. He pictured her curving hips, her
mound of pubic hair, her naked thighs and legs...He felt his heart beating heavily in his chest and felt his mouth become dry.

Khalil stared out to the north. The lights of Tripoli, twenty kilometers distant, were bright enough to be visible through the blowing
Ghabli. Beyond Tripoli lay the blackness of the Mediterranean. Around
Al Azziziyah was rolling arid land, some olive groves, date trees, a few
goatherd shelters, an occasional watering hole.

Asad Khalil peered over the parapet down into the compound. All was quiet below—there were no guards visible nor any vehicles at this hour. The only activity would be around Colonel Gadhafi's residence and around the headquarters area that housed the command, control, and communication buildings. There was no special alert tonight, but Khalil had a premonition that something was not right.

Asad Khalil looked again at his watch. It was exactly 2:00 A.M. and Bahira had not arrived. Khalil knelt down in the corner of the parapet, below the line of sight of anyone on the ground. In the corner he had unrolled his *sajjafiamda*, his prayer mat, and placed on it a copy of the Koran. If they came for him, they would find him praying and reading the Koran. That might save him. But more likely, they would guess correctly that the Koran was a ruse and his *sajjafiamda* was for the naked body of Bahira. If they suspected that, then his blasphemy would be dealt with in a way that would make him wish for beheading. And Bahira... They would most likely stone her to death.

And still, he did not run back to his mother's house. He was determined to meet whatever fate came up those stairs.

He thought of how he'd first noticed Bahira at her father's house. Captain Habib Nadir, like Khalil's own father, was a favorite of Colonel Gadhafi. The three families were close. Khalil's father, like Bahira's father, had been active in the resistance to the Italian occupation; Khalil's father had worked for the British during the Second World War, while Bahira's father had worked for the Germans. But what did that matter? Italians, Germans, British—they were all infidels and they were owed no loyalty. His father and Bahira's father had joked about how they had both helped the Christians kill one another.

Khalil thought a moment about his father, Captain Karim Khalil. He had been dead five years now, murdered on the street in Paris by agents of the Israeli Mossad. The Western radio broadcasts had reported that the murder was probably committed by a rival Islamic faction, or perhaps even by fellow Libyans in some sort of political power play. No arrest had been made. But Colonel Gadhafi, who was far wiser than any of his enemies, had explained to his people that Captain Karim Khalil had been murdered by the Israelis and everything else was a lie.

Asad Khalil believed this. He had to believe. He missed his father, but took comfort from the fact that his father had died a martyr's death at the hands of the Zionists. Of course, doubts did creep into his head, but the Great Man himself had spoken and that was the end of it.

Khalil nodded to himself as he knelt in the corner of the roof. He looked at his watch, then at the doorway of the tin shed ten meters away. She was late, or she had not been able to slip out of her house, or she'd overslept, or she had decided not to risk her life to be with him. Or, worst of all, she'd been caught and even now was betraying him to the military police.

Khalil considered his special relationship with the Great Leader. He had no doubt that Colonel Gadhafi was fond of him and his brothers and sisters. The Colonel had let them stay on in their house in the privileged compound of Al Azziziyah, he had seen to it that his mother had a pension, and that he and his siblings were educated.

And only six months ago, the Colonel had said to him, "You are marked to avenge your father's death."

Asad Khalil had been filled with pride and joy and replied to his surrogate father, "I am ready to serve you and to serve Allah."

The Colonel had smiled and said, "We are not ready for you, Asad. Another year or two, and we will begin training you to be a freedom fighter."

And now Asad was risking everything—his life, his honor, his family—all for what? For a woman. It made no sense, but...There was the other thing...The thing he knew but could not bring himself to think...The thing with his mother and with Moammar Gadhafi...Yes, there was something there, and he knew what it was, and it was the same thing that had put him here on the roof waiting for Bahira.

He reasoned that if the relationship between his mother and the Great Leader was not a sin, then not all sex outside of marriage was sinful. Moammar Gadhafi would not do anything sinful, anything outside the Sharia, the accepted way. Therefore, Asad Khalil, if caught, would take his case directly to the Great Leader and explain his confusion concerning these matters. He would explain that it was Bahira's father who had brought home the magazine from Germany that showed photos of naked men and women, and it was this filth from the West that had corrupted him.

Bahira had found the magazine hidden beneath bags of rice in their house and had stolen it and showed it to Khalil. They had looked at the photographs together—a sin that would have gotten them both whipped if they'd been caught. But instead of the photographs filling them with disgust and shame, it was these pictures that had been the cause of their speaking of the unspeakable. She had said to him, "I want to show myself to you like these women. I want to show you all that I have. I want to see you, Asad, and feel your flesh."

And so, Satan had entered her and through her had entered him. He had read the story of Adam and Eve in the Hebrew book of Genesis, and had been told by his *mousyed*, his spiritual teacher, that women were weak and lustful and had committed the original sin and would lure men to sin if men did not remain strong.

And yet...he thought, even great men like the Colonel could be corrupted by women. He would explain that to the Colonel if he were caught. Perhaps they would not stone Bahira to death and would let them off with a whipping.

The night was cool and Khalil shivered. He remained kneeling on his prayer mat, Koran in his hands. At ten minutes after two, there was a noise on the stairs, and he looked up to see a dark outline standing at the opening of the tin shed. He said softly, "Allah, be merciful."

Chapter 15

Lieutenant Chip Wiggins said to Lieutenant Bill Satherwaite, "We're getting a strong crosswind. There's that south wind that blows out of the desert. What's it called?"

"It's called the south wind that blows out of the desert."

"Right. Anyway, that'll be a good tailwind getting the hell out of there—plus, we'll be four bombs lighter."

Satherwaite mumbled a reply.

Wiggins stared out the windscreen into the dark night. He had no idea if he'd see the sun rise on this day. But he knew that if they accomplished their mission, they'd be heroes—but nameless heroes. For this was no ordinary war—this was a war against international terrorists whose reach went beyond the Middle East, and thus the names of the pilots on this mission would never be released to the press or the public, and would be classified top secret for all time. Something about that rubbed Wiggins the wrong way; it was an admission that the bad guys could reach out, right into the heartland of America, and exact a revenge against the pilots and crew or their families. On the other hand, even though there would be no parades or public awards ceremonies, this anonymity made him a little more comfortable. Better to be an unnamed hero than a named terrorist target.

They continued east over the Mediterranean. Wiggins thought about how many wars had been fought around this ancient sea and especially on the shores of North Africa—the Phoenicians, the Egyptians, the Greeks, the Carthaginians, the Romans, the Arabs, on and on for thousands of years right up until the Second World War—the Italians, the German Afrika Korps, the British, the Americans... The sea and the sand of North Africa was a mass grave of soldiers, sailors, and airmen. *To the shores of Tripoli*, he said to himself, aware that he was not the only flier that night to think those words. *We will fight our country's battles...*

Satherwaite asked, "Time till turn?"

Wiggins came out of his reverie and checked his position. "Twelve minutes."

"Keep the clock."

"Roger."

Twelve minutes later, the formation began a ninety-degree turn to the south. The entire air armada, minus tankers, was on a course toward the Libyan coast. Satherwaite pushed his throttles forward and the F-III gathered speed.

Bill Satherwaite scanned the clock and the flight instruments. They were approaching the aerial gate where the attack preparations and profiles would begin. He noted his indicated air speed at true four hundred eighty knots and his altitude at twenty-five thousand feet. They were less than two hundred miles from the coast and headed dead-on for Tripoli. He heard a series of radio clicks, which he acknowledged in kind, and with the rest of his squadron began his descent.

Satherwaite was inclined to start the final checklists right then, but he knew that it was a little early, that it was possible to get yourself peaked too soon, and that was not a smart way to go into combat. He waited.

Wiggins cleared his throat, and over the interphone it sounded like a roar and gave them both a start. Wiggins said, "One hundred miles to feet dry," using the aviator's term for land.

"Roger."

They both looked at the radar screen, but there was nothing coming out of Libya to greet and meet them. They leveled off at a mere three hundred feet above sea level.

"Eighty miles."

"Okay, let's get started on the attack review."

"Ready."

Satherwaite and Wiggins began the litanies of the checklist and reviews. Just as they were finished, Wiggins looked up and saw the lights of Tripoli straight ahead. "Tally-ho." Satherwaite looked up, too, and nodded. He moved the hydraulic wing position lever, and the out-stretched wings of the F-III began to sweep further aft, like the wings of a hawk who's spotted his meal on the ground.

Wiggins noticed that his heart had speeded up a little, and he realized he was very thirsty.

Satherwaite increased power again as the F-IIIs approached the coast in formation. Their run-in altitude remained at three hundred feet, and they'd been told there were no radio towers or skyscrapers that high to worry about. Their run-in speed was now five hundred knots. It was zero-one-fifty hours. In a few minutes, they'd break formation and head toward their individual targets in and around Tripoli.

Wiggins listened closely to the silence in his headset, then heard a warbling tone that indicated a radar lock-on. *Oh, shit.* He looked quickly at his radar homing and warning screen and said, with as cool a tone as he was able to fake, "SAM alert at one o'clock."

Satherwaite nodded. "I guess they're awake."

"I'd like to kick that briefing officer in the nuts."

"He's not the problem and neither are those missiles."

"Right…" The F-III was flying too low and fast for the missiles to score a hit, but now at three hundred feet, they were squarely in the killing zone of the anti-aircraft guns.

Wiggins watched two missiles rise up on his radar screen, and he hoped these Soviet-made pieces of junk really couldn't track them at their speed and altitude. A few seconds later, Wiggins visually spotted the two missiles off their starboard side streaking upward into the night sky with their fiery tails burning red and orange.

Satherwaite commented dryly, "A waste of expensive rocket fuel."

It was Wiggins' turn not to reply. He was, in fact, finally speechless. In total contrast, Satherwaite was now chatty and was going on about the shape of the coastline and the city of Tripoli and other inconsequential matters. Wiggins wanted to tell him to shut up and fly.

They crossed over the coast and below them lay Tripoli. Satherwaite noted that despite the air raid in progress, the streetlights were still on. "Idiots." He caught a glimpse of the Arch of Marcus Aurelius and said to Wiggins, "There's your arch. Nine o'clock."

But Wiggins had lost interest in history and concentrated on the moment. "Turn."

Satherwaite peeled out of the formation and began his run-in toward Al Azziziyah. "How do you say that word?"

"What?"

"Where we're going."

Wiggins felt sweat forming around his neck as he divided his attention between the instruments, the radar, and the visuals outside his windscreen. "Holy shit! Triple-A!"

"Are you sure? I thought it was Al-something."

Wiggins didn't like or appreciate Satherwaite's sudden cockpit humor. He snapped back, "Al Azziziyah. What fucking difference does it make?"

"Right," Satherwaite replied. "Tomorrow they'll call it rubble." He laughed.

Wiggins laughed, too, despite the fact that he was scared out of his mind. Arcs of anti-aircraft tracers cut through the black night much too close to their aircraft. He couldn't believe he was actually being shot at. This really sucked. But it was also a rush.

Satherwaite said, "Al Azziziyah, dead-on. Ready."

"Rubble," replied Wiggins. "Rubble, rubble, toil and trouble. Ready to release. Fuck you, Moammar."

Chapter 16

Asad." MMMMMMMMMMMMMMMMMMMMMMMM Asad Khalil's heart almost stopped. "Yes...yes, over here." He asked quietly, "Are you alone?"

"Of course." Bahira walked toward his voice, then saw him kneeling on the prayer rug.

"Stay low," he whispered hoarsely.

She crouched below the parapet as she moved toward him, then knelt on the prayer rug in front of him. "Is everything all right?"

"Yes. But you are late."

"I had to avoid the guards. The Great Leader—"

"Yes, I know." Asad Khalil looked at Bahira in the moonlight. She was wearing the flowing white robe that was a young woman's customary garment in the evenings, and she also wore her veil and scarf. She was three years older than he and had reached an age when most women in Libya were married or betrothed. But her father had turned down many suitors, and the most ardent of them had been exiled from Tripoli. Asad Khalil knew that if his own father were alive, the families would certainly have agreed to a marriage between Asad and Bahira. But though his father was a hero and a martyr, the fact was that he was dead and the Khalil family had little status except as favored pensioners of the Great Leader. Of course, there was a connection between the Great Leader and Asad's mother, but that was a hidden sin and of no help.

They knelt facing each other and neither spoke. Bahira's eyes went to the Koran lying at the corner of the rug, then she seemed to notice the rug itself. She stared at Asad, whose look seemed to say, "If we are to commit the sin of fornication, what difference does it make if we also commit a blasphemy?"

Bahira nodded in agreement to the silent understanding.

Bahira Nadir took the initiative and pulled aside the veil that covered her face. She smiled, but Khalil thought it was more a smile of embarrassment at being without her veil, less than a meter away from a man.

She slid the scarf off her head and unfastened her hair, which fell in long curly strands over her shoulders.

Asad Khalil took a deep breath and stared into Bahira's eyes. She was beautiful, he thought, though he had little with which to compare. He cleared his throat and said to her, "You are very beautiful."

She smiled, reached out and took his hands in hers.

Khalil had never held the hands of a woman and was surprised at how small and soft Bahira's hands were. Her skin was warm, warmer than his, probably the result of her exertions in traveling the three hundred meters between her home and this place. He also noticed that her hands were dry, while his were moist. He moved closer to her on his knees and smelled now a flowered scent coming from her. He discovered as he moved that he was fully aroused.

Neither of them seemed to know what to do next. Finally, Bahira let go of his hands and began caressing his face. He did the same to her face. She moved closer to him and their bodies touched, then they embraced and he could feel her breasts beneath her robe. Asad Khalil was wild with desire, but a part of his brain was elsewhere—a primitive instinct was telling him to be alert.

Before he knew what was happening, Bahira had moved back and was unfastening her robe.

Khalil watched her and listened for signs of danger. If they were discovered now, they were dead. He heard her saying, "Asad. What are you waiting for?"

He looked at her kneeling before him. She was completely naked now and he stared at her breasts, then her pubic hair, then her thighs, and finally back at her face.

"Asad."

He pulled his short tunic over his head, then slipped his pants and undershorts down to his ankles and kicked them off.

She stared at his face, her eyes avoiding his erect penis, but then her eyes glanced downward at him.

Asad didn't know what to do next. He thought he would know—he understood the position they would assume, but he was not sure how to arrive at it.

Bahira again took the initiative and lay down on her back on the prayer mat, her garments beneath her head.

Asad nearly lunged forward and found himself on top of her and felt her firm breasts and warm skin beneath his own. He felt her legs parting and sensed the tip of his penis touching warm, wet flesh. In an instant, he was half inside her. She cried out softly in pain. He thrust further, past the resistance, and entered her fully. Before he could move, he felt her hips rise and fall, rise and fall, and between two heartbeats he released himself inside of her.

He lay motionless catching his breath, but she continued the rising and falling of her hips though Asad didn't know why she continued after he was satisfied. She started to moan and breathe heavily, then began saying his name, "Asad, Asad, Asad…"

He rolled off her and lay on his back looking at the night sky. The half-moon was rising in the east, the stars seemed dull over the lighted compound, a poor, pale imitation of the brilliant stars over the open desert.

"Asad."

He did not answer. His mind could not yet comprehend what he had just done.

She moved closer to him so that their shoulders and legs were touching, but the desire was gone in him.

She said, "Are you angry?"

"No." He sat up. "We should get dressed."

She sat up also and put her head on his shoulder.

He wanted to move away from her, but he didn't. Unhappy thoughts began to creep into his mind. What if she became pregnant? What if she wanted to do this again? The next time they would be caught for sure, or she would become pregnant. In either case, one or both of them might die. The law was not clear on some things, and it was usually the families that decided how the disgrace was to be dealt with. Knowing her father, he could imagine no mercy for either of them. For some reason that he couldn't comprehend, he blurted out, "My mother has been with the Great Leader."

Bahira did not reply.

Khalil was angry at himself for revealing this secret. He didn't know why he had and didn't know what he felt for this woman. He was dimly aware that the desire for her would return again and for that reason he knew he should be polite. Still, he wished he were anywhere else but here. He eyed his clothing at the far end of the prayer mat. He noticed, too, a dark stain on the prayer mat where she had lain.

Bahira put her arm around him and with her other hand stroked his thigh. She said, "Do you think we would be allowed to marry?"

"Perhaps." But he didn't think so. He glanced at her hand on his thigh, then noticed the blood on his penis. He realized he should have brought water for washing.

She said, "Will you speak to my father?"

"Yes," he replied, but he didn't know if he would. A marriage to Bahira Nadir, daughter of Captain Habib Nadir, would be a good thing, but it might be dangerous to ask. He wondered if the old women would examine her and find that she had lost her virginity. He wondered if she were pregnant. He wondered a lot of things, not least of all if he would go unpunished for this sin. He said, "We should go."

But she made no move to leave his side.

So they remained sitting together. Khalil was getting restless.

She began to speak, but he said, "Be still." He had the disquieting feeling that something was happening that he needed to be aware of.

His mother had once told him that like his namesake, the lion, he had been blessed with a sixth sense, or second sight, as it was also called by the old women. He had assumed that everyone could sense danger or know that an enemy was nearby without seeing or hearing anything. But he had come to understand that this feeling was a special gift, and he realized now that what he had sensed all night had nothing to do with Bahira, or the military police, or being caught in fornication; it had to do with something else, but he didn't know what it was yet. All he knew for certain was that something was wrong out there.

Chip Wiggins tried to ignore the streaks of tracer rounds sailing past his canopy. He had no point of reference in his life or in his training for what was happening. The whole scene around him was so surreal that he couldn't process it as mortal danger. He concentrated on the display screens that made up the flight console in front of him. He cleared his throat and said to Satherwaite, "We're on the money."

Satherwaite acknowledged, with no inflection in his voice.

Wiggins said, "Less than two minutes to target."

"Roger."

Satherwaite knew he was supposed to kick in the afterburners now for a power boost, but to do so would cause a very long and very visible trail of bright exhaust behind his aircraft, which would draw every gun muzzle in his direction. There wasn't supposed to be this much ground fire, but there was and he had to make a decision.

Wiggins said, "Afterburners, Bill."

Satherwaite hesitated. The attack plan called for the extra speed of the afterburners, or he stood a good chance that his squadron mate— Remit 22—who was only thirty seconds behind him, would be climbing up his ass.

"Bill."

"Right." Satherwaite kicked in the afterburners, and the F-111F shot forward. He pulled back on his stick and the nose rose. Satherwaite glanced above his flight panel for a brief second and saw an elaborate display of lethal trajectories pass off to their port side. "Those assholes can't shoot straight."

Wiggins wasn't so sure about that. He said, "On track, thirty seconds to release."

Bahira held her lover's arm. "What is wrong, Asad?"

"Be quiet." He listened intently and thought he heard someone shout in the far distance. A vehicle started its engine close by. He scrambled toward his clothes and pulled his tunic on, then stood, peeking over the parapet. His eyes scanned the compound below, then something on the horizon caught his attention, and he looked north and east toward Tripoli.

Bahira was beside him now, clutching her clothes to her breasts. "What is it?" she asked insistently.

"I don't know. Be still." Something was terribly wrong, but whatever it was could not be seen or heard yet, though he felt it now, very strongly. He stared into the night and listened.

Bahira, too, peeked over the parapet. "Guards?"

"No. Something…out there…" Then he saw it—incandescent trails of bright fire curving up from the glow of the city of Tripoli into the dark sky above the Mediterranean.

Bahira saw them, too, and asked, "What is that?"

"Missiles." *In the name of Allah, the merciful…* "Missiles, and anti-aircraft fire."

Bahira grabbed his arm. "Asad…what is happening?"

"Enemy attack."

"No! No! Oh, please…" She dropped to the floor and began pulling on her clothes. "We must get to the shelters."

"Yes." He pulled on his pants and shoes, forgetting his undershorts.

Suddenly, the ear-splitting shriek of an air raid siren filled the night air. Men began to shout and run out of the surrounding buildings, engines started, the streets filled with noise.

Bahira began running barefoot toward the stair shed, but Khalil caught up with her and pulled her down. "Wait! You can't be seen running from this building. Let the others get to the shelters first."

She looked at him. She trusted his judgment and she nodded.

Satisfied that she would stay where she was, Khalil ran back to the parapet and looked toward the city. "In the name of Allah…" Flames were erupting in Tripoli, and he could now hear and feel the distant explosions like rolling desert thunder.

Then something else caught his eye, and he saw a shadowy blur hurtling toward him, backlighted by the lights and fires of Tripoli. From the blur trailed an enormous plume of red and white, and Khalil knew he was looking at the hot exhaust gases of a jet aircraft coming right at him. He stood frozen in terror and not even a scream could rise from his throat.

Bill Satherwaite again took his eyes off the electronic displays and grabbed another quick glimpse through his windscreen. Out of the darkness in front of them he could recognize the aerial view of Al Azziziyah that he'd seen a hundred times in satellite photos.

Wiggins said, "Stand by."

Satherwaite shifted his attention back to the screens and concentrated on his flying and on the bomb-toss pattern that he would execute in a few seconds.

Wiggins said, "Three, two, one, drop."

Satherwaite felt the aircraft lighten immediately and fought for control as he began the high-speed evasive maneuvers that would get them the hell out of there.

Wiggins was now working the controls that guided the two-thousand-pound laser-smart bombs on their paths to their pre-assigned targets. Wiggins said, "Tracking...good picture...got it...steering...steering...impact! One, two, three, four. Beautiful."

They could not hear the four bombs detonating inside the Al Azziziyah compound, but both of them could imagine the sound and the flash of the explosions. Satherwaite said, "We're outta here."

Wiggins added, "Bye-bye, Mr. Arabian guy."

Asad could do nothing but stare at the incredible thing streaking toward him with fire belching out of its tail.

Suddenly, the attacking jet pulled straight up into the night sky, and its roar drowned out everything except Bahira Nadir's scream.

The jet disappeared, and the sound subsided, but Bahira continued to scream and scream.

Khalil shouted to her, "Be quiet!" He glanced down into the street and saw two soldiers looking up toward him. He ducked below the parapet. Bahira was sobbing now.

As Khalil contemplated his next move, the roof beneath his feet jumped and threw him face down. The next thing he was aware of was the sound of an enormous explosion close by. Then there was another explosion, then another, then another. He covered his ears with his hands. The earth shook, he could feel the air pressure change, and his ears popped and his mouth opened in a silent scream. A rush of heat swept over him, the sky turned blood red, and pieces of rock, rubble, and earth began to fall from the heavens. *Allah, be merciful. Spare me...* The world was being destroyed around him. He had no air in his lungs, and he fought to get his breath. Everything was strangely quiet, and he realized he was deaf. He also realized that he had wet himself.

Little by little, his hearing returned, and he could hear Bahira screaming again, an outpouring of pure, unmitigated terror. She scrambled to her feet and staggered over to the far parapet and began screaming down into the courtyard below.

"Shut up!" He ran to her and grabbed for her arm, but she got away from him and began running around the rubble-strewn perimeter of the roof, shrieking at the top of her lungs.

Four more explosions erupted at the far east end of the compound.

Khalil spotted men on the adjoining roof setting up an anti-aircraft machine gun. Bahira saw them, too, and threw up her arms to them, shouting, "Help! Help!"

They saw her, but continued setting up the machine gun.

"Help me! Help!"

Khalil grabbed her from behind and pulled her down to the concrete roof. "Shut up!"

She fought with him, and he was amazed at her strength. She continued to scream, broke free of his arms and clawed at his face, opening gashes along his cheeks and neck.

Suddenly, the machine gun on the next building opened fire, and the staccato sound mixed with the wailing siren and the thuds of explosions in the distance. Red tracer rounds streaked up from the machine gun and this caused Bahira to scream again.

Khalil put his hand over her mouth, but she bit his finger, then brought her knee up into his groin and he rocked backwards.

She was completely hysterical, and he could see no way to calm her down.

But there was a way.

He put his hands around her neck and throat and squeezed.

The F-III streaked southward over the desert, then Satherwaite banked hard to starboard and executed a hundred-and-fifty-degree turn that would bring them back over the coast a hundred kilometers west of Tripoli.

Wiggins said, "Nice flying, Skipper."

Satherwaite didn't acknowledge, but said, "Keep an eye out for the Libyan Air Force, Chip."

Wiggins adjusted the knobs on his radar screen. "Clear skies. Gadhafi's pilots are washing their underwear about now."

"We hope." The F-III had no air-to-air missiles, and the idiots who designed it hadn't even put a Gatling gun on board, so their only defense against another jet was speed and maneuver. "We hope," he repeated. Satherwaite sent out a radio signal indicating that Karma 57 was among the living.

They sat in silence waiting for the other signals. Finally, the radio signals began coming in: Remit 22, with Terry Waycliff piloting and Bill Hambrecht as wizo; Remit 61, with Bob Callum piloting, Steve Cox, wizo; Elton 38, with Paul Grey piloting, Jim McCoy, wizo.

Their whole flight had made it.

Wiggins said, "I hope the other guys did okay."

Satherwaite nodded. So far, this was a perfect mission and that made him feel good. He liked it when everything went as planned. Aside from the missiles and the Triple-A, which in any case had not done him or his flight mates any harm, this could have been a live-bomb training mission over the Mojave Desert. Satherwaite jotted an entry in his log. "Piece of cake."

"Milk run," Wiggins agreed.

*   *   *

Asad Khalil kept squeezing, and this had the intended effect of making her stop screaming. She looked at him with wide bulging eyes. He squeezed harder, and she began to thrash around beneath him. He squeezed even harder and the thrashing turned to muscle spasms, then even those stopped. He kept the pressure on her throat and looked into Bahira's eyes, which were wide open and unblinking.

He counted to sixty and released his hands from her neck. He had solved the problem of the present and all the problems of the future with one relatively simple act.

He stood, put his Koran on the prayer mat, rolled it and tied it, put it over his shoulder and went down the stairs and out the building into the street.

All the lights in the compound were out, and he made his way through the darkness toward his home. With every step he took away from the building where Bahira lay dead on the roof, he was that much more removed, physically and mentally, from any involvement with the dead girl.

A building in front of him was in ruins and by the light of the burning structure, he saw dead soldiers lying all around him. A man's face stared up at him, the white skin reddened by the reflected flames. The man's eyes had popped out of his skull and blood ran from his eye sockets, his nose, his ears, and his mouth. Khalil fought down the nausea in his churning stomach, but he caught a whiff of burning flesh and vomited.

He rested a moment, then pushed on, still carrying his prayer mat.

He wanted to pray, but the Koran specifically prohibited a man from praying after he had intercourse with a woman, unless he first washed himself, including his face and hands.

He saw a ruptured cistern pouring water down the side of a building, and he stopped to wash his face and hands, then washed the blood and urine from his genitals.

He moved on, reciting long passages from the Koran, praying for the safety of his mother, sisters, and brothers.

He saw fires raging from the direction he was headed, and he began running.

This night, he reflected, had begun in sin and ended in hell. Lust led to sin, sin led to death. Hellfires raged all around him. The Great Satan himself had delivered punishment to him and to Bahira. But Allah the merciful had spared his life, and as he ran he prayed that Allah had also spared his family.

As an afterthought, he also prayed for Bahira's family and for the Great Leader.

As Asad Khalil, age sixteen, ran through the ruins of Al Azziziyah, he understood that he had been tested by Satan and by Allah, and that from this night of sin, death, and fire he would emerge a man.

Chapter 17

Asad Khalil continued running toward his home. There were more people in this quarter of the compound—soldiers, women, a few children, and they were running, or walking slowly as if stunned; some he realized were on their knees praying.

Khalil turned a corner and stopped dead in his tracks. The row of attached stucco houses where he lived looked strangely different. Then he realized there were no shutters on the windows, and he noticed debris strewn in the open square in front of the houses. But even more strange was the fact that moonlight came through the open windows and doors. He suddenly realized that the roofs had collapsed into the buildings and blown out the doors, windows, and shutters. *Allah, I beg of you, please, no...*

He felt as if he were going to faint, then he took a deep breath and ran toward his house, stumbling over pieces of concrete, dropping his prayer mat, finally reaching the doorway opening. He hesitated, then rushed inside to what had been the front room.

The entire flat roof had collapsed into the room, covering the tile floor, the rugs, and the furniture with broken slabs of concrete, wooden beams, and stucco. Khalil looked upward at the open sky. *In the name of the most merciful...*

He took another deep breath and tried to get himself under control. On the far wall was the wood and tile cabinet that his father had built. Khalil made his way across the rubble to the cabinet, whose doors had been flung open. He found the flashlight inside and switched it on.

He swept the powerful, narrow beam around the room, seeing now the full extent of the damage. A framed photograph of the Great Leader still hung on the wall and this somehow reassured Khalil.

He knew he had to go into the bedrooms, but he couldn't bring himself to face what might be there.

Finally, he told himself, *You must be a man. You must see if they are dead or alive.*

He moved toward an arched opening that led further back into the house. The cooking and eating room had suffered the same damage as the front room. Khalil noticed that his mother's dishes and ceramic bowls had all fallen off their shelves.

He passed through the destruction into a small inner courtyard where three doors led to the three bedrooms. Khalil pushed on the door to the room that he shared with his two brothers, Esam, age five, and Qadir, age fourteen. Esam was the posthumous son of his father, always sickly, and was indulged by his sisters and mother. The Great Leader himself had sent for a European doctor once to examine him during one of his illnesses. Qadir, only two years younger than Asad, was big for his age and sometimes mistaken as his twin. Asad Khalil had hopes and dreams that Qadir and he would join the Army together, become great warriors, and eventually become Army commanders and aides to the Great Leader.

Asad Khalil held on to this image as he pushed on the door, which encountered some obstruction on the other side and held fast. He pushed harder and managed to squeeze himself through the narrow opening into his room.

There were three single beds in the small room—his own, which was flattened under a slab of concrete, Qadir's bed, which was also buried in concrete rubble, and Esam's bed, across which Khalil could see a huge rafter.

Khalil scrambled over the rubble to Esam's bed and knelt beside it. The heavy timber had landed lengthwise on the bed, and beneath the timber, under the blanket, was Esam's crushed and lifeless body. Khalil put his hands over his face and wept.

He got himself under control and turned toward Qadir's bed. The entire bed was buried under a section of concrete and stucco roof. Khalil's flashlight played over the mound of debris, and he saw a hand and arm protruding from the concrete pieces. He reached out and grasped the hand, then quickly let go of the dead flesh.

He let out a long, plaintive wail and threw himself across the mound of debris covering Qadir's bed. He cried for a minute or two, but then realized he had to find the others. He stumbled to his feet.

Before he left the room, he turned and again shone the flashlight on his bed and stared transfixed by the single slab of concrete that had flattened the bed where he had lain only hours before.

Khalil crossed the small courtyard and pushed on the splintered door of his sisters' room. The door had come unfastened from its hinges and fell inward.

His sisters, Adara, age nine, and Lina, age eleven, shared a double bed. Adara was a happy child and Khalil favored her, acting as more her father than her older brother. Lina was serious and studious, a joy to her teachers.

Khalil could not bring himself to shine his light on the bed or even to look at it. He stood with his eyes closed, prayed, then opened his eyes and put the beam of light on the double bed. He let out a gasp. The bed was overturned, and the entire room looked like it had been shaken by a giant. Khalil saw now that the rear outside wall had been blown in, and he could smell the powerful acrid stench of explosives. The bomb had detonated not far from here, he knew, and some of the explosion had blown down the wall and filled the room with fire and smoke. Everything was charred, tossed about, and reduced to unrecognizable pieces.

He stepped over the rubble near the door, took a few paces, then stopped, frozen, one leg in front of the other. At the end of the flashlight's beam was a severed head, the face blackened and charred, the hair nearly all singed off. Khalil couldn't tell if it was Lina or Adara.

He turned and ran toward the door, tripped, fell, scrambled across the rubble on all fours, and felt his hand coming into contact with bone and flesh.

He found himself lying in the small courtyard, curled into a ball, unwilling and unable to move.

In the distance, he could hear sirens, vehicles, people shouting, and, closer by, women wailing. Khalil knew there would be many funerals in the next few days, many graves to be dug, prayers to be said, and survivors to be comforted.

He lay there, numb with grief at the loss of his two brothers and two sisters. Finally, he tried to stand, but succeeded only in crawling toward the door of his mother's room. The door, he realized, was gone, blown away without a trace.

Khalil got to his feet and entered the room. The floor was relatively free of debris, and he saw that the roof had held, though everything in the room looked as if it had been moved toward the far wall, including the bed. Khalil saw that the curtains and shutters had been blown out of the two narrow-slit windows, and he realized that the force of the explosion outside had entered these windows and filled the room with a violent blast.

He hurried to his mother's bed, which had been pushed against the wall. He saw her lying there, her blanket and pillow gone and her night dress and sheets covered with gray dust.

At first he thought she was sleeping or just knocked senseless by the force of the collision with the wall. But then he noticed the blood around her mouth and the blood that had run from her ears. He remembered how his own ears and lungs had almost burst from the concussion of the bombs, and he knew what had happened to his mother.

He shook her. "Mother! Mother!" He continued to shake her. "Mother!"

Faridah Khalil opened her eyes and tried to focus on her oldest son. She began to speak, but coughed up foamy blood.

"Mother! It is Asad!"

She gave a slight nod.

"Mother, I am going to get help—"

She grabbed his arm with surprising strength and shook her head. She pulled on his arm, and he understood she wanted him closer.

Asad Khalil bent over so that his face was only inches from that of his mother.

She tried to speak again, but coughed up more blood, which Khalil could now smell. She kept her grip on him and he said, "Mother, you will be all right. I will go for a doctor."

"No!"

He was surprised to hear her voice, which sounded nothing like his mother's voice. He worried that there was damage done inside of her and that she was bleeding internally. He thought he might be able to save her if he could get her to the compound hospital. But she would not let him go. She knew she was dying and she wanted him close when she took her last breath.

She whispered in his ear, "Qadir...Esam...Lina...Adara...?"

"Yes...They are all right. They are...They...will be..." He found himself weeping so hard he couldn't continue.

Faridah whispered, "My poor children...my poor family..."

Khalil let out a long wailing sound, then screamed out, "Allah, why have you deserted us?" Khalil wept on his mother's breast, felt her heart-beat beneath his cheek, and heard her whisper, "My poor family..." Then her heart stopped, and Asad Khalil remained very still, listening for it, waiting for her chest to rise and fall again. He waited.

He lay on her breasts a long time, then he stood and walked out of her room. He wandered in a trance through the rubble of his home, and found himself outside in front of the house. He stood looking at the scene of chaos around him. Someone yelled nearby, "The whole Atiyeh family is dead!"

Men cursed, women wept, children screamed, ambulances came, stretchers took people away, a truck passed by, loaded with white-shrouded bodies.

He heard a man say that the Great Leader's house nearby had been hit by a bomb. The Great Leader had escaped, but members of his family had been killed.

Asad Khalil stood and listened to all that was said around him and noticed some of what was happening, but everything seemed very far away.

He began walking aimlessly and was almost hit by a speeding fire truck. He kept walking and found himself back near the munitions building where Bahira lay dead on the roof. He wondered if her family had survived. In any case, whoever was looking for her would be looking through the rubble in the area of the living quarters. It would be days or weeks before she was found on the roof, and by then the body would be...It would be assumed she died of concussion.

Asad Khalil found to his astonishment that he was still thinking clearly about certain things despite his grief.

He moved quickly away from the munitions building, not wanting any further association with that place.

He walked, alone with his thoughts, alone in the world. He said to himself, "My whole family are martyrs for Islam. I have succumbed to a temptation outside the Sharia and because of that I was not in my bed, and I have been spared the fate of my family. But Bahira succumbed to the same temptation and has suffered a different fate." He tried to make sense of all this and asked Allah to help him understand the meaning of this night.

The Ghabli whistled through the camp, blowing up dust and sand. The night was colder now and the moon had set, leaving the blacked out camp in total darkness. He had never felt so alone, so frightened, so helpless. "Allah, please, make me understand..." He lay face down on the black road facing toward Mecca. He prayed, he asked for an omen, he asked for guidance, he tried to think clearly.

He had no doubt who it was that had brought such destruction on them. There had been rumors for months that the madman, Reagan, would attack them, and now it had happened. He had an image of his mother speaking to him. *My poor family must be avenged.* Yes, that's what she had said, or was about to say.

Suddenly, in a flash of understanding, it became clear to him that he had been chosen to avenge not only his family, but his nation, his religion, and the Great Leader. He would be Allah's instrument for revenge. He, Asad Khalil, had nothing left to lose and nothing left to live for, unless he took up the Jihad and carried the Holy War to the shores of the enemy.

Asad Khalil's sixteen-year-old mind was now set and focused on simple revenge and retribution. He would go to America and slice the throats of everyone who had taken part in this cowardly attack. An eye for an eye, a tooth for a tooth. This was the Arab death feud, the blood feud, more ancient even than the Koran or Jihad, as ancient as the Ghabli. He said aloud, "I swear to Allah that I will avenge this night."

*   *   *

Lieutenant Bill Satherwaite asked his weapons officer, "All bull's-eyes?"

"Yeah," Chip Wiggins replied. "Well, one of them may have over-shot..." Wiggins added, "Hit something though. A line of, like, smaller buildings..."

"Good. As long as you didn't hit the Arch of Mario."

"Marcus."

"Whatever. You owe me dinner, Chip."

"No, you owe *me* dinner."

"You missed a bull's-eye. You buy."

"Okay, I'll buy if you fly back over the Arch of Marcus Aurelius."

"I flew *in* over the Arch. You missed it." Satherwaite added, "See it when you come back as a tourist."

Chip Wiggins had no intention of ever coming back to Libya, except in a fighter plane.

They flew on over the desert, and suddenly the coast streaked by below, and they were over the Mediterranean. They didn't need radio silence any longer, and Satherwaite transmitted, "Feet wet." They headed for the rendezvous point with the rest of their squadron.

Wiggins remarked, "We won't hear from Moammar for a while." He added, "Maybe not ever again."

Satherwaite shrugged. He was not unaware that these surgical strikes had a purpose beyond testing his flying ability. He understood that there would be political and diplomatic problems after this. But he was more interested in the locker room chatter back at Lakenheath. He looked forward to the debriefings. He thought fleetingly about the four 2,000-pound laser-guided bombs they had let loose, and he hoped everyone down there had enough warning to get into their shelters. He really didn't want to hurt anyone.

Wiggins broke into his thoughts and said, "By dawn, Radio Libya will report that we hit six hospitals, seven orphanages, and ten mosques."

Satherwaite didn't respond.

"Two thousand civilians dead—all women and children."

"How's the fuel?"

"About two hours."

"Good. Did you have fun?"

"Yeah, until the Triple-A."

Satherwaite replied, "You didn't want to bomb a defenseless target, did you?"

Wiggins laughed, then said, "Hey, we're combat veterans."

"That we are."

Wiggins stayed silent awhile, then asked, "I wonder if they're going to retaliate." He added, "I mean, they screw us, we screw them, they screw us, we screw them...where does it end?"

BOOK THREE

America, April 15, The Present

Terrible he rode alone
With his Yemen sword for aid;
Ornament, it carried none
But the notches on the blade.

—"The Death Feud"
An Arab war song

Chapter 18

Asad Khalil, recently arrived by air from Paris, and the only survivor of Trans-Continental Flight 175, sat comfortably in the back of a New York City taxi cab. He stared out the right side window, noticing the tall buildings set back from the highway. He noticed, too, that many of the cars here in America were bigger than in Europe, or in Libya. The weather was pleasant, but as in Europe, there was too much humidity for a man used to the arid climate of North Africa. Also, as in Europe, there was much green vegetation. The Koran promised a Paradise of greenery, flowing streams, eternal shade, fruits, wine, and women. It was curious, he thought, that the lands of the infidels seemed to resemble Paradise. But the resemblance, he knew, was only superficial. Or perhaps, Europe and America *was* the Paradise promised in the Koran, awaiting only the coming of Islam.

Asad Khalil turned his attention to the taxi driver, Gamal Jabbar, his compatriot, whose photo and name were prominently displayed on a license mounted on the dashboard.

Libyan Intelligence in Tripoli had told Khalil that his driver would be one of five men. There were many Muslim taxi drivers in New York City, and many of them could be persuaded to do a small favor, even though they were not chosen freedom fighters. Khalil's case officer in Tripoli, who he knew as Malik—the King, or the Master—had said with a smile, "Many drivers have relatives in Libya."

Khalil asked Gamal Jabbar, "What is this road?"

Jabbar replied in Libyan-accented Arabic, "This is called the Belt Parkway. You see, the Atlantic Ocean is over there. This part of the city is known as Brooklyn. Many of our co-religionists live here."

"I know that. Why are *you* here?"

Jabbar did not like the tone or the implication of the question, but he had a prepared answer and replied, "Just to make money in this accursed land. I will return to Libya and my family in six months."

Khalil knew this wasn't true—not because he thought Jabbar was lying—but because Jabbar would be dead within the hour.

Khalil looked out the window at the ocean on his left, then at the tall apartment buildings on his right, and then toward the distant skyline of Manhattan to his front. He had spent enough time in Europe not to be overly impressed with what he saw here. The lands of the infidels were populous and prosperous, but the people had turned away from their God and were weak. People who believed in nothing but filling their bellies and their wallets were no match for the Islamic fighters.

Khalil said to Jabbar, "Do you adhere to your faith here, Jabbar?"

"Yes, of course. There is a mosque near my home. I have maintained my faith."

"Good. And for what you are doing today, you are assured a place in Paradise."

Jabbar did not reply.

Khalil sat back in his seat and reflected on the last hour of this important day.

Getting out of the airport's service area and into this taxi and onto this highway had been very simple, but Khalil knew that it might not have been so easy ten or fifteen minutes later. He had been surprised on board the aircraft when he heard the tall man in the suit say, "Crime Scene," and then the man looked at him and ordered him off the spiral staircase. Khalil wondered how the police knew so soon that a crime had been committed. Perhaps, he thought, the fireman on board had said something on his radio. But Khalil and Yusef Haddad, his accomplice, had been careful not to leave any obvious evidence of a crime. In fact, Khalil thought, he had gone through the difficulty of breaking Haddad's neck so as not to leave evidence of a gunshot or knife wound.

There were other possibilities, Khalil thought. Perhaps the fireman had noticed the missing thumbs of the Federal agents. Or perhaps because the fireman was out of radio contact for a short time, the police became suspicious.

Khalil had not planned to kill the fireman, but he had no choice when the man tried to open the lavatory door. His only regret in killing the fireman was that another piece of evidence had been created at a critical moment in his plans.

In any case, the situation had changed quickly when that man in the suit came aboard, and Khalil then had to move more quickly. He smiled at the thought of that man telling him to get down from the staircase, which was exactly what he had been doing anyway. Getting off the aircraft had been not only simple—he'd actually been ordered to leave.

Getting into the baggage truck, whose engine was running, and driving off in the confusion had been even less of a problem. In fact, he'd had dozens of unoccupied vehicles to choose from, which is what he'd been told by Libyan Intelligence, who had a friend working as a baggage handler for Trans-Continental airlines.

Khalil's map of the airport had come from a Web site source, and the location of the place called the Conquistador Club had been accurately identified by Boutros, the man who had preceded him in February. Libyan Intelligence had made Khalil rehearse the route from the security area to the Conquistador Club, and Khalil could have made the drive blindfolded after a hundred rehearsals on mock roads laid out near Tripoli.

He thought about Boutros, whom he had met only once—not about the man himself, but about how easily Boutros had deceived the Americans in Paris, in New York, and then in Washington. The American Intelligence people were not stupid, but they were arrogant, and arrogance led to overconfidence, and thus carelessness.

Khalil said to Jabbar, "You are aware of the significance of this day."

"Of course. I am from Tripoli. I was a boy when the American bombers came. A curse be unto them."

"Did you suffer personally in the attack?"

"I lost an uncle at Benghazi. My father's brother. His death saddens me even now."

Khalil was amazed at how many Libyans had lost friends and

relatives in the bombing that had killed fewer than a hundred people. Khalil had long ago assumed they were all lying. Now he was probably in the presence of another liar.

Khalil did not often speak of his own suffering from that air attack, and he would never reveal such a thing outside Libya. But since Jabbar would soon pose no security risk, Khalil said to him, "My entire family was killed at Al Azziziyah."

Jabbar sat in silence a moment, then said, "My friend, I weep for you."

"My mother, my two sisters, my two brothers."

Again silence, then Jabbar said, "Yes, yes. I recall. The family of..."

"Khalil."

"Yes, yes. They were all martyred at Al Azziziyah." Jabbar turned his head to look at his non-paying passenger, "Sir, may Allah avenge your suffering. May God give you peace and strength until you see your family again in Paradise."

Jabbar went on, heaping praise, blessings, and sympathy on Asad Khalil.

Khalil's mind returned to earlier in the day, and again he thought of the tall man in the suit, and the woman in the blue jacket who seemed to be his accomplice. The Americans, like the Europeans, made women into men and the men became more like women. This was an insult to God and to God's creation. Woman was made of the rib of Adam, to be his helpmate, not to be his equal.

In any case, when that man and woman came on board, the situation had changed quickly. In fact, he had considered avoiding the place called the Conquistador Club—the secret headquarters of the Federal agents—but it was a target that he could not resist, a treat he had savored in his mind since February when Boutros had reported its existence to Malik. Malik had said to Khalil, "This is a tempting dish offered to you on your arrival. But it will not be as filling to you as those dishes served cold. Make your decision carefully and wisely. Kill only what you can eat, or what you can hide for later."

Khalil remembered those words, but had decided to take the risk and kill those who believed they were his jailers.

Khalil considered that what had happened on the aircraft was of little consequence. Poison gas was an almost cowardly way to kill, but it had been part of the plan. The bombs that Khalil had detonated in Europe gave him little satisfaction, though he appreciated the symbolism of killing those people in a manner similar to the way his family had been killed by the cowardly American pilots.

The killing of the American Air Force officer in England with the ax had given him the greatest satisfaction. He still recalled the man walking to his car in the dark parking lot, aware that someone was behind him. He remembered the officer turning to him and saying, "Can I help you?"

Khalil smiled. *Yes, you can help me, Colonel Hambrecht.* Then Khalil had said to the man, "Al Azziziyah," and he would never forget the expression on the man's face before Khalil swung the ax from under his trench coat and hit the man with the blade, almost severing his arm. And then Khalil took his time, chopping at the man's limbs, ribs, genitals, holding off the fatal blow to his heart until he was sure the man had suffered enough pain to be in extreme agony, but not so much pain as to become unconscious. Then he delivered the ax blow to the sternum, which split it open as the blade cut into his heart. The American colonel still had enough blood in him to produce a small geyser, which Khalil hoped the man could see and feel before he died.

Khalil had been sure to remove Colonel Hambrecht's wallet and watch to make it look like a robbery, though the ax murder clearly did not look like part of a simple robbery. Still, it put questions in the minds of the police, who had to label the murder as a possible robbery, but possibly political.

Khalil's next thought was of the three American schoolchildren in Brussels, waiting for a bus. There were supposed to be four—one for each of his sisters and brothers—but there were only three that morning. A female adult was with them, probably the mother of one or two. Khalil had stopped his car, got out, and shot each child in the chest and head, smiled at the woman, got back in the car, and drove off.

Malik had been angry with him for leaving a witness alive who saw his face, but Khalil had no doubt that the woman would remember nothing for the rest of her life, except the three children dying in her arms. This was how he had avenged the death of his mother.

Khalil thought a moment about Malik, his mentor, his master, almost his father. Malik's own father, Numair—the Panther—was a hero in the war of independence against the Italians. Numair had been captured by the Italian Army and hanged when Malik was just a boy. Malik and Khalil shared, and were bonded by, the loss of their fathers to the infidels, and both had sworn revenge.

Malik—whose real name was unknown—had, after his father had been hanged, offered to spy for the British against the Italians and the Germans as the armies of the three countries killed one another across the length of Libya. Malik had also spied for the Germans against the British, and his combined spying on the armies of both sides had ensured greater slaughter. When the Americans arrived, Malik found yet another employer who trusted him. Khalil recalled that Malik once told him of the time he led an American patrol into a German ambush, then returned to the American lines and revealed to them the location of the German ambush party.

Khalil had been in awe of Malik's duplicity and of his death toll without firing a shot himself.

Asad Khalil had been trained in the killing arts by many good men, but it had been Malik who taught him how to think, to act, to deceive, to understand the mind of the Westerner, and to use that knowledge to avenge all those who believed in Allah and who had been killed over the centuries by the Christian infidels.

Malik had told Asad Khalil, "You have the strength and courage of a lion. You have been taught to kill with the speed and ferocity of a lion. I will teach you to be as cunning as a lion. For without cunning, Asad, you will be an early martyr."

Malik was old now, nearly seventy years on this earth, but he had lived long enough to see many triumphs of Islam over the West. He had told Khalil, on the day before Khalil went to Paris, "God willing, you will reach America, and the enemies of Islam and of our Great Leader will fall before you. God has ordained your mission, and God will keep you safe until you return. But you must help God, a bit, by remembering all you have been taught and all you have learned. God himself has put in your hand the names of our enemies, and he has done so that you may slay them all. Be driven by revenge, but do not be blinded by hate. The lion does not hate. The lion kills all who threaten him or have tormented him. The lion also kills when he is hungry. Your soul has been hungry since that night when your family was taken from you. Your mother's blood calls to you, Asad. The innocent blood of Esam, Qadir, Adara, and Lina calls out to you. And your father, Karim, who was my friend, will be watching you from heaven. Go, my son, and return in glory. I will be waiting for you."

Khalil almost felt tears forming in his eyes as he thought of Malik's words. He sat quietly for a while, as the taxi moved through traffic, thinking, praying, thanking God for his good fortune so far. He had no doubt that he was at the beginning of the end of his long journey that had begun on the rooftop of Al Azziziyah so long ago on this very date.

The thought of the rooftop brought back an unpleasant memory— the memory of Bahira—and he tried to put this out of his mind, but her face kept returning to him. They had found her body two weeks later, so badly decomposed that no one knew how she died, and no one could guess why she had been on that roof so far from her house in Al Azziziyah.

Asad Khalil, in his naïveté, imagined that the authorities would connect him to Bahira's death, and he lived in mortal fear of being accused of fornication, blasphemy, and murder. But those around him mistook his agitated state for grief over the loss of his family. He *was* grief-stricken, but he was perhaps slightly more frightened of having his head severed from his body. He did not fear death itself, he told himself over and over again—what he feared was a shameful death, an early death that would keep him from his mission of revenge.

They did not come for him to kill him, they came to him with pity and respect. The Great Leader himself had attended the funeral of the Khalil family, and Asad had attended the funeral of Hana, the Gadhafis' eighteen-month-old adopted daughter, who had been killed in the air raid. Khalil had also visited the hospital to see the Great Leader's wife,

Safia, who had been wounded in the attack, as well as two of the Gadhafi sons, all of whom recovered. Praise be to Allah.

And two weeks later, Asad had attended the funeral of Bahira, but after so many funerals, he felt numb, without grief or guilt.

A doctor had explained that Bahira Nadir could have been killed by concussion or simply by fright, and she was thus joined with the other martyrs in Paradise. Asad Khalil saw no reason to confess to anything that would shame her memory or her family.

Regarding the Nadirs, the fact that the rest of the family had survived the bombing had caused Khalil to feel something like anger toward them. Envy, perhaps. But at least with Bahira's death, they could feel part of what he felt from losing everyone he loved. In fact, the Nadir family had been very good to him after the shared tragedy, and he'd lived with them for a while. It was during this time with the Nadirs—as he shared their home and their food—that he'd learned how to overpower his guilt at having killed and shamed their daughter. What happened on the roof was Bahira's fault alone. She had been fortunate to be honored as a martyr after her shameless and immodest behavior.

Khalil looked out the window and saw a huge gray bridge in front of him. He asked Jabbar, "What is that?"

Jabbar replied, "That is called the Verrazano Bridge. It will take us to Staten Island, then we cross another bridge to New Jersey." Jabbar added, "There is much water here and many bridges." He had driven a few of his countrymen over the years—some immigrants, some businessmen, some tourists—some on other business like this man, Asad Khalil, in the rear of his taxi. Nearly all of the Libyans he'd driven were amazed at the tall buildings, the bridges, the highways, and the green expanses. But this man didn't seem amazed or impressed, just curious. He said to Khalil, "Is this your first time in America?"

"Yes, and my last."

They drove over the long bridge and at the crown of the bridge, Jabbar said, "If you look that way, sir, to your right, you will see lower Manhattan, what they call the Financial District. You will notice the two very tall and identical towers."

Khalil looked at the massive buildings of lower Manhattan, which seemed to rise out of the water. He saw the two towers of the World Trade Center and appreciated Jabbar pointing them out. Khalil said, "Maybe next time."

Jabbar smiled and replied, "God willing."

In truth, Gamal Jabbar thought the bombing of the one tower was a horrible thing, but he knew what to say and who to say it to. In truth, too, the man in the back made him uneasy, though he couldn't say why. Maybe it was the man's eyes. They moved around too much. And the man spoke only occasionally, then lapsed into silence. With almost any Arabic speaker, the conversation in the taxi would have been ceaseless and good-hearted. With this man, conversation was difficult. Christians and Jews spoke more to him than this compatriot.

Jabbar slowed his vehicle as he approached the toll booths on the Staten Island side of the bridge. Jabbar said quickly to Khalil, "This is not a police or customs checkpoint. I have to pay here for the use of the bridge."

Khalil laughed and replied, "I know that. I have spent time in Europe. Do you think I'm an illiterate desert tribesman?"

"No, sir. But sometimes our countrymen get nervous."

"Your bad driving is the only thing that makes me nervous."

They both laughed.

Jabbar said to his passenger, "I have an electronic pass that will permit me to go through the toll booth without having to stop and pay an attendant. But if you wish to have no record of this crossing, then I must stop and pay cash."

Khalil wanted neither a record of the crossing nor did he want to approach a booth with a person in it. The record, he knew, would be permanent, and might be used to trace his route to New Jersey, because when they found Jabbar dead in his taxi, they might connect him to Asad Khalil. Khalil said to Jabbar, "Pay in cash."

Khalil put an English language newspaper in front of his face as Jabbar slowed down and approached the toll booth at the shortest line.

Jabbar pulled up to the booth, paid the toll in cash without exchanging a word with the toll attendant, then accelerated onto a wide highway.

Khalil lowered the newspaper. They were not yet looking for him, or if they were, they had not yet put out an alert this far from the airport. He wondered if they had concluded that the dead body of Yusef Haddad was not the dead body of Asad Khalil. Haddad had been chosen as an accomplice because he bore a slight resemblance to Khalil, and Khalil also wondered if Haddad had guessed his fate.

The sun was low on the horizon now and within two hours it would be dark. Khalil preferred the darkness for the next part of his journey.

He had been told that the American police were numerous and well equipped, and that they would have his photo and description within half an hour of his leaving the airport. But he had also been told that the automobile was his best means of escape. There were too many of them to stop and search, which was not the case in Libya. Khalil would avoid what were called choke points—airports, bus stations, train stations, hotels, houses of his compatriots, and certain roads, bridges, and tunnels where the toll takers or police might have his photo. This bridge was one such place, but he was certain that the speed of his escape had gotten him through the net that was not yet fully in place. And if they made the net tighter around New York City, it didn't matter because he was nearly out of the area, and would never return to this place. And if they made the net larger, which they would, then the net would be looser, and he could easily slip through it at any point in his journey. Many police, yes. But many people, too.

Malik had told him, "Twenty years ago, an Arab might have been noticed in an American city, but today, you might not even be noticed in a small town. The only thing an American man notices is a beautiful woman." They had both laughed at that. Malik had added, "And the only things an American woman notices are how other women dress and the clothes in shop windows."

They exited the highway onto another highway, heading south. The taxi maintained a safe speed and soon Khalil saw another bridge rising to his front.

Jabbar said, "There is no toll from this direction on this bridge. On the other side of the bridge is the state of New Jersey."

Khalil didn't reply. His thoughts went back to his escape. "Speed," they had told him at his intelligence briefing in Tripoli. "Speed. Fugitives tend to move slowly and carefully, and that's how they get caught. Speed, simplicity, and boldness. Get in the taxi and keep going. No one will stop you as long as the taxi driver does not go too fast or too slow. Make the driver assure you that there are no problems with his brake lights or signal lights. The American police will stop you for that. Sit in the rear of the taxi. There will be an English language newspaper there. All our drivers are familiar with American driving and laws. They are all licensed taxi drivers."

Malik had further instructed him, "If you are stopped by the police for any reason, assume it has nothing to do with you. Sit in the taxi, let the driver talk. Most American policemen travel alone. If the policeman speaks to you, answer in English with respect, but not fear. The policeman may not search you or the driver or the vehicle without a legal reason. This is the law in America. Even if he searches the taxi, he will not search you, unless he is certain you are someone he is seeking. If he asks you to get out of the taxi, he intends to search you. Leave the taxi, draw your pistol, and shoot him. He will not have his gun drawn, unless he is already certain you are Asad Khalil. If that is the case, may Allah protect you. And be certain to have your bulletproof vest on. They will give this to you in Paris to protect you from assassins. Use it against them. Use the Federal agents' guns against them."

Khalil nodded to himself. They were very thorough in Libya. The Great Leader's intelligence organization was small, but well financed and well trained by the old KGB. The godless Russians had been knowledgeable, but they had faith in nothing, which was why their state had collapsed so suddenly and so totally. The Great Leader still made use of the former KGB men, hiring them like whores to service the Islamic fighters. Khalil himself had been trained partly by Russians, some Bulgarians, and even some Afghani, who the American CIA had trained to fight the Russians. It was like the war which Malik had fought between the Germans and Italians on one side and the British and the Americans on the other. The infidels fought and killed one another and trained Islamic fighters to help them—not understanding that they were sowing the seeds of their further destruction.

Jabbar crossed the bridge and turned the taxi off the highway onto a street of houses that looked, even to Khalil, like poor homes. "What is this place?"

"It is called Perth Amboy."

"How much longer?"

"Ten minutes, sir."

"And there is no problem with this automobile being noticed in this other state?"

"No. One may drive freely from state to state. Only if I go too far from New York might someone notice a taxi so far from the city. To journey a long distance by taxi can be expensive." Jabbar added, "But of course you should pay no attention to this taxi meter. I leave it on because it is the law."

"There are many small laws here."

"Yes, you must obey the small laws so you can more easily break the big ones."

They both laughed.

Khalil pulled out the wallet in the breast pocket of the dark gray suit jacket that Gamal Jabbar had given him. He checked his passport, which had his photo showing him wearing glasses and a short mustache. It was a clever photo, but he was concerned about the mustache. In Tripoli, where they had taken the photo, they told him, "Yusef Haddad will give you a false mustache and eyeglasses. It is necessary as a disguise, but if the police search you, they will test your mustache, and when they see that the mustache is false, they will know that everything else is false."

Khalil put his fingers to the mustache, then tugged on it. It was firmly fixed, but, yes, it could be discovered to be false. In any event, he had no intention of letting a policeman get close enough to pull on his mustache.

He had the glasses, given to him by Haddad, in his breast pocket. He didn't need glasses, but these were bifocals so that he could see with them on, and they would also pass as legitimate reading glasses.

He looked at the passport again. His name was Hefni Badr and he was an Egyptian, which was good, because if he were questioned by an Arab-American who worked for the police, a Libyan could pass for an Egyptian. Khalil had spent many months in Egypt and felt confident that he could convince even an Egyptian-American that they were countrymen.

The passport also gave his religion as Muslim, his occupation as schoolteacher, which he could easily impersonate, and his residence in El Minya, a city on the Nile that few Westerners or even Egyptians were familiar with, but this was a place where he'd spent a month for the explicit purpose of reinforcing what was called his legend—his false life.

Khalil checked through the wallet and found five hundred dollars in American money—not too much to draw attention, but enough to meet his needs. He also found some Egyptian money, an Egyptian internal identification card, an Egyptian bank card in his assumed name, and an American Express card, also in his assumed name, that Libyan Intelligence told him would work in any American scanner.

Also in his breast pocket was an international driver's license in the name of Hefni Badr, with a photo similar to the one on his passport.

Jabbar was glancing in his rearview mirror and said to him, "Is everything in order, sir?"

Khalil replied, "I hope I never have to discover if it is."

Again, they both laughed.

Khalil put everything back in his breast pocket. If he were stopped at this time, he could probably deceive an ordinary policeman. But why should he bother to be an actor just because he wore a disguise? Despite what they'd told him in Libya, his first reaction—not his last—would be to pull both his pistols and kill anyone who posed a threat to him.

Khalil opened the black overnight bag that Jabbar had placed for him in the back seat. He rummaged through the big bag, finding toilet articles, underwear, a few ties, a sports shirt, a pen and a blank notebook, American coins, a cheap camera of the type a tourist might have, two plastic bottles of mineral water, and a small copy of the Koran, printed in Cairo.

There was nothing in the bag that could compromise him—no invisible writing, no microdots, not even a new pistol. Everything he needed to know was in his head. Everything he needed to use would be provided or acquired along the way. The only thing that could connect him, Hefni

Badr, to Asad Khalil were the two Federal agents' Glock pistols. In Tripoli, they had told him to dispose of the pistols as soon as possible, and his taxi driver would give him a new pistol. But he had replied, "If I'm stopped, what difference does it make what pistol I have with me? I wish to use the enemy's weapons until I complete my mission or until I die." They did not argue with him, and there was no pistol in the black bag.

There *were* two items in the bag that could possibly compromise him: the first was a tube of toothpaste that was actually gum for his false mustache. The second was a can of foot powder, an Egyptian brand that was in fact colored with a gray tint. Khalil twisted the cap and sprinkled the powder in his hair, then combed it through as he looked at himself in a small hand mirror. The results were amazing—turning his jet black hair to a salt-and-pepper gray. He restyled his swept-back hair into a part on the left side, put on his glasses, then said to Jabbar, "Well, what do you think?"

Jabbar glanced in his rearview mirror and said, "What has become of the passenger I picked up at the airport? What have you done with him, Mr. Badr?"

They both laughed, but then Jabbar realized he should not have drawn attention to the fact that he knew the fictitious name of his passenger, and he fell silent. Jabbar looked in his rearview mirror and saw this man's dark eyes staring at him.

Khalil turned to look out the window. They were still in an area that seemed less prosperous than any he had seen in Europe, but there were many good cars parked on the streets, which surprised him.

Jabbar said, "Look there, sir. That is the highway you will need to drive on—it is called the New Jersey Turnpike. That is the entrance to the highway, there. You will take a ticket from a machine and pay a toll when you get off. The highway goes north and south, so you must get into the proper lane."

Khalil noted that Jabbar did not ask him which way he was going to travel. Jabbar understood that the less he knew, the better for everyone. But Jabbar already knew too much.

Khalil asked Jabbar, "Do you know what happened at the airport today?"

"Which airport, sir?"

"The one we came from."

"No, I do not."

"Well, you will hear about it on the radio."

Jabbar did not reply.

Khalil opened one of the bottles of mineral water, drank half of it, then tipped the bottle and poured the remainder on the floor.

They pulled into a huge parking lot with a sign that said PARK AND RIDE. Jabbar explained, "People drive their cars here and take a bus into Manhattan—into the city. But today is Saturday, so there are not many cars."

Khalil looked around at the expanses of crumbling blacktop surrounded by a chain-link fence. There were about fifty cars parked within white lines, but the parking lot could hold hundreds more. He noted, too, that there were no people in view.

Jabbar put his taxi in a parking space and said, "There, sir, do you see that black car straight ahead?"

Khalil followed Jabbar's gaze to a large black automobile parked a few rows ahead of them. "Yes."

"Here are the keys." Without looking at Khalil, Jabbar passed the keys over the seat. Jabbar said, "All of your rental papers are in the glove box. The car is rented in the name on your passport for one week, so after that time, the car agency may become concerned. The car was rented at Newark Airport, in New Jersey, but the license plates are from New York. This is of no concern. That is all I have been instructed to tell you, sir. But if you would like, I can lead you back to the highway."

"That won't be necessary."

"May Allah bless your visit, sir. May you return safely to our homeland."

Khalil already had the .40 caliber Glock in his hand. He put the muzzle of the Glock into the opening of the empty plastic bottle and pushed the bottom of the bottle against the rear of the driver's seat. He fired a shot through the back of the seat into Gamal Jabbar's upper spine, so that if it missed the spinal column, it would penetrate the heart from the rear. The plastic bottle muffled the blast of the gun.

Jabbar's body lurched forward, but his harness belt held him upright.

Smoke poured from the bottle's neck and from the bullet hole in the bottom. Khalil loved the smell of burnt cordite and inhaled it through his nostrils. He said, "Thank you for the water."

Khalil considered a second shot, but then he saw Jabbar's body start to twitch in a way that a man could not fake. Khalil waited half a minute, listening to Jabbar's gurgling.

As he waited for Jabbar to die, he found the empty .40 caliber shell casing and put it in his pocket, then put the plastic bottle in his overnight bag.

Gamal Jabbar finally stopped twitching, gurgling, and breathing, and sat motionless.

Khalil looked around to be certain they were alone in the lot, then he reached over the seat and quickly took Jabbar's wallet from his pocket, then unfastened the man's seat belt and pushed him down below the dashboard. He turned off the ignition and took the keys out.

Asad Khalil removed his black overnight bag, got out of the taxi, closed and locked the doors, then walked to the black car, which was called a Mercury Marquis. The key fit, he entered the car, and started it, remembering his seat belt. He moved out of the quiet parking lot onto the street. He recalled a line from the Hebrew scripture. *A lion is in the streets*. He smiled.

Chapter 19

An FBI guy named Hal Roberts met Kate, Ted, and me in the lobby of 26 Federal Plaza.

When someone meets you in the lobby of your workplace, it's either an honor, or you're in trouble. Mr. Roberts was not smiling, and this was my first clue that we were not going to receive letters of commendation.

We got on the elevator, and Roberts used his key for the twenty-eighth floor. We rode up in silence.

Twenty-six Federal Plaza is home to various government agencies, most of them no more than innocuous tax eaters. But floors twenty-two through twenty-eight are not innocuous and are accessible only by key. I was given a key when I started this job, and the guy who gave it to me said, "I'd like to get the thumbprint pad here. You can forget your key, or lose it, but you can't forget or lose your thumb." Actually, you can lose your thumb.

My work floor was twenty-six where I had a piece of a cube farm, along with other ex-NYPD and active-duty NYPD. Also on the twenty-sixth floor were a few suits, as cops referred to the FBI. This is a bit of a misnomer, since many of the NYPD types wear suits, and about a third of the FBI types are female and don't wear suits. But I learned long ago never to question the jargon of an organization; somewhere in the jargon is a clue to the mind-sets of the people who work there.

Anyway, we got to the top floor where the celestial beings dwelt, and we were ushered into a corner office facing southeast. The name on the door said JACK KOENIG, known by his translated and transposed name as King Jack. Mr. Koenig's actual title was Special Agent in Charge, SAC for short, and he was in charge of the entire Anti-Terrorist Task Force. His dominion extended throughout the five boroughs of New York City, the surrounding counties of New Jersey and Connecticut, as well as nearby upstate New York and the two counties of Long Island— Nassau and Suffolk. It was in this latter county, on the east end of Long Island, where I had first run into Sir Ted and Sir George, to continue the metaphor, knights-errant, who turned out to be fools. In any case, I had no doubt that King Jack did not like things going wrong in his kingdom.

His Highness had a big office with a big desk. There was also a couch and three club chairs around a coffee table. There were built-in bookshelves and an Arthurian round table and chairs, but no throne.

His Majesty was not in, and Mr. Roberts said, "Make yourselves at home, put your feet up on the coffee table, and lay on the couch if you like." Actually, Mr. Roberts did not say this—Mr. Roberts said, "Wait here," and left.

I wondered if I had time to get to my desk and check my hiring contract.

I should mention that since this is a Joint Anti-Terrorist Task Force, there is a New York City police captain who shares this command with Jack Koenig. The captain is named David Stein, a Jewish gent with a law degree, and in the eyes of the Police Commissioner, a man with enough brains to hold his own against the overeducated Feds. Captain Stein has a tough job, but he's slick, sharp, and just diplomatic enough to keep the Feds happy while still protecting the interests of the NYPD men and women under him. People like me who are ex-NYPD Contract Agents are in a sort of gray area, and no one looks out for our interests, but neither do I have the problems of career officers, so it's a wash.

Anyway, regarding Captain Stein, he's a former Intelligence Unit guy who worked on a lot of cases involving Islamic extremists, including the murder of Rabbi Meir Kahane, and he's a natural for this job. Not to read too much into the Jewish thing, but he clearly has a personal problem with Islamic extremists. The Anti-Terrorist Task Force, of course, covers all terrorist organizations, but you don't have to be a rocket scientist to figure out where most of the focus was.

In any case, I wondered if I'd be seeing Captain Stein tonight. I hoped so—we needed another cop in the room.

Kate and Ted put Phil's and Peter's briefcases on the round table without comment. I recalled occasions when I had to remove the shield, gun, and credentials of men I knew and return them to the precinct. It's not unlike when ancient warriors would take the swords and shields of their fallen comrades and bring them home. In this case, however, the weapons were missing. I opened the briefcases to be sure the cell phones were off. It's disturbing when a dead person's phone rings.

Anyway, regarding Jack Koenig, I'd met him only once when I was hired, and I found him to be fairly intelligent, quiet, and thoughtful. He was known as a hard-ass and had a sarcastic side to him, which I admired greatly. I recalled that he'd said to me, apropos of my professorship at John Jay, "Those who can, do—those who can't, teach." To which I'd replied, "Those who have taken three bullets on the job don't have to explain their second careers." After a moment of frosty silence, he smiled and said, "Welcome to the ATTF."

Despite the smile and welcome, I had the impression he was a wee bit pissed at me. Maybe he'd forgotten the incident.

We stood in the office with the plush blue carpet, and I glanced at Kate, who seemed a little anxious. I looked at Ted Nash, who, of course, did not call Jack his Special Agent in Charge. Mr. CIA had his own bosses, housed across the street at 290 Broadway, and I'd have given a month's pay to see him on the carpet at 290. But that would never happen.

Some of the ATTF, by the way, is located at 290 Broadway, a newer and nicer building than Federal Plaza, and rumor has it that the separation of forces is not the result of an administrative space problem, but a planned strategy in the event someone decided to test out their advanced chemistry class on one of the Federal buildings. Personally, I think it's just a planning screwup and bureaucratic jockeying, but this kind of organization lends itself to top security explanations for common stupidity.

If you're wondering why Ted, Kate, and John were not conversing, it's because we figured that the office was bugged. When two or more people are left alone in someone else's office, just assume you're on the air. Testing, one, two, three. I did say, however, for the record, "Nice office. Mr. Koenig has really good taste."

Ted and Kate ignored me.

I glanced at my watch. It was nearly 7:00 P.M., and I suspected that Mr. Koenig was not happy about having to return to the office on a Saturday evening. I wasn't too thrilled with the idea either, but anti-terrorism is a full-time job. As we used to say in the Homicide Squad, "When a murderer's day ends, our day begins."

Anyway, I went to the window and looked out to the east. This part of lower Manhattan is jam-packed with courthouses, and further to the east was One Police Plaza, my former headquarters where I'd had good visits and bad visits. Beyond Police Plaza was the Brooklyn Bridge from whence we'd come, and which crossed over the East River itself, which separated Manhattan Island from Long Island.

I could not actually see Kennedy Airport from here, but I could see the glow of its lights, and I noticed in the sky above the Atlantic Ocean what appeared to be a string of bright stars, like a new constellation, but which were actually approaching aircraft. Apparently the runways were open again.

Out in the harbor, to the south, was Ellis Island, through which millions of immigrants had passed, including my Irish ancestors. And to the south of Ellis Island in the middle of the bay stood the Statue of Liberty, all lit up, holding her torch high, welcoming the world. She was on just about every terrorist's hit list, but so far, so good. She was still standing.

All in all, it was a spectacular evening view from up here—the city, the lighted bridges, the river, the clear April sky, and the nearly full moon rising in the east above the flatlands of Brooklyn.

I turned and looked southwest through the big window of the corner office. The most dominant features out there were the Twin Towers of the World Trade Center, soaring a quarter mile into the sky, a hundred and ten stories of glass, concrete, and steel.

The towers were about half a mile away, but they were so massive that they looked as if they were across the street. The towers were designated the North Tower and the South Tower, but on Friday, February 26, 1993, at 12:17 and 36 seconds P.M., the South Tower almost became known as the Missing Tower.

Mr. Koenig's desk was arranged so that every time he looked out the window, he could see these towers, and he could contemplate what some Arab gentlemen had prayed for when they had driven an explosive-filled van into the basement parking garage—namely, the collapse of the South Tower and the death of over fifty thousand people in the tower and on the ground.

And if the South Tower had collapsed just right and hit the North Tower, there would have been another forty or fifty thousand dead.

As it turned out, the structure held, and the death toll was six, with over a thousand injured. The subterranean explosion took out the police station located in the basement and left a cavern where the multi-layered underground parking garage had been. What could have been the biggest loss of American life since World War II turned out to be a loud and clear wake-up call. America had become the front lines.

It occurred to me that Mr. Koenig could have rearranged his furniture or put blinds on the windows, but it said something about the man that he chose to look at these buildings every workday. I don't know if he cursed the security lapses that had led to the tragedy, or if he thanked God every morning that a hundred thousand lives had been spared. Probably he did both, and probably, too, these towers, plus the Statue of Liberty and Wall Street and everything else that Jack Koenig surveyed from up here, haunted his sleep every night.

King Jack had not actually been in charge of the ATTF when the bomb blew in 1993, but he was in charge now, and he might think about rearranging his desk Monday morning to look toward Kennedy Airport. Indeed, it was lonely at the top, but the view was supposed to be good. For Jack Koenig, however, there were no good views from here.

The subject of my thoughts entered his office at that moment and caught me staring out at the World Trade Center. He asked me, "Are they still standing, Professor?"

Apparently he had a good memory for snotty subordinates. I replied, "Yes, sir."

"Well, that's good news." He looked at Kate and Nash and motioned us all to the seating area. Nash and Kate sat on the couch, I sat in one of the three club chairs, while Mr. Koenig remained standing.

Jack Koenig was a tall man of about fifty years old. He had short, steely-gray hair, steely-gray eyes, a steely-gray Saturday stubble, a steely jaw, and stood like he had a steel rod up his ass that he was about to transfer to someone else's ass. All in all, he was not an avuncular type, and his mood looked understandably dark.

Mr. Koenig was dressed in casual slacks, a blue sports shirt, and loafers, but on him nothing looked casual, sporty, or loafish.

Hal Roberts entered the office and sat in the second club chair, across from me. Jack Koenig didn't seem inclined to sit and relax.

Mr. Roberts had a long yellow legal pad and a pencil. I thought perhaps he was going to take drink orders, but I was being too optimistic.

Mr. Koenig began without preamble and asked us, "Can one of you explain to me how a cuffed and guarded suspected terrorist managed to kill three hundred men, women, and children aboard an American airliner, including his two armed escorts, and two Federal Air Marshals on board, a Port Authority Emergency Service man, and then proceed to a secret and secure Federal facility where he murdered an ATTF secretary, the FBI duty officer, and an NYPD member of your team?" He looked at each of us. "Would anyone care to take a shot at an explanation?"

If I were at Police Plaza instead of Federal Plaza, I would have answered a sarcastic question like that by saying, "Can you imagine how much worse it could have been if the perp *wasn't* cuffed?" But this was not the time, place, or occasion for flippancy. A lot of innocent people were dead, and it was the job of the living to explain why. Nevertheless, King Jack was not getting off to a good start with his subjects.

Needless to say, no one answered the question, which seemed to be rhetorical. It's a good idea to let the boss vent awhile. To his credit, he vented only for another minute or so, then sat down and stared off out the window. His view was toward the financial district, so there were no unhappy associations attached to that scene, unless he happened to own Trans-Continental stock.

Jack Koenig, by the way, was FBI, and I'm sure that Ted Nash did not like being spoken to in such a manner by an FBI guy. I, as a quasi-civilian, didn't like it either, but Koenig was the boss, and we were all part of the Task Force. The Team. Kate, being FBI, was in a career-threatening position, and so was George Foster, but George had chosen the easy job and stayed behind with the bodies.

King Jack seemed to be trying to get himself under control. Finally, he looked at Ted Nash and said, "I'm sorry about Peter Gorman. Did you know him?"

Nash nodded.

Koenig looked at Kate and said, "You were a friend of Phil Hundry."

"Yes."

Koenig looked at me and said, "I'm sure you've lost friends on the job. You know how hard that is."

"I do. Nick Monti had become my friend."

Jack Koenig stared off into space again, contemplating many things, I'm sure. It was a time for respectful silence, and we gave it about a minute, but everyone knew that we had to get back to business quickly.

I asked, perhaps undiplomatically, "Will Captain Stein be joining us?"

Koenig looked at me a moment and finally said, "He's taken direct charge of the stakeout and surveillance teams and has no time for meetings."

You never know what the bosses are actually up to, or what kind of palace struggle is going on, and it's best not to give a shit. I yawned to indicate that I just lost interest in both my question and Koenig's answer.

Koenig turned to Kate and said, "Okay, tell me what happened. From the top."

Kate seemed prepared for the question and went through the events of the day, chronologically, objectively, and quickly, but without rushing.

Koenig listened without interrupting. Roberts took notes. Somewhere an audiotape was spinning.

Kate mentioned my insistence on going out to the aircraft, and the fact that neither she nor Foster thought it was necessary.

Koenig's face remained impassive, neither approving nor disapproving throughout the narrative. He didn't raise an eyebrow, didn't frown, didn't wince, didn't nod or shake his head, and for sure never smiled. He was an expert listener and nothing in his manner or demeanor encouraged or discouraged his witness.

Kate got to the part where I went back into the dome of the 747 and discovered that Hundry's and Gorman's thumbs were missing. She stopped there and collected herself. Koenig glanced at me, and though he didn't give me any sign of approval, I knew that I was going to stay on the case.

Kate moved on with the sequence of events, giving only the facts, leaving the speculation and theories for later, if and when Koenig asked for them. Kate Mayfield had an amazing memory for detail, and an astonishing ability to refrain from coloring and slanting facts. I mean, in similar situations when I was on the carpet in front of the bosses, I would try not to color or slant, unless I was protecting a bud, but I have been known to have memory lapses.

Kate concluded with, "George decided to stay and take charge of the scene. We all concurred, and we asked Officer Simpson to drive us here."

I glanced at my watch. Kate's narrative had taken forty minutes. It was now nearly 8:00 P.M., the time when my brain usually needs alcohol.

Jack Koenig sat back in his chair, and I could see he was processing the facts. He said, "It seems as though Khalil was just a step or two ahead of us."

I decided to reply and said, "That's all it takes in a race. Second place is just the first loser."

Mr. Koenig regarded me a moment and repeated, "Second place is the first loser. Where did you get that?"

"I think the Bible."

Koenig said to Roberts, "Take a break," and Mr. Roberts put down his pencil.

Koenig said to me, "I understand you've put in a transfer request for the IRA section."

I cleared my throat and replied, "Well, I did, but—"

"Do you have some personal grudge against the Irish Republican Army?"

"No, actually, I—"

Kate spoke up and said, "John and I discussed this earlier, and he has withdrawn the request."

That's not exactly what I said to her, but it sounded better than my racist and sexist remarks regarding Muslims. I glanced at Kate and our eyes met.

Koenig informed me, "I reviewed the Plum Island case last fall."

I didn't reply.

"I read the case report prepared by Ted Nash and George Foster, and the report that was written by a Detective Beth Penrose of the Suffolk County Homicide Division." He added, "There seemed to be some differences of opinion and fact between the ATTF report and the Suffolk County Police report. Most of the differences had to do with your role in the case."

"I had no official role in the case."

"Nevertheless, you solved the case."

"I had a lot of time on my hands. Maybe I need a hobby."

He didn't smile. He said, "Detective Penrose's report was perhaps colored by your relationship with her."

"I had no relationship with her at the time."

"But you did when she wrote her final report."

"Excuse me, Mr. Koenig, I've been through this with the NYPD Internal Affairs—"

"Oh, they have people who investigate affairs?"

This, I realized, was a joke and I chuckled, a second or two late.

"Also," he continued, "Ted and George's report may have been colored by the fact that you pissed them off."

I glanced at Nash, who seemed totally aloof, as usual, as though Koenig was talking about another Ted Nash.

Koenig said, "I was fascinated by your ability to get to the heart of a very complex case that had eluded everyone else."

"It was standard detective work," I said modestly, hoping that Mr. Koenig would say, "No, my boy, you're brilliant."

But he didn't say that. He said, "That's why we hire NYPD detectives. They bring something different to the table."

"Like donuts," I suggested.

Mr. Koenig was neither amused nor annoyed. He said, "They bring to the table a degree of common sense, street smarts, and an insight into the criminal mind that is slightly different from that of an FBI or CIA agent. Do you agree?"

"Absolutely."

"It is an article of faith in the ATTF that the whole is greater than the sum of the parts. Synergy. Right?"

"Right."

"This is only possible through mutual respect and cooperation."

"I was just about to say that."

He regarded me a moment and asked, "Do you want to stay on this case?"

"Yes. I do."

He leaned toward me and looked in my eyes. He said, "I don't want to see any grandstanding, I don't want to hear about any shitty attitudes, and I want complete loyalty from you, Mr. Corey, or so help me God, I'll have your head stuffed and mounted on my desk. Agreed?"

My goodness. The guy sounded like my ex-bosses. There must be something about me that brings out the nasties in people. Anyway, I mulled over the contract amendment. Could I be a loyal and cooperative team player? No, but I wanted the job. I realized that Mr. Koenig hadn't demanded that I cease my sarcasm or dull my rapier wit, and I took this as either approval or an oversight on his part. I crossed my fingers and said, "Agreed."

"Good." He put out his hand and we shook. He said, "You're on."

I was going to say, "You won't regret it, sir," but I thought maybe he would, so I just said, "I'll do my best."

Koenig took a folder from Roberts and began leafing through it. I regarded Jack Koenig a moment and decided I should not underestimate him. He didn't get to this corner office because Uncle Sam was his mother's brother. He got here for all the usual reasons of hard work, long hours, intelligence, training, belief in his mission, good leadership skills, and probably patriotism. But a lot of people in the FBI had the same skills and qualifications.

What distinguished Jack Koenig from other talented men and women was his willingness to accept responsibility for catastrophes that he'd been hired to prevent. What happened this afternoon was bad enough, but somewhere out there was a bad guy—Asad Khalil, and others like him—who wanted to nuke midtown Manhattan, or poison the water supply, or wipe out the population with microorganisms. Jack Koenig knew this, we all knew this. But Koenig was ready to carry this burden and take the final rap if and when it happened. Like today.

Koenig looked at Ted, Kate, and me, then nodded to Roberts, who picked up his pencil. The John Corey job interview and attitude adjustment period was over, and Part Two of the JFK disaster was about to begin.

Koenig said to Kate, "I find it hard to believe that Flight One-Seven-Five was without radio contact for over two hours, and none of you knew about it."

Kate replied, "Our only contact with the airline was through the gate agent, who knew very little. We'll have to re-evaluate that procedure."

"That's a good idea." He added, "You should also be in direct contact with Air Traffic Control and Tower Control, and the Port Authority police command center."

"Yes, sir."

"If that flight had been hijacked in the air, it could have been in Cuba or Libya before you knew about it."

"Yes, sir." She added, "Ted had the foresight to have the name and phone number of the Tower Supervisor."

Koenig glanced at Nash and said, "Yes. Good thinking. But you should have called him sooner."

Nash didn't reply. I had the impression that Nash would say nothing that Mr. Roberts could jot down on his legal pad.

Koenig continued, "It would appear that our February defector was on a dry run to see what our procedures are. I think we all suspected that after he bolted, hence the extra precautions this time." Koenig added, "If the February defector had been blindfolded, he wouldn't have seen the Conquistador Club, its location, or...how to unlock the door. So, maybe we should start blindfolding all non-authorized personnel, including so-called defectors and informants." He added, "Also, you'll recall that the February defector was brought in on a Saturday and saw how few people were at the Conquistador Club on a weekend."

Part Two, it seemed, was a review of policies and procedures, also called Closing the Cage After the Lion Escapes. Mr. Koenig went on in this vein for some time, speaking mostly to Kate, who was filling in for our fearless leader, George Foster.

"All right," said Mr. Koenig, "the first indication you had that everything was not going as planned was when Ted called the Tower Control Supervisor, a Mr. Stavros."

Kate nodded. "That's when John wanted to go out to the aircraft, but Ted, George, and I—"

"I've already noted that," said Mr. Koenig. I sort of wanted to hear it again, but Koenig pushed on and asked Ted Nash a direct and interesting question. He looked at Nash and said, "Did you anticipate a problem with this assignment?"

Nash replied, "No."

I thought otherwise, despite old Ted's crap about only the truth is spoken here. CIA types are so into deceit, deception, double and triple crosses, paranoia, and bullshit, that you never knew what they knew, when they knew it, and what they were making up. This doesn't make them bad guys, and in fact you have to admire their world-class bullshit. I mean, a CIA guy would lie to a priest in a confessional. But admiration aside, it's not easy to work with them if you're not one of them.

In any case, Jack Koenig had asked the question and thereby raised the issue, but he let it go and said to me, "By the way, while I admire your initiative, when you got in that Port Authority car and crossed the runways, you lied to your superiors and broke every rule in the book. I'll let this pass, but don't let it happen again."

I was a little pissed off now and I said, "If we'd acted about ten minutes sooner, maybe Khalil would be in custody right now, charged with murder. If you'd instructed Hundry and Gorman to call and report on their cell phones or the airphone, we'd have known there was a problem when we didn't hear from them. If we'd been in direct contact with Air Traffic Control, we'd have been told the aircraft was out of radio contact for hours. If you hadn't welcomed this February bozo with open arms, what happened today wouldn't have happened." I stood and announced, "Unless you need me for something important, I'm going home."

When I used to pull this stunt with my bosses, someone would say, "Don't let the door hit you in the ass on your way out." But Mr. Koenig said softly, "We need you for something important. Please sit down."

Okay, so I sat. If I was back at Homicide North, this is when one of the bosses opens his desk and passes around the seltzer bottle of vodka to cool everyone down. But I didn't expect any rule-bending here in a place where they hung warning posters in the corridors about drinking, smoking, sexual harassment, and thought crimes.

Anyway, we all sat there a moment, engaged, I guess, in Zen meditation, calming our nerves without nasty alcohol.

Mr. Koenig went on with his agenda and asked me, "You called George Foster on Kate's mobile phone and instructed him to put out a citywide."

"That's right."

He went through the sequence and content of my cell phone calls to George Foster, then said, "So you went back to the dome, and saw that Phil's and Peter's thumbs had been severed. You understood what that meant."

"What else could it mean?"

"Right. I congratulate you on an incredible piece of deductive reasoning...I mean...to go back and look for...their thumbs." He looked at me and asked, "How did you come to that thought, Mr. Corey?"

"I really don't know. Sometimes things pop into my head."

"Really? Do you usually act on things that pop into your head?"

"Well, if they're weird enough. You know, like severed thumbs. You have to go with that."

"I see. And you called the Conquistador Club, and Nancy Tate didn't answer."

I said, "I think we've been through this."

Koenig ignored this and said, "She was, in fact, dead by that time."

"Yes. That's why she didn't answer."

"And Nick Monti was also dead by that time."

"He was probably in the process of dying at that time. It takes a while with chest wounds."

Out of nowhere, Koenig asked me, "Where did you get wounded?"

"On West One Hundred and Second Street."

"I mean, *where?*"

I knew what he meant, but I don't like to discuss anatomy in mixed company. I replied, "There wasn't much brain damage."

He looked doubtful, but dropped that subject and looked at Ted. "Do you have anything to add?"

"No, I don't."

"Do you think that John and Kate missed any opportunities?"

Ted Nash considered this loaded question and replied, "I think we all underestimated Asad Khalil."

Koenig nodded. "I think we did. But we won't do that again."

Nash added, "We all have to stop thinking of these people as idiots. That will get us into a lot of trouble."

Koenig didn't reply.

Nash continued, "If I may say so, there is an attitudinal problem in the FBI and the NYPD Intelligence Unit regarding Islamic extremists. Part of this problem stems from racial attitudes. The Arabs and other ethnic groups in the Islamic world are not stupid or cowardly. Their armies or air forces may not impress us, but Mideastern terrorist organizations have scored some major hits around the world, in Israel and America. I've worked with Mossad, and they have a healthier respect for Islamic terrorists than we do. These extremists may not all be top-notch, but even bunglers can score once in a while. And sometimes you get an Asad Khalil."

Needless to say, King Jack did not enjoy the lecture, but he appreciated its message. And that made Jack Koenig brighter than the average boss. I, too, was hearing what Nash was saying, and so did Kate. The CIA, despite my bad attitude toward its representative, had many strengths. One of its strengths was supposed to be in the area of enemy capability assessment, but they tended to overestimate the enemy, which was good for the CIA budget. I mean, the first inkling they had of the collapse of the Soviet Union was from the newspapers.

On the other hand, there was some truth in what Ted Nash was saying. It's never a good idea to think of people who look, talk, and act differently from you as clowns. Especially when they want to kill you.

Jack Koenig said to Nash, "I think everyone's attitudes are changing, but I agree with you that we still have some problems in that area. After today, we'll see some improvement in how we perceive our opponents."

Now that Mr. Nash had made his philosophical point, he returned to the specific subject and said, "It's my belief, as Kate told you earlier, that Khalil has left the country. Khalil is headed now to a Mideastern country on a Mideastern carrier. He will eventually wind up in Libya again where he'll be debriefed and honored. We may never see him again, or we may see his handiwork a year from now. In the meantime, this is a matter best handled through international diplomacy and by international intelligence agencies."

Koenig looked at Nash awhile. I had the distinct impression they were not fond of each other. Koenig said, "But you don't mind, Ted, if we continue to pursue leads here?"

"Of course not."

My, my. The fangs were bared for a brief moment. I thought we were a team.

Mr. Koenig suggested to Mr. Nash, "Since you have firsthand knowledge of this case, why don't you request a reassignment back to your agency? You would be invaluable to them on this case. Perhaps an overseas assignment."

Nash got the drift and replied, "If you feel you can spare me here, I'd like to go to Langley tonight or tomorrow and discuss that idea with them. I think it's a good idea."

"So do I," said Jack Koenig.

It looked to me as though Ted Nash was about to disappear from my life, which made me very happy. On the other hand, I might miss old Ted. Then again, maybe I wouldn't. People like Nash who disappear have a habit of reappearing when you least expect or want them to.

The polite but pissy exchange between Ted Nash and Jack Koenig seemed to be finished.

I mentally lit a cigar, drank some Scotch, and told a dirty joke to myself while Kate and Jack chatted. How do these people function without alcohol? How can they talk without swearing? But Koenig did let a few profanities slip out now and then. There was hope for him. In fact, Jack Koenig might have made a good cop, which is about the highest praise I can offer.

There was a knock on the door and it opened. A young man stood in the doorway and said, "Mr. Koenig. There's a call for you that you may want to take out here."

Koenig stood, excused himself, and walked to the door. I noticed that the outer area, which had been empty and dark when we arrived, was now all lit up, and I saw men and women at their desks or walking around. A police station is never dark, quiet, or empty, but the Feds try to keep normal work hours, trusting in a few duty officers and beepers to turn out the troops when the poopy hits the paddles.

Anyway, Jack disappeared, and I turned to Hal Roberts and suggested, "Why don't you find us some coffee?"

Mr. Roberts did not like being sent for coffee, but Kate and Ted seconded my suggestion, and Roberts got up and left.

I regarded Kate a moment. Despite the day's events, she looked as fresh and alert as if it were 9:00 A.M. instead of 9:00 P.M. I myself felt my ass dragging. I'm about ten years older than Ms. Mayfield, and I haven't fully recovered from my near-death experience, so that might explain the difference in our energy levels. But it didn't explain why her clothes and hair were so neat and why she smelled good. I felt, and probably looked, crumpled, and I needed a shower about now.

Nash looked dapper and awake, but that's the way mannequins always looked. Also, he hadn't done anything physical today. Certainly he hadn't had a wild ride around the airport or climbed through an aircraft full of corpses.

But back to Kate. She had her legs crossed, and I noticed for the first time what good legs they were. Actually, I may have noticed this about a month ago in the first nanosecond after meeting her, but I'm trying to modify my NYPD piggishness. I have not hit on one single— or married—female in the ATTF. I was actually getting a reputation as a man who was either devoted to duty, or was devoted to some off-scene girlfriend, or was gay, or who had a low libido, or who perhaps had been hit below the belt by one of those bullets.

In any case, a whole new world was opening up to me now. Women in the office talked to me about their boyfriends and husbands, asked me if I liked their new hairstyles, and generally treated me in a gender-neutral manner. The girls haven't yet asked me to go shopping with them or shared recipes with me, but maybe I'll be invited to a baby shower. The old John Corey is dead, buried under a ton of politically correct memos from Washington. John Corey, NYPD Homicide, is history. Special Contract Agent John Corey, ATTF, has emerged. I feel clean, baptized in Potomac holy water, reborn and accepted into the ranks of the pure angelic hosts with whom I work.

But back to Kate. Her skirt had ridden above her knees, and I was treated to this incredible left thigh. I realized she was looking at me, and I tore my eyes away from her legs and looked at her face. Her lips were fuller than I'd thought, pouty and expressive. Those ice blue eyes were looking deep into my soul.

Kate said to me, "You look like you need coffee."

I cleared my throat and my mind and replied, "I actually need a drink."

She said, "I'll buy you one later."

I glanced at my watch and said, "I'm usually in bed by ten."

She smiled, but didn't reply. My heart was pounding.

Meanwhile, Nash was being Nash, totally unconnected, as inscrutable as a Tibetan monk on quaaludes. It occurred to me again that maybe the guy was not aloof. Maybe he was stupid. Maybe he had the IQ of a toaster oven, but he was bright enough not to let on.

Mr. Roberts returned with a tray on which was a carafe and four coffee mugs. He set this down on the table without comment and didn't even offer to pour. I took the carafe and poured three mugs of hot coffee. Kate, Ted, and I each took a mug and sipped.

We all stood and went to the windows, each of us lost in our own thoughts as we stared out into the city.

I looked east, out toward Long Island. There was a nice cottage out there, about ninety miles and a world away from here, and in the cottage was Beth Penrose, sitting in front of a fire, sipping tea or maybe brandy. It wasn't a good idea to dwell on those kinds of things, but I remembered what my ex-wife once said to me, "A man like you, John, does only what he wants to do. You want to be a cop, so don't complain about the job. When you're ready, you'll give it up. But you're not ready."

Indeed not. But at times like this, the idiot students at John Jay were looking good.

I glanced at Kate and saw she was looking at me. I smiled. She smiled. We both turned back to our views.

For most of my professional life, I had done work that was considered important. Everyone in this room knew that special feeling. But it took its toll on the mind and on the spirit, and sometimes, as in my case, on the body.

Yet, something kept pushing me on. My ex had concluded, "You'll never die of boredom, John, but you will die on this job. Half of you is dead already."

Not true. Simply not true. What was true was that I was addicted to the adrenaline rush.

Also, I actually felt good about protecting society. That's not something you'd say in the squad room, but it was a fact and a factor.

Maybe after this case was over, I'd think about all this. Maybe it was time to put down the gun and the shield and get out of harm's way, time to make my exit.

Chapter 20

Asad Khalil continued on through a residential neighborhood. The Mercury Marquis was big, bigger than anything he'd ever driven, but it handled well enough.

Khalil did not go to the toll highway called the New Jersey Turnpike. He had no intention of going through any toll booths. As he had requested in Tripoli, the rented automobile had a global positioning system, which he'd used in Europe. This one was called a Satellite Navigator, and it was slightly different from the ones he was used to, but it had the entire U.S. roadway system in its database, and as he drove slowly through the streets, he accessed the directions to Highway I.

Within a few minutes he was on the highway heading south. This was a busy road, he noticed, with many commercial establishments on either side.

He noticed that some automobiles coming toward him had their headlights on, so he put on his headlights.

After a mile or so, he dropped Jabbar's keys out the window, then removed Jabbar's cash from his wallet, counting eighty-seven dollars. He went through Jabbar's wallet as he drove, ripping up what could be ripped and dropping small pieces out the window. The credit cards and plasticized driving license presented a problem, but Khalil managed to bend and break them all, and let them fall out the window. The wallet now contained nothing except a color photograph of the Jabbar family—Gamal Jabbar, a wife, two sons, a daughter, and an elderly woman. Khalil regarded the photograph as he drove. He had been able to retrieve a few photographs from the ruins of his home in Al Azziziyah, including a few photographs of his father in uniform. These images were precious to him, and there would be no further photographs of the family of Khalil.

Asad Khalil tore the Jabbar family photograph in four pieces and let it fly out the window, followed by the wallet, then the plastic bottle, and finally the shell casing. All the evidence was now strewn over many miles of the highway and would attract no attention.

Khalil reached over, opened the glove box, and pulled out a stack of papers—rental forms, maps, some advertisements and other papers that had little purpose. The Americans, he saw, like the Europeans, loved useless papers.

He glanced through the rental agreement and confirmed that the name on the agreement matched his passport.

He turned his attention back to the road. There were many bad drivers on the road here. He saw very young people driving, and very old people driving, and many women were driving. No one seemed to drive well. They drove better in Europe, except for Italy. The drivers in Tripoli were like Italian drivers. Khalil realized he could drive badly here and not be noticed.

He looked at his gas gauge and saw that it read FULL.

A police car came into view in his side mirror and stayed behind him for a while. Khalil maintained his speed and did not change lanes. He resisted glancing too often in the sideview or rearview mirrors. That would make the policeman suspicious. Khalil put on his bifocal glasses.

After a full five minutes, the police car pulled into the outside lane and came alongside of him. Khalil noticed that the policeman didn't even give him a glance. Soon, the police car was ahead of him.

Khalil settled back and paid attention to the traffic. They had told him in Tripoli that there would be much traffic on a Saturday night, many people visited or went to restaurants or movie theaters or shopping malls. This was not too different from Europe, except for the shopping malls.

In Tripoli they also told him that in the more rural areas, the police were looking at cars that might be driven by dealers of drugs. This could be a problem, they warned him, as the police sometimes looked for drivers who were of the black or Spanish race, and they might stop an Arab man by mistake or even on purpose. But at night, it was difficult to see who was driving, and now the sun was setting.

Asad Khalil thought for a minute about Gamal Jabbar. He took no pleasure in killing a fellow Muslim, but each believer in Islam was expected to fight, or to sacrifice, or to be martyred in the Jihad against the West. Too many Muslims, such as Gamal Jabbar, did nothing except send money back to their homelands. Jabbar did not actually deserve death, Khalil thought, but death became the only possibility. Asad Khalil was on a holy mission, and others had to sacrifice so that he could do what they couldn't do—kill the infidel. His only other thought about Gamal Jabbar was a passing concern that the man could have survived the single bullet. But Khalil had seen that twitching before, and heard that gurgling. The man was dead. "May Allah take him into Paradise this very night."

The sun was setting, but it was not practical to stop to perform the Salat. He had been given dispensation from the mullah for the time he was engaged in the Jihad. But he would not fail to say his prayers. In his mind, he prostrated himself on his prayer rug and faced Mecca. He recited, "God is most great! I bear witness that there is no God but Allah. I bear witness that Muhammad is the Messenger of God. Hasten to Salat! Hasten to success! God is most great. There is no God but Allah!"

He recited random passages from the Koran, "Kill the aggressors wherever you find them. Drive them out of the places from which they drove you...Fight them until Allah's religion is supreme...Fight for the cause of Allah with the devotion due to him...Permission to take up arms is hereby given to those who are attacked...Allah has the power to grant them victory...Believers, fear Allah as you rightly should, and when death comes, die true Muslims...If you have suffered a defeat, so did the enemy. We alternate these victories among mankind so that Allah may know true believers and choose martyrs from among you, and that he may test the faithful and annihilate the infidels. Allah is the supreme Plotter."

Satisfied that he had fulfilled his obligations, he felt at peace as he drove through the strange land, surrounded by enemies and infidels.

Then, he recalled the ancient Arab war song, and he sang the song called "The Death Feud." "Terrible he rode alone with his Yemen sword for aid; ornament, it carried none but the notches on the blade."

Chapter 21

Jack Koenig returned with some papers in his hand that looked like faxes. We all sat and he said to us, "I spoke to the crime lab supervisor at JFK. They have a preliminary report—" he tapped the papers on the coffee table "—of the scenes of the aircraft and the Conquistador Club." He added, "I also spoke to George, who has offered to transfer out of the ATTF and out of New York."

He let that hang there for a few seconds, then asked Kate, "Yes? No?"

"No."

Koenig addressed Kate and me and said, "Can you two speculate or guess as to what happened on the aircraft before it landed?"

Kate said, "John is the detective."

Koenig said to me, "You're on, Detective."

I should point out here that the FBI uses the term "investigator" to describe what amounts to a detective—so I didn't know if I was being honored or patronized. In any case, this is partly what I was hired for, of course, and I'm good at this stuff. But Koenig made no secret of the fact that he just got some answers to the questions he was asking. So, rather than make an idiot of myself, I asked Koenig, "I assume they found those two oxygen bottles in the dome coat closet."

"Yes, they did. But as you discovered, both had their valves open, so all that's left are the residual amounts after the pressures equalized. That should be enough for the lab to get a good reading on what was in each, but even before that happens we can assume that one was oxygen and the other wasn't." He said to me, "Proceed."

"Okay...about two hours outside of New York, Air Traffic Control lost contact with Trans-Continental One-Seven-Five. So, it was then that the guy with the medical oxygen bottles, probably sitting in Business Class in the dome—"

"Correct," said Mr. Koenig. "His name was Yusef Haddad. Seat Two A."

"Okay, this guy—what's his name?"

"Yusef Haddad. Means Joe Smith. He's on the manifest with a Jordanian passport and medical oxygen required for emphysema. The passport's probably a fake, so was the emphysema, and so was one of the oxygen bottles."

"Right. Okay, Joe Smith, Business Class Jordanian in Seat Two A. This guy is breathing the real oxygen, then he reaches down and opens the valve of the second bottle. A gas escapes and gets into the closed air-conditioning system of the aircraft."

"Correct. What kind of gas?"

"Well, it was something nasty like cyanide."

"Very good. It was most probably a hemotoxin, maybe a military form of cyanide. The victims basically suffocated. Like I said, the lab is analyzing the remnants in each cylinder, plus the blood and tissue of the victims. They should be able to identify the particular gas pretty soon. Not that it really matters. But that's the way they work. Anyway, within ten minutes, all the air on board is recirculated. So everyone got a dose of this gas except Yusef Haddad, who was still breathing pure oxygen." He looked at me and said, "Tell me how Khalil escaped death."

"Well, I'm not sure of the sequence of events, but…I'm thinking that Khalil was in the lav when the gas escaped. The lavatory might be less toxic than the cabin air."

"In fact," Koenig said, "it is not. But the exhaust flow of air from the lav is vented directly out of the aircraft, which is why everyone in the cabins can't smell it when someone sits on the potty."

Interesting. I mean, I once took an AeroMexico flight to Cancun where they served a lunch consisting of twenty-two different bean dishes, and I was surprised the plane didn't explode in midair. I said, "So the lav is toxic, and Khalil is breathing as little as possible and maybe has a wet paper towel over his face. Haddad has to make his move very quickly and get to Khalil, either with his own oxygen or one of those small oxygen bottles that are carried on board for medical emergencies."

Koenig nodded, but said nothing.

Kate said, "What I don't understand is how Haddad and Asad Khalil knew that the aircraft was pre-programmed to land itself."

Koenig replied, "I'm not sure either. We're checking that out." He looked at me and said, "Continue."

"Okay, so within ten minutes, there are only two people alive on board the aircraft—Asad Khalil and his accomplice, Yusef Haddad. Haddad finds the handcuff keys on Peter Gorman and uncuffs Khalil in the lav. The poison gas is eventually vented, and after they're certain that the air is safe to breathe, maybe fifteen minutes, they get off the oxygen. Kate and I didn't see the aircraft's emergency oxygen bottle lying around, so I assume that Haddad or Khalil put it back where it's usually stored. Then they put Haddad's medical oxygen in the dome coat closet where we found it."

"Yes," Koenig replied, "they wanted everything to look fairly normal when the aircraft was first boarded at JFK. Assuming Peter or Phil had died near the lav, they also put that person's body back in his seat. Continue, Mr. Corey."

I continued, "Okay, Khalil must not have killed Haddad immediately because Haddad's body was warmer than everyone else's. So these two guys tidy up things, maybe go through Phil's and Peter's belongings, take their guns, then probably go down to First and Coach and make sure everyone is dead. At some point, Khalil doesn't need any more company, and he breaks Haddad's neck, as Kate discovered. He puts Haddad next to Phil, cuffs him, and puts the sleeping mask on him." I added, "Somewhere along the line, Khalil took the thumbs."

"Correct," Koenig said. "The lab found a knife in the dome galley with traces of wiped blood, and they found the napkin used to wipe the knife hidden in the galley trash. Had anyone who first boarded seen a bloody knife, that would have gotten some attention. Had you or Kate seen it, you'd have come to the conclusion you came to even sooner."

"Right." What you first see when you arrive at a crime scene is often what the perpetrator wants you to see. Further investigation, however, turns up the ropes and pulleys behind the scenery.

Koenig looked at us and said, "At some point, while the aircraft was being towed, Sergeant Andy McGill of the Port Authority Emergency Service unit made a final transmission to his people."

We all nodded. I said, "McGill and Khalil may have stumbled on each other by accident."

Koenig regarded his faxes and said, "Preliminary evidence—blood, brain, and bone tissue—suggests that McGill was killed between the galley and the lav—facing the lav. Some tissue was sprayed into the galley, some of it landing on the dead flight attendant, although someone made an attempt to wipe it up, which is why you may not have noticed it," Koenig said pointedly. He added, "So maybe McGill opened the lav door and discovered Asad Khalil. Also, forensic found a lap blanket with a hole and burn marks, indicating that the blanket was used to muffle the sound of the gunshot."

I nodded. It's always amazing what the forensic people can tell you very quickly, and how quickly a detective can make deductions and re-create the crime. It didn't matter that this was a terrorist incident—a crime scene is a crime scene. Murder was murder. The only thing missing was the murderer.

Koenig continued, "Regarding Khalil's escape from the aircraft, we can assume he knew what the procedure would be at JFK. With the pilots dead, any Emergency Service personnel entering the aircraft would shut down the engines. At that point, a tow truck would be summoned and the aircraft would be taken to the security area. You know the rest."

Indeed we did.

Koenig added, "Also, we found what we assume was Yusef Haddad's hang-up garment bag. Under a suit was a blue Trans-Continental baggage handler's jumpsuit that was meant for Mr. Haddad. There was, in that garment bag, undoubtedly a second jumpsuit for Asad Khalil, and he had it on at some point, knowing that baggage handlers would come aboard to collect carry-on luggage."

He looked at Kate, then at me and asked, "Did either of you notice anyone who looked suspicious? You knew something was wrong, yet Khalil got away."

I replied, "I think he was gone when we got there."

"He may have been. Then again, maybe he wasn't. Maybe you bumped into him."

Kate said, "I think we would have recognized him."

"Do you? Not if he was wearing a baggage handler's jumpsuit, combed his hair differently, was wearing glasses and a phony mustache. But maybe he saw *you*. Maybe at some point he realized there were Federal agents or detectives on board. Think about that. Try to recall what happened and who you saw on the aircraft and in that security area."

Okay, Jack, I'll think about it. Thanks for mentioning it.

Koenig continued, "In any case, Khalil got into an empty baggage truck and drove off. At this point, most men who'd just pulled off one of the most ballsy moves—excuse my language—one of the most audacious moves in terrorist history, would get to the international terminal, get out of that jumpsuit under which was street clothing, and get on an outbound flight for Sandland—forgive my characterization of the Middle East. But no, Asad Khalil is not going home. Not yet. He has to make a stop at the Conquistador Club first. The rest, as they say, is history."

No one spoke for a full minute, then Koenig observed, "This is a very resourceful, clever, and bold individual. He exploits situations quickly and without hesitation or fear of getting caught. He relies on other people being either preoccupied or unaware that there is a psychopathic killer in their midsts. Speed, savagery, and shock. Decisiveness, daring, and deception. Understand?"

We all understood. If I had the inclination, I could tell Jack Koenig about ten or fifteen such killers I'd come across over the years. The really good psychotic killers were just as Koenig described. You couldn't believe the stuff they got away with. You couldn't believe how stupid and trusting their victims were.

Mr. Koenig continued his thoughts and said, "There are other scenarios regarding how Khalil's plan might work out. The worst scenario for him was that the aircraft simply crashed and killed everyone on board, including Khalil. He would have accepted that, I think, and called it a win."

We all sort of nodded. The boss was on.

"Another possibility," Koenig continued, "is that he'd get caught on the ground and be identified as the killer. That would also be okay with him. He'd still be a hero in Tripoli."

Again, we nodded, starting to appreciate not only Koenig, but also Khalil.

Koenig said, "Yet another possibility is that he escapes from the aircraft, but is not able to carry out his mission at the Conquistador Club. In any case, Asad Khalil couldn't lose once Yusef Haddad was on board with his medical oxygen and poison gas. In fact, even if Yusef Haddad had been stopped before he boarded the aircraft in Paris, Asad Khalil would still have wound up in the Conquistador Club, though he'd be guarded and cuffed. But who knows how that would have played out later?"

Everyone thought about Asad Khalil back at the Conquistador Club as planned. At what point would this guy go psychotic?

Mr. Koenig concluded with, "Other scenarios aside, Asad Khalil hit a grand-slam home run. He cleared the bases, and he's on the way to home plate—whether that means a safe house in America, or back to Libya, we don't know yet." He added, "But we'll play it as though he's close by and waiting to hit again."

Since we were out of facts and into speculation, I speculated, "I think this guy is a loner, and he won't be turning up at the usual watched houses or hanging around the local mosque with the usual suspects."

Kate concurred and added, "He may have one contact here, maybe the February guy, or someone else. Assuming he needs no help after the initial contact, we can expect to find another accomplice's body somewhere, soon. I'm also assuming he had a man at JFK to help get him out of there and that could be the guy who turns up dead. We should give the NYPD a heads-up on that."

Koenig nodded. He looked at Nash. "Why do you think he's gone?"

Nash didn't reply for a second or two, giving the impression that he was tired of casting pearls before swine. Finally, he leaned forward and looked at each of us. He said, "We've described Khalil's entrance into this country as grand and dramatic. And Mr. Koenig is correct that no matter how any of those scenarios played out, Khalil was a winner. He was ready to sacrifice his life in the service of Allah and join his brethren in Paradise. This was one hell of a risky way to sneak into a hostile country."

"We know that," Koenig said.

"Hear me out, Mr. Koenig. This is important, and actually some good news. All right, back this thing up and postulate that Asad Khalil was coming to America to blow up this building, or the one across the street, or all of New York City, or Washington. Postulate a nuclear device hidden somewhere, or more likely a ton of toxic gas or a thousand liters of anthrax. If Asad Khalil was the man who was supposed to deliver any of these weapons of mass death and destruction, then he would have come into Canada or Mexico on a false passport and slipped easily over the border to accomplish this important mission. He would not have arrived as he did with the high risk of getting caught or killed. What we saw today was a classical Seagull Mission…" He looked around at us and explained, "You know, a person flies in, makes a lot of noise, craps all over everything, then flies out. Mr. Khalil was on a Seagull Mission. Mission accomplished. He's gone."

So, we all thought about Seagull Missions. Old Ted had spoken and revealed that he had the IQ of at least a VCR. This was irrefutable logic. The silence in the room told me that everyone had finally seen the incandescent brilliance of Nash's mind at work.

Koenig nodded and said, "Makes sense to me."

Kate nodded, too, and said, "I think Ted is right. What Khalil was sent here to do, he did. There's no second act to come. His mission ended at JFK, and he was perfectly positioned to take any one of dozens of late afternoon flights out."

Koenig looked at me. "Mr. Corey?"

I, too, nodded. "Makes sense to me. Ted makes a strong case for his theory."

Koenig thought a moment and said, "Still, we have to proceed as if Khalil may still be in this country. We've notified every law enforcement agency in the U.S. and in Canada. We've also called up every ATTF agent we could find tonight, and we're staking out every place where a Mideast terrorist might turn up. We've also alerted the Port Authority police, NYPD, New Jersey, Connecticut, suburban counties, and so forth. The more time that goes by, the bigger the search area gets. If he's hiding out, perhaps waiting to get out of the country, we may still nab him close by. Containment is the first priority."

Nash informed us, "I called Langley from JFK, and they put out a high-priority watch-and-detain at all international airports where we have assets." He looked at me. "That means people who work for us, with us, or *are* us."

"Thank you. I read spy novels."

So, that was it. Asad Khalil was either already out of the country, or was in hiding, waiting to get out. This really did make the most sense, considering what happened today and how it happened.

There were, however, a few things that bothered me, a detail or two that didn't fit. The first and most obvious was the question of why Asad Khalil had turned himself in to the CIA liaison guy at the Paris Embassy. A much simpler plan would have been for Khalil to just get on board Trans-Continental Flight 175 with a false passport, the way Joe Smith, his accomplice, did. The same poison gas plan would have worked better if Khalil was not in cuffs, and not guarded by two armed Federal agents.

The thing Nash was missing was the human element, which is what you'd expect Nash to miss. You had to understand Asad Khalil to understand what he was up to. He didn't want to be another anonymous terrorist. He wanted to walk into the Paris Embassy, get himself cuffed and guarded, then escape like Houdini. This was still an in-your-fucking-face act on his part—not a Seagull Mission. He wanted to read what we knew about him, he wanted to cut off thumbs and go to the Conquistador Club and murder anyone who was there. It was definitely a high-risk operation, but what was unique about it was the personal nature of it. It was, in fact, an insult, a humiliation, like an ancient warrior riding alone into an enemy camp and raping the chief's wife.

The only question in my mind was whether or not Asad Khalil was finished fucking the Americans. I didn't think he was—the guy was on a roll—but I agreed with Nash now, that Khalil didn't have a nuke that needed to be detonated, or poison gas or germs that needed to be spread. I was going with a gut feeling that Asad Khalil—the Lion—was in America to push more shit in our faces, up close and personal. I would not have been completely surprised if he showed up on the twenty-eighth floor and cut some throats and broke some necks.

So, it was time to share this feeling with my teammates, time to reveal my ace to King Jack, if you'll pardon the metaphor or whatever the hell that is.

But my colleagues were chatting about something else, and while I waited for an opportunity to talk, I had second thoughts about these things that bothered me and this feeling that Asad Khalil was trying keys to the elevator about now. So I let it go for the time being and tuned back in.

Kate was saying to Jack Koenig, "Obviously Khalil read everything in Phil's and Peter's briefcases."

Koenig replied, too matter-of-factly I thought, "They didn't have much with them."

Kate pointed out, "Asad Khalil now has our dossier on Asad Khalil."

"There wasn't that much in it," Koenig said. "Not much he didn't already know about himself."

Kate pressed the point. "But now he knows how little we know."

"All right. I get it. Anything else?"

"Yes . . . in the dossier was a memo from Zach Weber. It was just an operations memo, but it was addressed to George Foster, Kate Mayfield, Ted Nash, Nick Monti, and John Corey."

Holy shit! I never thought of that.

Jack Koenig, in his understated way, said, "Well, then, be careful."

Thanks, Jack.

He added, "But I doubt if Khalil . . ." He thought about it, then advised us, "We know what this man is capable of. But we don't know what he plans to do. I don't think you're in his plans."

Kate had another thought about that and said, "We agreed that we shouldn't underestimate this man."

"Neither should we overestimate him," Koenig replied curtly.

There's a switch—the FBI, like the CIA, usually overestimates everything. It's good for their budget *and* their image. But I kept that thought to myself.

Kate continued, "We have rarely seen a terrorist act like this. Most acts of terrorism are either random or remote, such as bombings. This man is suspected of personally murdering people in Europe, and I don't have to tell you what he just did here. There's something about this guy that bothers me, aside from the obvious."

"And what do you think that is?" Mr. Koenig asked.

"I don't know," she replied. "But unlike most terrorists, Khalil has shown a lot of intelligence and courage."

Koenig commented, "Like a lion."

"Yes, like a lion. But we shouldn't get too metaphorical. He's a man, and he's a killer, and that makes him more dangerous than any lion."

Kate Mayfield was coming close to the heart of the matter, closer to an understanding of Asad Khalil. But she didn't say anything else, and no one ran with her thoughts.

We discussed the personality types of killers for a minute or two, and the FBI is really good at this kind of psychological profiling. A lot of it sounded psychobabbly to me, but some of it was on the mark. I offered my assessment and said, "I get the feeling that Khalil has a hard-on for Americans."

"Excuse me?" said Mr. Koenig. "A *what?*"

I regretted my lapse into station house jargon and I clarified my noun. "He has more than a philosophical or political agenda. He has a burning hatred for Americans as people." I added, "I think in light of today's events, we can assume that some or all of the suspicions and allegations contained in Khalil's dossier are, in fact, true. If so, then he murdered an American Air Force officer with an ax. He shot down three innocent American schoolkids in Brussels. If we can figure out why, then maybe we can figure out what's bothering this guy, and maybe what's next and who's next."

Nash piped in and said, "He's also targeted the Brits. We think he exploded a bomb in the British Embassy in Rome. So, your theory about him having a—an obsession with killing only Americans doesn't hold up."

I replied, "If he did bomb that British Embassy, then there's a connection. He doesn't like Brits *or* Americans. Connections are always clues."

Nash sort of laughed at me. I really don't like it when people do that.

Koenig looked at Nash. "You disagree with Mr. Corey?"

Nash replied, "Mr. Corey is mixing police work and intelligence work. The model for one doesn't necessarily apply as the model for the other."

"Not necessarily," Koenig said. "But sometimes."

Nash shrugged, then said, "Even if Asad Khalil was targeting only Americans, that doesn't make him unique. In fact, quite the opposite. Most terrorists target America and Americans. That's our reward for being Number One, for being pro-Israel, for the Gulf War, and for our worldwide anti-terrorist operations."

Koenig nodded, but said, "Still, there's the matter of Khalil's unique style—his up-close, personal, insulting, and humiliating modus operandi."

Nash again shrugged. "So what? That's his style, and even if it were a clue to his future plans, we couldn't head him off. We're not going to catch him on a mission. He has a million targets, and he chooses the target, the time, and the place. Seagull Missions."

No one replied.

Ted Nash concluded, "In any event, you know that I'm convinced that what happened today *was* the mission, and that Khalil is gone. He may strike next in Europe, where he's apparently struck before and where he knows the terrain, and where security is not always consistent. And yes, he may come back here someday. But for now, the lion is full, to continue the metaphor. He's on his way back to his lair in Libya, and he won't come out again until he's hungry."

I thought about offering my Dracula metaphor—the ship arriving like magic with a dead crew and passengers, and Drac slipping into a totally clueless country full of porky people with good veins and all that. But Mr. Koenig seemed to think I was a logical guy with good instincts and no metaphorical thoughts. So I bagged the Dracula thing and said, "Not to be contrary, but based on what we saw today, I still think that Khalil is within fifty miles of where we're sitting. I have a ten-dollar bet with Ted that we hear from him soon."

Mr. Koenig managed a smile. "Do you? You'd better let me hold the money. Ted's leaving for overseas."

Koenig wasn't kidding and held out his hand. Nash and I each put ten bucks in his hand, which he pocketed.

Kate sort of rolled her eyes. Boys will be boys.

Jack Koenig looked at me and said, "So, Khalil is out there somewhere, and he has your name, Mr. Corey. Do you think you're now on his menu?"

I guess we were back to lion metaphors and I got the meaning, which I didn't like.

Koenig informed me, "Sometimes the hunters become the hunted." He looked at Nash. "For instance, a Mideast terrorist murdered two men in the parking lot of CIA headquarters."

Ted Nash looked as if he'd rather forget that. He replied, "The victims were both CIA employees, but they were random targets. The killer didn't know them. The institution was the target."

Jack Koenig didn't reply. He said to Kate, Ted, and me, "If Asad Khalil is still in this country, you were not the reason he came here originally, but you may now be on his list of targets. Actually, I see this as an opportunity."

I leaned forward. "Excuse me? What opportunity?"

"Well, I hate to use the word bait, but—"

"Bad idea. Let's drop that."

He didn't want to drop it and got back to the lion metaphor. "You have this rogue lion who's eating villagers. And you have these hunters, who almost caught the lion. The lion is angry at the hunters, and he makes the fatal mistake of going after the hunters. Right?"

Nash seemed amused. Kate seemed to be considering it.

Koenig said, "We'll put out a news story about John and Kate, and maybe even use your pictures, although we'd never do that normally.

Khalil will think it's standard to use names and photos of agents in America, and he won't suspect a trap. Right?"

I said, "I don't think that's in my contract."

Koenig continued, "We won't and can't use Ted's name and photo because his agency would never allow that. George is married and has children, and we won't take that risk. But you, John, and you, Kate, are single and you live alone—correct?"

Kate nodded.

I said, "Why don't we shelve this idea for a while?"

"Because if you're correct, Mr. Corey, and Khalil is still in this country and close to where we sit, he may be tempted to go for a target of opportunity before he moves on to his next target, which could be far bigger than what he's already done. That's why. I'm trying to head off another mass murder. Sometimes an individual has to put himself or herself in harm's way for the greater safety and security of the nation. Don't you agree?"

Kate said, "I agree. It's worth a try."

I'd gotten myself into a lose-lose situation. I said, "Great idea. Why didn't I think of that?"

Nash observed, "And if John is wrong, and Khalil is out of the country, John only loses ten dollars. If Khalil is *in* the country, John wins ten dollars, but... well, let's not think about that."

Ted Nash was really enjoying himself for the first time that I can remember. I mean, old stoic Ted was grinning at the prospect of John Corey getting his throat slashed by some psychotic camel jockey. Even Mr. Roberts was trying to suppress a grin. Funny what turns people on.

The meeting went on for a while longer. We were now into the public relations problems, which could be sticky with three hundred people dead on board the aircraft, people murdered on the ground, and the perp at large.

Jack Koenig concluded with, "The next few days are going to be very difficult. The news media are generally friendly toward us, as we saw in the World Trade Center case and the TWA case. But we have to control the news a little. Also, we have to go to Washington tomorrow and assure those people that we are on top of things. I want everyone to go home and get some sleep. Meet me at the US Airways shuttle at La Guardia for the first flight at seven A.M. George will stay at the Conquistador Club and supervise the crime scene." He stood and we all stood with him. He said, "Despite the outcome of today's assignment, you all did a fine job." He surprised me by saying, "Pray for the dead." We all shook hands, even Mr. Roberts. Kate, Ted, and I left.

As we walked through the twenty-eighth floor, I felt a lot of eyes on us.

Chapter 22

Asad Khalil knew he had to cross the Delaware River at a bridge with no toll, and he had been instructed to continue on Highway I to the city of Trenton where there were two such bridges. He programmed the Satellite Navigator as he drove. It would have been easier if the man who had rented the car had programmed the Satellite Navigator, or asked the car rental agency to do it, but that was a dangerous convenience. Khalil's last and only need for assistance, and last point where he could be traced, was Gamal Jabbar in the parking lot.

Khalil exited Highway I onto Interstate 95. This was a good road, much like the German Autobahn, he thought, except the vehicles moved more slowly here. The Interstate took him around the city of Trenton. He saw, near an exit, a brown sign saying WASHINGTON CROSSING STATE PARK. He recalled that his Russian training officer, Boris, a former KGB man who had lived in America, had said to him, "You will be crossing the Delaware River near where George Washington crossed two hundred years ago by boat. He didn't want to pay a toll either."

Khalil did not always understand Boris' humor, but Boris was the one man in Tripoli who could be counted on to give good advice about America and Americans.

Khalil crossed the toll-free bridge into the state of Pennsylvania. He continued on I-95 heading south, as the Satellite Navigator instructed.

The sun was fully set now, and it was dark. Soon, he found that I-95 went through the city of Philadelphia. There was much traffic, and he had to slow down. He could see tall lighted buildings and at one point he drove parallel to the Delaware River, then he passed the airport.

This was not the fastest or most direct route to his destination, but it was a heavily traveled route, without tolls, and therefore the safest route for him.

Soon, the city was behind him, and the vehicles began moving more quickly.

He let his thoughts turn to other matters. His first thought was that this day of April 15 had begun well, and by now in Tripoli, the Great Leader knew that Asad Khalil had arrived in America and that hundreds had been slain to avenge this day, and that more would die in the coming days.

The Great Leader would be pleased, and soon all of Tripoli and all of Libya would know that a blow had been struck to redeem the nation's honor. Malik would be awake, even at this early morning hour in Tripoli, and he would also know by now, and he would bless Asad Khalil and pray for him.

Khalil wondered if the Americans would retaliate against his country. It was difficult to guess what this American President would do. The Great Satan, Reagan, had at least been predictable. This President was sometimes weak, sometimes strong.

In any case, even retaliation would be good. It would awaken all of Libya and all of Islam.

Khalil turned on the radio and heard people talking about their sexual problems. He set the frequency to a news station and listened for ten minutes before the story of the aircraft came on. He listened carefully to the man speaking, then to other people speaking about what they called the tragedy. It was clear to Khalil that the authorities either did not know what happened, or they knew and they were hiding it. In either case, even if the police were in a high state of alert, the general population was not. This made things much easier for him.

Asad Khalil continued south on Route I-95. The dashboard clock told him it was 8:10 P.M. There was still traffic on the road, enough so that his car would not attract attention. He passed several exits that led to rest stops, brightly lit places in which he could see cars, people, and gasoline pumps. But his fuel gauge read over half full and he wasn't hungry. He took the second liter bottle of water from the overnight bag, finished the water, then urinated in the bottle, screwed the cap back on and put the bottle under the passenger seat. He was, he realized, tired, but not so tired as to fall asleep. He'd slept well on the aircraft.

They had told him in Tripoli to try to drive through the night—that the more distance he put between himself and what he had left behind, the better his chances would be to escape detection. Soon, he would be in yet another jurisdiction—Delaware—and the more jurisdictions he was from New York and New Jersey, they'd told him, the less likely it would be that the local police would be alerted.

In any case, the police had no idea what they were looking for. Certainly they didn't know to look for a black Mercury Marquis heading south on any one of many roads. Only a random stop by a patrol car would be a problem, and even then, Khalil knew that his papers were in order. He'd been stopped twice in Europe, where they always demanded to see a passport and at times a visa as well as all the papers for the rental car. Both times he had been sent on his way. Here, according to his people in Tripoli, they wanted to see only a driver's license and a registration for the car, and they wanted to know if you had been drinking alcohol. His religion forbade alcohol, but he was not supposed to say this—say only, "No." But again, he could not conceive of a situation with the police that would last too long before one of them was dead.

Also, as they had told him, the police usually drove alone, which he found somewhat incredible. Boris, who had spent five years in America, had given him instructions for when he was out of the taxi and driving on his own. Boris had said, "Stay in your car. The policeman will come to you and lean into your window or order you out of the car. One bullet to his head, and you are on your way. But he has radioed your license plate number to his headquarters before he stopped you, and he may have a video camera on his dashboard recording the event. So, you must abandon your automobile as soon as possible and find other transportation. You will have no contacts to help you, Asad. You are on your own until you reach the West Coast of America."

Khalil had recalled replying, "I have been on my own since the fifteenth of April, nineteen eighty-six."

At twenty minutes after 9:00 P.M., Khalil crossed into the state of Delaware. Within fifteen minutes, I-95 turned into the John F. Kennedy

Memorial Highway, which was a toll road, so Khalil exited onto Route 40, which paralleled the Interstate south and west toward Baltimore. Within half an hour, he crossed into the state of Maryland.

Less than an hour later, he was on an Interstate that took him in a circle around the city of Baltimore, then back to I-95, which had no toll at this point. He continued south.

He had no idea why some roads and bridges were free while others had tolls. In Tripoli, they had no idea either. But his instructions had been clear—avoid toll booths.

Boris said, "They will, at some point, have a photograph of you at each place where you must pay."

Khalil saw a large green and white sign that gave distances to various cities, and he saw the one he wanted: WASHINGTON, D.C., 35 MILES. He smiled. He was close to his destination.

It was nearly midnight, but there was still some traffic on this road that connected the two large cities. In fact, he thought, there was an amazing number of vehicles on the roads, even after dark. It was no wonder why the Americans needed so much oil. He had once read that the Americans burned more oil in one day than Libya did in one year. Soon they would suck the earth dry of all petroleum, then they could walk or ride camels. He laughed.

At 12:30 A.M., he intersected the road called the Capital Beltway and entered it going south. He looked at his odometer and saw he'd traveled nearly three hundred miles in six hours.

He exited the Beltway at an exit called Suitland Parkway, near Andrews Air Force Base, and drove along a road that passed through shopping malls and large stores. His Satellite Navigator actually gave him the names of some lodging places, but he had no intention of stopping at well-known places. As he cruised slowly, he took the plastic bottle of urine and threw it out the side window.

He drove by a few motels, then saw one that looked sufficiently unpleasing. A lighted sign said VACANCIES.

Khalil pulled into the parking lot, which was almost empty. He took off his tie, put on his glasses, and exited the Mercury, locking the door. He stretched for a second, then strode into the small motel office.

A young man behind the counter was sitting and watching television. The young man stood and said, "Yes?"

"I need a room for two days."

"Eighty dollars, plus tax."

Khalil put two fifty-dollar bills on the counter.

The clerk was used to cash guests and said, "I need a hundred dollars for a security deposit. You get it back when you check out."

Khalil put two more fifties on the counter.

The young man gave him a registration card, and Khalil filled it out, using the name Ramon Vasquez. He put down the correct make and model of the automobile as he was told to do because it might be checked later when he was in his room. Khalil also put down the correct license plate number and pushed the card to the clerk.

The clerk gave him a key on a plastic tag, his change, and a receipt for his hundred dollars. He said, "Unit Fifteen. To your right when you walk out. Toward the end. Checkout is at eleven."

"Thank you."

Khalil turned and left the small office. He went to his car and drove to the unit marked 15 on the door.

He took his overnight bag, locked the car, and entered the room, turning on the light switch, which illuminated a lamp.

Khalil locked the door and bolted it. The room was furnished very simply, he noted, but there was a television, which he turned on.

He undressed and went into the bathroom, carrying his overnight bag, his bulletproof vest, and the two .40 caliber Glocks.

He relieved himself, then opened his overnight bag and took out the toiletries. He peeled his mustache off, then brushed his teeth and shaved. He showered quickly, his pistols on the sink nearby.

Khalil dried himself, took the overnight bag, pistols, and bulletproof vest and re-entered the bedroom. He dressed again, putting on clean undershorts, undershirt, a different tie, and socks from the overnight bag. He also put on the bulletproof vest. He got out the tube of toothpaste with gum for his mustache, and he stood in front of the bedroom mirror and reaffixed the mustache.

Khalil found the television remote control, sat on the bed, and changed channels until he found a news station. This was a taped replay of an earlier news broadcast, he understood, but it might be useful.

He watched for fifteen minutes, then the newsman said, "More on the tragedy at Kennedy Airport this afternoon."

A scene of the airport came on the screen. He recognized a view of the security area off in the distance. He could see the tall tail and the dome of the 747 rising above the steel wall.

The man's voice was saying, "The death toll is mounting as airport and airline officials confirm that toxic fumes, apparently from unauthorized cargo in the cargo hold, have killed at least two hundred people aboard Trans-Continental Flight One-Seven-Five."

The newsman went on awhile, but there was nothing to be learned from this report.

The scene then went to the arrivals terminal where friends and relatives of the victims were weeping. There were many reporters with microphones, Khalil noted, all trying to get interviews with the weeping people. Khalil found this odd. If they thought it was an accident, what difference did it make what these weeping people said? What did they know? Nothing. If the Americans were admitting to a terrorist attack, then certainly these hysterical people should be filmed for propaganda purposes. But as far as he could tell, the reporters only wanted to know about friends and family on the flight. Many of those interviewed, Khalil realized, were still hoping that those they were waiting for had survived. Khalil could tell them with absolute certainty that they had not.

Khalil kept watching, fascinated by the idiocy of these people, especially the reporters.

He wanted to see if anyone spoke of the fireman on board whom he had murdered, but it was not mentioned. Neither did anyone say anything about the Conquistador Club, but Khalil knew there would be no mention of that.

He waited for his picture to come on the screen, but it did not. Instead, the scene shifted again to the newsroom where the newsman was saying, "There is still speculation that this aircraft landed itself. We have with us a former American Airlines 747 pilot, Captain Fred Eames. Welcome."

Captain Eames nodded, and the reporter asked him, "Captain, is it possible that this aircraft landed itself—with no human hand at the control?"

Captain Eames replied, "Yes, it is possible. Matter of fact, it is thoroughly routine." The pilot added, "Almost all aircraft can fly a pre-programmed route, but the newest generation of airliners can also automatically control the landing gear, flaps, and brakes, making a totally automatic landing a routine operation. It's done every day. The computers, however, do not control the reverse thrusters, so that an aircraft landing on autopilot needs more runway than it normally would—but at JFK, this isn't a problem."

The man went on awhile. Asad Khalil listened, though he wasn't that interested. What interested him was that no Federal agents were on the television, and there was no mention of him and no photo. He guessed that the government had decided not to tell what they knew. Not yet. By the time they did, Khalil would be well on his way toward completing his mission. The first twenty-four hours were the most critical, he knew. After that, his chances of being caught decreased with each passing day.

The story of the deaths on board the aircraft ended, and another story came on. He watched to see if there was any news of the death of Gamal Jabbar, but there was not.

Asad Khalil shut off the television. When he had driven to Room 15, he had looked at the Mercury's compass and determined which way was east.

He got off the bed, prostrated himself, facing Mecca, and said his evening prayers.

He then lay in his bed, fully clothed, and fell into a light sleep.

Chapter 23

Kate Mayfield, Ted Nash, and I exited 26 Federal Plaza and stood on Broadway.

There weren't many people around, and the evening had cooled off.

No one said anything, which didn't mean there was nothing to say. It meant, I think, that we were completely alone for the first time, the three of us who had blown it big-time despite Koenig's kind parting words, and we didn't want to talk about it.

There's never a taxi or a cop around when you need one, and we stood there, getting cold. Finally, Kate said, "You guys want a drink?"

Nash replied, "No, thanks. I have to be on the phone half the night with Langley."

She looked at me. "John?"

I needed a drink, but I wanted to be alone. I said, "No, thanks. I'm going to get some sleep." I didn't see any taxis, so I said, "I'm taking the subway. Anyone need subway directions?"

Nash, who probably didn't even know there *was* a subway in New York City, replied, "I'll wait for a taxi."

Kate said to me, "I'll share a taxi with Ted."

"Okay. See you at La Guardia."

I walked to the corner and glanced up at the Twin Towers before I turned east on Duane Street.

To my front rose the fourteen-story building called One Police Plaza, and a wave of nostalgia passed over me, followed by a sort of montage of my old life—the Police Academy, rookie cop, street cop, plainclothes cop, then the gold detective shield. Before I'd abruptly left the job, I'd passed the sergeant's exam, and I was about to be promoted from the list. But circumstances beyond my control cut it short. Act Two was teaching at John Jay. This, the ATTF, was the third and final act of a sometimes brilliant, sometimes not so brilliant career.

I turned north up Centre Street and continued on, past the court-houses, through Chinatown and past my subway entrance.

Maybe one of the unspoken thoughts that Nash, Kate, and I had out on the sidewalk was the thought that Asad Khalil was gunning for us. In reality, with few exceptions, no one, not organized crime, not sub-versive groups, not even the drug kings ever went after a Federal agent in America. But we were starting to see something different here with the extremist Islamic groups. There had been incidents, like the CIA park-ing lot killing, which were unsettling peeks into the future. And that future had arrived today on Flight 175.

I was in Little Italy now, and my feet found their way to Giulio's Restaurant on Mott Street. I entered the restaurant and went to the bar.

The restaurant was full on this Saturday night, mostly parties of six and bigger. There were Manhattan trendies, some bridge and tunnel types from the burbs, a few actual Little Italy families, and some tour-ists from places where people have blond hair. I didn't see any goom-bahs, who mostly avoided Little Italy on weekends when people came to see goombahs.

I recalled, however, that a Mafia don was whacked here on a Friday night about ten years ago. Actually, he was whacked out on the sidewalk, but re-entered the restaurant through the plate glass window, having been lifted off his feet by a shotgun blast fired by some other goom-bah's designated hitter. As I recall, the don didn't actually die because he was wearing a Little Italy T-shirt—a bulletproof vest—but he was murdered later by some married lady that he was porking.

Anyway, I didn't recognize the bartender, or anyone at the bar or at the tables. During the week, I might have run into some of my old buds, but not tonight, which was fine.

I ordered a double Dewar's, straight up with a Bud chaser. No use wasting time.

I banged back the Dewar's and sipped on the beer.

Above the bar was a TV with its sound off. At the bottom of the screen, where stock prices usually run continuously during the week, there was a running line of sports scores. On the screen itself was a Mafia sitcom called *The Sopranos*, which everyone at the bar was watching. The Mafia guys I know love this show.

After a few rounds, when I was feeling better, I left and caught a taxi, which are plentiful in Little Italy, and went back to my condominium on East 72nd Street.

I live in a clean, modern high rise with a terrific view of the East River, and my apartment shows none of the funkiness associated with unmarried New York City detectives. My life is messy, but my digs are clean. This is partly the result of my starter marriage, which lasted about two years. Her name was Robin, and she had been an Assistant District Attorney in the Manhattan DA's office, which is how I'd met her. Most female ADAs marry other attorneys. Robin married a cop. We were married by a judge, but I should have asked for a jury.

Anyway, as often happens with sharp ADAs, Robin was offered and took a job with a law firm that specialized in defending the scumbags she and I were trying to put away. The money got good, but the marriage got bad. Philosophical differences of the irreconcilable sort. I got the condo. The vig is very high.

Alfred, my night doorman, greeted me and held the door open.

I checked my mailbox, which was full of junk mail. I was half expecting a letter bomb from Ted Nash, but so far he was showing admirable restraint.

I took the elevator up and entered my apartment, taking minimal precautions. Even I had trouble getting past Alfred for the first month or two of my marriage. He didn't like the idea that I was sleeping with my wife, who he'd taken a liking to. Anyway, Robin and I had both briefed Alfred and the other doormen that we were associated with law enforcement, and that we had enemies. All the doormen understood, and their Christmas and Easter bonuses reflected our appreciation of their loyalty, discretion, and vigilance. On the other hand, since my divorce, I think Alfred would give my keys to Jack the Ripper for a twenty-buck tip.

Anyway, I went through the living room with the big terrace and

into the den where I turned on the TV to CNN. The TV wasn't working right and needed some percussive maintenance, which I performed
by smacking it three times with my hand. A snowy picture appeared, but
CNN was doing a financial report.

I went to the phone and hit the message button on my answering
machine. Beth Penrose, at 7:16, said, "Hi, John. I have a feeling you
were at JFK today. I remember you said something about that. That was
terrible—tragic. My God...anyway, if you're on that, good luck. Sorry
we couldn't get together tonight. Call when you can."

That's one advantage of a cop going out with a cop. Both parties
understand. I don't think there are any other advantages.

The second message was from my former partner, Dom Fanelli. He
said, "Holy shit. Did I hear right that you caught the squeal at JFK? I
told you not to take that job. Call me."

"You *got* me the job, you stupid greaseball."

There were a few other messages from friends and family, all
inquiring about the JFK thing and my connection to it. All of a sudden
I was back on everyone's radar screen. Not bad for a guy who everyone
thought had crashed and burned a year ago.

The last message, just ten minutes before I'd gotten home, was from
Kate Mayfield. She said, "This is Kate. I thought you'd be home by now.
Okay...well, call if you want to talk...I'm home...I don't think I can
get to sleep. So call anytime...talk to you."

Well, I wasn't going to have any problem getting to sleep. But I
wanted to catch the news first, so I took off my jacket and shoes, loos-
ened my tie, and fell into my favorite chair. The financial guy was still
on. I was drifting, half aware of the phone ringing, but I ignored it.

Next thing I knew, I was sitting in a big jet aircraft, trying to get out
of my seat, but something was holding me down. I noticed that everyone
around me was fast asleep, except for a guy standing in the aisle. The
guy had a big bloody knife in his hand, and he was coming right toward
me. I went for my gun, but it wasn't in my holster. The guy raised the
knife, and I sprang out of my chair.

The VCR clock said 5:17. I had barely enough time to shower,
change, and get to La Guardia.

As I undressed, I turned on the radio in my bedroom, which was tuned to 1010 WINS, all news.

The guy on the radio was talking about the Trans-Continental tragedy. I turned up the volume and jumped in the shower.

As I soaped up, I could hear pieces of the story above the sound of the water. The guy was saying something about Gadhafi and about the American air raid on Libya in 1986.

It seemed to me that people were starting to put things together.

I sort of remembered the air raid in '86, and I recalled that the NYPD and Port Authority cops had been put on alert in case some shit splattered back here. But other than some overtime, I couldn't remember anything special happening.

But I guess it happened yesterday. These people had long memories. My partner, Dom Fanelli, once told me a joke—Italian Alzheimer's is where you forget everything except who you have to kill.

No doubt this also applied to the Arabs. But it didn't seem as funny when you put it that way.

BOOK FOUR

America, The Present

...we stirred among the Christians enmity and hatred, which shall endure until the Day of Resurrection.... Believers, take neither Jews nor Christians for friends.

—The Koran, Sura V, "The Table"

Chapter 24

April 15 sucked, and April 16 wasn't going to be much better.

"Good morning, Mr. Corey," said Alfred, my doorman, who had a taxi waiting for me.

"Good morning, Alfred."

He said, "The weather report is good. La Guardia, correct?" He opened the rear door for me and said to the driver, "La Guardia."

I got into the taxi, which pulled away, and said to the driver, "You have a newspaper?"

He took one off the front seat and handed it back to me. It was in Russian or Greek. He laughed.

The day was going downhill already.

I said to the guy, "I'm late. Step on it. Capisce? Pedal to the metal."

He showed no signs of breaking the law, so I took out my Fed creds and pushed them in front of his face. "Move it."

The taxi accelerated. If I'd had my piece with me, I'd have put the muzzle in his ear, but he seemed to be with the program. I'm not a morning person, by the way.

Traffic was light at this hour on a Sunday morning, and we made good time up the FDR Drive and over the Triborough Bridge. When we got to La Guardia, I said, "US Airways terminal."

He pulled up to the terminal, I paid him, and gave him his newspaper back, saying, "Here's your tip."

I got out and checked my watch. I had about ten minutes before flight time. This was cutting it close, but I had no luggage, and no gun to declare.

Outside the terminal, I noticed two Port Authority uniformed cops eyeing everyone as though they'd arrived in a car bomb. Obviously, the word was out, and I hoped everyone had a photo of Asad Khalil.

Inside the terminal at the ticket counter, the guy asked if I had a ticket or a reservation. Actually, I had lots of reservations about this flight, but this was not the place for flippancy. I said, "Corey, John."

He found me on the computer, then printed my ticket. The guy asked for a photo ID, and I gave him my New York State driver's license instead of my Fed creds, which always brings up the question of a gun. One reason I had chosen not to carry this morning was because I was running late and didn't have time to mess around with filling out paperwork. Also, I was traveling with armed people who would protect me. I think. On the other hand, whenever you think you don't need your gun, you do. But there was another, important reason I'd chosen not to carry. More on that later.

Anyway, the ticket guy asked me if I'd packed my own luggage, and I told him I had no luggage, and he gave me my ticket and said, "Have a good flight," as though I had some input into the thing.

If I'd had more time, I would have replied, "May Allah give us a good tailwind."

There was also a Port Authority cop at the metal detector and the line was slow. I walked through and my brass balls didn't set the bell off.

As I moved with haste toward my gate, I ruminated over this increased security. On the one hand, a lot of cops were going to earn a lot of overtime in the next month or so, and the Mayor would have a fit and try to shake down Washington for Federal bucks, explaining that this was their fault.

On the other hand, these domestic transportation terminal operations rarely turned up who you were looking for, but you had to do it anyway. It made life difficult for fugitives trying to get around the country. But if Asad Khalil had half a brain, he'd be doing what most perps do who are on the run—hole up somewhere until the heat is off, or get a clean car and disappear on the highways. Or, of course, he may have already caught a Camel Air flight to Sandland yesterday.

I gave the gate agent my ticket, went down the jetway, and boarded the shuttle to Cuckooland.

The stewardess said, "You just made it."

"My lucky day."

"Light flight. Take any seat."

"How about that guy's seat over there?"

"Any *empty* seat, sir. Please be seated."

I moved down the aisle and saw that the plane was half empty, and I took a seat by myself, away from Kate Mayfield and Ted Nash, who were sitting together, and Jack Koenig, who was across the aisle from them. I did, however, mumble, "Morning" as I made my way to the back of the aircraft. I envied George Foster for not having to make this flight.

I hadn't thought to grab a free magazine at the gate, and someone had swiped the magazines in the pockets in front of me, so I sat there and read the emergency evacuation card until the plane took off.

Halfway through the flight, while I was dozing, Koenig walked by on his way to the lav and threw the front section of the Sunday *Times* on my lap.

I cleared my mind and read the headline, which said, *Three Hundred Dead on JFK Flight.* That was an eye-opener on a Sunday morning.

I read the *Times* story, which was sketchy and a little inaccurate, a result, no doubt, of the spinmeisters at work. The bottom line was that the Federal Aviation Agency and the National Transportation Safety Board were not releasing many details, except to say that unidentified toxic fumes had overcome the passengers and crew. There was no mention that the autopilot had actually landed the aircraft, no mention of any murders or terrorists, and for sure no mention of the Conquistador Club. And, thank God, no mention of anyone named John Corey.

Tomorrow's news, however, would be more specific. The details would be spooned out in manageable doses, like cod liver oil with a little honey, a day at a time, until the public got used to it and then had its attention distracted by something else.

Anyway, the one-hour flight was uneventful, except for a bad cup of coffee. As we came into Ronald Reagan National Airport, we followed the Potomac River, and I had a spectacular view of the Jefferson Memorial with all the cherry blossoms in bloom, the Mall, the Capitol, and all those other white stone buildings that project power, power, power. It occurred to me for the first time that I worked for some of those people down there.

Anyway, we landed and deplaned on schedule. I noticed that Koenig was wearing a Federal blue suit and carried a briefcase. Nash had on yet another continental-cut suit and also carried a briefcase, no doubt hand-crafted of yak hide by Tibetan freedom fighters in the Himalayas. Kate was also wearing a blue suit, but it looked better on her than on Jack. She also carried a briefcase, and I had the thought that I was supposed to carry a briefcase. My attire for the day was a dove gray suit that my ex bought me from Barney's. With tax and tip, it probably ran close to two thousand bucks. She has that kind of money. It comes from defending drug dealers, hit men, white-collar criminals, and other high-income felons. So why do I wear this suit? I wear it, I think, as a cynical statement. Also, it fits very well and looks expensive.

But back to the airport. A car and driver met us and took us on a ride to FBI Headquarters, aka the J. Edgar Hoover Building.

There wasn't a lot of chatter in the car, but finally Jack Koenig, sitting up front with the driver, turned to us and said, "I apologize if this meeting interferes with your worship services."

The FBI, of course, pays lip service to church attendance, and maybe it wasn't just lip service. I couldn't imagine my old bosses saying anything like that, and I was at a loss for a reply.

Kate replied, "That's all right," whatever that means.

Nash mumbled something that sounded like he was giving us all a dispensation.

I'm not a habitual churchgoer, but I said, "J. Edgar is up there watching over us."

Koenig shot me an unpleasant look and turned back to the front.

Long day. Long, long day.

Chapter 25

At 5:30 a.m., Asad Khalil rose, took a wet towel from the bathroom and wiped all the surfaces where he might have left fingerprints. He prostrated himself on the floor, said his morning prayers, and left the motel room. He put his overnight bag in the Mercury, and walked back to the motel office, carrying the wet towel.

The young desk clerk was sleeping in his chair and the television was still on.

Khalil came around the counter with the towel-wrapped Glock in his hand. He put the pistol to the man's head and pulled the trigger. The young clerk and the wheeled chair flew into the counter. Khalil pushed the young man's body beneath the counter and took his wallet from his hip pocket, then took the money out of the cash drawer. He found the stack of registration slips and receipt copies, and put them all in his pocket, then wiped his key tag with the wet towel and returned his key to the keyboard.

He looked up at the security camera, which he'd noticed earlier and which had recorded not only his arrival but also the entire murder and robbery. He followed the wire to a small back room where he found the video recorder. He pulled the tape out and put it in his pocket, then went back to the counter where he found an electrical switch marked MOTEL SIGN. He shut it off, then shut off the lights in the office, walked out the door, and went back to his car.

There was a damp fog hanging in the air, which obscured everything beyond a few meters. Khalil pulled out of the parking lot without headlights and didn't turn them on until he was fifty meters down the road.

He re-traced his route and approached the Capital Beltway. Before he entered, he pulled into the big parking lot of a strip mall, found a storm sewer drain, and pushed the registration cards, receipts, and video cassette through the metal grate. He took the cash out of the clerk's wallet and threw the wallet into the drain.

He got back into his car and entered the Capital Beltway.

It was six in the morning and a faint dusk came out of the east illuminating the fog. There was little traffic on the road on this Sunday morning, and neither did Khalil see any police cars.

He followed the Beltway south, then it curved west and crossed the Potomac River, then continued west until it went north and crossed the Potomac again. He was circling the city of Washington, like a lion, he thought, stalking his prey.

Khalil programmed the Satellite Navigator with the address he needed in Washington and exited the Beltway at Pennsylvania Avenue.

He continued on Pennsylvania Avenue, heading directly into the heart of the enemy capital.

At 7:00 A.M. he drove up to Capitol Hill. The fog had lifted, and the huge white-domed Capitol Building sat in the morning sunshine. Khalil drove around the Capitol, then stopped and parked near the southeast side. He removed his camera from the overnight bag and took photos of the sunlit building. He noticed a young couple about fifty meters away doing the same. This photography was not necessary, he knew, and he could have passed the time elsewhere, but he thought these photographs would amuse his compatriots in Tripoli.

He could see police cars within the gated area around the Capitol Building, but none on the street around him.

At 7:25 A.M., he got back in his car and drove the few blocks to Constitution Avenue. He drove slowly down the tree-lined street of town houses and located number 415. A car was parked in the narrow driveway, and he saw a light on in the third-floor window. He kept going, circled around the block, and parked his car a half block from the house.

Khalil put both Glocks in his jacket pockets, and waited, watching the house.

At 7:45 A.M., a middle-aged man and woman came out the front door. The lady was well dressed and the man wore the blue uniform of an Air Force general. Khalil smiled.

They had told him in Tripoli that General Terrance Waycliff was a man of habit, and his habit was to attend religious services at the National Cathedral every Sunday morning. The General would almost always attend the 8:15 service, but had been known to attend the 9:30 service. This morning it was the 8:15 service, and Khalil was pleased that he didn't have to waste another hour somewhere.

Khalil watched the General escort his wife to their car. The man was tall and slender, and though his hair was gray, he walked like a younger man. In 1986, Khalil knew, General Waycliff had been Captain Waycliff, and the radio call sign on his F-111 had been Remit 22. Captain Waycliff's fighter-bomber had been one of the four in the attack squadron that had bombed Al Azziziyah. Captain Waycliff's weapons officer had been Colonel—then Captain—William Hambrecht, who had met his fate in London in January. Now General Waycliff would meet a similar fate in Washington.

Khalil watched as the General opened the door for his wife, then went around, got into the driver's side, and backed out of the driveway.

Khalil could have killed both of them right there and then on this quiet Sunday morning, but he chose to do it another way.

Khalil straightened his tie, then exited and locked his car.

He walked to the front door of the General's house and pushed the doorbell. He heard chimes ringing inside the house.

He heard footsteps and kept back from the door so his face could be seen though the peephole. Khalil heard the metallic scrape of what he thought was a chain being put on the door, then the door opened a crack, and he could see the hanging chain and a young woman's face. She started to say something, but Khalil slammed his shoulder into the door. The chain snapped and the door swung in, knocking the woman to the floor. Khalil was inside in a second and closed the door behind him as he pulled his pistol. "Silence."

The young woman lay on the marble floor, a look of terror in her eyes.

He motioned her to her feet and she stood. He regarded her a moment. She was a small woman, dressed in a robe, barefoot, and her complexion was dark. This was the housekeeper, according to his information, and no one else lived in the house. To be certain, he asked, "Who is home?"

She replied in accented English, "General home."

Khalil smiled. "No. General is not home. Is General's children home?"

She shook her head, and he could see she was trembling.

Khalil smelled coffee coming from somewhere and said to her, "Kitchen."

She turned hesitatingly and walked through the long foyer of the town house to the kitchen in the rear, Khalil behind her.

Khalil looked around the big kitchen and saw two plates and two coffee cups on the round table near a big, curved window in the rear.

Khalil said to her, "Basement. Downstairs." He motioned down.

She pointed to a wooden door in the wall. He said, "You go down."

She went to the door, opened it, turned on a light switch, and went down the basement stairs. Khalil followed.

The basement was filled with boxes and cartons, and Khalil looked around. He found a door and opened it, revealing a small room that held the heating unit. He motioned the young woman inside, and as she passed him and took a step into the boiler room, Khalil fired a single shot into the back of her head where the skull met the spinal column. She fell forward and was dead before she hit the floor.

Khalil closed the door and went upstairs into the kitchen. He found a carton of milk in the refrigerator and drank the entire contents from the carton, then threw it in a trash bin. He also found containers of yogurt and he removed two from the refrigerator, took a coffee spoon from the table, and ate both yogurts quickly. He didn't realize how hungry he was until he smelled food.

Khalil went back through the foyer to the front door. He unhooked the metal slide from the hanging chain and pressed the slide and its screws back into the wooden frame from which it had been torn. He left the door locked, but unchained, so that the General and his wife could let themselves in.

He looked around the ground floor, finding only a large dining room off the kitchen, a sitting room across the foyer, and a small lavatory.

He went up the stairs to the second floor where a large living room took up the entire floor of the town house, and he could see that no one was there. He continued up the stairs to the third floor where the bedrooms were. He checked each of the bedrooms. Two of the bedrooms were obviously for the General's children, a girl and a boy, and Khalil found himself wishing they were home and sleeping. But the rooms were empty. The third room seemed to be for guests, and the fourth bedroom was the master bedroom.

Khalil proceeded up to the fourth floor, which held a large den and a very small bedroom, which he guessed was that of the housekeeper.

Khalil looked around the wood-paneled den, noting all the military memorabilia on the walls, on the desk, and on a side table.

A model of an F-III hung on nylon strings from the ceiling, its nose pointed down, its swing wings swept back as though it were diving in for an attack. Khalil noticed four silver bombs under its wings. He pulled the model from its strings and with his hands crushed and ripped it apart, letting the plastic pieces fall to the floor where he ground them into the carpet with his foot. "May God damn you all to hell."

He got himself under control and continued his examination of the den. On the wall was a black-and-white photo of eight men, standing in front of an F-III fighter-bomber. The photo had a printed caption which read LAKENHEATH, APRIL 13, 1987. Khalil read it again. This was not the correct year of the bombing attack, but then he realized that the names of these men as well as their mission were secret, and thus the general misdated the photograph, even here in his private office. Clearly, Khalil thought, these cowardly men gained no honor from what they had done.

Khalil moved to the large mahogany desk and examined the odds and ends on the desktop. He found the General's daybook and opened it to Sunday, April 16. The General had noted, "Church, 8:15, National."

There were no further entries for Sunday, Khalil noted, so perhaps no one would notice that the General was missing until he failed to report to work.

Khalil looked at Monday and saw that the General had a meeting at 10:00 A.M. By that time, another of the General's squadron mates would be dead.

Khalil looked at the entry for April 15, the anniversary of the attack, and read, "Nine A.M., conference call, squadron."

Khalil nodded. So, they stayed in communication. This could be a problem, especially as they began to die, one after the other. But Khalil had expected that some of them might still be in communication. If he acted quickly enough, by the time they realized they were all dying, they would all be dead.

He found the General's personal telephone book beside his phone and opened it. He quickly scanned the book and saw the names of the other men in the photograph. Khalil noted with satisfaction that Colonel Hambrecht's entry was marked DECEASED. He also noted that the address of the man called Chip Wiggins was crossed out with a red question mark beside his name.

Khalil considered taking the telephone book, but its absence would be noted by the police, and this would call into question the motive for the murder that was about to take place.

He put the telephone book back on the desk, then wiped it and the leather daybook with a handkerchief.

He opened the desk drawers. In the middle drawer he discovered a silver-plated .45 caliber automatic pistol. He checked to see that the magazine was fully loaded, then slid back the mechanism, and chambered a round. He moved the safety to the off position and put the pistol in his waistband.

Khalil walked to the door, then stopped, turned around, and carefully picked up the pieces of the F-III model, putting them into a wastebasket.

He then went back down to the third floor and ransacked each of the bedrooms, taking money, jewelry, watches, and even a few of the General's military decorations. He put everything into a pillowcase, then went down to the kitchen on the first floor, carrying the pillowcase. He found a carton of orange juice in the refrigerator, and sat at the General's kitchen table.

The wall clock said five minutes to nine. The General and his wife would be home by nine-thirty if, indeed, they were people of habit and punctuality. By nine-forty-five, they would both be dead.

Chapter 26

We crossed the Potomac River by way of some bridge and got into the city. There wasn't much traffic at 8:30 A.M. on a Sunday, but we saw a few joggers and bicyclists as well as some tourist families on spring break, the kids looking stunned at being rousted out of bed at this hour.

As we drove, the Capitol Building loomed up to our front, and I wondered if the full Congress had been briefed yet. When the shit hits the fan, the Executive Branch likes to present the Congress with a done deal, then ask for their blessings. For all I knew, there were already warplanes heading for Libya. But that wasn't my problem.

We got onto Pennsylvania Avenue where the J. Edgar Hoover Building is located, not far from its parent company, the Justice Department.

We stopped in front of the Hoover Building, a uniquely ugly concrete slab structure whose size and shape defy description.

I'd actually been here once for a seminar, and I'd gotten a tour. You have to take the tour, especially through their cherished museum, or you don't get lunch.

Anyway, the front of the building is seven stories high, to conform to height restrictions on Pennsylvania Avenue, but the rear is eleven stories high. The building contains about two and a half million square feet, bigger than the old KGB Headquarters in Moscow, and is probably the biggest law enforcement building in the world. About eight thousand people work in the building, mostly support types and lab people. About a thousand actual agents also work in the building, and I don't envy them, any more than I envied the cops who work at One Police

Plaza. Job happiness is directly proportional to the distance you are from the home office.

We pulled up in front of the building and entered a small lobby that looked out onto a courtyard.

As we waited for our host, I wandered over toward the courtyard, which had a fountain and park benches and which I remembered from last time. There was a bronze inscription carved into the wall above the benches, a quote from J. Edgar Hoover, and it said, "The most effective weapon against crime is cooperation...the efforts of all law enforcement agencies with the support and understanding of the American people." Good quote. Better than the unofficial FBI motto which was, "We can do no wrong."

There I go again. I tried to adjust my attitude. But it's a male ego thing. Too many alpha males in law enforcement.

Anyway, there were the usual photos on one wall—the President, the Attorney General, the Director of the FBI, and so forth. The photos were friendly-looking and hung in a chain-of-command grouping so that, hopefully, no one would mistake them for America's Most Wanted Criminals.

In fact, there was another entrance, a visitor's entrance where guided tours began, and in that entrance were the Ten Most Wanted mug shots on display. Incredibly, three fugitives had been arrested as a result of visitors recognizing the photos. I had no doubt that by now, Asad Khalil's photo was in the number one spot. Maybe someone taking a tour would say, "Hey, I rent a room to that guy." Maybe not.

Anyway, the reason I'd been here about five years ago was for a seminar on serial killers. There were homicide dicks invited from around the country, and they were all a little nuts, like me. We put on a skit for the FBI called Cereal Killers, and brought in boxes of Wheaties, Cheerios, Grape Nuts, and so on that had been knifed, shot, strangled, and drowned. We thought it was pretty funny, but the FBI psychologists thought we needed help.

Back to the unhappy present at FBI Headquarters. It wasn't a normal workday, of course, and the building seemed mostly empty, but I had no doubt that the Counterterrorist section was around and about today. I hoped they didn't blame us for screwing up their Sunday.

Jack, Kate, and Ted declared their weapons at the security desk, and I had to admit I wasn't carrying, which is sort of a no-no. But I informed the security guy, "My hands are registered as lethal weapons." The guy looked at Jack, who tried to make believe I wasn't with him.

Anyway, before 9:00 A.M. we were escorted to a nice conference room on the third floor where we were offered coffee and introduced to six guys and two women. The guys were all named Bob, Bill, and Jim, or maybe that's what it sounded like. The two women were named Jane and Jean. Everyone wore blue.

What could have been a long, tense day turned out to be worse. Not that anyone was hostile or reproachful—they were polite and sympathetic—but I had the distinct feeling that I was back in grade school and I was in the principal's office. Johnny, do you think the next time a terrorist comes to America, you can remember what we taught you?

I'm glad I didn't bring my gun—I would have capped the whole bunch of them.

We didn't stay in the same conference room the whole time, but moved around a lot to different offices, a traveling dog and pony show, going through the same act for different audiences.

The interior of the building, by the way, was as stark as the outside. The walls are painted linen white and the doors are charcoal gray. Someone once told me that J. Edgar had banned pictures on the walls, and there still weren't any pictures. Anyone who hangs a picture dies a mysterious death.

As I said, the building has a weird shape, and it's not easy to figure out where you are half the time. Now and then, we passed a glass wall where we could look into a lab, or some other place where people worked. Although it was Sunday, a few people were bent over microscopes or computer terminals, or fooling around with glass beakers. A lot of what looked like windows here are two-way mirrors where the people you're seeing can't see you. And a lot of what looks like mirrors are also two-way where people on the other side can see you checking your teeth for poppy seeds.

The whole morning was basically a series of debriefings where we did most of the talking, and people nodded and listened. Half the time, I didn't know who we were talking to; a few times I thought we were directed to the wrong room because the people we were talking to seemed surprised or confused, like they'd come into the office to catch up on something and four people from New York burst in and started talking about poison gas and a guy called the Lion. Well, maybe I exaggerate, but after three hours of us telling different people the same thing, it all started to get blurry.

Now and then someone asked us a specific question of fact, and once in a while we were asked to express opinions or theories. But not once did anyone tell us anything that *they* knew. That was for after lunch, we were told, and only if we ate all our vegetables.

Chapter 27

Asad Khalil heard the front door open, then heard a man and woman talking. The woman's voice called out, "Rosa, we're home."

Khalil finished the coffee he was drinking and listened to the closet door open and close. Then, the voices got louder as they approached through the hallway.

Khalil stood and moved to the side of the doorway. He drew the General's Colt .45 automatic and listened closely. He heard two sets of footsteps on the marble floor coming toward him.

The General and his wife walked into the big kitchen. The General headed to the refrigerator, the woman to the electric coffeepot on the counter. They both had their backs to him, and he waited for them to notice him against the wall. He tucked the pistol in his jacket pocket and held it there.

The woman took two cups from the cupboard and poured coffee for both of them. The General was still looking in the refrigerator. He said, "Where's the milk?"

"It's in there," said Mrs. Waycliff.

She turned to walk to the kitchen table, saw Khalil, let out a startled cry, and dropped both cups to the floor.

The General spun around, looked at his wife, then followed her stare and found himself looking at a tall man in a suit. He took a breath and said, "Who are you?"

"I am a messenger."

"Who let you in?"

"Your servant."

"Where is she?"

"She went out to buy milk."

"Okay," General Waycliff snapped, "get the hell out of here, or I'll call the police."

"Did you enjoy your church service?"

Gail Waycliff said, "Please leave. If you leave now, we won't call the police."

Khalil ignored her and said, "I, too, am a religious man. I have studied the Hebrew testament as well as the Christian testament and, of course, the Koran."

At this last word, General Waycliff suddenly began to understand who this intruder might be.

Khalil continued, "Are you familiar with the Koran? No? But you read the Hebrew testament. So, why don't Christians read the word of God, which was revealed to the Prophet Muhammad? Praise be unto him."

"Look...I don't know who you are—"

"Of course you do."

"All right...I know who you are—"

"Yes, I am your worst nightmare. And you were once my worst nightmare."

"What are you talking about—?"

"You are General Terrance Waycliff, and I believe you work at the Pentagon. Correct?"

"That's none of your business. I'm telling you to leave. Now."

Khalil didn't reply. He just looked at the General standing before him in his blue uniform. Finally, Khalil said, "I see that you are highly decorated, General."

General Waycliff said to his wife, "Gail, call the police."

The woman stood frozen a moment, then moved toward the kitchen table where a phone hung on the wall.

Khalil said, "Don't touch the telephone."

She looked back at her husband, who said, "Call the police." General Waycliff took a step toward the intruder.

Khalil drew the automatic pistol from his jacket.

Gail Waycliff gasped.

General Waycliff let out a sound of surprise and stopped in his tracks.

Khalil said, "This is actually your gun, General." He held it up as though examining it and said, "It's very beautiful. It has, I believe, a nickel or silver plating, ivory handles, and your name inscribed on it."

General Waycliff did not reply.

Khalil looked back at the General and said, "It is my understanding that there were no medals issued for the Libyan raid. Is that true?" He looked at Waycliff, and for the first time saw fear in the man's eyes.

Khalil continued, "I'm speaking of the April fifteen, nineteen eighty-six, raid. Or was it nineteen eighty-seven?"

The General glanced at his wife, who was staring at him. They both knew where this was headed now. Gail Waycliff moved across the kitchen and stood beside her husband.

Khalil appreciated her bravery in the face of death.

No one spoke for a full minute. Khalil relished the moment and took pleasure at the sight of the Americans waiting for their death.

But Asad Khalil wasn't quite finished. He said to the General, "Correct me if I'm wrong, but you were Remit Twenty-two. Yes?"

The General didn't reply.

Khalil said, "Your flight of four F-IIIs attacked Al Azziziyah. Correct?"

Again, the General said nothing.

"And you're wondering how I discovered this secret."

General Waycliff cleared his throat and said, "Yes. I am."

Khalil smiled and said, "If I tell you, then I have to kill you." He laughed.

The General managed to say, "That's what you're going to do anyway."

"Perhaps. Perhaps not."

Gail Waycliff asked Khalil, "Where is Rosa?"

"What a good mistress you are to worry about your servant."

Mrs. Waycliff snapped, "Where is she?"

"She is where you know she is."

"You bastard."

Asad Khalil was not used to being spoken to that way by anyone, least of all a woman. He would have shot her right then, but he controlled himself and said, "In fact, I am not a bastard. I had a mother and father who were married to each other. My father was murdered by your allies, the Israelis. My mother was killed in your bombing raid on Al Azziziyah. And so were my two brothers and my two sisters." He looked at Gail Waycliff and said, "And it's quite possible that it was one of your husband's bombs, Mrs. Waycliff, that killed them. So, what have you to say to that?"

Gail Waycliff took a deep breath and replied, "Then all I can say is that I'm sorry. We're both sorry for you."

"Yes? Well, thank you for your sympathy."

General Waycliff looked directly at Khalil and said in an angry tone, "I'm not at all sorry. Your leader, Gadhafi, is an international terrorist. He's murdered dozens of innocent men, women, and children. The base at Al Azziziyah was a command center for international terrorism, and it was Gadhafi who put the civilians in harm's way by housing them in a military target. And if you know so much, you also know that only military targets were bombed all over Libya, and the few civilian casualties were accidental. You know that, so don't pretend that murdering anyone in cold blood is justified."

Khalil stared at General Waycliff and actually seemed to be considering his words. Finally, he said, "And the bomb that was dropped on Colonel Gadhafi's house in Al Azziziyah? You know, General—the one that killed his daughter and wounded his wife and injured his two sons. Was that an accident? Did your smart bombs go astray? Answer me."

"I have nothing more to say to you."

Khalil shook his head and said, "No, you do not." He raised his pistol and pointed it at General Waycliff. "You have no idea how long I've waited for this moment."

The General stepped in front of his wife and said, "Let her go."

"Ridiculous. My only regret is that your children are not home."

"*Bastard!*" The General sprang forward and lunged at Khalil.

Khalil fired a single shot into the General's service ribbons on his left breast.

The force of the low-velocity blunt-nosed .45 bullet stopped the General's forward motion and lifted him off his feet. He fell backwards onto the tile floor with a thud.

Gail Waycliff screamed and ran toward her husband.

Khalil held his fire and let her kneel beside her dying husband. She was stroking his forehead and sobbing. Blood foamed out of the bullet hole, and Khalil saw that he had missed the man's heart and hit the lung, which was good. The General would drown slowly in his own blood.

Gail Waycliff pushed the palm of her hand over the wound, and Khalil had the impression she was trained to recognize and treat a sucking chest wound. But perhaps, he thought, it was just instinct.

He watched for a half minute, interested, but disinterested.

The General was very much alive and was trying to speak, though he was choking on his blood.

Khalil stepped closer and looked at the General's face. Their eyes met.

Khalil said, "I could have killed you with an ax, the way I killed Colonel Hambrecht. But you were very brave and I respect that. So, you will not suffer much longer. I can't promise the same for your other squadron mates."

General Waycliff tried to speak, but pink, foamy blood erupted from his mouth. Finally, he managed to say to his weeping wife, "Gail…"

Khalil put the muzzle of the automatic to the side of Gail Waycliff's head, above her ear, and fired a shot through the skull and brain.

She toppled over beside her husband.

General Waycliff's hand reached out to touch his wife, then he picked his head up to look at her.

Khalil watched for a few seconds, then said to General Waycliff, "She died in far less pain than my mother."

General Waycliff turned his head and looked at Asad Khalil. Terrance Waycliff's eyes were wide open and blood frothed at his lips. He said, "Enough…" He coughed. "…enough killing…go back…"

"I'm not finished here. I'll go home when your friends are all dead."

The General lay on the floor, but said nothing further. His hand found his wife's hand, and he squeezed it.

Khalil waited, but the man was taking his time dying. Finally, Khalil crouched beside the couple and removed the General's watch and his Air Force Academy ring, then found the General's wallet in his hip pocket. He also took Mrs. Waycliff's watch and rings, then ripped her pearl necklace off.

He remained crouched beside them, then put his fingers over the General's chest wound where the blood covered his service ribbons. Khalil took his hand away and put his fingers to his lips, licking the blood off, savoring the blood and the moment.

General Waycliff's eyes moved, and he watched in horror as the man licked the blood from his fingers. He tried to speak, but began coughing again, spitting up more blood.

Khalil kept his eyes fixed on the General's eyes, and they stared at each other. Finally, the General began breathing in short, wheezing spasms. Then, the breathing stopped. Khalil felt the man's heart, then his wrist, then the artery in his neck. Satisfied that General Terrance Waycliff was finally dead, Khalil stood and looked down at both bodies. He said, "May you burn in hell."

Chapter 28

By noon, even Kate, Ted, and Jack looked thoroughly debriefed. In fact, if we'd been any more debriefed, all we'd have left in our heads were empty sinus cavities. I mean, jeez, these people knew how to get the last piece of information out of you without resorting to electric shock.

Anyway, it was now lunchtime in Hooverland, and they left us alone for lunch, thank God, but advised us to dine in the company cafeteria. They didn't give us lunch vouchers, so we actually had to pay for the privilege, though as I recall the chow was government-subsidized.

The cafeteria-style lunchroom was pleasant enough, but there was a reduced Sunday menu. What was offered tended toward healthy and wholesome—a salad bar, yogurt, vegetables, fruit juices, and herbal teas. I had a tuna salad and a cup of coffee that tasted like embalming fluid.

The people around us appeared to be the cast of a J. Edgar Hoover training film called *Good Grooming Leads to More Arrests*.

There were only a few black guys in the lunchroom, looking like chocolate chips in a bowl of oatmeal. Washington may be the capital of cultural diversity, but change comes slowly in some organizations. I wondered what the bosses here actually thought of the ATTF in New York, in particular the NYPD guys, who when assembled look like the alien bar scene in *Star Wars*.

Anyway, maybe I was being uncharitable toward my hosts. The FBI was actually a pretty good law enforcement agency whose main problem was image. The politically correct crowd didn't like them, the media could swing either way, but the public for the most part still adored them. Other law enforcement agencies were impressed by their work, envious of their power and money, and pissed off at their arrogance. It's not easy being great.

Jack Koenig, eating a salad, said, "I can't tell if the ATTF is going to stay on the case, or if the Counterterrorism section here is going to take it away from us."

Kate commented, "This is precisely the kind of case we were created for."

I guess it was. But parent organizations don't always like their weird offspring. The Army, for instance, never liked its own Special Forces with its fruity green berets. The NYPD never liked its anti-crime unit made up of guys who looked and dressed like derelicts and muggers. The spit-and-polish establishment neither trusts nor understands its own down-and-dirty special units, and they don't give a rat's ass how effective the irregular troops are. Weird people, *especially* when they're effective, are a threat to the status quo.

Kate added, "We have a good track record in New York."

Koenig thought a moment, then replied, "I suppose it depends on where Khalil is, or where they think he is. Probably they'll let us work the New York metro area without interference. Overseas will go to the CIA, and the rest of the country and Canada will go to Washington."

Ted Nash said nothing, and neither did I. Nash was holding so many cards so close to his chest that he didn't need a bib for his yogurt. I was holding no cards, and I was totally clueless about how these people carved up the turf. But I did know that ATTF people, based in the New York metro area, often were sent to different parts of the country or even the world when a case began in New York. In fact, one of the things that Dom Fanelli told me when he was pushing this job on me was that ATTF people went to Paris a lot to wine, dine, and seduce French women and recruit them to spy on suspicious Arabs. I didn't actually believe this, but I knew there was a possibility of hitting the Federal expense account hard for a trip to Europe. But enough about patriotism. The question was, If it happens on your turf, do you follow it to the ends of the earth? Or do you stop at the border?

The most frustrating homicide case I could remember was three years ago, when a rapist-murderer was loose on the East Side, and we couldn't get a fix on the guy. Then he goes down to Georgia for a week to see a friend, and some local yokel cop stops him for DWI, and the local yokels have a brand-new computer bought with Federal bucks and for no reason other than boredom, they run the guy's prints through to the FBI, and lo and behold, they match the prints we found at a crime scene. So we get an extradition order, and yours truly has to go down to Hominy Grits, Georgia, to extradite the perp, and I have to put up with twenty-four hours of Police Chief Corn Pone ribbing me about all kinds of crap, mostly about New York City, plus I got lessons in criminal investigation and how to spot a killer and if I ever needed any help again, just give him a call. That sucked big-time.

But back to the lunchroom at FBI Headquarters. I could tell by Koenig's musings that he wasn't sure the ATTF was in a strong position to pursue or resolve this case. He said, "If Khalil is caught in Europe, two or three countries will want a crack at him before we get him, unless the U.S. government can persuade a friendly country that he should be extradited here for what amounts to a crime of mass murder."

Though some of this legal stuff seemed to be for my benefit, I already knew most of this. I was a cop for almost twenty years, I taught at John Jay for five years, and I lived with a lawyer for almost two years. In fact, that was the only time in my life that I got to fuck a lawyer, rather than vice versa.

Anyway, Koenig's major concern was that we had dropped the ball at the goal line, and we were about to be sent to the showers. Actually, this was my concern, too.

To make matters worse, one of our team, Ted Nash by name, was about to get traded back to the team he started with. And this team had a better shot at winning this kind of game. An image of Police Chief Corn Pone flashed through my mind, but now he had Ted Nash's face, and he was pointing to Asad Khalil behind bars and saying to me, "See, Corey, I got him. Let me tell you how I did it. I was in this café on Rue St. Germaine—that's Paris, Corey—and I was talking to an asset." And then I pulled my gun and capped him.

In fact, Ted was babbling, and I tuned in. Ted was saying, "I'm going to Paris tomorrow to talk to our embassy people. It's a good idea to begin where it began, then work backwards from there." He went on.

I wondered if I could sever his windpipe with my salad fork.

Kate and Jack chatted a bit about jurisdiction, extradition, Federal and state indictments, and so forth. Lawyer crap. Kate said to me, "I'm sure it's the same with the police. The officers who start the case work it through to the end, which keeps the chain of evidence unbroken and makes the testimony of the case officers less open to attack by the defense."

And so on. I mean, jeez, we haven't even caught this scumbag yet and they're perfecting a case. This is what happens when lawyers become cops. This is the crap I had to put up with when I dealt with ADAs and District Attorney investigators. This country is sinking in legalities, which I guess is okay when you're dealing with your average all-American criminal. I mean, you need to keep an eye on the Constitution and make sure no one gets railroaded. But somebody should invent a different kind of court with different rules for somebody like Asad Khalil. The guy doesn't even pay taxes, except maybe sales tax.

Anyway, as the lunch hour ended, Mr. Koenig said to us, "You all did a fine job this morning. I know this is not pleasant, but we're here to help and to be useful. I'm very proud of the three of you."

I felt the tuna turn in my tummy. But Kate seemed pleased. Ted didn't give a rat's ass, which meant we finally had something in common.

Chapter 29

Asad Khalil retraced his route to the Beltway, and by 10:15 A.M. he was traveling south on Interstate 95, away from the city of Washington. There were, he knew, no further tolls on the roads or the bridges between here and his destination.

As he drove, he rummaged through the pillowcase and extracted the loose cash he'd found in the General's bedroom, the cash from the General's wallet, and the cash from the handbag of the General's wife, which he had taken from the foyer. All together, there was close to $200. The money from the motel office had been $440, but some of that had been his. Gamal Jabbar's wallet had contained less than $100. He made a quick calculation in his mind and added up a total of about $1,100. Certainly, he thought, this would be enough for the next few days.

He approached a bridge that crossed a small river and pulled his car over into the narrow emergency shoulder, putting his flasher lights on. Khalil got out of the car quickly, carrying the tied pillowcase, which contained the General's pistol and the valuables from his house. Khalil moved to the rail of the bridge, looked both ways, then looked down into the river to be sure there was no boat below, and let the bag fall over the railing.

He got back into his car and continued. He would have liked to keep some souvenirs of his visit, especially the General's ring and the photos of his children. But he knew from past experience in Europe that he needed to be able to survive a random and cursory search. He had no intention of allowing such a search, but it could happen, and he had to be prepared for such a possibility.

He took the first exit he saw and drove off the ramp where three service stations appeared before him. He pulled into the one called Exxon and drove to the line of gasoline pumps marked SELF-SERVICE. This was not different from Europe, they told him, and he could use the bank credit card he had with him, but he didn't want to leave a paper trail this early in his mission, so he decided to pay in cash.

He completed the refueling procedure, then went to a glass booth where he put two twenty-dollar bills through the small opening. The man glanced at him, and Khalil thought the quick look was not friendly. The man put his change on the ledge and announced the amount, then turned away from him. Asad took the change and went back to his car and got in.

He drove back to the Interstate and continued south.

This was the state of Virginia, he knew, and he noticed that the trees were more fully leafed here than in New York or New Jersey. His digital outside thermometer told him it was seventy-six degrees Fahrenheit. He pushed a button on the console and the temperature was displayed as twenty-five degrees Celsius. This was a pleasant temperature, he thought, but there was too much humidity here.

He continued on, keeping up with traffic that moved at over seventy-five miles per hour, much faster than north of Washington, and ten miles an hour faster than the posted speed limit. One of his briefing officers in Tripoli, Boris, the Russian KGB man who had lived five years in America, had told him, "The police in the South are known to stop vehicles that have license plates from the North. Especially from New York."

Khalil had asked why, and Boris told him, "There was a great civil war between the North and the South in which the South was defeated. They harbor much animosity because of this."

He'd inquired, "When was this civil war?"

"Over a hundred years ago." Boris explained the war to him briefly, then added, "The Americans forgive their foreign enemies in ten years, but they don't forgive each other so quickly." Boris added, "But if you stay on the Interstate highway, it will be better. This is a route heavily traveled by people from the North, who take their vacation in Florida. Your automobile will not attract undue attention."

The Russian further informed him, "Many people from New York are Jews, and the police in the South may stop a car from New York for that reason." The Russian had laughed and told him, "If they stop you, tell them you don't like Jews either."

Khalil thought about all of this. They had tried to make light of his driving in the South, but clearly they knew less about this place than they knew of the territory between New York and Washington. Clearly, too, this was a place that could cause him problems. He thought of the gasoline attendant, thought of his New York license plates, and also thought of his appearance. Boris had also told him, "There are not many races of people in the South—mostly they are black Africans or Europeans. To them, you look like neither. But when you get to Florida, it will be better. There are many races in Florida, and many skin colors. They may think you are South American, but many people in Florida speak Spanish and you do not. So, if you need to explain yourself, say you are Brazilian. In Brazil, they speak Portuguese and very few Americans speak that language. But if it is the police you are talking to, then you are Egyptian, just as it says on all your identification."

Khalil reflected on Boris' advice. In Europe, there were many visitors, businessmen, and residents from Arabic countries, but in America, outside of the area of New York, his appearance might be noticed, despite what Malik had said to the contrary.

Khalil had discussed this with Malik, who told him, "Don't let that idiot Russian worry you. In America you only have to smile, don't look suspicious, keep your hands out of your pockets, carry an American newspaper or magazine, tip fifteen percent, don't stand too close when you speak, bathe often, and tell everyone to have a good day."

Khalil smiled at the image of Malik telling him about Americans. Malik had concluded his assessment of Americans by saying, "They are like Europeans, but their thinking is more simple. Be direct, but not abrupt. Be friendly, but not familiar. They have a limited knowledge of geography and other cultures, less so than the Europeans. So if you want to be a Greek, be a Greek. Your Italian is good, so be from Sardinia. They've never heard of the place anyway."

Khalil directed his attention back to the road. The Sunday

afternoon traffic was sometimes heavy, sometimes light. There were few trucks on the road because it was the Christian Sabbath. The scenes on either side of the road were mostly of fields and forest with many pine trees. Occasionally, he would see what appeared to be a factory or a warehouse, but like the Autobahn, this road did not come close to cities or areas of population. It was difficult to imagine here that America held over 250 million people. His own country held not even five million, yet Libya had given the Americans much to worry about since the Great Leader had deposed the stupid King Idris many years ago.

Khalil finally let his thoughts go back to the house of General Waycliff. He had been saving these thoughts, like a sweet dessert, to be enjoyed at his leisure.

He re-created the entire scene in his mind, and tried to imagine how he might have gotten more pleasure from it. Perhaps, he thought, he should have made the General beg for his life, or made the wife get on her knees and kiss his feet. But he had the impression that they wouldn't beg. In fact, he had extracted all he could from them, and any further attempts to make them plead for mercy would have been unsatisfying. They knew they were going to die as soon as he revealed his purpose in being there.

He thought, however, that he could have made their deaths more painful, but he was restricted by the necessity of making the murders look as though they were part of a theft. He needed time to complete his mission before the American Intelligence organizations began to comprehend what was happening.

Asad Khalil knew that at any point in his visits to the men of the Al Azziziyah squadron, the police could be waiting for him. He accepted this possibility and took comfort in what he had already accomplished in Europe, at the New York airport, and now at the house of General Waycliff.

It would be good if he could complete his list, but if he could not, then someone else would. He would like to return to Libya, but it was not important that he do so. To die in the land of the infidel on his Jihad was a triumph and an honor. His place in Paradise was already secure.

Asad Khalil felt as good at this moment as he'd ever felt since that terrible night.

Bahira. I am doing this for you as well.

He approached the city of Richmond, and the traffic became heavier. He had to follow the signs that took him in a circle around the city, on a highway called I-295, then finally back to I-95, heading south again.

At 1:15 P.M., he saw a sign that said WELCOME TO NORTH CAROLINA.

He looked around, but noticed little difference from the state of Virginia. The Russian had warned him that the police in North Carolina were slightly more suspicious than the police in Virginia. The police in the next state, South Carolina, would be even more likely to stop him for no reason, and so would the police in Georgia.

The Russian had also said the police in the South sometimes traveled in pairs, and sometimes drew their weapons when they stopped a vehicle. Therefore, shooting them would be more difficult.

Boris had also warned him not to offer a policeman a bribe if he were stopped for a driving violation. They would most likely arrest him, according to the Russian. This, Khalil reflected, was the same as in Europe, but not in Libya where a few dinars would satisfy a policeman.

He continued on the wide, nearly straight Interstate highway. The vehicle was quiet and powerful and had a large fuel tank. But he could tell by the computer that he would have to refuel two more times before his destination.

He thought about the man he would visit next. Lieutenant Paul Grey, pilot of the F-III known as Elton 38.

It had taken over a decade and many millions of dollars before Libyan Intelligence gained access to this list of eight men. It had taken years longer to locate each of these murderers. One of them, Lieutenant Steven Cox, the weapons officer on the aircraft known as Remit 61, was beyond his reach, having been killed on a mission in the Gulf War. Khalil did not feel cheated, but was happy in the knowledge that Lieutenant Cox had died at the hands of Islamic fighters.

Asad Khalil's first victim, Colonel Hambrecht, had been sent home to America in small pieces in January. The body of his second victim, General Waycliff, was still warm, and the man's blood was inside Khalil's body.

That left five.

By this evening, Lieutenant Paul Grey would join his three squadron mates in hell.

Then there would be four.

Khalil knew that Libyan Intelligence had learned some of the names of the other pilots from other squadrons who had bombed Benghazi and Tripoli, but those men would be dealt with at another time. Asad Khalil had been given the honor of striking the first blow, of personally avenging the death of his own family, the death of the Great Leader's daughter, and the injuries suffered by the Great Leader's wife and sons.

Khalil had no doubt that the Americans had long forgotten April 15, 1986. They had bombed so many places since then that this incident was considered of little importance. In the Gulf War, tens of thousands of Iraqis had perished at the hands of the Americans and their allies, and the Iraqi leader, Hussein, had done little to avenge the death of his martyrs. But the Libyans were not like the Iraqis. The Great Leader, Gadhafi, never forgot an insult, a betrayal, or the death of a martyr.

He wondered what Lieutenant Paul Grey was doing at this moment. He wondered, too, if this man was one of the ones that General Waycliff had telephoned yesterday. Khalil had no idea if the surviving men all kept in contact, but according to the General's date book, there had been a conference call on April 15. And as for the frequency of their contact, having spoken only two days ago, it was unlikely they would speak again unless someone notified them of General Waycliff's death. Certainly Mrs. Waycliff was not going to notify them. In fact, it might be twenty-four hours before the bodies were even discovered.

Khalil also wondered if the death of the Waycliffs and their servant would be regarded as a robbery and murder. He thought that the police, like police everywhere, would look on the scene as a common crime. But if the intelligence organization became involved, they might see things differently.

In any case, even if they did, they had no reason to think first of Libya. The General's career had been long and varied, and his assignment to the Pentagon raised many other possibilities in the event that anyone was suspicious of a political murder.

The most important circumstance that Khalil knew he had on his side was the fact that almost no one knew that these fliers had participated in the April 15 raid. There were no references to the raid even in their personnel files, as Libyan and Soviet Intelligence had discovered. There was, in fact, only a list, and the list was classified top secret. The secrecy had protected these men for over a decade. But now that same secrecy would make it very difficult for the authorities to make a connection between what happened at Lakenheath, England, Washington, D.C., and soon, Daytona Beach, Florida.

But the men themselves knew what they had in common, and that had always been a problem. Khalil could only pray that God would keep his enemies in ignorance. That, plus speed and deception, would ensure that he would be able to kill all of them, or at least most of them.

Malik had said to him, "Asad—they tell me you have a sixth sense, that you can *feel* danger before you can see it, smell it, or hear it. Is that true?"

Khalil had replied, "I think I have this gift." He then told Malik of the night of the raid—leaving out the part about Bahira. He'd said to Malik, "I was on a roof praying, and before the first aircraft even arrived, I felt the presence of danger. I had a vision of monstrous and terrible birds of prey descending through the Ghabli toward our country. I ran home to tell my family…but it was too late."

Malik had nodded and said, "The Great Leader, as you know, goes into the desert to pray, and visions come to him as well."

Khalil knew this. He knew that Moammar Gadhafi had been born in the desert into a nomadic family. Those born in the desert to nomads were twice blessed, and many of them had powers that those who had been born in the cities and towns on the coast did not have. Khalil was vaguely aware that the mysticism of the desert people preceded the coming of Islam, and that some considered these beliefs to be blasphemy. For that reason, Asad Khalil, who had been born in the Kufra oasis—neither coast nor desert—did not often speak of his sixth sense.

But Malik knew of it and said to him, "When you feel danger, it is not cowardly to run. Even the lion runs at danger. That is why God gave him more speed than he needs to run down his prey. You must listen to your instincts. If you do not, this sixth sense of yours will leave you. If you ever feel that you have lost this power, then you must make up for it with more cunning and more caution."

Khalil thought he understood what Malik was saying.

But then Malik said, bluntly, "You may die in America, or you may escape from America. But you cannot be captured in America."

Khalil had not responded.

Malik continued, "I know you are brave and would never betray our country or our God, or our Great Leader, even under torture. But if they get their hands on you, alive, that is all the proof they will need to retaliate against our country. The Great Leader himself has asked me to tell you that you must take your own life if capture becomes imminent."

Khalil recalled being surprised at this. He had no intention of being captured, and would gladly take his own life if he thought it was necessary.

But he had envisioned a situation where he might be captured alive. He thought this would be acceptable, even beneficial to the cause. He could then tell the world who he was, how he had suffered, and what he had done to avenge that night of hell. This would excite all of Islam, redeem the honor of his country, and humiliate the Americans.

But Malik had rejected that possibility, and the Great Leader himself had prohibited such an ending to his Jihad.

Khalil thought about this. He understood why the Great Leader would not want to invite another American air strike. But that was, after all, the nature of the blood feud. It was like a circle—a circle of blood and death without end. The more blood, the better. The more martyrs, the more God would be pleased, and the more united would Islam become.

Khalil put these thoughts out of his mind, knowing that the Great Leader had a strategy that could only be comprehended by those chosen few around him. Khalil thought that someday he might be taken into the inner circle, but for now, he would serve as one of many Mujahadeen— the Islamic Freedom Fighters.

Khalil drew his thoughts from the past and projected them into the future. He went into a trance-like state, which was not difficult on this straight, uninteresting highway. He projected his mind hours and miles ahead, to this place called Daytona Beach. He visualized the house he had seen in the photographs, and the face of the man called Paul Grey. He tried to envision or sense any danger ahead, but he felt no peril lurking, no trap ready to spring closed on him. In fact, he had a vision of Paul Grey running naked through the desert, the Ghabli, blinding him as a huge and hungry desert lion ran behind him, closing the distance with every stride.

Asad Khalil smiled and praised God.

Chapter 30

After lunch, we made our way to a small, windowless briefing room on the fourth floor where we heard a short lecture about terrorism in general, and Mideast terrorism in particular. There was a slide show with maps, photos, and diagrams of terrorist organizations, and a handout listing suggested readings.

I thought this was a joke, but it wasn't. Nevertheless, I asked our instructor, a guy named Bill, I think, who wore a blue suit, "Are we killing time before something important happens?"

Bill seemed a little put off and replied, "This presentation was designed to reinforce your commitment and to give you an overview of the global terrorist network." And so on.

He explained to us the challenges we faced in the post–Cold War world, and informed us that international terrorism was here to stay. This was not exactly news to me, but I made an entry in my notebook, in case there was a test later.

The FBI, by the way, is broken up into seven sections—Civil Rights, Drugs, Investigative Support, Organized Crime, Violent Crime, White-Collar Crime, and Counterterrorism, which is a growth industry that didn't even exist twenty-five years ago when I was a rookie cop.

Bill was not explaining all of this to us—I already knew this, and I also knew that the White House was not a happy house this morning, though the rest of the country had no clue yet that the U.S. had suffered the worst terrorist attack since Oklahoma City. More importantly, this attack hadn't come from some homegrown yahoo, but from the deserts of North Africa.

Bill was flapping his gums about the history of Mideast terrorism, and I made notes in my book to call Beth Penrose, call my parents in

Florida, call Dom Fanelli, buy club soda, pick up my suits at the cleaner, call the TV repair guy, and so forth.

Bill kept talking. Kate was listening; Ted was drifting.

Jack Koenig, who was King Jack in New York metro, was not king here, I saw. In fact, he was just another loyal princeling in the Imperial Capital. I noticed that the D.C. types referred to New York as a field office, which didn't go down well with this particular New Yorker.

Anyway, Bill left and a man and woman came in. The lady's name was Jane, and the guy's name was Jim. They wore blue.

Jane said, "Thank you for coming."

I'd finally had enough and said, "Did we have a choice?"

"No," she smiled, "you didn't."

Jim said, "You must be Detective Corey."

I must be.

Anyway, Jane and Jim did a little duet, and the name of the song was Libya. This was a little more interesting than the last show, and we paid attention. They spoke about Moammar Gadhafi, about his relationship with the U.S., about his state-sponsored terrorism, and about the U.S. raid on Libya on April 15, 1986.

Jane said, "The suspected perpetrator of yesterday's incident, Asad Khalil, is believed to be a Libyan, though he sometimes travels under passports of other Mideast countries." Suddenly, a photo of Asad Khalil came on the screen. Jane continued, "This is the picture that was transmitted to you from Paris. I have a better quality shot for you, which I'll hand out later. We also took more photos in Paris."

A series of photos came on the screen, showing Khalil in various candid poses sitting in an office. Obviously, he didn't know he was on Candid Camera.

Jane said, "The embassy intelligence people took these in Paris while Khalil was being debriefed. They treated him as a legitimate defector because that's how he presented himself to the embassy."

"Was he searched?" I asked.

"Only superficially. He was patted down and went through a metal detector."

"He wasn't strip-searched?"

"No," Jane replied. "We don't want to turn an informant or defector into a hostile prisoner."

"Some people enjoy having someone look up their ass. You don't know until you ask."

Even old Ted chuckled at that one.

Jane replied, coolly, "The Arab people are quite modest when it comes to nudity, displays of flesh, and such. They would be outraged and humiliated if subjected to a body search."

"But the guy could have cyanide pills up his butt and could have offed himself or slipped an embassy guy a lethal dose."

Jane fixed me with a frosty stare and said, "The intelligence community is not as stupid as you may think."

And with that, a series of photos came on the screen. The photos showed Khalil in a bathroom. He was undressing, taking a shower, going to the potty, and so forth.

Jane said, "This was a hidden camera, of course. We also have videotapes of the same scenes, Mr. Corey, if you're interested."

"I'll pass on that."

I looked at the photo on the screen now. It was a full frontal nude of Asad Khalil stepping out of the shower. He was a powerfully built man, about six feet tall, very hairy, no visible scars or tattoos, and hung like a donkey. I said to Kate, "I'll get that one framed for you."

This didn't go over well with this bunch. The room became noticeably cooler, and I thought I was going to be asked to stand in the hall. But Jane went on, "While Mr. Khalil was in a deep sleep—caused by a naturally occurring sedative in his milk—" she smiled, conspiratorially, "—some embassy personnel searched and vacuumed fibers from his clothing. They also took fingerprints and footprints, swabbed epithelial cells from his mouth for DNA printing, took hair samples, and even got dental imprints." Jane looked at me and said, "Did we miss anything, Mr. Corey?"

"I guess not. I didn't know milk could put you out like that."

Jane continued, "All of this forensic product will be made available to you. A preliminary report on the clothing, which was a gray suit, shirt, tie, black shoes, and underwear, indicates that everything was made in America, which is interesting, since American clothing is not common in Europe or in the Middle East. We suspect, therefore, that Khalil wanted to blend in with an urban American population very soon after his arrival."

That's what I thought.

Jane continued, "There is an alternate theory, which is simply that Khalil, carrying a false passport from Haddad, went to the International Arrivals and Departures terminal where a ticket was waiting for him under his false passport name at the ticket counter of a Mideast airline, or perhaps any airline. Or, Yusef Haddad gave Khalil his ticket on board Flight One-Seven-Five."

Jane looked at us and said, "I understand you've considered both theories—Khalil stayed, Khalil is gone. Both are plausible. What we know for sure is that Yusef Haddad stayed. We're trying to establish his true identity, and determine what his connections are." She added, "Consider a man so ruthless—I mean Khalil—that he would murder his accomplice, murder a man who risked his own life to get Khalil into the country. Think about Asad Khalil breaking Haddad's neck, then sitting alone in a planeload of corpses, hoping that the aircraft's autopilot would land him at the airport. Then, instead of fleeing, he goes to the Conquistador Club and murders three of our people. To say that Khalil is ruthless and heartless is to define only a part of his personality. Khalil is also unbelievably fearless and brazen. Something very potent is driving him."

No doubt about it. I consider myself fearless and brazen, but it was time for me to admit to myself that I could not have done what Asad Khalil did. Only once in my career had I met an adversary who I thought had more balls than I did. When I finally killed him, I felt I wasn't worthy of having killed him; like a hunter with a high-powered rifle who kills a lion knows that the lion was the more worthy and braver of the two.

Jane hit the video projector button. A blown-up color photo appeared on the screen showing a man's face in profile. Jane said, "You'll see here, in this enhanced photo of Khalil's left cheek, three faint, parallel scars. He has three similar ones on his right cheek. Our pathologist says they are not burns or wounds made by shrapnel or a knife. They are, in fact, typical of wounds made by human fingernails or animal claws—parallel and slightly jagged lacerations. These are the only identifying scars on his body."

I asked, "Can we assume that these scars were caused by a lady's fingernails?"

"You can assume whatever you please, Mr. Corey. I point these out as identifying features in the event he's changed his outward appearance."

"Thank you."

"And along those lines, the people in Paris tattooed three small dots on Asad Khalil's body. One is located on his inner right earlobe..." She treated us to a close-up photo. "...one between the big toe and the second toe of his right foot..." Again, a weird photo. "...and the last is close to his anus. Right side."

She continued, "In the event you have a suspect, or if you find a body, this might be quick identification to be followed up by fingerprints, or a dental impressions check if necessary."

It was Jim's turn, and he said, "The setup for this operation is actually simple when you examine it. Going from one relatively open country to another is not that difficult. Yusef Haddad was flying Business Class and that always makes things easier, including bringing your garment bag and dealing with medical oxygen. Haddad is well dressed, he probably speaks enough French to understand what they're saying at De Gaulle, and he probably speaks enough English not to be a nuisance to the flight attendants on Trans-Continental."

I raised my hand. "May I ask a question?"

"Of course."

"How did Yusef Haddad know what flight Asad Khalil would be on?"

"Well, Mr. Corey, that is the question, isn't it."

"Yeah, it's been on my mind."

"Well, the answer is unfortunately simple. We almost always use Trans-Continental, our flag carrier airline, with whom we have a reduced Business Class fare arrangement, but more importantly, we have a security liaison person who works with Trans-Continental. We get people on and off aircraft quickly and with minimum fuss. Apparently, someone knew about this arrangement, which is not exactly top secret."

"But how did Haddad know that Khalil would be on *that* flight?"

"An obvious security breach within the Trans-Continental operation at De Gaulle. In other words, an employee at Trans-Continental in Paris, perhaps an Arab employee, of which there are many in Paris, tipped off Yusef Haddad. In fact, if you back it up further, Khalil defected in Paris and not in some other city *because* there was a security breach there. In fact," he added, "for security reasons, American air carriers have a policy that prohibits bringing your own medical oxygen on board. You have to put in a reservation for oxygen, and for a small fee it's delivered to you before you board. Obviously, someone thought about this potential security problem years ago. In this case, however, one of the airline employees swapped a canister of poison gas for one of the oxygen canisters."

I commented, "Both canisters looked the same to me. I guess one of them was marked."

"In fact, the oxygen had a small zigzag scratch in the paint. The poison gas didn't."

I pictured Yusef Haddad saying to himself, "Let me see now...oxygen is scratched, poison gas is not...or was it the other way around...?"

Jim said to me, "Something funny, Mr. Corey?"

I explained my silly thought, but only Nash laughed.

Jim referred to some notes, then said, "Regarding the gas, we have a preliminary report on that. I'm not an expert, but they tell me that there are four major types of toxic gas—choking, blister, blood, and nerve. The gas used on Flight One-Seven-Five was undoubtedly a blood agent—probably an advanced or modified cyanide chloride compound. This type of gas is very volatile and dissipates quickly in the ambient air. According to our chemical experts, the passengers may have noticed something that smelled like bitter almonds or even peach pits, but unless they were familiar with cyanide, they would not be alarmed."

Jim looked at us and saw he had everyone's attention, for a change. I've had the same experience in my class at John Jay. As soon as the students start to drift, I come up with something that has to do with murder or sex. Gets everyone's attention.

Jim was into the gas and continued, "Here's what we think happened.

Asad Khalil asked to use the lavatory. He was, of course, accompanied by Phil Hundry or Peter Gorman. Whoever accompanied him checked out the lavatory as they would do each time Khalil asked to use it. They wanted to be sure that no one was trying to pull a Michael Corleone—" He looked at us and said, unnecessarily, "You know, where someone slips a gun into the rest room. So Phil or Peter check the trash...and perhaps they also checked behind the maintenance panel under the sink. In that space, someone could hide something. In fact, someone did. But what was hidden looked innocuous and would not seem to Phil or Peter as something that shouldn't be there. What was there was a small oxygen bottle and mask of the type that is in each galley on every aircraft in the world. This is therapeutic oxygen for passengers in distress. But it's never put under the sink in a lav. Yet, if you don't know airline procedures, you wouldn't be aware of that. So even if Phil or Peter saw the oxygen bottle, they wouldn't have thought anything of it."

Again, Jim paused for effect and continued his narrative. He informed us, "Someone, most probably a cleaning person or maintenance person at De Gaulle, put that oxygen canister under the sink in the dome lav before takeoff. When Phil or Peter let Khalil into the lav, they left him cuffed and told him not to lock the door. Standard procedure. When Khalil was in the lav, this was the signal for Haddad to release the gas in his second canister. At some point, people began to show signs of distress. But by the time anyone realized they were in trouble, it was too late. The autopilot is always engaged during the flight, so the aircraft flew on."

Jim concluded, "Khalil, who was breathing the oxygen from the airline canister under the sink, came out of the lav after he was certain everyone was unconscious or dead. At this point Khalil and Haddad had over two hours to tidy things up, including uncuffing Khalil, putting the Federal escort back in his seat, putting Haddad's medical oxygen in the coat closet, and so forth. Khalil knew that he needed a few critical minutes on the ground to effect his escape by donning Trans-Continental luggage handlers' jumpsuits and mingling with the people who boarded the aircraft in the security area. That's why he wanted everything to appear as normal as possible for the Emergency Service personnel who would board the aircraft at the end of the runway. Khalil needed to be sure that the aircraft did not look like a crime scene, and that the aircraft was towed to the security enclosure where personnel other than Emergency Service would be allowed to board."

Jim finished, then Jane took over again, then Jim, then Jane, and so on. It was pushing four o'clock, and I needed a break.

We were doing Q&A now and Kate asked, "How did Khalil and Haddad know that the 747 was pre-programmed to land at JFK?"

Jim answered, "Trans-Continental has a company policy requiring pilots to program the computer for the entire flight before take-off, and that includes landing information. This is no secret. This has been reported in detail in any number of aviation magazines. Plus, there's the security breach at Trans-Continental at De Gaulle."

He added, "One thing that no one trusts a computer to do is engage the reverse thrusters because if the computer screws up and engages the reverse thrusters during flight, the engines or some other major parts of the airplane will rip off. Reverse thrusters have to be engaged manually, after landing, with as little automatic interface as possible. It's a safety feature, and it's maybe the only thing a human pilot still has to do, except say 'Welcome to New York,' or whatever, and taxi to the gate." He added, jocularly, "I guess the computers could do that, too. In any case, when that 747 landed at JFK without reverse thrusters, it was an indication that there was a problem."

Koenig said, "I didn't think runways were assigned until the flight was close to the airport."

Jim replied, "Correct, but the pilots generally know what runways are being used. The pre-programming is not meant to take the place of a pilot landing by hand and by radio instructions. It's just a procedural backup. The pilot I talked to tells me that it makes their onboard computer calculations more accurate en route." He added, "And as it turned out, Runway Four-Right—the pre-programmed runway—was still being used yesterday at Flight One-Seven-Five's arrival time."

Amazing, I thought. Absolutely amazing. I need a computer like that for my car so I can sleep behind the wheel.

Jim continued, "I'll tell you what else the perpetrators knew about. They knew the Emergency Service procedure at JFK. It's pretty much the

same at all American airports. The procedures at JFK are more sophisticated than at a lot of airports, but this is not top secret stuff. Articles
have been written about Guns and Hoses, and manuals are available.
None of this is hard to come by. Only the hijack security area is not well
known, but it's not top secret either."

I think Jim and Jane needed a break from me, and when Jim finished, Jane said, "Take a fifteen-minute break. Rest rooms and coffee
bar at the end of the corridor."

We all got up and left quickly, before they changed their minds.

Ted, Kate, Jack, and I chatted awhile, and I discovered that Jim and
Jane were actually named Scott and Lisa. But to me, they would always
be Jim and Jane. Everyone here was Jane and Jim, except Bob, Bill, and
Jean. And they all wore blue, and they played squash in the basement,
and jogged along the Potomac, and had houses in suburban Virginia, and
went to church on Sundays, except when the turds hit the turbines, like
today. The married ones had kids, and the kids were terrific, and they
sold candy bars to raise money for soccer equipment, and so forth.

On one level, you had to like these people. I mean, they did represent the ideal, or at least the American ideal as they saw it. The agents
were good at their jobs, they had a worldwide reputation for honesty,
sobriety, loyalty, and intelligence. So what if most of them were lawyers?
Jack Koenig, for instance, was a good guy who just happened to have the
misfortune of being a lawyer. Kate, too, was all right for a lawyer. I liked
her lipstick today. Sort of a pale, frosty pink.

Anyway, so maybe I was a little envious of family-and-church-
oriented people. Somewhere in the back of my mind was a house with a
white picket fence, a loving wife, two kids and a dog, and a nine-to-five
job where no one wanted to kill me.

I thought again of Beth Penrose out on Long Island. I thought of
the weekend house she'd bought on the North Fork, near the sea and the
vineyards. I wasn't feeling particularly well today, and the reasons why
were too scary to contemplate.

Chapter 31

Asad Khalil looked at his fuel gauge, which read one-quarter full. His dashboard clock said 2:13 P.M. He had traveled nearly three hundred miles since Washington, and he noted that this powerful automobile used more fuel than any vehicle he had driven in Europe or Libya.

He was neither hungry nor thirsty, or perhaps he was, but he knew how to suppress these feelings. His training had conditioned him to go for long periods without food, sleep, or water. Thirst was the most difficult need to ignore, but he had once gone six days in the desert without water and without becoming delirious, so he knew what his mind and body were capable of.

A white convertible automobile came abreast of him in the left lane, and he saw in the automobile four young women. They were laughing and talking, and Khalil noted that they were all light-haired though their skin was brown from the sun. Three of them wore T-shirts, but the fourth, in the rear closest to him, wore only the top of a pink bathing suit. He had once seen a beach in the south of France where the women wore no tops at all, and their bare breasts were exposed for the world to see.

In Libya, this would have gotten them a whipping and perhaps several years in jail. He couldn't say precisely what the punishment would be because such a thing had never happened.

The girl with the pink top looked at him, smiled and waved. The other girls looked, too, waved and laughed.

Khalil accelerated.

They accelerated with him and kept abreast of him. He noted that he was traveling at seventy-six miles per hour. He eased off the accelerator and his speed dropped back to sixty-five. They did the same and kept waving at him. One of them shouted something to him, but he could not hear her.

Khalil didn't know what to do. He felt, for the first time since he'd landed, that he was not in control of the situation. He let off on the accelerator again, and they did the same.

He considered getting off at the next exit, but they might follow. He accelerated, and they kept up with him, still laughing and waving.

He knew he was or would soon be attracting attention, and he felt sweat forming on his brow.

Suddenly, a police car with two men in it appeared in his sideview mirror, and Khalil realized he was traveling at eighty miles per hour and the car with the women was still right beside him. "Filthy whores!"

The police car veered into the outside lane behind the convertible and the convertible sped up. Khalil let off the accelerator and the police car drew up beside him. He put his right hand in his jacket pocket and wrapped his fingers around the butt of the Glock, keeping his head and eyes straight ahead on the road.

The police car passed him, then moved into his lane without signaling, and accelerated up to the convertible. Khalil eased off more on the accelerator and watched. The driver of the police car seemed to be speaking to the young women in the convertible. They all waved and the police car sped off.

The convertible was a hundred meters in front of him now, and its occupants seemed to have lost interest in him. He maintained a speed of sixty-five miles per hour, and the distance between the two cars widened. The police car, he noticed, had disappeared over a rise in the road.

Khalil took a deep breath. He thought about the incident, but only vaguely comprehended it.

He recalled something Boris had told him. "My friend, many American women will find you handsome. American women will not be as openly and honestly sexual as European women, but they may try to strike up an acquaintance. They think they can be friendly to a man without being provocative and without calling attention to the obvious differences between the sexes. In Russia, as in Europe, we find this idiotic. Why would you want to speak to a woman if not for sex? But in America, especially with the younger women, they will talk to you, even make sexual talk, drink with you, dance with you, even invite you to their homes, but will then tell you that they will not have sex with you."

Khalil found this difficult to believe. In any case, he'd told Boris, "I will have nothing to do with women while I'm on my mission."

Boris had laughed at him and said, "My good Muslim friend, sex is part of the mission. You may as well have some fun while you're risking your life. Surely, you have seen James Bond movies."

Khalil had not, and told the Russian, "Perhaps if the KGB had paid more attention to the mission and less attention to women, there would still be a KGB."

The Russian had not liked this reply, but told Khalil, "In any event, women *can* be a distraction. And even if you do not look for them, they may find you. You must learn to handle such situations."

"I have no intention of getting into such situations. My time in America is limited, and so are my occasions to speak to Americans."

"Still, things happen."

Khalil nodded to himself. Such a situation just occurred, and he had not handled it well.

He thought about the four young women, scantily dressed, in the convertible car. Aside from his confusion about what to do, he recognized and admitted to a strange desire, a longing to sleep naked with a woman.

In Tripoli, this was almost impossible without danger. In Germany, there were Turkish prostitutes everywhere, but he could not bring himself to buy the body of a fellow Muslim. He had contented himself in France with African prostitutes but only when they assured him that they were not Muslim. In Italy, there were the refugees from the former Yugoslavia and Albania, but many of these women were also Muslim. He recalled, once, being with an Albanian woman who he discovered was Muslim. He had beaten her so badly he wondered if she'd survived.

Malik had said to him, "When you return, it will be time for you to marry. You will have your pick of the daughters from the best families in Libya." In fact, Malik had mentioned one by name—Alima Nadir, the youngest sister of Bahira, who was now nineteen years old, and still without a husband.

He thought of Alima; even though veiled, he sensed she was not as beautiful as Bahira, but he also sensed in her the same brashness he had liked and also disliked in Bahira. Yes, he would and could marry her. Captain Nadir, who would have disapproved of his attentions to Bahira, would now welcome Asad Khalil as a hero of Islam, the pride of the fatherland, and a prized son-in-law.

A light blinked on his dashboard, and a small chime sounded. His eyes scanned the instruments, and he saw he was low on fuel.

At the next exit, he drove off the ramp onto a local road and into a Shell Oil station.

Again, he chose not to use his credit card and went to a pump marked SELF-SERVICE, CASH. He put on his eyeglasses and got out of the Mercury. He chose high-octane gasoline and filled the tank, which took twenty-two gallons. He tried to convert this into liters and estimated the liters at about a hundred. He marveled at the arrogance, or perhaps the stupidity, of the Americans for being the last nation on earth not to use the metric system.

Khalil replaced the pump nozzle and noticed that there was no glass booth where he could pay. He realized he had to go into the small office, and he cursed himself for not noticing this.

He walked to the office of the gasoline station and went inside.

A man sat on a stool behind a small counter, dressed in blue jeans and a T-shirt, watching television and smoking a cigarette.

The man looked at him, then looked at a digital display board and said, "That'll be twenty-eight eighty-five."

Khalil put two twenty-dollar bills on the counter.

As the man made change, he said, "Need anything else?"

"No."

"Ah got cold drinks right there in the frigerator."

Khalil had difficulty understanding this man's accent. He replied, "No, thank you."

The man counted his change out and looked at Khalil. "Where you from, bud?"

"From...New York."

"Yeah? Long drive. Where you headin'?"

"To Atlanta."

"You don't want to miss I-20 this side of Florence."

Khalil took his change. "Yes, thank you." He noticed that the television was showing a baseball game.

The man saw him glance at the television and said, "Braves are leadin' New York, two-zip, bottom of the second." He added, "Gonna kick some Yankee ass today."

Asad Khalil nodded, though he had no idea what the man was talking about. He felt sweat forming on his brow again and realized it was very humid here. He said, "Have a good day." He turned and walked out of the office to his car.

He got in and glanced back at the big window of the office to see if the man was watching him, but the man was looking again at the television.

Khalil drove quickly, but not too quickly, out of the gasoline station.

Asad Khalil got back on I-95 and continued south.

He realized that his greatest danger was the television. If they began to broadcast his photo—and they could be doing that even now—then he was not entirely safe anywhere in America. He was certain that the police all over the country had his photograph by now, but he had no intention of having any contact with the police. He did, however, need to have contact with a small number of Americans. He flipped his sun visor down and studied his face in the visor mirror, still wearing his eyeglasses. With his hair parted and the gray added, the false mustache, and the glasses, he was fairly certain that he didn't look like any photo that existed of him. But they had shown him in Tripoli what the Americans could do with a computer, adding a mustache or beard, adding eyeglasses, making his hair shorter, lighter, or combing it differently. He did not think that the average person was so observant as to see through even the thinnest of disguises. The man in the gasoline station had obviously not recognized him because if he had, Khalil would have seen it in the man's eyes immediately, and the man would now be dead.

But what if the gas station had been filled with people?

Khalil glanced at his image one more time, and it suddenly came to him that there was no photograph of him smiling. He had to smile. They had told him that several times in Tripoli. Smile. He smiled into the mirror and was astonished at how different he looked, even to himself. He smiled again, then flipped the visor back.

He continued driving and continued to think about his photograph on television. Perhaps that would not be a problem.

They had also told him in Tripoli that, for some reason, the Americans placed the photographs of fugitive criminals in all post offices. He didn't know why the Americans chose post offices to display the photographs of fugitives, but he had no business in post offices, so it was of no concern.

He thought, too, that if he and his intelligence officers had reasoned and planned correctly, then the Americans believed that Asad Khalil had flown out of the country, directly from the airport in New York. There had been much debate about this. The Russian, Boris, had said, "It doesn't matter what they think. The FBI and local police will be looking for you in America, and the CIA and their foreign colleagues will be looking for you in the rest of the world. So, we must create the illusion that you are back in Europe."

Khalil nodded to himself. Boris understood the game of intrigue very well. He had played this game with the Americans for over twenty years. But Boris once had unlimited resources for his game, and Libya did not. Still, they agreed with him and had created another Asad Khalil, who would commit some act of terrorism somewhere in Europe, probably in the next day or two. This might or might not fool the Americans.

Malik had said, "The American Intelligence people of my generation were incredibly naive and unsophisticated. But they have been engaged in the world long enough to have developed the cynicism of an Arab and the sophistication of a European and the duplicity of an Oriental. Also, they have developed very advanced technology of their own. We should not underestimate them, but neither should we overestimate them. They can be fooled, but they can also pretend they are being fooled. So, yes, we can create another Asad Khalil in Europe for a week or so, and they will pretend to be looking for him there, while all the time they know he's still in America. The real Asad Khalil should not count on anything except himself. We will do what we can to cause a distraction, but you, Asad, should live every moment in America as though they are five minutes behind you."

Asad Khalil thought of both Boris and Malik, two very different men. Malik did what he did out of his love for God, for Islam, for his country, and for the Great Leader, not to mention a hate for the West. Boris worked for money and did not especially hate the Americans or the West. Also, Boris had no God, no leader, and, in reality, no country. Malik had once described Boris as pitiable, but Asad thought of him as pitiful. Yet, Boris himself seemed happy enough, neither bitter nor defeated. He once said, "Russia will rise again. It is inevitable."

In any case, these two very different men worked well together, and each had taught him something that the other barely comprehended. Asad preferred Malik, of course, but Boris could be counted on to tell the entire truth. In fact, Boris had told him privately, "Your Great Leader doesn't want another American bomb falling on his tent, so don't expect much help if you're caught. If you make it back here, you'll be treated well. But if it appears that you're trapped in America and can't get out, the next Libyan you see will be your executioner."

Khalil reflected on that, but dismissed it as old-line Soviet thinking. The Islamic fighters neither betrayed nor abandoned one another. God would not be pleased with that.

Khalil turned his attention back to the road. This was a big country, and because it was so big and diverse, it was easy to hide or to blend in, whichever one needed to do at the moment. But its size was also a problem, and unlike Europe, there were not many borders one could cross to escape. Libya was a long way from here. Also, Khalil hadn't fully realized that the English he understood was not the English spoken here in the South. But he recalled that Boris had mentioned this and told him that Florida English was closer to what Khalil could understand.

He again thought about Lieutenant Paul Grey, and recalled the photograph of the man's house, a very nice villa with palm trees. He thought, too, of General Waycliff's house. These two murderers had gone home and lived good lives with wives and children, after destroying the life of Asad Khalil without a passing thought. If, indeed, there was a hell, then Asad Khalil knew the names of three of its inhabitants—Lieutenant Steven Cox, killed in the Gulf, and Colonel William Hambrecht and General Terrance Waycliff, killed by Asad Khalil. If they were speaking to one another now, the last two could discuss with the first how they died, and they could all wonder who would be the next of their squadron mates that Asad Khalil would choose to join them.

Khalil said aloud, "Be patient, gentlemen, you will know soon enough. And soon after, you will all be reunited again."

Chapter 32

The break was over, and we returned to our briefing room. Jim and Jane were gone, and in their place was an Arab-looking gentleman. I thought at first that this guy had gotten lost on his way to a mosque or something, or maybe he'd kidnapped Jim and Jane and was holding them hostage. Before I could put a choke hold on the intruder, he smiled and introduced himself as Abbah Ibin Abdellah, which he was nice enough to write on the chalkboard. At least his name wasn't Bob, Bill, or Jim. He did say, however, "Call me Ben," which fit in with the diminutive-naming system here.

Mr. Abdellah—Ben—wore a too-heavy tweed suit, not blue, and one of those checkered racing flags on his head. This was my first clue that he might not be from around here.

Ben sat with us and smiled again. He was about fifty, a little tubby, wore a beard, eyeglasses, thinning hair, good choppers, and smelled okay. Three demerits for that one, Detective Corey.

There was and there wasn't a little awkwardness in the room. I mean, Jack, Kate, Ted, and I were sophisticated, worldly, and all that. We'd all worked and socialized with Mideast types, but for some reason this afternoon there was a little tension in the air.

Ben began by saying, "What a terrible tragedy."

No one replied, and he continued, "I am a Special Contract Agent for the Bureau."

This meant that, like me, he was hired for some specialty, and I guessed it wasn't fashion consultant. At least he wasn't a lawyer.

He said, "The Deputy Director thought it might be a good idea if I made myself available to you."

Koenig asked, "Available for what?"

Mr. Abdellah looked at Koenig and replied, "I am a professor of Mideast political studies at George Washington University. My specialized area is the study of various groups who have an extremist agenda."

"Terrorist groups," Koenig prompted.

"Yes. For want of a better word."

I said helpfully, "How about psychotics and murderers? Those are better words."

Professor Abdellah looked cool, like he'd been through this before. He was well spoken, looked intelligent, and had a quiet manner about him. Nothing that happened yesterday was his fault, of course. But Ibin Abdellah had a tough job this afternoon.

He continued, "I myself am an Egyptian, but I have a good understanding of the Libyans. They're an interesting people, descended in part from the ancient Carthaginians. Afterward came the Romans, who added their bloodlines, and there have always been Egyptians in Libya. Following the Romans came the Vandals from Spain, who in turn were conquered by the Byzantines, who were conquered by the Arab people from the Arabian Peninsula, who brought the Islamic religion with them. The Libyans consider themselves Arab, but Libya has always had such a small population that every invading group has left their genes behind."

I misunderstood at first and thought he said "jeans," but then I got it.

Professor Abdellah got us up and running on Libyans, gave us some insights into Libyan culture, customs, and so forth. He had a whole bunch of handouts, including a glossary of words that were uniquely Libyan in case we cared, plus a glossary of Libyan cooking, which I didn't think I'd stick up in my kitchen. He said, "The Libyans love pasta. That's the result of the Italian occupation."

I loved pasta, too, so maybe I'd bump into Asad Khalil in Giulio's. Maybe not.

We received from the professor a short biography of Moammar Gadhafi and an online printout of a few *Encyclopedia Britannica* pages on Libya. He also presented us with a lot of pamphlets on Islamic culture and religion.

Professor Abdellah said to us, "Muslims, Christians, and Jews all trace their origins to the prophet and patriarch Abraham. The Prophet Muhammad is descended from Abraham's oldest son, Ishmael, and Moses and Jesus are descended from Isaac," he informed us, and added, "Peace be upon them all."

I mean, I didn't know whether to make the sign of the cross, face Mecca, or call my friend Jack Weinstein.

Ben went on about Jesus, Moses, Mary, the Archangel Gabriel, Muhammad, Allah, and so on. These guys all knew and liked each other. Incredible. This was interesting, but it wasn't getting me an inch closer to Asad Khalil.

Mr. Abdellah addressed Kate and said, "Contrary to popular myth, Islam actually elevates the status of women. Muslims do not blame women for violating the Forbidden Tree, as Christians and Jews do. Nor is their suffering in pregnancy and childbirth a punishment for that act."

Kate replied, coolly, "That's certainly an enlightened concept."

Undeterred by the Ice Queen, Ben continued, "Women who marry under Islamic law may keep their own family name. They may own property and dispose of property."

Sounds like my ex. Maybe she was a Muslim.

Ben said, "Regarding the veiling of women, this is a cultural practice in some countries, but does not reflect the teaching of Islam."

Kate inquired, "What about the stoning to death of women caught in adultery?"

"Also a cultural practice in some Muslim countries, but not in most."

I looked at my pamphlets to see if those countries were listed. I mean, what if Kate and I got sent to Jordan or someplace, and we got caught doing the dirty deed in our hotel? Would I be traveling home alone? But I couldn't find a list, and I thought it best not to ask Professor Abdellah for one.

Anyway, Ben prattled on a bit, and he was a very nice man, very polite, very knowledgeable, and really sincere. Nevertheless, I had the feeling I'd stepped through one of those two-way mirrors. And this was all being recorded and maybe videotaped by the boys in blue. This place was totally nuts.

I mean, I guess there was a reason for this lesson in Islam 101, but maybe we could accomplish the mission without being so sensitive to the other side. I tried to picture a scene before the D-Day invasion, and some paratrooper general is saying to his troops, "Okay, men, tomorrow's reading will be Goethe and Schiller. And don't forget tomorrow night will be a Wagner concert at Hangar Twelve. This is mandatory. The mess hall is serving sauerbraten tonight. Guten appetit."

Yeah, right.

Professor Abdellah said to us, "To catch this man, Asad Khalil, it would be helpful to understand him. Start first with his name—Asad. The Lion. An Islamic given name is not only a convention, it is also a definiens of the person—it defines the bearer of the name, though it may do so only partially. Many men and women from Islamic countries try to emulate their namesakes."

"So," I suggested, "we should start by looking around zoos."

Ben thought this was funny and chuckled. He went along with the joke and said, "Look for a man who likes to kill zebras." He looked into my eyes and said, "A man who likes to kill."

No one said anything, and Ben continued. "The Libyans are an isolated people, a nation isolated even from other Islamic countries. Their leader, Moammar Gadhafi, has assumed almost mystical powers in the minds of many Libyans. If Asad Khalil is working directly for Libyan Intelligence, then he is working directly for Moammar Gadhafi. He has been given a sacred mission, and he will pursue that mission with religious zeal."

Ben let that sink in, then continued, "The Palestinians, by contrast, are more sophisticated, more worldly. They are clever, they have a political agenda, and their main enemy is Israel. The Iraqis as well as the Iranians have become distrustful of their leaders. The Libyans, on the other hand, idolize Gadhafi, and they do what he says, though Gadhafi has changed courses and changed enemies often. In fact, if this is a Libyan operation, there seems to be no specific reason for it. Aside from making anti-American statements, Gadhafi has not been very active in the extremist movement since the American bombing of Libya, and Libya's retaliation, which was the bombing of Pan Am Flight One-Oh-Three over Lockerbie, Scotland, in nineteen eighty-eight." Ben added, "In other words, Gadhafi considers his blood feud with the U.S. as finished. His honor has been satisfied, the bombing of Libya, which caused the death of his adopted daughter, is avenged. I can't conceive of why he would want to renew this feud."

No one offered any reasons, and Ben said, "However, the Libyans have an expression, much like the French expression, which says, 'Revenge tastes better served on a cold plate.' You understand?"

I guess we did, and Ben went on, "So, perhaps Gadhafi does not consider some old feud fully settled. Look for Gadhafi's reason to send Khalil to America, and you might discover why Khalil did what he did, and whether or not the feud is over."

Kate said, "The feud has just begun."

Professor Abdellah shook his head. "It began long ago. A blood feud is only over when the last man is standing."

I guess this meant I had job security until I got whacked. I said to Ben, "Maybe it's Khalil's feud, and not Gadhafi's."

He shrugged. "Who knows? Find the man, and he will be happy to tell you. Even if you don't find him, he will eventually tell you why he did what he did. It's important to Khalil that you know."

Professor Abdellah stood and gave each of us his card. He said, "If I may be of any further assistance, please don't hesitate to call me. I can fly to New York if you wish."

Jack Koenig stood also and said, "We have people in New York—such as yourself—whom we rely on for background and cultural information. But we thank you for your time and your expertise."

Professor Abdellah collected his odds and ends and moved toward the door. He informed us, "I hold a high-security clearance. You should not hesitate to confer with me." He left.

None of us spoke for a minute or so. This was partly because the room was bugged, but partly because the session with Ibin—call me Ben—Abdellah was bizarre.

Indeed, the world was changing, the country was changing. America was not and had never been a country of one race, one religion, one culture. The glue that held us together was to some extent language, but even that was a little shaky. Also, we shared a central belief in law and justice, political freedom and religious tolerance. Someone like Abbah Ibin Abdellah was either a loyal and patriotic American and valuable special agent, or he was a security risk. He was almost undoubtedly the former. But that one percent doubt, like in a marriage, gets bigger in your imagination. *You should not hesitate to confer with me.*

Jim and Jane returned, and I was happy to see they hadn't been kidnapped by Ben. They were now joined by another boy and girl whose names were Bob and Jean, or something close to that.

This session was called "What's next?"

This was more of a brainstorming session, which is better than a blamestorm, and we were all invited to share and contribute. We discussed Khalil's next move, and I was pleased to discover that my theory was getting some play.

Bob summed it up with, "We think that Asad Khalil's alleged terrorist acts in Europe were a prelude to his coming to America. Notice that only American and British targets were involved in Europe. Notice, too, that there were never any demands issued, no notes left, no calls to the news media before or after an attack, and no credit taken by Khalil or by any organization. All we have is a string of attacks on people and places that are American or, in one case, British. This would seem to fit the profile of a man who has a private and personal grudge, as opposed to a political or religious mission or agenda, which he wants to publicize."

Bob did a whole profile thing on Khalil, comparing and contrasting him to a few American mad-bomber types in the past who had a grudge against their old employer or against technology or people who screwed up the environment, and so forth. Bob said, "In the perpetrator's mind, he is not evil, he is an instrument for justice. What he's doing, he thinks, is morally correct and justified."

Bob went on, "As for Asad Khalil, we didn't show you all the photos of him in the guest room at the embassy, but there are photos of him on the floor, praying toward Mecca. So, we have a man here who is religious, but conveniently forgets the parts of his religion that prohibit the killing of innocent people. In fact, Asad Khalil most probably has convinced himself that he is on a Jihad, a holy war, and that the ends justify the means."

Bob made the April 15 anniversary connection to the American air raid on Libya, and said, "For this reason, if for no other reason, we believe that Asad Khalil is Libyan, working for or with the Libyans. But be advised that the World Trade Center bombing happened on the second anniversary date of when U.S. forces ousted Iraqi forces from Kuwait City. And the perpetrators of this bombing were almost all non-Iraqi. In fact, most of them were Palestinians. So, you have to consider Pan-Arabism in these cases. The Arab nations have a lot of differences among themselves, but what keeps the extremists in each country united is their hatred for America, and for Israel. The date of April fifteen is a clue to who was behind yesterday's attack, but it is not proof."

True enough. But if it looks like a duck, walks like a duck, and quacks like a duck, then odds are it's a duck, not a seagull. But you had to keep an open mind.

I asked, "Excuse me, sir. Do any of Khalil's victims have anything in common?"

"No, they really don't. Not yet, anyway. Certainly no one on board that flight had much in common, except their destination. But a very clever person might create red herrings by targeting a few people who are not in any way connected to his real targets. We've seen this with domestic bombers who try to throw us off by exploding a device where we least expected it."

I wasn't so sure about that.

Bob continued, "We have contacted every overseas law enforcement and intelligence agency for anything they may have on this Asad Khalil. We've sent his fingerprints out as well as photographs. But so far—and this is early innings—no one seems to have anything on him, other than what you've read in the dossier. This man seems to have no contacts among known extremist organizations here or anywhere in the world. He is a lone wolf, but we know he couldn't pull off this stuff by himself. Therefore, we think he is being run directly by Libyan Intelligence, who are heavily influenced by the old KGB. The Libyans trained

him, financed him, sent him on a few European missions to see what he
was made of, then concocted this plan where Khalil would turn himself
in to the American Embassy in Paris. As you know, there was a similar
defection in February, which we believe was a dry run."

Jack Koenig reminded Bob, "The ATTF in New York delivered
this February defector to the FBI and the CIA here in Washington, and
someone let him walk away."

Bob replied, "I have no firsthand knowledge of that, but that's
correct."

Jack pressed on, "If the February guy hadn't gotten away, the April
guy—Khalil—would never have arrived the way he did."

"That's true," Bob said. "But I assure you, he would have arrived
one way or another."

Koenig asked, "Do you have any leads on the February defector? If
we could find him—"

"He's dead," Bob informed us. "The Maryland State Police
reported a burned and decomposed body found in the woods outside of
Silver Spring. No ID, no clothes, fingerprints burned, face burned. They
called the FBI Missing Persons, who in turn knew that the Counterterrorist section had a missing defector. Our tattoos did not survive, but we
were able to match the dental imprints to the imprints we took of this
guy while he was our guest in Paris. So, that's that."

No one spoke for a few seconds, then Jack said, "No one told me
about that."

Bob replied, "You should take that up with the Deputy Director in
charge of Counterterrorist operations."

"Thank you."

Bob concluded with, "Meanwhile, we have legitimate Libyan defectors here and in Europe, and we're questioning them about any knowledge they may have of Asad Khalil. Libya is a country of only five million
people, so we may turn up something about Khalil, if that's his real family name. So far, we haven't learned anything about Asad Khalil from
emigrés or defectors. However, we do know that a man named Karim
Khalil, a Libyan who held the rank of Army captain, was murdered in
Paris in nineteen eighty-one. The Sûreté tells us that Karim Khalil was

probably murdered by his own people, and the Libyan government tried
to pin it on Mossad." Bob continued, "The French believe that Moammar Gadhafi was the lover of Captain Khalil's wife, Faridah, and that's
why Gadhafi got rid of him." Bob smiled and said, "But I emphasize that
is a French explanation. Cherchez la femme."

We all chuckled. Those crazy Frenchmen. Everything had to do
with boom, boom, boom.

Bob continued, "We're trying to determine if Asad Khalil is related
to Captain Karim Khalil. Asad is old enough to be Karim's son or maybe
nephew. But even if we establish a relationship, that may not be significant to this case."

I suggested, "Why don't we ask the news media to put out that story
about Mr. Gadhafi and Mrs. Khalil, and Gadhafi getting rid of Karim
Khalil to make his love life easier. Then, if Asad is Karim's son, he'll
read this or hear it on the news, and he'll go home and kill Gadhafi—
his father's killer. That's what a good Arab would do. The blood feud.
Right? Wouldn't that be great?"

Bob thought a moment, cleared his throat and said, "I'll pass that
along."

Ted Nash picked up the ball, as I knew he would. He said, "That's
actually not a bad idea."

Bob was clearly out of his depth with this kind of thinking. He said,
"Let's find out first if a family relationship exists. This kind of...psy-
chological operation could well backfire. But we'll put it on the agenda
for the next Counterterrorism meeting."

Jean spoke and introduced herself by another name. She said, "My
responsibility in this case is to review all of the cases in Europe that we
believe Asad Khalil was connected to. We don't want to duplicate the
work of the CIA—" she nodded to Super-Agent Nash "—but now that
Asad Khalil is here, or was here, the FBI needs to familiarize themselves
with Khalil's overseas activities."

Jean went on, talking about interservice cooperation, international
cooperation, and so forth.

Clearly, Asad Khalil, who had been no more than a suspected terrorist, was now the most wanted terrorist in the world since Carlos,

the Jackal. The Lion had arrived. The Lion, I was certain, was absolutely thrilled and flattered by all the attention. What he had done in Europe, bad as it was, did not make him a major player in today's world of headline-grabbing terrorism. Certainly he had not come to the attention of the American public in a big way. His name had never been mentioned in the news; only his deeds had been reported, and the only one that caused a stir, as far as I could recall, was the murder of the three American kids in Belgium. Soon, when the true story broke of what happened yesterday, Asad Khalil's photo would be everywhere. This would make life outside Libya difficult for him, which was why a lot of people thought he'd run home. But I thought he would like nothing better than beating us at his game on our home field.

Jean concluded her talk with, "We'll stay closely in touch with the ATTF in New York. All information will be shared by us with you, and by you with us. Information is like gold in our business—everyone wants it, and no one wants to share it. So let's say that we're not sharing—we're borrowing from one another, and all accounts will be settled at the end."

I really couldn't resist a zinger, and I said, "Ma'am, you have my assurance that if Asad Khalil turns up dead in the woods in Central Park, we'll let you know."

Ted Nash laughed. I was beginning to like this guy. In this milieu, we had more in common with each other than we had in common with the nice and neat people in this building. There's a depressing thought.

Bob asked us, "Any questions?"

I asked, "Where do the X-Files people hang out?"

Koenig said, "Stow it, Corey."

"Yes, sir."

Anyway, it was nearly 6:00 P.M., and I figured we were through since we weren't told to bring toothbrushes. But no, we all moved to a big conference room with a table the length of a football field.

About thirty people drifted in, most of whom we'd already met today at various stations of the cross.

The Deputy Director of Counterterrorism made an appearance, gave a five-minute sermon, then ascended to heaven or somewhere.

We spent almost two hours in conference, mostly rehashing the ten-hour day, exchanging gold nuggets, and coming up with a plan of attack, and so forth.

Each of us got a thick dossier containing photos, contact names and numbers, and even recaps of what was said today, which must have been tape-recorded, transcribed, edited, and typed as the day progressed. Truly, this was a world-class organization.

Kate was kind enough to put all my papers in her attaché case, which now bulged. She advised me, "Always bring an attaché case. There are always handouts." She added, "An attaché case is a tax-deductible item."

The big conference ended, and everyone filed out into the corridor. We did a little chitchat here and there, but basically it was over. I could almost smell the air on Pennsylvania Avenue. Car, airport, 9:00 P.M. shuttle, 10:00 P.M. at La Guardia, home before the eleven o'clock news. I remembered some leftover Chinese food in the fridge and tried to determine how old it was.

Just then, a guy in a blue suit named Bob or Bill came up to us and asked if we'd like to follow him and go to see the Deputy Director.

This was the proverbial straw that broke the proverbial camel's back, and I replied, "No."

But "no" wasn't an option.

The good news was that Ted Nash was not invited into the inner sanctum, but he didn't seem put off. He said, "I have to get to Langley tonight."

We all hugged, promised to write and stay in touch, and blew kisses as we parted. With any luck, I'd never see Ted Nash again.

So, Jack, Kate, and I with our escort got on the elevator and went up to the seventh floor and were shown into a dark, paneled office with a big desk, behind which was the Deputy Director of Counterterrorist operations.

The sun was gone from the heavens, and the room was lit by a single green-shaded lamp on the Deputy Director's desk. The effect of the dim lighting at waist level was that no one could see anyone's face clearly. This was really dramatic, like a scene in a Mafia flick where don Goombah decides who gets whacked.

Anyway, we shook hands all around—hands were easy to find near the lamp—then we sat.

The Deputy Director went through a little spiel about yesterday and today, then got to tomorrow. He was brief. He said, "The ATTF in New York metro is in a unique position to work this case. We won't interfere, and we won't send you anyone you don't ask for. At least for now. This department will, of course, take on the responsibility for everything outside of your operational area. We'll keep you well informed on anything that turns up. We'll try to work closely with the CIA, and we'll brief you on that as well. I suggest you proceed as though Khalil is still in New York. Turn the place upside down and inside out. Lean heavily on your sources and offer money when you need to. I'll authorize a budget of one hundred thousand dollars for buying information. The Justice Department will offer a one-million-dollar reward for the arrest of Asad Khalil. That should put some heat on him vis-à-vis his compatriots in the U.S. Questions?"

Jack said, "No, sir."

"Good. Oh, and one more thing." He looked at me, then at Kate. He said, "Think about how you might lure Asad Khalil into a trap."

I replied, "You mean think about me using myself as bait."

"I didn't say that. I just said think of the best way to lure Asad Khalil into a trap. Whatever the best way is, you'll think of it."

Kate said, "John and I will talk it over."

"Good." He stood. "Thank you for giving up your Sunday." He added, "Jack, I'd like to speak to you a moment."

We pressed the flesh again, and Kate and I were out. We were escorted to the elevator by the guy in the blue suit, and he wished us good luck and good hunting.

In the lobby, we were met by a security guy, who invited us to sit. Kate and I sat, but said nothing.

I didn't know or care what Jack and the Deputy Director were talking about, as long as it wasn't me—and I was certain they had more important things to discuss than me or my behavior. Actually, I wasn't that bad today, and I had a few gold stars for almost saving the game yesterday. But that only goes so far.

I looked at Kate, and she looked at me. Here, in the Ministry of Love, even face crimes were noted, so we didn't reveal anything except steadfast optimism. I didn't even look at her crossed legs.

Ten minutes later Jack appeared and informed us, "I'm staying the night. You two go on, and I'll see you tomorrow." He added, "Brief George in the morning. I'll assemble all the teams tomorrow at some point, and we'll get everyone up-to-date, and see if they've turned up any leads, then we'll decide how to proceed."

Kate said, "John and I will stop at Federal Plaza tonight and see what's happening."

What?

"Good," Jack said. "But don't burn out. This will be a long race, and as Mr. Corey says, 'Second place is the first loser.'" He looked at us and pronounced, "You both did very well today." He said to me, "I hope you have a better appreciation of the FBI."

"Absolutely. Great bunch of guys and girls. Women. I'm not sure about Ben, though."

"Ben is fine," Jack said. "It's Ted you should keep an eye on."

My goodness.

So, we all shook hands and off we went, Kate and I with the security guy down into the basement garage, where a car whisked us to the airport.

In the car, I asked, "How did I do?"

"Borderline."

"I thought I did fine."

"That's scary."

"I'm trying."

"You're very trying."

Chapter 33

Asad Khalil saw a sign that said WELCOME TO SOUTH CAROLINA—THE PALMETTO STATE.

He didn't understand what that last line meant, but he understood the next sign that said DRIVE CAREFULLY—STATE LAWS STRICTLY ENFORCED.

He looked at his dashboard and saw that it was 4:10 P.M. The temperature remained at twenty-five degrees Celsius.

Forty minutes later, he saw the exits for Florence and for I-20 to Columbia and Atlanta. He had memorized parts of a road map of the South, so that he could give false but plausible destinations for anyone who asked. Now that he was passing the Interstate highway for Columbia and Atlanta, his next false destination would be Charleston or Savannah.

In any case, he had a good road map in the glove box, and he had the Satellite Navigator, if he needed to refresh his memory.

Khalil noticed that the traffic was heavier around this city of Florence, and he welcomed the other vehicles after so many miles of feeling exposed.

Strangely, he'd seen no police vehicles except the one that appeared at the worst possible moment when the four whores had come up beside him.

He knew, however, that there were unmarked police cars on the road, though he never noticed such a vehicle with police in it.

His driving had become more assured since leaving New Jersey, and he was able to mimic the driving habits of those around him. There were an amazing number of old people driving, he'd noticed—something one rarely saw in Europe or Libya. The elderly drove very badly.

There were also many young people with cars—again, something he rarely saw in Europe or Libya. The young, too, drove badly, but in a different way than the elderly.

Also, many women drove in America. There were women drivers in Europe, but not as many as here. Incredibly, he'd seen women driving men here, a thing he rarely saw in Europe, and never saw in Libya where almost no women drove at all. The women drivers, he decided, were competent but sometimes erratic, and often aggressive—like the whores who had been driving in North Carolina.

Asad Khalil believed that American men had lost control of their women. He recalled the words of the Koran, "Men have authority over women because Allah has made the one superior to the other, and because men spend their wealth to maintain women. Good women are obedient. They guard their unseen parts because Allah has guarded them. As for those women from whom you fear disobedience, admonish them and send them to beds apart, and beat them. Then, if they obey you, do nothing further against them."

Khalil couldn't comprehend how Western women had gained so much power and influence, reversing the natural order of God and nature, but he suspected that it had to do with democracy, where each vote was counted equally.

For some reason, his mind returned to the aircraft, to the time when it had been moved to the security area. He thought again of the man and the woman he had seen, both wearing badges, both giving orders as though they were equal. His mind could not grasp the idea of two people of the opposite sex working in concert, speaking to one another, touching, perhaps even sharing meals. And more amazing was the fact that the female was a police officer and was undoubtedly armed. He wondered how the parents of these women had allowed their daughters to be so brazen and masculine.

He recalled his first trip to Europe—Paris—and thought back at how shocked and offended he had been at the looseness and boldness of the women. Over the years, he had become almost accustomed to European women, but every time he went back to Europe—and now in America—he was newly offended and incredulous.

Western women walked alone, spoke to strange men, worked in shops and offices, exposed their flesh, and even argued with men. Khalil recalled the scripture stories of Sodom and Gomorrah, and of Babylon, before the coming of Islam. He knew that these cities had fallen because of the iniquities and sexual looseness of the women. Surely all of Europe and America would someday suffer the same fate. How could their civilization survive if the women behaved like whores, or like slaves who had overturned their masters?

Whatever God these people believed in, or did not believe in, had abandoned them, and would one day destroy them. But for now, for some reason he could not fathom, these immoral nations were powerful. Therefore, it fell to him, Asad Khalil, and others like him to deliver the punishment of his God, until their own God, the one God of Abraham and Isaac, delivered salvation or death.

Khalil continued on, ignoring the feeling of thirst that was growing in him.

He turned on the radio and scanned the frequencies. Some frequencies had a strange music, which a man on the radio called country-western. Some frequencies had music such as he'd heard on the radio north of Washington. A large number of frequencies were broadcasting what Khalil identified as Christian services or religious music. One man was reading from the Christian testament and the Hebrew testament. The man's accent and tonation was so odd that Khalil would not have understood a word he was saying if not for the fact that he recognized many of the passages. He listened for a while, but the man would often stop reading the scripture, then begin talking about the scripture, and Khalil could understand only half of what he was saying. This was interesting, but confusing. He changed the frequencies until he found a news station.

The newsman spoke understandable English, and Khalil listened to twenty minutes of the man speaking about rapes, robberies, and murders, then about politics, then about the news of the world.

Finally, the man said, "The National Transportation Safety Board and the FAA have issued a joint statement regarding the tragic incident at John F. Kennedy Airport in New York. According to the statement, there were no survivors of the tragedy. Federal officials say that the pilots may have been able to land the aircraft before they succumbed to toxic fumes, or they may have programmed the aircraft's flight computer to make an unassisted landing when they realized they were being overcome by fumes. FAA officials are not saying if there are any recorded radio transmissions from the pilots, but one unidentified official is calling the pilots heroes for getting the aircraft on the ground without endangering the safety of anyone at or near the airport. The FAA and the Safety Board are calling the tragedy an accident, but the investigation of the cause is continuing. Again, it is now official—there were no survivors on Trans-Continental Flight One-Seven-Five from Paris, and the death toll is estimated at three hundred and fourteen, crew and passengers. More on this story as it develops."

Khalil turned off the radio. Certainly, by this time, he thought, the technologically advanced Americans knew all there was to know about what happened on board Flight 175. He wondered why they were delaying telling the full truth, and he suspected that it was because of national pride as well as the natural tendency of intelligence agencies to hide their own mistakes.

In any case, if the radio news was not reporting a terrorist attack, then his photograph was not yet being broadcast on the television.

Khalil wished there had been a faster way to get to Washington, and to Florida. But this was the safest way.

In Tripoli, they had discussed alternative means of travel. But to go to Washington by air would have meant going to the other New York airport called La Guardia, and the police there would have been alerted by the time he got there. The same was true if Libyan Intelligence had chosen the high-speed train. It would have been necessary to go into the heart of the city to the place called Pennsylvania Station, and the police there would have been alerted by the time he got there. And in any case, the train schedule was not convenient.

Regarding his trip from Washington to Florida, air travel was possible, but it would have to be a private aircraft. Boris had considered this, but decided that it was dangerous. He had explained, "They are very attentive to security in Washington, and the citizens there consume too much news. If your photograph is broadcast on television or placed in the newspapers, you could be recognized by an alert citizen or even the private pilot. We will save the private flight for later, Asad. So, you must drive. It is the safest way, the best way to get you accustomed to the country, and it will give you time to assess the situation. Speed is good—but you don't want to fly into a trap. Trust my judgment on this. I lived among these people for five years. Their attention span is short. They confuse reality with drama. If you *are* recognized from a television photograph, they'll confuse you with a TV star, or perhaps Omar Sharif and ask for your autograph."

Everyone laughed when Boris had finished. Clearly, Boris had a degree of contempt for the American people, but Boris made certain that Asad Khalil understood that he had a high regard for the American Intelligence services, and even the local police, in some cases.

In any event, Boris, Malik, and the others had planned his itinerary with a mixture of speed and deliberation, boldness and caution, shrewdness and simplicity. Boris had warned him, however, "There are no alternative plans along the way, except at Kennedy Airport, where more than one driver has been assigned in the event that one meets with misfortune. The unlucky one will drive you to your rental car." Boris thought this was amusing, though no one else did. In fact, Boris had ignored the unsmiling faces around him at the last meeting and said, "Considering what will happen to your first two traveling companions, Haddad and the taxi driver, please don't ask me to take a trip with you."

Again, no one smiled. But Boris didn't seem to care and laughed. Boris would not be laughing much longer, however. Boris would soon be dead.

Khalil crossed a long bridge on a large lake called Lake Marion. Khalil knew that only about fifty miles to the south lived William Satherwaite, former United States Air Force lieutenant, and murderer. Asad Khalil had an appointment with this man on the following day, but for now, William Satherwaite was unaware of how close death was.

Khalil continued on and at 7:05 P.M., he saw a sign that said WEL-COME TO GEORGIA—THE PEACH STATE.

Khalil knew what peaches were, but why a state would want to identify with this fruit was a mystery.

He regarded his fuel gauge and saw that it was below a quarter full. He debated with himself about stopping now, or waiting until it got darker.

As he thought about this, he realized he was approaching Savannah, and the traffic got heavier, which meant the gasoline stations would have many customers, so he waited.

As the sun sank lower in the western sky, Asad Khalil recited a verse from the Koran, "Believers, do not make friends with any men other than your own people. They will corrupt you. They desire nothing but your ruin. Their hatred is clear from what they say, but more violent is the hatred in their hearts."

Truly, Khalil thought, this was the inspired word of God as revealed to the Prophet Muhammad.

At seven-thirty, he realized he was very low on fuel, but there seemed to be few exits on this section of the highway.

Finally, an exit sign appeared, and he turned onto the ramp. He was surprised to see that there was only one gasoline station, and it was closed. He proceeded west on a narrow road until he came to a small town named Cox, the same name as the pilot who died in the Gulf War. Khalil took this as an omen, though he didn't know if the omen was good or bad.

The small town seemed almost deserted, but he saw a lighted gasoline station at the edge of the town and drove into it.

He put his glasses on and exited the Mercury. It was warm and humid, he noticed, and a great many insects flew around the lights above the pumps.

He decided to use his credit card in the pump, but saw that there was no place for a card. In fact, it appeared that he was not supposed to pump his own fuel. These pumps looked older and more primitive than the ones he was used to. He hesitated a moment, then noticed a tall, thin man wearing blue jeans and a tan shirt coming out of the office of the small building. The man said, "Help you, bub?"

"I need to refuel my automobile." Asad Khalil recalled his advice to himself and smiled.

The tall man looked at him, then at the Mercury and the license plate, then back at his customer. The man said, "You need what?"

"Gasoline."

"Yeah? Any kind in particular?"

"Yes, high test, please."

The man took the nozzle from one of the pumps and pulled the hose to the Mercury. He began refueling, and Khalil realized they would be standing together a long time.

The man said, "Where you headin'?"

"I am going to the resort on Jekyll Island."

"You don't say."

"Excuse me?"

"Y'all dressed pretty fancy for Jekyll Island."

"Yes. I had a business meeting in Atlanta."

"What kinda business you in?"

"I am a banker."

"Yeah? You dress like a banker."

"Yes."

"Where you from?"

"New York."

The man laughed. "Yeah? You don't look like a damn Yankee."

Khalil was having trouble following some of this. He said, "I am not a baseball player."

The man laughed again. "That's a good one. If you had a pinstripe suit on, I'd think you was a Yankee ball-playin' banker."

Khalil smiled.

The man asked, "Where you from before New York?"

"Sardinia."

"Where the hell is that?"

"It is an island in the Mediterranean."

"If you say so. You come on I-Ninety-five?"

"Yes."

"That Phillips station closed?"

"Yes."

"Thought so. That fool ain't gonna make a buck if he closes so early. Much traffic on Ninety-five?"

"Not very much."

The man finished pumping and said, "You musta been near dry."

"Yes."

"Check the oil?"

"No, thank you."

"Cash or credit? I prefer cash."

"Yes, cash." Khalil took out his wallet.

The man squinted at the pump under the dim overhead light and said, "Twenty-nine eighty-five'll do it."

Khalil gave him two twenties.

The man said, "Got to get change. Right back. Don't go nowhere."

He turned and walked away. Khalil saw a holster and pistol attached to the rear of the man's belt. Khalil followed him.

Inside the small office, Khalil asked, "Do you have food or beverage here?"

The man opened the cash register and said, "Got that Coke machine out there and got them vending machines in here. You need some change?"

"Yes."

The man gave him his change and included several dollars' worth of quarters. Khalil put the change in the side pocket of his suit coat. The man asked, "You know how to get to Jekyll Island?"

"I have directions and a map."

"Yeah? Where you stayin' there?"

"Holiday Inn."

"Didn't think there was a Holiday Inn there."

Neither man spoke. Khalil turned and went to the vending machine. He put his hand in his pocket, removed two quarters, and put them in the slot. He pulled a knob and a small bag of salted peanuts dropped into the tray. Khalil reached again into his pocket.

There was a strip of mirror on the machine at eye level, and Khalil saw the man reaching behind his back with his right hand.

Asad Khalil pulled his Glock out of his pocket, spun around, and fired a single bullet between the man's eyes, shattering the plate glass behind him.

The tall man's knees folded, and he fell face down.

Khalil quickly removed the man's wallet and saw pinned inside a badge that read COX PD—DEPUTY. He cursed his bad luck, then removed the cash from the man's wallet, then the cash from the register, a total of only about a hundred dollars.

Khalil removed the spent .40 caliber shell casing. They had told him in Libya that this was an unusual caliber bullet, used mostly by Federal agents, and therefore he should take care not to leave something so interesting behind.

Khalil noticed a half-open door that led to a small toilet. He grabbed the man's left ankle and pulled him into the toilet. Before he left, he urinated and left the dirty toilet unflushed, then shut the door and said, "Have a nice day."

There was a newspaper on the desk, and Khalil threw it on the floor over the small pool of blood.

He found a set of switches and shut them all off, putting the entire station in darkness.

He left the office, closed the door, and went to the Coke machine. He put three quarters in and selected a Fanta orange, then walked quickly back to the Mercury.

Khalil got inside, started the engine, and made a U-turn back onto the small road that led to the Interstate.

Within fifteen minutes, he was back on I-95, going south. He accelerated to seventy-five miles an hour, keeping up with the light traffic around him. He ate the peanuts and drank the Fanta. Within an hour, he saw a large sign that said WELCOME TO FLORIDA—THE SUNSHINE STATE.

He kept on I-95, and near Jacksonville, the traffic got heavier. He exited at the sign for Jacksonville International Airport and followed the signs toward the airport. He looked at his Satellite Navigator and assured himself he was on the correct route.

He glanced at his dashboard clock. It was nearly 10:00 P.M.

He allowed himself a minute to reflect on the incident at the gasoline station in the village called Cox. *The man was a policeman, but he worked at the gasoline station.* This could have meant that he was an undercover policeman. But Khalil seemed to recall something he'd been told or had read about American policemen in small towns—some of them were volunteers and were called deputies. Yes, it was coming back to him now. These men liked to carry guns, and they worked for no pay, and were more inquisitive than even the regular police. In fact, that man was too inquisitive, and his life had been hanging by a thread as he pumped the gasoline and asked too many questions. What had stretched the thread was the gun on his belt. What had broken the thread was the last question about the Holiday Inn. Whether the man had reached for the gun or not, he had already asked one question too many, and Asad Khalil had run out of correct answers.

Chapter 34

We weren't going to make the 9:00 P.M. US Airways shuttle, so we went to Delta and caught their nine-thirty shuttle to La Guardia. The plane was half full if you're an optimist, or half empty if you own Delta stock. Kate and I took seats in the rear.

The 727 took off, and I occupied myself with a view of Washington. I could see the Washington Monument all lit up, the Capitol, the White House, the Lincoln and Jefferson memorials and all that. I couldn't see the J. Edgar Hoover Building, but the place was still in my head, and I said, "This takes some getting used to."

"You mean the FBI has to get used to you?"

I chuckled.

The stewardess, aka the flight attendant, came by. She knew from the manifest that we were Federal agents, so she didn't offer us cocktails, but asked if we'd like a soft drink.

Kate said, "Bottled water, please."

"And for you, sir?"

"Double Scotch. Can't fly on one wing."

"I'm sorry, Mr. Corey, I'm not allowed to serve armed personnel."

This was the moment I'd been waiting for all day, and I said, "I'm not armed. Check the manifest, or you can search me in the lav."

She didn't seem inclined to accompany me to the lav, but she did check the manifest, and said, "Oh...I see..."

"I'd rather drink than carry a gun."

She smiled and put two little bottles of Scotch on my tray with a plastic cup of ice. "On the house."

"On the plane."

"Whatever."

After she moved off, I offered Kate a Scotch.

She replied, "I can't."

"Oh, don't be such a goody-two-shoes. Have a drink."

"Do not try to corrupt me, Mr. Corey."

"I hate to be corrupt alone. I'll hold your gun."

"Cut it out." She drank her water.

I poured both Scotches over the ice and sipped. I smacked my lips. *"Ahhh.* Really good."

"Fuck off."

My goodness.

We sat in silence awhile, then she said to me, "Did you get things squared with your friend on Long Island?"

This was a loaded question, and I considered my reply. John Corey is loyal to friends and lovers, but the essence of loyalty is reciprocity. And Beth Penrose, for all her interest in yours truly, hadn't shown a great deal of loyalty. I think what she wanted from me was what the ladies call commitment, and then she'd be loyal. But men want loyalty first, then they might consider commitment. These were opposing concepts and not likely to be resolved unless one or the other party had a sex change operation. In any case, I wondered why Kate had asked the question. Actually, I didn't wonder at all. I finally replied, "I left a message on her answering machine."

"Is she the understanding type?"

"No, but she's a cop, and this stuff she understands."

"Good. It might be a while before you have any free time."

"I'll send her an e-mail to that effect."

"You know, when the ATTF worked the TWA explosion, they worked around the clock, seven days a week."

"And that wasn't even a terrorist attack," I pointed out.

She didn't reply. No one in the know replied to questions about TWA, and there were still unanswered questions. At least with this case, we knew who, what, where, when, and how. We weren't sure of why, or what next, but we'd know before too long.

Kate asked me, "What happened with your marriage?"

I spotted a trend in these questions, but if you think being a detective makes a guy wise to the ways of women, think again. I did, however, suspect a motive in Ms. Mayfield's questions that went beyond idle curiosity. I replied, "She was a lawyer."

She didn't speak for a few seconds, then said, "And that's why it didn't work out?"

"Yes."

"Didn't you know she was a lawyer before you married her?"

"I thought I could get her to reform."

Kate laughed.

It was my turn, and I asked her, "Have you ever been married?"

"No."

"Why not?"

"That's a personal question."

I thought we were doing personal questions. Actually, we were when I was on the receiving end. I refused to play this game and found a Delta magazine in the seat pocket.

She said, "I've moved around a lot."

I studied the Delta world routes map. Maybe I should go to Rome when this was all over. See the Pope. Delta didn't go to Libya, I saw. I thought about those guys on the air raid in 1986 who flew those little jet fighters from somewhere in England, around France and Spain, over the Mediterranean, and on to Libya. Wow. That was some flight, according to my map. And no one was serving Scotch. How did they take a leak?

"Did you hear me?"

"Sorry, no."

"I *said*, do you have children?"

"Children? Oh, no. The marriage was never consummated. She didn't believe in post-marital sex."

"Really? Well, for someone your age, that shouldn't have been a hardship."

My goodness. I said, "Can we change the subject?"

"What would you like to talk about?"

Actually, nothing. Except maybe Kate Mayfield, but that subject was trouble. I said, "We should discuss what we learned today."

"Okay." So we discussed what we learned today, what happened yesterday, and what we were going to do tomorrow.

We approached New York, and I was glad to see it was still there, and that the lights were on.

As we came into La Guardia, Kate asked me, "Are you coming with me to Federal Plaza?"

"If you'd like."

"I would. Then we can go for dinner."

I looked at my watch. It was 10:30 P.M. and by the time we got to Federal Plaza and left, it would be near midnight. I said, "It's a bit late to eat."

"Then drinks."

"Sounds good."

The plane touched down and as it decelerated on the runway, I asked myself the question that all men ask in these situations, which is, "Am I reading these signals right?"

If I wasn't, I could be in professional trouble, and if I was, I could get into personal trouble. I thought I should wait and see. In other words, when it comes to women, I played it safe.

We deplaned, got outside, got into a taxi, and went to Federal Plaza via the Brooklyn-Queens Expressway and the Brooklyn Bridge.

As we crossed the Brooklyn Bridge, I asked Kate, "Do you like New York?"

"No. Do you?"

"Of course."

"Why? This place is crazy."

"Washington is crazy. New York is eccentric and interesting."

"New York is crazy. I'm sorry I took this assignment. None of the FBI people like it. It's too expensive, and our cost-of-living allowance barely covers the extra expenses."

"Then why did you take this assignment?"

"For the same reasons that military people take hardship assignments and volunteer for combat. It's a quick career boost. You have to do New York and D.C. at least once to get ahead." She added, "And it's challenging. Also, bizarre and unbelievable things happen here. You can go on to any of the other fifty-five field offices around the country, and you'll have New York stories to tell the rest of your life."

"Well," I said, "I think New York gets a bad rap. Look, I'm a New Yorker. Am I weird?"

I didn't catch her reply, maybe because the cabbie was screaming at a pedestrian and the pedestrian was screaming back. They spoke different languages, so the exchange didn't last as long as it might have.

We pulled up to Federal Plaza, and Kate paid the driver. We went to the after-hours door on the south side, and Kate opened it by means of a security code keypad. Kate had her keys for the elevator, and we went up to the twenty-seventh floor where some of the suits hung out.

There were a dozen people there, looking tired, unhappy, and worried. Phones were ringing, faxes were dinging, and a moronic computer voice was telling people, "You've got mail!" Kate chatted with everyone, then checked her phone messages, her e-mail, then checked the commo for the day and so forth. There was an e-mail from George Foster, which said, "Meeting—as per Jack—twenty-eighth-floor conference room, 0800 hours." Unbelievable. Koenig, in D.C., calls an 8:00 A.M. meeting in New York. These people were either tireless or scared shitless. Probably the latter, in which case, you can't get much sleep anyway.

Kate asked me, "Do you want to check your desk?"

My desk in the cubicle farm was a floor below, and I really didn't think I'd have anything different down there than Kate had up here, so I said, "I'll check it tomorrow when I arrive at five."

She poked around awhile longer, and I stood there feeling close to useless, so I said, "I'm going home."

She put down whatever she was reading and said, "No, you're buying me a drink." She added, "Do you want your papers from my attaché case?"

"I'll get them tomorrow."

"We can look at some of this stuff later, if you'd like."

This sounded like an invitation to spend a long night together, and I hesitated, then said, "That's all right."

She put the attaché case under her desk.

So we left and found ourselves in the dark, quiet street again, cabless and this time I was gunless. I really don't need my gun to make me feel safe and secure, and New York has become a pretty safe city, but it's nice to have a little something on you when you suspect that a terrorist is trying to murder you. But Kate was carrying, so I said, "Let's walk."

We walked. There's not much open at this hour on a Sunday night, not even in the city that never sleeps, but Chinatown is usually half awake on Sunday night, so I headed that way.

We didn't exactly walk arm in arm, but Kate walked close to me and our shoulders kept brushing, and now and then she put her hand on my arm or shoulder as we chatted. Obviously, the woman liked me, but maybe she was just horny. I don't like being taken advantage of by horny women, but it happens.

Anyway, we got to this place in Chinatown that I knew, called the New Dragon. Years ago, over dinner with some other cops, I had asked the proprietor, Mr. Chung, what happened to the Old Dragon and he confided to us, "You're eating him!" whereupon he burst into peals of laughter and ran off into the kitchen.

Anyway, the place had a small bar and cocktail area, which was still full of people and cigarette smoke. We found two chairs at a cocktail table. The clientele looked like they were heavies in a Bruce Lee movie without subtitles.

Kate looked around and said, "You know this place?"

"I used to come here."

"Everyone's speaking Chinese."

"I'm not. You're not."

"Everyone else."

"I think they're Chinese."

"You're a wise-ass."

"Thank you."

A cocktail waitress came over, but I didn't know her. She was friendly, smiley, and informed us that the kitchen was still open. I ordered dim sum and Scotch for the table.

Kate asked me, "What's dim sum? Straight answer."

"Like . . . appetizers. Dumplings and stuff. Goes good with Scotch whiskey."

Kate looked around again and said, "This is exotic."

"They don't think so."

"Sometimes I feel like a real hick here."

"How long have you been here?"

"Eight months."

The drinks came, we chatted, more drinks came, I yawned. The dim sum came, and Kate seemed to enjoy it. A third round of drinks came, and my eyes were getting crossed. Kate seemed alert and awake.

I asked the waitress to call us a taxi, and I paid the tab. We went outside on to Pell Street and the cool air felt good. While we waited for the cab, I asked her, "Where do you live?"

"On East Eighty-sixth Street. That's supposed to be a good neighborhood."

"It's a fine neighborhood."

"I took the apartment from the guy I replaced. He went to Dallas. I heard from him. He says he sort of misses New York, but he's happy in Dallas."

"And New York is happy he's in Dallas."

She laughed. "You're funny. George told me you had a New York mouth."

"Actually, I have my mother's mouth."

The cab came and we got in. I said to the driver, "Two stops. First on...East Eighty-sixth."

Kate gave the driver the address, and we were off through the tiny streets of Chinatown, then up Bowery.

We rode mostly in silence, and within twenty minutes were in front of Kate's building, a modern high rise with a doorman. Even if she had a studio apartment, this was a little pricey, her cost-of-living allowance notwithstanding. But in my experience, Wendy Wasp from Wichita would choose a good building in a good neighborhood and cut down on luxuries such as food and clothes.

So, we stood there a moment on the sidewalk, and she said, "Would you like to come in?"

New Yorkers say "up," people from the hinterlands say "in." In any case, my heart got the message and began racing. I've been here before. I looked at her and said, "Can I take a rain check?"

"Sure." She smiled. "See you at five."

"Maybe a little after five. Like eight."

She smiled again. "Good night." She turned and the doorman greeted her as he held the door open.

I watched her move through the lobby, then turned and got into my cab. "East Seventy-second Street," I said and gave him the number.

The cabbie, a guy with a turban from someplace else, said to me in good English, "Maybe not my business, but I think the lady wanted you to go with her."

"Yeah?"

"Yeah."

I stared out the window as we drove down Second Avenue. Strange day. Tomorrow would be totally unpleasant and tense. Then again, maybe there wouldn't be any tomorrow, or any day after. I considered telling the cabbie to turn around and go back. I said to the cabbie, apropos of his turban, "Are you a genie?"

He laughed. "Yeah. And this is a magic carpet, and you get three wishes."

"Okay."

I made three wishes to myself, but the genie said, "You have to tell me, or I can't make them come true."

So I told him, "World peace, inner peace, and an understanding of women."

"The first two are no problem." He laughed again. "If you get the last one, give me a call."

We got to my condo, and I overtipped the genie, who advised me, "Ask her out again."

He drove off.

Alfred was still on duty for some reason. I can never figure out these doormen's schedules, which are more erratic than mine. Alfred greeted me, "Good evening, Mr. Corey. Did you have a good day?"

"I had an interesting day, Alfred."

I took the elevator up to the twentieth floor, opened my door, and went inside, taking minimal precautions, and, in fact, hoping I'd be knocked over the head like in the movies and wake up next month.

I didn't check my answering machine, but got undressed and fell into bed. I thought I was exhausted, but I discovered that I was wound up like a clock spring.

I stared at the ceiling, contemplating life and death, love and hate, fate and chance, fear and bravery, and stuff like that. I thought about Kate and Ted, Jack and George, the people in blue suits, a genie in a bottle, and finally Nick Monti and Nancy Tate, both of whom I was going to miss. And Meg, the duty officer, who I didn't know, but whose family and friends would miss her. I thought about Asad Khalil, and I wondered if I would have the opportunity to send him straight to hell.

I got to sleep, but I had one nightmare after the other. The days and nights were becoming the same.

Chapter 35

Asad Khalil found himself on a busy road lined with motels, car rentals, and fast food restaurants. A huge aircraft was landing at the nearby airport.

They had told him in Tripoli to find a motel near the Jacksonville International Airport, where neither his appearance nor his license plate would attract attention.

He saw a pleasant-looking place called Sheraton, a name he recognized from Europe, and he pulled into the parking lot, then drove up to the sign that said MOTOR INN—REGISTRATION.

He straightened his tie, brushed his hair with his fingers, put on his glasses, and went inside.

The young woman behind the registration counter smiled and said, "Good evening."

He smiled and returned the greeting. He could see that there were passageways in the lobby, and one of them said BAR-LOUNGE-RESTAURANT. He heard music and laughter coming through the door.

He said to the woman, "I would like a room for one night, please."

"Yes, sir. Standard or deluxe?"

"Deluxe."

She gave him a registration form and pen and said, "How would you like to pay for that, sir?"

"American Express." He took out his wallet and handed her the credit card as he filled out the registration form.

Boris had told him that the better the establishment, the fewer problems there would be, especially if he used the credit card. He hadn't wanted to leave a paper trail, but Boris assured him that if he used the card sparingly, it would be safe.

The woman handed him a credit card slip with the impression of his card on it and gave him back his American Express card. He signed the slip and pocketed his card.

Khalil completed the registration form, leaving blank the spaces concerning his vehicle, which they had told him in Tripoli he could ignore in the finer establishments. He was also told that, unlike Europe, there was no space for his passport number on the registration form, and the clerk would not even ask to see it. Apparently, it was an insult to be taken for a foreigner, no matter how foreign one looked. Or perhaps, as Boris said, "The only passport you need in America is American Express."

In any case, the desk clerk glanced at his registration form and asked nothing further of him. She said, "Welcome to the Sheraton, Mr...."

"Bay-dear," he pronounced.

"Mr. Bay-dear. Here's your electronic keycard to Room One-Nineteen, ground floor, to your right as you leave the lobby." She went on in a monotone, "This is your guest folder and here's your room number on the folder. The bar and restaurant are right through that door, we have a fitness center and a swimming pool, checkout time is eleven A.M., breakfast is served in the main dining room from six to eleven A.M., room service is available from six A.M. to midnight, the dining room is closing for dinner shortly, the bar and lounge are open until one A.M., and light snacks are available. There is a mini-bar in your room. Would you like a wake-up call?"

Khalil understood her accent, but barely understood all this useless information. He did understand wake-up calls and said, "Yes, I have a flight at nine A.M., so perhaps six A.M. would be good."

She was looking at him, openly, unlike a Libyan woman, who avoided eye contact with men. He maintained eye contact with her, as he was told to do to avoid suspicion, but also to see if she showed any hint that she knew who he was. But she seemed completely unaware of his true identity.

She said, "Yes, sir, wake-up call at six A.M. Would you like express checkout?"

He had been told to say yes if asked that question, that this type of checkout would mean he did not have to return to the desk. He replied, "Yes, please."

"A copy of your bill will be placed under your door by seven A.M. Is there anything else I can help you with?"

"No, thank you."

"Have a pleasant stay."

"Thank you." He smiled, took his folder, turned and left the lobby.

This had gone well, better than the last time he checked into the motel outside of Washington, he reflected, and had to kill the desk clerk. He smiled again.

Asad Khalil got into his car and drove to the door marked 119 where a parking space sat empty. He retrieved his overnight bag, got out of the car, locked it, and went to the door. He put his keycard into the slot, and the door lock hummed and clicked as a green light came on, reminding him of the Conquistador Club.

He went inside and closed and bolted the door behind him.

Khalil inspected the room, closets, and bathroom, which were clean and modern, but perhaps too comfortable for his taste. He preferred austere surroundings, especially for this Jihad. As a religious man once told him, "Allah will hear you as well if you pray in a mosque with a full belly or the desert with an empty belly—but if you want to hear Allah, go hungry to the desert."

That advice notwithstanding, Khalil was hungry. He'd had very little to eat since the day before he turned himself into the American Embassy in Paris, which was nearly a week ago.

He glanced at the room service menu, but decided not to invite another look at his face. Very few people had seen him up close, and most of them were dead.

He opened the mini-bar and found a can of orange juice, a plastic bottle of Vittel water, a jar of mixed nuts, and a bar of Toblerone chocolate, which he always enjoyed in Europe.

He sat in the armchair facing the door, still fully dressed with both Glocks in his pockets. He ate and drank slowly.

As he ate, he thought back to his short stay at the American Embassy in Paris. They had been suspicious of him, but not hostile. A military officer and a man in civilian clothes had initially questioned him, and the next day, two other men—who had identified themselves only as Philip and Peter— had arrived from America, telling him they would escort him safely to Washington. Khalil knew this was a lie on both counts—they would go to New York, not Washington, and neither Philip nor Peter would arrive safely.

The night before his departure, they had drugged him, as Boutros said they would, and Khalil had allowed that, so as not to arouse suspicion. He wasn't certain what they had done to him while he was drugged, but it was of no importance. He had been drugged by Libyan Intelligence in Tripoli and questioned, to see if he was able to withstand the effects of these so-called truth drugs. He had passed this test with no problems.

He had been told that the Americans would probably not subject him to a lie detector test in the embassy—the diplomats wanted him out of the embassy as soon as possible. But if asked to take such a test, he should refuse and demand to go to America or to be released. In any case, the Americans had acted predictably and gotten him out of the embassy and out of Paris as quickly as possible.

As Malik had said, "You are wanted for questioning by the French, the Germans, the Italians, and the British. The Americans know this and want you for themselves only. They will get you out of Europe as soon as possible. They almost always take the most sensitive cases to New York, so they can deny that they are holding a defector or a spy in Washington. There are, I think, other psychological and perhaps practical reasons why they go to New York. Eventually, they intend to take you to Washington—but I think you can get there without their help."

Everyone in the room had laughed at Malik's humor. Malik was very eloquent, and also used humor to make his point. Khalil did not always appreciate the humor of Malik or Boris, but the humor was at the expense of the Americans or the Europeans, so he tolerated it.

Malik had also said, "If, however, our friend who works for Trans-Continental Airlines in Paris informs us that you *are* going to Washington, then Haddad, your traveling companion, who is in need of oxygen, will be on *that* flight. The procedures at Dulles Airport will be the same—the aircraft will be towed to a security area, and you will proceed as though you are in New York." Malik had given him a rendezvous point at Dulles Airport where he would meet his taxi and driver, who would take him to his rental car, and from there—after silencing the driver—he would stay in a motel until Sunday morning, then go into the city and visit General Waycliff before or after church.

Asad Khalil had been impressed with the thoroughness and cleverness of his intelligence service. They had thought of everything, and they had alternate plans if the Americans changed their methods of operation. More importantly, his Libyan operation officers had stressed to him that even the best of plans could not be carried out without a true Islamic freedom fighter, such as Asad Khalil, nor without the help of Allah.

Boris, of course, had told him that the plan was mostly Boris', and that Allah had nothing to do with the plan or its success. But Boris *had* agreed that Asad Khalil was an exceptional agent. In fact, Boris had said to the Libyan Intelligence officers, "If you had more men like Asad Khalil, you wouldn't fail so much."

Boris was digging his own grave with his mouth, Khalil reflected, but he was fairly certain that at some point Boris knew this, which was why he was drunk so often.

Boris had needed a steady supply of women and vodka, which was supplied to him, and money, which was sent to a Swiss bank for Boris' family. The Russian, even when intoxicated, was very clever and very helpful, and he was smart enough to know that he was not going to leave Tripoli alive. He once said to Malik, "If I have an accident here, promise me you will ship my body home."

Malik had replied, "You will have no accident here, my friend. We will watch you closely."

To which Boris had replied, *"Yob vas,"* which in English meant, Fuck you, and which Boris used too often.

Khalil finished his small meal and turned on the television, sipping the Vitelle from the bottle. When he finished the water, he put the empty plastic bottle in his overnight bag.

It was now almost 11:00 P.M., and while he waited for the 11 o'clock news, he used the remote control to switch channels. On one channel, two bare-breasted women were in a small pool of steaming and churning water and were becoming intimate with each other. Khalil switched to another channel, then switched back to see the two women.

He watched, transfixed, as the women—one blond, one dark-haired—stood in this hot water and caressed each other. A third woman, an African, appeared at the edge of this whirling pool. She was completely naked, but some sort of electronic distortion was covering her pudenda as she walked down a set of stairs into the pool.

The three women said very little, Khalil noticed, but laughed too much as they splashed water on one another. Khalil thought they acted like half-wits, but he continued to watch.

A fourth woman with red hair was walking backwards down the stairs so that he could see her bare buttocks and back as she lowered herself into the water. Soon, all four women were rubbing and stroking one another, kissing and embracing. Khalil sat very still, but he realized that he had become aroused, and he shifted uncomfortably in his chair.

He understood that he should not be watching this, that this was the worst sort of Western decadence, that all the holy scriptures of the Hebrews, Christians, and Muslims defined these acts as unnatural and unholy. And yet, these women, who were touching one another in an unclean way, aroused him and caused his mind to have lustful and impure thoughts.

He pictured himself naked in the pool with them.

He came out of his reverie and noticed on the digital clock that it was already four minutes past eleven. As he began switching channels, he cursed himself, cursed his weakness, and cursed the satanic forces that were loose in this accursed land.

He found a news program and stopped.

A female newscaster was saying, "This is the man who authorities say is a prime suspect in an unnamed terrorist attack in the United States—"

A color photo captioned ASAD KHALIL came on the screen, and Asad Khalil stood quickly and knelt in front of the television, studying the photo. He had never seen this color photo of himself, and suspected that it had been taken secretly in the Paris Embassy, while he was being interrogated. In fact, he noticed that the suit was the same as the one he wore now, and the tie was the one he had worn in Paris, but which he'd changed.

The woman said, "Please look at this photograph carefully, and notify the authorities if you see this man. He is considered armed and dangerous, and no one should attempt to confront or detain him. Call the police, or call the FBI. Here are two toll-free numbers you can call—" Two phone numbers came on the screen below his photo. "—the first number is for anonymous tips that you can leave on a tape recorder, the second number is the hotline manned by FBI personnel. Both numbers are open twenty-four hours a day, seven days a week. Also, the Justice Department has offered a *one-million*-dollar reward for information that leads to the arrest of this suspect."

Another photograph of Asad Khalil came on the screen, but with a slightly different expression on his face, and again Khalil recognized it as a Paris Embassy photograph.

The newswoman was saying, "Again, please study this photograph—Federal authorities are asking your help in locating this man, Asad Khalil. He speaks English, Arabic, and some French, German, and Italian. He is suspected of being an international terrorist, and he may now be in the U.S. We have no further information on this individual, but we will be reporting to you as soon as we have more details."

All the while, Asad Khalil's face stared out of the television at Asad Khalil.

Another news story came on, and Khalil pushed the Mute button, then went to the wall mirror, put on his bifocals, and stared at himself.

Asad Khalil, the Libyan on television, had black, swept-back hair. Hefni Badr, the Egyptian in Jacksonville, Florida, had grayish hair, parted to the side.

Asad Khalil on television had dark eyes. Hefni Badr in Jacksonville wore bifocals, and his eyes looked blurred to an observer.

Asad Khalil on television was clean-shaven. Hefni Badr wore a graying mustache.

Asad Khalil on television was not smiling. Hefni Badr in the mirror *was* smiling, because he did not look like Asad Khalil.

He said his prayers and went to bed.

Chapter 36

I made it to the 8:00 A.M. meeting on the twenty-eighth floor of Federal Plaza, feeling virtuous about not having spent the night with Kate Mayfield. In fact, I was able to look her right in the eye and say, "Good morning."

She returned my greeting, and I thought I heard the word "schmuck," but maybe I was just feeling like one.

We stood around this long conference table in a windowless room and made chitchat until the meeting was called to order.

The walls of the room were adorned with blown-up photos of Asad Khalil, in various shots taken in Paris. There were also two photos labeled YUSEF HADDAD. One was subtitled MORGUE SHOT, the other PASSPORT PHOTO. The morgue shot actually looked better than the passport photo.

There were also a few photos of the February defector, whose name turned out to be Boutros Dharr, and whose status was dead.

I have this theory that all these guys were mean because they had silly names—like a boy named Sue.

Anyway, I counted ten coffee cups and ten legal pads on the table and deduced that there would be ten people at this meeting. On each legal pad was written a name, and I further deduced that I was supposed to sit in front of the pad with my name. So I sat. There were four carafes of coffee on the table, and I poured myself some coffee, then pushed the carafe across the table to Kate, who was sitting directly opposite me.

She was dressed in a blue pinstripe business suit today, looking a little more severe than she'd looked in her blue blazer and knee-length skirt on Saturday. Her lipstick was a sort of coral pink. She smiled at me.

I smiled at her. Anyway, back to the Anti-Terrorist Task Force meeting.

Everyone was taking their seat now. At one end of the table was Jack Koenig, very recently arrived from D.C. and wearing the same suit he'd worn yesterday.

At the other end of the table was Captain David Stein, NYPD, the co-commander of the New York Anti-Terrorist Task Force. Stein and Koenig could both think they were sitting at the head of the table.

Sitting to my left was Mike O'Leary of the NYPD Intelligence Unit, and I noted that the name on his pad was the same as his name, which made me optimistic about the Police Intelligence Unit.

To my immediate right was Special Agent Alan Parker, FBI, ATTF. Alan is our public relations guy. He's in his mid-twenties, but looks about thirteen. He's a world-class bullshitter, and that's what we needed in this case.

To Parker's right, near Koenig, was Captain Henry Wydrzynski, Deputy Chief of Detectives with the Port Authority police. I'd met this guy a few times when I was an NYPD detective, and he seemed like an okay guy, except for his name, which looked like the third line of an eye chart. I mean, somebody should buy this guy a vowel.

Across from me were Kate and three other people—at the far end, next to Captain Stein, was Robert Moody, NYPD Chief of Detectives. Moody was the NYPD's first black Chief of Detectives, and was, in fact, my former boss, before my near death and resuscitation. I don't have to tell you that being the commanding officer of a few thousand guys like me is not an easy job. I've met Chief Moody on a few occasions, and he seems to not dislike me, which is as good as it gets with me and bosses.

Sitting to Kate's left was Sergeant Gabriel Haytham, NYPD/ATTF, an Arab gent.

Sitting next to Gabriel, to Koenig's right, was an unknown man, but it was only his name that was unknown. I had no doubt that this nattily dressed gentleman was CIA. It's funny how I can spot them; they affect this sort of slightly bored nonchalance, they spend too much money on clothes, and they always look like they have to be someplace more important than where they are.

In any case, I had been feeling a little empty since I didn't have Ted Nash to kick around any longer. I was feeling better now that I might have someone to take his place.

Regarding Mr. Ted Nash, I pictured him packing his silk undies for his trip to Paris. I also pictured him back in my life at some point, as I said. I recalled Koenig's words—*It's Ted you should keep an eye on.* Jack Koenig did not make statements like that lightly.

Also missing was George Foster, whose job it was to mind the store. He was at the Conquistador Club and would probably stay there for a long time. George's assignment, in the parlance of criminal investigation, was to act as the "Host," or the coordinator of the crime scene, he being a witness to, and actual participant in, the events. Better George than me, I guess.

Aside from Nash and Foster, also missing from this group was Nick Monti. Thus, Jack Koenig began the meeting by proposing a moment of silence for Nick, as well as Phil, Peter, the two Federal Marshals on board Flight 175, Andy McGill of the Port Authority Emergency Service unit, Nancy Tate, and the duty officer, Meg Collins, and all the victims of Flight 175.

We did the moment of silence, and Jack called the meeting to order. It was exactly 8:00 A.M.

Jack first introduced the gentleman to his left by saying, "With us this morning is Edward Harris of the Central Intelligence Agency."

No shit. I mean, all Jack had to say was, "This is Edward Harris from you-know-where."

Jack did add, "Mr. Harris is with the agency's Counterterrorism section."

Harris acknowledged the intro by moving his pencil back and forth like a windshield wiper. Très cool. Also, these guys, unlike the FBI, almost always used their full names. There was no Ed in Edward Harris. Ted Nash seemed to be an exception to this rule. I suddenly had this bright idea to call him Teddy next time I saw him.

I should point out that normally I would not be at a meeting at this level, and neither would Kate. But having been witnesses to, and participants in, the events that had brought us all together, Kate and I were included. How good is *that?*

Jack Koenig announced, "As some of you may know, a decision was made in Washington yesterday afternoon to put out a brief statement to the news media, along with photographs of Asad Khalil. The statement says only that he is a suspect in a case involving international terrorism, and is wanted by Federal authorities. No mention was made of Flight One-Seven-Five. The statement and his photographs appeared on most eleven o'clock TV news broadcasts. Some of you may have seen it last night. Today's newspapers will carry the photos and the statement."

No one commented aloud, but the expressions on everyone's face said, "It's about fucking time."

Captain David Stein asserted his co-commandership and stood unbidden by King Jack. Captain Stein announced, "We will set up an Incident Command Center on the twenty-sixth floor. Everyone who is assigned to this case will move themselves and their pertinent files there. Everything associated with this case will be in, or come through, the ICC—files, photos, maps, charts, leads, evidence, interview transcripts—the whole nine yards. Until further notice, there are only three places that the ATTF people will be—in the ICC, in bed, or out in the field. Don't spend too long in bed." He looked around the room and added, "Anybody who needs to go to the funerals can go. Questions?"

No one seemed to have any questions, so he continued, "The Mideast section will have fifty ATTF agents directly assigned to this case, from all law enforcement agencies who make up our task force. Another hundred or so men and women will be attached to the case in the New York metropolitan area, plus there are hundreds of other agents working this case in the U.S. and abroad."

And so on.

Next up to bat was Lieutenant Mike O'Leary of the NYPD Intelligence Unit. He spoke a few words about Nick Monti, who was an Intell guy, and in true Irish tradition, told a funny Nick Monti anecdote, which he probably made up.

There aren't that many municipal police forces with their own intelligence organizations, but New York City, home to every weirdo political movement on the planet, needs such an outfit.

The NYPD Intelligence Unit was founded during the Red Scare, and they used to hound and harass the local commies, who actually liked being persecuted by the cops. No one else paid any attention to them except the FBI.

The old Red Squad morphed into what it is today, and they're not bad at what they do, but they have limitations. Also, they don't really like the ATTF, which they consider competition, but Mike O'Leary assured everyone that his organization was on the case and would cooperate fully. I knew in my guts that if his people got a lead, we'd never hear about it. But to be fair, if the FBI got a lead, O'Leary would never hear about it either.

Lieutenant O'Leary blessed us all and sat down. The Irish are beautiful bullshitters. I mean, you know they're lying, they know you know they're lying, but they do it with so much charm, conviction, and energy that everyone feels kind of good about it.

Next up was Robert Moody, NYPD Chief of Detectives. He was saying, "My detectives will keep their eyes and ears open on this case while working other cases, and I assure you that the four thousand men and women in my command will carry with them at all times a photo of the alleged perpetrator, and will forward all leads to the ATTF Incident Command Center."

Bullshit.

Chief Moody concluded with, "If he's anywhere in the five boroughs, we have a good chance of knowing about it, and we'll pick him up."

The subtext here was that Moody would love to collar Khalil before the Feds even got a lead, and let them find out about it in the morning papers.

Captain Stein thanked Inspector Moody and added, "I also have assurances from the Police Commissioner that all uniformed officers will be briefed before their duty tours. Also, today, the Commissioner is meeting with all the Police Commissioners from the surrounding suburban counties and municipalities, seeking their full cooperation and support. This means that over seventy thousand law enforcement officers in the metropolitan area are looking for the same man. This is, in effect, the single biggest manhunt in the history of the New York metropolitan area."

I noticed that Alan Parker was making copious notes, maybe to use in a news release, or maybe he was writing a TV mini-series. I don't particularly trust writers.

Stein said, "Meanwhile, our first focus is the Mideastern community," and turned it over to Gabriel Haytham.

Haytham stood and looked around the room. As the only Arab and Muslim person present, he could have been a little paranoid, but after years of working with the NYPD Intelligence Unit, and now with the ATTF, Sergeant Gabriel Haytham was cool. He once confided to me, "My real name is Jibril—means Gabriel in Arabic. But don't let that get around—I'm trying to pass as a WASP."

I like a guy with a sense of humor, and Gabe needed a very good sense of humor and sense of self to do what he was doing. I mean, it's not too difficult being an Arab-American in New York, but being an Arab-American Muslim assigned to the Mideast section of the Anti-Terrorist Task Force took big balloons. I wonder what Gabriel tells his buddies down at the mosque? Like, "Hey, Abdul, I busted two Salami-Salamis last night." Not likely.

Sergeant Haytham was the commander of the stakeout units, the NYPD detectives assigned to the ATTF who did the actual legwork, keeping track of people who were suspected of having ties to extremist organizations. These guys sat for hours outside of apartments and houses, took photos, used long-range audio detection equipment and tape recorders, and followed people in cars, subways, taxis, trains, buses, and on foot—stuff that the FBI guys couldn't or wouldn't do. The job sucked, but it was the meat and potatoes of the ATTF. A lot of time and money went into this, and the Mideast community wasn't too happy about being under the eye all the time, but, as the saying goes, "If you haven't done anything wrong, you have nothing to worry about."

Anyway, Gabriel was informing us, "Between about five P.M. Saturday and now, the stakeout people dropped their cover, and they turned the city inside out and upside down. We managed to get consent searches and blanket search warrants that covered everything except the Mayor's bedroom. We questioned about eight hundred people in their homes, in station houses, on the street, in their places of business, and here—civic leaders, suspects, regular Yusefs, and even Muslim religious leaders."

I couldn't resist saying to Gabe, "If we don't hear from at least twenty Arab League civil rights lawyers by noon, you're not doing your job."

Everyone got a good chuckle out of that one. Even Kate laughed.

Gabe said to me, "Hey, we sweated the Arab League lawyers, too. They're hiring Jewish lawyers to file suit."

Again, everyone laughed, but the laughter was a little strained. This was, after all, a bit awkward. But a little humor goes a long way toward dealing with touchy subjects. I mean, there was a lot of cultural diversity in the room, and we hadn't even heard from the Polish guy, Captain Wydrzynski, yet. I had a great Polish joke, but maybe I'd hold it for another time.

Gabriel went on without blowing his horn too much and had to admit, "I've got to tell you, we have not one single lead. Not a glimmer. Not even the regular crap of somebody trying to pin a bum rap on their father-in-law. No one wants to touch this one. But we've got another thousand or so people to question, and we've got a hundred more places to search. Also, we're doubling back on some people and places. We're putting maximum heat on the Mideast community, and, yeah, we may be stepping on some civil rights, but we'll worry about that later." He added, "We're not torturing anybody."

Koenig remarked dryly, "Washington will appreciate your restraint."

Gabriel said to Jack, "Most of these people come from countries where police beatings are used before the first question is asked. The people we're talking to get confused if you don't at least get a little physical with them."

Koenig cleared his throat and said, "I don't think we need to hear that. In any case, Sergeant, we don't—"

Sergeant Haytham interrupted, "We've got over three hundred corpses lying in city and hospital morgues. And we don't know how many more dead are yet to come. I don't want one more corpse on my watch."

Koenig considered a moment, but with the hidden microphone in mind, said nothing.

Sergeant Gabriel Haytham sat.

There was a stillness in the room. Everyone probably had the same thought, which was that Sergeant Gabriel Haytham could get away with some rough stuff regarding his co-religionists. This, of course, may have been one of the reasons that Sergeant Haytham had been picked for his job. Also, he was good at what he did. Most of the successes of the ATTF were the result of the NYPD stakeout guys. All the other stuff—walk-in informants, foreign intelligence sources, phone tips, convicted snitches, and such—didn't get as much information as the guys out on the bricks.

Port Authority Captain Wydrzynski got up and informed us, "All the Port Authority police, plus all toll takers and other PA personnel at transportation terminals have been given a photograph of Asad Khalil, plus a memo explaining that this fugitive is now the most wanted man in America. We tried to play down the Flight One-Seven-Five connection—as per orders—but the word is out."

Captain Wydrzynski went on a bit. This was one of those cases where the Port Authority police played a big role. Fugitives on the run would eventually cross the path of a ticket agent, or a toll taker, or a Port Authority cop at a bus terminal or airport. Therefore, it was important that these people were up and running, and motivated.

As for Henry Wydrzynski, I didn't know the guy, but—well, okay, here's the joke. This Polish guy goes into the optometrist's office, and the optometrist says to the guy, "Can you read that chart?" And the guy says, "Sure, I know all those guys."

Anyway, though I didn't know Captain Wydrzynski, I knew that like most Port Authority cops, he had a little attitude. What they wanted was recognition and respect, so most smart NYPD, like me, gave it to them. They were good, they were helpful, and they were useful. If you messed with them, they'd find a way to screw you big-time, like putting a thousand bucks charge on your E-Z Pass or something.

Wydrzynski was a big guy in an ill-fitting suit, like seven pounds of Polish sausage stuffed into a five-pound casing. He also seemed to lack any charm or diplomacy, and I liked that.

Jack Koenig asked Captain Eye-Chart, "When was the photo of Khalil in the hands of your people?"

Captain Wydrzynski replied, "We had hundreds of these photos made up as soon as we could. As each batch was copied, we sent patrol cars out to the bridges, tunnels, airports, bus stations, and so forth. Also, we faxed photos to every place that has a fax machine, and we did the same over the Internet." He looked around the room and said, "I'd guess that by nine P.M. Saturday, everybody in our command had a copy of Khalil's photo. Sooner, in some cases. But I gotta tell you, the quality of the photo sucked."

Captain Stein said, "So, conceivably, Asad Khalil could have boarded a flight, or taken a bus, or crossed a bridge or tunnel before nine P.M., and not been noticed."

"That's right," Wydrzynski replied. He added, "We did get the word and photo out to the airports first, but if the fugitive was quick, he could have boarded a flight—especially at JFK where he already was."

No one had any comment on that.

Captain Wydrzynski continued, "I've got over a hundred detectives out there trying to find out if this guy left the greater New York, New Jersey metropolitan area by way of a Port Authority facility. But you know, there're sixteen million people in New York metro, and if this guy had a disguise or phony ID, or an accomplice, or whatever, he could have slipped out. This is not a police state."

Again, no one said anything for a few seconds, then Koenig inquired, "How about the piers?"

"Yeah," Wydrzynski said. "On the off-chance that this guy had a ticket for a slow boat to Arabia, my office notified Customs and Immigration people at all the cruise line piers, plus piers where cargo and private ships are docked. I sent detectives around with photo packs, too. But so far, no Khalil. We'll keep the piers under the eye."

Everyone asked Wydrzynski questions, and it was clear that this kid brother agency was all of a sudden important. Wydrzynski managed to mention the fact that one of the dead, Andy McGill, was a Port Authority cop, and though his men needed no motivation other than patriotism and professionalism, McGill's death had hit the PA cops hard.

Wydrzynski got tired of being put on the spot and turned the tables a little by saying, "You know, I think that Asad Khalil's photo should have been on every television station within half an hour of the crime. I know there were other considerations, but unless we go completely public with this thing, this guy is going to get away."

Jack Koenig said, "There is a high likelihood that he's already gone. In fact, he probably took the first Mideast carrier out of JFK before the bodies were cold. Washington believes that, and therefore made the decision that we would keep this within the law enforcement community until the public could be fully apprised of the nature of the Trans-Continental tragedy."

Kate spoke up and said, "I agree with Captain Wydrzynski. There was no reason to hide these facts other than to cover our own... whatever."

Captain Stein also agreed and said, "I think Washington panicked and made the wrong decision. We went along with it, and now we're trying to find a guy who has a two-day head start."

Koenig tried to spin this a little and said, "Well, Khalil's photo is out to the media *now*. But the point is moot if Khalil flew out quickly." Koenig looked at some papers in front of him and said, "There were four flights leaving JFK that he could have made before the Port Authority police were alerted." He rattled off the names of four Mideastern carriers and their departure times. He added, "And of course there were also other overseas flights as well as some domestic and Caribbean flights that wouldn't have required a passport to board, where any kind of photo ID would have been sufficient."

Koenig concluded with, "Of course, we had people on the other end—Los Angeles and the Caribbean and so forth, waiting for the aircraft. But no one fitting his description deplaned."

We all mulled that over. I saw Kate looking at me, which I guess meant she wanted me to stick my neck out. I'm only here on a contract anyway, so I said, "I think Khalil is in New York. If he's not in New York, then he's someplace else in this country."

Captain Stein asked me, "Why do you think that?"

"Because he's not finished."

"Okay," Stein asked, "what is it that he needs to finish?"

"I have no idea."

"Well," said Stein, "he made a hell of a good start."

"And that's all it is," I replied. "There's more to come."

Captain Stein, like me, sometimes lapses into station house speech and commented, "I fucking well hope not."

I was about to reply, but Mr. CIA spoke for the first time and asked me, "Why are you so certain that Asad Khalil is still in this country?"

I looked at Mr. Harris, who was staring at me. I considered several replies, all of them starting and ending with "Fuck you," but then I decided to give Mr. Harris the benefit of the doubt and treat him with courtesy. I said, "Well, sir, I just have this gut feeling, based on Asad Khalil's personality type, that he is the sort of man who doesn't quit while he's ahead. He only quits when he's finished, and he's not finished. How do I know that, you ask? Well, I was thinking that a guy like this could have continued to cause damage to American interests abroad, and get away with it like he has for years. But instead, he decided to come here, to America, and cause more damage. So, did he just stop by for an hour or so? Was this a Seagull Mission?"

I looked around at the uninitiated, and explained, "That's where a guy flies in, shits on everybody, then flies out."

A few people chuckled, and I continued, "No, this was not a Seagull Mission. It was a ... well, a Dracula mission."

I seemed to have everyone's attention, so I continued. "Count Dracula could have sucked blood in Transylvania for three hundred years and kept getting away with it. But, no, he wants to sail to England. Right? But why? To suck the blood of the ship's crew? No. There was something in *England* that the Count wanted. Right? Well, what did he want? He wanted this babe—the one he saw in Jonathan Harker's photo. Right? What was her name? Anyway, he has the hots for the babe, and the babe is in England. You follow? Likewise, Khalil didn't come here to kill everybody on that plane or everybody in the Conquistador Club. Those people were just appetizers, a little blood sucking before he got to the main meal. All we have to do is to identify and locate the babe—or Khalil's equivalent—and we've got him. You follow?"

There was this long silence in the room, and some people, who'd been staring at me, turned away. I thought that maybe Koenig or Stein were going to put me on medical leave or something. Kate was staring down at her pad.

Finally, Edward Harris, gentleman that he was, said to me, "Thank you, Mr. Corey. That was an interesting analysis. Analogy. Whatever."

A few people chuckled.

I said, "I have a ten-dollar bet with Ted Nash that I'm right. You wanna bet?"

Harris looked like he wanted to leave, but he was a good sport and said, "Sure. Make it twenty."

"You're on. Give Mr. Koenig a twenty."

Harris hesitated, then pulled a twenty out of his wallet and slid it to Koenig, who pocketed it.

I passed a twenty down the table.

Interagency meetings can really be boring, but not when I'm there. I mean, I hate bureaucrats who are so colorless and careful that you couldn't even remember them an hour after the meeting. Aside from that, I wanted each and every person in that room to remember that we were there on the assumption that Khalil might still be in the country. As soon as they started to believe he was gone, they'd get lazy and sloppy, and let the overseas guys do the work. Sometimes you've got to be a little weird to make the point. I'm good at weird.

In fact, Koenig, who was not a fool, said, "Thank you, Mr. Corey, for that persuasive argument. I think there's a fifty-fifty chance you're right."

Kate was looking up from her pad now and said, "Actually, I think Mr. Corey *is* right." She glanced at me, and our eyes met for half a second.

If we'd slept together, my face would have turned red, but no one in that room—all of them trained face readers—could detect an ounce of post-coital complicity. Boy, I really made the right move last night. Really. Right?

Captain Stein broke the silence and said to Edward Harris, "Is there anything you'd like to share with us?"

Harris shook his head and said, "I was recently assigned to this case, and I haven't yet been briefed. You all know more than I do."

Everyone had the exact same simultaneous thought, which was "Bullshit." But no one said anything.

Harris did say to me, however, "The lady's name was Mina."

"Right. It was on the tip of my tongue."

So, we all chatted for another ten or fifteen minutes, then Koenig glanced at his watch and said, "Last but not least, we'll hear from Alan."

Special Agent Alan Parker stood. He's kind of short for his age, unless maybe he really is thirteen. Alan said, "Let me be very frank—"

Everyone groaned.

Alan seemed confused, then got it and chuckled. He began again, "Let me...well, first of all, the people in Washington, who wanted to manage the flow of information—"

Captain Stein interrupted and said, "Speak English."

"What? Oh...okay...the people who wanted to keep a lid on this—"

"Who is that?" Stein demanded.

"Who? Well...some people in the administration."

"Like who?"

"I don't know. Really. But I guess the National Security Council. Not the FBI."

Captain Stein, who knows about these things, pointed out, "The Director of the FBI is a member of the National Security Council, Alan."

"Really? Anyway, whoever these people are have decided that it's time to begin full disclosure. Not all at once, but within the next seventy-two hours. Like a third of what we know each day, for the next three days."

Captain Stein, who has a sarcastic streak, inquired, "Like nouns today, verbs tomorrow, and everything else on Wednesday?"

Alan forced a chuckle and said, "No, but I have a three-part news release, and I'll pass out the first part to everyone today."

Stein said, "We want it all within the next ten minutes. Continue."

Alan said, "Please understand that I don't make the news, and I don't decide which facts are made public. I just do what I'm told. But I *am* the clearinghouse for news items, so I'd appreciate it if people didn't give interviews or hold press conferences without first checking with my office." He further advised us, "It's very important that the media and the public are kept informed, but it's more important that they only know what we want them to know."

Alan didn't seem to see any contradiction in that statement, which was scary.

Anyway, Alan was babbling on about the importance of news as another weapon in our arsenal and so forth, and I thought he was going to say something about using me and Kate as bait, or about Gadhafi laying the wood to Asad's mommy and putting that out to the press, but he didn't touch on any of that. Instead, he told anecdotal stories about how leaked news got people killed, tipped off suspects, ruined operations, and caused all sorts of problems including obesity, impotence, and bad breath.

Alan concluded with, "It's true that the public has a right to know, but it's not true that we have a duty to tell them anything."

He sat.

No one seemed certain they understood what Alan was saying, so to clarify, Jack Koenig said, "No one should speak to the press." He added, however, "This afternoon, there will be a joint press conference of the NYPD and the FBI, followed by another joint press conference that will include the Governor of New York, the Mayor of New York City, the NYPD Commissioner, and others. Someone, at some point, in some manner, will announce what a lot of people already know or suspect, which is that Flight One-Seven-Five was the subject of an international terrorist attack. The President and members of the National Security Council will go on TV tonight and announce the same thing. There will be a media feeding frenzy for a few days, and your respective offices will get many phone calls. Please refer everyone to Alan, who gets paid to talk to the press."

Koenig then reminded everyone that there was a million-dollar reward for information leading to the arrest of Asad Khalil, plus Federal money available for buying information.

We tidied up a few loose ends and Jack Koenig concluded, "I realize that interagency cooperation is challenging, but if ever there was an occasion for everyone to pull together, to share information, and to show goodwill, this is the occasion. When we catch this guy, I assure you, there'll be enough credit to go around."

I heard NYPD Chief of Detectives Robert Moody mumble something like, "There's a first."

Captain David Stein stood and said, "We don't want to find out later that we had a tip on this guy that got lost in the bureaucracy, like what happened with the Trade Center bombing. Remember, the ATTF is the clearinghouse for all information. Remember, too, every law enforcement agency in this country, Canada, and Mexico has the particulars on this guy, and every tip will be forwarded here. Plus, now that Khalil's face is on TV, we can count on a couple hundred million citizens to be on the lookout. So, if this guy is still on this continent, we might get lucky."

I thought of Police Chief Corn Pone in Hominy Grits, Georgia. I imagined getting a direct phone call from him saying, "Mornin', John. I hear y'all been lookin' for this Ay-rab, Khalil what's-his-name. Well, John, we got this feller right here in the pokey, and we'll hold him for you till you get here. Hurry on down—this boy won't eat pork, and he's starvin' to death."

Stein said to me, "Something funny, Detective?"

"No, sir. My mind was wandering."

"Yeah? Tell us about where it wandered to."

"Well…"

"Let's hear it, Mr. Corey."

So, rather than share my stupid Police Chief Corn Pone reverie, which is maybe funny only to me, I quickly came up with a joke apropos to the meeting. I said, "Okay…The Attorney General wants to find out who's the best law enforcement agency—the FBI, the CIA, or the NYPD. Okay? So she calls a group from each organization to meet her outside D.C., and she lets a rabbit loose in the woods, and says to the FBI guys, 'Okay, go find the rabbit.'" I looked at my audience, who were wearing neutral expressions, except for Mike O'Leary, who was smiling in anticipation.

I continued, "The FBI guys go in and two hours later, they come out without the rabbit, but of course call a big press conference and they say, 'We lab-tested every twig and leaf in the woods, we questioned two hundred witnesses, and we have concluded that the rabbit broke no federal laws, and we let him go.' The Attorney General says, 'Bullshit. You never found the rabbit.' So then the CIA guys go in"—I glanced at Mr. Harris—"and an hour later, they also come out without the rabbit, but they say, 'The FBI was wrong. We found the rabbit, and he confessed to a conspiracy. We debriefed the rabbit, and we turned the rabbit around, and he is now a double agent working for us.' The Attorney General says, 'Bullshit. You never found the rabbit.' So then the NYPD guys go in and fifteen minutes later, this bear comes stumbling out of the woods, and the bear has taken a really bad beating, and the bear throws his arms up in the air and yells out, 'All right! I'm a rabbit! I'm a rabbit!'"

O'Leary, Haytham, Moody, and Wydrzynski let out a big laugh. Captain Stein tried not to smile. Jack Koenig was not smiling, and therefore neither was Alan Parker. Mr. Harris, too, did not seem amused. Kate...well, Kate was getting used to me, I think.

Captain Stein said, "Thank you, Mr. Corey. I'm sorry I asked." David Stein concluded the meeting with a few words of motivation. "If this bastard strikes again in New York metro, most of us here should think about calling their pension office. Meeting adjourned."

Chapter 37

On Monday morning at 6:00 A.M., Asad Khalil answered the ringing telephone and a voice said, "Good morning."

Khalil started to reply, but the voice continued without pause, and Khalil realized it was a recorded message. The voice said, "This is your six A.M. wake-up call. Today's temperature will get into the high seventies, clear skies, chance of a passing shower late in the day. Have a nice day, and thank you for choosing Sheraton."

Khalil hung up the phone and the words *Yob vas* came into his mind. He got out of bed, and carried the two Glocks into the bathroom. He shaved, brushed his teeth, used the toilet and showered, then touched up the gray, and combed his hair with a part, using the wall-mounted hair dryer.

As in Europe, he reflected, there were many luxuries in America, many recorded voices, soft mattresses, hot water at the turn of a faucet tap, and rooms without insects or rodents. A civilization such as this could not produce good infantrymen, he thought, which was why the Americans had reinvented warfare. Push-button war. Laser-guided bombs and missiles. Cowardly warfare, such as they had visited on his country.

The man he was going to see today, Paul Grey, was an old practitioner of cowardly bombing, and now had become an expert in this game of remote-control killing, and had become a rich merchant of death. Soon, he would be a dead merchant of death.

Khalil went into the bedroom, prostrated himself on the floor facing Mecca, and said his morning prayers. When he had completed the required prayers, he prayed, "May God give me the life of Paul Grey this day, and the life of William Satherwaite tomorrow. May God speed me on my journey and bless this Jihad with victory."

He rose and dressed himself in his bulletproof vest, clean shirt and underwear, and gray suit.

Khalil opened the Jacksonville telephone directory to the section he had been told to look under—AIRCRAFT CHARTER, RENTAL & LEASING SERVICES. He copied several telephone numbers on a piece of notepaper and put it in his pocket.

Under his door was an envelope, which contained his bill, and a slip of paper informing him that his newspaper was outside his door. He peered through the peephole, saw no one, and unbolted and opened his door. On the doormat was a newspaper, and he retrieved it, then closed and rebolted his door.

Khalil stood by the light of the desk lamp and stared at the first page. There, staring back at him, were two color photographs of himself—a full-face view and a profile. The caption read: *Wanted—Asad Khalil, Libyan, age approximately 30, height six feet, speaks English, Arabic, some French, Italian, and German. Armed and dangerous.*

Khalil took the newspaper to the bathroom mirror and held it up to the left of his face. He put his bifocals on and peered through the clear tops of the lenses. His eyes shifted back and forth between the photographs and his own face. He made several facial expressions, then stepped back from the mirror, and turned his head slightly to one side so he could see his profile in the wraparound wall mirror.

He put the newspaper down, closed his eyes, and created a mental image of himself and the photographs. The one feature that stood out in his mind was his thin, hooked nose with the flaring nostrils, and he had mentioned this to Boris once.

Boris had told him, "There are many racial characteristics in America. In some urban areas, there are Americans who can tell the difference between a Vietnamese and a Cambodian, for instance, or between a Filipino and a Mexican. But when the person is from the Mediterranean region, then even the most astute observer has difficulty. You could be an Israeli, an Egyptian, a Sicilian, a Greek, a Sardinian, a Maltese, a Spaniard, or perhaps even a Libyan." Boris, who stank of vodka that day, had laughed at his own joke and added, "The Mediterranean Sea connected the ancient world—it did not divide people, as it does today, and there was much fucking going on before the coming of Jesus and Muhammad." Boris laughed again and said, "Peace be unto them."

Khalil clearly recalled that he would have killed Boris right then and there had Malik not been present. Malik had been standing behind Boris, and Malik had shaken his head and at the same time made a cutting motion across his throat.

Boris had not seen this, but he must have known what Malik was doing, because he said, "Oh, yes, I have blasphemed again. May Allah, Muhammad, Jesus, and Abraham forgive me. My only god is vodka. My saints and prophets are deutsche marks, Swiss francs, and dollars. The only temple I enter is the vagina of a woman. My only sacrament is fucking. May God help me."

Whereupon Boris began weeping like a woman and left the room.

On another occasion, Boris had said to Asad, "Stay out of the sun for a month before you go to America. Wash your face and hands with a bleaching soap that you will be given. In America, lighter is better. Also, when your skin darkens from the sun, those scars on your face are more visible."

Boris had asked, "Where did you get those scars?"

Khalil replied truthfully, "A woman."

Boris had laughed and slapped Khalil on the back. "So, my holy friend, you've gotten close enough to a woman for her to scratch your face. Did you fuck her?"

In a rare moment of candor, because Malik was not present, Khalil had replied, "Yes, I did."

"Did she scratch you before or after you fucked her?"

"After."

Boris had collapsed into a chair, laughing so hard he could barely speak, but finally he said, "They don't always scratch your face after you fuck them. Look at *my* face. Try it again. It may go better next time."

Boris was still laughing when Khalil came up to him and put his lips to Boris' ear and said, "After she scratched me, I strangled her to death with my bare hands."

Boris had stopped laughing and their eyes met. Boris said, "I'm sure you did. I'm sure you did."

Khalil opened his eyes and looked at himself in the bathroom mirror of the Sheraton Motor Inn. The scars that Bahira had inflicted on him were not so visible, and his hooked nose was perhaps not so distinguishing a feature now that he wore eyeglasses and a mustache.

In any case, he had no choice but to go forward, confident that Allah would blind his enemies, and that his enemies would blind themselves by their own stupidity, and by the American inability to focus on anything for more than a few seconds.

Khalil took the newspaper back to the desk and, still standing, he read the front-page story.

His spoken English was good, but his ability to read this difficult language was not so good. The Latin letters confused him, the spelling seemed to have no logic to it, the phonetics of letter groupings, such as "ght" and "ough," provided no clue to their pronunciation, and the language of the journalists seemed totally unrelated to the spoken language.

He struggled through the story, and was able to comprehend that the American government had admitted that a terrorist attack had taken place. Some details were provided, but not, Khalil thought, the most interesting details, nor the most embarrassing facts.

There was an entire page listing the three hundred and seven dead passengers, and a separate listing of the crew. Missing from all these names was a passenger called Yusef Haddad.

The names of the people whom he had personally killed were listed under a caption titled *Killed in the Line of Duty.*

Khalil noted that his escorts, whom he knew only as Philip and Peter, were surnamed Hundry and Gorman. They were also listed as *Killed in the Line of Duty,* as were a man and woman identified as Federal Marshals, who Khalil had not known were on board.

Khalil thought a moment about his two escorts. They had been polite to him, even solicitous. They had made certain he was comfortable and had everything he needed. They had apologized for the handcuffs and offered to let him remove his bulletproof vest during the flight, an offer that he declined.

But for all their good manners, Khalil had detected a degree of condescension in Hundry, who had identified himself as an agent of the Federal Bureau of Investigation. Hundry had been not only condescending, but at times contemptuous, and once or twice had revealed a moment of hostility.

The other one, Gorman, had not identified himself beyond his name, which he gave only as Peter. But Khalil had no doubt that this man was an agent of the Central Intelligence Agency. Gorman had shown no hostility, and in fact, seemed to treat Asad Khalil as an equal, perhaps as a fellow intelligence officer.

Hundry and Gorman had taken turns sitting in the seat beside their prisoner, or their defector, as they referred to him. When Peter Gorman sat beside him, Khalil took the opportunity to reveal to Gorman his activities in Europe. Gorman had been at first incredulous, but finally impressed. He had said to Asad Khalil, "You are either a good liar, or an excellent assassin. We'll find out which you are."

To which Khalil had replied, "I am both, and you will never discover what is a lie, and what is the truth."

Gorman said, "Don't bet on it."

Then, the two agents would confer quietly for a few minutes, and then Hundry would sit beside him. Hundry would try to make Khalil tell him what he told Gorman. But Khalil would only talk to him about Islam, his culture, and his country.

Khalil smiled, even now, at this little game that had kept him amused during the flight. Finally, even the two agents found it amusing, and they made a joke of it. But clearly, they realized they were in the presence of a man who should not be treated with condescension.

And finally, just as Yusef Haddad went into the lavatory, which was the signal for Khalil to ask permission to use the facility, Asad Khalil said to Gorman, "I killed Colonel Hambrecht in England as the first part of my mission."

"What mission?" Gorman asked.

"My mission to kill all seven surviving American pilots who participated in the air raid on Al Azziziyah on April fifteen, nineteen eighty-six." He added, "My family all died in that attack."

Gorman had remained silent for a long moment, then said, "I'm sorry about your family." He added, "I thought those pilots' names were classified as top secret."

"Of course they are," Khalil had replied. "But top secrets can be revealed—they just cost more money."

Then, Gorman had said something that even now bothered Khalil. Gorman said, "I have a secret for you, too, Mr. Khalil. It concerns your mother and father. And other personal matters."

Khalil, against his better judgment, was baited into asking, "What is it?"

"You will know in New York. After you tell us what *we* want to know."

Yusef Haddad had exited the lavatory, and there was not a minute to spare to pursue this. Khalil requested permission to use the lavatory. A few minutes later, Peter Gorman took his secret and Khalil's secret to the grave with him.

Asad Khalil scanned the newspaper again, but there was little of interest beyond the one-million-dollar reward, which he thought was not much money, considering all the people he had killed. In fact, it was almost an insult to the families of the dead, and certainly a personal insult to himself.

He threw the newspaper in the trash can, gathered his overnight bag, looked out the peephole again, then opened the door and went directly to his car.

He got in, started the engine, and drove out of the parking lot of the Sheraton Motor Inn, back on to the highway.

It was 7:30 A.M., the sky was clear, and the traffic was light.

He drove to a shopping strip that was dominated by a huge supermarket called Winn-Dixie. They had told him in Tripoli that coin telephones could usually be found at gasoline stations or near supermarkets, and sometimes in post offices, as was the case in Libya and Europe. But the post office was a place he needed to avoid. He saw a row of telephones against the wall of the supermarket near the doorways, and parked his car in the nearly empty lot. He found coins in the overnight bag, put one of the pistols in his pocket, got out of the car, and went to one of the telephones.

He looked at the numbers he had written down and dialed the first one.

A woman answered, "Alpha Aviation Services."

He said, "I would like to hire an aircraft and pilot to take me to Daytona Beach."

"Yes, sir. When would you like to go?"

"I have a nine-thirty A.M. appointment in Daytona Beach."

"Where are you now?"

"I am calling from Jacksonville Airport."

"Okay, then you should get here as soon as possible. We're located at Craig Municipal Airport. Do you know where that is?"

"No, but I'm coming by taxi."

"Okay. How many passengers, sir?"

"Just myself."

"Okay...and will this be round-trip?"

"Yes, but the wait will be short."

"Okay...I can't give you an exact price, but it's about three hundred dollars round-trip, plus waiting time. Any landing or parking fees are additional."

"Yes, all right."

"Your name, sir?"

"Demitrious Poulos." He spelled it for her.

"Okay, Mr. Poulos, when you get to Craig Municipal, tell the driver we're, like, at the end of the row of hangars on the north side of the field. Okay? Big sign. Alpha Aviation Services. Ask anyone."

"Thank you. Have a nice day."

"You, too."

He hung up.

They had assured him in Tripoli that renting an aircraft and pilot in America was easier than renting an automobile. With an automobile, you needed a credit card, a driver's license, and you had to be a certain age. But with a piloted aircraft, you were asked no more questions than if you were taking a taxi. Boris had told him, "What the Americans call General Aviation—private flying—is not subject to close government scrutiny as it is in Libya or my country. You need no identification. I have done this many times myself. This is an occasion when cash is better than a credit card. They can avoid taxes if you pay cash, and their record keeping of cash is not so meticulous."

Khalil nodded to himself. His journey was becoming less difficult. He put a coin in the telephone and dialed a number that he'd memorized.

A voice answered, "Grey Simulation Software. This is Paul Grey."

Khalil took a long breath and replied, "Mr. Grey, this is Colonel Itzak Hurok of the Israeli Embassy."

"Oh, yes, been waiting for your call."

"Someone from Washington has spoken to you?"

"Yes, of course. They said nine-thirty. Where are you now?"

"Jacksonville. I have just landed."

"Oh, well, it's going to take you about two and a half hours to get here."

"I have a private aircraft waiting for me at the Municipal Airport, and I understand that you live at an airport."

Paul Grey laughed and said, "Well, you could say that. It's called a fly-in community. Spruce Creek, outside of Daytona Beach. Listen, Colonel, I have an idea. Why don't I fly to Craig and pick you up in my plane? Meet me in the lounge. It's less than an hour flight. I can be airborne in ten minutes. Then I can fly you right back to Jacksonville International in time for your flight back to Washington. How's that?"

Khalil had not anticipated this and had to think quickly. He said, "I have already engaged a car to drive me to the Municipal Airport, and my embassy has prepaid for the aircraft. In any case, I am instructed to accept no favors. You understand."

"Sure. I understand that. But you have to have a cold beer when you get here."

"I am looking forward to it."

"Okay. Make sure the pilot has the info he needs to land at Spruce Creek. Any problem, just call me here before take-off."

"I will do that."

"And when you land, give me a call from the fuel and maintenance facility at the center of the airport, and I'll come over and pick you up with my golf cart. Okay?"

"Thank you." He said, "As my colleague told you, there is a degree of discretion in my visit."

"Huh? Oh, yeah. Right. I'm alone."

"Good."

Paul Grey said, "I have a hell of a show set up for you."

And I for you, Captain Grey. "I look forward to it."

Khalil hung up and got into the Mercury. He programmed the Satellite Navigator for Craig Municipal Airport, and got onto the highway.

He headed east from the north side of Jacksonville, followed the instructions of the Satellite Navigator, and within twenty minutes approached the entrance to the airport.

As they said in Tripoli, there were no guards at the gate, and he drove straight through, following the road that led to the buildings around the Control Tower.

The sun glared here, as it did in Libya, he thought, and the land was flat and featureless, except for clusters of pine trees.

The buildings were mostly hangars, but there was a small terminal building and a car rental agency. He saw a sign that said FLORIDA AIR NATIONAL GUARD, which sounded military and which caused him some anxiety. Also, he hadn't realized that individual states had their own military. But he thought perhaps he was misinterpreting the sign. Boris had told him, "In America, the meaning of many signs is not clearly understood, even by the Americans. If you misinterpret a sign and make a transgression, do not panic, do not attempt to flee, and do not kill anyone. Simply apologize and explain that the sign was not clear, or you did not see it. Even the police will accept that explanation. The only signs Americans see and understand are signs that say Sale, Free, or Sex. I once saw a road sign in Arizona that said, 'Free Sex—Speed Limit Forty Miles an Hour.' You understand?"

Khalil did not, and Boris had to explain it to him.

In any case, Khalil avoided the area that said AIR NATIONAL GUARD, and soon saw the large sign that said ALPHA AVIATION SERVICES.

He also noticed that there were many license plates of different colors in the parking lot near the car rental agency, so that his New York plates did not stand out.

He pulled the Mercury into an empty space some distance from where he needed to be, took his overnight bag that contained the second Glock and the spare magazines, exited the car, locked it, and began his walk to Alpha Aviation.

It was very humid here, very glaring, and he realized he could wear sunglasses as many people did. But they had told him in Tripoli that many Americans considered it rude to wear sunglasses when speaking to another person. The Southern police, however, often wore sunglasses while speaking to you, according to Boris, and they meant it, not as rudeness, but as a demonstration of their power and masculinity. Khalil had questioned Boris about this, but even Boris had to admit he didn't understand the nuances.

Khalil looked around the airport, shielding his eyes with his hand. Most of the aircraft he saw were small, single-or two-engine propeller planes, and a good number of medium-sized jet aircraft, many of which had the names of what seemed to be corporations on them.

A small aircraft was taking off from a distant runway, and a few aircraft were taxiing slowly out to the runways. There were a lot of engine noises around him, and the smell of petroleum hung in the still air.

Asad Khalil walked to the glass door of the Alpha Aviation Services office, opened it, and strode inside. A blast of frigid air hit him, causing him to catch his breath.

A heavy, middle-aged woman behind a long counter stood at her desk and said, "Good morning. Can I help you?"

"Yes. My name is Demitrious Poulos, and I called—"

"Yes, sir. You spoke to me. How would you like to pay for this flight, sir?"

"Cash."

"Okay, why don't you give me five hundred now, and we'll adjust it when you return."

"Yes." Khalil counted out five hundred dollars, and the woman gave him a receipt.

She said, "Have a seat, sir, and I'll call the pilot."

Khalil sat in the reception area of the small office. It was quieter in here, but the air was too cold.

The woman was on the telephone. Khalil noticed two newspapers on the low coffee table in front of him. One paper was the *Florida Times-Union* that he had seen in the hotel. The other was called *USA Today*. Both front pages had his photographs displayed in color. He picked up the *USA Today* and read the article, glancing over the paper at the woman, whose head he could see beyond the counter.

He was fully prepared to kill her or the pilot, or anyone whose eyes and face betrayed the slightest hint of recognition.

The article in *USA Today* was, if anything, less clear than the other newspaper, though the words were more simple. There was a small color map that showed the route of Trans-Continental Flight 175 from Paris to New York. Khalil wondered why this was important or necessary.

A few minutes later, a side door opened, and a slim woman in her middle twenties entered the office. She was dressed in khaki slacks, a pullover shirt, and wore sunglasses. Her blond hair was short, and at first Khalil thought it was a boy, then realized his mistake. In fact, Khalil noticed, she was not unattractive.

The woman walked toward him and inquired, "Mr. Poulos?"

"Yes." Khalil stood, folded his paper so that his photo wasn't showing, and put it down over the other newspaper.

The woman removed her sunglasses, and they made eye contact.

The woman smiled, thereby saving her own life and the life of the woman behind the counter. The woman standing before him said, "Hi, I'm Stacy Moll. I'll be your pilot today."

Khalil was speechless for a moment, then nodded and noticed the woman had her hand stretched toward him. He reached out and took her hand, hoping that she couldn't see the flush he felt in his face.

She released his hand and asked, "You got any luggage besides that bag?"

"No. That is all."

"Okay. You got to use the plumbing or anything?"

"Oh…no…"

"Good. Hey, you smoke?"

"No."

"Then I need a fix here." She took a pack of cigarettes out of her breast pocket and lit one with a book of matches. She said, "Just be a

minute. You want a candy bar or something?" She puffed on the cigarette as she spoke. "Sunglasses? Got some over there. They come in
handy when you're flying."

Khalil looked toward the counter and noticed a display of sunglasses. He examined them and took a pair, on which was a tag that
said $24.95. Khalil couldn't understand this American pricing, where
everything was a few pennies short of a full dollar. He removed his bifocals, put on the sunglasses, and looked at himself in the small mirror
attached to the display. He smiled. "Yes, I will take these."

The woman behind the counter said, "Just give me twenty-five, and
I'll take care of Florida for you."

Khalil had no idea what she was talking about, but took two
twenty-dollar bills from his wallet and gave them to her.

She gave him his change and said, "Give me the glasses, and I'll cut
off the tag."

He hesitated, but could see no way to refuse this request. He took
off the glasses, but she didn't look at him as she snipped the plastic
thread that held the price tag. She handed the glasses back to him, and
he put them on quickly, watching her face the whole time.

The female pilot said to him, "Okay, got my fix."

He turned toward her and saw she was carrying his overnight bag.
He said, "I will carry that."

"Nope. That's my job. You're the customer. Ready?"

Khalil had been told they had to file a flight plan, but the female
pilot was already at the door.

He walked to the door, and the woman behind the counter said,
"Have a nice flight."

"Thank you. Have a nice day."

The female pilot held the door open for him, and they walked out
into the heat and sunshine. The sunglasses made it easier to see.

She said, "Follow me."

He walked beside her as they made their way toward a small aircraft
parked close to the office.

She said, "Where you from? Russia?"

"Greece."

"Yeah? I thought Demitrious was Russian."

"Demitri is Russian. Demitrious is from Greece."

"You don't look Russian."

"No. Poulos. From Athens."

"You fly into Jacksonville?"

"Yes, Jacksonville International Airport."

"Right from Athens?"

"No. From Athens to Washington."

"Right. Hey, you hot in that suit? Take your tie and jacket off."

"I am fine. It is much hotter where I come from."

"No kidding?"

"Allow me to carry the bag."

"No problem."

They reached the aircraft and the woman asked, "You need the bag, or should I stow it in the passenger compartment?"

"I need the bag." He added, "There are delicate terra-cottas in the bag."

"Say what?"

"Ancient vases. I am a dealer in antiquities."

"No kidding? Okay, I'll try not to sit on the bag." She laughed and put the bag down gently on the tarmac.

Khalil looked at the small blue and white aircraft.

Stacy Moll said, "Okay, FYI, this is a Piper Cherokee. I use it mostly for flight instruction, but I make short charter flights with it. Hey, you have a problem with a female pilot?"

"No. I am sure you are competent."

"I'm better than competent. I'm great."

He nodded, but felt his face flush again. He wondered if there was a way to kill this brazen woman without jeopardizing his future plans. Malik had said to him, "You may have a desire to kill rather than a *need* to kill. Remember, the lion has no desire to kill, only a need to kill. With every killing, there is a risk. With every risk, the danger increases. Kill who you must, but never kill for sport or in anger."

The woman said to him, "Hey, you look good in shades—sunglasses."

He nodded. "Thank you."

She said, "She's all ready to go. I gave her a complete pre-flight check. You ready?"

"Yes."

"You a nervous flier?"

Khalil had the urge to tell her he'd arrived in America in an aircraft with two dead pilots, but instead he said, "I have flown often."

"Good." She hopped onto the right wing, opened the Piper's door, and reached her hand out. "Give me the bag."

He handed the bag up to her, and she placed it on the back seat, then reached out her hand to him and said, "Put your left foot on that little step and use the handhold on the fuselage." She pointed to the protruding bracket just above the rear window. "I've got to get in first—this is the only door—then you slide in after me." She got into the aircraft.

He climbed up on the wing as she said, then eased himself down into the aircraft's right front seat. He turned and looked at her. Their faces were only inches apart, and she smiled at him. "Comfortable?"

"Yes."

He reached behind him and placed the black bag on his lap.

She fastened her harness and told him to do the same. He managed to fasten his belt with the bag still on his lap.

She said, "You want to keep that bag on your lap?"

"Just until we are in the air."

"You need a pill or something?"

I need to be close to my weapons until we are safely out of here. "The vases are delicate. May I ask you—do we need to file a flight plan? Or has it been filed?"

She pointed out the window and said, "Chamber of Commerce blue skies. Don't need a flight plan."

She handed him a headset with a boom microphone, and he put it on. She put hers on and said, "Calling Demitrious. How do you hear me, Demitrious?"

He cleared his throat and said, "I can hear you."

"Same. This is better than screaming over the engine noise. Hey, can I call you Demitrious?"

"Yes."

"I'm Stacy."

"Yes."

She put on her sunglasses, started the engine, and they began to taxi out. She said, "We're using Runway Fourteen today. Blue skies all the way to Daytona Beach, no turbulence reported by anyone, good southerly wind, and the best damned pilot in Florida at the controls."

He nodded.

She stopped at the end of Runway Fourteen, reached across him to close and lock the door, did an engine check, then broadcast, "Piper One-Five Whiskey, ready for take-off."

The Control Tower broadcast, "Cleared for take-off, One-Five Whiskey."

Stacy Moll ran up the engine, released the brake, and they began rolling down the runway. Within twenty seconds, the aircraft lifted off and climbed out.

She turned the Piper thirty degrees to the right to a heading of one hundred seventy degrees, almost due south, then punched some buttons on the panel, explaining to Khalil, "This is the Global Positioning Satellite Navigation radio. You know how that works?"

"Yes. I have one in my automobile. In Greece."

She laughed. "Good. You're in charge of the GPS, Demitrious."

"Yes?"

"Just kidding. Hey, do you want me to shut up, or do you want company?"

He found himself saying, "I would enjoy company."

"Good. But tell me if I'm talking too much, and I'll shut up."

He nodded.

She said, "Our flight time to Daytona Beach Airport is forty to fifty minutes. Maybe less."

He replied, "It is not actually to Daytona Beach Airport that I wish to go."

She glanced at him and asked, "Where exactly do you wish to go?"

"It is a place called Spruce Creek. Do you know it?"

"Sure. Pishy-poshy fly-in community. I'll reprogram." She hit some buttons on the console.

He said, "I am sorry if there was confusion."

"No problem. This is easier than the big airport, especially on a perfect day like this."

"Good."

She settled back in her seat, scanned her control panel, and said, "Eighty-four nautical miles, flight time forty-one minutes, expected fuel burn nine and a half gallons. Piece of cake."

"No, thank you."

She looked at him, then laughed. "No, I mean... it's like slang. Piece of cake. Means, like, no problem."

He nodded.

"I'll keep the slang down to a minimum. If you can't understand me, say, 'Stacy, talk English.'"

"Yes."

"Okay, we're climbing through twenty-five hundred feet, passing due east of Jacksonville Naval Air Station. You can see it down there. Take a look. The other air field to the west was called Cecil Field, also Navy, but that's been decommissioned. Do you see any jet fighters out here? They're doing some practice crap on most days. Keep a lookout. Last thing I need is some jet-jockey up my ass—pardon my French."

"French?"

"Forget it." She said, "Hey, none of my business, but why are you going to Spruce Creek?"

"I have a business appointment there. A collector of Greek antiquities."

"Okay. About an hour on the ground?"

"Perhaps less. No more."

"Take as long as you need. I'm free all day."

"It will not take long."

"You know where you need to go when we hit the ground?"

"Yes. I have the information."

"You ever been there? Spruce Creek?"

"No."

"Pishy-poshy. That means people with too much money. Well, they don't all have big bucks, but lots of them have their noses in the air. You know? Lots of doctors, lawyers, and businessmen who think they know how to fly. But you've also got lots of commercial airline pilots—active and retired. They know how to fly the big stuff, but sometimes they get themselves killed in their little sports planes. Sorry, I'm not supposed to talk about crashing to the customers." She laughed again.

Khalil smiled.

She continued, "Anyway, at Spruce Creek you also got some retired military guys. Real 'Right Stuff' kind of macho types. You know? I mean, they think they're God's gift to women. Understand?"

"Yes."

"Hey, the guy you're going to see wouldn't be named Jim Marcus, would it?"

"No."

"Whew! Good. I used to date that idiot. Former Navy, now a US Airways pilot. My father was a military jet pilot. Told me never to date a pilot. Good advice. Hey, what's the difference between a pig and a pilot? Give up? A pig won't stay up all night to screw a pilot." She laughed. "Sorry. You didn't get it anyway. Right? Anyway, if I never see that SOB again, it will be too soon. Okay, enough of my problems. Down there on the left—you can't see it now, but on the way back you can—is Saint Augustine. Oldest settlement in America. I mean, European settlement. The Indians were here first. Right? Gotta remember my PC."

Khalil asked, "Do retired military pilots in America have much money?"

"Well...depends. They get a good pension if they have enough time in service, and enough rank. Like maybe a colonel—in the Navy, that would be a captain. They do okay if they saved a little and didn't piss away all of their pay. A lot of them go into some kind of related business. You know? Like working for a private company that makes parts or weapons for military aircraft. They got connections, and they talk the talk. Some of them do some corporate jet flying. Big shots like to hire ex-military guys. Macho male crap. Old boys network. The CEOs want somebody who dropped bombs on some poor bastards. They tell all their friends—like, my pilot is Colonel Smith, who bombed the crap out of the Yugos, or the Iraquis. You know?"

"Or the Libyans."

"We never bombed the Libyans. Did we?"

"I think so. Many years ago."

"Yeah? I don't remember that one. We gotta stop doing that. Pisses people off."

"Yes."

The Piper continued south.

Stacy Moll said, "We just passed Palatka. Okay, if you look out to your right, you'll see the Navy bombing range. See that big wasted area down there? We can't get any closer because it's restricted airspace. But you can see the target areas. Hey! They're bombing today. Did you see that guy swoop in, then climb straight up? *Wow!* Haven't seen that in about a year. Keep an eye out for these hotshots. They usually come in high, and they release way up there, but sometimes they practice low run-ins—like they do when they're ducking under enemy radar. You know? Then you have to watch out. Hey—look! See that? That's another guy making a low run. Wow. You see any aircraft?"

Asad Khalil's heart was beating heavily in his chest. He closed his eyes and through the blackness he saw the burning red plume of the attack jet coming toward him, the indistinct blur of the aircraft itself, backlighted by the glow of Tripoli. The jet fighter was not more than an arm's length from his face, or perhaps that was how he recalled it with the passage of time. The fighter had suddenly risen straight up into the air, and seconds later, four ear-splitting explosions erupted, and the world around him was destroyed.

"Demitrious? Demitrious? You okay?"

He was aware that his hands were covering his face, and sweat was pouring from his skin. The woman was shaking his shoulder.

He put his hands down, took a deep breath, and said, "Yes, I am fine."

"You sure? If you get pukey, I've got a barf bag handy."

"I am fine. Thank you."

"You want some water? I have water in the back."

He shook his head. "I am fine now."

"Okay."

They continued south over rural Florida. After a few minutes, Khalil said, "I am feeling much better."

"Yeah? Maybe you shouldn't look down. You know? Vertigo. How do you say that in Greek? Vertigo."

"Vertigo. It is the same."

"No kidding? That means I speak Greek."

He looked at her, and she glanced at him. She said, "Just kidding."

"Of course." *If you spoke Greek, you would know that I do not.*

She said, "Out there to the left—don't look—is Daytona Beach. You can see the big hotels on the beach. Don't look. How's your tummy?"

"I am fine."

"Good. We're starting our descent. Might get a little choppy."

The Piper descended toward one thousand feet, and the lower they went, the more turbulence they experienced. Stacy Moll asked, "How we doing?"

"Fine."

"Good. It won't get much bumpier than this. Just some low-altitude turbulence." She dialed in a frequency on her radio and clicked her transmitter three times. An automated female voice came on the air and said, "Spruce Creek Airport advisory, wind one hundred ninety degrees at nine knots, altimeter three-zero-two-four."

Stacy Moll changed frequencies and transmitted, "Spruce Creek traffic, Piper One-Five Whiskey is two miles west, to enter downwind for Runway Two-Three."

Khalil asked, "To whom are you speaking?"

"Just announcing our position to other aircraft who might be in the area. But I don't see anyone, and no one is saying anything on this frequency. So we'll head right in." She added, "There's no tower at Spruce Creek, which is six miles south of Daytona Beach International. I'm staying low and west of Daytona so I can just skirt around their radar and not have to talk to them. Understand?"

He nodded. "So...there is no...record of our arrival?"

"Nope. Why do you ask?"

"In my country, there is a record of all aircraft."

"This is a private airfield." She began a slow, banking turn. She said, "It's a guard-gate community. You know? If you drive in, the Nazi at the gate wants to strip-search you unless you've been cleared by one of the residents inside. Even then, you get the once-over and the third degree."

Khalil nodded. He knew this, which was why he was arriving by air.

Stacy Moll went on, "I used to drive here once in a while to see Mr. Wonderful, and the idiot sometimes forgot to tell the Nazi I was coming. You know? I mean, Mr. Wonderful is going to get lai—he's going to...anyway, you'd think he'd remember I was coming. Right? So, whenever I could, I'd just fly in. I mean, you could be an ax murderer, but if you have an airplane, you fly right in. Maybe they should put in anti-aircraft guns. You know? And you need a password for the automated voice. Friend or foe? If you don't have the password, they open fire and blow you out of the sky." She laughed. "Someday I'm going to drop a bomb on Mr. Wonderful's fricking house. Maybe right in his pool when he's swimming in the raw. Him and his newest. Men. God, they piss me off. Can't live with 'em, can't live without them. You married?"

"No."

She didn't respond to that, but said, "See the country club there? Golf course, tennis courts, private hangars right next to some of the houses, swimming pools—these twits have themselves a good deal. You know? See that big yellow house there? Look. That belongs to a famous movie star who likes to fly his own jet. I'll bet the good old boys here don't like him much, but I'll bet the ladies do. See that big white house with the pool? That belongs to a New York real estate tycoon who owns a Citation twin-engine jet. I met him once. Nice guy. He's Jewish. The boys probably like him about as much as they like the movie star. I'm looking for this other house...guy named...can't remember, but he's a US Airways pilot, wrote a couple of airplane novels...can't remember the names...he was a friend of Mr. Wonderful. Wanted to put me in one of his books. What was *that* going to cost me? *Jeez.* Men."

Khalil looked at the expanse of large houses below, the palm trees, the swimming pools, the green lawns, and the aircraft parked near some of the homes. The man who may have murdered his family was down there, waiting for him with a smile and a beer. Khalil could almost taste his blood.

Stacy said, "Okay, everybody shut up for the next few seconds." The

Piper drifted down toward a runway marked 23, the engine became quieter, the runway seemed to rise upward, and the aircraft touched down gently. "Great landing." She laughed, then slowed the aircraft down quickly with the wheel brakes. "I had a rough landing last week in a bad crosswind, and the wise-ass customer asked me, 'Did we land, or were we shot down?'" She laughed again.

They stopped adjacent to the center taxiway, then exited the runway. Stacy asked, "Where's this guy going to meet you?"

"At his home. He lives on a taxiway."

"Oh, yeah? Big bucks. You know where to go?"

Khalil reached into his black bag and pulled out a sheet of paper on which was a computer-generated map titled COURTESY MAP—SPRUCE CREEK, FLORIDA.

Stacy took it from him and glanced at it. "Okay...what's this guy's address?"

"It is Yankee Taxiway. At the very far end."

"That's not far from where Mr. Wonderful lives. Okay...let's make like a taxi cab." She reached across her passenger, popped open the door to vent the cockpit, which was already becoming too warm, then glanced at the map in her lap and began taxiing the Piper. She said, "Okay, here's the fueling area and maintenance hangars of Spruce Creek Aviation... here's Beech Boulevard..." She taxied onto a wide concrete road and said, "Some of these things are taxiways only, some are for vehicles only, and some are for planes *and* vehicles. Like I want to share a road with some idiot's SUV—right? Keep an eye out for golf carts. The golfers are stupider than the SUV owners...okay, here's Cessna Boulevard...clever names, right?" She turned left on Cessna, then right on Tango Taxiway, then left on Tango East. She took off her sunglasses and said, "Look at these houses."

Khalil was doing just that. Passing on both sides of them were the backs of expensive taxiway homes, with large private hangars, enclosed swimming pools, and palm trees, which reminded him of his homeland. He said, "There are many palm trees here, but none in Jacksonville."

"Oh, they don't grow here naturally. These idiots bring them up from south Florida. You know? This is north Florida, but they think they need to have palm trees around them. I'm surprised they don't keep flamingos chained in the yard."

Khalil didn't reply, but once again thought of Paul Grey, whom he would be meeting in a few short minutes. Indeed, this murderer had gone to Paradise before he died, while Asad Khalil had lived in hell. Soon this situation would be reversed.

Stacy Moll said, "Okay, here's Mike Taxiway..." She turned the Piper right onto the narrow asphalt strip.

A number of the hangar doors were open, and Khalil noticed many types of aircraft—small single-engine aircraft, such as he was in, strange aircraft with one wing above another, and medium-sized jet aircraft. He asked, "Do these aircraft have any military purpose?"

She laughed. "No, these are boys' toys. Understand? I fly to make a living. Most of these clowns fly just to give themselves something to do, or to impress their friends. Hey, I'm going to school for jet training. Big bucks, but some guy is paying for it...wants me to be his corporate jet pilot. You know? Some of the big shots want military guys, like I said, but some of them want...like a toy inside the toy. Get it?"

"Excuse me?"

"*Where* you from?"

"Greece."

"Yeah? I thought the Greek millionaires...anyway, here we are— Yankee Taxiway." She veered to the right, and the taxiway ended at a concrete apron attached to a large hangar. On the hangar wall was a small sign that said PAUL GREY.

The hangar was open, revealing a twin-engine aircraft, a Mercedes-Benz convertible, a staircase that led to a loft, and a golf cart. She said, "This guy has *all* the toys. That's a Beech Baron, a Model 58, and it looks pretty new. Big buckeroos. You selling him something?"

"Yes. The vases."

"Yeah? They expensive?"

"Very."

"Good. He's got the dough. The money. Hey, is this guy married?"

"No, he is not."

"Ask him if he needs a co-pilot." She laughed.

She shut down the Piper's engine. "You've got to get out first, unless you want me crawling over your lap." She laughed. "Just take it nice and easy. I'll hold your bag." She took the bag off his lap.

He exited the aircraft onto the skidproof section of the wing. She handed the bag to him, and he placed it on the wing. Khalil stepped off the aft end of the Piper's wing and dropped onto the concrete. He turned and retrieved his bag from the wing.

Stacy followed him and jumped off the low wing onto the concrete, but lost her balance and found herself stumbling forward into her passenger. "Oops." She bumped into Khalil and held his shoulder to steady herself. His sunglasses slipped off, and Asad Khalil stood less than six inches from Stacy Moll, face-to-face. She looked into his eyes, and he stared back at her.

Finally, she smiled and said, "Sorry."

Khalil stooped down, retrieved his sunglasses, and put them on.

She took her cigarettes out of her pocket and lit one. She said, "I'll wait here in the hangar where it's shady. I'm going to help myself to something to drink in his refrigerator and use the bathroom in the hangar. They all have toilets and refrigerators. Sometimes kitchens and offices. So when the missus kicks their butts out, they don't have far to go." She laughed. "Tell this guy I'm taking a Coke. I'll leave a buck."

"Yes."

She said, "Hey, Mr. Wonderful is a short walk from here. Maybe I should go say hello."

"Perhaps you should stay here." He added, "This should not take long."

"Yeah. Just kidding. I'd probably put a crimp in his fuel line if he wasn't around."

Khalil turned toward the concrete footpath that led toward the house.

She called out, "Good luck. Squeeze him hard. Make him pay in blood."

Khalil looked over his shoulder. "Excuse me?"

"Means make him pay a lot."

"Yes. I will make him pay in blood."

He followed the path through some shrubbery until it came to a screen door that led to a large screened-in pool. He tried the door and it was open. He entered the pool area, noting the lounge chairs, a small serving counter, and a flotation device in the pool.

There was another door, and he stepped up to it. Inside, he could see a large kitchen area. He looked at his watch and saw that it was nine-ten.

He pushed the doorbell button and waited. Birds sang in the nearby trees, some sort of creature made a croaking sound, and a small aircraft circled overhead.

After a full minute, a man dressed in tan pants and a blue shirt came to the door and looked at him through the glass.

Khalil smiled.

The man opened the door and said, "Colonel Hurok?"

"Yes. Captain Grey?"

"Yes, sir. Just *Mister* Grey. Call me Paul. Come on in."

Asad Khalil entered the large kitchen of Mr. Paul Grey. The house was air-conditioned, but not uncomfortably cold.

Paul Grey said, "Can I take that bag?"

"No need."

Paul Grey glanced at his wall clock and said, "You're a little early, but no problem. I'm all set."

"Good."

"How did you get to the house?"

"I instructed my pilot to use the taxiways."

"Oh... how did you know what taxiways to use?"

"Mr. Grey, there is little that my organization does not know about you. That is why I am here. You have been chosen."

"Okay. Sounds good to me. How about a beer?"

"Just bottled water, please."

Khalil watched Paul Grey as he retrieved a container of juice and a plastic bottle of mineral water from the refrigerator, then went to the cupboard for two glasses. Paul Grey was not tall, but he seemed to be in excellent physical condition. His skin was as brown as a Berber's, and like General Waycliff, his hair was gray, but his face was not old.

Paul Grey asked, "Where's your pilot?"

"She is sheltering from the sun in your hangar. She asked if it was permissible to use your toilet there, and to have something to drink."

"Sure. No problem. You got a lady pilot?"

"Yes."

"Maybe she wants to come in and look at this demonstration. It's awesome."

"No. As I said, we must be discreet."

"Of course. Sorry."

Khalil added, "I told her I was a Greek selling you antique Greek vases." He hefted his black bag and smiled.

Paul Grey smiled back and said, "Good cover. I guess you could be Greek."

"Why not?"

Grey handed Khalil a glass of mineral water.

Khalil said, "No glass." He explained, "I am kosher. No offense, but I cannot use non-kosher items. Sorry."

"Not a problem." Grey retrieved another plastic bottle of mineral water and gave it to his guest.

Khalil took it and said, "Also, I have a condition of my eyes and must wear these dark glasses."

Grey held up his glass of orange juice and said, "Welcome, Colonel Hurok."

They touched glass to bottle and drank. Grey said, "Well, come on in to my war room, Colonel, and we can get started."

Khalil followed Paul Grey through the rambling house. Khalil commented, "A very beautiful home."

"Thank you. I was lucky enough to buy during a slight downturn in the market—I only had to pay twice what it was worth." Grey laughed.

They entered a large room, and Paul Grey slid the pocket door closed behind them. "No one will disturb us."

"There is someone in the house?"

"Only the cleaning lady. She won't bother us in here."

Khalil looked around the large room, which seemed to be a combination of a sitting room and an office. Everything appeared to be expensive—the plush carpet, the wood furniture, the electronics against the far wall. He saw four computer screens, with keyboards and other controls, in front of each screen.

Paul Grey said, "Let me take that bag for you."

Khalil said, "I'll put this down with my water."

Paul Grey indicated a low coffee table, on which was a newspaper. Grey and Khalil put their drinks down on the table, and Khalil placed his bag on the floor, then said, "Do you mind if I look around the room?"

"Not at all."

Khalil moved to a wall on which hung photographs and paintings of many different aircraft, including a realistic painting of an F-III fighter jet, which Khalil studied.

Paul Grey said, "I had that done from a photograph. I flew F-IIIs for a lot of years."

"Yes, I know that."

Paul Grey didn't reply.

Khalil studied a wall that displayed many citations, letters of commendation, and a framed, glass-enclosed case in which nine military medals were mounted.

Grey said, "I received many of those medals for my part in the Gulf War. But I guess you know that, too."

"Yes. And my government appreciates your service on our behalf."

Khalil walked to a shelf unit that held books and plastic models of various aircraft. Paul Grey came up beside him and took a book off the shelf. "Here—you'll appreciate this one. It was written by General Gideon Shaudar. He signed it for me."

Khalil took the book, which had a fighter aircraft on the cover, and saw that it was in Hebrew.

Paul Grey said, "Look at the inscription."

Asad Khalil opened the book to the back, which, as he knew, was the beginning of the book in Hebrew as it was in Arabic, and saw that the inscription was in English, but there were also Hebrew characters, which he could not read.

Paul Grey said, "Finally, someone who can translate the Hebrew for me."

Asad Khalil stared at the Hebrew writing and said, "It is actually an Arabic proverb, which we Israelis are also fond of—'He who is the enemy of my enemy is my friend.'" Khalil handed the book back to Grey and remarked, "Very appropriate."

Paul Grey shelved the book and said, "Let's sit a minute before we start." He motioned Khalil to an upholstered chair beside the coffee table. Khalil sat and Paul Grey sat opposite him.

Paul Grey sipped on his orange juice. Khalil drank from his bottle of water. Grey said, "Please understand, Colonel, that the software demonstration I'm going to show you could be considered classified material. But as I understand it, I can show it to a representative of a friendly government. But when it comes to the question of purchasing it, then we have to get clearance."

"I understand that. My people are already working on that." He added, "I appreciate the security. We would not want this software to fall into the hands of...let's say, our mutual enemies." He smiled.

Paul Grey returned the smile and said, "If you mean certain Mid-eastern nations, I doubt they'd be able to put this to any practical use. To be honest with you, Colonel, those people don't have the brains they were born with."

Khalil smiled again and said, "Never underestimate an enemy."

"I try not to, but if you'd been in my cockpit in the Gulf, you'd think you were flying against a bunch of crop dusters." He added, "That doesn't bring much credit on me, but I'm talking to a pro, so I'll be honest."

Khalil replied, "As my colleagues told you, though I am the embassy air attaché officer, I'm afraid I have no combat experience in attack aircraft. My area of expertise is training and operations, so I cannot regale you with any heroic war stories."

Grey nodded.

Khalil regarded his host for a moment. He could have killed him the minute he opened the kitchen door, or any time since then, but the killing would be almost meaningless without some pleasant trifling. Malik had said to him, "All members of the cat family toy with their captured prey before killing them. Take your time. Savor the moment. It will not come again."

Khalil nodded toward the newspaper on the coffee table and said, "You've read what has been revealed about Flight One-Seven-Five?"

Grey glanced down at the newspaper. "Yes...some heads are going to roll over that. I mean, how the hell did those Libyan clowns pull that off? A bomb on board is one thing—but gas? And then the guy escapes and kills a bunch of Federal agents. I see the hand of Moammar Gadhafi in this."

"Yes? Perhaps. It's unfortunate that the bomb you dropped on his residence at Al Azziziyah didn't kill him."

Paul Grey did not reply for a few seconds, then said, "I had no part in that mission, Colonel, and if your intelligence service thinks I did, they're wrong."

Asad Khalil waved his hand in a placating gesture. "No, no, Captain—I did not mean you, personally. I meant the American Air Force."

"Oh...sorry..."

"However," Khalil continued, "if you *were* on that mission, then I congratulate you, and thank you on behalf of the Israeli people."

Paul Grey remained expressionless, then stood and said, "Why don't we move over here and have a look?"

Khalil stood, took his bag, and followed Paul Grey to the far side of the room where two leather swivel chairs sat facing two screens.

Paul Grey said, "First, I'll show you a demonstration of the software, just using this joystick and the keyboard. Next, we'll move to those other two chairs where we'll enter the world of virtual reality." He moved to the two more elaborate chairs with no TV screens in front of them. He said, "Here we use computer modeling and simulation to enable a person to interact with an artificial three-dimensional visual and other sensory environments. Are you familiar with this?"

Khalil did not reply.

Paul Grey hesitated a moment, then continued, "Virtual reality applications immerse the user in a computer-generated environment that simulates reality through the use of interactive devices which send and receive information. These devices are typically goggles, helmets, gloves, or even body suits. Here I have two helmets with a stereoscopic screen for each eye where you can view animated images of a simulated environment. The illusion of being there—telepresence—is effected by motion sensors that pick up the user's movements and adjust the view on the screens accordingly, usually in real time." Paul Grey looked at his potential customer, but could see no sign of comprehension or non-comprehension behind the sunglasses.

Paul Grey continued, "Here you see I've set up a generic fighter-bomber cockpit, complete with rudder pedals, throttles, control stick, bomb release triggers, and so forth. Since you have no experience with fighter craft, you won't be able to fly this thing, but you can experience a bomb run just by putting on the stereoscopic helmet while I fly."

Asad Khalil looked at the elaborate paraphernalia around him, then said, "Yes, we have similar capabilities in our Air Force."

"I know you do. But the software that has recently been developed is years ahead of existing software. Let's sit in front of the monitors, and I'll give you a quick look before we move on to virtual reality."

They moved back to the other side of the room, and Paul Grey indicated one of the two leather swivel chairs with a console between them, and a keyboard in front of each chair. Khalil sat.

Paul Grey, still standing, said, "These are seats from an old F-III that I put swivel legs on. Just to get us in the spirit."

"Not very comfortable."

"No, they're not. I once flew—I've flown long distances in those seats. Can I hang your jacket?"

"No, thank you. I am not accustomed to the air conditioning."

"You may want to take your sunglasses off when I dim the room."

"Yes."

Paul Grey sat in the aircraft seat beside Khalil and picked up a remote control from the console, hit two buttons, and the lights dimmed as heavy blackout curtains drew closed over the large windows. Khalil removed his sunglasses. They sat silently in the darkness for a second, watching the lights of the electronics around them.

The image screen brightened and showed the cockpit and windshield of an advanced jet attack fighter. Paul Grey said, "This is the cockpit of the F-16, but several other aircraft can be used in this simulation. You have some of these aircraft in your armory. The first simulation that I'll show you is of an aerial toss-bombing mission. Fighter pilots who spend ten or fifteen hours with this relatively inexpensive software are that many hours ahead of a pilot who goes cold into a flight training program. This can save millions of dollars per pilot."

The view through the windshield of the simulated cockpit suddenly changed from blue sky to a green horizon. Paul Grey said, "Now, I'm just using this joystick with a few additional controls and the keyboard, but the software can be interfaced with the actual controls of most modern American attack aircraft which are placed in a virtual reality ground simulator, which we'll see later."

"This is very interesting."

Paul Grey said, "Now, the targets programmed into the software are mostly imaginary targets—generic stuff—bridges, airfields, anti-aircraft emplacements, and missile sites—they shoot back at you—" He laughed, and continued, "But I have some real targets pre-programmed in, plus other real targets can be programmed if there's some aerial recon, or satellite shots of it."

"I understand."

"Good. Let's take out a bridge."

The view through the computer-generated windshield changed from a featureless horizon to computer-generated hills and valleys, through which a river flowed. In the distance, coming up fast, was a bridge on which was a simulated column of moving tanks and trucks.

Paul Grey said, "Hold on." The horizon disappeared and turned to blue sky as the simulated jet climbed into the air. A radar screen in the cockpit now filled the right-hand viewing screen, and Grey said in a rapid tone of voice, "This is what the pilot would be paying close attention to at this point. See the radar image of the bridge? The computer has completely isolated it from the background clutter. See the cross-hairs? Right on. Release—one, two, three, four—"

Now the screen in front of Khalil showed a close-up overhead view of the simulated bridge with the simulated armored column crossing it. Four huge explosions, complete with deafening sound, erupted from the speakers as the bridge and the vehicles disintegrated into a fiery ball.

The bridge began to collapse, and a few vehicles fell off the structure, then the simulation froze. Paul Grey said, "That's as much blood and guts as I wanted to program into the show. I don't want to be accused of loving this stuff."

"But it must give you some enjoyment."

Paul Grey did not reply.

The screen went blank and the room was dark.

Both men sat in the darkness awhile, then Grey said, "Most of the programs don't show such graphic detail. Most just give the pilot his bomb score and the results of the damage. In fact, Colonel, I don't enjoy war."

"I didn't mean to be offensive."

The lights brightened slightly, and Paul Grey turned his head toward his guest. He said, "May I see some sort of credentials?"

"Of course. But let's first move to the virtual reality seats, and destroy a real target with women and children. Perhaps...well, do you have, for instance, a Libyan target? Specifically, Al Azziziyah?"

Paul Grey stood and took a deep breath. "Who the hell are you?"

Asad Khalil stood also, his plastic water bottle in one hand, his other hand in the pocket of his suit jacket. "I am—as God said to Moses—who I am. I am who I am. What a remarkable response to a stupid question. Who else could it have been, but God? But I suppose Moses was nervous, not stupid. A nervous man says, 'Who are you?' when what he really means is one of two things—I hope you *are* who I think you are, or I hope you are *not* who I think you are. So, who do you think I am, if not Colonel Itzak Hurok of the Israeli Embassy?"

Paul Grey did not reply.

"I'll give you a hint. Look at me without my sunglasses. Picture me without the mustache. Who am I?"

Paul Grey shook his head.

"Don't pretend to be stupid, Captain. You know who I am."

Again, Paul Grey shook his head, but this time took a step back from his visitor, focusing on Khalil's hand in his pocket. Asad Khalil said, "Our lives crossed once, on the fifteenth of April, in nineteen eighty-six. You were a lieutenant piloting an F-III attack aircraft out of

Lakenheath Airbase, call sign Elton thirty-eight. I was a boy of sixteen, who lived a pleasant life with my mother, two brothers, and two sisters in the place called Al Azziziyah. They all died that night. So, that's who I am. Now, why do you think I am here?"

Paul Grey cleared his throat and said, "If you are a military man, you understand war, and you understand that orders must be obeyed—"

"Shut up. I am not a military man, but I am an Islamic freedom fighter. In fact, it was you and your fellow murderers who made me what I am. And now, I have arrived at your beautiful home to avenge the poor martyrs of Al Azziziyah, and all of Libya." Khalil pulled the pistol out of his pocket and pointed it at Paul Grey.

Paul Grey's eyes darted around the room, as though he were looking for an escape.

Khalil said to him, "Look at *me*, Captain Paul Grey. Look at *me*. I am reality. Not your stupid, bloodless virtual reality. I am flesh-and-blood reality. I shoot back."

Paul Grey's eyes went back to Asad Khalil.

Khalil said, "My name is Asad Khalil, and you can take that to hell with you."

"Look...Mr. Khalil—" He stared at Khalil and recognition dawned in his eyes.

Khalil said, "Yes, I am *that* Asad Khalil, who arrived on Flight One-Five-Five. The man who your government is looking for. They should have looked here, or at the home of the late General Waycliff and his late wife."

"Oh, my God..."

"Or the home of Mr. Satherwaite, who I will visit next, or Mr. Wiggins, or Mr. McCoy, or Colonel Callum. But I'm happy to see that neither you nor they have reached any such conclusions."

"How did you know...?"

"All secrets are for sale. Your compatriots in Washington betrayed you all for money."

"No."

"No? Then perhaps it was the late Colonel Hambrecht, your squadron mate, who sold you to me."

"No...did you...did you..."

"Yes, I killed him. With an ax. You will not suffer such physical pain as he did—just mental pain, as you stand there and contemplate your sins and your punishment."

Paul Grey did not reply.

Asad Khalil said, "Your knees are shaking, Captain. You can release your bladder if you wish. I won't be offended."

Paul Grey drew a deep breath and said, "Look, your information was wrong. I wasn't on that mission. I—"

"Oh. Then forgive me. I'll be leaving." He smiled, then tipped his bottle of water, and let it pour on the carpet.

Paul Grey focused on the water splashing on the floor, then looked back at Asad Khalil, and an expression of puzzlement crossed his face.

Khalil had the Glock close to his body, the muzzle pushed into the neck of the plastic bottle.

Paul Grey saw the bottom of the bottle pointing toward him, then saw that Khalil held the gun behind it, and he understood what that meant. He threw out his hands in a protective gesture. "No!"

Khalil fired a single shot through the bottle, hitting Paul Grey in the abdomen.

Grey doubled over and stumbled backwards until he sank to his knees. He grabbed his abdomen with both hands, trying to stem the flow of blood, then looked down and saw the blood seeping between his fingers. He looked up at Khalil, who was walking toward him. "Stop...no..."

Khalil aimed the Glock with the contrived silencer and said, "I have no more time for you. You don't have the brains you were born with." He fired a single shot into Paul Grey's forehead, blowing his brains out the back of his skull. Khalil turned before Paul Grey hit the floor and retrieved the two shell casings as he heard the body fall on the carpet.

Khalil then went to an open safe sitting between two of the viewing screens. Inside, he found a stack of computer disks, which he put into his black bag, then extracted the disk from the computer that Paul Grey had been using. He said, "Thank you, Mr. Grey, for the demonstration. But war is not a video game in my country."

He looked around the room and found Paul Grey's appointment

book on his desk. It was opened to that day, and the notation said, "Col. H.—9:30." He flipped to April 15 and read, "Conf. call—Squadron— A.M." He closed the appointment book and left it on the desk. *Let the police wonder who this Colonel H. is, and let them think this mysterious colonel stole some military secrets from his victim.*

Asad Khalil flipped through the Rolodex and extracted the cards for the remaining squadron members—Callum, McCoy, Satherwaite, and Wiggins. On each card were addresses, telephone numbers, and notations about wives and children.

Khalil also took the card of General Terrance and Mrs. Gail Waycliff, formerly of Washington, D.C., now residing in hell.

He also found the card for Steven Cox, and saw that it was marked in red letters, "K.I.A.," which he knew to mean killed in action. There was on the card the name of a woman, "Linda," and the notation "Remarried Charles Dwyer," followed by an address and telephone number.

The card for William Hambrecht had an address in England that was crossed out and replaced by an address in a place called Ann Arbor, Michigan, and the notation "Dec'd," followed by the date that Khalil had killed him. There was another woman's name, "Rose," and the names of two more females and a male with the word "Children."

Asad Khalil put all the cards in his pocket, thinking he could make use of this information someday. He was pleased that Paul Grey was such a meticulous record keeper.

Asad Khalil put his plastic bottle under his arm and held his pistol in his other hand. He slung his black bag over his shoulder and opened the sliding door. He could hear a vacuum cleaner running somewhere. He closed the door and followed the sound.

He found the cleaning woman in the living room, her back to him, and she did not hear him as he stepped up behind her. The vacuum cleaner was very loud, and there was also music playing somewhere, so he didn't bother with the plastic bottle, but simply put the pistol close to the back of her neck as she pushed and pulled the vacuum cleaner. He now heard that she was singing as she worked. He pulled the trigger, and she stumbled forward, then fell on the carpet beside the overturned vacuum cleaner.

Khalil put the Glock in his pocket, placed the bottle in his bag, righted the vacuum cleaner but left it running, and recovered the shell casing. He found his way to the kitchen, then out the back door.

He put on his sunglasses and retraced his route past the swimming pool, out of the screened enclosure, down the shrub-constricted path to the open area of the hangar. He noticed that the aircraft he'd arrived in was now pointing back to the taxiway.

He did not see his pilot and went quickly to the hangar. He looked inside, but did not see her there, then heard talking coming from the loft overhead.

He went toward the staircase, then realized the talking was coming from a television or radio. He had forgotten the woman's name, so he called up, "Hello! Hello!"

The talking stopped, and Stacy Moll leaned over the half wall of the loft and looked down. "All done?"

"All done."

"Be right down." She disappeared, then reappeared on the staircase and came down to the hangar floor. She said, "Ready to roll?"

"Yes. Ready."

She walked out of the hangar, and he followed. She said, "You can eat off the floor in that hangar. This guy is an anal retentive. Maybe he's gay. You think he's gay?"

"Excuse me?"

"Never mind." She walked to the passenger side of the Piper, and he followed. She asked, "Did he buy the vases?"

"Yes, he did."

"Great. Hey, I wanted to see them. He buy them all?"

"Yes, he did."

"Too bad. I mean, good for you. You get your price?"

"I did."

"Great." She scrambled up on the wing and reached down for his bag, which Khalil handed her. She said, "Doesn't feel much lighter."

"He gave me some bottles of water for the trip back."

She opened the side door and put the bag in the rear and said, "I hope he gave you cash, too."

"Of course."

She got into the aircraft, then slid across to the left seat. Khalil followed her, sat in the right seat of the small cockpit, then buckled himself in. Even with the door still open, it was very hot in the cockpit, and Khalil felt sweat forming on his face.

She started the engine, taxied off the apron, and turned right on the taxiway. She put the headset on and motioned for Khalil to do the same.

He didn't want to listen to this woman any longer, but he did as she instructed. Her voice came through the earphones and she said, "I took a Coke and put a buck in the fridge. You tell him?"

"I did."

"Protocol. You understand? Lots of protocol in the flying game. You can borrow what you need without asking, but you have to leave a note. You can take a beer or a Coke, but you have to leave a buck. What does this guy Grey do for a living?"

"Nothing."

"Where'd he get his money?"

"It is not my business to ask."

"Yeah. Me neither."

They continued taxiing out to the airfield, and when they reached it, Stacy Moll glanced up at the wind sock, then taxied to the end of Runway Twenty-three. She then reached across Asad Khalil and closed and locked the door.

She made a broadcast to other aircraft, visually checked the skies around her, then ran up the engine. She released the brake, and they rolled down the runway.

The Piper lifted off and at five hundred feet, she began to turn to the north, back toward Craig Municipal Airport in Jacksonville.

They stayed low for the first few minutes, then resumed a climb. The Piper settled into a cruise altitude of thirty-five hundred feet at one hundred forty knots. Stacy Moll said, "Flight time to Craig, thirty-eight more minutes."

Khalil didn't reply.

They flew on in silence awhile, then she asked, "Where you headed after this?"

"I have an early afternoon flight to Washington, then back to Athens."

"You came all the way here just for this?"

"Yes."

"Jeez. I hope it was worth it."

"It was."

"Maybe I should get into the Greek vase business."

"There is some risk involved."

"Yeah? Oh, like—like, these vases aren't supposed to leave your country."

"It's best if you discussed this flight with no one. I have said too much already."

"Mum's the word."

"Excuse me?"

"My lips are sealed."

"Yes. Good. I will be back in a week. I would like to engage your services once again."

"No problem. Next time, stay awhile, and we can have a drink."

"That would be pleasant."

They flew in silence for the next ten minutes, then she said, "Next time, just call from the airport, and someone will pick you up. You don't have to take a taxi."

"Thank you."

"In fact, if you want, I can drive you back to the airport."

"That's very kind of you."

"No problem." She said, "Just fax or call a day or two before you come, and I'll be sure I'm available. Or make the reservation when we get back to the office."

"I will do that."

"Good. Here's my card." She took a card out of her breast pocket and gave it to him.

She made conversation with her passenger as they flew, and he made appropriate responses.

As they began their descent, he asked her, "Did you make contact with your friend at Spruce Creek?"

"Well...I thought about calling him and telling him I was a couple of blocks away...but then I said to myself, Screw him. He doesn't deserve a call. Someday, I'll fly in low and drop a live alligator in his pool." She laughed. "I know a guy who did that once to his ex-girlfriend, but the gator hit the roof and died on impact. Waste of a good gator."

Khalil found himself smiling at this image.

She noticed he was smiling and chuckled. "Good one, right?"

They approached Craig Municipal Airport, and she radioed the Tower for landing instructions.

The Tower cleared her for landing, and within five minutes they were lined up with the runway, and a few minutes later they were on the ground.

They taxied back to Alpha Aviation Services, and Stacy Moll cut the engine fifty feet from the office.

Khalil retrieved his bag, and they both got out and began the walk to the building. She said, "Enjoy your flight?"

"Very much."

"Good. I don't always talk so much, but I enjoyed your company."

"Thank you. You were a pleasant companion. And a very good pilot."

"Thanks."

Before they reached the office, he said to her, "Would it be permissible if I asked you not to mention Spruce Creek?"

She glanced at him and said, "Sure. No problem. Same price as Daytona Beach."

"Thank you."

They entered the office, and the woman at the desk stood and came to the counter. "Good flight?"

Khalil replied, "Yes, very good."

The woman examined some paperwork on a clipboard, then looked at her watch and made some notations. She said, "Okay, three-fifty should cover it." She counted out one hundred fifty dollars and handed it to him. She said, "You can keep the five-hundred-dollar receipt—for business." She winked conspiratorially.

Khalil put the money in his pocket.

Stacy Moll said, "I'm going to run Mr. Poulos back to Jacksonville Airport, unless you have something for me."

"Nope—sorry, honey."

"That's okay. I'll take care of the Piper when I get back."

The woman said to her customer, "Thank you for using Alpha. Call us again."

Stacy asked Khalil, "You want to reserve for next week?"

"Yes. The same time, one week from today. The same destination. Daytona Beach."

The woman made a note on a piece of paper and said, "You got it."

Khalil said, "And I wish for this lady as the pilot."

The woman smiled and said, "You must be a glutton for punishment."

"Excuse me?"

"She can talk your ear off. Okay, see you next week." She said to Stacy Moll, "Thanks for taking Mr. Poulos back."

"No problem."

Asad Khalil and Stacy Moll went out into the hot sunshine. She said, "My car's over there."

He followed her to a small convertible with the top up. She unlocked the doors with a remote control and asked him, "Top up or down?"

"The way it is."

"Right. Stay here until I get it cooled off." She got inside, started the engine, and turned up the air conditioner, waited a minute, then said, "Okay."

He got in the passenger seat and she said, "Buckle up. It's the law."

He buckled his seat belt.

She closed her door, put the car in gear, and drove toward the exit. She asked, "What time's your flight?"

"One P.M."

"You're okay for time." She exited the airport and began accelerating. She said, "I don't drive as good as I fly."

"A little slower, please."

"Sure." She eased off the gas. She asked, "Mind if I smoke?"

"Not at all."

She pushed the car lighter in, fingered a cigarette out of her pocket, and asked him, "Want one?"

"No, thank you."

"These things are going to kill me."

"Perhaps."

The lighter popped out, and she lit her cigarette. She said, "There's a great Greek restaurant in Jacksonville. Spiro's. When you're in next week, maybe we can go there."

"That would be nice. I'll arrange to stay overnight."

"Yeah. What's the rush? Life is short."

"Indeed, it is."

"What's the name of that eggplant stuff? Moo-something. Moo-la-ka? What's it called?"

"I don't know."

She glanced at him. "You know. It's a famous Greek dish. Moo. Moo-something. Eggplant, fried in olive oil with goat cheese. You know?"

He replied, "There is much cooking from the provinces that I have never heard of. I am an Athenian."

"Yeah? So's this guy who owns the restaurant."

"Then I think perhaps he invents things for American tastes and invents a name for his creations."

She laughed. "Wouldn't be surprised. That happened to me in Italy once. They never heard of what I wanted."

They were on a stretch of semi-rural highway, and Khalil said, "I am embarrassed to say that I should have used the lavatory at your office."

"Huh? Oh, you got to take a leak? No problem. Gas station up the road."

"Perhaps here, if you don't mind. There is some urgency."

"Gotcha." She pulled off onto a farm road and stopped the car. She said, "Take care of business. I won't peek."

"Thank you." He got out of the car, walked a few feet toward a clump of bushes, and urinated. He put his right hand in his pocket and walked back toward the car and stood at the open door.

She said, "Feel better?"

He didn't reply.

"Jump in."

Again, he didn't reply.

"You okay? Demitrious?"

He took a long breath and noticed that his heart was pounding.

She got out of the car quickly, came around and took his arm. "Hey, you okay?"

He looked at her and said, "I…yes. I am fine."

"You want some water? You got that water in your bag?"

He drew a long breath and said, "No. I am fine." He forced a smile and said, "Ready to roll."

She smiled back at him and said, "Good. Let's roll."

They both got in the car, and she turned back onto the main road.

Asad Khalil sat in silence, trying to comprehend why he hadn't killed her. He satisfied himself with the explanation that, as Malik said, each killing entails a risk, and perhaps this killing was not necessary. There was another reason he hadn't killed her, but he did not want to think about what it was.

They got to Jacksonville International Airport, and she pulled up to the international departure area. "Here we are."

"Thank you." He asked, "Is it appropriate that I give you a tip?"

"Nah. Buy me dinner."

"Yes. Next week." He opened the door and got out.

She said, "Have a good flight home. See you next week."

"Yes." He took the black bag from the car, started to close the door, then said, "I enjoyed our conversation."

"You mean my monologue?" She laughed. "See you later, alligator."

"Excuse me?"

"You say, 'After a while, crocodile.'"

"I say…?"

She laughed. "Remember—dinner at Spiro's. I want you to order in Greek."

"Yes. Have a good day." He closed the door.

She lowered the window and said, "Moussaka."

"Excuse me?"

"The Greek dish. Moussaka."

"Yes, of course."

She waved and sped off. He watched her car until it was out of sight, then went to a line of taxis and took the first one.

The driver asked, "Where to?"

"Craig Municipal Airport."

"You got it."

The taxi drove him back to Craig Municipal Airport, and Khalil directed him to a car rental agency close to his parked Mercury. He paid the driver, waited until he was gone, then walked to his car.

He got in, started the engine, and opened the windows.

Asad Khalil drove out of the municipal airport, programming his Satellite Navigator for Moncks Corner, South Carolina. He said to himself, "Now I will pay a long overdue visit to Lieutenant William Satherwaite, who is expecting me, but not expecting to die today."

Chapter 38

By mid-afternoon Monday, I'd moved my stuff to the Incident Command Center along with about forty other men and women.

The ICC is set up in this big commo room, which reminded me of the room in the Conquistador Club. There was a real buzz in the place, like everyone was on uppers, and the phones were ringing, faxes were going off, computer terminals were all lit up, and so forth. I'm not exactly familiar with a lot of the new technology, and my idea of high tech is a flashlight and a phone, but my brain works just fine. Anyway, Kate and I had desks that faced each other in a small, chest-high cubicle, which was kind of neat, I guess, but a little awkward.

So, I was all settled in, and I was reading a huge stack of memos and interrogation reports, plus some of the crap I'd picked up in D.C. the day before. This is not my idea of working a case, but there wasn't much else I could do at the moment. I mean, in a regular homicide case, I'd be out on the street, or down at the morgue, or bugging the medical examiner or the forensic people, and generally making life miserable for a lot of people so that my life could be better.

Kate looked up from her desk and said to me, "Did you see this memo about funerals?"

"No, I didn't."

She glanced at a memo in her hand and read me the arrangements. Nick Monti was being waked at a funeral home in Queens, and his full Inspector's Funeral would be on Tuesday. Phil Hundry and Peter Gorman were being shipped back to their hometowns out of state. Meg Collins, the duty officer, was to be waked in New Jersey and buried on Wednesday. The arrangements for Andy McGill and Nancy Tate were to be announced, and I guessed that the medical examiner had held things up.

I've been at nearly every wake, burial, and memorial service of everyone I've ever worked with, and never missed one where the person was killed in the line of duty. But I didn't have time for the dead just now, and I said to Kate, "I'll skip the wakes and burials."

She nodded, but said nothing.

We kept at the reading, answered a few phone calls, and read some faxes. I managed to access my e-mail, but other than something called the Monday Funnies, there wasn't much interesting. We drank coffee, swapped ideas and theories with the people around us, and generally spun our wheels, waiting for something.

As new people arrived in the room, they glanced at Kate and me— we were sort of minor celebrities, I guess, being the only two people in the room who had been eyewitnesses to the biggest mass murder in American history. Living eyewitnesses, I should say.

Jack Koenig entered the room and came over to us. He sat so that he was below the cubicle partition, and said, "I just got a top secret communiqué from Langley—at six-thirteen P.M., German time, a man answering the description of Asad Khalil shot to death an American banker in Frankfurt. The gunman escaped. But the four eyewitnesses described the gunman as Arab-looking, so the German police showed them Khalil's photo, and they all ID'ed him."

I was, to say the least, stunned. Crushed. I saw my whole career down the toilet. I miscalculated, and when you do that, you have to wonder if you've totally lost whatever it was that you had.

I glanced at Kate and saw that she, too, was shocked. She really had believed that Khalil was still in the U.S.

My mind raced ahead to my resignation and badly attended retirement party. This was a bad end to things. You don't recover professionally from blowing the biggest case in the world. I stood and said to Jack, "Well…that's it…I guess…I mean…" For the first time in my life, I felt like a loser, like a totally incompetent blowhard, an idiot and a fool.

Jack said softly, "Sit down."

"No, I'm out of here. Sorry guys."

I grabbed my jacket, and went out into the long corridor, my mind not working and my body just sort of moving like an out-of-body experience, like when I was bleeding to death in the ambulance.

I didn't even recall getting to the elevator, but there I was, waiting for the doors to open. To make matters worse, I'd lost a total of thirty dollars to the CIA.

All of a sudden, Kate and Jack were beside me. Jack said, "Listen, you're not to breathe a word of this to anyone."

I couldn't understand what he was saying.

Jack Koenig went on, "The ID is not positive—How can it be? Right? So, we need everyone to keep working this case as if Khalil may still be here. Understand? Only a handful of people know about this Frankfurt thing. I thought I owed it to you to tell you. But not even Stein knows about this. John? You have to keep this to yourself."

I nodded.

"And you can't do anything to arouse suspicion. In other words, you can't resign."

"Yes, I can."

Kate said, "John, you can't do that. You've got to do this one last thing. You have to carry on as if nothing has happened."

"I can't. I'm not good at playacting. And what's the point?"

Jack said, "The point is not to ruin everyone's morale and enthusiasm. Look, we don't know if this guy in Frankfurt really was Khalil." He tried to make a joke and said, "Why would Dracula go to Germany?"

I didn't want to be reminded of my stupid Dracula analogy, but I tried to clear my head and think rationally. Finally, I said, "Maybe it was a plant. A look-alike."

Koenig nodded. "That's right. We don't know."

The elevator came, the doors opened, but I didn't get in. In fact, I realized Kate was holding my arm.

Koenig said, "I'm offering you two the opportunity to fly to Frankfurt tonight and join the American team there—FBI, CIA, and German police and German Intelligence people. I think you should go." He added, "I will accompany you for a day or two."

I didn't reply.

Finally, Kate said, "I think we should go. John?"

"Yeah...I guess...better than being here..."

Koenig looked at his watch and said, "There's an eight-ten P.M. Lufthansa out of JFK to Frankfurt. Arrives tomorrow morning. Ted will meet us at—"

"Nash? Nash is there? I thought he was in Paris."

"I guess he was. But he's on his way to Frankfurt now."

I nodded. Something smelled funny.

Koenig said, "Okay, let's wrap it up here and be at JFK no later than seven P.M. Lufthansa, eight-ten flight to Frankfurt. Tickets will be waiting for us. Pack for a long stay." He turned and walked back to the ICC.

Kate stood there awhile, then said, "John, what I like about you is your optimism. You don't let anything get you down. You see problems as a challenge, not as a—"

"I don't need a pep talk."

"Okay."

We both walked toward the ICC. Kate said, "That's very good of Jack to send us to Frankfurt. Have you been to Frankfurt?"

"No."

"I've been a few times." She added, "This trip could take us all over Europe, following leads. Can you break away on short notice without too much inconvenience?"

There seemed to be other questions hidden in that question, but I replied simply, "No problem."

We got to the ICC, and we went to our desks. I packed some papers in my attaché case, and threw junk in my desk drawers. I wanted to call Beth Penrose, but I thought it might be better if I waited until I got home.

Kate finished up at her desk and said, "I'm going to go home and pack. You leaving now?"

"No...I can pack in five minutes. I'll meet you at JFK."

"See you later." She took a few steps, then came back and put her face close to mine. She said, "If Khalil is here, you were right. If he's in Europe, you'll be there. Okay?"

I noticed a few people looking at us. I said to her, "Thanks."

She left.

I sat at my desk and contemplated this turn of events, trying to identify the smell in my nostrils. Even if Khalil had left the country, why and how had he gotten to Europe? Even a guy like that would head home for a pat on the back. And clipping a banker was not exactly a strong Second Act after what he'd done here. And yet... I was really burning up the neurons on this one. It's easy to outfox yourself when you're too smart for your own good.

I mean, the brain is a remarkable thing. It is the only cognitive organ in the human body, except for a man's penis. So, I sat there and put my brain in overdrive. My other controlling organ was saying, "Go to Europe with Kate and get laid. There's nothing in New York for you, John." But the higher areas of my intellect were saying, "Someone's trying to get rid of you." Now, I don't necessarily mean someone was trying to get me overseas to have me whacked. But maybe someone was trying to get me away from where the action was. Maybe this Khalil thing in Frankfurt was made up, either by the Libyans, or by the CIA. It really sucks when you don't know what's real and what's made up, who your friends are, and who your enemies are—like Ted Nash.

Sometimes I envy people with diminished mental capacity. Like my Uncle Bertie, who's senile. He can hide his own Easter eggs. You know?

But I wasn't where Uncle Bertie was yet. I had too many synapses opening and closing, and the wiring was burning up with information, theories, possibilities, and suspicions.

I stood to leave, then sat down again, then stood again. This looked weird, so I moved toward the door with my briefcase, determined to make my decision before I left for the airport. I was leaning toward Frankfurt at that moment.

I got to the elevators, and coming toward me was Gabriel Haytham. He saw me and motioned me toward him. I went to where he was standing, and he said in a soft voice, "I think I have a live one for you."

"Meaning?"

"I got a guy in an interrogation room—this guy is a Libyan, and he made contact with one of our stakeout teams—"

"You mean he's a volunteer?"

"Yeah. Just like that. He has no prior problems with us, no history as an informant, he's not on any list or anything. Regular Yusef, whose name is Fadi Aswad—"

"Why do all your names sound like the starting lineup of the Knicks?"

Gabriel laughed. "Hey, try the Chinatown task force. Their names sound like the noise a pinball machine makes. Look, this guy Aswad is a taxi driver, and this guy has a brother-in-law, another Libyan, named Gamal Jabbar. Jabbar drives a taxi, too. We Arabs all drive taxis, right?"

"Right."

"So, early Saturday morning, Gamal Jabbar calls his brother-in-law, Fadi Aswad, and tells him that he's going to be gone for the whole day, that he has a special fare he has to pick up at JFK and that he's not happy about this fare."

"I'm listening."

"Gamal also says that if he's late getting home, that Fadi should call his wife, who's Fadi's sister, and reassure her that everything is okay."

"And?"

"Well, you have to understand the Arabs."

"I'm trying."

"What Gamal was saying to his brother-in-law—"

"Yeah, I get it. Like, I may be more than a little late."

"Right. Like I may be dead."

I asked, "So where's Gamal?"

"Dead. But Fadi doesn't know that. I just got off the horn with Homicide. Perth Amboy cops got a call this morning from an early commuter, who went to some Park and Ride about six-thirty A.M., sunrise, and he sees this yellow cab with New York plates. He thinks this is strange, and as he's walking to the bus shelter, he peeks inside and sees a guy half on the floor on the driver's side. Doors are locked. He gets on his cell phone and calls Nine-One-One."

I said, "Let's go talk to Fadi."

"Right. But I think I squeezed him dry. In Arabic."

"Let me try English."

We walked down the corridor, and I said to Gabe, "Why'd you come to me with this?"

"Why not? You need some points." He added, "Fuck the FBI."

"Amen."

We stopped in front of the door of an interrogation room. Gabe said, "I got a preliminary forensic report over the phone. This guy Gamal was killed with a single bullet that was fired through the back of his seat which severed his spinal column and nicked his right ventricle, exiting into the dashboard."

"Forty caliber?"

"Right. Bullet is deformed, but definitely a forty. The guy's been dead since about Saturday late afternoon, early evening."

"Did anyone check his E-Z Pass?"

"Yeah, but there's no toll records on his account for Saturday. Gamal lived in Brooklyn, apparently went to JFK, and wound up in New Jersey. You can't get there without paying a toll, so he paid cash and maybe his passenger was sitting behind a newspaper or something. We won't be able to trace his route, but the mileage on his meter checks out for a trip from JFK to where we found him and his taxi. We don't have a positive ID on the guy yet, but his hack license looks like the deceased."

"Anything else?"

"That's all the important stuff."

I opened the door and we entered a small interrogation room. Sitting at a table was Fadi Aswad, dressed in jeans, running shoes, and a green sweatshirt. He was puffing on a cigarette, the ashtray was overflowing, and the room was thick with smoke. This is a federally correct no-smoking building, of course, but if you're a suspect or a witness to a major crime, you may smoke.

There was another ATTF/NYPD guy in the room, watching the witness for signs that he might kill himself more quickly than by smoking, and making sure he didn't stroll away, down the elevator and out, as happened once.

Fadi stood as soon as he saw Gabriel Haytham, and I liked that. I have to get my witnesses and suspects to stand when I enter a room.

Anyway, the ATTF guy left, and Gabriel introduced me to my star witness. "Fadi, this is Colonel John."

Jesus. I must have done really well on the sergeant's exam.

Fadi sort of bowed his head, but said nothing.

I invited us all to sit, and we sat. I put my briefcase on the table so Fadi could see it. Third World types equate briefcases with power, for some reason.

Fadi was a voluntary witness, and thus had to be treated well. His nose appeared unbroken and there were no visible contusions on his face. Just kidding. But I knew that Gabe could be rough at times.

Gabe took Fadi's cigarette pack and offered me one. I noticed that the cigarettes were Camels, which I found funny for some reason. You know—camels, Arabs. Anyway, I took a cigarette and so did Gabe. We lit up with Fadi's lighter, but I didn't inhale. Honest. I did not inhale.

There was a tape recorder on the table, and Gabe hit the button, then said to Fadi, "Tell the Colonel what you told me."

Fadi looked anxious to please, but he also looked scared shitless. I mean, you almost never get an Arab walk-in unless they're trying to fuck someone else, or if there's a reward to be had, or if they were agents provocateurs, to use a French and CIA term. In any case, the guy who he was telling us about, Gamal Jabbar, was dead, so part of this guy's story checked out already, though he didn't know it yet.

Anyway, Fadi's English was okay, but he lost me a few times. Now and then, he'd slip into Arabic, then turn to Gabe, who translated.

Finally, he finished his story and chain-lit another cigarette.

We sat there for a full minute, and I let him sweat a little. I mean, he really *was* sweating.

I leaned toward him and asked slowly, "Why are you telling us this?"

He took a deep breath and sucked about half the smoke in the room into his lungs. He replied, "I am worried about my sister's husband."

"Has Gamal ever disappeared before?"

"No. He is not that type."

I continued the interrogation, alternating hard and soft questions.

I tend to be blunt during interrogations. It saves time and keeps the witness or suspect off-balance. But I knew from my brief training and experience with Mideast types that they are masters at beating around the bush, talking in circumlocution, answering a question with a question, engaging in seemingly endless theoretical discussions, and so forth. Maybe that's why the police in some of their countries beat the shit out of them. But I played the game, and we had a nice, non-productive half hour of chitchat, both of us wondering what in the world could have happened to Gamal Jabbar.

Gabe seemed to appreciate my cultural sensitivity, but even he was getting a little impatient.

The bottom line here was that we had a lead, a break, really. You always know that something is going to pop up, but you're always surprised when it actually does.

I strongly suspected that Gamal Jabbar picked up Asad Khalil at JFK, took him to the Park and Ride at Perth Amboy, New Jersey, then got a slug in his back for his trouble. My main questions were: Where did Khalil go next, and how did he get there?

I said to Fadi Aswad, "Are you certain that Gamal didn't say to you that he was picking up a fellow Libyan?"

"Well, sir, he did not say that. But it is possible. I say this because I do not think my brother-in-law would accept such a special fare from, let us say, a Palestinian, or an Iraqi. My brother-in-law, sir, was a Libyan patriot, but he was not much involved in the politics of other countries who share our faith in Allah—may peace be unto him. So, sir, if you are asking me if his special passenger was someone other than a Libyan, or if in fact he was a Libyan, in either case, I could not be certain, but then I must ask myself, 'Why would he go to such lengths to accommodate a man who was not a Libyan?' Do you see my point, sir?"

Holy shit. My head was spinning, and my eyes were rolling. I couldn't even remember the fucking question.

I looked at my watch. I could still catch the flight, but why should I?

I asked Fadi, "And Gamal did not say where his destination was to be?"

"No, sir."

I was a little thrown off by the short-form answer. I asked, "He didn't mention Newark Airport?"

"No, sir, he did not."

I leaned toward Fadi and said, "Look, you didn't contact the ATTF to report a missing brother-in-law. You obviously know who we are and what we do and this isn't family court, my friend. Capisce?"

"Sir?"

"Here's a direct question, and I want a one-word answer. Do you think your brother-in-law's disappearance has anything to do with what happened with the Trans-Continental flight at Kennedy Airport Saturday? Yes or no?"

"Well, sir, I have been thinking about this possibility—"

"Yes or no?"

He lowered his eyes and said, "Yes."

"You understand that your brother-in-law, your sister's husband, may have met with a misfortune?"

He nodded.

"You know that he thought he might be killed?"

"Yes."

"Is it possible he left any other clue—any other—" I looked at Gabe, who asked the question in Arabic.

Fadi replied in Arabic, and Gabe translated, "Gamal said to Fadi that Fadi should look after his family if something happened to him. Gamal said to Fadi that he had no choice but to take this special fare, and that Allah in his mercy would see him safely home."

No one spoke for a while. I could see that Fadi was visibly upset.

I used the time to think about this. In one way, we had nothing of any immediate use. We just had Khalil's movements from JFK to Perth Amboy, if indeed it was Khalil who was in Gamal's taxi. And if it was, all we knew for sure was that Khalil had probably murdered Gamal and then left Gamal's taxi and disappeared. But where did he disappear to? To Newark Airport? How did he get there? Another taxi? Or was there an accomplice with a private car waiting for him at the Park and Ride? Or maybe a rental car? And which direction did he go? In any case, he'd slipped through the net and was no longer in the New York metro area.

I looked at Fadi Aswad and asked him, "Does anyone know you contacted us?"

He shook his head.

"Not even your wife?"

He looked at me like I was nuts. He said, "I do not speak to my wife of such things. Why would you tell a woman or a child of such things?"

"Good point." I stood. "Okay, Fadi, you did the right thing by coming to us. Uncle Sam loves you. Go back to work and act like nothing has happened. Okay?"

He nodded.

"Also, I've got some bad news for you—your brother-in-law has been murdered."

He stood and tried to speak, then looked at Gabe, who spoke to him in Arabic. Fadi slumped into his chair and buried his face in his hands.

I said to Gabe, "Tell him not to say anything when the Homicide guys come around. Give him your card and tell him to show that to the detectives and have them call ATTF."

Gabe nodded and spoke to Fadi in Arabic, then gave him his card.

It occurred to me that I once had been a homicide cop, but here I was telling a witness not to talk to NYPD Homicide and to call the Feds instead. The transformation was nearly complete. Scary.

I took my briefcase, Gabe and I left the room, and the ATTF guy went in. Fadi's statement would be reduced to writing, and he would sign it before he left.

Out in the corridor, I said, "Keep a twenty-four-hour stakeout on him, his family, and his sister, and so forth."

"Done."

"Make sure no one sees him leaving this building."

"We always do."

"Right. And send a few guys over to One PP and see if there are any more dead cabbies around."

"I already asked. They're checking."

"Good. Am I insulting your intelligence?"

"Just a little."

I smiled for the first time that day. I said to Gabe, "Thanks for this. I owe you one."

"Right. So, what do you think?"

"I think what I always thought. Khalil is in America and he's not hiding out. He's on the move. He's on a mission."

"That's what I think. What's the mission?"

"Beats me, Gabe. Think about it. Hey, are you Libyan?"

"No, there aren't many Libyans here. It's a small country with a small immigrant community in the U.S." He added, "I'm actually Palestinian."

Against my better judgment, I asked him, "Don't you find this a little awkward? Stressful?"

He shrugged. "It's okay most of the time. I'm an American. Second generation. My daughter wears shorts and makeup, talks back to me, and pals around with Jews."

I smiled, then looked at him. I asked, "You ever get any threats from anyone?"

"Now and then. But they know it's not a good idea to whack a cop who's cross-designated as a Federal officer."

I would have agreed with that before Saturday. I said, "Okay, let's ask the NYPD and suburban cops to start running through the records of all car rental agencies, looking for Arab-sounding names. It's a long shot, and it's going to take a week or more, but we're not doing much else anyway. Also, I think you personally should go talk to the recent widow and see if maybe Mr. Jabbar confided in her. Also, start talking to Jabbar's friends and relatives. What we have here is our first lead, Gabe, and it may go somewhere, but I'm not real optimistic."

Gabe observed, "Assuming it was Khalil who killed Gamal Jabbar, then all we have is a cold trail, a dead witness, and a dead end in Perth Amboy. Dying in New Jersey is redundant."

I laughed. "Right. Where's the taxi?"

"Jersey State Police are going over it. Undoubtedly, we'll get enough forensic out of the car to use in putting a court case together—if we ever get that far."

I nodded. Fibers, fingerprints, maybe a ballistic match to one of the .40 caliber Glocks that belonged to Hundry and Gorman. Standard police work. I've seen murder trials where the physical evidence took a week to present to the jury. As I teach at John Jay, you almost always need physical evidence to *convict* a suspect, but you don't always need physical evidence to catch him.

With this case, we *started* with the name of the murderer, his photo, fingerprints, DNA samples, even pictures of him taking a crap—plus, we had a ton of forensic evidence to link him to the crimes at JFK. No problem there. The problem was that Asad Khalil was one quick and slippery sonofabitch. The guy had balls and brains, he was ruthless, and he had the advantage of being able to pick and choose his movements.

Gabe said, "We've been focusing on the Libyan community anyway, but maybe now with one of their people murdered, they'll open up a little." He added, "On the other hand, we may get the opposite reaction."

"Maybe. But I don't think Khalil has many accomplices in this country—not many live ones, anyway."

"Probably not. Okay, Corey, I got work to do. I'll keep you informed. And you'll pass this information on to the proper people, ASAP, and tell them a transcript of these interviews with Fadi is on the way. Okay?"

"Right. And, by the way, let's see that some of those Federal information bucks go to Fadi Aswad—for cigarettes and tranquilizers."

"Will do. See you later." He turned and went back to the interrogation room.

I went back to the ICC, which was still buzzing though it was past 6:00 P.M. already. I put down my briefcase and called Kate's apartment, but her voice mail informed me, "I'm not in. Please leave a cogent message."

So I left a cogent message in case she accessed her voice mail, then I called her cell phone, but she didn't answer. I called Jack Koenig's home number on Long Island, but his wife said he'd left for the airport. I tried his cell phone, but no luck.

I next called Beth Penrose at home, got her answering machine, and said, "I'm on this case around the clock. I may have to do some traveling. I love this job. I love my life. I love my bosses. I love my new office. Here's my new phone number." I gave her my direct number in the ICC and said, "Hey, I miss you. Speak to you soon." I hung up, realizing I meant to say, "I love you." But...anyway, I then dialed Captain Stein and asked his secretary for an immediate appointment. She informed me that Captain Stein was attending several meetings and press conferences. I left an ambiguous and confusing message, which even I didn't understand.

So, having fulfilled my requirement to keep everyone informed, I sat there and twiddled my thumbs. Everyone around me looked busy, but I'm not good at looking busy if I'm not busy.

I waded through more papers on my desk, but I was already overloaded with useless information. There was nothing for me to do out on the street, so I stayed in the Incident Command Center in case something popped. I figured I'd hang in there until two or three in the morning. Maybe the President wanted to talk to me, and since I had to leave a forwarding number wherever I went, I shouldn't be caught at home, or in Giulio's having a beer.

I realized I hadn't yet typed my Incident Report, regarding everything that happened at JFK. I was a little pissed that some flunk in Koenig's office kept sending me e-mails about it, and rejected my suggestion that I simply sign a transcript of the tape-recorded meeting in Koenig's office, or the two dozen meetings in D.C. No, they wanted *my* report, in *my* words. The Feds suck. I addressed my word processor and began: *SUBJECT—Fucking Incident Report.*

Someone walked by and put a sealed envelope on my desk marked URGENT FAX—YOUR EYES ONLY, and I opened it and read it. It was a preliminary report about the shooting in Frankfurt. The victim was a man named Sol Leibowitz, described as a Jewish-American investment banker with the Bank of New York. I read the brief summary of what happened to this unfortunate man and concluded that Mr. Leibowitz was just in the wrong place at the wrong time. There are thousands of American bankers in Europe at any given moment, Jewish or otherwise, and I was certain that this guy was just a soft target for a third-rate gunman who bore a resemblance to Asad Khalil. But this incident had caused some doubts and confusion in the minds of people who thrive on doubt and confusion.

Two other important papers landed on my desk—two take-out menus—one Italian, one Chinese.

My phone rang, and it was Kate. She said, "What the hell are you doing *there?*"

"I'm reading take-out menus. Where are you?"

"Where do you think I am? I'm at the airport, John. Jack and I are in the Business Class lounge, waiting for you. We have your ticket. Are you packed? Do you have your passport?"

"No. Listen—"

"Hold on."

I could hear her talking to Jack Koenig. She came back on the line and said, "Jack says you *must* go with us. He can get you on without your passport. Get here before the flight leaves. That's an order."

"Calm down and listen to me. I think we've got a lead here." I briefed her about Gabe Haytham, Fadi Aswad, and Gamal Jabbar.

She listened without interrupting, then said, "Hold on."

She came back on the phone and said, "That still doesn't prove that Khalil didn't get on a flight out of Newark and fly to Europe."

"Come on, Kate. The guy was already at an airport, less than a half mile from the International Terminal. Within ten minutes of the Port Authority cops being alerted at JFK, the Port Authority cops at Newark were also alerted. It's an hour ride between JFK and Newark. We're talking about Asad the Lion, not Asad the Turkey."

"Hold on."

Again I could hear her talking to Koenig. She came back on the line and said, "Jack says the MO and the description of the assailant in Frankfurt fit—"

"Put him on."

Koenig came on the line and started getting pissy with me.

I cut him off and said, "Jack, the reason the MO and the description fit is because they are trying to trick us. Asad Khalil just pulled off the crime of the century, and he did not fly to Germany to whack a banker, for Christ's sake. And if he was going to Newark Airport, why did he whack his cab driver before he got there? Does not compute, Jack. Now, you go to Frankfurt if you want, but I'll stay here. Send me a postcard, and bring me back a dozen real frankfurters and some of that hot German mustard. Thanks." I hung up before he could fire me.

I bagged the Incident Report, since I was probably fired, and I went back to my desk work, again wading through stacks of background stuff, reports from various agencies, all of whom had nothing to report. Finally I got to the half ton of paperwork that related to Saturday's incident—forensic, Port Authority police, an FAA complaint with my name prominently featured, photos of dead people in their seats, the toxicology report—it was indeed a cyanide compound—and so forth.

Somewhere in these piles of papers might be a clue to something, but so far all I saw was the work product of people with tunnel vision and access to a word processor with spell check.

Which reminded me that they'd hold my paycheck until I turned in a report, so I swiveled in my chair and again addressed my keyboard and monitor screen. I began my report with a joke about a French Foreign Legionnaire and a camel, then deleted it and tried again.

At about a quarter to nine, Kate walked in and sat at her desk facing me. She watched me as I typed, but said nothing. After a few minutes of being watched, I was starting to make spelling errors, so I looked up at her and said, "How was Frankfurt?"

She didn't reply, and I could see she was a little pissed. I know that look.

I asked, "Where's Jack?"

"He went to Frankfurt."

"Good. Am I fired?"

"No, but you're going to wish you were."

"I don't respond well to threats."

"What *do* you respond to?"

"Not much. Maybe a cocked pistol pointed at my head. Yeah, that usually gets my attention."

"Tell me again about the interrogation."

So, I went through it again, in more detail, and Kate asked lots of questions. She's very bright, which was why she was sitting in the ICC rather than on a Lufthansa flight to Frankfurt.

She said, "So, you think Khalil left the Park and Ride in a car?"

"I think so."

"Why not a commuter bus to Manhattan?"

"I thought about that. That's why people go to the Park and Ride—to catch a commuter bus to Manhattan. But it seems a little excessive to murder your taxi driver while you're waiting for the bus. In fact, I'll bet if Khalil had asked Jabbar to *drive* him to Manhattan, Jabbar would have."

"Don't get sarcastic with me, John. You're on thin ice."

"Yes, ma'am."

She ruminated a moment, then said, "Okay, so there was a getaway car parked in the Park and Ride. It wouldn't attract any attention, and would be relatively safe there. Jabbar drives Khalil to the lot, Khalil fires a single bullet—forty caliber—through Jabbar's spine, killing him, then gets in this other car. Is there a driver? An accomplice?"

"I don't think so. Why does he need a driver? He's a loner. He's probably driven in Europe. He just needs the keys and papers to the car, which he may have gotten from Jabbar. Jabbar, of course, has now seen too much, and he gets whacked. In the getaway car, or maybe in Jabbar's taxi, would be an overnight bag with some necessities, money, false identity, and maybe a disguise. That's why Khalil took nothing from Phil or Peter. Asad Khalil is now somebody else, and he's on the great American highway system."

"Where is he headed?"

"I don't know. But by now, if he drove with minimum sleep, he could be across the Mexican border. Or he could even be on the West Coast. Fifty hours' driving time at sixty-five miles an hour is a radius of over three thousand miles, and the square miles are—let's see, is that pi r squared?"

"I get the point."

"Good. So, assuming we have a killer loose on the highways, and assuming he wants to do something other than see Disney World, then we have to just wait to see what he does next. There's not much else we can do at this point, except to hope that somebody recognizes this guy."

She nodded, then stood. She said, "I have a taxi waiting outside with my luggage. I'm going home to unpack."

"Can I help?"

"I'll hold the cab." She left.

I sat there a few minutes, during which time my phone rang and someone plopped more papers on my desk.

I was trying to figure out why I said, "Can I help?" I have to learn to keep my mouth shut.

There are times when I'd rather face an armed homicidal maniac than face another night in a lady's apartment. At least with the homicidal maniac, you know where you stand, and the conversation is understandably brief and to the point.

My phone was ringing again, and in fact phones were ringing all over the big room, and it was getting on my nerves.

Anyway, as good as I am about getting into the heads of killers and predicting their moves, I am absolutely clueless about sexual involvements—I don't know how I get into them, what I'm supposed to do when I'm in them, *why* I'm in them, and how to get out of them. Usually, though, I know who the other person is. I'm good at remembering names, even at 6:00 A.M.

I'm also good at smelling trouble, and this was trouble. Also, I'd been straight as an arrow since my involvement with Beth Penrose, and I didn't want to complicate that relationship or complicate my life.

So, I made the decision to go downstairs and tell Kate I decided to go home. I got up, took my jacket and briefcase, and went downstairs and got into the cab with her.

Chapter 39

Asad Khalil continued north on I-95, retracing his route from Jacksonville, across the Georgia border, then into South Carolina. Along his route, he disposed of the computer disks from Paul Grey's office.

As he drove, he thought about his morning activities. Certainly by this evening, someone would be looking for the cleaning woman, or for Paul Grey. At some point, someone would discover the bodies. The assumed motive for Grey's murder would be the theft of the sensitive software. This was all as planned. What wasn't well thought out, he realized, was the problem of his pilot. Quite possibly, by this evening or tomorrow morning, the murders in Spruce Creek would come to the attention of someone at Alpha Aviation Services, and, of course, his female pilot, who would certainly recall the name Paul Grey. Khalil had not realized that the man's name would be on the hangar.

This woman would call the police and suggest that she may have some knowledge of this crime. In Libya, no one would call the police with any information that would bring them into contact with the authorities. But Boris had been fairly certain that this could happen in America.

Khalil nodded to himself as he drove. Boris had told him to use his judgment regarding the pilot, pointing out, "If you kill the pilot, then you must also kill everyone else who knew of your flight and who saw your face. Dead men cannot go to the police. But the more corpses you leave around, the more determined the police will become to find the murderer. A single murder of a man in his house for the purpose of theft does not cause too much interest. You may be fortunate enough to have it go unnoticed in Jacksonville."

Again, Khalil nodded. But he'd had to kill the cleaning woman, just as he'd done in Washington, in order to give him more time to distance himself from the killing. Someone should tell Boris that Americans did not like to clean their own homes.

In any case, the police were looking for a thief, not Asad Khalil. Also, they were not looking for his automobile, and if the pilot called the police, they would be looking for a Greek on his way to Athens via Washington, D.C. All of this depended on how stupid the police were.

There was the other possibility, of course—the female pilot, seeing the front page of the newspapers, might actually realize who her passenger had been... Undoubtedly, he should have killed her, but he had not. He had spared her life, he told himself, not out of pity, but because of what Boris and even Malik had said about too many killings. Boris was not only cautious, but also too concerned about the lives of the enemies of Islam. Boris had not wanted to gas the aircraft full of people, for instance, and had called this "an insane act of mass murder."

Malik had reminded him, "Your former government killed over twenty million of your own people since your revolution. All of Islam has not killed that many people since the time of Muhammad. Please do not preach to us. We have a long way to go to equal your accomplishments."

Boris had not replied to this.

As he drove along I-95, Khalil put these recollections out of his mind, and thought once again of Paul Grey. He had not died as well as the brave General Waycliff and his brave wife. Yet, he had not died begging for his life. Khalil thought perhaps he should try a different method with William Satherwaite. They told him in Libya that the former Lieutenant Satherwaite had experienced some misfortunes in life, and Boris had said, "Killing him might be doing him a favor." To which Khalil had replied, "No man wants to die. Killing him will be as pleasurable for me as killing the rest of them."

Khalil looked at his dashboard clock—it was 3:05 P.M. He looked at his Satellite Navigator. Soon he would be leaving I-95 for a road called ALT 17 that would take him directly to the place called Moncks Corner.

Once again his thoughts returned to the morning. These dealings with the female pilot had a disturbing effect on him, but he couldn't completely comprehend what had caused him such indecision and confusion. There were good reasons to kill her, and good reasons not to kill her. He recalled that she had said to the woman behind the counter, "I'll be back to take care of the Piper."

Thus, if she hadn't returned, they would be looking for her, and for him. Unless, of course, the woman behind the counter had the thought that her pilot and her customer decided to...be together. Yes, he could see that thought in the woman's face and the way she acted. However, the woman eventually might become concerned and call the police. So perhaps it had been better not to kill the female pilot.

As he drove, a vision of the pilot filled his mind, and he saw her smiling, talking to him, helping him into the aircraft—touching him. Those thoughts continued running through his mind, even as he tried to rid himself of her image. He found her business card in his pocket and looked at it. It had her home phone number written in pen above the business number of Alpha Aviation. He put the card back in his pocket.

He saw his exit at the last moment and swerved into the right lane, then onto the exit ramp for ALT 17.

He found himself on a two-lane road, much different from the Interstate. There were houses and farms on both sides of the road, small villages, gasoline stations, and pine forests. A compatriot had traveled this route on Khalil's behalf some months ago and reported, "This is the most dangerous of roads because of the drivers who are insane, and because of the police who have motorcycles and who watch everyone pass by."

Khalil heeded this warning and tried to drive so as not to attract attention. He passed through a number of villages and saw a police car and a motorcycle in two of them.

But it was a short distance to his destination—sixty kilometers, or forty miles, and within the hour, he was approaching the town of Moncks Corner.

✳   ✳   ✳

Bill Satherwaite sat with his feet on his cluttered desk in a small concrete block building at Berkeley County Airport, Moncks Corner, South Carolina. He had the grimy handset of a cheap telephone cradled between his ear and shoulder, and he listened to Jim McCoy's voice at the other end. Satherwaite glanced at the anemic air-conditioner stuck through the wall. The fan was clattering, and a trickle of cold air was coming out the vent. It was only April, and it was already close to ninety degrees outside. *Damned hellhole.*

Jim McCoy said, "Have you heard from Paul? He was going to call you."

Satherwaite replied, "Nah. Sorry I couldn't get on the conference call Saturday. Had a busy day."

"That's okay," said McCoy. "I just thought I'd call you and see how you were doing."

"Doing fine." Satherwaite glanced at the desk drawer beneath where his feet were propped up. In the drawer, he knew, was a mostly full bottle of Jack Daniel's. He glanced at the wall clock: 4:10 P.M. Somewhere in the world it was past 5:00 P.M.; time for one small drink—except that the charter customer was supposed to be here by 4:00 P.M. Satherwaite said, "Did I tell you I flew down to see Paul a few months ago?"

"Yes, you did—"

"Yeah. You ought to see his setup. Big house, pool, hangar, twin Beech, hot and cold running babes." He laughed and added, "Shit, when they saw my old Apache coming in, they tried to wave me off." He laughed.

McCoy took the opportunity to say, "Paul was a little concerned about the Apache."

"Yeah? Paul's an old lady, if you want my opinion. How many times did he piss us off wasting time checking everything a hundred times? Guys who are too damned careful get into accidents." He added, "The Apache passes FAA inspection."

"Just passing it on, Bill."

"Yeah." He kept staring at the drawer, then swung his legs off the desk, sat upright in his swivel chair, leaned forward, and opened the desk drawer. He said to Jim McCoy, "Hey, you really got to get down there and see Paul's setup."

In fact, Jim McCoy had been down to Spruce Creek a number of times, but he didn't want to mention that to Bill Satherwaite, who'd been invited just once, though Satherwaite was only about an hour-and-a-half flight time away. "Yes, I'd like to—"

"Incredible house and stuff. But you should see what he's working on. Virtual fucking reality. Jesus, we sat there all night drinking, bombing the shit out of everything." He laughed. "We did the Al Azziziyah run five times. Fucking incredible. By the fifth run, we were so shit-faced we couldn't even hit the fucking ground." He broke into peals of laughter.

Jim McCoy laughed, too, but his laughter was forced. McCoy really didn't want to hear the same story again that he'd heard a half dozen times since Paul had invited Satherwaite down to Spruce Creek for a long weekend. It had been, Paul told him afterward, a *particularly* long weekend. Up until that time, none of the guys had quite understood how much Bill Satherwaite had deteriorated in the past seven years since they'd last gotten together in an informal reunion of the flight crews from the squadron. Now, everyone knew.

Bill Satherwaite caught his breath and said, "Hey, wizo, remember when I waited too long to kick in my afterburners, and Terry almost climbed up my ass?" He laughed again and put the bottle on his desk.

Jim McCoy, sitting in his office at the Cradle of Aviation Museum on Long Island, didn't reply. He had trouble connecting the Bill Satherwaite he had known with the Bill Satherwaite at the other end of the line. The old Bill Satherwaite was as good a pilot and officer as there was in the Air Force. But ever since his too-early retirement, Bill Satherwaite had been on a steep glide slope toward the ground. Being a Gadhafi-killer had become increasingly more important to him as the years went by. He told his war stories incessantly to anyone who would listen, and now he was even telling them to the guys who flew the mission with him. And every year these stories got a little more dramatic, and every year his role in their little twelve-minute war got a little grander.

Jim McCoy was concerned about Bill Satherwaite's bragging about the raid. No one was supposed to mention that they'd been part of that mission, and certainly no one was supposed to mention other pilots' names. McCoy had told Satherwaite numerous times to watch what he said, and Satherwaite had assured him that he'd only used their radio code names or first names when he discussed the raid. McCoy had warned him, "Don't even say *you* were on that raid, Bill. Stop talking about it."

To which Bill Satherwaite had always replied, "Hey, I'm proud of what I did. And don't worry about it. Those stupid ragheads aren't coming to Moncks Corner, South Carolina, to even the score. Chill out."

Jim McCoy thought he should mention this again, but what good would it do?

McCoy often wished that his old squadron mate had stayed in the Air Force at least until the Gulf War. Maybe if Bill had participated in the Gulf War, life would somehow have been better for him.

As he spoke into the phone, Bill Satherwaite kept an eye on the clock and an eye on the door. Finally, he spun the top off the bourbon bottle and took a quick slug without missing a beat in his war story. He said, "And fucking Chip—slept all the way there, I wake him up, he tosses four, and goes back to sleep." He howled with laughter.

McCoy's patience was wearing thin, and he reminded Satherwaite, "You said he never shut up all the way to Libya."

"Yeah, never shut his mouth."

McCoy realized that Satherwaite didn't see any inconsistencies in his stories, so he said, "Okay, buddy, let's stay in touch."

"Don't go yet. I'm waiting for a charter. Guy needs to go to Philly, then overnight and back here. Hey, how's the job going?"

"Not bad. This is a world-class facility. Not finished yet, but we've got a great sampling of aircraft. We've got an F-III, and we've even got a model of the Spirit of St. Louis. Lindbergh took off from Roosevelt Field just a few miles from here. You have to come up and see it. I'll put you in the F-III."

"Yeah? Why's it a cradle?"

"Cradle of Aviation. Long Island is called the Cradle of Aviation."

"How about Kitty Hawk?"

"I don't ask—I'm not rocking the cradle." He laughed and said, "Fly up one of these days. Go into Long Island MacArthur, and I'll pick you up."

"Yeah. One of these days. Hey, how's Terry doing?"

Jim McCoy wanted to get off the phone, but old comrades-in-arms had to be indulged, though not for too much longer. He replied, "He sends his regards."

"Bullshit."

"He did," McCoy replied, trying to sound sincere. Bill Satherwaite was nobody's favorite anymore—probably never was—but they had shared the Holy Sacrament of Baptism by Fire, and the Warrior Ethos—or what was left of it in America—demanded that those bonds remain intact until the last man took his last breath.

Everyone in the squadron tried to accommodate Bill Satherwaite—except for Terry Waycliff—and the other guys had given the General a silent pass on that assignment.

Satherwaite said, "Is Terry still sucking Pentagon dick?"

McCoy replied, "Terry is still in the Pentagon. We expect that he'll retire out of there."

"Fuck him."

"I'll be sure to give him your best."

Satherwaite laughed. "Yeah. You know what that guy's problem was? He was a general even back when he was a lieutenant. Know what I mean?"

McCoy replied, "You know, Bill, a lot of people said the same about you. I mean that as a compliment."

"If that's a compliment, then I don't need any insults. Terry had it in for me—always competing with everybody. Broke my balls about me not kicking in the goddamned afterburners—wrote a snitch note about it, blamed me for the stray fucking bomb instead of blaming Wiggins—"

"Hold on, Bill. That's out of line."

Bill Satherwaite took another swig of bourbon, suppressed a belch, and said, "Yeah...okay...sorry..."

"That's okay. Forget it." McCoy thought about Terry Waycliff and

Bill Satherwaite. Bill was not even in the Air Force Reserve, and for that reason he would normally have lost his post commissary privileges and that would have been the ultimate blow for Satherwaite—losing his discount liquor privileges at Charleston Air Base. But Terry Waycliff had pulled some strings—unknown to Bill Satherwaite—and got him a PX card. McCoy said, "We had Bob on the conference call, too."

Bill Satherwaite squirmed in his chair. Thinking about Bob Callum and his cancer was not something that he did on a voluntary basis—or ever, for that matter. Callum had made colonel, and the last that Satherwaite knew, he was still working as a ground instructor at the Air Force Academy at Colorado Springs. He asked McCoy, "He still working?"

"He is. Same place. Give him a call."

"I will. Tough break." He thought a moment, then said, "You survive a war, you die of something worse."

"He may beat it."

"Yeah. And last but not least, my little shit of a wizo—how's Chip?"

"Couldn't reach him," McCoy replied. "Last letter I sent to him in California got returned with no forwarding address. Phone is disconnected, no info available."

"Just like Wiggins to forget to keep his paperwork up to date. I really had to work to keep that guy in line. Always had to remind him to do everything."

"Chip never changes."

"You can say that again."

McCoy thought about Chip Wiggins. The last time he'd spoken to him was April 15 of the previous year. Wiggins had taken flying lessons when he left the Air Force and was now a pilot, flying cargo for various small airlines. Everyone liked Chip Wiggins, but he was not good about attention to detail, such as change-of-address cards.

Jim McCoy, Terry Waycliff, and Paul Grey had shared the thought that Wiggins didn't keep in touch because he was a pilot now, but hadn't been a pilot back then. Also, he had been in Satherwaite's crew, and that was probably reason enough to be ambivalent about the past. Jim McCoy said, "I'll try to track him down. You know, I don't think Chip even knows about Willie yet."

Satherwaite took another drink of bourbon, glanced at the clock, then at the door. Regarding the late Colonel Hambrecht, he said, "Chip liked Willie. He should be told."

"Right. I'll do my best." McCoy didn't know what else to say, knowing that Bill Satherwaite wouldn't put a stamp on an envelope to keep the group in contact, and that the work of maintaining everyone's whereabouts had mostly been his and Terry's.

In fact, ever since he'd gotten the job as Director of the Long Island Cradle of Aviation Museum, Jim McCoy had become the unofficial corresponding secretary of their little unofficial group. The guys found it convenient to use him as a rallying point—he had the office assets to keep in touch by telephone, mail, e-mail, and fax. Terry Waycliff was sort of their President, but his Pentagon job made him unavailable most of the time, and Jim McCoy never called him unless it was important. Soon, they'd all be old men and have plenty of time to stay in touch if they wanted to.

McCoy said to Satherwaite, "Did you say you have a charter?"

"Yeah. Guy's late."

"Bill, have you been drinking?"

"Are you crazy? Before a flight? I'm a pro, for God's sake."

"Okay..." McCoy thought that Bill was lying about drinking, so he hoped that Bill Satherwaite was also lying about having a customer. He took a moment to reflect on the old squadron—Steve Cox, killed in the Gulf; Willie Hambrecht, murdered in England; Terry Waycliff, completing a brilliant military career; Paul Grey, a successful civilian; Bob Callum, sick with cancer in Colorado; Chip Wiggins, missing in action, but presumed well; Bill Satherwaite, a ghost of his former self; and finally, himself, Jim McCoy, museum director—good job, bad pay. Out of eight men, two were dead, one was dying of cancer, one was dying of life, one was missing, and three were okay for the moment. He said to Bill Satherwaite in a soft tone of voice, "We should all fly out to see Bob. We shouldn't delay. I'll put it together. You've got to be there, Bill. Okay?"

Bill Satherwaite remained quiet for a few seconds, then said, "Okay. Can do. Can do."

"Take it easy, buddy."

"Yeah...you, too." Satherwaite put the phone down and rubbed his eyes, which were moist. He took another drink, then put the bottle in his overnight bag.

Bill Satherwaite stood and looked around his shabby office. On the far wall was a state of South Carolina flag and a Confederate flag that a lot of people found offensive, which was why he kept it there. The whole country had gone to hell, he thought, politically correct faggots were in charge, and even though Bill Satherwaite was from Indiana, he liked the South—except for the heat and the humidity—he liked their attitudes, and he liked his Confederate flag. "Fuck 'em."

On the side wall was a large aeronautical plotting chart, and beside the chart was an old poster, faded and wrinkled from the humidity. It was a photograph of Moammar Gadhafi with a big bull's-eye drawn around his head. Satherwaite picked up a dart from his cluttered desk and flung it at the poster. The dart hit the middle of Gadhafi's forehead, and Satherwaite yelled, "Yeah! Fuck you!"

Bill Satherwaite went to the window of his small office and looked out into the bright sunshine. "Nice day for flying." Out on the runway, one of his two aircraft, the Cherokee 140 trainer, was just lifting off, and in the afternoon heat and turbulence, the small airplane's wings wobbled as the student pilot strained to gain altitude.

He watched the Cherokee disappear as it continued its wobbly climb. He was glad he didn't have to be in the cockpit with this kid, who had no balls, no feel for aviation, and too much money. Back when he was an Air Force student pilot, they just axed out the dead wood. Now, he had to cater to them. And this kid would never see a minute of combat—he wanted to fly to impress his main hump. The country was going down the toilet, fast.

To make the day worse, his customer was some stupid foreigner, probably an illegal alien running drugs up to the hopheads in Philly, and the bastard was late. At least the guy wouldn't say anything if he smelled the bourbon. He'd probably think it was an American soft drink. He laughed.

He walked back to his desk and checked out a note he'd made. *Alessandro Fanini*. Sounded like a spic or a greaseball. "Yeah, a wop. That's not so bad. Better than some Pedro from south of the border."

"Good afternoon."

Satherwaite spun around and saw a tall man wearing dark sun-glasses standing at the open door. The man said, "Alessandro Fanini. I apologize for my lateness."

Satherwaite wondered if the guy had heard him. He glanced at the wall clock and said, "Only half an hour. No problem."

The two men walked toward each other, and Satherwaite put out his hand. They shook, and Khalil said, "I was delayed at my last appointment in Charleston."

"No problem." Bill Satherwaite saw that the man carried a large black canvas bag and was dressed in a gray suit. He asked, "You got any other luggage?"

"I have left my luggage in my hotel in Charleston."

"Good. You don't mind my jeans and T-shirt, I hope."

"Not at all. Whatever is comfortable. But as I said, we will be staying overnight."

"Yeah. I got an overnight bag." He motioned to an Air Force bag on the dirty floor. He said, "My girlfriend will be here later to watch the store and lock up."

"Good. You should be back by midday tomorrow."

"Whatever."

"I have left my rental car near the main building. It will be safe there?"

"Sure." Satherwaite walked to a sagging bookshelf and scooped up a stack of rolled charts, then retrieved his overnight bag. "Ready?" He followed his customer's gaze, which was fixed on the poster of Gadhafi. Satherwaite grinned and said, "You know who that is?"

Asad Khalil replied, "Of course. My country has had many confrontations with that man."

"Yeah? You got into it with Mr. Moammar Shithead Gadhafi?"

"Yes. He has threatened us many times."

"Yeah? Well, for your information, I almost killed that bastard once."

"Yes?"

Satherwaite asked, "You're from Italy?"

"I am from Sicily."

"No shit? I could've wound up there once if I'd run out of gas."

"Excuse me?"

"It's a long story. I'm not allowed to talk about it. Forget it."

"As you wish."

"Okay, if you open that door for me, we're outta here."

"Oh, one more thing. There has been a slight change in my plans that may necessitate some change on your part."

"Like what?"

"My company has ordered me to New York."

"Yeah? I don't like flying to New York, Mr...."

"Fanini."

"Yeah. Too much traffic, too much bullshit."

"I am willing to pay extra."

"It's not the money, it's the bullshit. Which airport?"

"It is called MacArthur. You know of it?"

"Oh, yeah. Never been there, but it's okay. A suburban airport out on Long Island. We can do that, but it's extra."

"Of course."

Satherwaite put his things down on the desk and looked for another chart on the shelf. He said, "Funny coincidence—I was just talking to a guy on Long Island. He wanted me to stop by—maybe I'll surprise him. Maybe I should call him."

"Perhaps a surprise would be better. Or call him when we land."

"Yeah. Let me get his phone numbers." Satherwaite flipped through a tattered Rolodex and extracted a card.

Khalil said, "Is he close to the airport?"

"I don't know. But he'll pick me up."

"You may take my rental car if you wish. I have a car reserved, as well as two motel rooms for us."

"Yeah. I was going to ask you about that. I don't share rooms with guys."

Khalil forced a smile and replied, "Neither do I."

"Good. As long as we got that straight. Hey, you want to pay up front? You get a discount for up-front cash."

"How much will this amount to?"

"Oh...now that it's MacArthur, plus the overnight and I lose some flight instructing time tomorrow, plus gas...let's say eight hundred in cash should do it."

"That sounds reasonable." Khalil took out his wallet and counted eight hundred dollars in cash, then added another hundred dollars to it and said, "Plus a tip for you."

"Thanks."

That was most of the cash that Khalil had, but he knew he would get it all back soon.

Bill Satherwaite counted the money and pocketed it. "Okay. Done deal."

"Good. I am ready."

"I gotta take a piss." Satherwaite opened a door and disappeared into the toilet.

Asad Khalil looked at the poster of the Great Leader and noticed the dart in the forehead. He removed the dart and said to himself, "Surely no one deserves to die more than this American pig."

Bill Satherwaite came out of the toilet, picked up his charts and bag, and said, "If there's no more changes, we can get moving."

Khalil said, "Do you have any beverages we can bring with us?"

"Yeah. I already put an ice chest in the plane. Got soda and beer— beer's for you if you want. I can't drink."

Khalil clearly smelled alcohol on the man's breath, but said, "Do you have bottled water?"

"No. Why spend money for water? Water is free." *Idiots and fairies buy bottled water.* "You want water?"

"It is not necessary." Khalil opened the door, and they went out into the sweltering air.

As they walked across the hot concrete ramp toward the Apache parked a hundred feet from the office, Satherwaite asked, "What kind of business you in, Mr. Panini?"

"Fanini. As my colleague told you when he called from New York, I am in the textile business. I am here to buy American cotton."

"Yeah? You came to the right place. Nothing's changed here since the Civil War, except now they have to pay the slaves." He laughed and added, "And some of the slaves are Spanish and white now. You ever see a cotton field? Talk about shit work. They can't find enough people to do it. Maybe they should import some stupid Arabs to pick cotton— they love the sun. Pay 'em in camel shit, and tell 'em they can take it to the bank for money." He laughed.

Khalil did not reply, but asked, "Do you need to file a flight plan?"

"No." Satherwaite pointed to the clear sky as they continued their walk toward the airplane. "There's a big-ass high-pressure area across the entire East Coast—great weather all the way." Thinking he might have a nervous passenger, he added, "The gods are shining on you, Mr. Fanini, 'cause we've got a great day for flying all the way to New York and, probably, when we come back tomorrow, too."

Khalil did not need to hear this man tell him that Allah had blessed the Jihad—he already knew it in the depths of his soul. He also knew that Mr. Satherwaite was not flying home tomorrow.

As they continued to walk, Satherwaite said, as if thinking to himself, "I might check in with New York approach control radar when we cut across the ocean south of Kennedy Airport on the direct route to Islip. They'll keep us away from airliners inbound to JFK."

Khalil thought a moment of how he had been inside an airliner on that very route only a few brief days ago, yet it now seemed almost an eternity.

Satherwaite added, "And I'll call Long Island Tower for a landing clearance. That's it." Satherwaite waved his hand around the nearly deserted Moncks Corner airfield. "Sure as hell don't have to talk to anyone to depart from here," he said with a laugh. "Hell, there's no one around to talk to, except my own student out there in my own piece-of-shit Cherokee. And that kid wouldn't know what to say if I called him on the radio anyway."

Khalil looked out to where the pilot was pointing at the small single-engine airplane that was now lined up and descending toward the landing runway, wobbling slightly from side to side. He could see that the airplane very closely resembled the type that he had chartered out of Jacksonville with the female pilot. The memory of her crept back into Khalil's thoughts, and he quickly pushed her image from his mind.

They stopped at an old blue and white two-engine Piper Apache. Satherwaite had earlier untied the ropes, removed the control locks, and put aside the wheel chocks. He had also checked the fuel. That was all he ever checked, anyway, he thought, mostly because there were so many things wrong with the old airplane that it was a waste of time finding anything more. Satherwaite said to his customer, "I checked it all out before you got here. Everything's in tip-top shape."

Asad Khalil regarded the old aircraft. He was glad it had two engines.

Satherwaite sensed some concern on the part of his paying customer and said, "This is a very basic machine, Mr. Fanini, and you can always depend on it to get you there and back."

"Yes?"

Satherwaite tried to see what the prissy foreigner saw. The Plexiglass windows of the 1954 airplane were a little dirty and crazed, and the paint on the fuselage was a bit faded—in fact, Satherwaite admitted, it was now hardly more than a hint of what it had previously been. He glanced at the foppishly dressed, sunglasses-wearing Mr. Fanini and gave him more encouragement. "There's nothing complex or fancy about it, but that means that nothing of importance can go wrong. The engines are good, and the flight controls are working fine. I used to fly military jets, and let me tell you, those things are so complex that you need an army of maintenance people just to launch on a simple one-hour mission." Satherwaite glanced beneath the right engine where a growing puddle of black oil had accumulated in the week since he'd last flown the Apache. "In fact, I took this to Key West and back yesterday. Flies like a homesick angel. Ready?"

"Yes."

"Good." Satherwaite threw his overnight bag on the wing, then with the charts under his arm, he climbed onto the Apache's right wing, opened the only door, and retrieved his bag. He threw his bag and the charts in the rear and said to his passenger, "Front or back?"

"I will sit in the front."

"Okay." Bill Satherwaite sometimes helped passengers up, but the tall guy looked like he could manage. Satherwaite climbed into the cockpit and maneuvered himself across the co-pilot's seat into the pilot's seat. It was hot in the cabin, and Satherwaite popped open the small vent window on his side, waiting for his passenger. He called out, "You coming?"

Asad Khalil placed his bag on the wing, climbed up onto the skid-proof surface, which was worn smooth, retrieved his bag, and slid into the co-pilot's seat, placing his bag on the seat behind him.

Satherwaite said, "Leave your door open a minute. Buckle up."

Khalil did as his pilot instructed.

Bill Satherwaite put on a headset, flipped some switches, then hit the starter for the left engine. After hesitating a few seconds, the prop began to swing around, and the old piston engine sputtered to life. Once the engine was running smoothly, Satherwaite hit the starter for the right engine, which fired up better than the left. "Okay...beautiful sound."

Khalil shouted over the sound of the engines, "It is very loud."

Satherwaite shouted back, "Yeah, well, your door and my window are open." He didn't tell his passenger that the door seal leaked, and it wouldn't be much quieter with it closed. He said, "Once we get up to cruise altitude, you can hear your mustache grow." He laughed and began taxiing out toward the runway. With the money in his pocket, he reflected, he didn't have to be overly nice to this greaseball. He asked, "Where'd you say you're from?"

"Sicily."

"Oh...yeah..." Satherwaite remembered that the Mafia was from Sicily. He glanced at his passenger as he taxied, and it suddenly dawned on him that this guy could be in the mob. He immediately regretted his high-handed manner and tried to make amends. "You comfortable, Mr. Fanini? Do you have any questions about the flight?"

"The time of the flight."

"Well, sir, if we get good tailwinds, which is what has been forecast, we'll be at MacArthur in about three and a half hours." He checked his watch. "That should put us on the ground about eight-thirty. How's that?"

"That will be fine. And must we refuel along the way?"

"Nope. I got extra tip tanks installed so I can go about seven hours, non-stop. We'll refuel in New York."

Khalil asked, "And you have no difficulty landing in the dark?"

"No, sir. It's a good airport. Airlines go there with jets. And I'm an experienced pilot."

"Good."

Satherwaite thought he'd smoothed things out with Mr. Fanini, and he smiled. He taxied the Apache to the end of the active runway. He glanced up and through his windshield. His student was going around again in the traffic pattern for Runway Twenty-three, doing touch-and-go landings in the crosswind and apparently not having any problems. He said, "That kid up there, he's a student pilot who needs a double-ball transplant. You know? American kids have gone way too soft. They need a kick in the ass. They need to become killers. They need to taste blood."

"Is that so?"

Satherwaite glanced at his passenger and said, "I mean, I saw combat and I can tell you, when the Triple-A is so thick you can't see the sky, and when the missiles are cruising alongside your cockpit, then you become a man real fast."

"You have experienced this?"

"Lots of times. Okay, here we go. Close your door." Satherwaite ran up his engines, checked his instruments, then looked around the airport. Only the Cherokee was there, and he was no conflict. Satherwaite taxied the Apache onto the runway, pushed up the power, and they began to roll. The aircraft picked up speed and with half the runway remaining, lifted off.

Satherwaite said nothing as he made adjustments in his throttles and controls. He banked the aircraft and turned to a course of 040 degrees as the plane continued to climb.

Khalil looked out the window at the green countryside below. He sensed that the aircraft was more sound than it looked, and that the pilot, too, was better than he looked. He said to his pilot, "What war did you fight in?"

Satherwaite put a piece of chewing gum in his mouth and said, "Lots of wars. The Gulf was the big one."

Khalil knew that this man had not fought in the Gulf War. In fact,

Asad Khalil knew more about Bill Satherwaite than Satherwaite knew about himself.

Satherwaite asked, "Want some gum?"

"No, thank you. And what type of aircraft did you fly?"

"Flew fighters."

"Yes? What is that?"

"Fighters. Fighter jets. Fighter-bombers. I flew lots of different kinds, but I ended up on something called the F-111."

"Can you discuss that—or is it a military secret?"

Satherwaite laughed. "No, sir, it's no secret. It's an old aircraft, long since retired from service. Just like me."

"Do you miss this experience?"

"I don't miss the chickenshit. That means the spit-and-polish—like saluting, and everybody looking up your butt all the time. And now they have *women* flying combat aircraft, for Christ's sake. I can't even *think* about that. And these bitches cause all kinds of goddamned problems with their sexual harassment bullshit—sorry, you got me started. Hey, how are the women where you come from? They know their place?"

"Very much so."

"Good. Maybe I'll go there. Sicily, right?"

"Yes."

"What do they speak there?"

"A dialect of Italian."

"I'll learn it and go there. They need pilots there?"

"Of course."

"Good." They were climbing through five thousand feet and the late afternoon sun was almost directly behind them, and that made the view ahead particularly clear and dramatic, Satherwaite thought. With the backlighting, the lush spring terrain took on an even deeper hue of colors, and created a clear line of demarcation against the distant blue of the coastal waters. A twenty-five-knot tailwind added to their ground speed, so they might make Long Island sooner than he'd estimated.

Somewhere in the back of Bill Satherwaite's mind was the thought that flying was more than a job. It was a calling, a brotherhood, an otherworldly experience, like some of those holy rollers in Moncks Corner felt in church. When he was in the sky, he felt better and had better feelings about himself. This, he realized, was as good as it was going to get. He said to his passenger, "I do miss combat."

"How can you miss something like that?"

"I don't know...I never felt so good in my life as when I saw those tracers and missiles around me." He added, "Well, maybe if I'd been hit, I wouldn't have felt so good about it. But those stupid bastards couldn't hit the floor with a stream of piss."

"What stupid...people?"

"Oh, let's just say the Arabs. Can't say which ones."

"Why not?"

"Military secret." He laughed. "Not the mission—just who was on the mission."

"Why is that?"

Bill Satherwaite glanced at his passenger, then replied, "It's a policy not to give out the names of pilots involved in a bombing mission. The government thinks these stupid camel jockeys are going to come to America and take revenge. Bullshit. But you know, the captain of the Vincennes—that was a warship in the Gulf that accidentally shot down an Iranian airliner—somebody planted a bomb in the skipper's car, his van—in California, no less. I mean, Jesus, that was scary—almost killed his wife."

Khalil nodded. He was very aware of this incident. The Iranians had shown, with the car bomb, that they did not accept the explanation or the apology. Khalil said, "In war, killing leads to more killing."

"No kidding? Anyway, the government thinks these camel jockeys could be dangerous to their big, brave warriors. Shit, I don't care who knows that I bombed the Arabs. Let them come looking for me. They'll wish they never found me."

"Yes...Do you arm yourself?"

Satherwaite glanced at his passenger and said, "Mrs. Satherwaite didn't raise an idiot."

"Excuse me?"

"I'm armed and dangerous."

Satherwaite continued, as they climbed through seven thousand feet. "But then, during the Gulf War, the stupid government wants good press, so they put these pilots on TV. I mean, Jesus, if they're afraid of the fucking Arabs, why are they parading these fighter pilots in front of TV cameras? I'll tell you why—they wanted big public support back home, so they put these pretty fly-boys on TV to smile and say how great this war is, and how everybody loves doing their fucking duty for God and Country. And for every guy they had on, they had about a hundred broads—I kid you not. Parading the pussy in front of the cameras to show how fucking politically correct the military is. Jesus, if you watched the war on CNN, you'd have thought the whole war was being fought by pussies. I'll bet that went over big with the Iraquis. You know? Thinking they were getting the shit kicked out of them by a bunch of broads." He laughed. "Jesus, I'm glad I'm out of there."

"I see that."

"Yeah. I get worked up. Sorry."

"I share your feeling about women doing the jobs of men."

"Good. We gotta stick together." He laughed again, thinking this guy wasn't so bad, despite the fact he was a foreigner, and maybe a little light in the loafers.

Khalil said, "Why do you have that poster on your wall?"

"To remind me of the time I almost put a bomb up his ass," Bill Satherwaite replied without a thought about security. "Actually, my mission didn't include his house. That was Jim and Paul's mission. They dropped one right on the bastard's house, but Gadhafi was sleeping outside in a tent, for God's sake. Fucking Arabs like their tents. Right? But his daughter got it, which was too bad, but war is war. Fucked up his wife, too, and a couple of his kids, but they lived. Nobody wants to kill women and children, but sometimes they're where they're not supposed to be. You know? I mean, if I was Gadhafi's kid, I'd keep a mile between me and Pop." He laughed.

Khalil took a deep breath and got himself under control. He asked, "And what was *your* mission?"

"I hit the commo center, a fuel depot, a barracks, and…something else. I can't remember. Why do you ask?"

"No reason. I find this fascinating."

"Yeah? Well, forget it all, Mr. Fanini. Like I said, I'm not supposed to talk about it."

"Of course."

They were at their cruise altitude of seventy-five hundred feet. Satherwaite pulled back on the power, and the engines got a little quieter.

Khalil said, "You will call your friend on Long Island?"

"Yeah. Probably."

"He was a military friend?"

"Yeah. He's the Director of an aviation museum now. Maybe if we have time in the morning, I'll shoot over there and check it out. You can come if you want. I'll show you my old F-111. They've got one there."

"That would be interesting."

"Yeah. I haven't seen one of those in lots of years."

"It will bring back memories."

"Yeah."

Khalil stared out at the landscape below. How ironic, he thought, that he'd just come from killing this man's comrade, and now this man was transporting him to where Asad Khalil would kill another of his comrades. He wondered if this man beside him would appreciate the irony.

Asad Khalil sat back and looked into the sky. As the sun began to set, he said his required prayers to himself and added, "God has blessed my Jihad, God has confused my enemies, God has delivered them to me—God is great."

Bill Satherwaite asked, "You say something?"

"I just thanked God for a good day, and asked him to bless my trip to America."

"Yeah? Ask him to do me a couple of favors, too."

"I did. He will."

Chapter 40

As the cab moved away from Federal Plaza, Kate asked me, "Are you coming in this time? Or do you need your sleep?"

This sounded a wee bit like a taunt, perhaps even a challenge to my manhood. The woman was learning what buttons to push. I said, "I'm coming up. You say 'up,' not 'in.'"

"Whatever."

We sat in the taxi in relative silence. Traffic was moderate, a passing April shower made the streets shine, and the taxi driver was from Croatia. I always ask. I'm doing a survey.

Anyway, we got to Kate's apartment house, and I paid the cab, which included the trip from JFK, and waiting time. I also carried her suitcase. There's no such thing as free sex, by the way.

The doorman opened the door, wondering, I'm sure, why Ms. Mayfield left with a suitcase and came back a few hours later with the same suitcase and a man. I hope it bothers him all night.

We went up the elevator and into her apartment on the fourteenth floor.

It was a small, basic white-wall rental, carpetless oak floors, and minimal modern furniture. There were no living plants, no wall art, no sculpture, no knickknacks, and thank God, no sign of a cat. A wall unit was crammed with books, a TV set, and a CD player, whose speakers were on the floor.

There was a sort of open galley kitchen into which Ms. Mayfield entered and opened a cupboard. She said, "Scotch?"

"Please." I put the suitcase and my briefcase down.

She put the Scotch bottle on the breakfast counter between the kitchen and the dining area that had no dining table. I sat on a stool at the breakfast counter, and she put down two glasses with ice and poured. "Soda?"

"No, thanks."

We touched glasses and drank. She poured again and finished another few ounces of Scotch.

She asked me, "Did you have dinner?"

"No. But I'm not hungry."

"Good. But I have some snacks." She opened a cupboard and took out some god-awful stuff—things in big cellophane bags with weird names like Crunch-Os. She ate a handful of orange caterpillars, or whatever.

She poured herself another Scotch, then went over to the CD and put on a disk. It was an old Billie Holiday.

She kicked off her shoes, then took off her suit jacket, revealing a nice white tailored blouse, a holstered Glock, and whatever. Not many people in law enforcement wear the shoulder rig anymore, and I wondered why she did. She threw the jacket on an armchair, then took off her holster and dropped it on the jacket. I waited for her to get even more comfortable, but that was it.

So, not wanting or needing an armed advantage, I took off my jacket and unstrapped my belt holster. She took the holster and jacket from me and put it on top of hers, then sat on the stool beside me. Being very professional, I talked about the advantages of the new federally issued .40 caliber Glock, and how it outperformed the 9mm model, and so forth. "It won't penetrate body armor, but it *will* knock down a man."

She seemed uninterested in this subject and said, "I need to get this apartment squared away."

"It looks fine."

"Do you live in a dump?"

"I used to. But I wound up in the marital residence. It's not bad."

"How'd you meet your wife?"

"Mail order."

She laughed.

"I sent for a cappuccino machine, but I think I wrote the item number wrong, and she showed up, UPS."

"You're weird." She looked at her watch. "I want to catch the eleven o'clock news later. There were three press conferences."

"Right."

She stood and said, "I'll check my answering machine, and tell the ICC I'm home." She looked at me and asked, "Should I say that you're here?"

"That's your call."

"They have to know where you are at all times with this case."

"I know that."

"Well? Are you staying?"

"That's also your call. Surprise me."

"Right." She turned and went through a door that led to her bedroom or office.

I sipped my Scotch, contemplating the length and purpose of my visit. I knew that if I finished my drink and left, then Ms. Mayfield and I would no longer be pals. If I stayed and did the deed, then Ms. Mayfield and I would also no longer be pals. I'd really gotten myself into a corner.

Anyway, she returned and said, "There was just that message from you." She sat down beside me again and stirred her Scotch and ice with her finger. "I called the ICC."

Finally, I asked, "Did you mention that I was here?"

"I did. The duty officer had it on speaker, and I could hear a cheer from the crowd."

I smiled.

She made another drink for herself, then rummaged around the cellophane bags, commenting, "I shouldn't have this junk in the house. I really can cook. But I don't. What do you do for meals at home?"

"I bring home roadkill."

"Do you like living alone?"

"Sometimes."

"I've never lived with anyone."

"Why not?"

"The job, I guess. The hours. Calls at all hours, trips here and there. Reassignments. Plus, you've got guns and classified documents in the house, but I guess that's not a big deal." She said, "The older guys tell me that years ago if a female agent lived with a guy, she was in trouble."

"Probably true."

"I don't think the guys got away with a lot either. The FBI has changed." She said, "You're an older guy. What was life like in the forties?"

I smiled, but that wasn't funny.

Ms. Mayfield had consumed four cocktails, but she seemed lucid enough.

We listened to "I Only Have Eyes for You" awhile and made small talk. She surprised me by saying, "I drink when I'm nervous. Sex always makes me nervous. I mean, first-time sex. Not sex itself. How about you?"

"Yeah...I get a little tense."

"You're not as tough as you act."

"That's my evil twin you're thinking of. James Corey."

"Who's the woman out on Long Island?"

"I told you. A homicide cop."

"Is it serious? I mean, I don't want to put you in an awkward situation."

I didn't reply.

She said, "A lot of the women in the office think you're sexy."

"Really? I've been on my best behavior."

"It doesn't matter what you do or say. It's how you walk and look."

"Am I blushing?"

"A little." She asked me, "Am I being too forward?"

I had a good standard answer to that and said, "No, you're being honest and up-front. I like a woman who can express her interest in a man without any of the hang-ups that society forces on women."

"Bullshit."

"Right. Pass the Scotch."

She took the bottle and walked over to the couch. "Let's watch the news."

I took my glass and sat on the couch. She turned off the CD, found the zapper, and turned on the CBS eleven o'clock news.

The lead story was Trans-Continental Flight 175 and the press conferences. The anchorwoman was saying, "We have some startling new developments regarding the tragedy of Flight One-Seven-Five at Kennedy Airport on Saturday. Today, in a joint press conference, the FBI and the New York City police announced what has been rumored for days—the deaths on board the Trans-Continental flight were the result of a terrorist attack and not an accident. The FBI has a prime suspect in the attack, a Libyan national, named Asad Khalil—" A photo of Khalil came on the screen and stayed there as the anchorlady continued. "This is the photo that we showed you last night and the person we reported was the object of a nationwide and worldwide manhunt. Now we have learned that he is the prime suspect in the Trans-Continental—"

Kate zapped to NBC and the story was basically the same, then she zapped to ABC, then CNN. She kept channel surfing, which when I do it is okay, but when someone else does it, especially a woman, is annoying.

Anyway, we caught the gist of the various news stories, then some tape of the first press conference came on, and Felix Mancuso, head of the New York FBI field office, was giving a few carefully considered details of the incident, followed by the Police Commissioner.

Then Jack Koenig came on and said a few words about the FBI and NYPD coordinating their efforts and so forth, but he didn't mention the Anti-Terrorist Task Force by name.

Koenig did not mention Peter Gorman or Phil Hundry, but he spoke of the deaths of Nick Monti, Nancy Tate, and Meg Collins, whom he identified as Federal law enforcement people, and he didn't mention the Conquistador Club, of course. His brief description of their deaths sounded as if they'd been killed in a shootout with the terrorist as he made his escape.

The tape of the joint FBI/NYPD press conference ended with a barrage of questions from reporters, but everyone of importance seemed to have disappeared, leaving little Alan Parker alone at the podium, looking like a deer caught in the headlights.

The anchorperson then introduced the story of the second press conference at City Hall, and there were snippets of the Mayor, the

Governor, and some other politicians, all of whom vowed to do something, though they were vague about what it was they were going to do. More importantly, they had the opportunity to get on TV.

Next was some videotape from Washington that featured the Director of the FBI and also the Deputy Director in charge of Counterterrorism, whom we'd met at FBI Headquarters. Everyone made a grim, but optimistic statement.

The Deputy Director took the opportunity to announce again the one-million-dollar reward for any information that led to the arrest of Asad Khalil. He didn't even say, "conviction," just arrest. For people in the know, this was unusual, and indicated a high degree of anxiety and desperation.

Anyway, following was a quick scene from the White House where the President made a carefully worded statement that I thought could be used for almost any occasion, including National Library Week.

I noted that the entire story, including long press conferences, had taken about seven minutes, which is a lot of airtime for network news. I mean, I have this funny skit in my head where an anchorguy reads the TelePrompTer in a monotone, and says, "A meteor is headed toward the earth and will destroy the planet on Wednesday," and then he turns to the sportscaster and says, "Hey, Bill, how about those Mets today?"

Perhaps I exaggerate, but here was a story of some importance, about which I had firsthand knowledge, and even I couldn't follow the kaleidoscope of images and sound bites.

But each of the networks promised a special report at eleven-thirty, and these in-depth reports were usually better. The regular news was more like coming attractions.

The bottom line, though, was that the cat was out of the bag, and Asad Khalil's mug was on the airwaves. This should have been done sooner, but better late than never.

Kate shut off the TV with the zapper and turned the CD on with the same zapper. Amazing.

I said, "I want to see tonight's X-Files rerun—this is the one where Mulder and Scully discover that his underwear is an alien life form."

She didn't reply.

The Moment had arrived.

She poured herself another Scotch, and I saw that her hand was actually shaking. She slid across the couch, and I put my arm around her. We sipped Scotch out of the same glass while we listened to sexy Billie Holiday singing "Solitude."

I cleared my throat and said, "Can we just be friends?"

"No. I don't even *like* you."

"Oh..."

Well, we kissed, and little Johnny became Big Bad John in about two seconds.

Before I knew it, all our clothes were scattered on the floor and across the coffee table, and we were lying naked on the couch, face-to-face on our sides.

If the FBI gave out medals for good bodies, Kate Mayfield would get a gold star encrusted with diamonds. I mean, I was too close to *see* her body, but like most men in these up-close, in-the-dark situations, I had developed the sense of touch of a blind person.

My hands ran over her thighs and buttocks, between her legs, and across her belly to her breasts. Her skin was smooth and cool, which I like, and her muscles had obviously all been gym-toned.

My own body, if anyone is interested, can be described as sinewy, but pliable. I once had a washboard tummy, but since I'd caught a slug in my groin area, I'd developed a little flab—sort of like a wet, rolled hand towel on the washboard.

Anyway, Kate's fingers passed over my right butt and stopped at the hard scar on my lower cheek. "What's that?"

"Exit wound."

"Where'd it enter?"

"Lower abdomen."

Her hand went to my groin area, and she searched around until she found the spot about three inches north and east of Mount Willie.

"Oooh...that was close."

"Any closer and we'd just be friends."

She laughed and embraced me in a hug so tight it squeezed the air out of my bad lung. *Jeez*—this woman was strong.

Somewhere in the back of my mind, I was pretty certain that Beth Penrose wouldn't approve of this. I do have a conscience, but Wee Willie Winkie has no conscience whatsoever, so to resolve the conflict, I shut off my main brain and let Willie take over.

We groped, kissed, hugged, and squeezed for about ten minutes. There's something exquisite about exploring a new naked body—the texture of the skin, the curves, the hills and valleys, the taste and the scent of a woman. I enjoy the foreplay, but Willie gets impatient, so I suggested we find the bedroom.

She replied, "No, do it to me here."

No problem. Well…a bit of a problem on the couch, but where there's a Willie, there's a way.

She climbed on top of me and within a heartbeat, we changed the nature of our professional relationship.

I lay on the couch while Kate went to the bathroom. I didn't know what kind of contraceptive she used, but I didn't see any cribs or playpens around the apartment, so I figured she had it under control.

She came back into the living room and turned on the lamp near the couch. She stood looking down at me, and I sat up. I could see her whole body now, and it was indeed exquisite, more full than I'd imagined it on the very few occasions that I'd undressed her in my mind. I also noticed that she was legally blond, top and bottom, but I figured that.

She knelt down in front of me and parted my legs. I noticed she had a wet washcloth in her hand, and she polished the rocket a little, which almost caused another launch. She commented, "Not bad for an old guy. You take Viagra?"

"No, I take saltpeter to keep it down."

She laughed, then bent over and put her face in my lap. I stroked her hair.

She picked her head up, and we held hands. She saw the scar on my chest and touched it, then moved her hand around to my back, and her fingers found the exit wound. "This bullet broke the front and back rib."

I guess FBI ladies know these things. Very clinical. But better than, "Oh, you poor dear, it must have been so painful."

She continued, "Now I can tell Jack where you were wounded." She laughed, then asked me, "Are you hungry?"

"Yes."

"Good. I'll scramble some eggs."

She went into the small kitchen, and I stood, tidying up the strewn clothes.

She called out, "Don't get dressed."

"I just wanted to put your bra and panties on for a minute."

She laughed again.

I watched her in the open kitchen, moving around in the nude, looking like a goddess performing sacred rituals in the temple.

I looked through the stack of CDs and found Willie Nelson, my favorite post-coital music.

Willie sang "Don't Get Around Much Anymore."

She said, "I like that one."

I looked up at the books on her shelves. You can usually tell something about a person by what they read. Most of Kate's books were training manuals, the sort of stuff you really have to read to stay on top of things in this business. There were also a lot of true-crime books, books about the FBI, terrorism, abnormal psychology, and that sort of thing. There were no novels, no classics, no poetry, no books of art or photography. This reinforced my original take on Ms. Mayfield as a dedicated professional, a team player, a lady who never colored outside the lines.

But obviously there was another side to this clean-cut cheerleader, and it wasn't very complicated; she liked men and she liked sex. But why did she like *me?* Maybe she wanted to tweak a few noses among her FBI colleagues by going out with a cop. Maybe she was tired of playing by the unwritten rules and the written directives. Maybe she was just horny. Who knows? A guy could go crazy trying to analyze why he'd been picked as a sexual partner.

The phone rang. Agents are supposed to have a separate line for official calls, but she didn't even look at the wall phone in the kitchen to see what line was lit up. It rang until her answering machine picked up.

I said to her, "Can I do anything?"

"Yes. Go comb your hair and wash the lipstick off your face."

"Right." I entered the bedroom and noticed that the bed was made. Why do women make the bed?

Anyway, the bedroom was as sparse as the living room, and I could have been in a motel room. Clearly Kate Mayfield had not made herself at home in Manhattan.

I went into the bathroom. As neat as the other rooms were, the bathroom looked like someone had been in there with a search warrant. I borrowed a comb from the cluttered vanity and combed my hair, then washed my face and gargled with mouthwash. I looked at myself in the mirror. I had bags under my bloodshot eyes, my skin was a little pale, and the scar on my chest looked white and hairless compared to the rest of my chest. Clearly there were a lot of hard miles on John Corey, and more to come. But my crankshaft was still working, even if my battery was run down.

Not wanting to stay too long in Mademoiselle's private quarters, I went back into the living room.

Kate had laid two plates of scrambled eggs and toast on the coffee table and two glasses of orange juice. I sat on the couch, she knelt on the floor opposite me, and we ate. I really was hungry.

She said, "I've been in New York eight months, and you're the first man I've been with."

"I could tell."

"How about you?"

"I haven't been with a man in years."

"Be serious."

"Well...what can I say? I'm seeing someone. You know that."

"Can we get rid of her?"

I laughed.

"I'm serious, John. I don't mind overlapping for a few weeks, but after that I feel like...you know."

I wasn't sure I did, but I said, "I understand completely."

We looked at each other for a long time. Finally, I realized I had to say something, so I said, "Look, Kate, I think you're just lonely. And busy. I'm not Mr. Right—I'm just Mr. Right Now, so—"

"Bullshit. I'm not *that* lonely or that busy. I have men hitting on me all the time. Your friend, Ted Nash, has asked me out ten times."

"What?" I dropped my fork. "That little turd—"

"He's not little."

"He's a turd."

"No, he isn't."

"That pisses me off. Did you go out with him?"

"Just dinner a few times. Interagency cooperation."

"Damn it, that pisses me off. Why are you laughing?"

She didn't tell me why she was laughing, but I guess I knew why.

I watched her, covering her face with her hand while she was trying to swallow scrambled eggs and laugh at the same time. I said, "If you choke, I don't know the Heimlich maneuver."

This made her laugh more.

Anyway, I changed the subject and asked her something about what she thought of the press conferences.

She answered, but I wasn't paying attention. I thought about Ted Nash, and about how he'd put the moves on Beth Penrose during the Plum Island case. Well, maybe it was mutual and it didn't amount to much anyway, but I have a low tolerance for competition. Somehow, I think Kate Mayfield figured that out, and might actually be using it on me.

Next, I thought of Beth Penrose, and to be honest, I was feeling a bit guilty. Whereas, Kate Mayfield didn't mind a few weeks overlap in regard to sexual involvements, I'm basically monogamous, preferring one headache at a time—except for a weekend in Atlantic City with these two sisters, but that's another story.

So, we sat there awhile, our bodies touching, and I picked at my eggs. I haven't had a meal with a woman in the nude in a long time, and I remembered that I used to really enjoy the experience. There's something about food and nudity, eating and sex, that goes together, if you think about it. It's primitive on the one hand, and very sensuous on the other.

Well, I was on the slippery slope into the abyss of love, companion-ship, and happiness—and you know where that leads. Misery.

But so what? You gotta go for it. I said to Kate, "I'll call Beth in the morning and tell her it's over."

"You don't have to do that. I'll do it for you." She laughed again.

Obviously Kate Mayfield was in a better post-coital mood than I was. I really *was* conflicted, confused, and a little scared. But I'd get it all sorted out in the morning.

She said to me, "Business. Tell me more about the informant."

So I told her again about my interrogation of Fadi Aswad, making me feel less guilty about cutting my workday short for food and sex.

She listened, taking it all in, then asked, "And you don't think he's a plant?"

"No. His brother-in-law is dead."

"Nevertheless, that could all be part of the plan. These people can be ruthless in ways that we can't comprehend."

I thought about that and asked her, "What would be the purpose of trying to make us think that Asad Khalil got to Perth Amboy by taxi?"

"So that we think he's on the road, and we stop looking for him in New York City."

"You're overworking this. If you'd seen Fadi Aswad, you'd know he was telling the truth. Gabe thought so, too, and I trust Gabe's instincts."

She said, "Fadi told the truth about what he knew. That doesn't prove it was Khalil in the taxi. But if it was, then the Frankfurt murder was a red herring and the Perth Amboy murder was the real thing."

"That's it." I rarely have brainstorming sessions in the nude with a colleague of the opposite sex, and it's not as enjoyable as it might seem. But I suppose it's better than a long conference table meeting.

I said, "Well, I saved you from having to spend a few weeks in Europe with Ted Nash."

"That's why I think you made this whole thing up. To get me back here."

I smiled.

She stayed silent a few seconds, then said, "Do you believe in fate?"

I thought about that. My chance encounter with the two Hispanic gentlemen on West 102nd Street a year ago had set off a chain of events that put me on convalescent leave, then to the Anti-Terrorist Task Force, then to here and now. I don't believe in predestination, fate, chance, or luck. I believe that a combination of free will and random chaos controls our destinies, that the world is sort of like a ladies' garment sale at Loehmann's. In any case, you had to be awake and alert at all times, ready and able to exercise your free will amidst an increasingly chaotic and dangerous environment.

"John?"

"No, I don't believe in fate. I don't think we were fated to meet, and I don't think we were fated to make love in your apartment. The meeting was random, the lovemaking was your idea. Great idea, by the way."

"Thank you. It's your turn to chase me."

"I know the rules. I always send flowers."

"Skip the flowers. Just be nice to me in public."

I have a writer friend who is wise in the ways of women, and he once told me, "Men talk to women so they can have sex with them, and women have sex with men so that men will talk to them." This seemed to work out for everyone, but I'm not sure how much talk I need to engage in after sex. With Kate Mayfield, the answer seemed to be, Lots.

"John?"

"Oh . . . well, if I'm nice to you in public, people will talk."

"Good. And the other idiots will stay away."

"What other idiots? Besides Nash?"

"It doesn't matter." She sat back and put her bare feet on the coffee table, stretched, yawned, and wiggled her toes. She said, "God, that felt good."

"I did my best."

"I mean the food."

"Oh." I glanced at the digital clock on the VCR and said, "I should leave."

"Not a chance. I haven't slept overnight with a man in so long I can't remember who ties who up."

I sort of chuckled. The thing about Kate Mayfield that attracted me, I guess, was that in public she looked and acted virginal and wholesome, but here ... well, you get the picture. This turns some men on, and I'm one of them.

I said, "I don't have a toothbrush."

"I have one of those Business Class airline toilet kits for men. It should have everything you need. I've been saving it."

"Which airline? I like the British Airways kit."

"I think it's Air France. There's a condom in it."

"Speaking of which—"

"Trust me. I work for the Federal government."

That may have been the funniest thing I'd heard in months.

She turned on the TV and lay on the couch with her head in my lap. I caressed her breasts, which caused my hydraulic lift to extend, and she craned her neck and head forward and said, "A few inches higher, please," then laughed. Anyway, we watched a lot of news reruns until about 2:00 A.M., plus a few specials on what was now called "The Flight 175 Terrorist Attack." The network news seemed to be trying to leave the name of their major advertiser, Trans-Continental, out of the unpleasantness. In fact, bizarre as it may seem, one of the networks had a Trans-Continental ad showing happy passengers in Coach Class, which is an oxymoron. I think they use midgets to make the seats look bigger. Also, notice how they never use Arab-looking passengers in the ads.

Anyway, regarding the news specials, the talking heads had been rousted from every corner of the planet, and they were babbling on about global terrorism, the history of Mideast terrorism, Libya, Muslim extremists, cyanide gas, autopilots, and on and on.

At about 3:00 A.M., we retired to the bedroom, carrying only our pistols and holsters with us. I said, "I sleep in the nude, but I wear my gun and holster."

She smiled and yawned, then put her shoulder holster on over her bare skin, and if you're into that kind of thing, it looks sexy. She looked in the mirror and said, "That looks weird. I mean, the tits and the gun."

"No comment."

She said to me, "That was my father's holster rig. I didn't want to tell him that shoulder holsters weren't used any longer. I put a new

Glock holster on the rig, and I wear it about once a week, and every time I go home."

I nodded. This told me something nice about Kate Mayfield.

She took off the holster and went to her answering machine on the night table and hit a button. The unmistakable voice of Ted Nash came on, and he said, "Kate, this is Ted—calling from Frankfurt. I've gotten word that you and Corey won't be joining us here. You should reconsider. I think you're both missing an opportunity. I think that taxi driver's murder was a red herring... Anyway, call me... it's after midnight in New York... I thought you'd be home... they said you'd left the office and were going home... Corey's not home, either. Okay, call me here until three or four A.M., your time. I'm at the Frankfurter Hof." He gave the number and said, "Or I'll try you later at the office. Let's talk."

Neither of us said anything, but somehow that guy's voice in Kate Mayfield's bedroom pissed me off, and I guess she sensed this because she said, "I'll talk to him later."

I said, "It's just three—nine there. You can catch him in his room staring at himself in the mirror."

She smiled, but said nothing.

I guess Ted and I had different theories, as usual. I thought the murder in Frankfurt was the red herring. And I was pretty certain that wily old Ted thought that, too, but he wanted me in Germany. Interesting. Well, if Ted says go to Point B, then I stay at Point A. Simple.

Kate was in bed now, motioning me to join her.

So I crawled into the sack, and we snuggled together, arms and legs intertwined. The sheets were cool and crisp, the pillow and mattress were firm, and so was Kate Mayfield. This was better than nodding off in my chair in front of the TV.

The big brain was falling asleep, but the little brain was wide awake, which sometimes happens. She got on top of me and buried the bishop. I totally passed out at some point, and had a very realistic dream about having sex with Kate Mayfield.

Chapter 41

Asad Khalil watched the countryside slip by beneath the aircraft as the old Piper Apache cruised at seventy-five hundred feet through clear skies, heading northeast, toward Long Island.

Bill Satherwaite informed his passenger, "We have a nice tailwind, so we're making good time."

"Excellent." *The tailwind has stolen some time from your life.*

Bill Satherwaite said, "So, as I was saying, this was the longest jet fighter attack mission ever attempted. And the F-111 isn't exactly comfortable."

Khalil sat quietly and listened.

Satherwaite continued, "The fucking French wouldn't let us fly over their country. But the Italians were okay—said we could abort in Sicily if we had to. So, in my book, you guys are okay."

"Thank you."

Norfolk, Virginia, was passing beneath them, and Satherwaite took the opportunity to point out the United States naval facility off the right wing. "Look—there's the fleet—you see those two aircraft carriers in their berths? See them?"

"Yes."

"Navy did a good job for us that night. They didn't see any action, but just knowing they were out there to cover us on our way back from the attack was a big confidence booster."

"Yes, I can understand that."

"But as it turned out, the chickenshit Libyan Air Force didn't follow us out after we'd completed our attack." He added, "Their pilots were probably hiding under their beds, pissing in their drawers." He laughed.

Khalil recalled his own episode of incontinence with shame and anger. He cleared his throat and said, "I seem to remember that one of the American aircraft was shot down by the Libyan Air Force."

"No way. They never got off the ground."

"But you lost an aircraft—correct?"

Satherwaite glanced at his passenger and said, "Yeah, we lost one aircraft, but a lot of us are pretty sure that the guy just screwed up his attack—he got too low and hit the water on his run-in to the beach."

"Perhaps he was shot down by a missile, or by anti-aircraft fire."

Again, Satherwaite glanced at his passenger. He said, "Their air defenses sucked. I mean, they had all this high-tech stuff from the Russkies, but they didn't have the brains or the balls to use it." Satherwaite reconsidered this remark, then added, "But there really *was* a lot of Triple-A and SAMs coming up at us. I had to take evasive action from the SAMs, you know, but with the Triple-A, all you can do is charge on, right through it."

"You were very brave."

"Hey, just doing my job."

"And you were the first aircraft to fly into Al Azziziyah?"

"Yeah. Lead aircraft...hey, did I say Al Azziziyah?"

"Yes, you did."

"Yeah?" Satherwaite didn't recall using that word, which he could hardly pronounce. "Anyway, my wizo—weapons officer—Chip...can't use last names—but he tosses four, scores three directs, and fucks up the last one, but he hit something."

"What did he hit?"

"I don't know. After-action satellite photos showed...maybe some barracks or houses—no secondary explosions, so it wasn't what he was supposed to hit, which was an old Italian munitions storage building. Who cares? He hit something. Hey, do you know how we get a body count? Satellite recon counts arms and legs and divides by four." He laughed.

Asad Khalil felt his heart beating rapidly, and he prayed to God for self-control. He took several deep breaths and closed his eyes. This man, he realized, had killed his family. He saw images of his brothers,

Esam and Qadir, his sisters, Adara and Lina, and his mother, smiling at him from Paradise, enfolding her four children in her arms. She was nodding, and her lips were moving—but he couldn't hear what she was saying, though he knew she was proud of him and was encouraging him to finish the task of avenging their deaths.

He opened his eyes and looked at the blue sky ahead of him. A single brilliant white cloud hung outside at eye level, and somehow he knew this cloud held his family.

He thought, too, of his father, whom he barely remembered, and said silently to him, "Father, I will make you proud."

Then, he thought of Bahira, and it suddenly struck him that this monster sitting next to him had actually been responsible for her death.

Bill Satherwaite said, "I wish I'd had the Gadhafi run. That was Paul's target, the lucky bastard. I mean, we weren't sure that Arab ass-hole would be in that military compound that night, but our G-2 guys thought he was. You're not supposed to assassinate heads of state. Some kind of stupid law—I think that pussy Carter signed the law. Can't try to kill heads of state. Bullshit. You can bomb the shit out of civilians, but you can't kill the boss. But Reagan had a ton more balls than pussy Carter, so Ronnie says, 'Go for it,' and Paul draws the hot ticket. You understand? His wizo was this guy Jim, who lives on Long Island. Paul finds Gadhafi's house, no problem, and Jim puts a big one right on target. Bye, bye house. But fucking Gadhafi is sleeping in a fucking tent out back or someplace—Did I tell you this? Anyway, he escapes with nothing more than shit and piss on himself."

Asad Khalil drew another deep breath and said, "But his daughter was killed, you said."

"Yeah…tough break. But typical of how this fucking world works. Right? I mean, they tried to kill Hitler with a bomb, a bunch of people around him get pureed, and fucking Hitler walks away with a singed mustache. So, what's God thinking? You know? This little girl gets killed, we look bad, and the head scumbag walks away."

Khalil did not reply.

"Hey, the other hot ticket was drawn by another squadron. Did I tell you about that? This other squadron has some targets right in Tripoli, and one of the targets is the French Embassy. Now, nobody ever admitted to that, and it was supposed to be a mistake, but one of our guys plants one right in the backyard of the French Embassy. Didn't want to kill anybody, and it was early A.M., so nobody should be around there, and nobody was. But think about that—we hit Gadhafi's house, and he's in the backyard. Then we hit the backyard of the French Embassy on purpose, but nobody's in the embassy anyway. See my point? What if it had been reversed? Allah was watching over that asshole that night. Makes you wonder."

Khalil felt his hands trembling, and his body began to shake. If they had been on the ground, he would have killed this blasphemous dog with his bare hands. He closed his eyes and prayed.

Satherwaite went on, "I mean, the French are our good buddies, our allies, but they went pussy on us and wouldn't let us fly over their territory, so we showed them that accidents can happen when flight crews have to fly extra hours and get a little tired." Satherwaite laughed hard. "Just an accident. *Excusez moi!*"

He laughed again and added, "Did Ronnie have balls or what? We need another guy like that in the White House. Bush was a fighter pilot. You know that? Got shot down by the Japs in the Pacific. He was an okay guy. Then we get that ball-less wonder from East Chicken Shit, Arkansas—you follow politics?"

Khalil opened his eyes and replied, "As a guest in your country, I do not make comments on American politics."

"Yeah? I guess not. Anyway, the fucking Libyans got what they deserved for bombing that disco."

Khalil stayed silent a moment, then commented, "This was all so long ago, yet you seem to remember it all quite well."

"Yeah...well, it's hard to forget a combat experience."

"I'm certain the people in Libya have not forgotten it either."

Satherwaite laughed. "I'm sure not. You know, the Arabs have long fucking memories. I mean, two years after we unloaded in Libya, they blow Pan Am One-Zero-Three out of the sky."

"As it says in the Hebrew scriptures, 'An eye for an eye, a tooth for a tooth.'"

"Yeah. I'm surprised we didn't get them back for that. Anyway, that wimp Gadhafi finally turned over the guys who planted the bomb. That kind of surprised me. I mean, what's his game?"

"What do you mean?"

"I mean, this scumbag must have a trick up his sleeve. You know? What's in it for him to turn over two of his own people, who he ordered to plant the bomb?"

Khalil replied, "Perhaps he felt great pressure to cooperate with the World Court."

"Yeah? But then what? Then he has to save face with his terror-ist Arab buddies, so he goes and pulls another stunt. You know? Like maybe what happened with that Trans-Continental flight was another Gadhafi stunt. The guy that they suspect is a Libyan. Right?"

"I am not very familiar with this incident."

"Me neither, to tell you the truth. The news sucks."

Khalil added, "But you may be right about this latest act of terrorism being revenge for the Libyans being compelled to surrender these indi-viduals. Or perhaps, the air raid on Libya has not been fully avenged."

"Who knows? Who gives a shit? You try to figure out those rag-heads, you'll go as crazy as them."

Khalil did not reply.

They flew on. Satherwaite seemed to lose interest in conversation and yawned a few times. They followed the coast of New Jersey as the sun sank lower. Khalil could see scattered lights below, and to his front he saw a bright glow on the ocean. He asked, "What is that?"

"Where? Oh...that's Atlantic City coming up. I've been there once. Great place if you like wine, women, and song."

Khali recognized this as a reference to a verse by the great Persian poet Omar Khayyafiaam. *A jug of wine, a loaf of bread and thou beside me sing-ing in the wilderness—Oh, wilderness is Paradise enough!* He said, "So, that is Paradise?"

Satherwaite laughed. "Yeah. Or hell. Depends on how the cards are running. You gamble?"

"No, I do not gamble."

"I thought the...the Sicilians were into gambling."

"We encourage others to gamble. The winners of the game are those who do not gamble themselves."

"You got a point there."

Satherwaite banked the aircraft to the right and set a new heading. He said, "We'll go out over the Atlantic and head in straight for Long Island. I'm beginning my descent now, so your ears may pop a little."

Khalil glanced at his watch. It was seven-fifteen, and the sun was barely visible on the western horizon. On the ground below, it was dark. He removed his sunglasses, put them in his breast pocket, and put on his bifocals. He said to his pilot, "I have been thinking of this coincidence that you have a friend on Long Island."

"Yeah?"

"I have a client on Long Island, whose name is also Jim."

"Can't be Jim McCoy."

"Yes, that is the name."

"He's a client of yours? Jim McCoy?"

"This is the man who is the director of an aviation museum?"

"*Yeah!* I'll be damned. How do you know him?"

"He buys cotton canvas from my factory in Sicily. This is a special cotton that is made for oil paintings, but it is excellent for use to cover the frames of the old aircraft in his museum."

"Well, I'll be damned. You sell canvas to Jim?"

"To his museum. I have never met him, but he was very pleased with the quality of my cotton canvas. It is not as heavy as sail canvas, and because it must be stretched over the wooden frames of the ancient aircraft, the lightness is desirable." Khalil tried to recall what else he'd been told in Tripoli, and continued, "And, of course, since it is made for artists, it has the ability to absorb the aircraft paint much better than sail canvas, which in any case is a rarity today, as most sails now are made from synthetic fibers."

"No shit?"

Khalil stayed silent a moment, then asked, "Perhaps we can visit Mr. McCoy this evening?"

Bill Satherwaite thought a moment, then said, "I guess so...I can give him a call..."

"I will not take advantage of your friendship with him and will make no business talk. I want only to see the aircraft on which my canvas has been used."

"Sure. I guess..."

"And, of course, for this favor, I would insist on giving you a small gift... perhaps five hundred dollars."

"Done. I'll call him at his office and see if he's still in."

"If not, perhaps you can call his home and ask for him to meet us at the museum."

"Sure. Jim would do that for me. He wanted to give me a tour anyway."

"Good. There may not be time in the morning." Khalil added, "In any case, I wish to donate two thousand square meters of canvas to the museum, for good publicity, and this will give me an opportunity to present my gift."

"Sure. Hey, what a coincidence. Small world."

"And it gets smaller each year." Khalil smiled to himself. It was not necessary that this pilot facilitate his meeting with former Lieutenant McCoy, but it made things somewhat easier. Khalil had McCoy's home address, and it didn't matter if he killed the man at home with his wife, or if he killed him in his office at the museum. The museum would be better, but only because of the symbolism of the act. The only thing of importance was that he, Asad Khalil, needed to be flying west tonight for the final portion of his business trip to America.

So far, he thought, everything was going as planned. In a day or two, someone in the American Intelligence services would make the connections between these seemingly unconnected deaths. But even if they did, Asad Khalil was prepared to die now, having already accomplished so much: Hambrecht, Waycliff, and Grey. If he could add McCoy, all the better. But if they were waiting for him at the airport, or at the museum, or at the home of McCoy, or at all three places, at least this pig sitting beside him would die. He glanced at his pilot and smiled. *You are dead, Lieutenant Satherwaite, but you don't know it.*

They were still descending toward Long Island, and Khalil could see the coastline ahead. There were many lights along the coast, and

Khalil now saw the tall buildings of New York City to his left. He asked, "We will fly near to Kennedy Airport?"

"No, but you can see it over there on the bay." Satherwaite pointed to a large, lighted expanse near the water. "See it?"

"Yes."

"We're at a thousand feet now, below the Kennedy arrival patterns, so we don't have to deal with that bullshit. Jesus Christ, those FAA Tower guys are assholes."

Khalil made no reply, but he was amazed at how much profanity this man used. His own countrymen used too much profanity, but never would they blaspheme as this godless pig did, using the name of the prophet Jesus in vain. In Libya, he would be whipped for blaspheming a prophet—killed if he used the name of Allah in vain.

Satherwaite glanced at his passenger and said, "So, you're really in the canvas business."

"Yes. What business did you think I was in?"

Satherwaite smiled and replied, "Well, to tell you the truth, I thought maybe you were in the mob business."

"What is that?"

"You know...Mafia."

Asad Khalil smiled. "I am an honest man, a merchant of textiles." He added, "Would a Mafia man ride in such an old aircraft?"

Satherwaite forced a laugh. "I guess not...but I got you here okay— didn't I?"

"We are not yet on the ground."

"We will be. I never killed anybody yet."

"But you did."

"Yeah...but I was paid to kill people. Now I get paid not to kill people." He laughed again and said, "The first one at the scene of a crash is the pilot. Do I look dead?"

Asad Khalil smiled again, but did not reply.

Satherwaite got on the radio and called MacArthur Tower. "Long Island Tower, Apache Six-Four Poppa is ten miles to the south at one thousand feet, VFR, landing at MacArthur." Satherwaite listened to the radioed reply from the Tower, then acknowledged receipt of the landing instructions.

A few minutes later, a large airport appeared to their front, and Satherwaite banked the aircraft and lined it up on Runway Twenty-four.

Khalil could see the main terminal building in the distance to his left, and to his right a group of hangars, near which were parked small aircraft. The airport was surrounded by trees, suburban housing, and highways.

According to his information, this airport was seventy-five kilometers east of Kennedy Airport, and because there were no international flights, the security was not excessive. In any case, he was flying in a private aircraft now and would be flying in a private jet later, and the security at the private end of the airport, as with all American private flying, was non-existent.

In fact, he thought, there was an irony here, and it was this: at least fifteen years before, according to his intelligence briefing, the American government had put commercial airports on a Security Level One status, and that high level of security had never been lifted. Therefore, private aircraft carrying unscreened passengers and crew could no longer taxi to a commercial terminal, as they had been able to do many years ago. Now, private aircraft were required to taxi to the place called General Aviation, where there was no security.

As a consequence, the very people that the Americans were concerned about—saboteurs, drug traffickers, freedom fighters, and lunatics—could fly about the country freely, so long as they flew in private aircraft and landed at private airfields—or as today, the private end of a commercial airport. No one, including this idiot pilot, would question why a passenger who needed to rent a car or take a taxi or was scheduled to fly a commercial aircraft would want to land so far from the main terminal; it simply wasn't allowed.

Asad Khalil murmured a word of thanks to the stupid bureaucrats who had made his mission easier.

The Apache settled smoothly and touched down. Khalil was surprised at how gentle the landing was, considering the apparent mental deterioration of the pilot.

Satherwaite said, "See? You're alive and well."

Khalil made no reply.

Satherwaite rolled out to the end of the runway and exited onto a taxi-way. They proceeded toward the private hangars he had seen from the air.

The sun had set and the airport was dark, except for the lights of the runways and the General Aviation buildings in the distance.

The Apache stopped near the cluster of buildings and hangars, far from the main terminal.

Khalil looked out the dirty Plexiglass for any signs of danger, any trap set for him. He was prepared to pull his pistol and order the pilot to take off again, but there seemed to be only normal activity around the hangars.

Satherwaite taxied up to the parking ramp and cut the engines. He said, "Okay, let's get out of this flying coffin." He laughed.

Both men unbuckled their flight harnesses and retrieved their over-night bags. Khalil unlatched the door and got out on the wing, his right hand in the jacket pocket that held the Glock. At the first sign that some-thing was wrong, he would put a bullet in the head of Bill Satherwaite, regretting only the missed opportunity to discuss with ex-Lieutenant Satherwaite the reason why he was about to die.

Khalil was no longer looking for danger, but was now trying to sense danger. He stood absolutely motionless, like a lion, sniffing the air.

Satherwaite said, "Hey. You okay? Just jump. Your feet are closer to the ground than your eyes. Jump."

Khalil looked around one last time and was satisfied that all was well. He jumped to the ground.

Satherwaite followed, stretched and yawned. He observed, "Nice and cool here." He said to Khalil, "I'll get a ramp attendant to run us over to the terminal. You can stay here."

"I will walk with you."

"Whatever."

They walked toward a nearby hangar and intercepted a ramp agent. Satherwaite said, "Hey, can you get us a ride to the terminal?"

The ramp agent replied, "That white van is heading to the termi-nal now."

"Terrific. Hey, I'll be overnight, leaving mid-morning, maybe later. Can you refuel me and paint the plane?" He laughed.

The ramp agent replied, "That thing needs more than paint, pal. Is your parking brake off?"

"Yeah."

"I'll tow it to a tie-down spot and refuel it there."

"All six tanks. Thanks."

Khalil and Satherwaite hurried over to the van. Satherwaite spoke to the driver, and they got in the rear. In the middle seats were a young man and an attractive blond woman.

Asad Khalil was not comfortable with this arrangement, but he knew from his training that he never would have gotten as far as the van if this were a trap. Still, he kept his hand in his pocket with his Glock.

The driver put the van in gear and began moving. Khalil could see the main terminal lit up about a kilometer away across the flat terrain.

They exited the airport, and Khalil asked the driver, "Where are you going?"

The driver replied, "The General Aviation and commercial end of the airport are separate. You can't cut across."

Khalil didn't reply.

No one spoke for a while, but then Satherwaite said to the couple in front of him, "You guys just fly in?"

The man turned his head and looked first at Khalil. Their eyes met, but in the darkness of the van, Khalil knew his features were not visible.

The man looked at Satherwaite and replied, "Yes, just got in from Atlantic City."

Satherwaite asked, "You get lucky?" He nodded toward the blonde, winked and smiled.

The man forced a smile in return and replied, "Luck has nothing to do with it." He turned back toward the front, and they continued in silence along a dark road.

The van re-entered the airport and pulled up to the main terminal. The young couple got out and walked toward the taxi stand.

Khalil said to the driver, "Excuse me, but I see that I have an automobile rental with Hertz, and it is Gold Card Service. So, I believe I can go directly to the Hertz parking."

"Yeah. Okay." The driver moved off and within a minute was in the small exclusive area reserved for Hertz Gold Card customers.

There were twenty numbered parking places beneath a long, illuminated metal canopy, and at each space was a name in lights. One of the light signs said BADR, and he walked toward it.

Satherwaite followed.

They got to the automobile, a black Lincoln Town Car, and Khalil opened the rear door and placed his bag on the seat.

Satherwaite said, "Is this your rental?"

"Yes. B-A-D-R is the company name."

"Oh...don't have to sign some papers or something?"

"It is a special service. It avoids long queues at the rental counter."

"Long what?"

"Lines. Please get in."

Satherwaite shrugged, opened the front passenger door, and slid in, throwing his overnight bag into the rear seat.

The keys were in the ignition, and Khalil started the car and turned on the headlights. He said to Satherwaite, "Please retrieve the papers from the glove box."

Satherwaite opened the compartment and took out the papers as Khalil drove toward the exit.

A woman at the exit booth opened her window and said, "May I see your rental agreement and driver's license, sir?"

Khalil took the rental papers from Satherwaite and handed them to the woman, who glanced at them. She peeled off one of the copies, and Khalil then handed her his Egyptian driver's license and his international driver's license. She studied them for a few seconds, took a quick look at Khalil, then handed them back with his copy of the rental papers. "Okay."

Khalil pulled out onto a main road and turned right as he'd been told to do. He put his driver's license in his breast pocket along with the rental agreement.

Satherwaite said, "That was pretty easy. So that's how the big shots do it."

"Excuse me?"

"Are you rich?"

"My company."

"That's good. You don't have to talk to some snotty bitch at the rental counter."

"Precisely."

"How far's the motel?"

"I thought perhaps we would telephone Mr. McCoy before we go to the motel. It is nearly eight P.M. already."

"Yeah…" Satherwaite glanced at the mobile phone on the console. "Yeah, why not?"

Khalil had noted the mobile phone unlock code on the rental paper and repeated it to Satherwaite. "Do you have your friend's telephone number?"

"Yeah."

Satherwaite took Jim McCoy's Rolodex card out of his pocket and turned on the courtesy light.

Before Satherwaite dialed, Khalil said, "Perhaps you should describe me only as a friend. I will introduce myself when we arrive." He added, "Please tell Mr. McCoy that your time here is short, and that you would very much like to see the museum tonight. If necessary, we can go to his home first. This vehicle has a Satellite Navigator, as you can see, and we need no directions to his home or to the museum. Please leave the telephone speaker on."

Satherwaite glanced at his driver, then at the global positioning display on the dashboard. He said, "Gotcha." He dialed the unlock code, then dialed Jim McCoy's home number.

Khalil heard the phone ringing over the speaker. On the third ring, a woman's voice answered, "Hello."

"Betty, this is Bill Satherwaite."

"Oh…hello, Bill. How are you?"

"I'm great. How are the kids?"

"Fine."

"Hey, is Jim there?" Before she could reply, Bill Satherwaite, who was used to people not being in for him, added quickly, "I have to speak to him for a minute. Kind of important."

"Oh...okay, let me see if he's off his other call."

"Thanks. I have a surprise for him. Tell him that."

"Just a moment."

The telephone went on hold.

Khalil understood the subtext of this conversation, and wanted to congratulate Mr. Satherwaite for using the correct words, but he just drove and smiled.

They were on an expressway now, heading west, toward Nassau County where the museum was located, and where Jim McCoy lived, and where he would die.

A voice came over the speaker. "Hey, Bill. What's up?"

Satherwaite smiled wide and said, "You're not going to believe this. Guess where I am?"

There was a silence on the phone, then Jim McCoy asked, "Where?"

"I just landed at MacArthur. Remember that Philly charter? Well, the guy had a change of plans, and I'm here."

"Great..."

"Jim, I have to fly out first thing tomorrow, so I thought maybe I could stop by the house, or maybe meet you at the museum."

"Well...I have—"

"Just for half an hour or so. We're on the road now. I'm calling from the car. I really want to see the F-111. We can pick you up."

"Who's with you?"

"Just a friend. A guy who flew up with me from South Carolina. He really wants to see some of the old stuff. We got a surprise for you. We won't keep you long, if you're busy." He added, "I know this is last-minute, but you said—"

"Yeah...okay, why don't we meet at the museum? Can you find it?"

"Yeah. We got GPS in the car."

"Where are you?"

Satherwaite glanced at Khalil, who said into the remote microphone, "We are on Interstate Four ninety-five, sir. We have just passed the exit for the Veterans Memorial Highway."

McCoy said, "Okay, you're on the Long Island Expressway, and you're about thirty minutes away with no traffic. I'll meet you at the main entrance to the museum. Look for a big fountain. Give me your cell phone number."

Satherwaite read the number off the telephone.

McCoy said, "If we somehow miss, I'll call you, or you call me. Here's my cell phone number." He gave his number and asked, "What are you driving?"

Satherwaite replied, "A big black Lincoln."

"Okay...Maybe I'll have a guard meet you at the entrance." He added in a lighter tone, "Rendezvous time, approximately twenty-one hundred hours, rendezvous point as instructed, commo established between all craft. See you later, Karma Five-Seven. Over."

"Roger, Elton Three-Eight. Out," said Satherwaite with a big grin. He pressed End and looked at Khalil. "No problem." He added, "Wait until you offer him two thousand yards of canvas for free. He'll buy us a drink."

"Meters."

"Right."

A few minutes passed in silence, then Bill Satherwaite said, "Uh... no rush, but I might go out later, and I could use a little extra cash."

"Oh, yes. Of course." Khalil reached into his breast pocket, extracted his billfold, and handed it to Satherwaite. "Take five hundred dollars."

"It might be better if you counted it."

"I am driving. I trust you."

Satherwaite shrugged, turned on the courtesy light, and opened the billfold. He took out a wad of bills and counted out five hundred dollars, or five hundred twenty; he couldn't be sure in the bad light. He said, "Hey, this leaves you about tapped out."

"I will go to a cash machine later."

Satherwaite handed Khalil his billfold and said, "You sure?"

"I am sure." He put the billfold back in his pocket as Satherwaite put the money in his wallet.

They drove west on the Expressway, and Khalil programmed the Satellite Navigator for the Cradle of Aviation Museum.

Within twenty minutes, they exited onto a southbound parkway, then got off the parkway at Exit M4, which said CRADLE OF AVIATION MUSEUM.

They followed the signs to Charles Lindbergh Boulevard, then turned right into a wide, tree-lined entrance drive. Ahead was a blue-and red-lighted fountain, beyond which was a massive glass and steel structure with a dome rising up behind it.

Khalil steered around the fountain and drove toward the main entrance.

A uniformed guard stood outside. Khalil stopped the car, and the guard said, "You can leave it right here."

Khalil shut off the ignition and exited the Lincoln. He retrieved his black bag from the rear.

Satherwaite, too, exited, but left his overnight bag in the Lincoln.

Khalil locked the car with the remote switch, and the guard said, "Welcome to the Cradle of Aviation Museum." He looked at Khalil and at Satherwaite. He said, "Mr. McCoy is waiting for you in his office. I'll take you in." He said to Khalil, "Do you need that bag, sir?"

"Yes, I have a gift for Mr. McCoy, and a camera."

"Fine."

Satherwaite looked around at the huge complex. To the right, attached to the modern building in front of them, were two vintage 1930s hangars, restored and repainted. "Hey, look at that."

The guard said, "This is the old Mitchel Army Air Force Base, which served as a training and air defense base from the thirties through the middle-sixties. These hangars have been left in place and restored to their original condition, and they hold most of our vintage aircraft. This new building in front of us houses the Visitor Center and the Grumman Imax Dome Theater. To the left is the Museum of Science and Technology and the TekSpace Astronautics Hall. Please follow me."

Khalil and Satherwaite followed the guard to the entrance doors. Khalil noted that the guard was unarmed.

They entered the building, which held a four-story-high atrium, and the guard said, "This is the Visitor Center, which, as you can see, has exhibit space, a museum shop over there, and the Red Planet Café right ahead."

Khalil and Satherwaite looked around the soaring atrium as the guard continued, "There's a Gyrodyne Rotorcycle, an experimental one-man Marine helicopter, vintage nineteen fifty-nine, and there's a Merlin hang glider, and a Veligdons sailplane built here on Long Island in nineteen eighty-one."

The guard continued his guided tour as they walked through the vast space. Their footsteps echoed off the granite floor. Khalil noted that most of the lighting was turned on, and he commented, "We are your only guests this evening?"

"Yes, sir. In fact, the museum is not officially opened yet, but we take small groups of potential donors through, plus we have a reception now and then for the fat cats." He laughed and added, "We'll be open in about six or eight months."

Satherwaite said, "So, we're getting a private tour."

"Yes, sir."

Satherwaite glanced at Khalil and winked.

They continued on and passed through a door that said PRIVATE— STAFF ONLY.

Beyond the door was a corridor, off which were office doors. The guard stopped at a door marked DIRECTOR, knocked, and opened the door. He said, "Have a good visit."

Satherwaite and Khalil stepped into a small reception area. Jim McCoy was sitting at the receptionist's desk, looking through some papers, which he put down. He stood and came around the desk, smiling, his hand extended. He said, "Bill, how the hell are you?"

"I'm fucking terrific."

Bill Satherwaite took his squadron mate's hand, and they stood looking at each other, smiling.

Khalil watched as the two men seemed to be attempting great joy.

Khalil noticed that McCoy did not look as fit as General Waycliff or Lieutenant Grey, but he looked much better than Satherwaite. McCoy, he noticed, was dressed in a suit, which highlighted the contrast between him and Satherwaite.

The two men spoke briefly, then Satherwaite turned and said, "Jim, this is...my passenger...Mr...."

"Fanini," said Asad Khalil. "Alessandro Fanini." He extended his hand, which Jim McCoy took. Khalil said, "I am a manufacturer of canvas cloth." He looked at Jim McCoy, and they made eye contact, but McCoy showed no sign of alarm. Yet, Khalil saw an intelligence in the man's eyes and realized that this man would not be nearly as stupid and trusting as Satherwaite.

Satherwaite said, "Mr. Fanini's company sold—"

Khalil interrupted and said, "My company supplies canvas for ancient aircraft. In gratitude for this private tour, I would like to send to you two thousand meters of fine cotton canvas." He added, "There is no obligation on your part."

Jim McCoy stayed silent a moment, then replied, "That's very generous of you...we accept all donations."

Khalil smiled and bowed his head.

Satherwaite said to Khalil, "Didn't you say—?"

Again Khalil interrupted and said, "Perhaps I can see some of the ancient aircraft and examine the quality of the canvas you are using. If it is better than mine, then I apologize for offering you my inferior cloth."

Satherwaite thought he understood that Mr. Fanini wanted him to shut his mouth for some reason. Jim McCoy thought he saw a sales pitch coming.

Jim McCoy said to Khalil, "Our vintage aircraft are not meant to leave the ground, so we tend to use a heavy-duty canvas."

"I see. Well, then I will ship to you our heaviest grade."

Satherwaite thought that this information seemed to be at odds with what Mr. Fanini had told him earlier, but he said nothing.

They made small talk for a few seconds. McCoy seemed a little put off by the fact that Bill Satherwaite had dragged along a stranger to their reunion. But, McCoy thought, this was typical Bill—totally clueless, completely without forethought or social skills. He smiled despite the situation and said, "Let's go see some flying machines." He said to Khalil, "You can leave that bag here."

"If you don't mind, I have a photographic camera as well as a video camera."

"Fine." McCoy led the way out into the corridor, back through the atrium and through a set of big doors that led to the hangars.

On the floor of the adjoining hangars were over fifty aircraft from various periods of history, including both world wars, the Korean Conflict, as well as modern jet fighters. Jim McCoy said, "Most, but not all, of these aircraft were made here on Long Island, including some Grumman Lunar Landing modules in the next hangar. All the restorations that you will see were accomplished with volunteer labor—men and women who worked in the aerospace industry here on Long Island, or in commercial or military aviation, who have put in thousands of hours of time in exchange for coffee, donuts, and their names on the wall in the atrium."

McCoy went on in a tone that betrayed the fact that this was a short tour. He said, "Hanging up there, as you can see, is a Ryan NYP, which was the original sistership of the Spirit of St. Louis, so we've taken the liberty of putting that name on the fuselage."

They walked as McCoy talked, bypassing many aircraft, which again revealed that this was not the tour that the major benefactors got. McCoy stopped in front of an old, yellow-painted biplane and said, "This is a Curtiss JN-4, called a Jenny, built in nineteen eighteen. This was Lindbergh's first aircraft."

Asad Khalil took his camera out of his bag and shot a few perfunctory photos. McCoy looked at Khalil and said, "You can feel the canvas if you wish."

Khalil touched the stiff, painted canvas and remarked, "Yes, I see what you mean. This is too heavy for flight. I will remember that when I send you my donation."

"Good. And over here is a Sperry Messenger, an Air Corps scout plane built in nineteen twenty-two, and there, in the far corner, are a bunch of Grumman World War Two fighters—the F4F Wildcat, F6F Hellcat, TBM Avenger—"

Khalil interrupted. "Excuse me, Mr. McCoy. I sense that time is short for all of us, and I am aware that Mr. Satherwaite would like to see his former fighter aircraft."

McCoy looked at his guest, nodded and said, "Good idea. Follow me."

They walked through a large opening into the second hangar, which held mostly jet aircraft as well as space exploration craft.

Khalil was amazed at all the artifacts of war gathered here. The Americans, he knew, liked to present themselves to the world as a peace-loving people. But it was clear, in this museum, that the art of war was the highest expression of their culture. Khalil did not fault them or judge them harshly regarding this; in fact, he was envious.

McCoy walked directly to the F-III, a shining silver, twin-engine aircraft with American Air Force insignia. The F-III's variable wings were in a swept-back position, and on the fuselage, under the pilot's side, was the name of the aircraft—*The Bouncing Betty*.

Jim McCoy said to Bill Satherwaite, "Well, here it is, buddy. Bring back any memories?"

Satherwaite stared at the sleek jet fighter, as if it were an angel, beckoning him to take her hand and fly.

No one spoke as Bill Satherwaite continued to stare, mesmerized by the vision of his past. Bill Satherwaite's eyes misted.

Jim McCoy was smiling. He said softly, "I named it after my wife."

Asad Khalil stared, recalling memories of his own.

Finally, Satherwaite approached the aircraft and touched its fuselage. He walked around the fighter, his fingers caressing the aluminum skin, his eyes taking in every detail of its perfect, sleek body.

He completed his walk-around, looked at McCoy and said, "We flew these, Jim. We actually flew these."

"Indeed, we did. A million years ago."

Asad Khalil turned away, giving the impression he was sensitive to this moment between old warriors, but in fact, he was sensitive only to his own moment, as their victim.

He heard the two men talking behind him, heard them laughing, heard words that brought joy to them. He closed his eyes and a memory of the blur coming toward him now took shape in his mind, and he could see this terrible war machine clearly, belching red fire from its tail like a demon from hell. He tried to block the memory of himself urinating in his trousers, but the memory was too strong, and he let it overtake him, knowing that this humiliation was about to be avenged.

He heard Satherwaite calling to him, and he turned around.

There was a rolling aluminum platform with a staircase beside the pilot's side of the fuselage now, and Satherwaite said to Asad Khalil, "Hey, can you shoot us in the cockpit?"

This was exactly what Khalil had in mind. Khalil said, "My pleasure."

Jim McCoy went first and climbed the staircase. The cockpit canopy was lifted, and McCoy lowered himself into the weapons officer's seat on the right. Satherwaite scrambled up the staircase, jumped into the pilot's seat, and let out a loud whooping sound. "Yoooweeey! Back in the saddle again. Let's kill some ragheads! Yeah!"

McCoy glanced at him disapprovingly, but said nothing to spoil his friend's moment.

Asad Khalil climbed the staircase.

Satherwaite said to McCoy, "Okay, wizo, we're off to Sandland. Hey, I wish you were with me that day instead of Chip. Fucking Chip can talk the balls off a brass bull." Satherwaite played with the controls, making mock engine noises. "Fire one, fire two." He smiled broadly. "Hell, I can remember the start-up drills as if we did them yesterday." He ran his hands across the cockpit controls, nodding in recognition. "I bet I could do the whole pre-take-off checklist from memory."

"I'll bet you could," McCoy said, indulging his friend.

Satherwaite said, "Okay, wizo, I want you to put one in that tent where Moammar is inside fucking a camel." He let out a loud laugh and made more engine noises.

Jim McCoy looked at Mr. Fanini, who stood on the platform at the top of the stairs. He forced a weak smile at his guest, wishing again that Satherwaite had come alone.

Asad Khalil raised his camera. He aimed it at the two men in the cockpit, and he said, "Are you ready?"

Satherwaite grinned into the camera. The flash went off. McCoy tried to keep a neutral expression as the flash went off again. Satherwaite raised his left hand and extended his middle finger as the flash went off yet again. McCoy said, "Okay—" The flash went off again. Satherwaite gripped McCoy's head playfully in an armlock and the flash went off once more. McCoy said, "Okay—" The flash went off again, then again. McCoy said, "Hey, that's enough—"

Asad Khalil dropped the camera into his black bag, and extracted the plastic bottle that he'd taken from the Sheraton. He said, "Just two more shots, gentlemen."

McCoy blinked to clear the flash from his eyes and looked at his guest. He blinked again and noticed the water bottle, which did not alarm him, but he also noticed a strange expression on Mr. Fanini's face. In an instant, he realized that something was terribly wrong.

Asad Khalil said, "So, gentlemen, you are having happy memories of your bombing mission?"

McCoy did not reply.

Satherwaite said, "This is a fucking gas. Hey, Mr. Fanini, crawl onto the nose and get a shot of us from the front."

Khalil did not move.

Jim McCoy said, "Okay, let's get out of here. Come on, Bill."

Khalil said, "Stay where you are."

McCoy stared at Asad Khalil, and his mouth suddenly went dry. Somewhere in the deepest recesses of his mind, he knew this day would come. Now, it was here.

Satherwaite said to Khalil, "Roll the stairs around and take some shots from the other side. Get a few standing on the ground, too, then—"

"Shut up."

"Huh?"

"Shut your mouth."

"Hey, who the fuck—" Satherwaite found himself staring into the muzzle of a pistol, held close to his customer's body.

McCoy said softly, "Oh, God...oh, no—"

Khalil smiled and said, "So, Mr. McCoy, you have already guessed that I am not a maker of canvas. Perhaps I am a maker of shrouds."

"Oh, mother of God..."

Bill Satherwaite seemed confused. He looked at McCoy, then at Khalil, trying to figure out what they knew that he didn't know. "What's going on?"

"Bill, shut up." McCoy said to Khalil, "This place is full of armed guards and security cameras. I suggest you leave now, and I won't—"

"Quiet! I will do the talking, and I promise I will be brief. I have another appointment, and this will not take long."

McCoy did not reply.

For once, Bill Satherwaite did not say anything, but a glimmer of understanding began to penetrate his mind.

Asad Khalil said, "On April fifteen, nineteen eighty-six, I was a young boy living with my family in the place called Al Azziziyah, a place that both of you know."

Satherwaite said, "You lived there? In Libya?"

"Silence!" Khalil continued, "Both of you flew into my country, dropped bombs on my people, killed my family—my two brothers and two sisters and my mother—then went back to England, where I presume you celebrated your murders. Now, you are both going to pay for your crimes."

Satherwaite finally realized that he was going to die. He looked at Jim McCoy sitting beside him and said, "Sorry, buddy—"

"Shut up." Khalil continued, "First of all, thank you for inviting me to this little reunion. Also, I want you to know that I have already killed Colonel Hambrecht, General Waycliff and his wife—"

McCoy said softly, "You bastard."

"—Paul Grey, and now both of you. Next...well, I must decide if I should waste a bullet on Colonel Callum and end his suffering. Next is Mr. Wiggins and then—"

Bill Satherwaite extended his middle finger toward Khalil and shouted, "Fuck you, raghead! Fuck you, fuck that camel-fucking boss of yours, fuck—"

Khalil put the neck of the plastic bottle over the muzzle of the Glock and fired a single shot at close range into Bill Satherwaite's forehead. The muffled shot echoed in the cavernous hangar as Satherwaite's head snapped back in a splash of blood and bone, then fell forward on his chest.

Jim McCoy sat frozen in his seat, then his lips started to move in prayer. He bowed his head, praying, then made the sign of the cross, and continued to pray through trembling lips.

"Look at me."

McCoy continued to pray, and Khalil heard the words, "...the valley of the shadow of death, I will fear no evil—"

"My favorite Hebrew psalm. For thou art with me—"

They finished the psalm together, "Thy rod and thy staff they comfort me. Thou preparest a table before me in the presence of mine enemies; thou anointest my head with oil; my cup runneth over. Surely goodness and mercy shall follow me all the days of my life; and I will dwell in the house of the Lord forever."

When they were finished, Asad Khalil said, "Amen," and fired a round through Jim McCoy's heart. He watched him die, and their eyes met, before Jim McCoy's eyes stopped seeing anything.

Khalil pocketed the pistol, put the plastic bottle back in his bag, and reached inside the cockpit, finding Satherwaite's wallet in the hip pocket of his jeans, and McCoy's wallet, covered with blood, in the breast pocket of his suit jacket. He put both wallets in his bag and wiped his fingers on Satherwaite's T-shirt. He felt around Satherwaite's body, but found no weapon and concluded that the man lied too much.

Khalil reached up and pulled down the Plexiglass canopy. "Good night, gentlemen. May you already be in hell, with your friends."

He came down from the staircase and gathered his two shell casings, then rolled the staircase away, near another aircraft.

Asad Khalil held his Glock in his jacket pocket, and walked quickly out of the hangar and back into the atrium. He didn't see the guard in the huge expanse, and did not see him outside through the glass doors.

He walked into the office area and heard a sound coming from behind a closed door. He opened the door and saw the guard sitting at a desk, listening to a radio, and reading a magazine called *Flying*. Behind the guard, fifteen numbered television monitors showed scenes of the vast museum complex, interior and exterior.

The guard looked up at his visitor and said, "You guys done?"

Khalil closed the door behind him, fired a bullet through the guard's head, then walked to the monitors as the guard fell off his chair.

Khalil scanned the monitors until he saw the one that showed images of the hangar with the modern jet aircraft. He saw changing scenes of the exhibition space, recognizing the rolling staircase, then the F-111 with its canopy down. He also saw images of the theater, the exterior doorways where his car was parked, and various images of the atrium lobby. No one else seemed to be in the building.

He found the video recorders stacked on a countertop and pushed the Stop button of each one, then extracted all fifteen tapes and put them in his bag. He knelt beside the guard, removed the dead man's wallet, found his shell casing, then left the security office and closed the door behind him.

Khalil walked quickly back through the atrium, and exited one of the front doors. He pulled on the door behind him and noted with pleasure that it was locked.

Khalil got into his rental car and drove off. He looked at the dashboard clock. It was 10:57 P.M.

He set his Satellite Navigator for Long Island MacArthur Airport, and within ten minutes was on the parkway heading north toward the Long Island Expressway.

He dwelt a moment on the last minutes in the lives of Mr. Satherwaite and Mr. McCoy. It occurred to him that one could never anticipate how a man was going to die. He found that interesting, and wondered how he would act in a similar situation. Satherwaite's final arrogance had surprised him, and it occurred to Khalil that the man had found some courage in the last few seconds of his life. Or perhaps the man had so much evil in him that those last words were not courage at all—but pure hate. Asad Khalil realized that he himself would probably act as Satherwaite had in a similar situation.

Khalil thought of McCoy. This man had reacted in a predictable way, assuming he was a religious man. Or he had quickly found God in the last minute of his life. One never knew. In any case, Khalil appreciated the man's choice of psalms.

Khalil swung off the parkway into the eastbound Long Island Expressway. There was not much traffic, and he kept up with the other vehicles, noting his speed on the speedometer's metric scale at ninety kilometers per hour.

He knew full well that his time was running out—that these double murders would attract much attention.

The appearance of a robbery was very suspect, he knew, and sometime this evening, Mrs. McCoy would call the police and report her husband was missing and that no one answered the telephone at the museum.

Her story of Mr. McCoy meeting an Air Force comrade would cause the police to worry far less than Mrs. McCoy was worrying. But at some point, the corpses would be discovered. It would be some time before the police thought to go to the airport to see about the aircraft that Satherwaite arrived in. In fact, if McCoy never mentioned his friend's method of arrival to his wife, it would never occur to the police to go to the airport at all.

In any case, no matter what Mrs. McCoy or the police did, Asad Khalil had time for his next act of vengeance.

Yet, as he drove, he felt, for the first time, the presence of danger, and he knew that somewhere, someone was stalking him. He was certain that his stalker did not know where he was, nor did his stalker completely comprehend his intentions. But Asad Khalil sensed that he, the Lion, was now being hunted, and that the unknown hunter understood, at the very least, the nature and substance of what he was hunting.

Khalil tried to conjure an image of this person—not his physical image, but his soul—but he could not penetrate this man's being, except for the strong force of danger that the man radiated.

Asad Khalil came out of his trance-like state. He reflected, now, on his trail of corpses. General Waycliff and his wife would have been found no later than late Monday morning. At some point, a member of the Waycliff family would attempt to contact the deceased General's old squadron mates. In fact, Khalil was surprised that by now, Monday evening, no one had telephoned McCoy. A telephone call to Paul Grey would not have found him able to come to the phone, nor would a call to Mr. Satherwaite be answered. But Khalil had the feeling that Mrs. McCoy, aside from her worry about her husband, might be given the additional worry, tonight or tomorrow, of a call from the Waycliff family or the Grey family, with the tragic news of the murders.

Soon, by tomorrow, he guessed, there would be many telephone calls, answered and unanswered. By tomorrow evening, his game would be drawing to a close. Perhaps sooner, perhaps later, if God was still with him.

Khalil saw a sign that said REST STOP, and he pulled off into a parking lot hidden from the road by trees. There were a few trucks parked in the big lot, as well as a few cars, but he parked away from them.

He retrieved Satherwaite's Air Force overnight bag from the rear seat, and examined the contents, finding a liquor bottle, some underwear, prophylactics, toiletries, and a T-shirt, which depicted a jet fighter and the words NUKES, NAPALM, BOMBS, AND ROCKETS—FREE DELIVERY.

Khalil took Satherwaite's bag and his own bag and walked into the woods behind the rest rooms. He retrieved all his money from Satherwaite's wallet, and the money from McCoy's wallet, which amounted to eighty-five dollars, and the guard's wallet, which contained less than twenty dollars, and put the bills in his wallet.

Khalil scattered the contents of all three wallets in the undergrowth, and threw the wallets into the woods. He also scattered the contents of Satherwaite's overnight bag, then flung the bag into a thicket of bushes. Finally, he removed the security videotapes from his overnight bag and threw them in different directions into the woods.

Khalil made his way back to his car, got in, and drove back onto the Expressway.

As he drove, he dropped the three .40 caliber shell casings onto the highway at intervals.

They had told him in Tripoli, "Do not waste too much time erasing fingerprints or worrying about other scientific evidence of your visits. By the time the police process all of this, you will be gone. But do not get caught with any evidence on your person. Even the most stupid policeman will become suspicious if he finds another man's wallet in your pocket."

Of course, there was the matter of the two Glocks, but Khalil did not consider that evidence—he considered the pistols as the last thing a policeman would see before he saw nothing at all. Still, it was good to divest himself of the other things, and to leave the automobile without obvious evidence in it.

He continued on, and his thoughts returned to home, to Malik, and Boris. He knew, as did Malik and Boris, that he could not play this game for very long. Malik had said to him, "It is not the game itself, my friend, it is how you choose to play it. You have chosen to have the Americans in Paris lay their hands on you, to make a grand entrance into America, to have them know who you are, what you look like, where and when you arrived. You yourself, Asad, have invented the rules of the game and made those rules more difficult for yourself. I understand why you do this, but you must understand that the odds are against you completing this mission, and you have only yourself to blame if you fall short of winning a complete victory."

To which Khalil recalled saying, "The Americans never go into battle unless they've done all they can to assure victory before the first shot is fired. This is like shooting a lion from a vehicle with a telescopic sight. It is not victory at all—only slaughter. There are tribesmen in Africa who have guns, but who still hunt the lion with spears. What good is a physical victory without a spiritual or moral victory? I have not made the odds go against me—I have simply made the odds even, so that no matter who wins this game, I am the winner."

Boris, who was present, commented, "Tell me that when you're rotting in an American jail, and all your American Air Force demons are leading happy lives."

Khalil recalled turning to Boris and saying, "I don't expect you to understand."

Boris had laughed and replied, "I understand, Mr. Lion. I understand quite well. And for your information, I don't care if you kill those pilots or not. But you'd better be sure you don't care either. If the hunt is more important than the kill, then take pictures of them as the sensitive Americans do on safari. But if you want to taste their blood, Mr. Lion, then you'd better think of another way to go to America."

In the end, Asad Khalil had examined his heart and his soul, and had come to the conclusion that he could have it both ways—his game, his rules, their blood.

Asad Khalil saw the sign for MacArthur Airport and drove onto the exit ramp.

Within ten minutes, he pulled the Lincoln into the long-term parking lot of the airport.

He exited and locked the car, taking his bag with him.

He did not bother wiping fingerprints from the car—if the game was up, it was up. He intended to do no more than the bare minimum to cover his tracks. He only needed another twenty-four hours, perhaps less, and if the police were even two steps behind him, they were one step too late.

He went to a bus shelter, and within a short time a minivan arrived and he got in. He said, "The main terminal, please."

The driver replied, "There's only one terminal, buddy, and you got it."

Within a few minutes, the van discharged him at the entrance to the nearly deserted terminal. Khalil walked to the taxi stand where a solitary taxi sat and said to the driver, "I need only to go to the General Aviation side of the airport. But I am prepared to pay you twenty dollars for your assistance."

"Jump in, sport."

Khalil got in the rear of the taxi and within ten minutes was at the far end of the airport. The driver asked, "Any place in particular?"

"That building there."

The driver pulled up in front of a small building that held the offices of several aviation services. Khalil gave the man a twenty-dollar bill and got out.

He was less than fifty meters from where he'd landed, and in fact, he saw Satherwaite's aircraft parked not far away.

He walked into the small building and found the office of Stewart Aviation.

A male clerk behind the counter stood and said, "Help you?"

"Yes, my name is Samuel Perleman, and I believe you have an aircraft reserved for me."

"Right. Midnight flight." The clerk looked at his watch. "You're a little early, but I think they're ready."

"Thank you." Khalil watched the young man's face, but saw no sign of recognition. The man did say, however, "Mr. Perleman, you've got something on your face and shirt."

Khalil knew immediately what that something was—the contents of Satherwaite's head. He said, "I'm afraid my eating habits are not so good."

The man smiled and said, "There's a washroom right over there." He pointed to a door on the right. "I'll give the pilots a call."

Khalil went into the washroom and looked at his face in the mirror. There were specks of reddish brown blood, grayish brain, and even a bone splinter on his shirt. One lens of his glasses had a few specks, and there was a spot or two on his face and tie.

He removed his glasses and washed his face and hands, being careful not to disturb his hair or mustache.

He dried his hands and face with a paper towel, wiped his shirt, tie, and glasses with the damp paper towel, then put on his glasses. He went back to the counter, carrying his black bag.

The clerk said, "Mr. Perleman, this charter has been prepaid by your company. All I need from you is to read this agreement and waiver and sign it where I put the X."

Khalil pretended to read the single printed page. He said, "It seems satisfactory." He signed it with the pen on the counter.

The clerk said, "You from Israel?"

"Yes. But I live here now."

"I've got relatives in Israel. They live in Gilgal on the West Bank. You know it?"

"Of course." Khalil recalled that Boris had told him, "Half of Israel is in the New York area on any given day. You'll attract no attention, except perhaps some Jews who want to discuss their relatives or their vacations with you. Study your maps and guidebooks of Israel."

Khalil said, "It is a medium-sized town thirty kilometers north of Jerusalem. Life there is difficult, surrounded by Palestinians. I congratulate your relatives on their bravery and stubbornness in staying there."

"Yeah. The place sucks. They should move to the coast." The clerk added, "Maybe someday we can learn to live with the Arabs."

"The Arabs are not easy to live with."

The clerk laughed. "I guess not. You should know."

"I know."

A middle-aged man in a nondescript blue uniform came into the office and greeted the clerk. "Evening, Dan."

The clerk said to the man, "Bob, this is Mr. Perleman, your passenger."

Khalil faced the man, who had his hand extended. Khalil was still mystified by American handshaking. Arab men shook hands, but not as many hands as American men shook, and certainly one did not touch a woman. Boris had advised him, "Don't worry about it. You're a foreigner."

Khalil took the pilot's hand, and the pilot said, "I'm Captain Fiske. Call me Bob. I'll be flying you to Denver tonight, then on to San Diego. Correct?"

"That is correct."

Khalil looked directly into the pilot's eyes, but the man did not make eye contact. The Americans, Khalil noticed, looked at you, but did not always see you. They would allow eye contact, but only for brief periods, unlike his countrymen, whose eyes never left you, unless they were of an inferior status, or, of course, if they were women. Also, the Americans kept their distance. At least one meter, as Boris had informed him. Any closer and they became uncomfortable, or even hostile.

Captain Fiske said, "The aircraft is ready. Do you have luggage, Mr. Perleman?"

"Just this bag."

"I'll take that for you."

Boris had suggested a polite American reply, and Khalil said, "Thank you, but I need the exercise."

The pilot smiled and walked toward the door. "Only you, correct, sir?"

"Correct."

The clerk called out as Khalil was leaving, "Shalom alekhem."

To which Khalil almost responded in Arabic, "Salaam alakum," but caught himself and said, "Shalom."

He followed the pilot toward a hangar, in front of which sat a small white jet aircraft, parked on the ramp. A few service people were departing from around the aircraft.

Again, Khalil noticed Satherwaite's aircraft and wondered how long beyond the expected departure tomorrow morning before they became concerned and began to investigate. Certainly not before the next day—and Khalil knew that he would be far away by then.

The pilot said, "We're flying that Lear 60 tonight. With just the three of us and light luggage, we're well below gross take-off weight, so I had all the fuel tanks filled to capacity. That means we can make Denver non-stop. Headwinds are light, and the flying weather between here and Denver is excellent. I'm planning a flight time of three hours and eighteen minutes. Denver temperature should be about forty degrees—five Celsius—when we land. We'll refuel in Denver. As I understand it, you may need to spend a few hours in Denver. Correct?"

"Correct."

"Okay, we should be landing in Denver a little before two A.M., Mountain Time. You understand that, sir?"

"I do. I will call my colleague from your airphone, which I have requested."

"Yes, sir. There's always an airphone on board. Okay, at some point, we'll be flying on to San Diego. Correct?"

"That's correct."

"They are at this time reporting slight turbulence over the Rockies and light rain in San Diego. But, of course, that can change. We'll keep you informed, if you wish."

Khalil did not reply, but he found himself annoyed at the American obsession with predicting the weather. In Libya, it was always hot and dry, some days more hot than others. The evenings were cool, the Ghabli blew in the spring. Allah made the weather, man experienced it. What was the point of trying to predict it, or talking about it? It could not be changed.

The pilot led him to the left side of the two-engine aircraft where two steps led to an open door.

The pilot motioned him forward, and Khalil climbed up the entrance steps and lowered his head to enter the craft.

The pilot was directly behind him and said, "Mr. Perleman, this is Terry Sanford, our co-pilot."

The co-pilot, who was sitting in the right-hand seat, turned his head and said, "Welcome aboard, sir."

"Good evening."

Captain Fiske motioned toward the cabin and said, "Take any seat, of course. There's the service bar where you'll find coffee, donuts, bagels, soft drinks, and more potent stuff." He chuckled. "There are newspapers and magazines in those racks. In the rear is the head—the lavatory. Make yourself comfortable."

"Thank you." Khalil moved to the last seat on the right in the six-seat cabin, sat, and put his bag in the aisle beside him.

He noticed that the pilot and co-pilot were busy with the cockpit instruments and speaking to each other.

Khalil looked at his watch. It was a few minutes past midnight. This had been a good day, he reflected. Three dead—five, if he counted Paul Grey's cleaning woman and the museum guard. But they should not be counted, and neither should the three hundred people aboard the Trans-Continental aircraft, nor the others who'd gotten in his way, or who needed to be silenced. There were only six people in America whose deaths had any meaning for him, and four of them were already dead by his hand. Two remained. Or so it would seem to the authorities if they came to the correct conclusions. But there was another man—

"Mr. Perleman? Sir?"

Asad Khalil looked up at the pilot standing near him. "Yes?"

"We're about to taxi, so please put your seat belt on."

Khalil fastened his belt as the pilot continued, "The airphone is at the service bar. The cord will reach any seat."

"Good."

"The other instrument mounted on the sidewall is the intercom. You can call us anytime by pressing that button and speaking."

"Thank you."

"Or, you can simply come up to the cockpit."

"I understand."

"Good. Is there anything I can help you with before I take my seat?"

"No, thank you."

"Okay, the emergency exit is there, and these windows have shades if you want to pull them down. After we get airborne, I'll let you know when you can unbuckle and move around."

"Thank you."

"See you later." The pilot turned, entered the cockpit, and closed the sliding partition between the cockpit and the cabin.

Khalil glanced out the small window as the aircraft taxied toward the runway. It was not so very long ago, he thought, that he'd landed here with a man who was now sitting dead in the pilot's seat of a warplane that had perhaps killed many people. Beside that dead man sat another murderer, who had paid for his crimes. It had been an exquisite moment, a fitting end to their bloodthirsty lives. But it was also a sign, a signature really, if anyone thought to read it properly. He regretted indulging himself in this symbolic act, but on reflection, he decided that he would not have changed one word, one moment, or one thing of what he'd done. "My cup runneth over." He smiled.

The Learjet came to a stop, and Khalil heard the engines grow louder. The aircraft seemed to tremble, then shot forward down the runway.

Within half a minute, they were in flight, and he heard the landing gear retracting beneath him. A few minutes later, the aircraft banked slightly as it continued to climb.

Some time later, the co-pilot's voice came over the speaker. "Mr. Perleman, you can move around if you'd like, but please keep your seat belt fastened while sitting. Your seat reclines all the way back if you want to get some sleep. We're passing lower Manhattan now if you'd like to take a look."

Khalil looked out his window. They were flying over the southern tip of Manhattan Island, and Asad Khalil could see the skyscrapers at the end of the water, including the Twin Towers of the World Trade Center.

They had told him in Tripoli that there was a building near the

Trade Center, called 26 Federal Plaza, where Boutros had been taken, and that if everything that could go wrong, went wrong, he, too, would be taken there.

Malik had said, "There is no escape from that place, my friend. Once you are there, you are theirs. Your next stop will be a government prison nearby, then a government courthouse, also nearby, then a prison somewhere in the frozen interior of the country, where you will spend the rest of your life. No one can help you there. We will not even acknowledge you as our own, or offer to exchange you for a captured infidel. There are many Mujahadeen in American prisons, but the authorities will not let you see them. You will live out your life alone in a strange land, amongst strangers, and you will never see your home again, nor hear your native tongue, nor be with a woman. You will be a lion in a cage, Asad, pacing the floor of your cell forever." Malik had added, "Or you can end your own life, which will be a victory for you, and for our cause, and a defeat for them." He asked, "Are you prepared for such a victory?"

To which Asad Khalil had replied, "If I am willing to sacrifice my life in battle, why would I not take my own life to escape capture and humiliation?"

Malik had nodded thoughtfully and noted, "For some, the one is easier than the other," whereupon Malik had handed him a razor blade and said, "This is one way." He added, "But you should not cut your wrists because they may be able to save your life. You must cut several main arteries." A doctor appeared and showed Khalil how to locate his carotid artery and femoral artery. The doctor said, "And just to be certain, also slice your wrists."

Another man took the place of the doctor, and this man instructed Khalil on how to fashion a noose from various materials, including a bedsheet, an electrical wire, and clothing.

After the demonstrations of suicide, Malik had said to Khalil, "We all must die, and we all would choose to die in Jihad by the hand of an enemy. But there are situations when we must die by our own hand. I assure you, Paradise awaits you at the end of either path."

Khalil looked again out the window of the Learjet and caught a last glimpse of New York City. He vowed that he would never see that place again. His last American destination was the place called California, then his final destination was Tripoli, or Paradise. In either case, he would be home.

Chapter 42

I woke up, and within a few seconds I knew where I was, who I was, and who I was sleeping with.

One often regrets the intemperance of an alcoholic evening. One often wishes one had awakened alone, somewhere else. Far away. But I didn't have that feeling this morning. In fact, I felt pretty good, though I resisted the temptation to run to the window and shout, "Wake up, New York! John Corey got laid!"

Anyway, the clock on the night stand said seven-fourteen.

I got quietly out of bed, went into the bathroom, and used the facilities. I found the Air France kit, shaved and brushed my teeth, then jumped in the shower.

Through the frosted glass shower door, I saw Kate come into the bathroom, then heard the toilet flush, then heard her brushing her teeth and gargling between yawns.

Having sex with a woman you barely know is one thing—spending the night is another. I'm real territorial about the bathroom.

Anyway, the shower door slid open and in walks Ms. Mayfield. Without even a by-your-leave, she nudges me away and stands under the shower. She said, "Wash my back."

I washed her back with my soapy washcloth.

"Ooooh, that feels good."

She turned around, and we embraced and kissed, the water cascading over our bodies.

Anyway, after soapy sex in the shower, we got out, dried off, and went into the bedroom, both wrapped in our bath towels. Her bedroom faced east and the sun was coming through the window. It looked like a nice day, but looks are deceptive.

She said, "I really enjoyed last night."

"Me, too."

"Will I see you again?"

"We work together."

"Right. You're the guy whose desk faces mine."

You never know what to expect in the morning, or what to say, but it's best to keep it light, which was what Kate Mayfield was doing. Five points.

Anyway, my clothes were elsewhere—in the living room, if my memory served me correctly, so I said, "I'll leave you to your painting and find my clothes."

"Everything is hung and pressed in the hall closet. I washed your underwear and socks."

"Thank you." Ten points. I retrieved my gun and holster and went into the living room where my clothes were still strewn around the floor. She must have dreamed about washing and ironing. Minus ten points.

I got dressed, unhappy about the day-old underwear. I'm obsessively clean for an alpha male, though, of course, I can rough it.

I went into the small kitchen and found a clean glass and poured myself an orange juice. The contents of the refrigerator, I noticed, were minimal, but there *was* yogurt. There's always yogurt. What is it with women and yogurt?

I picked up the kitchen wall phone and dialed my apartment, hearing my recorded voice say, "John Corey residence—the missus has flown the coop, so don't leave any messages for her." Maybe, after a year and a half, I should change the message. Anyway, I punched in my code and robo-voice said, "You have eight messages." The first was recorded last night from my ex, who said, "Change that stupid greeting message. Call me. I'm concerned."

And she was. And I would call her, when I got around to it.

There was another concerned message from Mom and Pop, who live in Florida, and who were by now resembling sun-dried tomatoes.

There was a message from my brother, who reads only *The Wall Street Journal*, but who must have heard something from Mom and Dad, who instructed him to call Black Sheep. That's my family nickname, and it has no negative connotations.

Two old buds from the job had also called inquiring about my possible involvement with Flight 175. There was also a message from my ex-partner, Dom Fanelli, who said, "Hey, goombah! Did I steer you straight on that job, or what? Holy shit! And you were worried about the two Pedros gunning for you? This raghead took out a whole plane and a bunch of Feds. Now he's probably looking for you. Are you having fun yet? You were spotted in Giulio's the other night, drinking alone. Buy a blond wig. Give me a call. You owe me a drink. Arrivederci."

I smiled despite myself and said, "Va fungole, Dom."

The next message was from Mr. Teddy Nash. He said, "Nash here—I think you should be in Frankfurt, Corey. I hope you're on the way. If not, where are you? You need to be in contact. Call me."

"Double va fungole, you little turd, you—" I realized this man was getting to me, and as Kate suggested at the airport, I shouldn't let that happen.

The last message was from Jack Koenig, at midnight, my time. He said, "Nash tried to reach you. You're not in the office, you've left no forwarding number, you don't answer your pager, and I guess you're not home. Call me back, ASAP."

I think Herr Koenig was too long in the Fatherland already.

Robo-voice said, "End of messages."

"Thank God."

I was glad not to hear Beth's voice, which would have increased my guilt quotient.

I went into the living room and sat on the couch, the scene of last night's crime. Well, one of the scenes.

Anyway, I flipped through the only magazine I could see, a copy of *Entertainment Weekly*. In the book section, I saw that Danielle Steel had her fourth book out this year, and it was only April. Maybe I could get her to write my Incident Report. But she might dwell a bit too long on what the corpses in First Class were wearing.

I flipped to another section and was prepared to read a story about

Barbra Streisand doing a charity concert to benefit Marxist Mayans in the Yucatan Peninsula, when, Voilà! Kate Mayfield appeared, powdered, coiffed, and dressed. That didn't take too long actually. Ten points.

I stood and said, "You look lovely."

"Thank you. But don't go sensitive and goo-goo on me. I liked you the way you were."

"And how was that?"

"Insensitive, loutish, self-centered, egotistical, rude, and sarcastic."

"I'll do my best." Twenty-five points.

She informed me, "Tonight, your place. I'll bring an overnight bag. Is that all right?"

"Of course." As long as the overnight bag didn't resemble three suitcases and four moving boxes. I really had to think this through.

She also informed me, "While you were in the bathroom last night, your pager beeped. I checked it. It was the Incident Command Center."

"Oh...you should have told me."

"I forgot. Don't worry about it."

I had a feeling I was handing over some mission control, and perhaps life control to Kate Mayfield. See what I mean? Minus five points.

She moved toward the door, and I followed. She said, "There's a cute little French café on Second Avenue."

"Good. Leave it there."

"Come on. My treat."

"There's a greasy coffee shop down the block."

"I asked first."

So, we gathered our briefcases and off we went, just like John and Jane Jones, off for a day at the office, except we were both carrying .40 caliber Glocks.

Kate was wearing black slacks, by the way, and a sort of Heinz Ketchup—colored blazer over a white blouse. I was wearing what I wore yesterday.

We took the elevator down to the lobby and exited the building. The doorman was the same guy from last night. Maybe they work an hour on and two hours off until they get in an eight-hour day. Anyway, the guy said, "Taxi, Ms. Mayfield?"

"No, thank you, Herbert, we're walking."

Herbert gave me a look that suggested that it should have been him, not me, in Apartment 1415.

It was a nice day, clear skies, a little cool, but no humidity. We walked east on 86th Street to Second Avenue, then turned south in the direction of my place, though we weren't going there. The motor traffic on the avenue was already heavy, and so was the pedestrian traffic. I said, apropos of nothing but my mood at the moment, "I love New York."

She replied, "I hate New York." She realized that this statement was pregnant with future problems, especially if *she* were pregnant, and she added, "But I could get to like it."

"No, you can't. No one does. But you can get used to it. Sometimes you'll love it, sometimes you'll hate it. You never like it."

She glanced at me, but did not comment on my profundity.

We came to a place called La-Something-de-Something. We went inside and were greeted warmly by a French lady on Prozac. She and Kate seemed to know each other, and they exchanged words in French. Get me out of here. Minus five points.

We sat at a table the size of my cuff links, on wire chairs made of coat hangers. The place looked like a Laura Ashley remnant sale, and smelled of warm butter, which makes my stomach turn. The clientele were all cross-dressers.

"Isn't this cute?"

"No."

The proprietress handed us tiny menus, handwritten in Sanskrit. There were thirty-two kinds of muffins and croissants, all unsuitable food for men. I asked Madame, "Can I get a bagel?"

"Non, monsieur."

"Eggs? Sausage?"

"Non, monsieur." She turned on her spiked heel and strode away. The Prozac was wearing off.

Kate said, "Try the strawberry croissant."

"Why?" Anyway, I ordered coffee, orange juice, and six brioches. I can handle brioche. They taste like my English Grandma's popovers. Kate ordered tea and a cherry croissant.

As we had our breakfast, she asked me, "Do you have any other information you'd like to share with me?"

"No. Just the murder in Perth Amboy."

"Any theories?"

"Nope. Come here often?"

"Most mornings. Any plan of action for today?"

"I need to pick up my dry cleaning. How about you?"

"I have to get up and running on all those things on my desk."

"Think about what's not on your desk."

"Such as?"

"Such as detailed information about Khalil's alleged victims in Europe. Unless I missed it, there's nothing on our desks. Nothing from Scotland Yard. Nothing from the Air Force CID or FBI."

"Okay...what are we looking for?"

"For a connection and a motive."

"There seems to be no connection, other than that the targets were British and American. That's also the motive," she pointed out.

"The one attack that sticks out is the ax murder of that American Air Force colonel in England."

"Colonel Hambrecht. Near Lakenheath Airbase."

"Right. This coffee's not bad."

"Why does it stand out?"

"It was up close and personal."

"So was the murder of those schoolchildren."

"They were shot. I'm talking about the ax. That's significant."

She looked at me and said, "Okay, Detective Corey. Tell me about it."

I played with my remaining brioche. I said, "A murder like that suggests a personal relationship."

"Okay. But we're not even sure that Khalil committed that murder."

"Right. It's mostly Interpol speculation. They've been tracking this guy. I waded through a half ton of paper yesterday while you and Jack were running up taxi bills to JFK. I found very little from Scotland Yard, or Air Force CID, or our CIA friends." I added, "And nothing from the FBI, who must have sent a team over to investigate the

Hambrecht murder as well as the murder of the American kids. So, why is this stuff missing?"

"Maybe because you missed it."

"I put in requests to the Incident File Room, and I'm still waiting."

"Don't get paranoid."

"Don't be so trusting."

She didn't reply immediately, then said, "I'm not."

I think we were in silent agreement that something stank here, but Agent Mayfield was not going to verbalize this.

Madame presented me with the bill, which I passed to Mademoiselle, who paid in cash. Five points. Madame made change from a hip purse, just like in Europe. How cool is that?

We left, and I hailed a cab. We got in, and I said, "Twenty-six Federal Plaza."

The man was clueless, and I gave him directions. "Where you from?"

"Albania."

When I was a kid, there were still cabbies around who were from old czarist Russia, all former nobility, if you believed their stories. At least they knew how to find an address.

We sat in silence a minute, then Kate said, "Maybe you should have gone home to change."

"I will, if you'd like. I'm a few blocks from here." I added, "We're almost neighbors."

She smiled, mulled it over, then said, "The hell with it. No one will notice."

"There are five hundred detectives and FBI people in the building. You don't think they'll notice?"

She laughed. "Who cares?"

I said, "We'll go in separately."

She took my hand, put her lips to my ear and said, "Fuck 'em."

I gave her a kiss on the cheek. She smelled good. She looked good. I liked her voice. I asked her, "Where are you from, exactly?"

"All over. I'm an FBI brat. Dad is retired. He was born in Cincinnati, Mom was born in Tennessee. We moved around a lot. One posting was in Venezuela. The FBI has lots of people in South America. J. Edgar tried to keep South America from the CIA. Did you know that?"

"I think so. Good old J. Edgar."

"He was very misunderstood, according to my father."

"I can relate to that."

She laughed.

I asked, "Are your parents proud of you?"

"Of course. Are your parents proud of *you?* Are they both alive?"

"Alive and well in Sarasota."

She smiled. "And...? Do they love you? Are they proud of you?"

"Absolutely. They have a pet name for me—Black Sheep."

She laughed. Two points.

Kate stayed quiet awhile, then said, "I had a long-term, long-distance relationship with another agent." She added, "I'm glad you and I are neighbors. It's easier. It's better."

Thinking of my own long-distance relationship with Beth Penrose, and my former marriage, I wasn't sure what was better. But I said, "Of course."

She further revealed, "I like older men."

I guess that meant me. I asked, "Why?"

"I like the pre-sensitive generation. Like my father. When men were men."

"Like Attila the Hun."

"You know what I mean."

"There's nothing wrong with the men of your generation, Kate. It's your job and the people on it. They're probably okay guys, too, but they work for the Federal government, which has become very strange."

"Maybe that's it. Jack is okay, for instance. He's older, and he acts normal half the time."

"Right."

She said, "I don't usually throw myself at men."

"I'm used to it."

She laughed. "Okay, enough morning-after talk."

"Good."

So, we made small talk—the kind of stuff that used to be pre-coital talk thirty years ago. The country has changed, mostly for the better, I think, but the sex thing has become more, rather than less, confusing. Maybe I'm the only one who's confused. I've dated women who are into the new/old concept of chastity and modesty as well as women who've switched mounts faster than a pony express rider. And it was hard to tell who was who by appearances, or even by what they said. The women have it easier—all men are pigs. It's that simple.

Anyway, you're not supposed to talk about classified stuff in the presence of civilians, even Albanian taxi drivers who pretend they don't speak English and don't know where Federal Plaza is—so we made small talk all the way downtown, getting to know each other.

I suggested we get out of the taxi a block before our destination and arrive separately. But Kate said, "No, this is fun. Let's see who notices and who leers." She added, "We haven't done anything wrong."

The FBI, of course, is not like most private employers, or even the NYPD for that matter, and they do keep an eye out for possible sexual conflicts and problems. Notice that Mulder and Scully still haven't gotten it on. I wonder if they get laid at all. Anyway, I was only working for the FBI on contract, so it wasn't my problem.

The taxi arrived at 26 Federal Plaza before 9:00 A.M., and I paid the driver.

We got out and entered the lobby together, but there weren't many of our colleagues around, and the ones we recognized didn't seem to notice that we'd arrived together, late, in the same cab, and that I hadn't changed my clothes. When you're doing it with a workmate, you think everyone knows, but usually people have more important things on their minds. If Koenig was around, however, he'd be on to us, and he'd be pissed. I know the type.

There was a newsstand in the lobby, and we bought the *Times*, the *Post*, the *Daily News*, and *USA Today*, despite the fact that all these newspapers and more are delivered to us five days a week. I like my newspapers fresh, unread, and unclipped.

As we waited for the elevator, I perused the headline story in the *Times*, which was the story about the newly admitted terrorist attack. A familiar name and face caught my eye, and I said, "Holy shit. Excuse my French. The brioches are repeating on me."

"What is it?"

I held up the newspaper. She stared at it and said, "Oh…"

To make a long article short, the *Times* printed my name, and then a photograph of me taken supposedly at JFK on Saturday, though I don't recall wearing that suit Saturday. It was obviously a doctored photo, and so were a few quotes from me that I didn't recall saying, except for one that said, "I think Khalil is still in the New York metropolitan area, and if he is, we'll find him." I didn't actually say that verbatim and not for public consumption. I made a mental note to punch little Alan Parker in the nose.

Kate was going through the *Daily News* and said, "Here's a quote from me. It says we came very close to capturing Asad Khalil at JFK, but he had accomplices at the airport and managed to evade us."

She looked up at me.

I said, "See? That's why we didn't have to talk to the press. Jack or Alan or somebody did the talking for us."

She shrugged, then said, "Well, we agreed to being…what's the word I'm looking for?"

"Bait. Where's *your* picture?"

"Maybe they'll run it tomorrow. Or this afternoon." She added, "I don't photograph that well." She laughed.

The elevator came, and we rode up with other people going to the ATTF offices. We all made small talk, except for the people reading the newspapers. One guy glanced at me, then back at his paper. He said, "Hey, you're on Khalil's Most Wanted List."

Everyone laughed. Why was I not finding this funny?

Someone else said, "Don't stand too close to Corey."

More laughter. The higher the elevator went, the stupider the jokes got. Even Kate chimed in and said, "I have a bottle of Lady Clairol blonde I can lend you."

Ha, ha, ha. If I weren't a gentleman, I'd have announced that Ms. Mayfield was a very natural blonde.

Anyway, we got off at the ICC on the twenty-sixth floor, and Kate said to me, "Sorry. That was funny."

"I must be missing the joke."

We walked toward the ICC. "Come on, John. You're not in any real danger."

"Then let's use your photo tomorrow."

"I don't care. I volunteered."

We went into the ICC and made our way toward our desks, greeting people as we went. No one made any amusing comments about my photo in the newspaper. It was all very professional here, and the elevator funnies were an aberration, a moment of unguarded un-FBI behavior. The elevator comedians were probably all reporting each other now for laughing. If this was my old Homicide squad room, they'd have a blown-up photo of me captioned, "Asad Khalil Is Looking for This Man—Can You Help?"

I sat at my desk. In reality, there was almost no chance that my photo in the papers, or even on television, was going to draw Khalil out, or that I would become his target. Unless I got too close to him.

Kate sat opposite me and began flipping through the paperwork on her desk. "My God, there are tons of stuff here."

"Most of it is garbage."

I scanned the *New York Times*, looking for the story of the murder of the American banker in Frankfurt. Finally, I found a small AP piece that gave only the barest details and made no mention of any Asad Khalil connection.

I assumed that the various authorities didn't want to help create confusion amongst the American citizenry and law enforcement people, who were looking for Khalil here.

I gave the newspaper to Kate, who read the article. She said, "They must be having some doubts about this." She added, "And they don't want to play into the hands of Libyan Intelligence, if that's what this murder is about."

"Right." Most of the homicides I've dealt with were committed by idiots. The international intelligence game is played by people who are so smart that they *act* like idiots. People like Ted Nash and his opponents.

Their brilliant schemes get so convoluted that half of them must wake up every morning trying to remember whose side they're on that week and what lie was the truth disguised as a lie disguised as the truth. No wonder Nash didn't say much—he used most of his mental energy trying to resolve conflicting reality. My motto is—Keep it simple, stupid.

Anyway, Kate reached for the telephone and said, "We need to call Jack."

"It's six hours earlier in Frankfurt. He's asleep."

"It's six hours *later*. He'll be in the field office."

"Whatever. Let him call us."

She hesitated, then put down the receiver.

We both read the headline stories in the newspapers, commenting to each other about how the media didn't have to be manipulated—they managed to get most of the pre-packaged news wrong anyway. Only the *Times*, to give the Gray Lady her due, got most of it right. But, as with my files, the important and interesting stuff was missing.

There were photos of Khalil again in all the newspapers, and a few doctored shots had him wearing glasses, a beard, a mustache, and grayish hair parted differently. This, of course, was supposed to alert the public to the possibility that the fugitive had changed his appearance. What it accomplished, however, was to make the public suspicious of innocent people with glasses, mustaches, and beards. Also, as a cop, I knew that the thinnest of disguises were usually effective, and even I might not be able to spot this guy in a crowd if he was smiling and wearing a mustache.

I perused the articles to see if anyone had taken my suggestions about making public the theory that Mrs. Khalil and Mr. Gadhafi were more than friends. But I didn't see any hint of that.

Despite my motto of keeping it simple, there are times when psychological warfare is good stuff, but underused by the military and by law enforcement—except when the cops question a suspect and use the old "good cop/bad cop" routine. In any case, you have to plant seeds of doubt and deception through the media, and hope the fugitive reads it and believes it, and that the good guys remember that it's bullshit.

On that subject, I was wondering if Mr. Khalil was reading about himself and seeing himself on TV. I tried to picture him somewhere, holed up in a cheap rooming house in an Arab neighborhood, eating canned goat meat, watching daytime TV, and reading the newspapers. But I couldn't picture that. I pictured him, instead, nattily dressed in his suit, out there in public, working on fucking us again.

If this case had a name, it would be called "The Case of the Missing Information." Some of the stuff missing in the news was missing because they didn't know it. But what was also missing was stuff they should have known or concluded. The most glaring thing missing was any reference to April 15, 1986. Some hotshot reporter with half a brain, or half a memory, or a modem, should have made this connection. Even newspaper reporters weren't that stupid, so I had to figure that the news was being managed a little. The press will cooperate with the Feds for a few days or a week, if they can be convinced that national security is at stake. On the other hand, maybe I was reading too much into what I wasn't reading. I asked Kate, "Why didn't any of these stories mention the anniversary date of the Libyan raid?"

She looked up from her desk and replied, "I guess someone asked them not to. It's not a good idea to give the other side the public relations it wants. They make a big deal of anniversary dates, but if we ignore it, they get frustrated."

Sounded good to me. There were a lot of considerations regarding an event of this magnitude. The bad actors were putting on a tragedy, but we weren't going to give them free advertising.

Anyway, there wasn't much new in the news, so I accessed my voice mail as Kate was now doing. I should have used the handset rather than the speaker because the first message was from Beth at 7:12 A.M. She said, "Hey, you. I called your place last night and this morning, but didn't leave a message. Where are you hiding? Call me at home until eight, then the office. Miss you. Big wet kiss. Bye."

Kate continued listening to her own voice mail, pretending not to hear. I said, as if to myself, "Got to call Mom back," but I didn't think that was going to fly.

Anyway, the next message was from Jack Koenig, who said, "Message for Corey and Mayfield. Call me." He gave a long phone number with lots of zeros and ones, and I guessed he wasn't back in his office down the hall.

There was a similar message from Teddy Nash, which I deleted.

There were no further messages, and I looked at new stuff on my desk.

After a few minutes, Kate looked up and said, "Who was that?"

"Jack and Ted."

"I mean the other one."

"Oh... Mom?"

She said something that sounded like "wool shirt," but I may have misunderstood. She stood and walked away from her desk.

So, I'm sitting there, sleep-deprived, the bullet hole in my abdomen aching, six undercooked brioches in my stomach, the last and final act of my career in trouble, and some crazed terrorist is drinking camel milk somewhere, staring at my picture in the papers. I could handle all of that. But did I need *this*? I mean, I thought I'd been up-front with Kate.

Just when I was having second thoughts about Ms. Mayfield, she returned with two mugs of coffee and put one on my desk. "Dark, one sugar. Right?"

"Right. No strychnine. Thanks."

"I can run out and get you an Egg McMuffin if you'd like. With cheese and sausage."

"No, thanks."

"A man on the move needs solid food."

"Actually, I'm just sitting here. Coffee is fine. Thanks."

"I'll bet you didn't take your vitamins this morning. Let me run out and get you some vitamins."

I was detecting a wee bit of taunting in Ms. Mayfield's tone, or maybe the word of the morning was baiting. Not only *was* I bait, I was *being* baited. I said, "Thanks, but coffee is all I need." I lowered my head and studied a memo in front of me.

She sat opposite me and sipped her coffee. I felt her eyes on me. I looked up at her, but those blue eyes, which were heavenly a little while ago, had turned to ice cubes.

We stared at each other, then finally she said, "Sorry," and went back to her paperwork.

I said, "I'll take care of it."

Without looking up, she replied, "You'd better."

After a minute or two, we got back to the business of catching the world's most wanted terrorist. She said, "There's a combined report from various police departments regarding car rentals in the metropolitan area...basically, thousands of cars are rented every day, but they're trying to isolate cars rented to people with Mideastern-sounding names. Sounds like a long shot."

"A very long shot. For all we know, Khalil is driving a car borrowed from a compatriot. Even if it is a rental car, his accomplices could use the name Smith if they had the proper ID."

"But the people renting it might not look like Smith."

"True...but they could use a Smith-looking guy, then whack him. Forget the car rentals."

"We got lucky with the Ryder van in the World Trade Center bombing. Solved the case."

"Forget the fucking World Trade Center bombing."

"Why?"

"Because, like an Army general who tries to relive his past successes in a new battle, you'll find that the bad guys are not trying to relive their past defeats."

"Is that what you tell your students at John Jay?"

"I sure do. It definitely applies to detective work. I've seen too many homicide cops try to solve Case B the way they solved Case A. Every case is unique. This one, especially."

"Thank you, Professor."

"Do what you want." I got surly and went back to my memos and reports. I hate paper.

I came across a sealed YOUR EYES ONLY envelope without a routing note. I opened it and saw it was from Gabe. It said: *I kept Fadi incommunicado yesterday, then went to the home of Gamal Jabbar and interviewed his wife, Cala. She claims no knowledge of her husband's activities, intentions, or his Saturday destination. But she did say that Jabbar had a visitor Friday night, that after the visitor left, Jabbar put a black canvas bag under their bed and instructed her not to touch it. She did not recognize the visitor, and heard nothing that was said. The next morning, her husband stayed home, which was unusual, as he normally worked on Saturdays. Jabbar left their Brooklyn apartment at 2:00 P.M., carrying the bag, and never returned. She characterizes his behavior as worried, nervous, sad, and distracted—as best I can translate from Arabic. Mrs. Jabbar seems resigned to the possibility that her husband is dead. I called Homicide and gave them the go-ahead to break the news to her and released Fadi for the same purpose. Speak to you later.*

I folded the memo and put it in my breast pocket.

Kate asked, "What was that?"

"I'll show you later."

"Why not now?"

"You need some plausible deniability before we speak to Jack."

"Jack is our boss. I trust Jack."

"So do I. But he's too close to Teddy right now."

"What are you talking about?"

"There are two games being played on the same field—the Lion's game, and somebody else's game."

"Whose game?"

"I don't know. I just have this feeling that something is not right."

"Well...if you mean that the CIA is in business for itself, that's not exactly news."

"Right. Keep an eye on Ted."

"Okay. Maybe I'll seduce him, and he'll confide in me."

"Good idea. But I saw him naked once, and he has a teeny weenie."

She looked at me and saw that I wasn't kidding. "When did you see him naked?"

"Bachelor party. He got carried away with the music and the strippers and before anyone could stop him—"

"Cut it out. When did you see him naked?"

"On Plum Island. After we left the biocontainment lab, we all had to shower out. That's what they call it. Showering out."

"Really?"

"Really. I don't think he showered thoroughly because later that day, his dick fell off."

She laughed, then thought a moment and observed, "I forgot you guys once worked a case together. George, too, right?"

"Right. George has a normal dick. For the record."

"Thank you for sharing." She mulled a bit, then said, "So, you came to distrust Ted on that case."

"It wasn't an evolving process. I didn't trust him three seconds after I met him."

"I see...so, you're a little suspicious of this coincidence of meeting him again."

"Perhaps a little. By the way, he actually threatened me on the Plum Island case."

"Threatened you in what way?"

"In the only way that matters."

"I don't believe that."

I shrugged. I further revealed to Ms. Mayfield, "He was interested in Beth Penrose, for your information."

"Oh! Cherchez la femme. Now it all makes sense. Case closed."

It may have been unwise of me to share that. I didn't reply to her illogical deductive reasoning.

She said, "So, here's a solution to both our problems. Ted and Beth. Let's get them together."

Somehow I'd gone from an anti-terrorist agent to a soap opera character. I said, to end the conversation, "Sounds like a plan."

"Good. Now give me the thing you just put in your pocket."

"It says my eyes only."

"Okay, read it to me."

I took Gabe's memo out of my pocket and sailed it across her desk. She read it to herself and said to me, "There's nothing much new in here that I shouldn't see, and nothing that I have to deny seeing." She added, "You're trying to control information, John. Information is power. We don't work like that here." She further observed, "You and Gabe and some other NYPD here are playing a little game of hide-it-from-the-Feds. This is a dangerous game." And so on. I got a three-minute lecture, ending with, "We don't need what amounts to a sub-rosa organization within our task force."

I replied, "I apologize for withholding the memo from you. I will share all future cop-to-cop memos with you. You can do whatever you want with them." I added, "I know that the FBI and the CIA share everything with me and with the other police detectives assigned to the ATTF. As J. Edgar Hoover said—"

"Okay. Enough. I get the point. But don't be secretive with *me.*"

We made eye contact, and we both smiled. You see what happens when you get involved with a workmate? I said, "I promise."

We both went back to our paperwork.

Kate said, "Here's the preliminary forensic report on the taxi found in Perth Amboy...wow...wool fibers found on the back seat match fibers taken from Khalil's suit in Paris."

I found the report quickly and read to myself as Kate read it aloud.

She said, "Clear polyethylene terephthalate embedded in the driver's seat and in the body...what the hell does that mean?"

"It means the gunman used a plastic bottle as a silencer."

"Really?"

"Really. I'm sure it's in one of those manuals on your shelves."

"I never read that...what else...? Okay, the spent rounds were definitely forty caliber...I guess that could mean he used...an agent's weapon."

"Probably."

"Fingerprints all over the car, but no match to Asad Khalil..."

We both read the report, but there was no conclusive evidence that Khalil had been in that taxi, except for the wool fibers, and that by itself was not conclusive of his presence at the scene. It only meant his suit, or a similar suit, was present. That's what a defense lawyer said once in court.

She thought awhile, then said, "He's in America."

"That's what I said *before* we learned about the Perth Amboy murder."

"The Frankfurt murder was a red herring."

"Right. That's why we're not following that scent. In fact, we're not following any scent. We lost the scent in Perth Amboy."

"Still, John, we know where he was Saturday night. What can we extrapolate from that?"

"Nothing." In fact, good, solid clues and verifiable facts often led nowhere. When the Federal indictment was eventually drawn up on Asad Khalil, we could add the name of Gamal Jabbar to the list of over three hundred men, women, and children he was suspected of murdering. But that didn't bring us an inch closer to capturing him.

We both went back to the papers on our desks. I started at the beginning, in Europe, and read what little was available on Khalil's suspected murders and other activities. Somewhere in Europe was a clue, but I wasn't seeing it.

Someone, not me, had requested the Air Force personnel file of Colonel William Hambrecht, also known as a service record, and I had a copy of it on my desk in a sealed envelope. The file, like all military personnel files, was marked CONFIDENTIAL.

I found it interesting that the file had been requested two days ago and had not been part of the original suspect file. In other words, Khalil turned himself in to the American Embassy in Paris on Thursday, and when they realized he was a suspect in Hambrecht's murder, then Hambrecht's Air Force file should have been here by Saturday—Monday latest. Here it was Tuesday, and this was the first I'd seen of the file. But maybe I was giving the Feds more credit than they deserved by thinking the file would have been one of their first priorities. Or, maybe somebody was trying to control information. As I had said to Kate, "Think about what's not on your desk." Someone had already done that, but I didn't know who, since there was no request tag attached to the Colonel Hambrecht file.

I said to Kate, "See if you have the personnel file of Colonel William Hambrecht." I held up the first page. "Looks like this."

Without glancing up, she said, "I know what it looks like. I requested it Friday, when I got the assignment to meet Khalil at the airport, and after I'd read his dossier. I read the file half an hour ago."

"I'm impressed. Daddy must have taught you well."

"Daddy taught me how to get ahead in my career. Mommy taught me how to be nosy."

I smiled, then opened the file. The first page contained personal information, next of kin, home address of record, place and date of birth, and so on. I saw that William Hambrecht was married to Rose and had three children, he would have been fifty-five years old in March, had he lived, his religion was Lutheran, his blood type was A positive, and so forth.

I flipped through the file pages. Most of it was written in a sort of cryptic military jargon and was basically a précis of a long and apparently distinguished career. I thought perhaps Colonel Hambrecht had been involved with Air Force Intelligence, which may have brought him into contact with extremist groups. But basically the guy had been a pilot, then a flight commander, a squadron commander, and a wing commander. He had distinguished himself in the Gulf War, had lots of awards, unit citations, and medals, lots of postings around the world, was attached to NATO in Brussels, then was assigned to the Royal Air Force Station Lakenheath in Suffolk, England, as a staff officer involved with training. Nothing unusual, except that he'd previously been stationed at Lakenheath in January 1984 until May 1986. Maybe he made an enemy there back then. Maybe he was screwing some local's wife, got reassigned, and when he came back over a decade later, the husband was still pissed. That would explain the ax. Maybe this murder had nothing to do with Asad Khalil.

Anyway, I kept reading. Military stuff is hard to read, and they write in acronyms, such as "Return to CONUS," which I know means Continental United States, and "DEROS," which is Date of Estimated Return from Overseas, and so forth.

I was getting a headache reading acronyms and abbreviations, but pressed on. There was nothing in here, and I was prepared to put the file aside, but on the last page was a line that read: "Deleted Info—REF DoD order 369215-25, Exec Order 279651-351-Purp. Nat. Sec. TOP SECRET." They never abbreviate Top or State Secret, and it's always capitalized just to make sure you understand.

I mulled this over. This is what is known as a footprint in the files. Things may be deleted for a variety of reasons, but nothing is totally lost in an Orwellian memory hole. The deleted information exists someplace—in another file marked TOP SECRET.

I kept staring at the footprint, but even Sherlock Holmes'

magnifying glass wouldn't help. There was no clue to what had been deleted, or when it had been deleted, or what time period it was missing from. But I knew who had deleted it and why. The who was the Department of Defense and the President of the United States. The reason was national security.

The order numbers would get someone access to the deleted information, but that someone was not me.

I thought about what might have been deleted and realized it could have been just about anything. Usually, it had to do with a secret mission, but in this case, it may have had something to do with Colonel Hambrecht's murder. Maybe both. Maybe neither. Maybe it had to do with screwing a local's wife.

There was also no hint if the deletion concerned honorable or dishonorable activities. But I would assume honorable, since his career seemed on track until the day someone mistook him for an oak tree.

Kate asked me, "So? What do you think?"

I looked up at her. "I found what's not here."

"Right. I already put in a request to Jack, who will put in a request up the chain to the Director, who will request the deleted information. That could take a few days. Maybe longer, though I marked it 'Urgent—Rush.'" She added, "This file is only marked 'Confidential,' and it took four days to get here. They're not real fast sometimes. 'Top Secret' takes longer."

I nodded.

She said, "Also, if someone upstairs thinks we have no need to know, or if they determine that the deleted information is irrelevant to our purposes, then we'll never see it." She added, "Or, it may be relevant, but too sensitive for us to see, and someone else will handle it. I'm not holding my breath."

I considered all this and pointed out, "Probably the deleted information is not relevant, unless it had to do with his murder. And if so, why is that top secret?"

She shrugged. "We may never know."

"That's not what I'm getting paid for."

She asked me, "What kind of clearance do you have?"

"About six foot, one inch. Sorry, old joke." She wasn't smiling. I said, "Only confidential. Working on secret."

"I have a secret clearance. But Jack has top secret, so he can see the deleted stuff if he has a need to know."

"How will he know if he has a need to know if he doesn't know what's deleted?"

"Someone with a need to know and a top secret clearance will tell him if he has a need to know."

"Who's on first?"

"Not you." She informed me, "The Federal government is not the NYPD. But I guess you figured that out."

"Murder is murder. The law is the law. Lesson One of my curriculum at John Jay." I picked up the telephone and dialed the Ann Arbor, Michigan, telephone number given in the file, which was noted as unlisted.

The number rang, and an answering machine picked up. The voice of a middle-aged woman, undoubtedly Mrs. Hambrecht, said, "This is the Hambrecht residence. We can't come to the phone right now, but please leave your name and telephone number, and we'll return your call as soon as possible."

If by "we" she meant Colonel Hambrecht, he wasn't coming to the phone ever. A beep sounded, and I said, "Mrs. Hambrecht, this is John Corey, calling on behalf of the Air Force. Please call me back as soon as possible regarding Colonel Hambrecht." I gave her my direct dial number and added, "Or call Ms. Mayfield." I gave her Kate's number, which she read to me from her telephone. I hung up.

In the event we weren't in, our voice mail would just say, "Corey, Task Force," or "Mayfield, Task Force," followed by a pleasant request to leave a name and number. That was vague enough and didn't use the upsetting word "Terrorist."

So, putting this unlikely lead out of my mind, I again began my Incident Report, which was a bit overdue. Assuming no one would ever read this, I thought I could get away with four pages, numbered one to fifty, with blank pages in between. In fact, I decided to start at the end, and typed, "So, in conclusion..."

Kate's phone rang, and it was Jack Koenig. After a few seconds, she said, "Pick up."

I hit the button for Kate's line and said, "Corey."

Mr. Koenig was in a cheery mood and said, "You're pissing me off."

"Yes, sir."

Kate held the phone away from her ear in a theatrical gesture.

Koenig continued, "You disobey an order to fly to Frankfurt, you don't return phone calls, and you were missing in action last night."

"Yes, sir."

"Where were you? You're supposed to stay in contact."

"Yes, sir."

"Well? Where were you?"

I have a really funny line for this question when I used to get asked it by one of my former bosses. I would say, "My date was arrested for prostitution, and I spent the night in court posting bail." But, as I say, these people lacked a sophisticated sense of humor, so I replied to Jack, "I have no excuse, sir."

Kate cut in and said, "I called the ICC and told the duty officer that Mr. Corey and I were in my apartment until further notice. I gave no further notice, and we were here by eight-forty-five A.M."

Silence. Then Jack said, "I see." He cleared his throat and informed us, "I'll be flying back to New York and should arrive in the office by eight P.M., New York time. Please be there, if it's not inconvenient."

We assured him it was no inconvenience. I took the opportunity to ask him, "Can you expedite Kate's request for the deleted information in the personnel file of Colonel Hambrecht?"

Again, silence. Then he said, "The Department of Defense has informed us that the information is not pertinent to his murder, and therefore not pertinent to this case."

"What is it pertinent to?" I asked.

Koenig replied, "Hambrecht had nuclear clearance. The deleted information pertains to that. It's standard operating procedure to delete nuclear stuff from a personnel file." He added, "Don't waste time on this."

"Okay." In fact, I knew this to be true from another case I had years ago that involved an Air Force officer.

Jack went on to other subjects, talking about the Perth Amboy murder and the forensics pertaining to it, asking about Gabe's lead, which I finessed, and how the case was going, and so forth. He also asked what was in the morning papers, and I informed him, "My photo."

"Did they get your address right?" He laughed. Kate laughed. I said to Jack, "You owe me one on that."

"Meaning?"

"Meaning that me being a target is beyond the call of duty. So, when I need a favor, you owe me one."

He informed me, "You're so many points in the hole, Corey, you're now about even. It's a wash."

Actually, I didn't think I was really a target, but I think Koenig thought so, which showed me a little of the FBI mind-set. So, I played on it and said, "Not a wash. Not by my reckoning."

"You guys know how to keep score, don't you?"

By "you guys," he meant cops, of course. I said, "You owe me."

"Okay. What do you want?"

"How about the truth?"

"I'm working on it."

This seemed to be an admission and acknowledgment that there was more to this than we knew. I said, "Remember the motto of our CIA friends—And ye shall know the truth and the truth shall make you free."

"The truth can make you dead. You're very clever, Corey. And this is not a secure line."

"Auf Wiedersehen," I said, and hung up. I went back to my Incident Report. *So, in conclusion...*

Kate spoke to Jack awhile longer, and read the brief article about the murder of Mr. Leibowitz in Frankfurt. They chatted awhile, then she hung up and said to me, "This is getting creepy."

I looked up from my keyboard and said, "Reminds me of an X-Files episode where Scully's goldfish try to kidnap her."

Ms. Mayfield may have thought I was indirectly making fun of the FBI, and didn't smile.

We went back to our tasks. *So, in conclusion...*

The phones were ringing all over the place, faxes were pinging, computer screens were glowing, telexes were doing whatever they do, clerks came around and plopped more stuff on people's desks, and so forth. This was truly the nerve center, the electronic brain of a far-flung operation. Unfortunately, the human brains in the room couldn't process all this fast enough, or quickly separate the useless from the useful.

I stood and said to Kate, "I'm going to find Gabe. Do you mind staying here so we don't miss Mrs. Hambrecht's call?"

"Sure. What is it you were going to ask her?"

"I'm not sure. Just put her in a good mood and have someone get me."

"Okay."

I left the ICC and went down to the interrogation rooms. I found Gabe talking to a few NYPD/ATTF detectives in the corridor.

He saw me, separated from the detectives, and came toward me. A steady stream of detectives were coming off the elevators or getting on, with Mideastern types in tow. He said, "You get my memo?"

"Yeah. Thanks."

"Hey, I saw your picture in the papers. So did every guy I've questioned today."

I ignored this and said to Gabe, "There are so many Arabs here, we ought to order prayer rugs and get a sign pointing toward Mecca."

"Done."

"Anything new?"

"Actually, yes. I called D.C. The metro cops, not the Bureau. I got to thinking that Mr. Khalil had no idea if he'd be brought to D.C., or to New York. So I inquired about any deceased or missing taxi drivers of Mideastern descent."

"And?"

"Got a missing person report. Guy named Dawud Faisal, taxi driver. Libyan. Went missing on Saturday."

"Maybe he went to get his name changed."

Gabe had learned to ignore me and continued, "I spoke to his wife—in Arabic, of course—and the wife said he went to Dulles for a fare and never came back. Sound a little familiar?"

I thought this over. As Gabe was suggesting, this driver may have been recruited to pick up Khalil in the event Khalil wound up in D.C. At some point, Khalil's organization, whether it was Libyan Intelligence or an extremist group, knew that their boy was going to New York. But Dawud Faisal knew too much already, and somewhere along the line, they whacked him or hopefully only kidnapped him for the duration of the mission. I said to Gabe, "Good thinking. What do we do with that information?"

"Nothing. Another dead end. But it does suggest an elaborate and well-planned operation. There's no Libyan Embassy in this country, but the Syrians have Libyans on staff in their embassy, who are Gadhafi henchmen. All Arabs look alike. Right? The CIA and FBI knows about this arrangement, but allows it to continue. Gives them some Libyans to watch. But somebody wasn't watching Friday night when someone went to Faisal's house with a black bag. That's what Mrs. Faisal said. Same as with Mrs. Jabbar—late-Friday-night visitor, black bag, husband looked worried. It all fits, but it's yesterday's news."

"Yeah. But it *does*, as you say, suggest a well-planned operation with accomplices in this country."

"Also yesterday's news."

"Right. Let me ask you something—as an Arab. Can you put yourself into this guy's head? What is this asshole up to?"

Gabe considered the politically incorrect question that suggested unfortunate racial stereotyping and replied, "Well, think about what he *didn't* do. He didn't sneak into this country anonymously. He got here at our expense—in more ways than one."

"Right. Go on."

"He's pushing camel shit in our faces. He enjoys that. But more than enjoying it, he's...how can I put this...? He's making a game of it, and he actually stacked the deck against himself, if you think about it."

"I thought about it. But why?"

"Well, it's an Arab thing." He smiled. "It's partly this feeling of inferiority regarding the West. The extremists plant bombs on planes, and stuff like that, but they know this isn't very brave, so now and then you get a guy who wants to show the infidels how a brave Mujahade acts."

"A who-ja-what?"

"An Islamic freedom fighter. There's a long tradition of the lone Arab horseman, like in the American West—a mean and lean motherfucker—to use an Arab word—who rides alone and will take on an army. There's a famous poem—'Terrible he rode alone with his Yemen sword for aid; ornament it carried none but the notches on the blade.' Get it?"

"I get it. So what's he up to?"

"I don't know. I'm just telling you who he is."

"Okay, but what's a guy like that *usually* up to?"

"He's up to about three hundred and twenty, and still counting."

"Yeah. Okay, good work, Gabe. How's Fadi doing?"

"Her name is now Maria, and she's a cleaning lady at St. Patrick's." He smiled.

"See you later." I turned to walk away, and Gabe said, "Khalil's going for the big one."

I turned around.

Gabe said, "If he showed up as a waiter at a presidential fund-raiser, I wouldn't be surprised. He's got a lot of hate toward somebody, who he thinks screwed him, or screwed Islam, or screwed Libya. He wants a personal confrontation."

"Go on."

He thought a moment and said, "The name of that poem is 'The Death Feud.'"

"I thought it was a love poem."

"It's a hate poem, my friend. It has to do with a *blood* feud, actually."

"Okay."

"An Arab can be motivated to great acts of bravery for God, and sometimes for country. But rarely for something abstract, like a political philosophy, and hardly ever for a political leader. They often don't trust their leaders."

"I must be an Arab."

"But there's something else that really motivates an Arab. A personal vendetta. You know? Like the Sicilians."

"I know."

"Like, if you kill my son or my father, or fuck my daughter or my wife, I'll hunt you down to the ends of the earth, if it takes me a lifetime, and I'll kill everyone you know or are related to until I get to you."

"I thought my wife's boss was fucking her. I sent him a case of champagne."

"Arabs don't think like that. Are you listening to me?"

"I get it. This could be a blood feud. A vendetta."

"Right. Could be. Also, Khalil doesn't care if he lives or dies trying to avenge the blood feud. It's only important that he tries. If he dies, he's still avenged, and he's going to Paradise."

"I'll try to help him get there."

Gabe said, "If and when you two meet, the one who recognizes the other last is the one who's going to Paradise." He laughed.

I left. Why does everyone find it funny that my picture was in the papers?

Back in the ICC, I got a fresh cup of coffee at the well-stocked coffee bar. There were croissants and brioche, muffins and cookies, but no donuts. Is this interagency cooperation?

Anyway, I mulled over what Gabe had said. While mulling, Kate came over to the coffee bar and said, "Mrs. Rose Hambrecht is on the telephone. I clarified who we are."

I put down my coffee mug and hurried to my desk. I picked up the receiver and said, "Mrs. Hambrecht, this is John Corey of the FBI Task Force."

A cultured voice replied, "What does this concern, Mr. Corey?"

Kate sat at her desk opposite me and picked up her telephone. I replied, "First, my deepest condolences on the death of your husband."

"Thank you."

"I've been assigned to do some follow-up work regarding his death."

"Murder."

"Yes, ma'am. I'm sure you're tired of answering questions—"

"I'll answer questions until his murderer is found."

"Thank you." You'd be surprised how many spouses don't give a rat's ass if the murderer of their departed honey-bun is found, notwithstanding the surviving spouse's hidden desire to personally thank the culprit. But Mrs. H. seemed to be a grieving widow, so this might go well. I winged it and said, "My records show that you've been questioned by the FBI, the Air Force CID, and Scotland Yard. Correct?"

"Correct. And by Air Force Intelligence, British MI-5, MI-6, and our CIA."

I looked at Kate, and we made eye contact. I said, "So that would seem to suggest that some people think there was a political motive for this murder."

"That's what I think. No one is telling me what *they* think."

"But your husband wasn't involved in politics, or in intelligence work, according to his personnel file."

"That's correct. He was always a pilot, a commander, and recently a staff officer."

I was trying to slide into the deleted information without spooking her, so I said contrarily, "We're now starting to think this was a random murder. Your husband was targeted by an extremist group simply because he wore an American military uniform."

"Nonsense."

I thought so, too, so I asked her, "Can you think of anything in his background that would make him a specific target of an extremist group?"

Silence, then, "Well...it has been suggested that his involvement in the Gulf War may have made him a target of Muslim extremists. The captain of the Vincennes—do you know about that?"

"No, ma'am."

So she explained it to me, and I did recall the attempted assassination. I asked, "So, it's possible that this was revenge for his part in the Gulf War?"

"Yes, it's possible...but there were so many fliers involved in that war. Thousands. And Bill was only a major then. So I never understood why *he* would be singled out."

"But some people suggested to you that he was."

"Yes. Some people did."

"But you're not sure of that."

"No. I'm not." She stayed silent awhile, and I let her think about what she *was* sure of. Finally, she said, "Then with the death of Terry and Gail Waycliff, how could anyone still think my husband's death was random, or connected to the Gulf War? Terry wasn't even *in* the Gulf."

I looked at Kate, who shrugged. I said, trying not to sound like I was clueless, "You think the Waycliffs' deaths were related to your husband's death?"

"Perhaps..."

If she thought so, then so did I. But she also thought I was informed, which I was not. I said, "Can you add anything to what we know about the Waycliffs' deaths?"

"Not much more than was in the papers."

"Which story did you read?"

"Which story? The Air Force Times. It was also reported in the Washington Post, of course. Why do you ask?"

I looked up at Kate, who was already on her computer banging away at the keyboard. I replied to Mrs. Hambrecht, "Some of the stories were inaccurate. How did you first hear of the deaths?"

"The Waycliff daughter—Sue—called me yesterday." She added, "They were apparently killed sometime Sunday."

I sat up in my chair. *Killed?* As in murdered? Kate's printer was spitting something out. I said to Mrs. Hambrecht, "Has anyone from the FBI or the Air Force spoken to you about this?"

"No. You're the first."

Kate was reading her printout and marking it. I motioned impatiently for her to hand it to me, but she kept reading it. I asked Mrs. Hambrecht, "Did their daughter indicate to you that she thought there was something suspicious about her parents' deaths?"

"Well, she was very distraught, as you can imagine. She said it appeared to be a robbery, but she sounded as though she wasn't sure." She added, "Their housekeeper was also murdered."

I was running out of generic questions and finally Kate handed me the printout. I said to Mrs. Hambrecht, "Please hold." I put her on hold.

Kate said, "We may have hit on something."

I quickly read the online news story from the *Washington Post*, discovering that Terrance Waycliff was an Air Force general, working in the Pentagon. Basically, it was reported as a straight homicide piece, saying that General and Mrs. Waycliff and a housekeeper were found shot to death in the Waycliffs' Capitol Hill town house late Monday morning by the General's adjutant, who became concerned when his boss didn't report for work at his Pentagon office and didn't answer his telephone or pager.

There was sign of forced entry—the door chain had been ripped from the jamb—and it appeared that the motive was robbery—there were valuables and cash missing. The General was in uniform and had apparently just returned from church, setting the time of the robbery and murder at about Sunday morning. The police were investigating.

I looked up at Kate and said, "What is the link between General Waycliff and Colonel Hambrecht?"

"I don't know. Find out."

"Right." I got back on the line and said to Mrs. Hambrecht, "Sorry. That was the Pentagon." Okay, Corey, give it a shot. I decided to be blunt and truthful and see what happened. I said to her, "Mrs. Hambrecht, let me be honest with you. I have your husband's personnel file in front of me. There is deleted information, and I'm having a difficult time accessing that information. I need to know what was deleted. I want to find out who killed your husband and why. Can you help me?"

There was a long silence, which I knew was not going to end. I said, "Please." I glanced up at Kate, who was nodding approvingly.

Finally, Mrs. Rose Hambrecht said to me, "My husband, along with General Waycliff, participated in a military operation. A bombing mission... Why don't you know this?"

All of a sudden I did know. What Gabe had said earlier was still in my head and when Rose Hambrecht said "bombing mission," it all came together like a key turning fifteen lock tumblers and opening a door. I said, "April fifteen, nineteen eighty-six."

"Yes. Do you see?"

"Yes, I do." I looked at Kate, who was sort of staring into space, thinking hard.

Mrs. Hambrecht further informed me, "There might even be a connection to that tragedy at Kennedy Airport, on the anniversary date, and what happened to the Waycliffs."

I took a deep breath and replied, "I'm not sure about that. But...tell me, has anyone else who was on that mission met with a misfortune?"

"There were dozens of men involved with that mission, and I can't account for all of them."

I thought a moment, then said, "But within your husband's unit?"

"If you mean his squadron, there were, I think, fifteen or sixteen aircraft in his squadron."

"And do you know if any of those men have met with a misfortune that could be viewed as suspicious?"

"I don't think so. I know that Steven Cox was killed in the Gulf, but I'm not certain about the others. The men in my husband's flight on that mission kept in touch, but I don't know about the rest of the squadron."

I was trying to remember Air Force terminology—flights, divisions, squadrons, air wings, and all that, but I was up in the air, so to speak. I said, "Forgive my ignorance, but how many aircraft and men are in a flight and a squadron?"

"It varies, according to the mission. But generally there are four or five aircraft in a flight, and perhaps twelve to eighteen in a squadron."

"I see...and how many aircraft were in your husband's flight on April fifteen, nineteen eighty-six?"

"Four."

"And these men...eight of them, correct?"

"Correct."

"These men..." I looked at Kate, who said into the telephone, "Mrs. Hambrecht, this is Kate Mayfield again. I'm wondering, too, about this connection. Why don't you tell us what you think so we can get quickly to the heart of the matter?"

Mrs. Hambrecht said, "I think I've said enough."

I didn't think so, and neither did Kate. She said, "Ma'am, we're trying to help solve your husband's murder. I know as a military wife that you're security-conscious, and so are we. I assure you, this is one time you can speak freely. Would you like us to come to Ann Arbor and speak to you in person?"

There was another silence, then Rose Hambrecht said, "No."

We waited through yet another silence, then Mrs. Hambrecht said, "All right...the four aircraft in my husband's flight of F-111s had the mission to bomb a military compound outside of Tripoli. It was called Al Azziziyah. You may recall from the news at that time that one of the aircraft dropped a bomb on the home of Moammar Gadhafi. That was the Al Azziziyah compound. Gadhafi escaped, but his adopted daughter was killed, and his wife and two sons were injured...I'm only telling you what has been reported. You can draw any conclusions you wish."

I looked up at Kate, who was again banging away at her keyboard, looking at her video screen, and I hoped she could spell Al Azziziyah and Moammar Gadhafi, or whatever she needed to get into this. I said to Mrs. Hambrecht, "You may have come to some conclusions of your own."

She replied, "When my husband was murdered, I thought that perhaps it had something to do with his Libyan mission. But the Air Force positively assured me that all the names of those men involved with the bombing of Libya were top secret for all time and could never be accessed. I accepted this, but thought perhaps that some person involved with that mission had spoken too freely, or perhaps...I don't know. But I put it out of my mind...until yesterday, when I learned that the Waycliffs had been murdered. It could be a coincidence..."

It could be, but it wasn't. I said, "So, of those eight men who bombed...what's it called?"

"Al Azziziyah. One died in the Gulf War, and my husband was murdered and so was Terry Waycliff."

I glanced again at Kate, who was printing out information. I asked Mrs. Hambrecht, "Who were the other five men on that mission? The Al Azziziyah mission?"

"I may not and will not tell you. Ever."

That was a pretty definite "no," so there wasn't any point in pursuing it. I did ask, however, "Can you at least tell me if those five men are alive?"

"They spoke on April fifteenth. Not all of them, but Terry called me afterward and said everyone he spoke to was well and sent their regards...except...one of them is very ill."

Kate and I made eye contact. Kate said into the phone, "Mrs. Hambrecht, can you give me a phone number where I can reach a member of the Waycliff family?"

She replied, "I suggest you call the Pentagon and ask for Terry's office. Someone there will be able to respond to your inquiries."

Kate said, "I'd rather speak to a family member."

"Then make that request through the Pentagon."

Obviously, Mrs. Hambrecht had her protocols down pat and probably regretted this phone conversation. The military was, to say the least, clannish. But Mrs. Hambrecht apparently had some second thoughts on the subject of clan loyalty, and it had occurred to her that loyalty was supposed to be reciprocal. I had no doubt that the Air Force and other government agencies had juked and jived her, and she knew it—or suspected it. Sensing that I'd come as far as I was going to get, I said to her, "Thank you, ma'am, for your cooperation. Let me assure you that we're doing everything possible to bring your husband's killer to justice."

She replied, "I've already been assured of that. It's been almost three months since..."

I'm a softie sometimes, and I tend to stick my neck out in these situations, so I said, "I think we're close to an answer." Again, I glanced at Kate, and saw she was giving me a kind smile.

Mrs. Hambrecht took a deep breath, which I could hear, and I thought she was starting to lose it. She said, "I pray to God you're right. I...I miss him..."

I didn't reply, but I had to wonder who would miss me if I checked out.

She got herself under control and said, "They killed him with an ax."

"Yes...I'll keep in touch."

"Thank you."

I hung up.

Kate and I stayed silent a moment, then she said, "That poor woman."

Not to mention poor William Hambrecht being chopped up. But women have a different take on these things. I took a deep breath and quickly felt my tough-guy self again. I said, "Well, I guess we know what top secret stuff was deleted by executive order and DoD order. And it wasn't nuclear clearance, as someone told our esteemed boss."

I left Kate to draw the conclusion that perhaps Jack Koenig was telling us less than he knew.

Kate didn't or wouldn't get into that and said to me, "You did a good job."

"You, too." I asked her, "What did you find online?"

She handed me some sheets of printout. I flipped through them, noting that they were mostly *New York Times* and *Washington Post* stories, dated after the April 15, 1986, raid.

I looked up at her and said, "It's starting to make sense, isn't it?"

She nodded and said, "It made sense from the beginning. We're not as smart as we think we are."

"Neither is anybody else around here. But solutions always look easy after you've come to them. Also, the Libyans aren't the only ones dragging red herrings around."

She didn't comment on my paranoia. She did say, however, "There are five men somewhere whose lives are in danger."

I replied, "It's now Tuesday. I doubt if all five men are still alive."

Chapter 43

Asad Khalil woke from his short sleep and looked out the porthole of the Learjet. There was mostly blackness on the ground, but he noticed small clusters of lights and had the sense that the aircraft was descending.

He looked at his watch, which was still on New York time: 3:16 A.M. If they were on schedule, they should be landing in Denver in twenty minutes. But he wasn't going to Denver. He picked up the airphone and with his credit card activated it and called a number he had committed to memory.

After three rings, a woman's voice came on the line, sounding as if she'd been woken from a sleep, as well she should have been at this hour. "Hello...? Hello? *Hello?*"

Khalil hung up. If Mrs. Robert Callum, wife of Colonel Robert Callum, was asleep in her bed at her home in Colorado Springs, then Asad Khalil had to assume that the authorities were not in her home and not waiting for him. Boris and Malik had both assured him of this; the Americans would take his intended victims into protective custody if the authorities had set a trap for him.

Khalil picked up the intercom handset and pressed the button. The co-pilot's voice came into the earpiece. "Yes, sir?"

Khalil said, "I have made a telephone call that will necessitate a change of plans. I must land at the airport in Colorado Springs."

"No problem, Mr. Perleman. It's only about seventy-five miles south of Denver. About ten minutes more flying time."

Khalil knew this, and Boris had assured him that midair changes in plans were not a problem. Boris had said, "For the amount of money you're costing the Libyan treasury, they'll fly you in circles if you want."

The co-pilot said, "I assume you want to land at the main municipal airport."

"Yes."

"I'll radio the necessary flight plan change, sir. No problem."

"Thank you." Khalil put the receiver back on its hook.

He stood, retrieved his black bag, and went into the small lavatory. After using the toilet, he removed the small travel kit from the overnight bag and shaved and brushed his teeth, keeping in mind all Boris' advice about American obsession with hygiene.

He examined himself closely in the lighted mirror and discovered yet another bone splinter, this one in his hair. He washed his hands and face and again tried to rub out the specks on his tie and shirt, but Mr. Satherwaite—or part of him—seemed intent on accompanying him on this flight. Khalil laughed. He found another tie in his black bag and changed ties.

Asad Khalil again went into the black bag and retrieved both Glock pistols. He ejected the magazines from each and replaced them with fully loaded magazines that he had taken from Hundry and Gorman. He chambered a round in each Glock and replaced them in the black bag.

Khalil left the lavatory and put the bag in the aisle beside his seat. He then went to the console, which he noticed had a built-in tape and CD player, as well as a bar. He doubted if there was any music to his liking and alcohol was forbidden. He found a can of orange juice in the small bar refrigerator, and contemplated the food in a clear plastic container. He picked up a round piece of bread, which he suspected was the bagel that the captain had referred to. Boris had the foresight to brief him on bagels. "It is a Jewish creation, but all Americans eat them. During your journey, when you have become Jewish, be certain you know what a bagel is. They can be sliced so that cheese or butter can be spread on them. They are kosher, so no pork lard is used in the baking, which will suit your religion as well." Boris had added, in his offensive way, "Pigs are cleaner than some of your countrymen I've seen in the souk."

Khalil's only regret about Boris' fate was that Malik had not given

Khalil permission to personally kill the Russian before Khalil began his Jihad. Malik had explained, "We need the Russian for mission control while you are away. And no, we will not save him for you. He will be eliminated as soon as we hear you are safely out of America. Ask nothing further about this matter."

It had occurred to Khalil that Boris might be spared because he was valuable. But Malik had assured him that the Russian knew too much and must be silenced. Yet, Khalil wondered, why he, Asad Khalil, who had suffered the insults of this infidel, wasn't given the pleasure of cutting Boris' throat? Khalil put this out of his mind and returned to his seat.

He ate the bagel, which tasted vaguely like unleavened pita, and drank his orange juice, which tasted of the metal can. His limited encounters with American food had convinced him that Americans had little sense of taste, or had great tolerance for bad taste.

Khalil felt the aircraft descending more rapidly now, and noticed that it was banking to the left. He looked out his window and saw in the far distance a great expanse of light, which he assumed to be the city of Denver. Beyond the city, clearly visible in the moonlight, was a wall of towering white-capped mountains rising toward the sky.

The aircraft made more maneuvers, then the intercom crackled. The voice of the co-pilot came into the cabin. "Mr. Perleman, we're beginning our descent into Colorado Springs Municipal Airport. Please fasten your seat belt in preparation for landing. Please acknowledge."

Khalil picked up the handset mounted on the bulkhead, pressed the button, and said, "I understand."

"Thank you, sir. We'll be on the ground within five minutes. Clear skies, temperature six degrees Celsius."

Khalil fastened his seat belt. He heard the landing gear being lowered and locked into place.

The small jet was very low now, flying straight and level, and within a few minutes, they crossed over the runway threshold and within seconds the aircraft touched down on a long, wide runway. The co-pilot said over the intercom, "Welcome to Colorado Springs."

Khalil had the irrational urge to tell the co-pilot to shut up. Asad

Khalil did not want to be in Colorado Springs—he wanted to be in Tripoli. He did not want to be welcomed anywhere in this godless country. He wanted only to kill who had to be killed and to go home.

The aircraft turned onto a taxiway, and the co-pilot slid back the partition and looked into the cabin. "Good morning."

Khalil did not reply.

The co-pilot said, "We'll taxi to the parking area and let you out before we refuel. Do you know how long you'll need here, sir?"

"Unfortunately, I do not. It may be as little as two hours. Perhaps less. On the other hand, the meeting may go well, then there are contracts to be signed, and probably breakfast. So, I may return here about nine o'clock. But no later."

"Fine. We're on your schedule." The co-pilot added, "We're at the corporate jet facility, sir. Is your party meeting you here?"

"I'm afraid not. I am to meet them at the main terminal, then proceed elsewhere. I will need transportation to the terminal."

"I'll see what I can do. It should be no problem."

The Learjet taxied toward a row of large hangars. Khalil unbuckled his seat belt and reached into his bag, keeping an eye on the pilots. He removed both Glocks and stuck them in his waistband behind each hip, so his suit jacket would cover them. He stood, took his bag, and walked toward the pilots. He bent at the knees so he could see through the windshield and side windows of the cockpit.

The captain said, "You might be more comfortable in your seat, sir."

"I wish to stay here."

"Yes, sir."

Khalil scanned the tarmac and the hangars. As in the Long Island airport, he saw nothing to cause him alarm. Also, the appearance of the pilots seemed normal.

The Learjet slowed and stopped on the parking ramp. A man and a woman in overalls appeared, but again, Khalil did not sense danger. But even if they were waiting for him, he would send some of them to hell before he ascended into Paradise.

He recalled that Malik had arrived one day at the training school with a *mursid*—a spiritual guide—who had said to Khalil, "If even the smallest portion of your Jihad is completed, you are assured a place in Paradise. God does not judge as men judge, but he judges what he sees in your heart, where men cannot see. As revealed in the holy scripture, 'If you should die or be slain in the cause of Allah, his forgiveness and his mercy would surely be better than all the riches the infidels amass.'" The *mursid* further assured him, "God does not count the number of enemies you slay for him—God counts only the enemies you swear with all your heart to slay."

Malik had thanked the *mursid*, and after the holy man had gone, Malik had clarified the man's guidance by saying, "God is more pleased when good intentions become great success. Try to kill all of them without getting yourself killed."

As Khalil stared out the cockpit windows, he thought he could do just that. He felt close to complete success in the worldly sense; in the spiritual sense, he already felt complete fulfillment.

The pilot shut down the engines and said, "We can deplane now, sir."

Khalil stood and moved back into the cabin as the co-pilot got out of his seat and went to the exit door, which he opened, causing a step to extend. The co-pilot exited the aircraft and held out his hand for Khalil.

Asad Khalil ignored the outstretched hand and stood in the doorway of the aircraft, searching the landscape before him. The facility was illuminated by large overhead lights, and there seemed to be few people around at this hour, which was not quite 2:00 A.M. local time.

As he stood in the doorway, the pilot remained in his seat, and Khalil knew he could escape if he had to.

He thought back to his training in Libya. He had been assured in Tripoli that the Americans had a standard operating procedure and would not use a sniper to kill him—unless he was barricaded and firing at them, and then only if he had no hostages. Also, they would be sure he was alone, in the open, before they would surround him with armed men—and even women—who would shout at him to raise his hands and surrender. These people would have bulletproof vests, as he himself had, and he understood that only a head shot would kill them or him.

He had practiced this situation in the camp outside of Tripoli, using men—but not women—dressed as police, or in suits, or some in paramilitary clothing. They all spoke a few words of English, and they would shout, "Freeze! Freeze! Hands up! Hands up! Get on the ground! Lay down! Lay down!"

He had been instructed to feign great fear and confusion. He would kneel instead of lying down, and they would draw closer, still shouting, as was their method. Then, as they drew into range, he would draw both pistols from his waistband and begin shooting. The .40 caliber Glock would not pierce body armor, but unlike the older 9mm, it would knock a man down and stun him.

To assure him of this, his trainers had demonstrated on a condemned prisoner. At twenty meters, they had fired a .40 caliber round from the Glock at the prisoner's chest, and the man, wearing a Kevlar vest, was knocked off his feet and lay stunned for a half minute, until he got up and was knocked down again by another round. They did this two more times, until the prisoner would not or could not get up again. A bullet to his head ended the demonstration.

Boris had told him, "Do not expect to win a gun battle. Americans pride themselves on good marksmanship. Guns are an important part of their culture, and the ownership of guns is actually guaranteed in their Constitution."

Khalil found this difficult to believe; Boris often invented things about the Americans, probably to impress and shock everyone.

In any case, they had practiced what Boris called the shoot-out many times, and Boris had concluded, "It is possible to escape from a shoot-out. It has been done. If you are not badly wounded, you simply run, my friend, like a lion, faster and further than they can run. They have been trained not to shoot when they run—they may hit an innocent person or each other. They may shoot and not run, or run and not shoot. In either case, put some distance between you and them, and you may very well escape."

Khalil recalled asking, "And what if they have a man with a sniper rifle?"

"Then," Boris replied, "expect to have your legs shot out from under you. They hesitate to kill with a sniper rifle, and pride themselves on bringing down a man without killing him." He added, "At that point, be sure you have a round left for yourself. You shouldn't miss your head at such close range." Boris had laughed, but said in a soft voice, "I wouldn't kill myself if I were you. Fuck Malik."

Asad Khalil noticed now that the co-pilot was still standing at the foot of the steps, attempting to keep a smile on his face while he waited patiently for his passenger.

The pilot had gotten out of his seat and was also waiting for Khalil to step out.

Khalil gripped his black bag with his left hand and kept his right hand free to draw his pistol. He stepped down onto the tarmac and stood close to the co-pilot.

The pilot followed and walked toward a man whose windbreaker said RAMP AGENT.

Khalil stayed close to the co-pilot, closer than the suggested one meter, but the co-pilot made no move to distance himself from his passenger. Khalil kept scanning the tarmac, the vehicles, the hangars, and the parked aircraft.

The pilot walked back to Khalil and said, "That gentleman will take you to the main terminal in his own car." The pilot added in a softer voice, "You may want to give him a tip, sir."

"How much?"

"Ten should do it."

Khalil was glad he'd asked. In Libya, ten dollars would buy a man for two days. Here, it would buy a ten-minute favor.

Khalil said to the pilots, "Thank you, gentlemen. If I don't return in approximately two hours, then you can expect me, as I said, about nine o'clock. No later."

Captain Fiske replied, "Understood. Please look for us in that building where there's a pilots' lounge."

Khalil joined the ramp agent and after a few words of introduction, they walked to a parking lot and got into the ramp agent's automobile. Khalil sat in the front beside the agent, though in Tripoli he would take the honored position in the rear. The Americans, Boris kept reminding him, were very democratic on the surface. "In my former classless workers state," Boris said, "everyone knew their place and stayed there. In America, the classes pretend to mix with each other. No one is happy with this, but when the occasions arise, the Americans become great egalitarians. However, they spend a good deal of time avoiding those occasions."

The ramp agent started his car and pulled out of the lot. He said to Khalil, "First time in Colorado Springs, Mr.…"

"Perleman. Yes."

"Where you from?"

"Israel."

"No kidding? I was there once. You live there?"

"Yes."

They followed a barrier road toward the municipal terminal.

"Too bad you can't stay around. This is a great place. Skiing, hiking, boating, horseback riding, hunting…well, hunting's kind of unpopular these days."

"Why?"

"People are down on guns, on killing."

"Really?"

"Some people. It's a big issue. You hunt?"

"I'm afraid not. I don't like the sight of blood."

"Well, then I'll keep my mouth shut."

They continued toward the terminal. The ramp agent, forgetting his promise, said, "Lots of military around here. The north side of this airfield is Peterson Air Force Base, and just south of here is Fort Carson. Army. Also, as you probably know, this is the home of the United States Air Force Academy. And in the mountains there to the left is NORAD—North American Air Defense Command—built right into Cheyenne Mountain. There's a thousand people who work deep inside that expensive hole. Yeah, lots of military around here. Real conservative. Now, north of Denver you got Boulder. Real liberal. The People's Republic of Boulder." He laughed, then continued, "Like I said, I was in Israel. My wife's real religious, and she dragged me to Jerusalem once. I don't mean dragged. Great city. We saw all the religious sites. You know? Hey, you're Jewish, right?"

"Of course."

"Sure. We took this tour, you know, to the Dome of the Rock. It's an Arab mosque, but it turns out that this was the main Jewish temple once. I guess you know that. I mean, Christ probably went there. He was Jewish. Now, it's a mosque." He looked at his passenger and said, "I think the Jews should take it back. That's what I think. They had it first. Then these Arabs come along and grab it, and build a mosque there. Why should the Arabs own it?"

"Because Muhammad ascended into heaven from that rock. Peace be unto him."

"Huh?"

Khalil cleared his throat and said, "This is what the Muslims believe."

"Oh...yeah. The guide said that. Hey, I shouldn't talk religion."

Khalil did not reply.

They pulled up to the front of the municipal terminal. Khalil opened his door and started to leave, then leaned back and gave the ramp agent a ten-dollar bill. "Thank you."

"Thank *you*. See you later."

Khalil got out of the automobile, and it pulled away. He saw that the terminal area was nearly deserted at this hour, but noted a taxi stand where two yellow vehicles sat parked.

He walked into the terminal, aware that a man alone at this hour would attract attention if anyone were there to notice. But he didn't even see a policeman. A man pushed a large broom over the tile floor, but did not look at him. They had stressed to him in Tripoli that municipal airports had much less security than international airports, and that even if the authorities were looking for him in America, the risks at these smaller airports would be minimal.

Khalil strode quickly and purposely through the main lobby, remembering from photos and diagrams where the business center and conference rooms were.

In an area just off the lobby, he saw a door marked CONFERENCE ROOM 2. Another sign said RESERVED. There was a keypad, and he punched in a code and opened the door.

He entered the room and closed the door behind him.

The room was equipped with a conference table, eight chairs, telephones, a fax machine, and a computer console. A coffee machine sat in a small alcove.

The computer screen had a message and he read, "Welcome Mr. Perleman—Have a successful meeting—Your friends at Neeley Conference Center Associates." Khalil didn't recall any such friends.

He put his bag on the floor and sat at the keyboard of the computer. He erased the message, then clicked the mouse until he got to his e-mail screen. He typed in his password and waited for the modem to access his account. He then read the one incoming message, which appeared on the screen in English addressed to Perleman, from Jerusalem: *We have reports that business is good with you. Sol's trip to Frankfurt has been terminated. Rival American firm in Frankfurt looking into this. No word here of rival American firm knowledge of your itinerary. Business in Colorado not necessary. Use judgment. California more important. Arrangements for return to Israel remain unchanged. Much success. See you soon. Reply requested. Mazel tov.* It was signed *Mordecai.*

Khalil switched screens to send his response. He typed slowly: *Reply your message in Colorado. Business good. California business soon.*

Khalil tried to fashion more English sentences, but it was not important that he do so. They had told him in Tripoli that any message would do, as long as it contained the word "business," which meant he was well, and not under the control of the Americans. He signed it *Perleman,* then sent his e-mail. He got out of his e-mail account, returned to the main screen, and shut off the computer.

He looked at his watch and saw it was 4:17 A.M. New York time, two hours earlier here.

The home of Colonel Robert Callum was in the foothills of the mountain range, less than half an hour from where he now sat. There was an all-night car rental agency less than ten minutes from the airport by taxi, and there was a car reserved for Samuel Perleman there.

Khalil stood and paced the room. *Business in Colorado not necessary. California more important.* But why couldn't he do both?

He thought about going back through the terminal, taking a taxi to the car rental agency, renting the car, then driving to the home of

Colonel Callum. There was some risk involved. There was always risk involved. But for the first time since he had walked into the American Embassy in Paris, Asad Khalil had a sense of...not danger, he thought, but urgency.

He continued pacing, weighing all the arguments for and against killing Colonel Callum—and, of course, his wife, and whoever else would be in the house.

The plan was simple, just as it had been at General Waycliff's house. He would wait here, where it was safe, then go to the car rental agency, then drive to the Colonel's rural home in the early morning. The Colonel or his wife exited the house each morning, no later than seven-thirty, and retrieved a newspaper from the mailbox at the end of the driveway, then re-entered the house. Like most military people, the Callums were punctual and habitual.

Once the door was open, the Callums were only five or ten minutes away from death, their remaining life-span depending entirely upon Asad Khalil's mood and patience.

He continued to pace the small room, like a lion, he thought, a lion such as the Romans kept in the arena at Leptis Magna, whose ruins he had seen near Tripoli. The lion knows from past experience that a man awaits him in the arena, and the lion becomes impatient. Surely he is hungry. The lion must be kept hungry. The lion also knows, from his past experience, that he always kills the man. What other experience could he know if he is still alive? But he also knows that he has encountered two kinds of men in the arena—the armed, and the unarmed. The armed fought for their lives, the unarmed prayed. They tasted equally well.

Khalil stopped pacing. He squatted on the floor, balancing himself on his haunches, as the Berber tribesmen did in the desert. He raised his head and closed his eyes, but did not pray. Instead, he transported himself into the night desert, and imagined a million brilliant stars in the black sky. He saw the full bright moon hanging over Kufra, his native oasis, and saw the palms swaying in the cool desert breeze. The desert was, as always, quiet.

He remained in the desert for a very long time, keeping the image unchanged, waiting for an unbidden image to appear out of the desert sands.

Time passed on earth, but stood still on the desert. Finally, a Messenger came out from the oasis, draped in cloths of black and white, illuminated by the moonlight, and casting a shadow on the sands as the figure moved toward him. The Messenger stood before him but did not speak, and Asad Khalil dared not speak.

Khalil could not see the Messenger's face, but heard now a voice. The voice said, "In the place where you are now, God will do your work for you. Go from that place to the other place across the mountains. The sands of time are running out. Satan is stirring."

Asad Khalil murmured a prayer of thanks, opened his eyes, and stood. He focused on the wall clock across the room and saw that over two hours had passed, though it seemed only minutes.

He gathered his black bag, left the room, and moved quickly through the deserted lobby.

Outside, he saw a solitary taxi occupied by a sleeping driver. He got into the rear of the taxi and slammed the door hard.

The taxi driver awoke with a start and mumbled some confused words.

Khalil said, "To the corporate jet facility. Quickly."

The driver started the engine, threw the vehicle into gear, and pulled away. "Where?"

Khalil repeated his destination and threw a twenty-dollar bill on the front seat beside the driver. "Quickly, please. I am late."

The driver sped up and got onto the barrier road. Within ten minutes, he was at the corporate jet facility.

Khalil said, "Over there."

The driver pulled up to a small building, and Khalil jumped out and walked rapidly into the building. He located the pilots' lounge, where he found both men asleep on couches. He shook the captain and said, "I am ready. We must leave soon."

Captain Fiske rose quickly to his feet. The co-pilot was already awake, and he stood, stretched, and yawned.

Khalil looked pointedly at his watch and said, "How long will it take to leave here?"

Captain Fiske cleared his throat and said, "Well...I've already made preliminary arrangements for our outbound flight plan...in the event we needed to depart suddenly—"

"Yes. Good. We need to depart suddenly. When can we depart?"

"Well, at this early hour, there's not much other air traffic, so we can take a few shortcuts with standard procedure. With luck, we should be able to taxi out in fifteen minutes."

"As soon as possible."

"Yes, sir." Captain Fiske walked over to a telephone and punched in a few numbers.

"Who are you calling?"

"Control Tower to activate my prior arrangements." Captain Fiske spoke to someone on the other end.

Khalil listened carefully to what the pilot said, but it seemed to be nothing more than technical talk. He looked at the pilot's face, then at the co-pilot, and both men seemed composed.

Captain Fiske said into the phone, "Okay. Thanks." He hung up and said to his passenger, "They promised to have our air traffic control departure clearance within fifteen minutes. The local Tower is already coordinating it with Denver Radar."

"I was under the impression that private flights could take off and land at their convenience."

Captain Fiske replied, "That's not true for private jets, sir, because of the altitudes at which we fly. Above eighteen thousand feet, instrument flight rules always apply."

"I see. Can we go now to the aircraft?"

"Sure."

Fiske led the way out of the lounge, followed by the co-pilot and Asad Khalil. They walked quickly through the cold night air toward the Learjet less than fifty meters away. Khalil stayed very close to his pilots, but he had the sense that there was no immediate danger.

The co-pilot opened the door of the Lear and entered, followed by Khalil, then by the captain.

The pilots took their seats and began their pre-flight checks as Khalil took his seat in the rear of the cabin.

Captain Fiske called back through the open partition, "We'll be under way shortly. Please fasten your seat belt."

Khalil did not reply.

A few minutes later, Fiske started both engines, and the co-pilot radioed, "Springs Tower—Lear Two-Five Echo is ready to taxi."

The Tower replied, "Roger, Lear Two-Five Echo, taxi to Runway Three-Five Left. I've got your clearance when you're ready."

"Go ahead with the clearance," the co-pilot said into the microphone, then began writing down what was being said on a pad in his lap.

Captain Fiske continued to taxi the Lear 60 to the end of Runway Three-Five Left, then wheeled the jet onto the runway centerline. "Here we go," Fiske said to no one in particular as he pushed the twin throttles full forward.

Within half a minute the jet nosed up, left the ground, and was climbing away rapidly from the lights of Colorado Springs below.

Khalil watched the pilots, who had not yet slid closed the partition door between the cockpit and cabin. After a minute, he glanced out the side window to his left and watched the mountains in the distance, which were still visible in the moonlight.

The co-pilot got on the intercom and said, "We need to continue on this northbound heading for a little while longer, sir, to get some altitude before we can turn westbound and on course. We've got those little hills over there to our left, called the Rockies." He laughed and added, "Some of those peaks are twelve thousand feet—about four thousand meters."

Khalil did not reply, but he looked at the foothills and mountains to their left as they continued on what was evidently a northerly heading. Somewhere down there, Colonel Robert Callum lay in bed, a terrible disease eating away at him. Khalil did not feel cheated, nor had he felt cheated when he'd learned that Steven Cox had died in the war against Iraq. God, he decided, wished to claim his share of the spoils of war.

Chapter 44

Kate and I spent the rest of the morning ringing the alarm bell, so to speak.

The Incident Command Center went from ant hill to beehive, if you'll pardon the insect analogy.

Kate and I fielded about a dozen calls from higher-ups, congratulating us, and so forth. Also, all the bosses wanted a private briefing from us, but we managed to put them off. They really didn't want any information—they wanted to say they were part of the solution, though, of course, they were becoming part of the problem.

Finally, I had to agree to a joint task force meeting, such as we'd had yesterday morning. But I was able to put it off until 5:00 P.M. by lying about having to stay by the phones for calls from my worldwide network of informants. In some respects, the bosses here resembled the NYPD brass when a big case was making the news. Photo ops with me and Kate couldn't be far off. In any case, by the time Jack Koenig returned from collecting frequent flier miles, the meeting would be over, and Jack would be pissed. Tough. I *told* him to stay here.

Within a half hour of our conversation with Mrs. Hambrecht, FBI agents were subpoenaing the phone records of Mrs. Hambrecht, and of course General Waycliff for April 15. At the same time, the good people in the J. Edgar Hoover Building were pushing hard to get the deleted information from Colonel Hambrecht's file, which I really didn't need now. But they were also trying to find the names of the surviving men in his flight who bombed Al Azziziyah, which we did need.

According to my e-mail, the FBI had immediately warned the Air Force and DoD that the men on the Al Azziziyah mission were in great and immediate danger, and that some degree of danger also existed for all the other men who flew the Libyan mission. The Air Force agreed to cooperate fully and quickly, of course, but in any bureaucracy, quickly is a relative term.

I didn't know if the CIA was being kept informed, but I hoped they were not. I still had this weird idea that the CIA knew some of this already. Okay, it's easy to get totally paranoid about those people, and half the time, as I keep reminding myself, they're not as smart or cunning as people think. But, as with any secret organization, they themselves sowed the seeds of mistrust and deception. Then they wonder why everybody thinks they're hiding something. What they're usually hiding is the fact that they don't know much. Sometimes I do the same thing, so how could I complain?

I never actually thought that the FBI—which is the heart of the Anti-Terrorist Task Force—knew more than they were telling us in New York. But I was convinced they knew, as Kate said, that the CIA was in business for itself. And they let it pass because, after all, we're all on the same team, and we're all on the side of the angels, and everybody has the best interests of the country at heart. The only problem was in defining best interests.

The good news was that Koenig and Nash were out of the country.

Anyway, during a little lull in the beehive activity, I looked at the printouts that Kate was still running from cyberspace.

I started with a *New York Times* story, dated March 11, 1989, headlined, "Blast Wrecks Van of Skipper Who Downed Iran Jet." This was about the *Vincennes* captain, and didn't seem pertinent, except as an example of what we suspected was happening now.

Kate handed me an Associated Press article, dated April 16, 1996, headlined, "Libya Seeks Trials Over 1986 Air Raids." I read aloud, "'Libya demanded Monday that the United States surrender the pilots and planners behind air raids on Libyan cities ten years ago, and Libyan leader, Moammar Gadhafi, insisted the United Nations take up the case.'" I looked at Kate and said, "I guess we didn't hand anyone over, and Gadhafi got impatient."

"Read on," she said.

I continued, " "We can't forget what happened," Gadhafi said on the anniversary of the U.S. attacks, which Libya said wounded over a hundred people, and killed thirty-seven, including Gadhafi's adopted daughter. "These children...are they animals, and Americans are human beings?" asked Gadhafi, in a CNN interview in the ruins of his bombed-out home, left standing a full decade after the raids.' " I looked up at Kate.

She said, "I'm guessing that Asad Khalil lived in this military compound with the Gadhafi family. Remember, there was a family connection, according to our files."

"Right." I thought about this and said, "Khalil would have been about fifteen or sixteen when the raid occurred. His father was already dead, but he must have had friends and family at this compound."

Kate nodded. "He's avenging them, and the Gadhafi family."

"Makes sense to me." I thought again about what Gabe had said earlier. I said to Kate, "Now we know what's motivating this guy, and I have to tell you...I mean, I don't sympathize with the bastard, but I understand."

She nodded. "I know." She added, "Khalil is more dangerous than we thought, if that's possible. Read on."

I read the end of the AP story, " 'Gadhafi spoke as Libya conducts ceremonies in remembrance of the U.S. raids on the Libyan capital, Tripoli, and on Benghazi. The raids were in retaliation for the bombing of the La Belle discotheque in Berlin on April five, nineteen eighty-six, which killed two U.S. servicemen. Libya's demands mirror U.S. insistence that Libya turn over to American or British courts two men wanted for the nineteen eighty-eight bombing of Pan Am Flight One-Oh-Three over Lockerbie, Scotland, which killed two hundred seventy people.' " I put the article aside and said, "Round and round it goes; where it stops, nobody knows."

"Indeed. A war without end. This is just another battle brought about by the last battle, which will lead to the next battle."

There's a depressing thought. I scanned a few more articles, and came across later articles about the captain of the *Vincennes* incident. As I said, there was no direct connection with Khalil, but I noticed an interesting progression of headlines, one of which, from the *New York Times*, read, "Bombing Inquiry Moving from State Terror Theory." The first of the succeeding articles indicated that maybe the Iranian government wasn't involved after all, and maybe no extremist groups were involved. Maybe it was a lone political weirdo, or maybe it was just a coincidence, or a personal grudge, leaving one wondering about who the captain or his wife pissed off down at the officers club. Bullshit. It was incredible how Washington spun these stories to calm people down and not get everyone worked up about Iranians, or Iraqis, or Libyans, or other countries who really didn't like us, and who got their own people worked up over the slightest incidents.

There must be some sort of great diplomatic strategy at work, but I didn't get it. By this time next month, Asad Khalil would be described as a lone malcontent, angry at the U.S. for smearing ink on his entry visa. If you don't think anyone knows what they're doing in the White House or the J. Edgar Hoover Building or the Pentagon or Langley, try the State Department—they're totally adrift with one oar in the water. Anyway, geopolitics aside, Asad Khalil was either done and gone, or heading toward his next victim. I said to Kate, "Any word on the crews of that mission?"

"No. But they won't necessarily tell us. By now, the FBI could have the survivors covered."

"I think they should tell us. In the NYPD, the investigating detective knows and is responsible for everything."

"I hate to be the bearer of bad news, John, but this is not the NYPD, and you'll be lucky if you even get a phone call telling you Khalil has been arrested."

This really sucked. I racked my brain for ways to get a piece of the action, but all I could think of was that Jack Koenig owed me a favor, though we disagreed on that obvious and simple fact. But Koenig wasn't around, and I had no pull or influence here, and no one else owed me anything. I asked Kate, "Have you slept with a supervisor who could do us a favor?"

"Not in New York."

"Washington?"

She seemed to be thinking about this, counting on her fingers and murmuring numbers until she reached seven, then said, "I think I called in all those favors." She laughed to show me she was just kidding.

Anyway, I flipped through a few more news articles that had arrived from another dimension. I'm not real sure how the Internet works, but it seems to tell you what you ask for, and it does what it's told, which is more than I can say for a lot of people I know.

I came across an article from the *Boston Globe* that was informative. It was dated April 20, 1986. It was a chronology of the events that led up to the American air attack. The first date of the crises was January 7. It said, "President Reagan accuses Libya of armed aggression against the United States, and orders economic sanctions against Libya, and orders all Americans out of that country. Western allies refuse to join the boycott. United States links Libya to an attack by Palestinian terrorists, December twenty-seven, nineteen eighty-five, on Rome and Vienna airports, which killed twenty people."

I continued reading, "January eleven, senior aide to Colonel Moammar Gadhafi says Libya will attempt to assassinate Reagan if United States attacks it. Gadhafi invites Reagan to visit him, saying a meeting might change Reagan's attitude."

I wouldn't have bet the rent money on that. I scanned the chronology and saw a definite pattern of two strong-willed macho males engaged in a pissing contest: "January 13, two Libyan jet fighters approach a U.S. Navy surveillance plane; February 5, Libya accuses U.S. of helping Israelis locate and bring down a Libyan plane, vows revenge; March 24, U.S. warplanes strike a Libyan missile site; March 25, U.S. forces hit four Libyan patrol boats; March 28, Gadhafi warns that military bases in Italy and Spain or any country aiding U.S. 6th Fleet would be targets for retaliation; April 2, bomb explodes on TWA flight en route from Rome to Athens, killing four persons—Palestinian group says it was in retaliation for U.S. attacks on Libya; April 5, bomb explodes in West Berlin disco, killing two U.S. servicemen; April 7, U.S. Ambassador to West Germany says U.S. has very clear evidence of Libyan involvement in disco bombing..." I looked down the page at the rest of the events that led up to April 15, 1986. No one could say they were surprised by the bombing raid, given the personalities involved, and, as we would say today in a gentler America, the misunderstandings brought about by unfortunate cultural and political stereotyping. The answer to the problem might well be in more immigration. At the rate we were going, most of the Middle East would be in Brooklyn within five years.

I picked up the last piece of cyber-news on my desk and scanned it. I said to Kate, "Hey, this is interesting. Did you see this April nineteen, nineteen eighty-six Associated Press interview with Mrs. Gadhafi?"

"Don't think so."

I read, " 'The wife of Libyan leader Moammar Gadhafi, who said her adopted daughter, Hana, eighteen months old, had been killed in the raid, spoke to reporters for the first time since the attack. Seated in front of her bomb-blasted home in Gadhafi's Tripoli headquarters complex, a crutch in her hand, her tone was sharp and defiant. Safia Gadhafi said she would forever consider the United States her enemy, "unless they give Reagan the death sentence." ' "

Kate commented, "It's rare for a woman in a fundamentalist Muslim country to make a public appearance."

"Well, if your house is blown up, you have to go out in public."

"I never thought of that. You're so clever."

"Thanks." I looked back at the article and read aloud, " 'She said, "If I ever find the U.S. pilot who dropped the bombs on my house, I will kill him myself." ' " I said to Kate, "So, there you have it. These people don't hide anything. The problem is, we take it as rhetoric, but they mean it literally, as Colonel Hambrecht and General Waycliff discovered."

She nodded.

I added, "I can't believe the hotshots in Washington didn't know this was coming, or didn't know it had arrived."

She didn't reply.

I continued reading, " 'As for her husband, he is no terrorist, she explained, because if he were, "I would not have children with him." ' " I commented, "Terrorists can make good fathers. That's a sexist statement."

Kate replied, "Can you just read the fucking article without stupid comments?"

"Yes, ma'am." I read, "'Libyan officials said two of Gadhafi's sons were injured in the bombing, one of whom is still in the hospital. Safia Gadhafi stated, "Some of my children are injured, some are scared. Maybe they have psychological damage."'"

Kate said, "Maybe some other children also had psychological damage."

"No maybes about it. I think we have a handle on how little Asad Khalil got fucked up in the head."

"I think so."

We both sat there, digesting yesterday's news. It's always good to know why—now we knew why. We also knew who, what, where, and when—Asad Khalil, assassination mission, in America, now. However, we didn't know precisely *where* he was, and *where* he would strike next. But we were close, and for the first time, I felt confident that we had the son-of-a-bitch. I said to Kate, "If he hasn't flown out of the country, he's ours."

She didn't comment on this optimistic remark, and given the history of Asad Khalil, I had a few doubts myself.

I thought again about Mrs. Gadhafi's remarks, and about the supposed relationship between the Gadhafis and the Khalils, which may have been closer than Mrs. Gadhafi knew. I thought, too, about the theory that Moammar had Captain Khalil killed in Paris long ago, and that Asad obviously didn't know or suspect this. I wondered, too, if little Asad knew that Uncle Moammar was sneaking out of his tent at night and tiptoeing across the sand to Mommy's tent. I had a college prof once who said that a lot of major world historical events have been influenced by sex, marital and illicit. I know this is true regarding my own history—so why not the history of the world?

I tried to imagine this Libyan elite, and they probably didn't differ much from other small autocracies where court intrigue, palace rumors, and power plays were the daily order of business.

I asked Kate, "Do you think Asad Khalil had family members killed in that attack?"

She replied, "If our information about the Khalil family relationship with the Gadhafis is correct, then we can assume the Khalils were in that compound—Al Azziziyah, where, according to Mrs. Hambrecht, four American aircraft dropped bombs. Khalil has killed, apparently, two men who bombed Al Azziziyah. He may have done that to avenge the Gadhafis, but, yes, I think he and his family were there, and I think he may have suffered a personal loss."

"That's what I think." I tried to picture this guy, Asad Khalil, being blown out of his bed at some early morning hour, being scared shitless as the world around him was reduced to rubble. He must have seen lots of dead bodies and pieces of bodies. I made the assumption that he'd lost family members, and I tried to imagine his state of mind—fright, shock, maybe survivor's guilt, then in the end, anger. Finally, at some point, he decided to get even. And he was in a good position to do that, being a victim as well as being part of the inner circle. Libyan Intelligence must have jumped on this kid like he was a new prophet. And Khalil himself...he's been carrying a grudge all his life, and since Saturday, he's been living his dream. His dream, our nightmare.

"What are you thinking about?"

"Khalil. How he got from there to here. He's been fantasizing about coming to America all his life, and we didn't know it, though we should have. And he's not here to start a new life, or to drive a taxi, or to escape persecution or economic misery. He is not who Emma Lazarus had in mind."

"Indeed not."

"And there are more of him out there."

"Indeed there are."

So, we remained at our posts, as we were told to do, but I'm not good at sitting and reading and answering dumb phone calls. I wanted to call Beth, but the situation across my desk had changed, so I e-mailed Ms. Penrose the following: *Can't talk now— Big break in case— May be out of town this p.m.— Thanks for big wet kiss.*

I hesitated at my keyboard. *So, in conclusion*...No, that wasn't good. Finally, I typed, *Need to talk to you— Will call soon.*

I hesitated again, then sent the message. "Need to talk," of course, says it all if you've been there. Lovers' shorthand, as per my wife. *John, we need to talk, i.e., fuck you.*

Kate asked, "Who are you e-mailing?"

"Beth Penrose."

Silence, then, "I hope you didn't use e-mail to tell her..."

"Uh...no..."

"That's really cold."

"How about a fax?"

"You have to tell her in person."

"In person? I don't even have the time to talk to *me* in person."

"Well...a phone call will do. I'll leave."

"No. I'll handle it later."

"Unless you don't want to. I understand."

I felt a headache coming on.

"Really. I understand if you've had second thoughts."

Why did I not believe this?

"What happened last night does not obligate you in any way. We're both adults. So, we'll just cool it awhile, and take it slow. Step at a time—"

"Are you out of clichés yet?"

"Go to hell." She stood and walked away.

I would have jumped up and followed her, but I think we'd already attracted some attention from our co-workers, so I just smiled and whistled "God Bless America" while members of the ATTF Anti-Sex League e-mailed Big Brother about a possible Sexcrime in progress.

Which reminded me that I needed clean undershorts. There was a men's shop close by, and I'd planned a quick stop there later. I was going to let Kate help me pick out a shirt and tie.

Anyway, back to the most wanted terrorist in America. I accessed my e-mail and saw a message from the Counterterrorism section in D.C. marked URGENT. The distribution was limited to only those in the Incident Command Center. I read from the screen: *Air Force informs us it may be difficult to ID pilots who flew Al Azziziyah mission. Records exist for full squadrons and larger units, but smaller sub-units need further research.*

I thought about this. It had the ring of truth, but I was so paranoid by now, I wouldn't believe an exit sign.

I read the remainder of the communiqué: *We have passed on to Air Force substance of Rose Hambrecht's telephone interview with New York agents, i.e., four aircraft, F-111s, on Al Azziziyah mission, eight airmen. General Waycliff murder, etc., see prior comm. on this. A.F. personnel and historian office are researching names, as per above para. Mrs. Hambrecht has been phone-contacted, but will not divulge names via phone. A general officer with escort has been dispatched from Wright-Patterson AFB, Dayton, Ohio, to Hambrecht home, Ann Arbor. Mrs. Hambrecht says she will divulge names to them, in person, with proper ID and waivers, etc. Will advise.*

I printed out the e-mail, circled URGENT in red, and threw it on Kate's desk.

I thought about this situation. First of all, Mrs. H. was a tough cookie and no phone threats, pleas, or cajoling were going to make her do what she'd been told not to do since she'd become an Air Force wife long ago.

Secondly, it occurred to me that, ironically, the security that had been put in place to protect these airmen from retaliation was the same security that had kept us from understanding what was going on, and now was hindering us from protecting them.

Also, it was obvious that the security had already been breached at some point. That's why Asad Khalil had a list of names, and we didn't. But what names did he have? Only those eight airmen on the Al Azziziyah mission? Probably. Those were the guys he wanted to whack. And did he have all eight names? Probably.

I ran this through my mind—eight men, one killed in the Gulf, one murdered in England, one murdered with his wife in their home on Capitol Hill, of all places. One had a serious illness, according to Mrs. Hambrecht. That left four probable victims—five, if the sick guy didn't die before Khalil killed him. But I had no doubt, as I'd said, that some of them were already dead. Maybe all of them, plus anyone around them who was in the wrong place at the wrong time, like Mrs. Waycliff and the housekeeper.

It's a little disturbing when your own country becomes the front lines. I don't pray often, and never for myself, but I prayed for those guys and their families. I prayed for the known dead, the probable dead, and the soon-to-be dead.

Then, I had a brilliant idea, checked my personal telephone book, and dialed a number.

Chapter 45

The Learjet continued its climb out of Colorado Springs. Asad Khalil moved to the port side of the aircraft and sat in the last seat. He stared out at the towering mountains as the aircraft continued north. It seemed to him that they had already climbed above the height of the tallest mountain, yet the aircraft continued straight ahead. In fact, he could now see the large, lighted expanse of Denver ahead.

He considered the possibility that the pilots may have been radioed a warning, and that they would feign a mechanical problem and land at some isolated airfield where the authorities were waiting for him. There was a quick and simple way to find out.

He stood and walked up the aisle to the cockpit. The partition was still open, and Khalil stood behind and between the two pilots. He said to them, "Are there any problems?"

Captain Fiske glanced over his shoulder and replied, "No, sir. Everything's fine."

Khalil studied the two pilots closely. He could always tell when someone was lying to him, or when someone was uneasy, no matter how good an actor that person thought he or she was. There appeared to be nothing in the manner of these two men that betrayed a problem, though he would like to have been able to see into their eyes.

Captain Fiske said, "We're beginning our turn west, over the mountains. We'll get some mountain turbulence, Mr. Perleman, so you may want to return to your seat."

Khalil turned and went back to his seat. The seat belt sign, which the captain had not used before, went on as a bell chimed.

The Lear banked to the left, then leveled off and continued on. Within a few minutes, the aircraft began to be buffeted by updrafts. Khalil could feel the jet continuing to gain altitude, its nose pointed up at a sharp angle.

The pilot came on the intercom and said, "We've just gotten our direct clearance for San Diego. En route time should be one hour and fifty minutes, which will put us on the ground at approximately six-fifteen A.M., California time. That's an hour earlier than Mountain Time, sir."

"Thank you. I think I understand the time zones now."

"Yes, sir."

In fact, Khalil thought, he had been traveling with the sun since Paris, and the earlier time changes had given him some extra hours, though he didn't particularly need them. His next time change would take him across the International Date Line, over the Pacific Ocean, and as Malik had said, "When you cross that line, the captain will announce this, and Mecca will be to the west, not in the east. Begin your prayers facing east, and end them facing west. God will hear you from both his ears, and you will be assured a safe journey home."

Khalil settled back in his leather seat, and his thoughts turned from Malik to Boris. It was Boris, he realized, who was more on his mind than Malik these last few days. Boris had been his primary briefing officer in regard to America and American customs, so it was natural now for Khalil to think more of Boris than of the others, who had trained his mind, body, and soul for this mission. Boris had trained him to understand the decadent culture in which Asad Khalil now found himself, though Boris did not always find American culture so decadent.

Boris had told him, "There are actually many cultures in America, from very high to very low. Also, there are many people, such as yourself, Asad, who believe deeply in God, and there are those who believe only in pleasure, money, and sex. There are patriots and those who show disloyalty to the central government. There are honest men and thieves. The average American is basically more honest than the thieving Libyans I've dealt with, despite your love of Allah. Do not underestimate the Americans—they've been underestimated by the British, the French, the Japanese warlords, Adolf Hitler, and by my former government. The British and French empires are gone, so is Hitler, the Japanese empire, and the Soviet empire. The Americans are still very much with us."

Khalil recalled replying to Boris, "The next century belongs to Islam."

Boris laughed and said, "You've been saying that for a thousand years. I'll tell you what is going to defeat you—your women. They are not going to put up with your nonsense much longer. The slaves will turn on their masters. I saw it happen in my country. One day your women will become tired of wearing veils, tired of being beaten, tired of being killed for fucking a man, tired of sitting home wasting their lives. When that day comes, people like you and your fucking mullahs had better be ready to negotiate."

"If you were a Muslim, that would be blasphemy, and I would kill you right now."

To which Boris had replied, "Yob vas," then buried his fist in Khalil's solar plexus and walked away, leaving Khalil doubled over, gasping for air.

Khalil recalled that neither man spoke of the incident again, but both knew that Boris was already a dead man, so the incident needed no further resolution; it was the equivalent of a condemned prisoner spitting in the eye of the man who would behead him.

The aircraft was still climbing and still being tossed about by the mountain winds. Khalil looked down and saw the moonlit peaks of the snowcapped mountains, but the moonlight did not penetrate into the dark valleys.

He again settled into his seat and again thought of Boris. Boris, for all his blasphemies, his drunkenness, and his arrogance, had proved to be a good teacher. Boris knew America and Americans. His knowledge, Khalil had once discovered, had not been entirely accumulated during his time in America; Boris, in fact, had once worked in a secret training camp in Russia, a KGB facility, called, Khalil remembered, Mrs. Ivanova's Charm School, where Russian spies had learned to become Americans.

Boris had mentioned this secret to him once, in a drunken moment, of course, and told him that this was one of the last great secrets that had never been revealed by the old KGB after the collapse of the Soviet Union. The Americans, too, according to Boris, wanted this secret forever buried. Khalil had no idea what Boris was talking about, and Boris would not mention it again, even after much prodding by Khalil.

In any case, during Boris' time in that school, he claimed to have come to an understanding of the American soul and psyche beyond anything he'd learned by living in America. In fact, Boris had once said, "There are times when I think I *am* an American. I remember once going to a baseball game in Baltimore, and when The Star-Spangled Banner was played, I stood and felt tears forming in my eyes." Boris added, "Of course, I still feel the same way when I hear The Internationale." He smiled and said, "Perhaps I have developed multiple personalities."

Khalil recalled telling Boris, "As long as you don't develop multiple loyalties, you will be much happier and much healthier."

The intercom crackled, breaking into Khalil's memories of Boris.

Captain Fiske said, "Mr. Perleman, I apologize for the turbulence, but this is typical of a mountain range."

Khalil wondered why the pilot would apologize for something that God, not he, controlled.

Captain Fiske continued, "The air should smooth out in about twenty minutes. Our flight plan tonight will take us southwest across Colorado, then over what is known as the Four Corners—the place where the state borders of Colorado, New Mexico, Arizona, and Utah come together. Then we continue southwest across the northern portion of Arizona. Unfortunately, you won't be able to see much after the moon sets, but you should be able to make out the desert and high plateaus."

Khalil had seen more desert in his life than these two had seen in their combined lives. He picked up his intercom and said, "Please let me know when we are passing over the Grand Canyon."

"Yes, sir. Hold on a moment...okay, in forty minutes we'll pass approximately fifty miles south of the South Rim. You may be able to see the general area of the Canyon from the right side, and certainly the high plateau beyond. But I'm afraid it won't be a very clear view from this altitude and distance."

Khalil had no interest at all in seeing the Grand Canyon. He was only assuring himself of a wake-up call in the event he fell asleep. He said, "Thank you. Don't hesitate to wake me when we approach the Canyon."

"Yes, sir."

Khalil tilted back his seat and closed his eyes. He thought again of Colonel Callum and was convinced he had made the correct decision in letting the Angel of Death deal with that murderer. He thought, too, of his next visit, to Lieutenant Wiggins. Wiggins, they had told him in Tripoli, was a man of erratic movements, unlike the men of habit and predictable existence that he had already killed. For this reason, and because Wiggins came at the end of his list, there would be someone in California to assist him. Khalil did not want or need assistance, but this portion of his mission was the most critical, the most dangerous, and also, as the world would soon discover, the most important.

Khalil felt himself falling into a sleep, and he dreamed again of a man who was stalking him. It was a confusing dream in which both he and the man were flying over the desert, Khalil in the lead, the man behind him, but out of sight—and flying over both of them was the Angel of Death that he had seen in the Kufra oasis. The Angel, he sensed, was contemplating which man he would touch and make fall to the earth.

This dream somehow transformed into a dream of him and the lady pilot flying naked, hand in hand, looking for a flat rooftop on which to alight so they could engage in carnal pleasure. Each building they saw below had been destroyed by a bomb.

The intercom crackled, and Khalil awoke with a start, sweat on his face, and his organ aroused.

The pilot said, "Grand Canyon coming up to your right, Mr. Perleman."

Khalil took a long breath, cleared his throat, and said into the intercom, "Thank you."

He rose and went into the lavatory. As he washed his face and hands in cold water, the dreams continued to run through his mind.

He returned to his seat and glanced out the window. The partial moon was nearly overhead, and the earth below was dimly visible.

He reached for the airphone and dialed a number from memory. A man's voice answered, "Hello."

Khalil said, "This is Perleman. I'm sorry to have awakened you."

The man replied, "This is Tannenbaum. It is no problem. I sleep alone."

"Good. I'm calling to see if we have business to do."

The man said, "The business climate is good here."

"And where are our competitors?"

"They are nowhere to be seen."

The rehearsed exchange complete, Khalil concluded with, "I look forward to our meeting."

"As planned."

Khalil hung up and drew a deep breath, then picked up the intercom.

The captain answered, "Yes, Mr. Perleman?"

Khalil said, "My phone call has necessitated another change of plans."

"Yes, sir."

Boris had said to Khalil, "Mr. Perleman should not be overly apologetic when he keeps changing his flight plans. Mr. Perleman is Jewish, and he is paying good money, and he wants service for his money. Business comes first—and everyone else's inconvenience is of no concern to him."

Khalil said to the pilot, "I need now to go to Santa Monica. I assume that is not a problem."

The pilot replied, "No, sir. There isn't much difference in flight time from our present position."

Khalil already knew that. "Good."

Captain Fiske continued, "There won't be any delay with Air Traffic Control at this hour."

"What is our flight time to Santa Monica?"

"I'm putting in the coordinates now, sir...okay, our flight time will be about forty minutes, which will get us near the municipal airport at about six A.M. We may have to slow up en route to be sure to land after six because of the noise curfew."

"I understand."

Twenty minutes later, the Learjet began its descent, and Khalil could see a low range of mountains in the soft glow of the sunrise behind them.

Captain Fiske came on the intercom and said, "We're beginning our descent, sir, so you may want to fasten your seat belt. Those are the San Bernardino Mountains ahead. Also, you can see the lights from the eastern edge of Los Angeles below. Santa Monica Airport is to your left front, near where the coast meets the ocean. We'll be on the ground in ten minutes."

Khalil did not reply. He felt the aircraft steepening its descent, and he could see enormous ribbons of lighted highways and roads below.

He set his wristwatch to California time, which was now 5:55 A.M.

He heard the pilot speaking on the radio, but could not hear the other end of the conversation because the pilots were listening on their earphones. They had not always used the earphones during the flight from New York, and Khalil had now and then been able to hear radio transmissions. He was not suspicious regarding the earphones, but it was worth noting in the event that other small deviations developed.

This flight had been planned in Tripoli so that his change of destination, announced over the Grand Canyon, would put him in Santa Monica no later—or even a few minutes earlier than if he'd landed in San Diego—and no earlier than the noise curfew allowed. If they were waiting for him in San Diego, and they discovered that he was going to Santa Monica, they had less than forty minutes to set a trap there. If it took longer to put the trap into place, the pilot would inform him of some delay, and Asad Khalil would make another request for a flight plan change, this time with a pistol to the pilot's head. Their alternate airport would be a small abandoned facility in the San Bernardino Mountains, only a few minutes' flying time from where they were now. A car with keys taped under the wheel well was waiting for him there. The authorities would soon learn who had the advantage—it was Asad Khalil in a private jet aircraft with a pistol.

They flew out over the ocean, then turned back toward the coast and continued their descent.

He waited for some indication of a delay in landing, but then he heard the Lear's landing gear being lowered, then watched the flaps extend from the back of the wing. Landing lights blinked on the tips of the wings and flashed into the cabin through the portholes.

All of these changes in flight plans, he knew, was no assurance that he would be safe on the ground. But since the possibility existed to change plans almost at will, it was decided to do so, if for no other reason than to make life more difficult for the Americans, if they were trying to trap him.

Malik had shown him two interesting films. In the first film, shown in slow motion, a lion was in full pursuit of a gazelle. The gazelle changed course to the left and Malik said, "Notice that the lion does not overcompensate in his turn to the left in order to intercept his prey. The lion knows that the gazelle can change direction quickly to the right, and the lion will overshoot his prey and lose him. The lion only changes directions at the same angle as his prey and follows directly behind him. He will not be fooled, and he knows that his speed will overtake even the gazelle, as long as he focuses on the animal's rear legs." The film ended with the lion leaping onto the haunches of the gazelle, who collapsed under the weight of his pursuer and waited quietly for his death.

The next film showed a lion being pursued across a grassy plain by a Land Rover in which two men and two women rode. The people in the vehicle, according to the narrator, were trying to get close enough to the lion to shoot a tranquilizing dart into him so that he could be captured for some scientific purpose.

This film, too, was in slow motion, and Khalil noticed that the lion at first tried to rely on its speed to outdistance the vehicle, but as the lion tired, he changed direction to the right, and the vehicle went to the right as well, but at a steeper angle, in order to intercept the lion. But the lion, who now was in the position of a gazelle, knew by instinct and experience what the vehicle was doing, and the lion suddenly veered to the left, and the vehicle found itself far to the right of the retreating lion. The film ended, and Khalil never knew if the lion escaped.

Malik had said, "The lion, when he is the hunter, remains focused on his prey. The lion, as the hunted, relies on his knowledge and instincts as a hunter to trick his pursuers. There are times when you must change directions to avoid your pursuers, and times when an unnecessary change of direction allows your prey to escape. The worst change of direction is that which leads you directly into a trap. Know when to change course, and when to increase your speed, and when to slow your pace if you smell danger ahead. Know, too, when to stop and blend into the bush. A gazelle who has escaped the lion quickly goes back to its mindless grazing. The gazelle is happy filling its belly with grass and not exerting itself. The lion still wants its meat, and will wait for the gazelle to get even fatter and slower."

The Learjet passed over the threshold of the runway, and Khalil looked out the porthole as the aircraft touched down on the concrete landing strip.

The Lear came to a quick stop, then exited onto a taxiway. A few minutes later, the Learjet taxied up to a nearly deserted General Aviation ramp.

Khalil watched closely through the cabin window, then stood, picked up his bag, walked to the front of the aircraft, and knelt behind the pilots. He scanned the scene through the cockpit windows and saw a man in front of them holding a set of lighted wands to guide the aircraft into a parking spot directly in front of the facility building.

Captain Fiske shut down the engines and said to his passenger, "Here we are, Mr. Perleman. Do you need a ride somewhere?"

"No. I am being met." *Though I don't know by whom.* Khalil continued to look through the cockpit windows.

The co-pilot, Sanford, unfastened his harness, stood, and excused himself as he slid past his passenger.

Sanford opened the cabin door and a soft breeze blew into the aircraft. Sanford then stepped out of the aircraft, and Asad Khalil followed him, ready to say good-bye, or to shoot the man in the head, depending on what happened in the next few seconds.

Captain Fiske also exited the aircraft, and the three men stood together in the cool dawn air. Khalil said, "I am to meet my colleague in the coffee shop."

"Yes, sir," said Captain Fiske. "There was a coffee shop in that two-story building last time I was here. Should be open now."

Khalil's eyes darted around at the hangars and the maintenance buildings, still in early morning shadow.

Captain Fiske said, "Over *there*, sir. That building with all the windows."

"Yes, I see it." He looked at his watch and said to Captain Fiske, "I will be driven to Burbank. How long will the drive be?"

Both pilots considered the question, then Terry Sanford replied, "Well, Burbank Airport is only about twelve miles north of here, so it shouldn't take long by car at this hour. Maybe twenty, thirty minutes."

In case the pilots were wondering, Khalil said, "Perhaps I should have gone directly to the airport there."

"Well, the noise curfew there lifts at seven A.M."

"Ah, then that's why my colleague instructed me to meet him here."

"Yes, sir. Probably."

In fact, Khalil knew all of this, and he smiled to himself at the thought of his pilots discovering sometime in the future that their passenger was not as ignorant as they themselves had been regarding his flight plans. He said to them, "Thank you." He addressed both men and said, "And I thank you for your assistance and your company."

Both pilots replied that it had been a pleasure having him on board. Khalil doubted their sincerity, but he gave each man a hundred dollars in cash and said, "I will request you both the next time I need your service."

They thanked Mr. Perleman, touched their caps, and walked off toward the open hangar.

Asad Khalil stood alone, exposed on the open ramp, and waited for the quiet to explode into screaming and running men. But nothing happened, which did not surprise him. He sensed no danger, and felt the presence of God in the rising sun.

He walked unhurriedly toward the glass building to the right of the hangar and entered.

He found the coffee shop and saw a man sitting alone at a table. The man wore jeans and a blue T-shirt and was reading the *Los Angeles Times*. Like himself, the man had Semitic features and was about his age. Asad Khalil approached the man and said, "Mr. Tannenbaum?"

The man stood. "Yes. Mr. Perleman?"

They shook hands, and the man who called himself Tannenbaum asked, "Would you like coffee?"

"I think we should go." Khalil exited the coffee shop.

The man paid for his coffee at the cash register and met Mr. Perleman outside the coffee shop. They left the building and began walking to the parking lot. Mr. Tannenbaum, still speaking English, inquired, "You have had a good journey?"

"If I had not, would I be here?"

The man didn't reply. He sensed that this compatriot walking beside him was not looking for companionship or idle talk.

Khalil asked, "Are you sure you weren't followed?"

"Yes, I'm certain. I am not involved in anything that would cause me to come to the attention of the authorities."

Khalil replied in Arabic, "You are not now involved in any such thing. Do not make any such assumptions, my friend."

The man answered in Arabic, "Of course. I apologize."

They approached a blue van parked in the lot. On the side of the van were the words RAPID DELIVERY SERVICE—LOCAL AND STATEWIDE—GUARANTEED SAME OR NEXT DAY DELIVERY, followed by a phone number.

The man unlocked the doors and got into the driver's seat. Khalil climbed into the passenger seat and glanced into the rear of the van where a dozen packages sat on the floor.

The man started the engine and said, "Please fasten your seat belt to avoid being stopped by the police."

Khalil fastened his seat belt, keeping his black bag on his lap. He said, "Route Four-Zero-Five, north."

The man put the van in gear and drove out of the lot, then out of the municipal airport. Within a few minutes, they were on a wide Interstate, heading north. Khalil and the driver both looked in their sideview mirrors as they gathered speed.

The sky had lightened, and Khalil looked around as they continued north. He saw exit signs for Century City, Twentieth Century-Fox Studios, West Hollywood, Beverly Hills, and something called UCLA. Khalil knew that Hollywood was where the American movies were made, but he had no interest in that subject, and his driver volunteered no information.

The driver said, "I have parcels in the rear addressed to Mr. Perleman." Khalil did not reply.

The driver added, "Of course I do not know what is in them, but I trust you will find everything you need."

Again, Khalil made no reply.

The driver remained quiet, and Khalil saw that the man was becoming uneasy, so Khalil addressed him by his real name and said, "So, Azim, you are from Benghazi."

"Yes."

"Do you miss your country?"

"Of course."

"And you miss your family. Your father, I believe, is still living in Libya."

Azim hesitated, then replied, "Yes."

"Soon you will be able to pay for a visit home, and you can shower your family with gifts."

"Yes."

They drove in silence awhile, both continuing to glance at the sideview mirrors.

They approached an interchange where the Interstate crossed the Ventura Freeway. To the east was Burbank and to the west led to Ventura. Azim said, "I was told you had the address of your meeting."

Khalil replied, "I was told *you* had the address."

Azim nearly ran the van off the road and began sputtering, "No... no... I know nothing... they told me—"

Khalil laughed and put his hand on Azim's shoulder. "Oh, yes. I forgot. I have the address. Take the exit for Ventura."

Azim forced a smile and a small laugh, then slowed into the right-hand lane and took the exit for Ventura.

Asad Khalil looked at the wide valley filled with houses and commercial buildings, then looked off at the high hills in the distance. He noted, too, the palm trees, which reminded him of home.

Khalil dismissed his thoughts of home and thought of his next meal. Elwood Wiggins had been an elusive prey, but eventually he had been located in Burbank, then had unexpectedly moved to the place called Ventura farther north, up the coast. In fact, this move was fateful, and placed Wiggins closer to where Asad Khalil intended to end his visit to America. Khalil could not doubt that the hand of Allah was moving the last few players of the game into place.

If Lieutenant Wiggins was at home, then Asad Khalil could finish this business today, and move on to unfinished business.

If Lieutenant Elwood Wiggins was not at home, then when he ultimately returned home, he would find in his house a hungry lion waiting to rip out his throat.

Khalil let out a small laugh, and Azim glanced at him and smiled, but Azim's smile quickly faded as he saw the expression that had accompanied the laugh. Azim felt the hairs on his neck rise as he stared at his passenger, who had seemed to transform from man to beast.

Chapter 46

I dialed a Washington, D.C., number and a voice came on the line. "Homicide. Detective Kellum."

I replied, "This is John Corey, NYPD, Homicide. I'm looking for Detective Calvin Childers."

"He has an alibi for that night."

Everyone's a comedian. I played the game and replied, "He's black, he's armed, and he's mine."

Kellum laughed and said, "Hold on."

I waited a minute and Calvin Childers came on the line. "Hey, John. How's it going in the Big Apple?"

"Just peachy, Cal. Same old shit." The pleasantries over, I said, "I'm actually working on the Trans-Continental thing."

"Well, whoop-de-doo. How'd you get a piece of *that?*"

"It's a long story. To tell you the truth, I'm working for the FBI now."

"I knew you'd amount to no good."

We both chuckled. Cal Childers and I had attended the previously mentioned seminar at FBI Headquarters some years ago, and we took a liking to each other for reasons that had to do mostly with our problems with authority and Feds. It was Cal who told me the stupid Attorney General joke. I said to him, "You ever find out who killed the Wheaties?"

He laughed and said, "Hey, were those guys stiff, or what? They sat there and never cracked a smile. You working for those turkeys?"

"I'm on a short contract and a shorter leash."

"Yeah. So, what can I do for you?"

"Well...you want me to be straight, or should I try to bullshit you so that the less you know the better?"

"Are we on the air?"

"Probably."

"You got a cell phone?"

"Sure do."

"Call me back." He gave me his direct dial. I hung up and said to Kate, who had returned from wherever it is that women stomp off to, "Excuse me. May I borrow your cell phone?"

She was doing something on her computer, and without a word or a glance, she reached into her jacket and handed me her cell phone.

"Thank you," I said. I dialed Calvin's direct number, he answered, and I said, "Okay. Are you working the General Waycliff case?"

"Nope. But I know the guys who are."

"Good. You guys got any leads?"

"No. Do you?"

"I have the name of the killer."

"Yeah? He in custody?"

"Not yet. That's why I need your help."

"Sure. Give me the name of the killer."

"Sure. Give me some help."

Cal laughed. "Okay, what do you need?"

"Here's the deal—I need the names of some guys who flew a bombing mission with the deceased General. I'll tell you straight, these names are top secret, and the Air Force and DoD are stonewalling, or dragging their feet, or maybe they don't know."

"Then how am I supposed to know?"

"Well, you can casually ask the family, or you can go to the deceased's house and look around. Look in his address book, or in his files. Maybe there's a photo, or something like that. I thought you were a detective."

"I'm a detective, not a fucking mind reader. Give me more."

"Right. The bombing mission was on a place in Libya called..." I looked at a news article on my desk and said, "Al Azziziyah—"

"I got a nephew named Al Azziziyah."

Did I say we both had a weird sense of humor? I said, "It's a *place*, Cal. In Libya. Near Tripoli."

"Oh, yeah, why didn't you say so? Now it's all clear."

"The thing is, I'm pretty sure that General Waycliff was murdered by this guy, Asad Khalil—"

"The guy who offed the whole plane?"

"That's the guy."

"What the hell's he doing in D.C.?"

"Murdering people. He's on the move. I think he wants to whack all the pilots and crew who participated in this raid on Al Azziziyah."

"No shit? Why?"

"Because he wants revenge. I think he lived in this place, and maybe some of those bombs killed people he knew. Understand?"

"Yeah...so now he's getting some payback."

"Right. The bombing mission was on April fifteen, nineteen eighty-six. There were four aircraft involved, F-111s, two-man crews, for a total of eight guys. One guy, a Colonel William Hambrecht, was ax-murdered near Lakenheath Airbase, in England, in January. Then there's General Waycliff, who was on the raid. Another guy, whose name I don't know, was killed in the Gulf War. So now you have two names—Hambrecht and Waycliff. Maybe there's a group photo or something."

"Got it." After a second or two, he said, "Why'd this guy wait so long to even the score?"

"He was a kid at the time. Now he's all grown up." I gave Cal a brief history of Asad Khalil, the defection in Paris, and other stuff that wasn't in the news.

Cal said, "Hey, if this perp was collared in Paris, you must have prints and stuff."

"Good point. Get the FBI lab to send you all they have. They even have fibers from the suit he might have been wearing in D.C. They also have DNA and some other stuff."

"No shit?"

"Yeah, they have that, too."

He laughed, then said, "We haven't turned up much at the murder scene, but if this guy Khalil did it, at least Forensics can know what they're looking for, when the FBI sends prints and fibers and all that."

"Right. Were the victims killed with a forty caliber?"

"No. A forty-five. The General had a military forty-five automatic, and it's missing, according to his daughter."

"I thought you weren't working this case."

"I'm not directly. But it's a big case. White folks, you know?"

"I know. Well, they can't pin this one on you."

He laughed again. "Tell you what—give me a few hours—"

"An hour, tops, Cal. There are other guys out there who need to be covered. We're probably too late for some of them already."

"Yeah, okay. I've got to get hold of the guys working the case, and I'll go over to the victim's house myself and call you from there. Okay?"

"I appreciate it." I gave him Kate's cell phone number and added, "Keep this to yourself."

He said, "You owe me."

"I already paid. Asad Khalil. That's your killer."

"It better be, buddy. I'm sticking my ass out with this."

"I'll cover you."

"Yeah. The FBI always covers the cops."

"I'm still a cop."

"You better be." He hung up. I put the cell phone down on my desk.

Kate looked up from her computer and said, "I heard all of that."

"Well, for the record, you didn't."

"It's okay. I think you're within bounds on that."

"That's a first."

"Don't get paranoid. You're allowed to explore all legitimate avenues of investigation."

"Even top secret stuff?"

"No. But it appears that the perpetrator has this information, and therefore it's already compromised."

"Are you sure?"

"Trust me. I'm a lawyer."

We both smiled. I guess we were pals again.

We had a sort of tenuous conversation, the kind that lovers have after a little misunderstanding about one of the parties not getting rid of someone that he or she was screwing. We segued from that issue to business.

Kate said, "If *we* can get those names and maybe addresses from your friend before Mrs. Hambrecht turns them over, or before the Air Force or DoD finds them, then we have a better shot at continuing to work this case." She added, "As opposed to Counterterrorism in Washington getting the names."

I looked at her. Clearly, Ms. Mayfield, team player, was re-thinking how the game should be played.

We made eye contact, and she smiled.

I said, "Yeah. I hate it when people take things from me that are mine."

She nodded, then said, "You're actually quite clever. I never thought to call D.C. Homicide."

"I'm a homicide cop. This is cop-to-cop. We do it all the time. Gabe just did it." I added, "You were the one who thought to request Colonel Hambrecht's file. See? We work well together. FBI, cops, synergy. It works really well. What a concept. Why didn't I get into this outfit ten years ago? When I think of all the time I wasted on the police force—"

"John, cool it."

"Yes, ma'am."

"I'm ordering lunch. What would you like?"

"Truffles on rye with béarnaise sauce, and pickles."

"How'd you like my fist down your throat?"

My goodness. I stood and stretched. "Let me take you out for lunch."

"Well...I don't—"

"Come on. I need to get out of here. We have beepers." I put Kate's cell phone in my pocket.

"All right." She stood and went over to the duty desk and told the woman there we'd be out and close by.

We exited the ICC and within a few minutes we were down on Broadway.

It was still a nice, sunny day and the sidewalks were crowded with lunch hour people, mostly government workers eating from vending carts or brown bags to save a few bucks. Cops aren't exactly overpaid, but we know how to treat ourselves well. When you're on the job, you never know what the future may bring, so you eat, drink, and make merry.

I didn't want to get too far from the Ministry of Truth, so I walked two blocks south to Chambers Street near City Hall.

As we walked, Kate said, "I'm sorry if I seemed a little…upset before. That's not like me."

"Forget it. The first few days can be tough."

"Exactly."

It doesn't get appreciably better, but why mention that and spoil the moment?

I directed Ms. Mayfield to a place called Ecco, and we entered. This is a sort of cozy place with the flavor of old New York, except for the prices. Ex and I used to come here since we both worked in the area, but I didn't mention that to Ms. Mayfield.

I was greeted by name by the maître d', which never fails to impress one's dining companions. The place was crowded, but we were escorted to a nice table for two near the front window. NYPD guys wearing suits and guns are treated well in New York restaurants, and I guess it's the same all over the world. Yet, I'd have no problem giving up the perks and status for a nice retirement someplace in Florida. Right?

Anyway, the place was full of politicos from City Hall and other city agencies. This is sort of a power place for the municipal elite on fat expense accounts; a place where the city's sales tax is recycled back into the private sector, momentarily, then cycled back to the city. It works really well.

Kate and I ordered glasses of eight-dollar wine from the proprietor, whose name was Enrico. White for the lady, red for the gentleman.

After Enrico left, Kate said, "You don't have to buy me an expensive lunch."

Of course I did. I said, however, "I really owe you a good lunch after that breakfast."

She laughed. The wine came, and I said to Enrico, "I might need to receive a fax here. Can you give me your number?"

"Of course, Mr. Corey." Whereupon he wrote the fax number on a cocktail napkin and left.

Kate and I touched glasses, and I said, "Slainté."

"What's that mean?"

"To your health. It's Gaelic. I'm half Irish."

"Which half?"

"The left side."

"I mean, mother or father?"

"Mother. Pop is mostly English. What a marriage that is. They send each other letter bombs."

She laughed and observed, "New Yorkers are so concerned with national origins. You don't see that all over the country."

"Really? That's boring."

"Like that joke you told about Italians and Jehovah's Witnesses. It took me a few seconds to get it."

"I have to introduce you to my ex-partner, Dom Fanelli. He's funnier than me."

And so forth. I've been here before, but this time it was different for some reason.

We studied the menus, as they say, me studying the right side, Kate studying the left side. The right side was a little steeper than I'd remembered it, but I was saved by the ringing cell phone. I took it out of my pocket and said, "Corey."

Calvin Childers' voice said, "Okay, I'm in the deceased's den, and there's a photograph here of eight guys in front of a jet fighter that someone tells me is an F-III. The date on the photo is April thirteen, and the year is nineteen eighty-seven, not eighty-six."

"Yeah... well, this was sort of a secret mission, so maybe—"

"Yeah. I got it. Okay, but none of the guys in the photo is ID'ed by name."

"Damn—"

"Hold on, sport. Calvin is on the case. So, then I find this big black-and-white photo labeled Forty-eighth Tactical Fighter Wing, Royal Air Force Station Lakenheath. And there's about fifty, sixty guys in the photo. And it's captioned with names, like first row, second row, and standing. So I put the magnifying glass to these faces, and I come up with the matches to the eight guys in the F-III photo. Then I go back to the big photo and get the names of those eight guys from the caption. Seven guys—I already know what Waycliff looks like. Okay, then I go into the deceased's personal phone book, and I get seven addresses and phone numbers."

I let out a deep breath and said, "Excellent. You want to fax those names and numbers to me?"

"What's in it for me?"

"Lunch in the White House. A medal. Whatever."

"Yeah. Probably time in Leavenworth. Okay, there's a fax machine here in the deceased's office. Give me your fax number."

I gave him the restaurant fax and said, "Thanks, buddy. Good job."

"Where do you think this guy Khalil is?"

"He's paying visits to those pilots. Any in the D.C. area?"

"No. Florida, South Carolina, New York—"

"Where in New York?"

"Let's see…guy named Jim McCoy…home is in a place called Woodbury, office is Long Island Cradle of Aviation Museum."

"Okay. What else?"

"You want me to fax this or read it?"

"Just fax it. And fax the eight-guy photo while you're at it. And note who's who on the photo. And while you're at it, send me a good photo on a shuttle flight, call me with the flight number, and I'll send an underemployed agent to pick it up."

"You're a pain in the butt, Corey. Okay, let me get out of here before I start attracting attention." He added, "This Khalil guy is a nasty dude, Corey. I'll also send you some of the photos of the crime scene."

"I'll send you some photos of a planeload of corpses."

"Watch your ass."

"I always do. See you at the White House." I hung up.

Kate looked at me, and I said, "We have all the names and addresses."

"I hope we're not too late."

"I'm sure we are."

I called over a waiter and said, "I need the check, and I need you to get me a fax out of your machine. Addressed to Corey."

He disappeared. I knocked off my wine, and Kate and I stood. I said, "I owe you lunch."

We moved toward the front door, the waiter came, I gave him a twenty, and he gave me a two-page handwritten fax and the faxed photo, which wasn't that clear.

Kate and I went out to Chambers Street, and as we walked quickly back to Federal Plaza, I read the alphabetized names aloud. "Bob Callum, Colorado Springs, Air Force Academy. Steve Cox, with a notation, KIA, Gulf, January nineteen ninety-one. Paul Grey, Daytona Beach/ Spruce Creek, Florida. Willie Hambrecht—we know about him. Jim McCoy in Woodbury—that's Long Island. Bill Satherwaite, Moncks Corner, South Carolina. Where the hell is that? And last, a guy named Chip Wiggins in Burbank, California, but Cal notes that this address and phone number were crossed out in Waycliff's book."

Kate said, "I'm trying to figure out Khalil's movements. He leaves Kennedy Airport by taxi, about 5:30 P.M., presumably in Gamal Jabbar's taxi. Does he then go to Jim McCoy's house with Jabbar driving him?"

"I don't know. We'll know when we call Jim McCoy."

I dialed Jim McCoy's home number on the cell phone as we walked, but all I got was an answering machine. Not wanting to leave too alarming a message, I said, "Mr. McCoy, this is John Corey from the FBI. We have reason to believe that…" *What?* The baddest motherfucker on the planet is gunning for your ass? "…that you may be the target of a man who is seeking revenge for your part in the nineteen eighty-six raid on Libya. Please notify your local police and also call the FBI office there on Long Island. Here's my direct number in Manhattan." I gave it to him and added, "Please be extremely cautious. I advise you and your family to move immediately to another location." I hit the End button and said to Kate, "He may think the call was a hoax, but maybe the word Libya will convince him. Note the time of my call."

She already had her pad out and was making notes. She said, "He may also never get that message."

"Let's not think about that. Think positive."

I stopped at a vending cart and said to the guy, "Two knishes, mustard and sauerkraut."

I then dialed the home number of Bill Satherwaite in South Carolina. I said to Kate, "I'm calling the potential victims at their homes first, before I call the local police. You can get hung up on the phone with the fuzz."

"Right."

"I'll call their respective offices next."

The phone rang and a recorded voice said, "Bill Satherwaite. Leave a message." So, I left a similar message to the one I left at the McCoy residence, ending with my advice to get out of town.

The street vendor heard my message and eyed me suspiciously as he handed me and Kate each a knish wrapped in wax paper. I gave him a ten.

Kate asked, "What's this?"

"Food. Kind of Jewish mashed potatoes. Fried. It's good." I dialed Paul Grey's home number in Florida, noting that his home and business address were the same.

Yet another answering machine instructed me to leave a message. I repeated my message, and the vendor guy stared at me as he handed me my change.

Kate and I continued walking. I tried Grey's office number and heard, "Grey Simulation Software. We're not able to come to the phone," and so forth. I didn't like the fact that no one seemed to be home, and Grey wasn't in his office. I left the same message, and again Kate made a note of it.

I then tried Satherwaite's business number, which was identified as Confederate Air Charter and Pilot Training. I got an answering machine with a sales pitch and a request to leave a number. I left my guarded message, which I noticed was becoming less guarded. I was tempted to scream into the phone, "Run for your life, buddy!" I hung up and said to Kate, "Where is everybody today?"

She didn't reply.

We were walking up Broadway, and Federal Plaza was a block away. I wolfed down half of my large knish in record time as I scanned the fax paper.

Kate took a bite out of the knish, made a face, and deposited it in a trash receptacle, without even offering it to me. My ex used to have the waiter take her half-finished food away without checking with me first. Not a good sign.

I decided to try the number of the Long Island Cradle of Aviation Museum, knowing I'd get a human voice. A woman answered the phone, "Museum."

I said, "Ma'am, this is John Corey, Federal Bureau of Investigation. I need to speak to Mr. James McCoy, the Director. It's urgent."

There was a long silence on the phone, and I knew what that meant. She said, "Mr. McCoy..." I heard a small sob. "...Mr. McCoy is dead."

I looked at Kate and shook my head. I threw my knish in the gutter and spoke as we walked quickly up the block. "How did he die, ma'am?"

"He was murdered."

"When?"

"Monday night. The police are all over the museum...no one is allowed in the building."

"Where are you, ma'am?"

"I'm in the Children's Museum next door. I'm Mr. McCoy's secretary, and his line now rings here, so that—"

"Okay. How was he murdered?"

"He...he was shot...in...one of the aircraft...there was another man with him...do you want to speak to the police?"

"Not yet. Do you know who the other man was?"

"No. Well, yes. Mrs. McCoy said he was an old friend, but I can't remember..."

I said, "Grey?"

"No."

"Satherwaite?"

"Yes. That's it. Satherwaite. Let me put the police on the phone."

"In a minute. You said he was shot in a *plane?*"

"Yes. He and his friend were sitting in a fighter...the F-III...and they were both...the guard, Mr. Bauer, was also murdered..."

"Okay. I'll call back."

I hung up and briefed Kate as we entered 26 Federal Plaza. While we waited for the elevator, I called Bob Callum's house in Colorado Springs and a woman answered, "Callum residence."

"Is this Mrs. Callum?"

"Yes. Who is this?"

"Is Mr. Callum home?"

"Colonel Callum. Who's calling?"

"This is John Corey, ma'am, of the FBI. I need to speak to your husband. It's urgent."

"He's not feeling well today. He's resting."

"But he's home."

"Yes. What is this about?"

The elevator came, but you can lose the signal on an elevator, so we didn't take it. I said to Mrs. Callum, "Ma'am, I'm going to put my partner on the line, Kate Mayfield. She can explain." I put the phone to my chest and said to Kate, "Women talk better to women."

I handed Kate the cell phone and said to her, "I'm going up." As I waited for the next elevator, I heard Kate introduce herself and say, "Mrs. Callum, we have reason to believe that your husband is in potential danger. Please listen, then as soon as I'm finished, I want you to call the police and the FBI, and call base security. Do you live on base?"

The elevator came and I got in, leaving the job in good hands.

Up on the twenty-sixth floor, I moved quickly to the ICC and got to my desk. I dialed the number of Chip Wiggins in Burbank, hoping to get a forwarding number, but a recording informed me that the number had been disconnected and there was no further information available.

I looked at the two fax sheets and noted that Waycliff, McCoy, and Satherwaite had already been murdered, Paul Grey wasn't coming to the phone, and Wiggins was missing. Hambrecht had been murdered in England in January, and I wondered if anyone at the time had thought about why. Steven Cox was the only one to die a natural death, if you consider killed in action as natural for a fighter pilot. Mrs. Hambrecht had indicated that one of the men was very ill, and I guessed that was Callum. The next reunion of these eight guys didn't need a big room.

I got on my computer, and remembering from past experience that homicides in some rural places in Florida are handled by the County Sheriff's Department, I discovered that Spruce Creek is in Volusia County. I got the phone number of the Sheriff's office and dialed, waiting for some cracker to answer. Meanwhile, I knew I was supposed to alert the Counterterrorism section in the Hoover Building ASAP, but a call like that could take an hour, followed by a mandatory written report, and my instinct was to call the potential victims first. In fact, it was more than instinct, it was my own standard operating procedure. If someone was looking to whack me, I'd want to be the first to know about it.

"Sheriff's Department, Deputy Foley speaking."

The guy sounded like he was from my neck of the woods.

"Sheriff, this is John Corey of the FBI field office in New York. I'm calling to report a murder threat against a Spruce Creek resident named Paul Grey—"

"Too late."

"Okay...when and where?"

"Can you identify yourself further?"

"Call me back through the switchboard here." I gave him the general number, and hung up.

About fifteen seconds later, the phone rang and it was Deputy Sheriff Foley. He said, "My computer says this is the number of the Anti-Terrorist Task Force."

"That's right."

"What's the angle?"

"I can't say until I hear what you have to say. National security."

"Yeah? What's that mean?"

This guy was definitely a New Yorker, and I played that card. "You from New York?"

"Yeah. How can you tell?"

"Wild guess. I was NYPD. Homicide. I'm double-dipping."

"I was a patrolman in the One-Oh-Six in Queens. Lots of NYPD down here, working and retired. I'm a Deputy Sheriff. Funny, right?"

"Hey, I might join you."

"They love NYPD here. They think we know what we're doing." He laughed.

So, the bonding over, I said to him, "Tell me about the murder."

"Okay. It took place in the victim's house. Home office. Monday. Coroner put the time of death about noon, but the air conditioner was on, so maybe earlier. Body discovered at about eight-fifteen P.M. by us, acting on a tip from a woman named Stacy Moll. She's a private pilot who flew a customer from Jacksonville Municipal Airport to the victim's home. The house is on an airstrip in this fly-in community called Spruce Creek, outside of Daytona Beach. The customer said he had business with the deceased."

"Indeed he did."

"Right. So this customer tells the lady pilot his name is Demitrious Poulos, an antiques dealer from Greece, but afterward, this woman sees this photo in the newspaper, and she thinks her customer was this guy Asad Khalil."

"She got that right."

"Jesus. I mean, we thought she was hallucinating, but then we find this guy dead...why'd Khalil want to whack this guy?"

"He has a thing about airplanes. I don't know. What else?"

"Well, two gunshot wounds, one abdomen, one head. Also, the cleaning lady got it, single shot to the back of the head."

"Did you recover slugs or shell casings?"

"Only the slugs. Three forty caliber."

"Okay. I guess you notified the FBI."

"Yeah. I mean, we didn't actually believe the Asad Khalil thing, but that aside, the victim seemed to be involved in some sort of defense work, and there could be some computer disks missing, according to the victim's girlfriend, who we located."

"But did you report the possible Khalil connection to the FBI?"

"We did. To the Jacksonville field office. They informed us they were getting Asad Khalil sightings every fifteen minutes." He added, "They didn't take it too seriously, but said they'd send an agent down. Still waiting."

"Right. So, after Spruce Creek, this lady pilot flew her customer where?"

"Back to Jacksonville Municipal, then drove him to Jacksonville International. The guy said he was flying back to Greece."

I thought that over and asked, "Did you notify the Jacksonville PD?"

"Of course. You think I forgot everything I know? They checked out the airport, manifests, ticket sales, and all that, but no Demitrious Poulos."

"Okay... how long did the perp stay in the house with the victim?"

"The pilot said about half an hour."

I nodded. I could almost re-create that conversation between Asad Khalil and Paul Grey.

I asked Sergeant Foley a few more questions and got a few more answers, but basically, that was it. Except that some FBI agents in Jacksonville were in deep shit, but they didn't know it yet. *Asad Khalil sightings every fifteen minutes*. But this one was real. I didn't know who Stacy Moll was, but I'd try to get her a few Federal bucks for good citizenship.

Deputy Foley asked me, "You closing in on this guy?"

"I think so."

"This is one bad motherfucker."

"Really."

"Hey, how's the weather in New York?"

"Perfect."

"Fucking hot here. By the way, the lady pilot said her customer would be back next week. Made a reservation to fly back to Spruce Creek."

"Don't hold your breath."

"Right. She also made a dinner date with him."

"Tell her she's lucky to be alive."

"Really."

"Thanks." I hung up and noted next to Paul Grey's name, "murdered," with the date and approximate time. That reunion just got smaller. In fact, maybe only Chip Wiggins would be there, unless Wiggins had moved east, and already had a visit from Asad Khalil. Bob Callum was still alive in Colorado, and I wondered if Khalil had left him alive because he knew the man was, according to Mrs. Hambrecht, very ill, or because Khalil simply hadn't gotten to Colorado yet. And where was Wiggins? If we could save Wiggins' life, that would be a small victory in a game where the score was Lion five, home team zip.

Kate came into the cubicle and sat at her desk. She said, "I stayed on the line with Mrs. Callum and held until she called the police and the Academy Provost Marshal on a second line. She said she has a gun and knows how to use it."

"Good."

"She said her husband was very ill. Cancer."

I nodded.

"Do you think Khalil knows that?"

"I'm trying to figure out what he *doesn't* know." I said to her, "I called the Daytona Beach police. Paul Grey was murdered Monday, about noon, maybe earlier."

"Oh, my God…"

I told her all of what Deputy Sheriff Foley told me, then said, "The way I figure it, Khalil got in Jabbar's taxi, did not go to McCoy's museum on Long Island, but got out of the area, which was smart, went directly to Perth Amboy, whacked Jabbar, got in a waiting car, drove to D.C., stayed someplace, went to Waycliff's house, whacked the General, his wife, and housekeeper, then somehow got to Jacksonville Municipal Airport, took a private plane to Spruce Creek, whacked Paul Grey and his cleaning lady, then flew back in the private plane to Jacksonville, then…I guess went to Moncks Corner…Satherwaite's business address is a charter flying service, so Khalil charters Satherwaite's plane with Satherwaite piloting, and they fly to Long Island for a reunion. Must have been an interesting flight. They get to Long Island, whack, whack, he does them both in the museum—in an F-III, no less, and also whacks the guard. Fucking incredible."

Kate nodded. "And where did he go next? How did he leave Long Island?"

"I guess he could have flown out of MacArthur. It's not international, so the security is not always tight. But maybe I see a pattern of private planes."

"I think that may be it. So he may be flying to Colorado Springs, or to California in a private plane." She added, "Most likely a jet."

"Maybe. But maybe he wants to quit while he's ahead, before he loses big-time, and he's now on his way to Sandland."

"We haven't given him much reason to lead him to believe he can't go for it all."

"Good point." I took a pencil and started adding up the known dead, not counting the gassed people on Flight 175. I said, "This guy is reducing the overpopulation on the East Coast." I put down my pencil and read, "Andy McGill, Nick, Nancy, and Meg Collins, Jabbar, Waycliff, wife, and housekeeper, Grey and cleaning lady, Satherwaite, McCoy, and a guard. That's unlucky thirteen."

"Don't forget Yusef Haddad."

"Right. Scumbag accomplice. Fourteen. And today's only Tuesday."

Kate didn't reply.

I handed her the fax sheets and said, "Except for Callum, who's covered, Wiggins is the last guy who is—or might be—alive and not covered."

She glanced at the fax sheets and asked me, "Did you try Wiggins?"

"Yeah. Phone disconnected. Let's try to get him through Burbank directory information."

She swiveled around and started banging away at her computer. "What's his real first name?"

"I don't know. See what you can do."

"Call Counterterrorism in D.C. while I play with this. Then call the L.A. field office. Then notify everyone here in the ICC by e-mail, or whatever you think is the quickest."

I didn't exactly jump to it. I was trying to think faster than Khalil was killing people. The knish, mustard, sauerkraut, and red wine were churning in my tummy.

I didn't see any immediate reason to alert my colleagues around me, or to alert Washington. I'd already established that four men were dead and didn't need cover. Callum was alive and covered. That left the problem of finding Wiggins, which Kate and I were more than equipped to handle. I said to her, "I'm going to call the FBI field office in Los Angeles. Or do you want to make that call?"

"I would if you knew how to use the computer better. I'll look for Wiggins." She added, "Ask for a man named Doug Sturgis. He's the Deputy Agent in Charge. Mention my name."

"Right." So I called the Los Angeles field office, identified myself as working with the New York Anti-Terrorist Task Force, which usually gets people's attention, and I asked for Doug Sturgis, who came on the line.

He asked me, "What can I do for you?"

I didn't want to confuse the guy with facts, nor did I want him on the horn with Washington, but I wanted him to help. I said, "Mr. Sturgis, we're looking for a male Caucasian named Chip Wiggins, first and middle name unknown, age about fifty, last known address is Burbank." I gave him the last known and added, "He's a possible witness in a high-profile case that might involve international terrorism."

"What case is that?"

Why is everyone so nosy? I replied, "The case is sensitive and under wraps at this time, and I'm sorry I'm not at liberty to identify it right now, but Wiggins may know something we need to know. All I need is for you to look for him and take him into protective custody, and call me ASAP." I gave him what little I had on Mr. Wiggins.

There was a silence, then Mr. Sturgis asked, "Who is targeting him? What group?"

"Let's say Mideast. And it's important that we find him before they find him. When I get more details, I'll call back."

Mr. Sturgis didn't seem inclined to do my bidding, so I said, "I'm working with Kate Mayfield on this."

"Oh."

"She said you were the man to call for help."

"All right. We'll do what we can." He repeated Wiggins' last known address and phone number, and said, "Give Kate my regards."

"Will do." I gave him my and Kate's direct dial numbers and said, "Thanks." I hung up and dialed LAPD Missing Persons. I ID'ed myself, asked for and got a supervisor, a Lieutenant Miles. I went through my slightly evasive rap and added, "You guys can do a lot better job than we can in locating a missing person."

Lieutenant Miles said, "This can't be the FBI I'm talking to."

I chuckled politely and informed him, "I used to be NYPD, Homicide. I'm here to teach basic law enforcement."

He laughed. "Okay. If we find him, we'll ask him to call you. That's all I can do if he's not a suspect in anything."

"I'd appreciate it if you'd escort him to your location. He's in some danger."

"Yeah? What kind of danger? Now we're talking danger."

"I'm talking national security, and that's all I can say at this time."

"Oh, now you're a Fed again."

"No, I'm a cop in a bind. I need this, and I can't say why."

"Okay. We'll put his picture on a milk carton. You have a photo?"

I took a deep breath and said, "It's not much of a photo, and it's very old, and I don't want posters in his old neighborhood either. We're trying to catch the guy who's trying to find him, not scare the guy off. Okay? By the way, I called the L.A. FBI office, an Agent Sturgis, and they're working on this, too. Whoever finds him first gets a gold medal."

"Wow. Why didn't you say so? We'll get right on it."

Cops can be pains in the ass. "But seriously, Lieutenant."

"Okay. I'll work this one and give you a call."

"Thanks." I gave him my and Kate's phone numbers.

"How's the weather in New York?"

"Snow and ice."

"Figures." He hung up.

Kate looked up from her computer and said to me, "You didn't have to be so secretive with our people, or with the LAPD."

"I wasn't secretive."

"Yes, you were."

"Well, it's not important that they know *why*, it's only important that they know *who*. Chip Wiggins is missing and needs to be found. That's all they need to know."

"They'd be more motivated if they knew *why*."

She was right, of course, but I was trying to think like a cop and act like a Fed, and all this national security crap was getting to me.

Kate went back to her computer and said, "I'm not finding anything in any of the Burbank or L.A. area directories."

"Tell the computer *why* you need to know."

"Fuck off, John." She added, "I am your boss. You'll keep me informed and listen to me."

Wow! I replied, in my I'm-outta-here tone, "If you don't like the way I'm handling this case, and you're not happy with my results so far——"

"Okay. Sorry. I'm just a little tense and tired. I was up all night." She smiled at me and winked.

I sort of smiled back. Ms. Mayfield had a tough side, too, and I'd be well advised to remember that. I said to her, "Sturgis says to say hello."

She didn't reply, but continued banging away at her computer and said, "This guy could have moved to Nome, Alaska, for all we know. I wish I had his Social Security number. Check your e-mail to see if we have any message from DoD or the Air Force regarding the personnel files of those eight guys."

"Yes, ma'am."

I punched up my e-mail, but aside from a lot of interoffice stuff, there was nothing there. I said to Kate, "Now that we have some names, we can specifically ask the Air Force for the Wiggins file."

"Right. I'll do that." She got on the phone, and I heard her making her way through some bureaucracy or another.

I said to no one in particular, "I hope Asad Khalil is having as much trouble finding Wiggins as we are." I got into my computer and tried a few avenues on the Information Highway, including the Air Force Web site. There was an MIA and a KIA section, and incredibly I found Steven Cox, killed in the Gulf War. But there was no section called "Guys on Secret Missions."

Kate put down her phone and announced, "It may take a while to get Wiggins' file. The Chip thing threw them. They want his service number or Social Security number. That's what *we* want."

"Right." I played with my computer, but aside from a good recipe for chocolate chip cookies, I wasn't getting much. I really prefer the telephone.

Kate kept bugging me to call the Counterterrorism office in D.C., and I kept putting it off because I *knew* it would be an hour conversation, followed by me on the shuttle to Washington. And in truth, with only one target still standing for Khalil, it was more important that I find Wiggins before Khalil did.

There are lots of ways to find a missing Joe Citizen in America— land of record-keeping, credit cards, driver's licenses, and all that. I've found people in less than an hour, though sometimes it can take a day or two. But sometimes you never find a person, even if that person was once Mr. Happy Homeowner with a wife and kids.

All I had on this guy was a nickname, a last name, a last known address, and the fact that he'd served in the Air Force.

I called the California Department of Motor Vehicles, and an unusually helpful civil servant gave me the name of an Elwood Wiggins in Burbank with the same last known address plus the date of birth. *Voilà!* Now I had a name, and a DoB that fit. I was getting a picture of this guy Chip, and I pictured a jerk-off who was totally irresponsible about keeping the world informed as to his whereabouts. On the other hand, that might be keeping him alive.

I said to Kate, "Try Elwood from now on. That's on his driver's license." I added, "DoB for Elwood is right for Chip—nineteen sixty. Not a son, not a father."

"Okay." She banged away at her computer, scanning telephone directories.

I called the Los Angeles County Coroner's Office to see if a Mr. Elwood "Chip" Wiggins had done me the favor of dying naturally. A clerk there informed me that a number of Wigginses had passed on in the last year, but not Elwood.

I said to Kate, "Coroner's office doesn't have a record of him."

She said, "You know, he could be out of L.A. County, out of the state, and out of the country. Try the Social Security Administration."

"I'd rather look for him on foot." I added, "Anyway, they'll want his Social Security number."

"Try the Veterans Administration, John."

"You try. But I'll tell you, this character probably doesn't keep anyone informed. I wish we had a hometown for him. Notify Air Force Personnel that we have the name Elwood, and date of birth. That may help their computer."

So, we worked the phones and computers for the next half hour. I called LAPD Missing Persons again and gave them Elwood and the date of birth, and did the same with my colleagues at the FBI L.A. office. But I was running out of clueless people to call. Finally, I had a thought and called Mrs. Rose Hambrecht.

She answered the telephone, and I re-introduced myself.

She informed me, "I've given all the information I had to a General Anderson from Wright-Patterson."

"Yes, ma'am. I don't have that information yet. But I have other information about the eight men on that Al Azziziyah mission, and I wanted to confirm some of it with you."

"Don't you people work in concert?"

No. "Yes, ma'am, but it takes a while, and I'm trying to do my job as quickly—"

"What do you want?"

"Well, I'm focusing on one person, a man named Chip Wiggins."

"Oh, Chip. He's a real character."

"Yes, ma'am. Would you know if his first name is Elwood?"

"I never knew his real first name. Only Chip."

"Okay, I have a Burbank, California, address for him." I read her the address and asked, "Is that what you have?"

"Let me get my phone book."

I held on while Mrs. Hambrecht went to find her phone book. I said to Kate, "How're we doing there?"

"Nothing. John, it's time we turned this problem over to the whole ICC. We've already delayed too long."

"I don't need fifty agents to call back the same people and agencies we've already called. If you need help, then you go ahead and put out an e-mail or however you alert all the troops. Meanwhile, I know how to find a fucking missing person."

"Excuse me?" said Mrs. Hambrecht, who was back on the line. "What did you say?"

"Uh…just clearing my throat." I cleared my throat.

She said, "I have the same address you have."

"Okay…would you know Mr. Wiggins' hometown?"

"No. I don't know much about him. I only remember him from Lakenheath on our first tour of duty there in the nineteen eighties. He's a very irresponsible officer."

"Yes, ma'am. But did Colonel Hambrecht keep in touch with him?"

"Yes. But not often. I know that they spoke last April, on the anniversary of..."

"Al Azziziyah."

"Yes."

I asked her a few more questions, but she didn't know anything, or like most people, she didn't think she knew anything. But you had to ask the right question. Unfortunately, I didn't know the right question.

Kate was listening on the line now and discovered that I was starting to run out of even stupid questions, and she covered the phone and said to me, "Ask her if she knows if he's *married?*"

Who cares? But I asked, "Do you know if he was married?"

"I don't think so. But he could have been. I've really told you all I know about him."

"Okay...well..."

Kate said, "What did he or does he do for a living?"

I asked Mrs. Hambrecht, "What did he or does he do for a living?"

"I don't...well. Actually, I do recall that my husband said Chip took flying lessons and became a pilot."

"He took flying lessons *after* he went on the bombing raid? Isn't that a little late? I mean—"

"Chip Wiggins was not a pilot," Mrs. Hambrecht informed me coolly. "He was a weapons officer. He dropped the bombs. And he navigated."

"I see...so—"

"He took flying lessons after he left the Air Force and became a cargo pilot, I believe. Yes, he couldn't get a job with an airline, so he flew cargo. I remember that now."

"Do you know what company he flew for?"

"No."

"Like FedEx, or UPS, or one of the big ones?"

"I don't think so. That's all I know."

"Well, thank you again, Mrs. Hambrecht. You've been very helpful. If you think of anything else regarding Chip Wiggins, please call me immediately." I again gave her my phone number.

She asked me, "What is this all about?"

"What do you think?"

"I think someone is trying to kill the pilots who flew that mission, and they started with my husband."

"Yes, ma'am."

"My God..."

"I'm...well, again, my condolences."

I heard her say softly, "This isn't right...this isn't fair...oh, poor William..."

"Please be cautious yourself. Just in case. Call the police and the FBI office closest to you."

She didn't reply, but I could hear her crying. I didn't know what to say, so I hung up.

Kate was already on another line, and she said to me, "I'm on with the FAA. They'll have a record of his pilot's license."

"Right. I hope he updated that, at least."

"He'd better, or he'd be in trouble with them, too."

I was glad it was still civil service business hours all over America, or we'd be sitting there playing computer games.

Kate said into the phone, "Yes, I'm still here. Okay..." She picked up a pen, which was hopeful, and wrote on a pad. She said, "As of when? Okay. That's very helpful. Thank you."

She hung up and said, "Ventura. That's a little north of Burbank. He sent a change-of-address about four weeks ago, but no phone number." She got online and announced to me, "He's not in the Ventura directory. I'll try an operator for directory assistance."

She called directory assistance and gave them the name Elwood Wiggins. She hung up and said, "Unlisted number." She added, "I'll have our office there get the number."

I looked at my watch. This had taken about an hour and fifteen minutes. If I'd gotten on the phone with Washington, I'd still be talking. I said to Kate, "Where's the closest FBI office to Ventura?"

"There's a small Resident Agent Office right in Ventura." She picked up the phone and said to me, "I hope we're not too late, and I hope they can set a trap for Khalil."

"Yeah." I stood. "I'll be back in about fifteen minutes."

"Where are you going?"

"Stein's office."

"More cop stuff?"

"Well, with Koenig over the Atlantic, Stein is the man. Be right back."

I hurried off, out of the ICC.

I took the elevator up. Captain Stein's office was located in the southwest corner of the twenty-eighth floor, and I had no doubt it had the exact same number of square feet as Mr. Koenig's southeast office.

I sort of barged past two secretaries and found myself in the middle of the room facing Captain Stein, who was sitting at his large desk, talking on the telephone. He saw me and got off the phone. He said, "This has *got* to be important, Corey, or your ass is in a sling." He motioned me to a chair across from his desk, and I sat.

We looked at each other, and we established that this was important. He opened his desk drawer, took out a seltzer bottle, and poured two vodkas in plastic cups. He handed one to me, and I drank about half of it. The Federal angels wept somewhere. He took a slug himself and said, "What do we got?"

"We got it all, Captain, or most of it. But we got it about seventy-two hours too late."

"Let's hear it."

So I told him, quickly, without regard to grammar or punctuation, cop-to-cop, if you will, my mouth in New York overdrive.

He listened, nodded, made no notes, then sat there when I finished and thought for a while. Finally, he said, "Four dead?"

"Five, counting Colonel Hambrecht. Fourteen counting everyone, not to mention everyone on board Trans-Continental Flight One-Seven-Five."

"That fuck."

"Yes, sir."

"We'll find this fuck."

"Yes, sir."

He thought a moment, then said, "And you didn't call anyone in Washington?"

"No, sir. The call would be better coming from you."

"Yeah." He thought awhile longer, then said, "Well, I guess we have one or two chances to collar this guy, assuming he didn't already get to this guy Wiggins, or, if he goes for Callum."

"Right."

"But maybe he's done, or he thinks it's getting hot around here, and he's out of the country already."

"Possible."

"Shit." Stein thought a moment and asked, "So the Ventura office is covering Wiggins' last known address?"

"Kate is working on it."

"And this guy Colonel Callum is covered?"

"Yes, sir."

"Are the Feds laying a trap for Khalil there?"

"I believe they're just covering the Callums. I'm thinking if Khalil knows this guy is dying, would he go for a dying man?"

Stein replied, "If the dying man dropped a bomb on him, I think he would. I'll call the FBI in Denver and strongly suggest they set a trap." He finished his vodka and I finished mine. I thought about asking for seconds.

Captain Stein looked up at his high ceiling awhile, then looked back at me and said, "You know, Corey, the Israelis took eighteen years to set- tle the score for the Munich Olympic massacre in nineteen seventy-two."

"Yes, sir."

"The Germans released the captured terrorists in exchange for the release of a hijacked Lufthansa flight. The Israeli Intelligence people systematically hunted down and assassinated each of those seven Black September terrorists who massacred the Israeli athletes. They got the last one in nineteen ninety-one."

"Yes, sir."

"They play a different game in the Mideast. There's no clock on the field. Ever."

"I see that."

Stein stayed silent a half minute or so, then said, "Did we do everything we could?"

"I think *we* did. I'm not sure about anyone else."

He didn't reply to that, but said, "Hey, good work. You like it here?"

"No."

"What do you want?"

"Back where I was."

"You can't go home again, my boy."

"Sure I can."

"I'll see what I can do. Meantime, you have enough writing to do to keep you busy through the weekend. I'll talk to you later." He stood, and I stood. He said, "Tell Ms. Mayfield I congratulate her, if it means anything from a cop."

"I'm sure it does."

"Okay, I've got a lot of calls to make. Scram."

I didn't scram. I said, "Let me fly out to California."

"Why?"

"I'd like to be in on the last act."

"Yeah? There's an army of police and FBI there by now. They don't need you."

"But I need to be there."

"Why not Colorado Springs? I'm thinking geography. Colorado's on the way to California, last time I checked."

"I'm tired of chasing this asshole. I want to be ahead of him."

"What if you go to California, and the FBI nabs him in Colorado Springs?"

"I can live with that."

"I doubt it. Okay, go wherever you want to go. You're better off out of here, anyway. I'll authorize it. Use your own credit card to save time. Don't get yourself killed. You have reports to write. Beat it before I change my mind."

I said, "I'll take my partner along."

"Whatever you want. You're the Golden Boy, for the moment. Hey, you watch the X-Files?"

"Sure do."

"How come he's not fucking her?"

"Beats me."

"Me, too." He put out his hand, and we shook.

On my way out the door, he called after me, "I'm proud of you, John. You're a good cop."

Captain Stein's office felt like a breath of fresh air in 26 Federal Plaza.

I went quickly back downstairs to the ICC, aware that I could be trapped here by a phone call, or an FBI boss. I went directly to Kate's desk and said, "Let's go." I took her arm.

"Where?"

"California."

"Really? Now?"

"Right now."

She stood. "Do I need——?"

"Nothing. Just your gun and shield."

"Badge. We say badge."

"I say walk faster."

She kept up with me as I walked toward the elevators. She asked, "Who authorized——?"

"Stein."

"Okay."

She thought a moment, then said, "Maybe we should go to Colorado Springs."

Maybe we should. But I didn't want an argument from my lady boss, so I said, "Stein only authorized California."

"Why?"

"I don't know. I think he wants me as far away as possible."

The elevator came, we got on, and rode down to the lobby, then walked out to Broadway. I hailed a taxi, and we both got in. I said to the driver, "JFK."

We pulled out into heavy downtown traffic.

I said to Kate, "What's the news from Ventura?"

"Well, our Ventura office got Wiggins' unlisted phone number, and they called Wiggins' house while I was on the phone. They got his answering machine, but didn't leave a detailed message. They just told him to call them the minute he got the message. Then, they sent some agents to his house, which they tell me is near the beach. Then they called for reinforcements from L.A." She added, "There are only a few people in the Ventura office."

"I hope they don't find him home and dead. What do they plan to do? Surround the house with tanks?"

"We are not as stupid as you think, John."

"That's reassuring."

"They'll check his house, interview neighbors, and, of course, lay a trap for Khalil."

I tried to picture a bunch of guys in blue suits running around a beachside neighborhood, knocking on doors and flashing Fed creds. That should cause a stampede of illegal aliens heading south. Meanwhile, if Asad Khalil was staking out the neighborhood, he might get a little suspicious. But to be fair, I wasn't sure how I'd handle this either.

I said to Kate, "Call Ventura again."

She took her cell phone and hit the buttons. The taxi was approaching the Brooklyn Bridge. I looked at my watch. It was just 3:00 P.M., noon in California. Or was it the other way around? I know it changes west of Eleventh Avenue.

Kate said into the cell phone, "This is Mayfield. Anything new?"

She listened awhile and said, "Okay, I'm flying to LAX. I'll call back later with my flight info. Meet me with a car at Arrivals and get me to the police helipad. Meet me with a car wherever you intend to land me in Ventura. Right. I'm authorizing it. Don't worry about it unless you don't do it. Then you have something to worry about." She hung up and looked at me. "See? I can be an arrogant asshole like you."

I smiled, then asked her, "So what's new in Ventura?"

"Well, the three available Ventura agents got to Wiggins' house, and they broke in on the possibility that he was dead inside. But he's not home. So, they're in the house, and they're using his phone book to call people where he might be or who might know where he is. If he's dead, he's not dead at home."

"Okay. He could be on a long flight."

"Could be. He flies for a living. Could be his day off. He could be at the beach."

"How's the weather in Ventura?"

"It's always the same. Sunny and seventy-two." She added, "I put in two years with the L.A. office about three years ago."

"How'd you like it?"

"It was okay. Not as interesting as New York."

We both smiled. I asked her, "Where the hell is Ventura?"

She told me, but I didn't quite understand the geography, or all the Spanish names she was throwing around.

We were over the Brooklyn Bridge, and the cabbie got on the southbound BQE, which is the Brooklyn-Queens Expressway, and may have once moved cars in an express-like fashion, but I've never seen that, except at 3:00 A.M. I flashed the Fed creds and said to the driver, "Step on it." I always say that even when I'm not late and I don't know where I'm going.

I asked the cabbie where he was from, and he told me he was from Jordan. That was a new one. Pakistan is way ahead, but Macedonia is starting to catch up. I said to Kate, "Stein said to congratulate you."

She didn't reply.

I said, "There's an outside chance I can get back on the job—on the police force."

Again, no reply, so I changed the subject and asked her, "Where do you think Khalil is?"

"California, Colorado Springs, or in transit."

"Maybe. But maybe he only worked the East Coast where he has some assets, then he got out, maybe with the help of some Mideast embassy. California and Colorado are a long way off."

"John, this guy didn't come halfway across the world to..." She glanced at the taxi driver and said, "...to eat part of a meal. You know that."

"Right. But I'm wondering how he's getting to L.A. The airports are dangerous for him."

"The big ones are. I once had a fugitive who went from L.A. to

Miami via small airports. He could have walked it faster, but he managed to give us the slip until we caught up with him in Miami."

"Right."

"And don't forget a private charter. I had a drug king once who chartered a private jet. A lot of them do that. No security points, no records of their flight, and they can go anywhere they can land."

"Maybe we should alert the local airports in the Ventura area."

"I suggested that to the Ventura office. They reminded me that there are dozens of small airports in the area, dozens more close by, and a private aircraft can land twenty-four hours a day at most of them. You'd need an army to watch every General Aviation facility, not to mention abandoned or unmanned landing fields."

"I guess." Kate seemed to know this stuff better than I did. I do cabs and subways. Half of my fugitives wind up going to their mother's house or their girlfriend's apartment or hanging around their favorite saloon. Most criminals, especially murderers, are really stupid. I like the smart ones better. They give me a little challenge and a lot of entertainment. I said to Kate, "Khalil pulled this off because of speed. Like a purse snatcher. He's no idiot, and he knows that we'd be on to his game within three, maybe four days."

"That's optimistic."

"Well, we got on to him in less than four days. Right?"

"Okay. And?"

"And...I don't know. Wiggins is either dead already, or he's someplace else. Like maybe he flew cargo to the East Coast, and Khalil knew this and nailed him already. Those agents in his house might be there for a long time waiting for Wiggins or Khalil to show up."

"Possible. You have any other ideas? You want to stay here in New York? You can go to that five o'clock meeting and listen to everyone tell you how brilliant you are."

"That's a cheap shot."

"And you don't want to miss the eight o'clock meeting tonight with Jack when he returns from Frankfurt."

I didn't reply.

"What do you want to do, John?"

"I don't know...this guy has me a little baffled. I'm trying to put myself in his head."

"Do you want my opinion?"

"Sure."

"I say we go to California."

"You said go to Frankfurt."

"I never said that. What do you want to do?"

"Call Ventura again."

"They have my cell phone number. They'll call me if anything develops."

"Call Denver."

"Why don't you buy your own cell phone?" She dialed the Denver FBI office and asked for an update. She listened, thanked them, and hung up. She said to me, "The Callums have been taken to housing at the Air Force Academy. We have agents staking out their off-post residence and waiting inside. Same as Ventura."

"Okay." We were on the Belt Parkway now, heading for Kennedy Airport. I was trying not to second-guess myself, trying to stay on the roll I was on, without blowing it at the end.

It's not easy being the man of the hour. Normally, I wouldn't confide all these doubts to anyone, but Kate and I were more than partners now. I said to her, "Call the L.A. office, and tell them to put a watch on consulate offices of countries that might help Khalil effect an escape. Also, make sure they're watching Wiggins' former Burbank house in case Khalil has old information and shows up there."

"I did that while you were talking to Stein. They informed me they already knew what to do. Get a little respect for the FBI, John. You're not the only genius in law enforcement."

I thought I was. But I guess I'm not alone. Still, there was something bothering me about how this was playing out. I was missing something, and I knew that I knew what it was, but I couldn't think of what it was. I ran the whole thing through my mind from Saturday to now, but whatever it was kept slipping away into a dark corner in my mind, not unlike how Asad Khalil kept slipping away.

Kate was on her cell phone to the woman at Fed Plaza who makes travel arrangements and was saying we needed info on first available non-stop flights to LAX and to Denver. She listened, glanced at her watch, then said, "Hold on." She said to me, "Where would you like to go?"

"Where Khalil is going."

"Where is he going?"

"L.A."

She got back on the phone and said, "Okay, Doris, can you book the American flight? No, I don't have an authorization number." She looked at me, and I pulled out my credit card. Kate took it and said to Doris, "We'll pay and put in for reimbursement." She gave Doris my credit card info, and added, "Make it First Class. And please call the L.A. office and advise them of our arrival. Thanks." She handed me my card. "For you, John, they'll pick up First Class."

"That may be true today, but by tomorrow they may not even pick up this cab ride."

"The government loves you."

"Where have I failed?"

Anyway, we got to JFK, and the driver said, "Which terminal?"

This is where I came in, on Saturday, with the same question. But this time I wasn't going to the Conquistador Club.

Kate said to the driver, "Terminal Nine."

We got to the American Airlines terminal, got out, I paid the cab, and we went inside to the ticket counter, where we got two First Class tickets in exchange for my available credit. We ID'ed ourselves and filled out Form SS-113 that identified our carry-on luggage as two Glock .40 caliber automatic pistols.

We had fifteen minutes to catch the flight, and I suggested a quick drink, but Kate looked at the departure board and said, "They're boarding now. We'll get a drink on board."

"We're carrying."

"Trust me. I've done this before."

Indeed, there was another side to Polly Perfect, which hadn't been revealed to me heretofore.

So, we flashed the creds and the Firearm Boarding Pass at the security point and got to the gate with minutes to spare.

The First Class flight attendant was in her late seventies or thereabouts, and she put her dentures in her mouth and welcomed us aboard. I asked her, "Is this a local or an express train?"

She seemed confused, and I recalled that seniority sometimes equaled senility.

Anyway, I was out of airline jokes, so we gave her our Firearm Boarding passes, and she looked at me as though wondering how I'd been licensed to carry. Kate gave her a reassuring smile. But perhaps this was all my imagination.

The flight attendant checked her manifest to assure herself of our identity, then went into the cockpit with the boarding passes, as per regulations, to inform the captain that two armed law enforcement people were on board, a nice lady and a weirdo, traveling together in First Class.

We found our seats, two bulkhead seats on the port side. First Class was half full, mostly people who looked like Angelenos going home, where they belonged.

Well, we weren't tarmacked too long, considering this was JFK, and we took off only fifteen minutes late, which the captain said we'd make up in the air, which is better, I guess, than making it up on the ground at LAX by taxiing to the gate at six hundred miles an hour while deploying the emergency chutes.

So, off we went, into the wild blue yonder, armed, motivated, and hopeful.

I said to Kate, "I forgot to buy clean underwear."

"I was about to mention that."

Ms. Mayfield was in a rare mood.

Another First Class flight attendant came around with newspapers, and I asked for the Long Island *Newsday*. I looked for and found a story about the Cradle of Aviation murders, which I read with interest. I noticed that this major Long Island story had no byline, which is sometimes a tip-off that the authorities were managing the story a little. In fact, there was no mention of Asad Khalil, and the motive for the murders was described as a possible robbery. Right. Standard armed robbery of a museum. I wondered if anyone was buying the museum robbery-homicide story. Specifically, I was wondering if Khalil would buy it if he saw it and believed that we were clueless. Worth a try, I guess.

I showed the story to Kate, who read it and said, "Khalil left a very clear message in that museum. That means he may be finished and heading home, or he has tremendous arrogance and contempt for the authorities, and he's saying, 'You won't figure this out until it's too late. Catch me if you can.'" She thought a moment, then said, "I hope it's the latter, and I hope he's going where we're going."

"If he is, he's probably there already. I just hope he's waiting until dark to make his next move."

She nodded.

Well, I needed a little drink or two, so I asked Kate to sweet-talk the grandma flight attendant into alcoholic beverages.

Kate informed me, "She won't serve us. We're armed."

"I thought you said—"

"I lied. I'm a lawyer. I said, 'Trust me.' That means I'm lying. How stupid can you be?" She laughed.

I was stunned.

She said, "Have a root beer."

"I'm going to have a fit."

She took my hand.

I calmed down and ordered a Virgin Mary.

The First Class meal wasn't too bad and the movie, starring John Travolta playing an Army CID guy, was terrific, despite a bad review that I recalled reading in Long Island's *Newsday*, written by John Anderson, a so-called movie critic, whose opinion I trusted to be the exact opposite of mine.

Kate and I held hands during the movie, just like kids in a theater. When the movie ended, I put my seat back and fell asleep.

As often happens, I had a revealing dream about what I couldn't think of when I was awake. I mean, the whole thing just came to me—what Khalil was up to, where he was going next, and what we had to do to catch him.

Unfortunately, when I woke up, I forgot most of the dream,

including the brilliant conclusions I'd come to. It's sort of like having a great sex dream and waking up realizing you still had a woody.

But I digress. We landed at LAX at 7:30 P.M., and for better or worse we were in California. This was either where we needed to be, or it wasn't. We'd soon find out.

BOOK FIVE

California, The Present

Go then and slay a man I shall name. When you return, my angels shall bear thee again to Paradise. And should you die, nevertheless they will carry you to Paradise.

—The Old Man of the Mountain, a thirteenth-century prophet, and founder of the Assassins

Chapter 47

We deplaned first, went outside, and were met by an FBI guy from the Los Angeles office, who drove us to the police heliport where a waiting FBI helicopter flew us to Ventura, wherever the hell that is.

Everything on the ground looked like Queens, except for the palm trees and the mountains. We flew a few miles out over some ocean, I guess, then along the coastline with some hefty hills just to our right. The sun sat right above the ocean, but instead of rising, like it does on *my* ocean, it was setting. Is this place weird, or what?

Within twenty-five minutes, we landed at a heliport at the community hospital on the east side of Ventura.

A blue Crown Victoria sedan was waiting for us, driven by a guy named Chuck. Chuck was dressed in tan pants and a sports coat and wore running shoes. Chuck claimed to be an FBI agent, but looked like a parking attendant; FBI, California version. But they all *think* the same because they all attended the same Manchurian Candidate school at Quantico.

Chuck asked us lots of questions as he drove us to the Ventura sub-office of the Federal Bureau of Investigation. I guess they don't handle that many international terrorist mass murder cases in Ventura. In fact, Kate had mentioned on the plane that this office had been closed once and recently re-opened, for some reason.

The office was located in a sort of modern office building surrounded by palm trees and parking lots. As we walked through the parking lot, I looked around. I smelled flowers in the air, and the temperature and humidity were perfect. The sun had almost set, but there was still a glow in the sky.

I asked Kate, "What does the FBI do here? Grow avocados?"

"Adjust your attitude."

"Sure." I pictured the agents here with blue Brooks Brothers suits, sandals, and no socks.

Anyway, we went into the building, up an elevator, and found a door that said FEDERAL BUREAU OF INVESTIGATION. They had their round coat-of-arms on the door, too, which said JUSTICE DEPARTMENT, and showed the standard scales of Justice, balanced, not tipped, and the motto FIDELITY, BRAVERY, INTEGRITY. Can't argue with that, but I said to Kate, "They should add, 'Politically Correct.'"

She'd gotten into the habit of ignoring me and rang the buzzer.

The door opened, and we were met by a nice lady agent named Cindy Lopez, who said, "Nothing new. We have three Ventura agents in the Wiggins house, joined by three agents from the L.A. office. There are two dozen L.A. and Ventura agents in the neighborhood, the local police have been alerted, and everyone is in radio and cell phone contact. We're still trying to locate Elwood Wiggins. We discovered from papers in his house that he flies for Pacific Cargo Services, and we visited them, but they informed us he's not scheduled to fly until Friday. But they mentioned he sometimes calls in sick on Friday. We have two agents at Pacific Cargo at Ventura County Airport in the event he shows up there. We've also assigned agents to locations where he's known to frequent. But we're developing a picture of this man as a free spirit whose movements are erratic."

"I like this guy."

Agent Lopez sort of smiled and continued, "His girlfriend is also missing. They are both known to be campers, and it's very possible they're camping."

"What's camping?" I asked.

Ms. Lopez looked at Ms. Mayfield. Ms. Mayfield looked at me. I said, "Oh, like in the woods. Tents and all that."

"Yes."

"Do you have a cell phone number for Wiggins or the girlfriend?"

"Yes. For both. But no one answers."

I thought a moment and decided that camping out was better than being dead, but not by much. I said to Ms. Lopez, "It sounds like you did a thorough job."

"I'm sure we have." She handed Kate a message slip and said, "Jack Koenig called from New York. He'd like you to call him back. He'll be there until midnight, New York time, then home."

I said to Kate, "We'll call him from the Wiggins house. When we have something to report."

She said, "We'll call now."

"How'd you like to be talking to Jack here when Khalil shows up at the Wiggins house?"

She nodded reluctantly and said to Cindy Lopez, "Okay, we'd like to go out to Wiggins' house."

"We're trying not to show too much activity there."

I replied, "Then we'll sit quietly on the couch."

She hesitated, then said, "If you go, we would appreciate it if you stayed at least until the early morning hours." She said pointedly, "We're trying to set a trap, not have an open house party."

I wanted to remind her that none of us would be at this juncture if it weren't for moi. But I resisted saying the obvious. You see how quickly a case can get away from you?

Kate, always the diplomat, replied to Agent Lopez, "You're in charge, and we're not here to get in the way."

Leaving Ms. Lopez to wonder why we *were* there. It's all ego, lady. I said, "Ms. Mayfield and I began this case with the tragedy at Kennedy Airport, so we'd like to see it through. We'll stay out of the way when we get to the Wiggins house."

I didn't think she believed me, but she said, "I would advise you to wear body armor. I have extras here I can loan you."

I had the urge to strip and show Ms. Lopez that bullets just passed through me with no effect. I said, "Thank you, but—"

Kate interrupted, "Thank you, we'll borrow the body armor." She informed Ms. Lopez, "Never ask a man if he wants a bulletproof vest or a pair of mittens. Just make him put it on."

Ms. Lopez smiled knowingly.

Well, I was feeling really special now, surrounded by nurturing, caring females who knew what was best for dopy little Johnny. But then I thought about Asad Khalil, and I hoped they had a vest in my size.

So off we went into their locked armament room behind a steel door. Inside the room were all the goodies—rifles, shotguns, stun grenades, handcuffs, and so on.

Ms. Lopez said, "You can try the vests on in the men's and ladies' rooms, if you wish."

Kate thanked Agent Lopez as she left.

I took off my tie, jacket, and shirt, and said to Kate, "I won't peek."

She took off her Heinz ketchup jacket and her blouse, and I peeked.

We both found our size and strapped on the body armor. I said, "This is just like a scene in the X-Files—"

"Stop with the fucking X-Files."

"But doesn't it bug you that those two never get it on?"

"She doesn't *love* him. She respects him and he respects her, and they don't want to lose or complicate that special relationship of trust."

"Say again?"

"Personally, I think they should be fucking by now."

We exited the armory and thanked Agent Lopez. Chuck, who had picked us up at the community hospital heliport, escorted us back out to the parking lot and drove us toward the house of Mr. Elwood "Chip" Wiggins.

A lot of thoughts ran through my mind as the car moved west toward the left coast. I'd come a long way to be here, but Mr. Asad Khalil had come a much longer way. His journey had begun in a place called Al Azziziyah somewhere in Libya, a long time ago. He and Chip Wiggins had, for a few brief minutes, shared a point in space and time on the night of April 15, 1986. Now, Asad Khalil wanted to repay the visit, and Mr. Wiggins didn't know he had company calling. Or, Chip Wiggins had already met Asad Khalil, and the business was finished. In that case, no one would show up at the Wiggins house, ever. But if Wiggins and Khalil had not yet met, I wondered who would be the first to come walking up the driveway.

The sunlight was almost gone, and the streetlights had come on.

As we approached Wiggins' neighborhood, Chuck radioed ahead to the stakeout units around Wiggins' house, so that they didn't get nervous or trigger-happy. Chuck then used his cell phone to call the agents inside the Wiggins house for the same reason, and I said, "Tell them to put coffee on."

Chuck didn't pass this along, and I could tell by his end of the phone conversation that the agents in the house weren't thrilled about the unexpected company. Fuck 'em. It's still my case.

Anyway, we drove through the long, straight streets of a suburban neighborhood that Chuck said was near the ocean, though I didn't see or smell the ocean. All the houses were on undersized lots, and the houses themselves were all single-story stucco boxes with attached garages and red-tile roofs, plus at least one palm tree per house. It didn't seem to be an expensive neighborhood, but in California, there was no way to tell, and neither did I care. I said to Chuck, "Were these houses always here, or did they come down in a mudslide from the mountains?"

Chuck chuckled and replied, "They slid down from the last earthquake, which preceded the wildfires."

I liked Chuck.

Happily, I didn't spot any of the stakeout units, and more happily, I didn't spot any kids around.

Chuck said, "That's the house on the right—second from the cross street."

"You mean the white stucco with the red-tile roof and the palm tree?"

"Yeah...they all...second from the end."

Kate, riding in the rear, kicked the back of my seat, which was some sort of signal, I guess.

Chuck said, "I'll stop, you exit, and off I go. Front door is unlocked."

I'd noticed when I got in the car that the interior lights had been disconnected, just like on the East Coast, which was reassuring. It was possible these people knew what they were doing.

The car stopped, Kate and I got out quickly, and without running moved up the broken concrete walkway. To the right of the door was a large picture window with the Venetian blinds shut. In my old neighborhood, the whole block would have been hip to the strange goings-on by this time, but this block looked like a scene from a 1950s B movie where everyone is dead from atomic radiation. Or maybe the Feds had evacuated the neighborhood.

So, I opened the door, and in we went. There was no foyer, and we found ourselves in a combination L-shaped living room/dining room, lit only by a single dim table lamp. A man and a woman stood in the middle of the room, wearing blue slacks and shirts, FBI nylon windbreakers with creds attached. They had big grins on their faces, and their hands were outstretched in greeting. Not really.

The man did say, "I'm Roger Fleming, and this is Kim Rhee."

Ms. Rhee was Oriental, now called East Asian, and by her name I guessed she was of Korean ethnicity. Roger was white bread and mayonnaise. I said, "I guess you know our names—I'm the one called Kate."

Agent Fleming did not smile and neither did Agent Rhee. Some people get all serious when they're waiting around for a deadly shootout. Cops tend to yuck it up, probably to cover their nervousness, but the Feds take *everything* seriously, including, I'm sure, a day at the beach.

Agent Rhee inquired, "How long will you be staying?"

I replied, "As long as it takes."

Kate said, "We don't intend to become involved with the actual apprehension of the suspect, if he shows up here, unless you need us. We're here only to help identify him, and to take a statement after he's apprehended. Also, we will escort him back to New York or Washington to answer a variety of Federal charges."

That wasn't exactly what I had in mind, but it was good for Fleming and Rhee to hear that one of us was sane.

Ms. Mayfield continued her mission statement and said, "If Mr. Wiggins shows up first, then we'll interview him and ask that he turn over the premises to us, then someone here can escort him to another location. In either case, we intend to remain in this house waiting for the suspect, who we believe is headed this way."

Ms. Rhee replied, "We have determined that six is the optimum number of agents we want in the house for safety and logistical reasons.

So if the suspect shows up at this location, we'll ask you to take a position in a back room, which we'll show you."

I said, "Look, Ms. Rhee, Mr. Fleming, we could all be here a long time, sharing the bathroom and bedrooms, so why don't we cut the shit and try to get along? Okay?"

No response.

Kate, to her credit, changed her tone and said, "We've worked this case since Asad Khalil landed in New York. We've seen over three hundred dead people aboard the aircraft he arrived in, we've had a member of our team murdered, our secretary murdered, and the duty officer murdered."

And so on. She put it to them, too nicely, I thought, but they got the message and actually nodded when Kate was finished.

Meanwhile, I looked around the living room, which was sparse, yet tasteless. Also, untidy, which I'd like to blame on the Feds, but which I thought was probably a reflection of Mr. Wiggins' attitude toward life.

Ms. Rhee offered to introduce us to her colleagues, and we followed her into the kitchen, while Mr. Fleming took up his position at the front picture window, peering through the Venetian blinds. High-tech. But, of course, someone on stakeout would tip us if anyone approached the house.

The kitchen was dimly lit by a soft fluorescent bulb under a cabinet, but I could see that the kitchen was circa 1955, and in it were another man and woman, also wearing the urban commando outfit of dark trousers, dark blue shirts, and nylon windbreakers. Their blue baseball caps sat on the counter. The man was seated at the small kitchen table, reading a stack of case reports with a flashlight. The woman was positioned at the back door, peering through the small door window.

Ms. Rhee introduced us to the gentleman, whose name, like my own, was Juan, though his last name was a mouthful of Spanish that I didn't catch. The lady was black, and her name was Edie. She gave us a wave as she continued to scope out the backyard.

We next went back through the L-shaped area and through a door into a small foyer, off of which were three doors, the smaller leading to a bathroom. In the larger of the rooms, a bedroom, a man dressed in a suit sat at a computer station and monitored his radio and two cell phones, while he played with Mr. Wiggins' PC. The only light in the room came from the monitor screen, and all the blinds were shut.

Ms. Rhee made the introductions, and the guy, whose name was Tom Stockwell, and whose ethnicity was pale, said to us, "I'm out of the L.A. office, and I'm the case agent for this detail."

I guess that left me out. I decided to be nice and said to Tom, "Ms. Mayfield and I are here to help, without being intrusive." How's that?

He replied, "How long you staying?"

"As long as it takes."

Kate briefed Tom by saying, "The suspect, as you should know, could be wearing body armor, and he has in his possession at least two weapons, forty caliber Glocks, which, like the body armor, he apparently took from the two agents on board the aircraft." She gave Tom a verbal report, and he listened attentively. She concluded with, "This man is extremely dangerous, and we don't expect taking him without a fight. But, of course, we need to take him alive."

Tom replied, "We have various non-lethal weapons and devices, such as the goo-gun and the projectile net, plus, of course, gas and—"

"Excuse me?" I said. "What's a goo-gun?"

"It's a big handheld device that squirts this goo that hardens immediately and immobilizes a person."

"Is this a California thing?"

"No, Mr. Corey. It's available nationwide." Tom added, "And we also have a net which we can fire and which ensnares the individual."

"Really? Do you have real guns, too?"

Tom ignored me and continued his briefing.

I interrupted and asked, "Have you evacuated the neighborhood?"

He replied, "We went through a lot of debate about that, but Washington agrees that to try to evacuate the neighborhood could be a problem."

"For whom?"

He explained, "First of all, there's the obvious problem of agents being seen making the notifications. Some people aren't home, and may come home later, so this could take all night. And the residents would be inconvenienced if they had to leave their homes for an indefinite period." He added, "We did, however, evacuate the houses on both sides and the back of this one, and there are agents in place at those houses."

The subtext here was that it was more important to capture Asad Khalil than it was to worry about taxpayers getting caught in a crossfire. I couldn't honestly say I disagreed with this.

Ms. Rhee added, "The stakeout people are instructed not to try to apprehend the suspect on the street, unless he senses danger and attempts to flee. Most likely, the apprehension will take place in or near this house. The suspect is most probably alone, and most probably armed with only two handguns. So, we don't expect there to be a large exchange of gunfire—or *any* gunfire—if we play it right." She looked at Kate and me and said, "The block will be sealed off to traffic if we determine that the suspect is approaching."

I personally thought the neighbors wouldn't even notice if there was a wild shoot-out on the front lawn if they had their TVs and stereos turned up loud enough. I said, "I agree, for what it's worth." But I had this mental image of a kid riding by on a bicycle at the worst possible moment. It happens. Boy, does it happen.

Kate said, "I assume the stakeout people have night vision devices."

"Of course."

So, we chatted awhile, and Kate made sure to tell Tom and Kim that she was once a California girl herself, and everyone agreed that we all had our acts together, except perhaps me, who felt a bit like the odd man out here.

Tom mentioned that Wiggins' former house in Burbank was also occupied and staked out by the FBI, and he informed us that the local police here and in Burbank were alerted but not asked for direct assistance.

At some point, I got tired of hearing how everything was covered nine ways from Sunday, and I asked, "Where's your sixth person?"

"In the garage. The garage is very cluttered, so Wiggins can't pull his car in there, but the door has an automatic opener, so Wiggins may enter that way on foot and come into the kitchen through the connecting door. That's probably what he'll do, since it's closest to where he'll pull his car into the driveway."

I yawned. I was a little jet-lagged, I guess, and I hadn't had much sleep in the last few days. What time was it in New York? Later? Earlier?

Tom also assured us that every effort was being made to locate Elwood Wiggins before he headed back to this house. He said, "For all we know, Khalil could try to take him while he's driving home. Wiggins drives a purple Jeep Grand Cherokee, which is not here, so we're alert for that vehicle."

I asked, "What does the girlfriend drive?"

Tom replied, "A white Ford Windstar, which is still at the girl-friend's house in Oxnard, which is also under surveillance."

Oxnard? Anyway, what could I say? These people had their act together, professionally speaking. Personally, I still thought they were dweebs.

I said, "I'm sure you've been briefed about Khalil's prior visits to Wiggins' now-deceased squadron mates. This indicates to me that Khalil may have more information about Chip Wiggins than we do. He's been looking for Wiggins a lot longer than we have." I added, for the record, "There's a strong possibility that Mr. Wiggins and Mr. Khalil have already met."

No one commented on that for a few seconds, then Tom said, "That doesn't change our job here. We wait and see if anyone shows up." He added, "There's an area-wide alert for Khalil and for Wiggins, of course, so we may get a happy call from the police telling us that one or the other or both have been found. Wiggins alive, and Khalil in cuffs."

I didn't want to be the bearer of further bad karma, but I couldn't picture Asad Khalil in cuffs.

Tom sat back at Wiggins' PC and said, "I'm trying to get a clue as to where Wiggins might be, from his computer. I've checked his e-mail to see if he corresponded with a state or national park, or reserved a camping space, something like that. We think he's camping..." he said, I guess to me, "...that's where you go out into the woods with a tent or a camper."

I concluded that Ms. Lopez and Tom had spoken.

I asked Tom, "Have you checked out Wiggins' underwear?"

He looked at me from his computer. "Excuse me?"

"If he wears medium boxers, I'd like to borrow a pair."

Tom thought about this a moment, then replied, "We've all brought changes of clothing, Mr. Corey. Perhaps someone—one of the men, I mean—can loan you a pair of shorts." He added, "You can't use Mr. Wiggins' underwear."

"Well, I'll ask him directly if he shows up."

"Good idea."

Kate, to her credit, wasn't trying to pretend she didn't know me. She said to Kim Rhee, "We'd like to see the garage and the rest of the house."

Ms. Rhee led us into the foyer and opened the door of a room that faced the backyard. The room, formerly a bedroom probably, was now an entertainment center that held a huge television, audio equipment, and enough speakers to start another earthquake. On the floor, I noticed six overnight bags. Ms. Rhee said, "You can use this room later. The couch pulls out into a bed." She added, "We'll all take turns getting some sleep if this goes through the night."

I used to think that my worst nightmare was Thanksgiving dinner with my family, but being trapped in a small house with FBI agents just took first place.

Ms. Rhee also showed us the small bathroom, leading me to wonder if she'd once been a Realtor. One thing I noticed that was missing from this house was any military memorabilia, which indicated to me that Elwood Wiggins did not want to be reminded of his service. Or maybe he just lost everything, which would be consistent with the profile we'd developed on him. *Or*, maybe we had the wrong house. It wouldn't be the first time the Feds got the address wrong. I thought about mentioning this last possibility to Ms. Rhee, but this is a touchy subject with them.

Anyway, we went back to the kitchen, and Ms. Rhee opened a door that revealed a cluttered garage. Sitting in a lawn chair behind some stacked cardboard boxes was a suntanned, blond-haired young man, obviously the junior agent, reading a newspaper by the light of the overhead fluorescent bulb. He stood and Ms. Rhee motioned him back in his seat, so that he was out of sight if the garage door suddenly opened electronically. She said to Kate and me, "This is Scott, who volunteered for garage duty." She actually smiled.

Scott, who looked like he'd just stepped off a surfboard, flashed his capped teeth and waved.

I said, "Like, yeah, dude, hang in there—you know?" Of course I didn't say that, but I really wanted to. Scott was my size, but he didn't look like the boxer shorts–type.

Ms. Rhee closed the door, and we stood in the kitchen with Edie and Juan. Ms. Rhee said, "We've stocked some frozen and canned food here so that no one has to come or go, if this lasts awhile." She added, pointedly, "We have six days of food for six people."

I had a sudden image of FBI agents turning cannibal when the food ran out, but I didn't share this thought. I was already on thin ice, or the California equivalent.

Juan said, "Now that we have two more mouths to feed, let's order pizza. I need my pizza."

Juan was okay, I decided. Unfortunately, he was a lot heftier than me, and also not the boxer shorts–type.

Edie said to me, "I cook a mean microwaved macaroni and cheese."

We all chuckled. This sucked. But so far, it was turning out a hell of a lot better than I could have expected twenty-four hours ago. Asad Khalil was within our grasp. Right? What could go wrong? Don't ask.

But at least if Wiggins was still alive, he had a good chance of staying alive.

Kate said she was going to call Jack Koenig and invited me to join her in the back room. I declined the opportunity, and she went off. I stayed in the kitchen, chatting with Edie and Juan.

Kate returned about fifteen minutes later and informed me, "Jack says hello and congratulations on a good piece of detective work. He wishes us luck."

"That's nice. Did you ask him how Frankfurt was?"

"We did not discuss Frankfurt."

"Where's Ted Nash?"

"Who cares?"

"I do."

Kate glanced at our colleagues and said softly, "Don't obsess on things of no importance."

"I just want to punch him in the nose. No big deal."

She ignored this and said, "Jack wants us to call him if something develops, of course. We're authorized to escort Khalil, dead or alive, to New York, rather than Washington. That's a major coup."

"I think Jack is counting his chickens before they're caught and cooked."

Again, she ignored me and said, "He's working with various local police forces to put together a clear picture of Asad Khalil's movements, his murders, and who his accomplices are or might have been."

"Good. That will keep him busy and off my back."

"That's exactly what I told him."

I think Ms. Mayfield was joshing me. Anyway, we didn't want to amuse our colleagues any further, so we ended the conversation.

Edie offered us coffee, and Kate, Kim, and I sat at the kitchen table with Edie, while Juan watched the back door. They were all very interested in everything that had happened since Saturday, asking us questions about things that hadn't appeared in the news or in their reports. They were curious about what the mood was at 26 Federal Plaza and what the bosses in Washington were saying, and all that. Law enforcement people, I decided, were the same all over, and despite the initial politely masked hostility upon our arrival, we were all getting along well—bonding and all that good stuff. I thought about leading everyone in a chorus of "Ventura Highway," or maybe "California, Here I Come." But I didn't want to overdo this West Coast moment.

It seemed that everyone knew I was ex-NYPD, so I guess they'd been warned, if that's the right word, or perhaps they just figured it out.

It was one of those times when things seem calm and normal, but everyone knows that a ringing telephone could stop the show and make your blood run cold. I've been there, and so had everyone else in that house. I guess I must thrive on this stuff because I wasn't thinking about my nice, safe classroom at John Jay. I was thinking of Asad Khalil, and I could almost taste the murdering bastard. In fact, I thought of Colonel Hambrecht being chopped to death with an ax, and the schoolkids in Brussels.

An hour went by, and the five agents took turns alternating guard posts. Kate and I volunteered to relieve them, but they seemed to want us in the kitchen.

Scott was at the table now and wanted to know about New York City. I tried to convince him that people surfed in the East River and everyone chuckled. I was tempted to tell my Attorney General joke, but it might be taken wrong.

Anyway, I was being modest about my contributions to the case, hardly mentioning that I'd figured out what Asad Khalil was up to, and glossing over my blinding brilliance regarding identifying the pilots who were marked for death.

On this subject, everyone was sort of glum, realizing that a lot of good guys, who had served their country, were now dead, murdered by a foreign agent. This was not supposed to happen.

It was close to 9:00 P.M. when a phone rang somewhere, and the talk stopped.

Tom came into the kitchen within seconds and said, "There's a blue delivery van cruising the neighborhood, single male occupant driving. The guys with the night vision say he fits the description of the suspect. Everyone take their posts."

Everyone was already up and moving, and Tom said to Kate and me, "Go into the TV room." He quickly left the kitchen as Kim Rhee went into the garage where Roger Fleming was now pulling duty. She left the door open, and I could see Roger crouched behind the cardboard boxes with his gun drawn. Kim pulled her piece and went to the garage door and stood to the side next to the lighted electric door opener.

Juan was at the back kitchen door, gun drawn, standing off to the side.

Kate and I went into the living room where Tom and Edie stood, guns drawn, on both sides of the front door. Scott was standing in front of the door, peering through the peephole. I couldn't help noticing that Scott had all his clothes off, except for a pair of baggy bathing trunks, in the back of which protruded the butt of a Glock. I guess this was the California version of undercover. In any case, I gave the guy credit for not wearing a bulletproof vest.

Tom saw us and again strongly suggested we retreat into the TV room, but he figured out quickly that we hadn't come three thousand miles to watch TV while the bust went down. He said, "Take cover, over here."

Kate moved beside Tom, who was to the left of the door, and drew her piece. I moved beside Edie, who was wedged against a small space between the door and the right-hand wall of the living room. The door would open toward us, and we would be behind it as it opened. There were enough guns drawn, so I didn't draw my Glock. I looked at Kate, who looked back at me, smiled and winked. My heart was pounding, but not, I'm afraid, for Kate Mayfield.

Tom had the cell phone to his ear, and he was listening. He said to us, "The van is slowing down a few doors away…"

Scott, at the peephole, said, "I see it. He's stopping in front of the house."

You could hear the breathing in the room, and despite all the backup and all the high-tech stuff and the bulletproof vests, there's still nothing quite like the moment when you're about to come face-to-face with an armed killer.

Scott, pretty cool, I thought, said, "A guy is getting out of the van… street side, can't see him…he's going to the rear…opening the doors… he's got a package…coming this way…fits the description…tall, Mid-eastern type…wearing jeans and a dark-collared shirt, carrying a small package in one hand…looking up and down the block…"

Tom was saying something into the cell phone, then put it in his pocket. He said to us, softly, "You all know what to do."

Actually, I missed that rehearsal.

Tom said, "Keep in mind, it could be an innocent delivery man… don't get too physical, but get him down and get the cuffs on him."

I wondered what happened to the goo-gun. I felt my face getting a little sweaty.

The doorbell rang. Scott waited about five seconds, then reached for the knob and opened the door. Before the door blocked my view, I saw Scott smiling as he said, "Something for me?"

"Mr. Wiggins?" said a voice with an accent.

"No," replied Scott, "I'm just housesitting. You want me to sign for that?"

"When will Mr. Wiggins be home?"

"Thursday. Maybe Friday. I can sign. It's okay."

"Okay. Please sign here."

I heard Scott say, "This pen doesn't write. Come on in."

Scott backed away from the door, and I couldn't help but think that if Scott were really a housesitter, he'd soon be dead and stinking in the back room while Asad Khalil waited for Mr. Wiggins to return home.

The tall, swarthy gentleman stepped a few feet into the living room, just clearing the door, which Edie kicked shut. Even without being briefed, I knew what was going to happen next. Before you could say abracadabra, Scott grabbed the guy's shirt and yanked him into the waiting crowd.

Within about four seconds, our visitor was pinned face down with me on his legs, Edie's foot on his neck, and Tom and Scott putting the cuffs on him.

Kate opened the door and signaled with a thumbs-up to whoever was watching through binoculars, then she ran down the walkway to the van, and I followed her.

We checked out the van, but there was no one in it. A few packages lay scattered on the floor, and Kate found a cell phone on the front seat, which she took.

Cars started appearing out of nowhere, screeching to a halt on the street in front of the house as agents jumped out, just like in the movies, although I don't see the need for the screeching. Kate said to them, "He's cuffed."

The garage door had opened, I noticed, and Roger and Kim were on the lawn now. Still no neighbors around. I had the unkind thought that if this were a movie being made, the crowds would be uncontrollable, as people shouted out offers to be an extra.

Anyway, as per SOP, the stakeout people all got back in their vehicles and began leaving to resume their watch of the house so as not to scare off any accomplice that might show up, not to mention upsetting

Mr. Wiggins, if he came home—or his neighbors, who might eventually notice.

Kate and I ran back into the house where the prisoner was now lying on his back, being closely searched by Edie and Scott, as Tom stood over the guy.

I looked at the man and was not overly surprised to discover that it wasn't Asad Khalil.

Chapter 48

Kate and I looked at each other, then at everyone around us. No one looked real happy.

Edie said, "He's clean."

The man was sort of blubbering, tears streaming down his face. If anyone had any doubts that this was not Asad Khalil, the blubbering clinched it.

Roger and Kim were in the living room now, and Kim said she was going to radio the stakeout units and tell them that the delivery guy wasn't our man, and to stay alert.

Scott had the guy's wallet and was rummaging through it. He asked the guy, "What's your name?"

The man tried to get himself under control and sobbed out something that sounded like a mixture of phlegm and snot.

Scott, holding the guy's driver's license with his photo said again, "Tell me your name."

"Azim Rahman."

"Where do you live?"

The man gave a Los Angeles address.

"What's your birth date?"

And so on. The guy got all the driver's license questions correct, which led him to believe he was about to be sent on his way. Wrong.

Tom started asking him questions that weren't on the driver's license, such as, "What are you doing here?"

"Please, sir, I have come to deliver a package."

Roger was examining the small package, but didn't open it, of course, in case it contained a little bomb. "What's in here?" Roger demanded.

"I do not know, sir."

Roger said to everyone, "There's no return address on this." He added, "I'll put this out back and call for a bomb disposal truck," and off he went, which made everyone a little happier.

Juan entered the living room, and by this time Azim Rahman was probably wondering why all these guys with FBI windbreakers were hanging around Mr. Wiggins' house. But maybe he knew why.

I looked at Tom's face and saw that he was worried. Knocking around a citizen, native-born or naturalized, was not good for the old career, not to mention the FBI image. Even knocking around an illegal alien could get you into hot water these days. I mean, we're all citizens of the world. Right?

On that thought, Tom asked Mr. Rahman, "You a citizen?"

"Yes, sir. I have taken the oath."

"Good for you," said Tom.

Tom asked Rahman a bunch of questions about his neighborhood in West Hollywood, which Rahman seemed able to answer, then he asked him a lot of other questions, sort of Civics 101 stuff, which Rahman answered not too badly. He even knew who the Governor of California was, which made me suspicious that he was a spy. But then he didn't know who his Congressman was, and I concluded he was a citizen.

Again, I looked at Kate, and she shook her head. I was feeling pretty low at that moment, and so was everyone else. Why don't things go as planned? Whose side was God on, anyway?

Edie had dialed the home phone number that Mr. Rahman had given her, and she confirmed that an answering machine answered "Rahman residence," and the voice sounded like the guy on the floor, despite the man's present emotional state.

Edie did say, however, that the phone number on the Rapid Delivery Service van was a non-working number. I suggested that the paint on the van looked new. Everyone stared at Azim Rahman.

He knew he was on the spot again, and explained, "I just start this business. It is new to me, maybe four weeks…"

Edie said, "So you painted a number on your van and hoped that the phone company would give you that number? Do we look stupid to you?"

I couldn't imagine how we looked to Mr. Rahman from his perspective on the floor. Position determines perspective, and when you're on the floor in cuffs with armed people standing over you, your perspective is different from that of the people standing around with the guns. Be that as it may, Mr. Rahman stuck to his story, most of which seemed plausible, except the business phone number bullshit.

So, by most appearances, what we had here was an honest immigrant pursuing the American Dream, and we had the poor bastard on the floor with a red bump on his forehead, for no other reason than the fact that he was of Mideastern descent. Shame, shame.

Mr. Rahman was getting himself under control and he said, "Please, I would like to call my lawyer."

Uh-oh. The magic words. It's axiomatic that if a suspect doesn't talk within the first five or ten minutes, when he's in shock, so to speak, he may never talk. My colleagues didn't pull it off in time.

I said, "Everyone here except me is a lawyer. Talk to these people."

"I wish to call my own lawyer."

I ignored him and asked, "Where you from?"

"West Hollywood."

I smiled and advised him, "Don't fuck with me, Azim. Where you *from?*"

He cleared his throat and said, "Libya."

No one said anything, but we glanced at one another, and Azim noticed our renewed interest in him.

I asked him, "Where did you pick up the package you were delivering?"

He exercised his right to remain silent.

Juan had gone out to the van, and he was back now and announced, "Those packages look like bullshit. All wrapped in the same brown paper, same tape, even the same fucking handwriting." He looked at Azim Rahman and said, "What kind of shit are you trying to pull?"

"Sir?"

Everyone started to browbeat poor Mr. Rahman again, threatening him with life in prison, followed by deportation, and Juan even offered him a kick in the nuts, which he refused.

At this point, with Mr. Rahman giving conflicting answers, we probably had enough to make a formal arrest, and I could see that Tom was leaning in that direction. Arrest meant the reading of rights, lawyers, and so forth, and the time had come to do the legal thing—it had actually passed a few minutes ago.

John Corey, however, being not quite so concerned with Federal guidelines or career, could take a few liberties. The bottom line was that if this guy was connected to Asad Khalil, it would be really good if we knew about it. Now.

So, having heard enough of Mr. Rahman's bullshit, I assisted him from the sitting to the supine position and sat astride him to be sure I had his attention. He turned his face away from mine, and I said, "Look at me. Look at me."

He turned his face back to me, and our eyes met.

I asked him, "Who sent you here?"

He didn't reply.

"If you tell us who sent you here, and where he is now, you will go free. If you don't tell us quickly, I will pour gasoline all over you and set you on fire." This, of course, was not a physical threat, but only an idiomatic expression that shouldn't be taken literally. "Who sent you here?"

Mr. Rahman remained silent.

I re-phrased my question in the form of a suggestion to Mr. Rahman and said, "I think you should tell me who sent you, and where he is." I should mention that I had my Glock out now and, for some reason, Mr. Rahman had put the muzzle in his mouth.

Mr. Rahman was properly terrified.

By this time, the Federal agents in the room, including Kate, had stepped away and were actually looking the other way, literally.

I informed Mr. Rahman, "I'm going to blow your fucking brains out, unless you answer my questions."

Mr. Rahman's eyes got very wide, and he was starting to comprehend that there was a difference between me and the others. He wasn't sure what the difference was, but to help him toward a complete understanding, I gave him a knee in the nuts.

He let out a groan.

The thing is, when you start this course of action, you better be real sure that the guy whose rights you may be infringing upon knows the answers to the questions he's being asked, and that he will give you those answers. Otherwise, contract agent or not, my ass was hanging out. But nothing succeeds like success, so I kneed him again to encourage him to share his knowledge with me.

A few of my colleagues left the room, leaving only Edie, Tom, and Kate to witness that Mr. Rahman was a voluntary witness whose cooperation was not coerced, and so forth.

I said to Mr. Rahman, "Look, asshole, you can go to jail for the rest of your fucking life, or maybe get the gas chamber as an accessory to murder. You understand that?"

He wasn't sucking on my automatic any longer, but still he refused to say anything.

I hate to leave marks, so I shoved my handkerchief down Mr. Rahman's throat and pinched his nostrils shut. He didn't seem able to breathe through his ears, and he began thrashing around, trying to get my two hundred pounds off his chest.

I heard Tom clear his throat.

I let Mr. Rahman turn a little blue, then took my fingers off his nose. He caught his breath in time to get another knee in his nuts.

I really wished that Gabe were there to instruct me on what worked, but he wasn't, and I didn't have much more time to mess around with this guy, so I held his nostrils again.

Without going into details, Mr. Azim Rahman saw the advantage of cooperating and indicated his willingness to do so. I pulled the handkerchief out of his mouth, and jerked him up into a sitting position. I asked him again, "Who sent you here?"

He sobbed a little, and I could see that he was very conflicted about all of this. I reminded him, "We can help you. We can save your life.

Talk to me, or I'll put you back in that fucking van, and you can go meet your friend and explain things to *him*. You want to do that? You want to go? I'll let you go."

He didn't seem to want to go, so I asked him again, "Who sent you?" I added, "I'm tired of asking you the same fucking question. Answer me!"

He sobbed a little more, caught his breath, cleared his throat, and replied in a barely audible voice, "I do not know his name...he...I only knew him as Mr. Perleman, but—"

"*Perleman?* Like in Jewish?"

"Yes...but he was not Jewish...he spoke my language..."

Kate already had a photo in her hand, and she shoved it in his face.

Mr. Rahman stared at the photo a long time, then nodded.

Voilà! I wasn't going to jail.

I asked, "Does he look like this now?"

He shook his head. "He has now glasses...a mustache...his hair is now gray..."

"Where is he?"

"I don't know. I don't know..."

"Okay, Azim, when was the last time you saw him, and where?"

"I...I met him at the airport—"

"Which airport?"

"The airport in Santa Monica."

"He flew in?"

"I don't know..."

"What time did you meet him?"

"Early...six in the morning..."

By now, with the rough stuff out of the way, and the witness cooperating, all six FBI folks were back in the living room, standing behind Mr. Rahman so as not to make him too nervous.

I, having secured the witness's cooperation and trust, was the person who would ask most of the questions now. I asked Mr. Rahman, "Where did you take this man?"

"I...took him...he wanted to drive...so we drove..."

"Where?"

"We drive up the coast road…"

"Why?"

"I do not know—"

"How long did you drive? Where did you go?"

"We drove to nowhere…we drive…perhaps an hour, or more, then we return here, and we find a shopping mall that was now open—"

"A *shopping mall?* What shopping mall?"

Mr. Rahman said he didn't know the mall because he was not from around here. But Kim, who was from the Ventura office, knew it by Rahman's description, and she quickly left the room to call the troops. But I had no doubt that Asad Khalil had not stuck around the mall all day.

I backtracked to the airport and asked Rahman, "You met him with your van?"

"Yes."

"At the main terminal?"

"No…at the other side. In a coffee shop…"

Further questioning revealed that Mr. Rahman met Mr. Khalil at the General Aviation side of Santa Monica Airport, leading me to believe that Khalil had arrived by private plane. Made sense.

Then, with time to kill until dark, the two Libyan gents took a nice scenic drive up the coast, then got back to Ventura where Mr. Khalil expressed a desire to do a little shopping, maybe get a bite to eat, and maybe buy a few souvenirs. I asked Rahman, "What was he wearing?"

"A suit and a tie."

"Color?"

"A gray…a dark gray suit."

"And what was he carrying? Luggage?"

"Only a bag, sir, which he disposed of as we drove. I drove him into a canyon."

I looked around. "What's a canyon?"

Tom explained. Sounded silly to me.

Back to Azim Rahman. I asked him, "Could you find this canyon again?"

"I…I don't know…perhaps…in the daytime…I will try…"

"You bet you will." I then asked him, "Did you give him anything? Did you have a package for him?"

"Yes, sir. Two packages. But I do not know what they contained."

Well, everyone there probably took the same course I did in something called Crateology, so I asked Mr. Rahman, "Describe the packages, the weight, size, all of that."

Mr. Rahman described a generic box, about the size of a microwave oven, except it was light, leading us all to believe it may have contained a change of clothes, and perhaps some documents. Crateology.

The second package was more interesting and scary. It was long. It was narrow. It was heavy. It did not contain a tie.

We all looked at one another. Even Azim Rahman knew what was in that package.

I turned my attention back to our star witness and asked him, "Did he also dispose of the packages, or does he still have them?"

"He has the packages."

I thought a moment and concluded that Asad Khalil was now decked out in new duds, had new identity papers, and had a sniper rifle broken down in some sort of innocuous-looking bag, like a backpack.

I inquired of Mr. Rahman, "This man sent you here to see if Mr. Wiggins was home?"

"Yes."

"You understand that this man is Asad Khalil, who killed everyone on board that aircraft that landed in New York."

Mr. Rahman claimed that he didn't make the connection, so I made it for him, and explained, "If you are helping this man, you will be shot, or hanged, or fried in the electric chair, or put to death by lethal injection, or put into the gas chamber. Or maybe we'll chop your head off. You understand?"

I thought he was going to faint.

I continued, "But if you help us capture Asad Khalil, you get a million-dollar reward." Not likely. "You saw that on television, didn't you?"

He nodded enthusiastically, giving away the fact that he knew who his passenger had been.

"So, Mr. Rahman, stop dragging your ass. I want your full cooperation."

"I am doing that, sir."

"Good. Who hired you to meet this man at the airport?"

He cleared his throat again and replied, "I do not know...truly, I do not know..." He then went into a convoluted explanation of a mysterious man who accosted him one day, about two weeks ago, at the gas station in Hollywood where Mr. Rahman actually worked. The man asked his assistance in aiding a compatriot and offered him ten thousand dollars, ten percent then, ninety percent later, and so forth. Classic recruiting by an intelligence agent—maybe twice removed—of some poor schmuck who needed cash and had relatives in the old country. Dead end, since Mr. Rahman was not going to ever see this guy again to collect his nine Gs. I said to Rahman, "These people would kill you before they would pay you. You know too much. You understand?"

He understood.

"They picked you out of the Libyan community because you look like Asad Khalil, and you were sent here to see if there was a trap waiting for him. Not just to see if Wiggins was here. You understand?"

He nodded.

"And look at you now. Are you sure these people are your friends?"

He shook his head. The poor guy looked miserable, and I was feeling badly about kneeing him in the balls and almost suffocating him. But he'd brought it on himself.

I said, "Okay, here's the big question, and your life depends on the answer. When, where, and how are you supposed to contact Asad Khalil?"

He took a long, deep breath and replied, "I am to call him."

"Okay. Let's call him. What's the number?"

Azim Rahman recited a telephone number, and Tom said, "That's a cell phone number."

Mr. Rahman agreed and said, "Yes, I gave this man a cell phone. I was instructed to buy two cell phones...the other is in my vehicle."

Kate had that cell phone, which had a Caller ID on it, and I assumed

Asad Khalil's cell phone also had a Caller ID. I asked Mr. Rahman, "What is the telephone company for these cell phones?"

He thought a moment, then replied, "Nextel."

"Are you sure?"

"Yes. I was instructed to use Nextel."

I looked at Tom, who shook his head, meaning they couldn't trace a Nextel call. In reality, it was difficult to trace *any* cell phone, though back at 26 Federal Plaza and One Police Plaza, we had these devices called Trigger Fish and Swamp Box that could at least tell you the general location of an AT&T or Bell Atlantic call. Mr. Rahman's friends had apparently ignored the enticements and bullying of the big carriers and taken advantage of an unadvertised feature of a smaller carrier, a feature known in the trade as the Fuck the Feds Feature. These people were not as stupid as some of their compatriots. Bad break for us, but there had been a lot of them, and this wasn't the last.

It was time to make Mr. Rahman more comfortable, so Tom uncuffed him. Rahman rubbed his wrists, and we helped him to his feet.

He seemed to have difficulty standing straight and complained about a pain in an unspecified area.

We sat Mr. Rahman down in a nice easy chair, and Kim went into the kitchen to get him a cup of coffee.

Everyone was a little more optimistic, though the chances of Azim Rahman bullshitting Asad Khalil into thinking everything was fine at the Wiggins house were pretty slim. But you never know. Even a smart guy like Khalil could be conned if he was obsessed with a goal, like murdering someone.

Kim returned with a black coffee, which Mr. Rahman sipped. Okay, coffee break is over. I said to our government witness, "Look at me, Azim. Is there a code word you're supposed to use for danger?"

He looked at me like I'd discovered the secret of the universe. He said, "Yes. This is so. If I am...as I am now...then I am to say the word 'Ventura' in my talk to him." He gave us a nice example, by using the word in a sentence like I had to do in school, and said, "Mr. Perleman, I have delivered the package to Ventura."

"Okay, make sure you don't say the word 'Ventura,' or I'll have to kill you."

He nodded vigorously.

So, Edie went into the kitchen to take the house phone off the hook, everyone shut off their cell phones, and if there had been a dog in the house, he would have gotten a nice walk.

I looked at my watch and saw that Mr. Rahman had been here about twenty minutes, which was not long enough to make Khalil nervous. I asked Azim, "Was there a specific time you were supposed to call?"

"Yes, sir. I was to deliver my package at nine P.M., then to drive ten minutes and make the telephone call from my van."

"Okay, tell him you got lost for a few minutes. Take a deep breath, relax, and think nice thoughts."

Mr. Rahman went into a deep-breathing meditation mode.

I asked him, "You watch the X-Files?"

I thought I heard Kate groan.

Mr. Rahman smiled and said, "Yes, I have watched this."

"Good. Scully and Mulder work for the FBI. Just like us. Do you like Scully and Mulder?"

"Yes."

"They're the good guys. Right? We're the good guys." He was polite enough not to bring up the subject of me knocking his nuts around. As long as he didn't forget it. I said, "And, we will make sure you are safely moved to wherever you want to live. I can get you out of California," I assured him. I asked, "Are you married?"

"Yes."

"Kids?"

"Five."

I'm glad he had the kids before he met me. I said, "You've heard of the Witness Protection Program. Right?"

"Yes."

"And you get some money. Right?"

"Yes."

"Okay. Are you supposed to meet this man after your telephone call?"

"Yes."

"Excellent. Where?"

"Where he says."

"Right. Make sure your telephone call leads to that meeting. Yes?"

I didn't get an enthusiastic response. I asked Mr. Rahman, "If all he needed from you was to come here and see if Wiggins was home, or to see if the police were here, why does he need to meet you again?"

Mr. Rahman had no idea, so I gave him an idea. "Because he wants to *kill* you, Azim. You know too much. Understand?"

Mr. Rahman swallowed hard and nodded.

I had some good news for him, and I said, "This man will be captured, and he will cause you no further trouble. If you do this for us, we will take you to lunch at the White House, and you will meet the President. Then we give you the money. Okay?"

"Okay."

I took Tom to the side and said softly, "Does anyone here speak Arabic?"

He shook his head and said, "Never needed an Arabic speaker in Ventura." He added, "Juan speaks Spanish."

"Close enough." I went back to Mr. Rahman and said, "Okay, dial the number. Keep the conversation in English. But if you can't, my friend Juan here understands a little Arabic, so don't fuck around. Dial."

Mr. Azim Rahman took a deep breath, cleared his throat yet again and said, "I need to smoke a cigarette."

Oh, shit! I heard a few groans. I said, "Does anyone here smoke?"

Mr. Rahman said, "You have taken my cigarettes."

I informed him, "You can't smoke your own, pal."

"Why may I not—"

"In case they're poison. I thought you watched the X-Files."

"Poison? They are not poison."

"Of course they are. Forget the cigarettes."

"I must have a cigarette. Please."

I know the feeling. I said to Tom, "I'll light one of his."

Tom produced Azim's cigarettes—not Camels—and in an act

of uncommon bravery, put one in his own mouth and flipped Azim's lighter. Tom said to Azim, "If this is poison, and it harms me, my friends will—"

I helped out and said, "We'll cut you up with knives and feed the pieces to a dog."

Azim looked at me. He said, "Please. I want only a cigarette."

Tom lit up, took a drag, coughed, didn't die, and handed the cigarette to Azim, who puffed away without dropping dead.

I said, "Okay, my friend. Time to make your telephone call. Keep it in English."

"I don't know if I can do that." He nursed the cigarette as he dialed the telephone, flipping the ash into his coffee cup. "I will try."

"Try hard. And make sure you understand where you have to meet him."

Rahman listened to the rings, which we could all hear, then Azim Rahman said into the telephone, "Yes, this is Tannenbaum."

Tannenbaum?

He listened, then said, "I'm sorry. I became lost."

He listened again, then suddenly the expression on his face changed, and he looked at us, then said something into the telephone. I have no idea what he said because it was in Arabic.

He continued the conversation in Arabic, making helpless shrugging gestures toward us. But Juan was cool, pretending to listen, nodding, even whispering in my ear. Juan whispered to me, "What the fuck is he saying?"

I made eye contact with Mr. Rahman, mouthed the word "Ventura" at him, and made a cutting gesture across my throat, which in Arabic or English or whatever is understandable.

He continued his conversation, and it was obvious, despite everyone's lack of Arabic, that Mr. Khalil was putting Mr. Rahman on the spot. In fact, Mr. Rahman began to sweat. Finally, he put the cell phone to his chest and said simply, "He's asking to speak to my new friends."

No one said anything.

Mr. Rahman looked very distraught and said to us, "I am sorry.

I tried. This man is too clever. He is asking me to sound the horn of my van. He knows. I did not tell him. Please. I do not want to speak to him."

So, I took the cell phone and found myself talking to Asad Khalil. I said, pleasantly, "Hello? Mr. Khalil?"

A deep voice replied, "Yes. And who are you?"

It's not a good idea to give a terrorist your name, so I said, "I am a friend of Mr. Wiggins."

"Are you? And where is Mr. Wiggins?"

"He's out and about. Where are *you*, sir?"

He laughed. Ha, ha. He said, "I, too, am out and about."

I had turned up the volume and was keeping the phone away from my face, and I had seven heads around me. We were all interested in what Asad Khalil had to say, but also everyone was listening for a background sound that might be a clue as to where he was. I said, "Why don't you come to Mr. Wiggins' house and wait for him here?"

"Perhaps I'll wait for him elsewhere."

This guy was smooth. I didn't want to lose him, so I resisted the temptation to call him a camel-fucking scumbag murderer. I felt my heart beating rapidly and took a breath.

"Hello? Are you there?"

I replied, "Yes, sir. Is there anything you'd like to tell me?"

"Perhaps. But I don't know who you are."

"I am with the Federal Bureau of Investigation."

There was a silence, then, "And do you have a name?"

"John. What would you like to tell me?"

"What would you like to know, John?"

"Well, I think I know almost everything there is to know. That's why I'm here. Right?"

He laughed. I hate it when scumbags do that. He said, "Let me tell you some things you may not know."

"Okay."

"My name, as you know, is Asad, from the family of Khalil. I once had a father, a mother, two brothers, and two sisters." He then proceeded to give me their names, and a few other details about his family, ending with, "They are all dead now."

He went on, talking about the night of April 15, 1986, as though it was still fresh in his mind, which I guess it was. He ended his story with, "The Americans killed my entire family."

I looked at Kate, and we nodded at each other. We'd gotten that part right, though it didn't matter much anymore. I said to Asad Khalil, "I sympathize with you, and I—"

"I don't need your sympathy." Then he said, "I have lived my life to avenge my family and my country."

This was going to be a difficult conversation, since we had so little in common, but I wanted to keep him on the line, so I used the techniques I'd learned in hostage negotiating class and said, "Well, I can certainly understand that. Now it may be time to tell the world your story."

"Not yet. My story is not finished."

"I see. Well, when it is, I'm sure you'd like to tell us all the details, and we'd like to give you an opportunity to do so."

"I don't need you to give me any opportunities. I make my own opportunities."

I took a deep breath. The standard stuff didn't seem to be working. But I tried again. "Look, Mr. Khalil, I'd like us to meet, to talk in person, alone—"

"I would welcome the opportunity to meet you alone. Perhaps we will someday."

"How about today?"

"Another day. I may come to your home someday, as I came to the homes of General Waycliff and Mr. Grey."

"Call before you come."

He laughed. Well, the asshole was toying with me, but that's okay. Part of the job. I didn't think this was going anywhere, but if he wanted to talk, that was fine. I said to him, "How do you think you're going to get out of the country, Mr. Khalil?"

"I don't know. What would you suggest?"

Asshole. "Well, how about we fly you to Libya in exchange for some people in Libya that we'd like to have here?"

"Who would you rather have in jail here more than me?"

Good point, asshole. "But if we catch up with you before you leave the country, we won't offer you such a good deal."

"You're insulting my intelligence. Good night."

"Hold on. You know, Mr. Khalil, I've been in this business for over twenty years, and you're the..." *Biggest scumbag.* "...the most clever man I've had to deal with."

"Perhaps to you, everyone seems clever."

I was about to lose it and took a deep breath and said, "Such as having that man killed in Frankfurt, so we would think it was you."

"That was clever, yes. But not so clever." He added, "And I congratulate you on keeping the newspeople in ignorance—or perhaps it was you who was ignorant."

"Well, a little of both. Hey, for the record, Mr. Khalil, did you...dispose of, I guess you'd say, anyone else we don't know about yet?"

"Actually, I did. A motel clerk near Washington, and a gas station attendant in South Carolina."

"Why'd you do that?"

"They saw my face."

"I see. Well, that's a good...but the lady pilot in Jacksonville saw your face, too."

There was a long pause, then Khalil replied, "So, you know a few details."

"Sure do. Gamal Jabbar. Yusef Haddad on board the airliner. Why don't you tell me about your travels and the people you've met along the way?"

He had no problem with that, and gave me a nice rundown on his travels by car and plane, the people he met and killed, where he'd stayed, things he'd seen and done, and all that. I thought maybe we could get a fix on him, if we could determine what false identity he'd used, but he burst my bubble and said, "I have a complete set of new identity, and I assure you I will have no problem leaving here."

"When are you leaving?"

"When I wish to leave." He then said, "My only regret, of course, is not being able to see Mr. Wiggins. As for Colonel Callum, may he suffer and die in agony."

My goodness. What a prick. I got a little testy and said, "You can thank me for saving Wiggins' life."

"Yes? And who are you?"

"I told you. John."

He stayed silent a moment, then said again, "Good night—"

"Hold on. I'm having a good time. Hey, did I tell you that I was one of the first Federal agents on board that aircraft?"

"Is that so?"

"You know what I'm wondering? I'm wondering if we saw one another. You think that's possible?"

"It is possible."

"I mean, you were wearing a blue Trans-Continental baggage handler's jumpsuit. Right?"

"Correct."

"Well, I was the guy in the light brown suit. I had this good-looking blonde with me." I winked at Kate. "You remember us?"

He didn't reply right away, then said, "Yes. I was standing on the spiral staircase." He laughed. "You told me to get off the aircraft. Thank you."

"Well, I'll be damned. Was that you? Small world."

Mr. Khalil picked up the ball and said, "In fact, I saw your photograph in the newspapers. You and the woman. Yes. And your name was mentioned in Mr. Weber's memo that I found in your Conquistador Club. Mr. John Corey and Miss Kate Mayfield. Of course."

"Hey, this is special. Really." *You prick.*

"In fact, Mr. Corey, I believe I had a dream about you. Yes, it was a dream, and a feeling...a presence, actually."

"No kidding? Were we having fun?"

"You were trying to capture me, but I was more clever and much faster than you."

"I had just the opposite dream. Hey, I'd really like to meet you and buy you a drink. You sound like a fun guy."

"I don't drink."

"You don't drink alcohol. You drink blood."

He laughed. "Yes, in fact, I licked the blood of General Waycliff."

"You're a mentally deranged camel-fucker. You know that?"

He thought about that and said, "Perhaps we *will* meet before I leave. That would be very nice. How can I reach you?"

I gave him my number at the ATTF and said, "Call anytime. If I'm not in, leave a message, and I'll get back to you."

"And your home number?"

"You don't need that. I'm at work most of the time."

"And please tell Mr. Rahman someone will be calling on him, and the same to Mr. Wiggins."

"You can forget that, sport. And by the way, when I catch up with you, I'm going to kick your balls into your mouth, then rip your head off, and shit down your neck."

"We'll see who catches who, Mr. Corey. And my regards to Miss Mayfield. Have a good day."

"Your mother was fucking Gadhafi. That's why Moammar had your father killed in Paris, you stupid—" The line was dead, and I stood there awhile, trying to get myself together. The room was really quiet.

Finally, Tom said, "You did a nice job."

"Yeah." I walked out of the living room, into the TV room to where I had spotted a bar, and poured myself a few inches of Scotch. I took a deep breath and drank it all.

Kate came into the room and asked softly, "You okay?"

"I will be soon. Want a drink?"

"Yes, but no thanks."

I poured another and stared off into space.

Kate said, "I think we can go now."

"Go where?"

"We'll find a motel and stay in Ventura, then check in tomorrow with the L.A. office. I still know some people there, and I'd like you to meet them."

I didn't reply.

She said, "Then, I'll show you around L.A., if you want, then back to New York."

I said, "He's here. He's very close to here."

"I know. So, we'll stay around a few days and see what develops."

"I want all car rental agencies checked, I want the Libyan community turned upside down, all ports of departure watched, the Mexican border under tight—"

"John, we know all of that. It's in the works right now. Same as New York."

I sat down and sipped my Scotch. "Damn it."

"Look, we saved Wiggins' life."

I stood. "I'm going to sweat Rahman a little more."

"He doesn't know anything more, and you know it."

I sat again and finished my Scotch. "Yeah...well, I guess I'm out of ideas." I looked at her. "What do you think?"

"I think it's time to leave these people to their work. Let's go."

I stood. "Do you think they'll let us play with the goo-gun?"

She laughed, the kind of laugh that's more a sigh of relief when someone you like is getting weird, then gets back to normal.

I said, "Okay. Let's blow this place."

We went back into the living room to wrap it up and say good night. Rahman had disappeared somewhere, and everyone was looking a little down. Tom said to Kate and me, "I called Chuck to give you a lift to a motel."

Just then, Tom's cell phone rang, and everyone became quiet. He put the phone to his ear and listened, then said, "Okay...okay...no, don't stop him...we'll handle it here." He hung up and said to us, "Elwood Wiggins is coming home." He added, "Lady in the car with him."

Tom said to everyone, "We'll all stay here in the living room, and let Mr. Wiggins and his friend enter his house—through the garage or the front door. When he sees us—"

"We all yell, 'Surprise!'" I suggested.

Tom actually smiled and said, "Bad idea. I will put him at ease and explain the situation."

I hate it when they faint, or bolt out the door. Half the time they think you're bill collectors.

Anyway, I didn't need to be around for this interesting moment, but then I decided I'd like to meet Chip Wiggins, just to satisfy my curiosity and see what he looked and sounded like. God, I'm convinced, looks after His most clueless and carefree creations.

A few minutes later, we could hear a car pull up in the driveway, the garage door opened, then closed, followed by the kitchen door opening, then a light went on in the kitchen.

We could hear Mr. Wiggins rummaging around the kitchen and opening the refrigerator. Finally, he said to his lady friend, "Hey, where did all this food come from?" Then, "Whose baseball hats are these? Hey, Sue, these hats say FBI."

Sue said, "I think someone was in here, Chip."

What was your first clue, sweetheart?

"Yeah," Chip agreed, maybe wondering if he had the right house.

We waited patiently for Mr. Wiggins to come into the living room. He said, "Stay here. I'll check it out."

Chip Wiggins walked into his living room and stopped dead in his tracks.

Tom said, "Please don't be alarmed." He held up his badge case. "FBI."

Chip Wiggins looked at the four men and four women standing in his living room. He said, "Wha...?"

Chip was wearing jeans, a T-shirt, and hiking boots, and looked fairly tan and fit, and younger than his age. Everyone in California looks tan and fit and young, except people like me, who are just passing through.

Tom said, "Mr. Wiggins, we'd like to talk to you for a few minutes."

"Hey, what's this about?"

The lady friend peeked around the door jamb and said, "Chip, what's happening?"

Chip explained to her where the FBI hats had come from.

After a minute or so, Chip was seated, the lady was escorted into the TV room by Edie, and Chip was relaxed, but curious. The lady, by the way, was a knockout, but I didn't notice.

Tom began by saying, "Mr. Wiggins, this matter concerns the bombing mission you participated in on April fifteen, nineteen eighty-six."

"Oh, shit."

"We took the liberty of entering your house based on information that a Libyan terrorist—"

"Oh, shit."

"—was in the area, and was looking to harm you."

"Oh, shit."

"We have the situation under control, but I'm afraid we're going to ask you to take some time off from work, and take a vacation."

"*Huh...?*"

"This man is still at large."

"Shit."

Tom gave Chip some of the background, then said, "I'm afraid we have some bad news for you. Some of your squadron mates have been murdered."

"*What?*"

"Killed by this man, Asad Khalil." Tom gave Chip a photograph of Khalil, which he encouraged Chip to look at and to keep.

Chip stared at the photograph, put it down and said, "Who was killed?"

Tom replied, "General Waycliff and his wife—"

"Oh, my God... Terry is dead? And Gail...?"

"Yes, sir. I'm sorry. Also, Paul Grey, William Satherwaite, and James McCoy."

"Oh, my God...oh, shit...oh..."

"And, as you may know, Colonel Hambrecht was murdered in England in January."

Chip got himself under control, and the realization dawned on him that he'd had a close call with the Grim Reaper. "Holy shit..." He stood and looked around, as if trying to spot a terrorist. He said, "Where is this guy?"

"We're trying to apprehend him," Tom assured Chip. "We can stay here tonight with you, though I don't think he'll show up here, or we'll wait until you pack, and escort you——"

"I'm outta here."

"Fine."

Chip Wiggins stood in deep thought for a moment, perhaps the deepest thinking he'd done in some time, and said, "You know, I always knew...I mean, I told Bill that day, after we'd released and were heading back...I told him those bastards weren't going to let that one go...oh, shit...Bill is dead?"

"Yes, sir."

"And Bob? Bob Callum?"

"He's under close protection."

I spoke up and said to Chip, "Why don't you go visit him?"

"Yeah...good idea. He's at the Air Force Academy?"

"Yes, sir," I said. "We can keep an eye on both of you there." And it's cheaper that way.

Well, no use hanging around, so Kate and I made our farewells, while Chip went off to pack. He looked like the kind of guy who'd loan you a pair of underwear, but he had enough on his mind.

Kate and I went outside and stood in the balmy air, waiting for Chuck. Kate observed, "Chip Wiggins is a very lucky man."

"No kidding. Did you see that babe?"

"Why do I even try to talk to you?"

"Sorry." I thought a moment, then said, "Why did he need the rifle?"

"Who? Oh, you mean Khalil."

"Yeah. Khalil. Why did he need the rifle?"

"We don't know it was a rifle."

"Let's say it was. Why did he need the rifle? Not to kill Chip in his house."

"That's true. But maybe he wanted to kill him someplace else. In the woods."

"No, this guy is up close and personal. I *know* he talks to his victims before he kills them. Why does he need the rifle? To kill someone he can't get close to. Someone he doesn't need to talk to."

"I think you have a point there."

The car came, and we got in——me in the front, Kate in the back, Chuck at the wheel. He said, "Tough break. You want a good motel?"

"Sure. With mirrors on the ceiling."

Someone behind me smacked my head.

So, off we went, toward the ocean, where Chuck said there were a few nice motels with an ocean view.

I asked Chuck, "Is there an all-night, drive-thru underwear place in the area?"

"A what?"

"You know. Like California has all these all-night, drive-thru places. I wondered if——"

Kate said, "John, shut up. Chuck, ignore him."

As we drove, Chuck and Kate talked about logistics and scheduling for the next day.

I was thinking about Mr. Asad Khalil and our conversation. I was trying to put myself into his disturbed mind, trying to think what I'd do next if I were him.

The one thing I was sure of was that Asad Khalil was *not* heading home. We would hear from him again. Soon.

Chapter 49

Chuck made a call from his cell phone and reserved us two rooms at a place called the Ventura Inn, on the beach. He used my credit card number, got the reduced government rate, and assured me it was a reimbursable expense.

Chuck handed a small paper bag to Kate and said, "I stopped and got you a toothbrush and toothpaste. If you need anything else, we can stop."

"This is fine."

"What did you get me?" I asked.

He produced another paper bag from under his seat and handed it to me, saying, "I got you some nails to chew on."

Chuckle, chuckle.

I opened the bag and found toothpaste, toothbrush, a razor, and a travel-size can of shaving cream. "Thanks."

"On the government."

"I'm overwhelmed."

"Right."

I put the stuff in my jacket pockets. Within ten minutes we reached a high-rise building, whose marquee announced itself as the Ventura Inn Beach Resort. Chuck pulled up to the reception doors and said, "Our office will be staffed all night, so if you need anything, give a call."

I said to Chuck, "If anything pops, make sure *you* call *us*, or I'll be very, very angry."

"You're the man, John. Tom was impressed with how you got that delivery guy to voluntarily cooperate."

I said, "A little psychology goes a long way."

"To tell you the truth, there're a lot of lotus-eaters out here. It's good to see a meat-eating dinosaur once in a while."

"Is that a compliment?"

"Sort of. So, what time do you want to be picked up in the morning?"

Kate replied, "Seven-thirty."

Chuck waved and drove off.

I said to her, "Are you crazy? That's four-thirty in the morning, New York time."

"It's *ten*-thirty A.M., New York time."

"Are you sure?"

She ignored me and walked into the motel lobby. I followed.

It was a pleasant place, and I could hear a piano playing through the lounge door.

The check-in guy greeted us warmly and informed us that he had deluxe ocean-view rooms for us on the twelfth floor. Nothing too good for the guardians of Western Civilization.

I asked him, "What ocean?"

"Pacific, sir."

"Do you have anything overlooking the Atlantic?"

He smiled.

Kate and I filled out the registration forms, and the guy made an impression of my American Express card, which I think let out a groan as it passed through the machine.

Kate took a photo out of her bag, along with her credentials, and said to the clerk, "Have you seen this man?"

The clerk seemed less happy than he'd been when he thought we were just passing through for the night. He stared at the photo of Asad Khalil, then replied, "No, ma'am."

Kate said, "Keep that. Call us if you see him." She added, "He's wanted for murder."

The clerk nodded and put the photo behind the counter.

Kate told him, "Pass it on to your relief person."

We got our keycards, and I suggested a drink in the lounge.

Kate said, "I'm exhausted. I'm going to sleep."

"It's only ten."

"It's one A.M. in New York. I'm tired."

I had this sudden unhappy thought that I was going to drink alone and sleep alone.

We went to the elevators and rode up in silence.

At about the tenth floor, Kate asked me, "Are you sulking?"

"Yes."

The elevator reached the top floor, and we got out. Kate said, "Well, I don't want you to sulk. Come into my room for a drink."

So, we went into her room, which was big, and with no luggage to unpack, we quickly made two Scotch and sodas from the mini-bar and retired to the balcony. She said, "Let's forget the case tonight."

"Okay." We sat in the two chairs with a round table between us and contemplated the moonlit ocean.

This somehow reminded me of my convalescent stay at my uncle's house on the water on eastern Long Island. It reminded me of the night Emma and I sat drinking cognac after a skinny-dip in the bay.

I was sliding into a bad mood and tried to get out of it.

Kate asked me, "What are you thinking about?"

"Life."

"Not a good idea." She said, "Did it ever occur to you that you're in this business, working long, hard hours because you don't want to have the time to think about your life?"

"Please."

"Listen to me. I really care for you, and I sense that you're looking for something."

"Clean underwear."

"You can *wash* your fucking underwear."

"I never thought of that."

"Look, John, I'm thirty-one years old, and I've never come close to getting married."

"I can't imagine why."

"Well, for your information, it wasn't for lack of offers."

"Gotcha."

"Do you think you'd get married again?"

"How far a fall do you think it is from this balcony?"

I thought she'd get angry over my flippancy, but instead, she laughed. Sometimes a guy can do no right, sometimes a guy can do no wrong. It has nothing to do with what a guy does; it has to do with the woman.

Kate said to me, "Anyway, you did a hell of a job today. I'm impressed. And I even learned a few things."

"Good. When you ram your knee into a guy's balls from that position, you may actually pop his nuts into his abdomen. So you have to be careful."

Smart lady that she was, she said, "I don't think you're a violent or sadistic man. I think you do what you have to do when you have to do it. And I think you don't like it. That's important."

See what I mean? I could do no wrong in Kate's eyes.

She'd put two more little bottles of Scotch in her jacket pocket, and she opened them and poured them in our glasses. After a minute or so, she said, "I...know about that thing that happened on Plum Island."

"What thing?"

"When you disemboweled that guy."

I took a deep breath, but didn't reply.

She let a few seconds pass, then said, "We all have a dark side. It's okay."

"Actually, I enjoyed it."

"No, you didn't."

"No, I didn't. But...there were extenuating circumstances."

"I know. He killed someone you cared for very much."

"Let's drop the subject."

"Sure. But I wanted you to know that I understand what happened and why."

"Good. I'll try not to do that again." See what I mean? I cut this guy's guts out, and it's okay. Actually, it *was* okay because he deserved it.

Anyway, we let that subject cool off awhile. We drank and stared at the mesmerizing ocean rolling toward the beach. You could hear the waves breaking softly against the shore. What a view. A breeze passed by, and I could smell the sea. I asked her, "You liked it here?"

"California is nice. The people are very friendly."

People often mistake spacey for friendly—but why ruin her memory? "Did you have a boyfriend here?"

"Sort of." She asked me, "Do you want my sexual history?"

"How long will that take?"

"Less than an hour."

I smiled.

She asked me, "Was your divorce nasty?"

"Not at all. The marriage was nasty."

"Why did you marry her?"

"She asked me."

"Can't you say no?"

"Well...I thought I was in love. Actually, she was an ADA, and we were on the side of the angels. Then she took a high-powered job as a criminal defense attorney. She changed."

"No, she didn't. The job changed. Could *you* be a criminal defense attorney? Could you be a criminal?"

"I see your point. But——"

"And she made a lot more money defending criminals than you did arresting them."

"Money had nothing to do——"

"I'm not saying what she does for a living is wrong. I'm saying that... what's her name?"

"Robin."

"Robin was not right for you even when she was an assistant district attorney."

"Good point. Can I jump now? Or is there more you need to tell me?"

"There is. Hold on. So, you meet Beth Penrose, who's on the same side of the law that you're on, and you're reacting against your ex-wife. You feel comfortable with a cop. Maybe less guilty. I'm sure it was no fun around the station house being married to a criminal defense attorney."

"I think that's enough."

"Actually, it's not. Then I came along. Perfect trophy. Right? FBI. Attorney. Your boss."

"Stop right there. Let me remind you that it was *you*——Forget it."

"Are you angry?"

"You're damned right I'm angry." I stood. "I gotta go."

She stood. "All right. Go. But you have to face some realities, John. You can't hide behind that tough-guy, wise-ass exterior forever.

Someday, maybe soon, you're going to retire, and then you have to live with the real John Corey. No gun. No badge—"

"Shield."

"No one to arrest. No one who needs you to protect them or to protect society. It'll just be you, and you don't even know who you are."

"Neither do you. This is California psychobabble bullshit, and you've only been here since seven-thirty. Good night."

I left the balcony, left her room, and went out into the corridor. I found my room next door and went in.

I kicked off my shoes, threw my jacket on the bed, and took off my holster, shirt, tie, and armored vest. Then I made a drink from the mini-bar.

I was pretty worked up and actually felt like crap. I mean, I knew what Kate was doing, and I knew it wasn't malicious, but I really didn't need to be prodded into confronting the monster in the mirror.

Ms. Mayfield, if I'd given her a few more minutes, would have painted a beautiful picture of how life could be if we were facing it together.

Women think the perfect husband is all they need for a perfect life. Wrong. First, there *are* no perfect husbands. Not even many good ones. Second, she was right about me, and I wasn't going to get any better by living with Kate Mayfield.

I decided to wash my underwear, go to bed, and never see Kate Mayfield again after this case was concluded.

There was a knock on my door. I looked through the peephole and opened the door.

She stepped inside, and we stood there looking at each other.

I can be really tough in these situations, and I didn't intend to give an inch, or to kiss and make up. I didn't even feel like sex anymore.

However, she was wearing a white terry cloth hotel robe, which she opened and let fall to the floor, revealing her perfect naked body.

I felt my resolve softening at the same rate Mr. Happy was getting hard.

She said, "I'm sorry to bother you, but my shower doesn't work. Could I use yours?"

"Help yourself."

She went into my bathroom, turned on the shower, and got in.

Well, I mean, what was I supposed to do? I got out of my pants, shorts, and socks, and got into the shower.

For purposes of propriety, in case there was a middle-of-the-night phone call from the FBI, she left my room at 1:00 A.M.

I didn't sleep particularly well and woke up at five-fifteen, which I guess was eight-fifteen on my body clock.

I went into the bathroom and saw that my undershorts were hanging on the retractable clothesline above the bathtub. They were clean, still damp, and someone had planted a lipstick kiss in a strategic spot.

I shaved, showered again, brushed my teeth and all that, then went out to the balcony and stood there naked in the breeze, looking at the dark ocean. The moon had set and the sky was full of stars. It doesn't get much better than this, I decided.

I stood there a long time because it felt good.

I heard the sliding glass door on the other side of the concrete partition open. I called out, "Good morning."

I heard her reply, "Good morning."

The partition jutted out beyond the balconies, so I couldn't peek around. I asked her, "Are you naked?"

"Yes. Are you?"

"Of course. This feels great."

"Meet me for breakfast in half an hour."

"Okay. Hey, thanks for washing my shorts."

"Don't get used to it."

We were talking sort of loud, and I had the feeling other guests were listening. I think she had the same thought because she said, "What did you say your name was?"

"John."

"Right. You're a good lay, John."

"Thanks. You, too."

So, there we were, two mature Federal agents, standing naked on hotel balconies with a partition between us, acting silly, the way new lovers act.

She called out, "Are you married?"

"No. How about you?"

"No."

So, what was my next line? Two simultaneous thoughts ran through my head. One, that I was being manipulated by a pro. Two, I loved it. Realizing that this moment and this setting was going to be remembered forever, I took a deep breath and asked, "Will you marry me?"

There was a long silence.

Finally, a woman's voice, not Kate's, called out, "Answer him!"

Kate called out, "Okay. I'll marry you."

Two people somewhere applauded. This was really dopey. I think I was actually embarrassed, which barely masked my sense of panic. What had I done?

I heard her sliding door close, so I couldn't qualify my proposal.

I went into my room, got dressed sans body armor, and went downstairs to the breakfast room where I got coffee and a copy of the *New York Times*, hot off the press.

There was continuing coverage of the Flight 175 tragedy, but it seemed like a rehash of events with a few new quotes from Federal, state, and local officials.

There was a small paragraph about Mr. Leibowitz's murder in Frankfurt and an obituary. He lived in Manhattan and had a wife and two children. It struck me again how random life could be. The guy goes to Frankfurt for business and gets clipped because some people need a red herring to make it look like a guy in America on a secret mission is back in Europe. *Whack.* Just like that, without regard to the victim's wife, kids, or anything. These people sucked.

There was also a little rehash of the double-murder of James McCoy and William Satherwaite at the Cradle of Aviation Museum. A Nassau Homicide detective was quoted as saying, "We're not ruling out the possibility that the motive for these murders may not have been robbery." Despite the tortured syntax, I could see that little Alan Parker was spooning out a third today, a third tomorrow, and the rest by the weekend.

Speaking of tortured syntax, I turned to Janet Maslin's movie review column. Some days I do the *Times* crossword puzzle, other days I try to understand what Ms. Maslin is trying to say. I can't do both on the same day without getting a headache.

Ms. Maslin was reviewing a box office smash, an action-adventure Mideast terrorist flick of all things, which I think she didn't like, but as I say, it's hard to follow her prose, or her reasoning. The movie was lowbrow, of course, and Ms. Maslin may think of herself as highbrow, but *somebody* from the *Times* had to go see this thing and tell everyone who loved it why it sucked. I made a mental note to see the movie.

Kate arrived and I stood and we pecked. We sat and looked at the menus, and I thought perhaps she'd forgotten the silly incident on the balconies. But then she put down her menu and asked, "When?"

"Uh...June?"

"Okay."

The waitress came by, and we both ordered pancakes.

I really wanted to read the *Times*, but I instinctively knew that my breakfast newspaper was a thing of the past.

We chatted briefly about the plans for the day, the case, the people we'd met at Chip Wiggins' house, and who I was going to be introduced to by Kate later in L.A.

The pancakes came and we ate. Kate said, "You'll like my father."

"I'm sure I will."

"He's about your age, maybe a little older."

"Well, that's good." I remembered a line from an old movie and said, "He raised a swell daughter."

"He did. My sister."

I chuckled.

She said, "You'll like my mother, too."

"Are you and she alike?"

"No. She's nice."

I chuckled again.

She said, "Is it all right if we get married in Minnesota? I have a big family."

"Great. Minnesota. Is that a city or a state?"

"I'm a Methodist. How about you?"

"Any kind of birth control is fine."

"My *religion*. Methodist."

"Oh…my mother's Catholic. My father's…some kind of Protestant. He never—"

"Then we can raise the children in a Protestant denomination."

"You have kids?"

"This is important, John. Pay attention."

"I am. I'm trying to…you know, shift gears."

She stopped eating and looked at me. "Are you totally panicked?"

"No, of course not."

"You look panicky."

"Just a little stomach acid. Comes with age."

"This is going to be all right. We are going to live happily ever after."

"Good. But you know, we haven't known each other that long—"

"We will by June," she said.

"Right. Good point."

"Do you love me?"

"Actually, I do, but love—"

"What if I got up and walked out of here? How would you feel? Relieved?"

"No. I'd feel awful."

"So? Why are you fighting how you feel?"

"Are we about to go into analysis again?"

"No. I'm just telling you like it is. I'm madly in love with you. I want to marry you. I want to have children with you. What else do you want me to say?"

"Say…I love New York in June."

"I hate New York. But for you, I'll live anywhere."

"New Jersey?"

"Don't push it."

Time for full disclosure, so I said, "Look, Kate, you should know that I'm a male chauvinist pig, a misogynist, and I tell sexist jokes."

"Your point is…?"

I saw I wasn't getting anywhere with this line of reasoning, so I said,

"Also, I have a bad attitude toward authority, and I'm always on the verge of career problems, and I'm broke, and I'm bad at handling money."

"That's why you need a good lawyer and a good accountant. That's me."

"Can I just hire you?"

"No. You have to marry me. I'm a full-service professional. Plus, I can prevent impotence."

No use arguing with a professional.

The light banter was over, and we looked at each other across the table. Finally, I said, "How do you *know* I'm the one for you?"

"How am I supposed to explain that? My heart beats faster when you're in the room. I love the sight, sound, smell, taste, and touch of you. You're a good lay."

"Thank you. You, too. Okay, I'm not going to bring up anything about careers, about you getting transferred, about living in New York, my paltry disability pension, our ten-year age difference—"

"Fourteen years."

"Right. I'm not going to fight this. I'm in love. Head over heels in love. If I blow this, I'll be miserable the rest of my life."

"You will be. Marrying me is the best thing for you. Trust me. I mean, really. Don't laugh. Look at me. Look into my eyes."

I did, and the panic was suddenly gone, and this weird feeling of peace flooded over me, just like I felt when I was bleeding to death on West 102nd Street. As soon as you stop fighting it—death or marriage—as soon as you let go and surrender, you see this radiant light and a chorus of singing angels bears you aloft, and a voice says, "Come along peacefully, or I'll have to handcuff you."

No, actually the voice says, "The fight is over, the suffering is ended, a new life, hopefully a little less fucked up than the last, is about to begin."

I took Kate's hand, and we looked into each other's eyes. I said, "I love you." And I really did.

Chapter 50

A t 7:30 A.M., Chuck picked us up in front of the Ventura Inn and informed us, "Nothing new."

Which wasn't completely true. I was now engaged to be married.

As we drove to the Ventura office, Chuck asked us, "Was the hotel okay?"

Kate answered him, "It was wonderful."

Chuck inquired, "Did you check out?"

Kate replied, "We did. We'll spend the next few days in L.A. Unless you've heard something different."

"Well...from what I hear, the bosses in Washington want you both at a major press conference tomorrow afternoon. They want you in D.C. tomorrow morning latest."

I asked, "What kind of press conference?"

"The big one. You know, where they spill it all. Everything about Flight One-Seven-Five, about Khalil, the Libyan raid in nineteen eighty-six, about Khalil killing the pilots who were on the raid, and then about what happened yesterday with Wiggins. Full disclosure. Asking for the public's cooperation and all that."

"Why," I wondered aloud, "do they need us at the press conference?"

"I think they need two heroes. Guy and a girl. The best and the brightest." He added, "One of you is very photogenic." He laughed. Ha, ha.

This day wasn't starting out well, despite it being seventy-two degrees and sunny again.

Chuck inquired, "Do we need to stop for anything? Underwear?"

"No. Drive."

A few minutes later, Chuck left us off in the parking lot of the Ventura FBI office and announced, "Surf's up. Gotta go."

I assumed he was joking. Anyway, we got out, carrying our body armor, and walked toward the building.

As we walked, I said to Kate, "This really sucks. I don't need to be put on display at a PR stunt."

"Press conference."

"Yeah. I've got work to do."

"Maybe we can use the press conference to announce our engagement."

Everyone's a comedian. It's probably my influence, but I wasn't in a funny mood that morning.

So, we went into the building, rode up the elevator, and rang the door buzzer. Cindy Lopez let us in again and informed us, "You need to call Jack Koenig."

If I never hear these words again, it will be too soon. I said to Kate, "You call."

Cindy informed me, "He wants to speak to *you*. There's an empty office over there."

Kate and I returned our vests, then went into the office, and I dialed Jack Koenig. It was just 8:00 A.M. in L.A., and I was reasonably certain it was 11:00 A.M. in New York.

Jack's secretary put me through, and Jack said, "Good morning."

I detected a note of pleasantness, which was scary. "Good morning." I put the call on speaker so that Kate could listen and talk. I said to Jack, "Kate's here."

"Hello, Kate."

"Hello, Jack."

"First," Jack said, "I want to congratulate you both on an outstanding job, a great piece of detective work, and from what I hear, John, a very effective interrogation technique regarding Mr. Azim Rahman."

"I kneed him in the balls, then tried to suffocate him. Old technique."

A brief silence, followed by, "Well, I spoke to the gentleman myself, and he seemed happy for the opportunity to be a government witness."

I yawned.

Jack continued, "I also spoke to Chip Wiggins and got some firsthand background on that Al Azziziyah raid. What a mission that was. But Wiggins did indicate that perhaps one of his bombs went a bit astray, and I wouldn't be surprised if it was that bomb that hit the Khalil house. Ironic, isn't it?"

"I guess."

"Did you know that this Al Azziziyah camp was dubbed Jihad University? It's true. It was and is a terrorist training center."

"Am I being coached for this idiotic press conference?"

"Not coached. Briefed."

"Jack, I don't give a shit what happened in that place in nineteen eighty-six. I don't give a rat's ass if Khalil's family was killed by mistake or on purpose. I have a perp to catch, and the perp is here, not in Washington."

"We don't know where the suspect is. For all we know, he may be in Libya, or back on the East Coast, and may very well be in Washington. Who knows? What I do know is that the Director of the FBI, and the Director of the Counterterrorism section, not to mention the Chief Executive Officer of the nation, want you in Washington tomorrow. So don't even *think* about pulling a disappearing act."

"Yes, sir."

"Good. My ass is on the line if you don't show up."

"I hear you."

Jack quit while he was ahead on that one and asked, "Kate, how are you?"

Kate spoke into the speaker and replied, "I'm fine. How's George?"

"George is well. He's still at the Conquistador Club, but he'll be back at Federal Plaza tomorrow." Jack added, "John, Captain Stein sends his regards and his compliments for a job well done."

"The perp is still at large, Jack."

"But you saved some lives. Captain Stein is proud of you. We're all proud of you."

And so forth. Chitchat, chitchat. But it's important to establish quasi-personal relationships in law enforcement. Everyone cares about everyone else as a person. This is good management, I guess, and fits nicely with the new touchy-feely America. I wondered if the CIA was like this. Which reminded me. I asked, "Where's Ted Nash?"

Jack replied, "I'm not sure. I left him in Frankfurt. He was going to Paris."

It occurred to me, not for the first time, that the CIA, upon whom so much once depended, was now being eclipsed by the FBI, whose mandate was domestic troublemakers. I mean, a guy like Nash or his colleagues could now vacation in Moscow with no more danger to themselves than bad food. An organization like that needs a purpose, and lacking a clear purpose these days, they were bound to get into mischief. Idle hands are the playthings of the devil, as my Protestant Grandma used to tell me.

Anyway, Jack and Kate were chewing the fat, and Jack asked a few leading questions about how Kate and I were getting on, and so forth.

Kate looked at me with that bursting-with-good-news look—so what could I do? I nodded.

Kate said to Jack, "John and I have some good news. We're engaged."

I thought I heard the phone hit the floor at the other end. There was a silence that lasted about two seconds longer than it should have. Good news for Jack would be that Kate Mayfield was filing a sexual harassment suit against me. But Jack is slick, and recovered nicely. He said, "Well…hey, that is good news. Congratulations. John, congratulations. This is very…sudden…"

I knew I had to say something, so, in my best male macho tone I said, "Time to settle down and tie the old knot. My bachelor days are over. Yes, sir. I finally found the right girl. Woman. I couldn't be happier." And so forth.

So, that out of the way, Jack briefed us on the momentous issue at hand and said, "We have people checking with the FAA about flight plans for private aircraft. We're concentrating on private jets. We actually turned up the flight plan and the pilots who flew Khalil across the country. We interviewed the pilots. They flew out of Islip on Long Island. This would have been right after Khalil murdered McCoy and Satherwaite at the museum. They stopped in Colorado Springs, Khalil deplaned, but we know he didn't kill Colonel Callum."

Jack went on about Khalil and his flight to Santa Monica. The pilots, according to Jack, were in shock now that they knew who their passenger was. This was interesting, but not that important. However, it did show Khalil to be resourceful and well financed. Plus, he could blend in okay. I said to Jack, "And you're trying to find out if Khalil has another private flight booked?"

"Yes. But there are hundreds of private jets filing flight plans every day. We're concentrating on non-corporate and foreign corporate charters, flights paid for by suspicious means and by non-repeat customers, and customers who may appear foreign, and so on. It's a long, long shot. But we have to give it a try."

"Right. How do you think this asshole is going to get out of the country?"

"Good question. Canadian security is tight and cooperative, but I can't say the same for our Mexican neighbors."

"I guess not with fifty thousand illegals crossing every month, not to mention tons of Mexican marching powder blowing across the border. Did you alert the DEA, Customs, and Immigration?"

"Of course. And they've assigned extra personnel and so have we. It's going to be a rough month for drug dealers and illegals. Also, we've alerted the Coast Guard. It's a short boat hop from southern California to the beaches of Mexico. We've done everything we can in cooperation with several local and Federal agencies—as well as our Mexican allies—to intercept the suspect if he tries to flee across the U.S.-Mexican border."

"Are you on TV now?"

"No. Why?"

"You sound like you're on TV."

"That's the way I talk. That's the way you should talk tomorrow afternoon. Keep the fuck word to a minimum."

I actually smiled.

So, we discussed the subject of the manhunt for a while, and finally Jack said, "John, it's taken care of. And it's out of your hands."

"Not quite. Look, I want to get back here as soon as this press conference is over tomorrow."

"That's a reasonable request. Let's see how you do at the press conference."

"One has nothing to do with the other."

"It does now."

"Okay. I get it."

"Good. Tell me about your phone conversation with Asad Khalil."

"Well, we didn't have a whole lot in common. Didn't someone brief you about that?"

"Yes, but I want to get a feeling from you about Khalil's mood, his state of mind, the possibility that he might be heading home or staying around. That sort of thing."

"Okay...I had the feeling I was talking to a man who was very much in control of himself and his emotions. Worse, he came across as though he were still in control of the situation, despite the fact that we fucked up his plans. I mean, that we *thwarted* his plans."

Jack stayed silent a moment, then said, "Go on."

"Well, if I had to bet, I'd bet that he was planning to stick around."

"Why?"

"I don't know. Just one of those feelings I get. By the way, speaking of bets, I want Nash's ten dollars, and his buddy Edward's twenty dollars."

"But you said Khalil was in the New York area."

"He *was*. Then he left, then he came back to Long Island. Point is, he didn't fly out to Sandland." I looked at Kate for support. This was important.

Kate said, "John is right. He won the bets."

Jack replied, "Okay. I'll accept Kate's impartial opinion." Ha, ha. Then Jack said, seriously, "So, John, you have a feeling now that Asad Khalil is still in your area?"

"I do."

"But this is just a feeling?"

"If you mean am I holding something back, I'm not. Even I know when to come clean. But...how can I put this?...well...Khalil said to me that he sort of felt my presence before he...this is stupid. Mystical Sandland stuff. But I sort of feel this guy's presence. You know?"

There was a long silence as Jack Koenig probably looked up the phone number of the Task Force psychiatric office. Finally, he said kindly, "Well, I've learned not to bet money against you."

I thought he was going to tell me to get some sleep, but instead he addressed Kate and asked, "Are you going to the L.A. office?"

She replied, "Yes. I think it's a good idea to say hello, establish a working relationship, and see if we can be of any help when we return."

"You have friends there, I understand."

"I do."

There may have been some subtext here regarding Kate's hour-long sexual history, but I wasn't jealous, and I wasn't going to be baited any longer. The hook was already in, the big fish had been reeled up and was now flopping around on the deck, gasping for air, to use an appropriate metaphor. So, Kate didn't need to use old boyfriends or suitors, such as Teddy, to get John to get off his ass and pop the question.

Jack and Kate chatted a minute about some people they knew in common in L.A., then Jack said, "Okay, pick a flight to Dulles, but no later than the red-eye."

Kate assured him we'd be on the red-eye at the latest.

Jack was about to sign off, but it was time for my Columbo moment and I said, "Oh, one more thing."

"Yes?"

"The rifle."

"What rifle?"

"The rifle that was in the long package."

"Oh...yes, I did question Mr. Rahman about that package. So has everyone else in L.A. and Washington."

"And?"

"Rahman and his family are under protective custody."

"Good. That's where they belong. And?"

"Well, the agents in L.A. made Rahman draw and describe the package. And they put together a box that Rahman says is the same size as the one he gave to Khalil, give or take an inch."

"And?"

"And, they put metal weights in the box until Rahman felt that the weight was about the same. Muscle memory. Are you familiar—"

"Yeah. And?"

"Well, it was an interesting experiment, but it proves nothing. Nylon and plastic stock rifles are light, older rifles are heavy. Hunting rifles are long, assault rifles are shorter. There's no way to determine if that was a rifle in the package."

"I understand that. Was this rifle long and heavy?"

"If it *was* a rifle, it was a long and heavy rifle."

"Like a hunting rifle, with a scope."

"That's right," Jack said.

"Okay, worst-case scenario. It's a long, accurate, hunting rifle with a scope. What is Khalil going to do with it?"

"The feeling is that this was a backup in the event that Wiggins was not at home. In other words, Khalil was prepared to hunt Wiggins as he camped in the woods."

"Really?"

"It's a theory. You have another theory?"

"Not at the moment. But I'm picturing Chip and his babe in the woods, camping out, and I'm wondering why Khalil, with new hiking duds, doesn't just go up to them and share a cup of coffee around the campfire, then casually mention that he's there to kill Chip and tell him why before he puts a forty caliber slug in his head. Capisce?"

Jack let a few seconds go by, then said, "Wiggins, as it turns out, was camping with about a dozen friends, so Khalil—"

"Doesn't wash, Jack. Khalil would do whatever he had to do to look Chip Wiggins in the eye before he killed him."

"Maybe. Okay, the other theory, which may make more sense, is that if this package contained a rifle, the rifle is to be used to help Khalil make his escape. For instance, if he had to take out a border patrol guy at the Mexican border, or if he got chased on the sea by a Coast Guard cutter. Something like that. He wants a long-range weapon for any situation that may arise during his escape from the U.S." Jack added, "He needed an accomplice anyway—Rahman—so why not have Rahman deliver a rifle along with whatever else he delivered? Rifles are easy to buy."

"They're not easy to hide."

"They can be broken down. I mean, we are not discounting the possibility that Asad Khalil has a sniper rifle and that he intends to kill someone, who he would have trouble getting within pistol range of. But it really doesn't fit his stated mission or his MO. You said so yourself. Up close and personal."

"Right. Actually, I think there was a patio furniture set in that box. You ever see how they pack that cheap shit in the discount stores? Ten-piece patio furniture set in a box no bigger than a shirt box. Six chairs, a table, umbrella, and two chaise lounges made in Taiwan. Put Slot A into Slot B. Okay, see you in D.C."

"Right. We'll make the travel arrangements here. I'll fax the flight info to the L.A. office. Press conference is at five P.M. at J. Edgar. I know John enjoyed his last visit there. And again, congratulations to both of you on a fine job and on your engagement. You set a date yet?"

Kate replied, "June."

"Good. Short engagements are best. I hope I'm invited."

"Of course you are," Kate assured him.

I hit the Disconnect button.

Kate and I sat silently for a minute, then she said to me, "I'm concerned about that rifle."

"And well you should be."

"I mean...I'm not the nervous type, but he could be gunning for us."

"Possibly. You want to borrow the Little Italy T-shirts again?"

"The what?"

"Bulletproof vests."

She laughed. "You have a way with words."

Anyway, we went back into the common area and had an informal stand-up meeting with the six people there, including Juan, Edie, and Kim. We drank some coffee, and Edie told us, "We're getting Mr. Rahman back from L.A. in about half an hour. We're going to take him out to look for the canyon where he took Khalil to drop that bag."

I nodded. Something about that bothered me, too. I realized that Khalil had to kill time at that early morning hour before the stores opened or whatever, but he really could have had Rahman just take him to a cheap motel. Why did he drive an hour north up the coast highway and ditch the bag?

Anyway, I didn't ask Cindy for the bulletproof vests and neither did Kate. I mean, all we were going to do today was drive around L.A. On the other hand, that may have been reason enough to have bulletproof vests. New York joke.

But Cindy did give us two nice overnight canvas bags with big FBI logos on them as souvenirs of our visit, and perhaps as a way of saying, "We don't want to see you again." But maybe I was projecting.

So, Kate and I put our few toiletries in our bags, and we were ready to go to the Los Angeles office. We discovered that there was no helicopter available, which is sometimes a tip-off that your stock is slipping. However, there was a car available, sans driver, and Cindy gave us the keys. Kate assured her that she knew the way. California people are really nice.

So, we all shook hands and promised to stay in touch, and we were invited back anytime, to which I replied, "We'll be back day after tomorrow." This had the same effect as if I'd broken wind.

Anyway, we left, found the blue government Ford Crown Victoria in the lot, and Kate slipped behind the wheel.

She seemed very excited about driving in California again, and informed me we'd take the scenic coast road to Santa Monica, via Santa Santa, then Las Santa Santos, then some other Santas. I didn't really give a rat's ass, but if she was happy, then I was happy. Right?

Chapter 51

We drove down this coastal highway, through Santa Oxnard, and south toward the City of Angels. The water was on our right, mountains to our left. Blue skies, blue water, blue car, Kate's blue eyes. Perfect.

Kate said it was about an hour's drive to the FBI field office on Wilshire Boulevard, near the UCLA campus in Westwood, and also near Beverly Hills.

I asked her, "Why isn't the office downtown? *Is* there a downtown?"

"There is, but the FBI seems to prefer certain neighborhoods over others."

"Like expensive, white, non–inner city neighborhoods."

"Sometimes. That's why I don't like lower Manhattan. It's incredibly congested."

"It's incredibly alive and interesting. I'm going to take you to Fraunces Tavern. You know, where Washington bid farewell to his officers. He got out on three-quarter disability."

"And went to live in Virginia. He couldn't stand the congestion."

So, we did the California–New York thing for a while as Kate drove. Then she asked me, "Are you happy?"

"Beyond happy."

"Good. You look less panicky."

"I have surrendered to the light." I said, "Tell me about the L.A. office. What did you do there?"

"It was an interesting assignment. It's the third largest field office in the country. About six hundred agents. Los Angeles is the bank robbery capital of the country. We had close to three thousand bank robberies a year, and—"

"Three *thousand?*"

"Yes. Mostly druggies. Small-time cash snatches. There are hundreds of small branch offices in L.A., plus there are all these freeways, so the robbers can make easy escapes. In New York, the robber would be sitting in a taxi for half an hour at a stop light. Anyway, this was more of a nuisance than anything else. Very few people got hurt. I was actually in my bank branch office once when it was getting robbed."

"How much did you get?"

She laughed. "I didn't get anything, but the perp got ten to twenty."

"You collared him?"

"I did."

"Tell me about it."

"No big deal. The guy was ahead of me in line, he passes a note to the teller, and she gets all nervous, so I knew what was coming down. She fills a bag with money, the guy turns to leave, and finds himself staring at my gun. It's a stupid crime. Small money, big Federal rap, and between the FBI and the police, we solved over seventy-five percent of the bank robberies."

We chatted about Kate's two years in L.A., and she said, "Also, it's the only field office in the country with two full-time media representatives. We got lots of high-profile cases that needed media fixes. Lots of celebrity stalker cases. I met a few movie stars, and once I had to live in this star's mansion and travel with him for a few weeks because someone had threatened his life, and it looked like a serious threat. Then there were the Asian organized crime syndicates. The only shoot-out I ever had was with a bunch of Korean smugglers. Those guys are tough cookies. But we have some Korean-Americans in the office who have penetrated the syndicates. Am I boring you?"

"No. This is more interesting than the X-Files. Who was the movie star?"

"Are you jealous?"

"Not at all." Maybe a little.

"It was some old guy. Pushing fifty." She laughed.

Why was I not having fun yet? Anyway, it appeared that Kate Mayfield was not the naive hick I thought she was. She'd been around the dark side of American life, and though she hadn't seen what I'd seen in twenty years on the job in New York, she'd seen more than your average Wendy Wasp from Wichita. In any case, I had the feeling that we had a lot of history to learn from each other. I was glad she didn't ask me about my sexual history because we'd be in Rio de Janeiro before I was finished. Just kidding.

All in all, it was a pleasant drive, she knew her way around, and before long we found ourselves on Wilshire Boulevard. Kate pulled into the big parking lot of a twenty-story, white office building, complete with flowers and palm trees. There's something about palm trees that makes me think nothing serious or deep is going on in the vicinity. I asked her, "Did you ever get involved with any Mideastern terrorism?"

"Not personally. There's not much of that here. I think they have one Mideast specialist." She added, "Now they have two more."

"Yeah. Right. You maybe. I don't know beans about Mideast terrorism."

She pulled the car into an empty space and shut the engine. "They *think* you do. You're on the Anti-Terrorist Task Force, Mideast section."

"Right. I forgot."

So, we got out of the car, walked into the building, and took the elevator up to the sixteenth floor.

The FBI had the whole floor, plus some other floors that they shared with other Justice Department agencies.

To make a long story short, the prodigal daughter had returned, there were hugs and kisses all around, and I noticed that the women seemed as happy to see Kate as were the men. This is a good sign, according to my ex, who explained it all to me once. I wish I'd been listening.

Anyway, we made the rounds of the offices, and I pumped a lot of hands and smiled so much my face hurt. I had the impression I was being shown off by…by my…fiancée. There, I said it. Actually, however, Kate didn't make any announcements along those lines.

Somewhere in this labyrinth of corridors, cubicles, cubby holes, and offices lurked a lover or two or maybe three, and I tried to spot the little shit or shits, but I wasn't getting any signals. I'm good at spotting people who are trying to fuck *me*, but not very good at spotting people who are, or have, fucked one another. To this day, I'm not sure if my wife was screwing her boss, for instance. They do travel a lot on business, but...it doesn't matter anymore, and it didn't matter then.

As my good luck would have it, the fellow I'd spoken to here on the telephone the other day, Mr. Sturgis, Deputy Agent in Charge of something, wanted to meet me, so we were escorted into his office.

Mr. Sturgis came around his desk and extended his hand, which I took as we exchanged greetings. His first name was Doug, and he wanted me to call him that. What else would I call him? Claude?

Anyway, Doug was a handsome gent, about my age, tan and fit, and well dressed. He looked at Kate, and they shook hands. He said, "Good to see you, Kate."

She replied, "It's nice to be back."

Bingo! This was the guy. I could tell by the way they looked at each other for a brief second. I think.

Anyway, there are many forms of hell on earth, but the most exquisitely hellish is going someplace where your spouse or lover knows everyone, and you know no one. Office parties, class reunions, stuff like that. And, of course, you're trying to figure out who had carnal knowledge of your mate, if for no other reason than to see if he or she at least had good taste and wasn't fucking the class clown or the office idiot.

Anyway, Sturgis offered us seats and we sat, though I wanted out of there.

He said to me, "You're exactly as I pictured you on the phone."

"You, too."

We left that alone and got on to business. Sturgis rambled on a bit, and I noticed that he had dandruff and small hands. Men with small hands often have small dicks. It's a fact.

He tried to be pleasant, but I was not. Finally, he sensed my mood and stood. Kate and I stood. He said, "Again, we thank you for your good work and your expertise in this matter. I can't say I'm confident that we'll apprehend this individual, but at least we've got him on the run, and he'll cause no further problems."

"I wouldn't bet on that," I said.

"Well, Mr. Corey, a man on the run can be a desperate man, but

Asad Khalil is not a common criminal. He's a professional. All he wants now is to escape and not draw any further attention to himself."

"He *is* a criminal, common or otherwise, and criminals do criminal things."

"Good point," he said dismissively. "We'll keep that in mind."

I thought I should tell this idiot to go fuck himself, but he already knew what I was thinking.

He said to Kate, "If you ever want to come back, put in for it, and I'll do all I can to see that it's done."

"That's very nice of you, Doug."

Barf.

Kate gave him a card and said, "My cell phone number is on there. Please have someone call me if anything develops. We're just taking some time off to sightsee. John's never been to L.A. We're taking the red-eye out tonight."

"I'll call you the minute anything develops. If you'd like, I'll give you a call later just to keep you up-to-date."

"I would appreciate that."

Barf.

They shook hands and bid adieu.

I forgot to shake hands on my way out, and Kate caught up to me in the corridor. She informed me, "You were rude to him."

"I was not."

"You *were.* You were being so charming to everyone, then you go and get nasty with a supervisor."

"I wasn't nasty. And I don't like supervisors." I added, "He pissed me off on the phone."

She dropped the subject, perhaps because she knew where it was headed. Of course, I may have been totally wrong about any amorous connections between Mr. Douglas Pindick and Kate Mayfield, but what if I weren't and what if I'd been all nice and smiley to Sturgis while he was thinking about the last time he'd screwed Kate Mayfield? Boy, what a fool I'd be. Better to play it safe and be nasty.

Anyway, as we walked down the corridor, it occurred to me that being in love had a lot of drawbacks.

Kate stopped by the commo room and got our flight information. She informed me, "United Flight Two-Zero-Four, leaves LAX at eleven-fifty-nine P.M., arrives Washington Dulles at seven-forty-eight A.M. Two Business Class reservations confirmed. We'll be met at Dulles."

"Then what?"

"It doesn't say."

"Maybe I have time to complain to my Congressman."

"About what?"

"About being off the job for a stupid press conference."

"I don't think a Congressman can relate to that. And on the subject of the press conference, they've faxed us some talking points."

I looked at the two-page fax. It wasn't signed, of course. These "suggestions" never are, and the person who's answering media questions is supposed to sound spontaneous.

In any case, Kate seemed to have run out of old friends, so we got on the elevator and rode down in silence.

Out in the parking lot, on the way to the car, she said to me, "That wasn't so bad, was it?"

"No, it wasn't. In fact, let's go back and do it again."

"Are you having a problem today?"

"Not me."

We got in the car and pulled out onto Wilshire Boulevard. She asked me, "Is there anything special you'd like to see?"

"New York."

"How about one of the movie studios?"

"How about your old apartment? I'd like to see where you lived."

"That's a good idea. Actually, I rented a house. Not far from here."

So, we drove through West Hollywood, which looked like an okay place, except everything was made of concrete and was painted in pastel colors, sort of like square Easter eggs.

Kate drove into a pleasant suburban neighborhood and drove past her former house, which was a small Spanish stucco job. I said, "Very nice."

We continued on to Beverly Hills, where the houses got bigger and bigger, then we cruised Rodeo Drive, and I caught a whiff of Giorgio perfume coming from the store of the same name. That stuff would keep a dead body from stinking.

We parked right on Rodeo Drive, and Kate took me to a nice open-air restaurant for lunch.

We lingered over lunch, as they say, with no appointments, no agenda, and not a worry in the world. Well, maybe a few.

I didn't mind killing time because I was killing it near to where Asad Khalil was last heard from. I kept waiting for Kate's phone to ring, hopefully with some news that would keep me from flying to Washington. I hated Washington, of course, and with good reason. My animus toward California was mostly illogical, and I was feeling ashamed of myself for my prejudices against a place I'd never been to. I said to Kate, "I can see why you'd like it here."

"It's very seductive."

"Right. Does it ever snow?"

"In the mountains. You can go from beach to mountains to desert in a few hours."

"How would you dress for a day like that?"

Chuckle, chuckle.

The California Chardonnay was good, and we slurped up a full bottle of it, disqualifying us from driving for a while. I paid the tab, which wasn't too bad, and we walked around downtown Beverly Hills, which is actually quite nice. I noticed, however, that the only pedestrians were hordes of Japanese tourists snapping pictures and making videotapes.

We walked and window-shopped. I pointed out to Kate that her ketchup-colored blazer and black slacks were getting a bit rumpled, and offered to buy her a new outfit. She said, "Good idea. But it will cost you a minimum of two thousand dollars on Rodeo Drive."

I cleared my throat and replied, "I'll buy you an iron."

She laughed.

I looked at a few dress shirts in the windows and the prices looked like area codes. But sport that I am, I bought a bag of homemade chocolates, which we ate while we walked. As I say, there weren't many pedestrians, so I wasn't surprised to discover that the Japanese tourists were videotaping Kate and me. I said to her, "They think you're a movie star."

"You're so sweet. *You're* the star. You're *my* star."

Normally, I would have blown the chocolates all over the sidewalk, but I was in love, walking on a cloud, love songs running through my head, and all that.

I said, "I've seen enough of L.A. Let's get a room somewhere."

"This isn't L.A. It's Beverly Hills. There's a lot I want to show you."

"There's a lot I want to see, but your clothes are covering it all." Isn't that romantic?

She seemed game, despite the fact that we were now engaged, and we got back in the car, doing a little tour on the way to someplace called Marina del Rey near the airport.

She found a nice motel on the water, and we checked in, carrying our canvas FBI bags to the room.

The view from our window was of the marina where lots of boats sat at anchor, and again I was reminded of my stay on eastern Long Island. If I learned anything there, it was not to get attached to any person, place, or thing. But what we learn and what we do are rarely the same thing.

I noticed that Kate was staring at me, so I smiled and said, "Thanks for a nice day."

She smiled in return, then thought a moment and said, "I would not have introduced you to Doug. He insisted on meeting you."

I nodded. "I understand. It's okay."

So, that was out of the way, with me acting with savoir faire. However, I made a mental note to knee Doug in the balls at the first opportunity. Kate gave me a big kiss.

Shortly thereafter, we were in bed, and, of course, her cell phone rang. It had to be answered, which meant I had to stop doing what I was doing. I rolled off, cursing the inventor of the cell phone.

Kate sat up, caught her breath, and answered the phone, "Mayfield." She listened, her hand over the mouthpiece as she took a few more breaths. She said, "Okay…yes…yes, we did…no, we're…just sitting by the water in Marina del Rey. Right…okay…I'll leave the car in the LAPD lot…right…thanks for calling. Yes. You, too. Bye." She hung up, then cleared her throat and said, "I hate when that happens."

I didn't reply.

She said, "Well, that was Doug. Nothing to report. But he said he'd have someone call us as late as half an hour before we board, if anything came up that might change our plans. Also, he heard from Washington, and short of Khalil being captured around here, we're to fly out tonight. However, if he is apprehended here, then we stay and do a press conference here."

She glanced at me, then continued, "We're the heroes of the moment, and we have to be where most of the cameras will be. Hollywood and Washington work the same way."

Again, she glanced at me and went on, "It's a little phony, and I don't like it, but with a case like this, you have to pay attention to the media. Quite frankly, the FBI could use a shot of good press."

She smiled at me and said, "Well, where were we?" She climbed on top and looked into my eyes. She said in a quiet voice, "Just fuck me. Okay? It's just you and me tonight. There's no world out there. There's no past and no future. Just now and just us."

The phone rang, which startled both of us out of our sleep. Kate picked up her cell phone, but a phone kept ringing, and we realized it was the room phone. I picked it up, and a voice said, "This is your ten-fifteen wake-up call. Have a good evening." I hung up. "Wake-up call."

We got out of bed, washed, got dressed, checked out of the motel, and got in the car. It was nearly 11:00 P.M., meaning 2:00 A.M. in New York, and my body clock was totally screwed up.

Kate got on the road, and we headed toward LAX only a few miles away. I could see jetliners taking off and heading west out over the ocean.

Kate said, "Do you want me to call the L.A. office?"

"No need."

"Okay. You know what I'm afraid of—that while we're airborne, Khalil will be apprehended. I really wanted to be in on that. So do you. Hello? Wake up."

"I'm thinking."

"Enough thinking. Talk to me."

We talked. She pulled into the airport and went to the LAPD

facility where a pleasant desk sergeant was actually expecting us and had a ride waiting to take us to the domestic terminal. I didn't think I could get used to all this nice shit.

Anyway, the young LAPD driver treated us like we were stars and wanted to talk about Asad Khalil. Kate indulged him, and I played NYPD and grunted out of the side of my mouth.

We got out of the car and were wished a good evening and a safe flight.

We went into the terminal and checked in at the United Airlines counter where our two Business Class tickets awaited us. Our Firearm Boarding passes were already filled out, needing only our signatures on the forms. The ticket agent informed us, "We start boarding in twenty minutes, but if you'd like, you can use the Red Carpet Club," and she gave us two passes for the club.

I was waiting for something really awful to happen now, the way New Yorkers do, but what could be worse than everyone smiling at you and wishing you all good things?

Anyway, we went to the Red Carpet Club and were buzzed in. A raven-haired goddess at the desk smiled and took our passes, then directed us to the lounge where the drinks were on the house. Of course, by now, I figured I had died and gone to California heaven.

I didn't feel like alcohol, despite the upcoming dry flight across the continent, so I went to the bar and got a Coke, and Kate took a bottled water from the bartender.

There were snacks at the bar, and I sat. Kate said, "Do you want to sit in the lounge?"

"No. I like bars."

She sat on the stool beside me. I drank my Coke, ate cheese and peanuts, and flipped through a newspaper.

She was looking at me in the bar mirror, and I caught her eye. All women look good to me in bar mirrors, but Kate *really* looked good. I smiled.

She smiled in return. She said, "I don't want an engagement ring. They're a waste of money."

"Can you give me the translation of that?"

"No, I really mean it. Stop being a wise-ass."

"You told me to stay the way I was."

"Not *exactly* the way you were."

"I see." Uh-oh.

Her phone rang, and she took it out of her purse and answered, "Mayfield." She listened, then said, "Okay. Thanks. See you in a few days." She put the phone in her pocket and said, "Duty officer. Nothing new. We are not saved by the bell."

"We should try to save ourselves from this flight."

"If we don't get on this flight, we are through. Heroes or no heroes."

"I know." I sat there and put my brain into overdrive. I said to Kate, "I think the rifle is the key."

"To what?"

"Hold on...something's coming..."

"What?"

I looked at my newspaper on the bar, and something started to seep into my brain. It wasn't anything to do with what was in the paper—it was the sports section. Newspaper. *What?* It was coming, then it slipped away again. *Come on, Corey. Get it.* This was like trying to get a brain erection except the brain kept getting soft.

"Are you okay?"

"I'm thinking."

"The flight is boarding."

"I'm thinking. Help me."

"How can I help you? I don't even know what you're thinking about."

"What is this bastard up to?"

The bartender asked, "Can I get you folks some fresh drinks?"

"Get lost."

"John!"

"Sorry," I said to the bartender, who was backing away.

"John, the flight is boarding."

"You go ahead. I'm staying here."

"Are you crazy?"

"No. Asad Khalil is crazy. I'm fine. Go catch your flight."

"I'm not leaving without you."

"Yes, you are. You're a career officer with a pension. I'm a contract guy, and I've got an NYPD pension. I'm okay on this. You're not. Don't break your father's heart. Go."

"No. Not without you. That's final."

"Now I'm under a lot of pressure."

"To do *what?*"

"Help me on this, Kate. Why does Khalil need a rifle?"

"To kill someone at long range."

"Right. Who?"

"You."

"No. Think newspaper."

"Okay. Newspaper. Someone important who's well guarded."

"Right. I keep thinking back to what Gabe said."

"What did Gabe say?"

"Lots of things. He said Khalil was going for the big one. He said, 'Terrible he rode alone...notches on his blade...'"

"What?"

"He said this was a blood feud..."

"We know that. Khalil has avenged the deaths of his family."

"Has he?"

"Yes. Except for Wiggins, and Callum, who's dying. Wiggins is beyond his reach—but he'll take you in exchange."

"He might want me, but I'm not a substitute for who he really wants, and neither were those people on board Flight One-Seven-Five or the people in the Conquistador Club. There's someone else on his original list...we're forgetting something."

"Do a word association."

"Okay...newspaper, Gabe, rifle, Khalil, bombing raid, Khalil, revenge—"

"Think back to when you first had this thought, John. Back in New York. That's what I do. I put myself back to where I was when I first had a—"

"That's it! I was reading those press clippings about the raid, and I had this thought...and then...I had this weird dream on the plane coming here...it had to do with a movie...an old western movie..."

A voice came over the intercom and announced, "Last call for boarding United Airlines Flight Two-Zero-Four to Washington Dulles Airport. Last call."

"Okay...here it comes. Mrs. Gadhafi. What did she say in that article?"

Kate thought a second, then replied, "She said...she would forever consider the United States her enemy...unless——" Kate looked at me. "Oh, my God...no, it can't be...is that possible?"

We looked at each other, and it was all clear. It was so clear that it was like glass, and we'd been looking right through it for days. I asked her, "Where does he live? He lives here. Right?"

"Bel Air."

I was off the stool now and didn't bother retrieving my canvas bag as I headed toward the club exit. Kate was right beside me. I asked her, "Where's Bel Air?"

"About fifteen, maybe twenty miles north of here. Right near Beverly Hills."

We were now back in the terminal and heading for the taxi stand outside. I said to her, "Get on your cell phone and call the office."

She hesitated, and I didn't blame her. I said, "Better safe than sorry. Right? Use just the right combination of concern and urgency."

We were outside the terminal, and she dialed a number, but it wasn't the FBI office. She said, "Doug? Sorry to bother you at this hour, but... yes, everything's fine..."

I didn't want to get into a taxi and have this conversation in earshot of the driver, so we stood away from the taxi stand.

Kate said, "Yes, we did miss the flight...please listen——"

"Give me the fucking phone."

She gave it to me, and I said, "This is Corey. Just listen. Here's a word for you——*Fatwah.* Like when a mullah puts a contract out on somebody. Okay? Listen. It is my belief, based on something which just popped into my head——and which is a product of five days of dealing with this shit——that Asad Khalil is going to assassinate Ronald Reagan."

Chapter 52

Off we went in the taxi to the LAPD airport station where our car hadn't yet been driven back to Ventura. So far, so good.

We got in the car and headed north toward the home of the Great Satan.

I mean, I don't think he's the Great Satan, and to the extent I have any political leanings, I'm an anarchist and I think all government and all politicians suck.

Also, of course, Ronald Reagan was a very old and very sick man, so who would want to kill him? Well, Asad Khalil for one, who lost a family as a result of Reagan's order to bomb Libya. Also, Mr. and Mrs. Gadhafi, who lost a daughter, not to mention losing a few months of sleep before the ringing in their ears stopped.

Kate was behind the wheel, driving fast on the San Something Freeway. She said, "Would Khalil really...? I mean, Reagan is..."

"Ronald Reagan may not remember the incident, but I assure you, Asad Khalil does."

"Right...I understand...but what if we're wrong?"

"What if we're not?"

She didn't reply.

I said, "Look, it fits, but even if we're wrong, we came to a really clever conclusion."

"How is it clever if it's wrong?"

"Just drive." I said, "Even if we're wrong, there's nothing lost."

"We just lost our fucking jobs."

"We can open a bed-and-breakfast."

"How the hell did I get involved with you?"

NELSON DeMILLE

"Drive."

We were clipping along at a good pace, but of course Douglas Doo-doo had already raised the alarm, and there were people in place at the Reagan house by now, so we weren't exactly the Seventh Cavalry riding to the rescue. I said to her, "How many Secret Service do you think he has there?"

"Not many."

"Why is that?"

"Well, as best I can recall from my limited dealings with the L.A. Secret Service office, the risk to the Reagans is assumed to go down every year, plus there are budget and manpower considerations." She added, "In fact, only a few years ago, some disturbed individual actually got on the grounds of their estate and into the house while they were home."

"Incredible."

"But they're not underprotected. They have a sort of discretionary fund, and they hire private guards to supplement the Secret Service detail. Plus, the local cops keep a close watch on the house. Also, the L.A. FBI office was always available when needed. Like now."

"Plus, we're on the way."

"Right. How much more protection can anyone want?"

"Depends on who's gunning for you."

She reminded me, "*We* did not have to miss that flight. Our phone call would have sufficed."

"I'll cover you."

"Don't do me any more favors, please." She added, "This is all your ego at work."

"I'm just trying to do the right thing. This is the right thing."

"No, it is not. The right thing is to follow orders."

"Think about how much more we can talk about at a press conference if we can collar Asad Khalil tonight."

"You're hopeless. Look, John, you do realize that if Khalil, or an accomplice, is staking out the Reagan house, and he sees that there is unusual activity there, then Khalil is gone forever, and we'll never know if your guess was correct. Basically, for us, it's a lose-lose situation."

"I know. But there's a chance that Khalil is waiting for another night and that the Reagan house is not being watched tonight by him or by an accomplice. Then, I assume, the Secret Service will try to do what the FBI did at Wiggins' house, and also at the Callum house."

"The Secret Service is in the protection business, John. Not the bait-and-trap business, especially if the bait is an ex-President."

"Well, obviously they have to move the Reagans to a safe location, and let the FBI set the trap without the bait. Right?"

"How did the Federal government get along all these years without you?"

I detected a bit of her sarcasm that I didn't expect now that we were engaged. Right? I asked her, "Do you know where the house is?"

"No, but I'll get directions when we get off the freeway."

"Why's it called a freeway?"

"It's free. I don't know. Why do they call the freeways parkways in New York?"

"They're parking lots. I don't know. Do you know what kind of setting this house is in? Rural? Suburban?"

"Bel Air is mostly semi-suburban. One-and two-acre estates, heavily treed. Friends of mine have driven past the Reagan house, and also those stupid star tours go past. I understand that the house is set on a few acres behind walls and can't be seen from the road."

"Does he have a good doorman?"

"We're about to find out."

We exited the freeway, and Kate got on the phone with the FBI office. She listened to and repeated a set of complicated directions, which I wrote down on my Marina del Rey hotel bill. Kate gave the duty officer our car description and the plate number.

The terrain in Bel Air was hilly, the roads looped around a lot, and there was enough vegetation to hide an army of snipers. Within fifteen minutes, we were on this heavily treed street called St. Cloud Road that had huge houses, most of which were barely visible behind fences, walls, and hedgerows.

I expected to see vehicles and people in front of the Reagan estate, but everything was quiet and dark. Maybe they really did know what they were doing.

All of a sudden, two guys popped out from some shrubbery and stopped us.

Next thing we knew, we had two passengers in the back seat, and we were being directed to proceed to a set of gates set into a stone wall.

The iron gates swung open automatically, and Kate drove through them and was directed to a parking area on the left, next to a big security gatehouse. This was really exciting if you're into history and all that. It would have been fun, too, if everyone didn't look so serious.

We got out of the car, and I looked around. You could just see the Reagan house, a ranch-type structure off in the distance, and a few lights were lit. There didn't seem to be many people around, but I was fairly confident that the place was now crawling with anti-sniper people and Secret Service people disguised as trees, rocks, or whatever these people do to blend in.

It was a moonlit night, what was called a hunter's moon in the days before infrared and starlight scopes made every night a hunter's night. In any case, the former President probably did not wander around at this hour, so I had to assume that Khalil also had a day scope and intended to wait until the Reagans took a morning stroll.

A balmy breeze blew the smell of flowering bushes across the lawn, and night birds chirped in the trees. Or, perhaps the trees were Secret Service people wearing perfume and chirping to each other.

We were politely asked to stand near our car, which we were doing, when lo and behold, Douglas Pindick came out of the security gatehouse and walked over to us.

Douglas got right to the point and said to me, "Tell me again why we're here."

I didn't like his tone, so I said, "Tell me why you *weren't* here yesterday. Do I have to do all the thinking for you?"

"You're out of line, mister."

"Ask me if I give a shit."

"That's enough insubordination from you."

"I'm just warming up."

Finally, Kate said, "Okay. Enough. Calm down." She said to Pindick, "Doug, why don't we step over here and talk?"

So, Kate and her friend moved out of earshot, and I stood there, royally pissed off about nothing. It was all male ego and posturing in front of the female of the species. Very primitive. I can rise above that. I should try it sometime.

Anyway, this Secret Service lady wearing regular street clothes came over to me and introduced herself as Lisa, and said she was in some sort of supervisory capacity. She was about forty, attractive, and friendly.

We chatted, and she seemed very curious about how I'd arrived at my conclusion that there was a death threat against the former President.

I told Lisa that I was having a drink in a bar, and it just popped into my head. She didn't like that explanation, so I expanded on it, mentioning that I was drinking Coke, and that I was really on top of the Asad Khalil case, and all that.

Not only was I being questioned, of course, I was being kept company so I wouldn't wander about. I asked her, "How many of these trees are really Secret Service people?"

She thought I was funny and replied, "All of them."

I asked her about the Reagans' neighbors and so forth, and she informed me the neighborhood was loaded with movie stars and other celebrities, the Reagans were nice to work for, and we were actually in the city of Los Angeles, though it looked to me like the movie set for a jungle plantation scene.

So, Lisa and I chitchatted while Kate spoke to her former lover and smoothed things over, telling him, I'm sure, that I was not as big an asshole as I appeared to be. I was really tired, physically and mentally, and this whole scene had an unreal quality to it.

Somewhere in my chatter to Lisa, she revealed to me, "The number of the Reagan house used to be six-six-six, but right after they bought it, they had it changed to six-six-eight."

I said, "You mean for security reasons?"

"No. Six-six-six is the sign of the devil, according to the Book of Revelation. Did you know that?"

"Uh..."

"So, Nancy, I guess, had it changed."

"I see...I should check my Amex card. I think I have triple sixes in there."

She laughed.

I had the feeling that Lisa might be helpful, so I turned on the charm, and we got on really well. In the middle of my being charming, Kate came back alone, and I introduced her to my new friend Lisa.

Kate wasn't that interested in Lisa, and she took my arm and moved me off a bit. She said to me, "We have to fly out first thing in the morning. We can still make the press conference."

"I know. It's three hours earlier in New York."

"John, shut up and listen. Also, the Director wants to speak to you. You could be in some trouble."

"What happened to hero?"

She ignored my question and said, "We're booked at an airport hotel and booked on an early morning flight to D.C. Let's go."

"Do I have time to kick Doug in the balls before I leave?"

"That's really not a good career move, John. Let's go."

"Okay." I walked back to Lisa and told her we had to leave, and she said she'd get the gates open for us. We went over to our car, and Lisa came with us. I really didn't want to leave, so I said to Lisa, "Hey, I'm feeling a little guilty about rousting everyone out of their beds. I really feel I should stay here with you guys until dawn. No problem. I'm happy to do it."

She replied, "Forget it."

Kate said to me, "Get in the car."

Lisa, who was my pal, thought she owed me an explanation for her perfunctory reply and said to me, "Mr. Corey, we have a carefully drawn up plan that's been in place since nineteen eighty-eight. I don't think you're part of that plan."

"This isn't nineteen eighty-eight. Also, this is not solely a protective mission. We're also trying to capture a trained killer."

"We know all of that. That's why we're here. Don't worry about it."

Kate said to me, "John, let's go."

I ignored Kate and said to Lisa, "Maybe we can go in the house where we'll be out of the way."

"Forget it."

"Just a quick drink with Ron and Nancy."

Lisa laughed.

Kate said again, "Let's go, John."

The Secret Service lady said, "They're not home anyway."

"Excuse me?"

"They're not home," Lisa repeated.

"Where are they?"

"I can't tell you."

"Okay. You mean you got them out of here already, and they're under close protective security in a secret location, like Fort Knox or something?"

Lisa looked around, then said, "This is actually not a secret. In fact, it was in the newspapers, but your friend back there, who you yelled at, doesn't want you to know."

"Know what?"

"Well, the Reagans left here yesterday and are spending a few days at Rancho del Cielo."

"Say what?"

"Rancho del Cielo. Ranch in the sky."

"You mean they're dead?"

She laughed. "No. That's his old ranch, north of here in the Santa Inez Mountains. The former Western White House."

"You're saying they're at this ranch. Right?"

"Right. This trip to the old ranch is sort of a...they're calling it the last round-up. He's very sick, you know."

"I know."

"She thought it might be good for him. He loved that ranch."

"Right. I remember that now. And this was in the papers?"

"There was a press release. Not all the news media picked it up. But the press is invited on Friday, which is the Reagans' last day there. Some photo ops and stuff. You know, the old man riding into the sunset. Kind of sad." She added, "I don't know about that press conference now."

"Gotcha. And you have people there now?"

"Of course." She said, as if to herself, "The man's got Alzheimer's. Who would want to kill him?"

"Well, *he* may have Alzheimer's, but the people who want to kill him have long memories."

"I hear you. It's under control."

"How big is this ranch?"

"Pretty big. About seven hundred acres."

"How many Secret Service guarded it when he was there as President?"

"About a hundred."

"And now?"

"I don't know. There were six today. We're trying to get another dozen up there. The Secret Service office here in L.A. isn't big. None of our offices are big. We get the manpower from the local police and from Washington when we need it."

Kate didn't seem so hot to trot now and asked Lisa, "Why don't you use the FBI?"

Lisa replied, "There are FBI on their way from Ventura. But they'll be posted near Santa Barbara. That's the closest town. We can't have non–Secret Service actually *on* the ranch who don't understand our modus operandi. People can get hurt."

Kate pointed out, "But if you don't have enough people, then the person you're protecting can get hurt."

She didn't reply.

I asked, "Why don't you get him out of there and into a safe location?"

Lisa looked around again and said, "Look, this is not considered a highly credible threat. But to answer your questions, there's only one narrow winding road into those mountains, and it's ambush heaven. The lighted presidential helipad is no longer there, but even if it were, the mountains are totally socked in with fog tonight, like they are most nights this time of year."

"Jesus. Whose idea was this?"

"You mean to go to Rancho del Cielo? I don't know. Probably seemed like a good idea at the time." She added, "Understand that this man, despite his past job, is a sick old man who hasn't been in the public eye for ten years. He hasn't done or said anything that would make him a target of assassination. In fact, we log more death threats against the White House pets than we do against this former President. I understand that the situation has possibly changed, and we'll react to that. Meanwhile, we've got three heads of state visiting L.A., two of whom are hated by half the world, and we're stretched pretty thin. We don't want to lose a visiting head of state from a friendly country, even if they are not nice people. I don't want to sound cold and heartless, but let's face it, Ronald Reagan is not that important."

"I think he is to Nancy. The kids. Look, Lisa, there's a psychological downside to having a former President whacked. Bad for morale. You know? Not to mention your job. So, try to get your bosses to take this seriously."

"We take it very seriously. We're doing all we can at the moment."

"Also, this presents an opportunity to capture the number one terrorist in America."

"We understand that. But understand that this theory of yours is not getting much play."

"Okay. Don't say I didn't warn everyone."

"We appreciate the warning."

I opened the car door, and Lisa asked us, "Are you going there?"

I replied, "No. Not in the mountains, in the dark. And we have to be in D.C. tomorrow. Hey, thanks."

"For what it's worth, I'm with you on this."

"See you at the Senate inquest."

I got into the car, and Kate was already behind the wheel. She pulled out of the parking area and onto the driveway. The gates opened automatically, and we moved out onto St. Cloud Road. Kate asked me, "Where to?"

"The Ranch in the Sky."

"Why did I even ask?"

Chapter 53

Off we went to Rancho del Cielo. But first, we had to get out of Santa Bel Air, and it took a while to get to a freeway entrance.

Kate asked me, "I already know the answer, but tell me why we're going to the Reagan ranch."

"Because ninety percent of life is just showing up."

"Try again."

"We have six hours to kill before our dawn flight. Might as well try to kill Asad Khalil while we're killing time."

She took a deep breath, smelling the flowers, I guess. She asked me, "And you think Khalil knows that Reagan is there, and that Khalil intends to kill him there. Right?"

"I think Khalil intended to kill Reagan in Bel Air, got some new information from someone when he got to California, had Aziz Rahman drive him north from Santa Monica to check out the terrain around the Reagan ranch, and to ditch his overnight bag that probably contained the Glocks and his false identity papers in a canyon. It fits, it makes sense, and if I'm wrong, I'm really in the wrong business."

She thought a moment, then said, "Okay, I'm with you on this, for better or for worse. That's what commitment is all about."

"Absolutely."

"And commitment is reciprocal."

"Hey, I'd take a bullet for you."

She looked at me, and we made eye contact in the dark car. She saw I was serious, and neither of us said the obvious, which was we might be about to find out. She did say, "Me, too."

Finally, she found the freeway entrance, and we got on, heading north on the San Diego Freeway. I asked her, "Do you know where the ranch is?"

"Somewhere in the Santa Inez Mountains near Santa Barbara."

"Where's Santa Barbara?"

"North of Ventura, south of Goleta."

"Got it. How long will it take?"

"Maybe two hours to Santa Barbara, depending on the fog. I don't know how to get to the ranch from there, but we'll find out."

"You want me to drive?"

"No."

"I can drive."

"I know how to drive, and I know the roads. Go to sleep."

"I'm having too much fun. Hey, if you want, we can stop at the Ventura office for body armor."

"I'm not anticipating a shoot-out. In fact, when we get to the ranch, we'll be politely asked to leave, just as we were in Bel Air. The Secret Service are very protective of their own turf." She added, "Especially with FBI involvement."

"I can relate to that."

She said, "We are not going to be given a piece of this, but if you want to be close to any possible action, then we're headed the right way."

"That's all I want. Call the Ventura office later and find out where the FBI folks are posted in Santa Barbara."

"Okay."

"Hey, this is a nice road. Really beautiful country here. Reminds me of those old cowboy movies. Gene Autry, Roy Rogers, Tom Mix."

"Never heard of them."

We drove on awhile, and I noticed it was 1:15 A.M. Long day.

We came to an interchange. To the east was Burbank and to the west Route 101, the Ventura Freeway, which Kate took. She said, "We're not taking the coast road this time because it may be fogged in. This is faster."

"You're the local."

So we headed west through what Kate said was the San Fernando Valley. How do these people keep all the Sans and Santas straight? I was really tired, and I yawned again.

"Go to sleep."

"No. I want to keep you company, to hear your voice."

"Okay. Listen to this—why were you so nasty to Doug?"

"Who's Doug? Oh, that guy. Do you mean in L.A. or in Bel Air?"

"Both."

"Well, in Bel Air, I was pissed off at him because he knew the Reagans weren't home, and he didn't tell us where they were."

"John, you didn't know that until *after* you were nasty to him."

"Let's not split hairs over the sequence of events."

She stayed silent awhile, then said, "I didn't *sleep* with him, I just went out with him." She added, "He's married. Happily married with two kids in college."

I saw no need to reply.

She pushed it a bit and said, "A little jealousy is all right, but you really—"

"Hold on. What do you call your stomping off back in New York?"

"That's totally different."

"Explain it to me, so I know."

"You're still involved with Beth. L.A. is history."

"Gotcha. Let's drop it."

"Okay." She took my hand and squeezed it.

So, I've been engaged for about twenty-four hours, and I didn't know how I was going to make it to June.

Anyway, we made nice talk for about half an hour, and I noticed that we were in the mountains or hills or whatever, and it was really dangerous-looking, but Kate seemed very assured behind the wheel.

She asked me, "Do you have a plan or something for when we get to Santa Barbara?"

"Not really. We'll wing it."

"Wing what?"

"I don't know. Something always pops up. Basically, we have to get to the ranch."

"Forget it, as your friend Lisa would say."

"Lisa who? Oh, that Secret Service woman."

"There are a lot of beautiful women in California."

"There's only *one* beautiful woman in California. You."

And so forth.

Kate's cell phone rang, and it could only be Douglas Pindick checking up on us after discovering that we hadn't checked into the designated airport hotel. I said, "Don't answer it."

"I have to answer it." And she did. It was, indeed, Señor Sin Cojones. Kate listened a few seconds, then said, "Well...we're on One-Oh-One, heading north." She listened, then replied, "That's right...we did discover that the Reagans are——" He obviously interrupted, and she listened.

I said, "Give me the phone."

She shook her head and continued to listen.

I was really pissed off because I knew he was chewing her out, and you don't do that to John Corey's fiancée, unless you're tired of living. I didn't want to grab the phone from her, so I sat and stewed. I also wondered why he wasn't asking to speak to me. No *cojones.*

Kate tried to say something a few times, but Doggy Dipshit kept interrupting. Finally, Kate butted into his little tirade and said, "Listen, Doug, I do *not* appreciate you withholding information from me and telling the Secret Service to withhold information. For *your* information, we were sent here by the co-commanders of the ATTF in New York, who have asked that the L.A. field office extend to us all courtesies and all aid and support necessary. The New York ATTF is the designated office on this case, and we are its representatives in L.A. I am, and have been, available by cell phone and beeper, and will remain so. All you need to know is that Mr. Corey and I will be on that flight this morning, unless we hear otherwise from our superiors in New York or Washington. And furthermore, it is not your business where I'm sleeping, or whom I'm sleeping with." She hung up.

I wanted to say, "Bravo," but it was best to say nothing.

We continued on in silence. A few minutes later, her cell phone rang again, and Kate answered it. I knew it couldn't be Douglas Dinky Dork because he wouldn't have the balls to call again. But I figured he'd called Washington and whined, and now Washington was calling us to pull the plug on our mission to the Reagan ranch. I was resigned to this.

Therefore, I was pleasantly surprised and relieved when Kate handed me the phone and said, "It's Paula Donnelly in the ICC. She has a gentleman on your direct line, who wants to speak to you and to you only." She added, unnecessarily, "Asad Khalil."

I put the phone to my ear and said to Paula, "This is Corey. Does this guy sound legit?"

Paula replied, "I'm not real sure what a mass murderer sounds like, but this guy said he spoke to you in Ventura and that you gave him your direct dial."

"That's the guy. Can you patch me through?"

"I can, but he doesn't want me to. He wants your number, so I'll give him Kate's cell phone number, if that's okay. I don't think he's going to give me his."

"Okay. Give him this number. Thanks, Paula." I hung up.

Neither Kate nor I spoke, and we waited for what seemed like a long time. Finally, her cell phone rang, and I answered it, "Corey."

Asad Khalil said, "Good evening, Mr. Corey, or should I say good morning?"

"Say whatever you want."

"Did I wake you?"

"That's okay. I had to get up to answer the phone, anyway."

There was a silence while he tried to figure out my sense of humor. I wasn't sure why he was calling me, but when someone calls you who has nothing to offer, that means they want something. I said to him, "So, what have you been up to since we last spoke?"

"I have been traveling. And yourself?"

"Me, too." I added, "Funny coincidence, I was just talking about you."

"I'm sure you speak of little else these days."

Asshole. "Hey, I've got a life. How about you?"

He didn't seem to understand the idiom and replied, "Of course, I am alive. Very much alive."

"Right. So, what can I do for you?"

"Where are you, Mr. Corey?"

"I'm in New York."

"Yes? I think I am calling a cell phone."

"Indeed you are. The cell phone is in New York, and I'm with it. Where are *you?*"

"In Libya."

"No kidding? You're coming across like you were down the block."

"Perhaps I *am.* Perhaps I am in New York."

"Perhaps you are. Look out the window and try to figure out where you are. You see camels, or yellow cabs?"

"Mr. Corey, I don't like your sense of humor, and it makes no difference where either of us is located, since we are both lying."

"Exactly. So, what is the purpose of this phone call? What do you need?"

"Do you think I only call you for favors? I just wanted to hear your voice."

"Well, that's really sweet of you. Have you been dreaming about me again?" I looked at Kate, who was keeping her eyes on the dark road. There was some ground fog now, and it was spooky out there. She glanced at me and winked.

Finally, Khalil replied, "In fact, I *have* been dreaming about you."

"Good one?"

"I dreamed that we met in a dark place, and that I emerged into the light, alone, covered with your blood."

"Really? What do you think that means?"

"You know what it means."

"Do you ever dream about *women?* You know, and wake up with a serious woody?"

Kate poked me in the ribs.

Khalil didn't answer my question, but changed the subject and said, "Actually, there may be a few things you can do for me."

"I knew it."

"First, please tell Mr. Wiggins that even if it takes another fifteen years, I will kill him."

"Come on, Asad. Isn't it time to forgive and get on—"

"Shut up."

My goodness.

"Second, Mr. Corey, the same goes for you and for Miss Mayfield."

I glanced at Kate, but she didn't seem to be able to hear Khalil's end of the conversation. I said to my disturbed caller, "You know, Asad, you can't solve all your problems with violence."

"Of course I can."

"He who lives by the sword shall die—"

"He who has the fastest sword will go on living. There is a poem in my language that I will try to translate for you. It is about a solitary and fearsome warrior, mounted on—"

"Hey, I know that one! My Arabic is a little rusty, but here's how it goes in English—" I cleared my throat and recited, " 'Terrible he rode alone with his Yemen sword for aid; ornament it carried none but the notches on the blade.' How's that?"

There was a long silence, then Khalil asked me, "Where did you learn that?"

"Bible study? No, let me think. An Arab friend." I added, to piss him off, "I have lots of Arab friends who work with me. They're working hard to find *you*."

Mr. Khalil thought about that and informed me, "They will all go to hell."

"And where are you going, pal?"

"Paradise."

"You're already in California."

"I am in Libya. I have completed my Jihad."

"Well, if you're in Libya, I'm not interested in this conversation, and we're running up the phone bill, so—"

"I will tell *you* when the conversation is ended."

"Then get to the point." Actually, I thought I knew what he wanted. More interestingly, during the silence, I heard a bird chirping somewhere, leading me to believe that Asad Khalil was not indoors, unless he owned a canary. I mean, I'm not good at bird calls, but I know what a bird sounds like, and this bird sounded like one of the nightbirds I'd heard in Bel Air. I was pretty sure this guy was still somewhere in the area, birds or no birds.

Anyway, Asad got down to the real purpose of his call and asked me, "What did you say to me when we last spoke?"

"I think I called you a camel-fucker. But I want to take that back because it's a racial slur, and as a Federal employee and an American, I—"

"About my mother and father."

"Oh, right. Yeah, well, the FBI—actually the CIA and their overseas friends—have some really reliable information that your mom was...how can I put this? Sort of like very good friends with Mr. Gadhafi. You know? Hey, we're men—right? We understand these things. Okay, so it's your mom, and maybe this is hard to hear, but she has needs and wants. Right? And you know...it gets kind of lonely with Pop out of town a lot...hey, you still there?"

"Go on."

"Right." I glanced at Kate, who was giving me a thumbs-up. I continued, "So look, Asad, I'm not being judgmental. Maybe Mom and Moammar didn't get together until *after* your father—oh, that's the other thing—your father. Are you sure you really, really want to hear this?"

"Go on."

"Okay. Well, the CIA again—they're a very smart bunch and they know stuff you wouldn't believe. I have this really good CIA friend, Ted, and Ted told me that your father—Karim was his name. Right? Anyway, you know what happened in Paris. But I guess what you don't know is that it wasn't the Israelis who whacked him—murdered him. In fact, Asad, it was...well, why dig up the past? Shit happens. You know? And I know how you are about holding a grudge, so why do you want to get yourself worked up again? Forget it."

There was a long silence, then he said, "Go on."

"Are you sure? I mean, you know how people are. They say, 'Go ahead. Tell me. I won't be mad at you.' Then, when you tell them bad news, they hate you. I don't want you to hate me."

"I don't hate you."

"But you want to kill me."

"Yes, but I don't hate you. You have done nothing to me."

"Of course I have. I fucked up your plans to whack Wiggins. Can't I get a little credit? Et tu, Brute?"

"Excuse me?"

"Latin. So, it's okay if you hate me, but why should I rub this in? I mean, what's in it for me to tell you about your dad?"

He mulled that over and replied, "If you tell me what you know, you have my word that I will not harm you or Miss Mayfield."

"And Wiggins."

"I will make no such promise. He is the walking dead."

"Well, okay. Better half a pita than none. So, where was I...? Oh, the Paris thing. Yeah, I don't want to speculate or sow seeds of doubt and distrust, but you have to ask yourself the question that all homicide cops ask themselves about a murder. The question is, Cui bono? That's Latin again. Not Italian. You speak Italian—right? Anyway, cui bono? Who gains? Who would gain from your father's death?"

"The Israelis, obviously."

"Come on, Asad. You're smarter than that. How many Libyan Army captains do the Israelis kill on the streets of Paris? The Israelis need a reason to whack someone. What did your father do to them? Tell me if you know."

I heard him clear his throat, then he replied, "He was an anti-Zionist."

"Like, who in Libya isn't? Come on, pal. Here's the sad truth. My CIA friends are positive that it was *not* the Israelis who killed Dad. In fact, the murder, according to Libyan defectors, was ordered by Mr. Moammar Gadhafi himself. Sorry."

He said nothing.

I went on, "That's the way it was. Was it a political difference between Dad and Moammar? Was it that somebody in Tripoli had it in for your father? Or was it because of Mom? Who knows? You tell me."

Silence.

"You still there? Asad?"

Asad Khalil said to me, "You are a filthy liar, and it will give me great pleasure to cut out your tongue before I slice your throat."

"See? I *knew* you'd be pissed. Try to do a favor and—Hello? Asad? Hello?"

I hit the End button and put the phone down on the seat between Kate and me. I took a deep breath.

We rode in silence awhile, then I gave Kate the gist of Khalil's end of the conversation, even telling her that he said he'd kill her. I concluded, "I don't think he likes us."

"Us? He doesn't like *you.* He wants to cut out your tongue and slit your throat."

"Hey, I have *friends* who want to do that."

We both laughed, trying to lighten the moment. She said, "Anyway, I think you handled him well. I mean, why should you be serious and professional?"

"The rule is, when the suspect has something *you* want, treat him with respect and importance. When he's calling for something *he* wants, jerk him around as much as you want."

"I don't remember that in the interrogator's manual."

"I'm rewriting the manual."

"I've noticed." She thought a moment, then said, "If he ever gets back to Libya, he's going to want some answers."

I replied, "If he asks questions like that in Libya, he's dead." I added, "He's either going to go into denial, or he's going to do in Libya what he's done here. This is a dangerous, driven man, a killing machine, whose life is dedicated to settling scores."

"And you just gave him a few more scores to settle."

"I hope so."

We drove on, and I noticed there was no traffic on the road at all. Only an idiot would be out on a night like this at this hour.

Kate said to me, "And you still think Khalil is in California?"

"I *know* he is. He's in the Santa whatever mountains, near or on the Reagan ranch."

She looked out the window at the black, fog-shrouded hills. "I hope he's not."

"I hope he is."

Chapter 54

Route 101 took us into Ventura, at which point the highway left the hills and became a coastal road. The fog was really thick, and we could barely see twenty feet in front of us.

I did see the lights of the Ventura Inn Beach Resort to our left and said to Kate, "That's where I got engaged."

"We'll come back here on our honeymoon."

"I was thinking of Atlantic City."

"Think again." After a few seconds, *she* thought again and said, "Whatever makes you happy."

"I'm happy if *you're* happy."

Anyway, we were doing only about forty miles an hour, and even that seemed too fast for the road conditions. I saw a sign that said SANTA BARBARA—30 MILES.

Kate turned on the radio, and we caught a news replay from an earlier broadcast. The news guy gave an update on the big story and said, "The FBI now confirms that the terrorist, who is responsible for the deaths of everyone aboard Flight One-Seven-Five at Kennedy Airport in New York, as well as four people at the airport, is still at large and has possibly killed as many as eight additional people as he flees from Federal and local law enforcement authorities."

The news guy went on, reading incredibly long and convoluted sentences. Finally, he wrapped it up with, "An FBI spokesperson confirms that there appears to be a connection between several of the people who have been targeted by Asad Khalil. There is a major press conference scheduled in Washington tomorrow afternoon to update this important and tragic story, and we will be there to cover this development."

I switched to an easy listening station.

Kate said, "Did I miss it, or did that guy not mention Wiggins?"

"He didn't. I guess the government is saving that for tomorrow."

"Actually, it's today. And we're not going to make that morning flight out of LAX."

I looked at the dashboard clock and saw it was 2:50 A.M. I yawned.

Kate unpocketed her cell phone and dialed. She said to me, "I'm calling the Ventura office."

Kate got Cindy Lopez on the line, and asked, "Any word from the ranch?" She listened and said, "That's good." What wasn't good was that apparently Douglas Rat-Fink had already called because Kate listened further, then replied, "I don't care what Doug said. All we're asking is that the agents from the Ventura office, who are in Santa Barbara, meet us in Santa Barbara, call the ranch, and tell the Secret Service we are driving to the ranch to meet with their detail." She listened again, then said, "Actually, John just spoke to Asad Khalil—yes, that's what I said. They have established some sort of rapport, and that would be invaluable if a situation developed. That's right. I'll hold." She covered the mouthpiece with her hand and said to me, "Cindy is calling the Secret Service detail at the ranch."

"Nice move, Mayfield."

"Thank you."

I suggested, "Do not let them mess us around with a telephone conference. We will not accept any calls from the Secret Service. Only a meeting in Santa Barbara, with FBI and/or Secret Service, followed by an invitation to the ranch."

She said, "You're going to get a piece of this if it kills you—aren't you?"

I replied, "I deserve a piece of it." I added, "Khalil not only murdered a lot of people who served their country, but he also threatened my life and your life. Not Jack's life, not Sturgis' life. *My* life, and yours. And let me remind you, it wasn't *my* idea to put my name and photo in the papers. Someone owes me, and it's time to pay."

She nodded, but didn't reply. Cindy Lopez came on the line. Kate listened, then said, "Forget it. We are not discussing this over an unsecured cell phone. Just tell me where we can meet them in Santa Barbara." She listened, then said, "Okay. Thanks. Yes, we will." She hung up and said to me, "Cindy says hello and when are you going back to New York?"

Everyone's a comedian. "What *else* did she say?"

Kate replied, "Well, the FBI detail is in a motel called the Sea Scape, north of Santa Barbara, not far from the mountain road that leads to the ranch. There are three people from the Ventura office there—Kim, Scott, and Edie. With them is a Secret Service man, who is acting as liaison. We are to go to the motel and tell them about your phone conversation with Khalil, and no, we cannot go to the ranch, but we can wait at the motel until dawn in case something develops and you're needed to chat with Khalil, by phone if he should call, or if he's apprehended, in person, in cuffs. Khalil in cuffs, not you."

"Got it." I added, "You understand we're going to the ranch."

"Take it up with the Secret Service guy at the motel."

We continued north, not making good time, but after a while, there were signs of civilization, and then a sign said WELCOME TO SANTA BARBARA.

The coast road passed through the south edge of the city, then veered north away from the coast. We continued north up Route 101 for about twenty more miles, and the road swung back to the coast. I said, "Did we miss that motel?"

"I don't think so. Call the motel."

I thought a moment, then said, "I think we should save time and just go on to the ranch."

"I don't think you understood our instructions, John."

"How can we find that road that goes to the ranch?"

"I have no idea."

We moved slowly through the fog, and I could sense, but not see, the ocean to our left. To our right, I could see that the ground rose, but I couldn't see the mountains that Kate said came right down to the sea in some places. In any case, there were very few roads that entered Route 101 at this point. In fact, I hadn't seen one in some time now.

Finally, to our left, was a flat, open piece of land between the road and the ocean, and through the fog was a lighted sign that said SEA SCAPE MOTEL.

Kate pulled into the lot and said, "Rooms one-sixteen and one-seventeen."

"Drive to the reception office first."

"Why?"

"I'll get us two more rooms and see if we can get some snacks and coffee."

She pulled up to the front office under a canopy, and I got out.

Inside, a desk clerk saw me through the glass door and buzzed me in. I guess I looked respectable in my suit, even if it was crumpled and smelled.

I went to the desk clerk and showed him my credentials. I said, "I think we have colleagues registered here. Rooms one-sixteen and one-seventeen."

"Yes, sir. Do you want me to call them?"

"No, I just need to leave them a message."

He gave me a pad and pencil, and I scribbled, "Kim, Scott, Edie— Sorry I couldn't stop by—See you in the morning—J.C." I gave the note to the clerk and said, "Call them about eight. Okay?" I slipped him a ten and said casually, "How can I find the road to the Reagan ranch?"

"Oh, it's not too hard to find. Go north another six tenths of a mile, and you'll see to your left Refugio State Park, and to your right is the beginning of the mountain road. Refugio Road. But you won't see a sign." He added, "I sure wouldn't try it tonight."

"Why not?"

"You can't *see* anything. Near the top, the road makes a lot of switchbacks, and it's real easy to zig when you should zag, and wind up in a ravine. Or worse."

"No problem. It's a government car."

He laughed, then looked at me and said, "So, the old man is home?"

"Just for a few days." I asked him, "Am I going to have trouble finding the ranch?"

"No. It's sort of at the end of the road. Bear left at the Y. There's another ranch to the right. You'll see some iron gates if you bear to the left." He again advised me, "It's a tough drive in the *daylight*. Most people have four-wheel drive." He looked at me to see if he was getting through, wanting, I'm sure, to give it his best shot so he could say to the State Police later, "I warned him." He said, "It will be light in three hours and some of this fog might burn off an hour or so after sunrise."

"Thanks, but I have six pounds of jelly beans I have to deliver before breakfast. See you later."

I left the reception area and got back to the car. I opened Kate's door and said, "Stretch a little. Leave it running."

She got out and stretched. "That feels good. Did you get us rooms?"

"They're full." I slid behind the wheel, closed the door, and lowered the window. I said, "I'm going to the ranch. You staying or coming?"

She started to say something, then let out a sigh of exasperation, came around to the passenger side and got in the car. "Do you know how to drive?"

"Sure." I drove back onto the coast road and turned north. I said, "Six tenths of a mile, Refugio State Park to the left, Refugio Road to the right. Keep an eye out."

She didn't reply. I think she was angry.

We saw the sign for the state park, then at the last second I saw a turnoff and cut the wheel right. Within a few minutes we were headed uphill on a narrow road. A few minutes later, the fog got worse, and we couldn't have seen the hood ornament if there had been one.

We didn't say much, but just crept along the road that was at least straight at this point as it went up a sort of ravine with walls of vegetation on either side.

Kate finally spoke and said, "They're just going to turn us back."

"Maybe. But I have to do this."

"I know."

"For the Gipper."

She laughed. "You're a total idiot. No, you're Don Quixote, tilting at windmills. I hope you're not showing off for me."

"I don't even want you along."

"Sure you do."

So, up we went, and the road got steeper and narrower, and the surface started to get rougher. "How did Ron and Nancy get up here? Helicopter?"

"I'm sure of it. This road is dangerous."

"The road is fine. It's the drop-offs on each side that are dangerous."

I was really tired, and I had trouble keeping awake, despite the fact that I was starting to become anxious about the road. I said to Kate, "I own a Jeep Grand Cherokee. I wish I had it now."

"It wouldn't matter if you had a tank. Do you see those drop-offs on either side of us?"

"No. Too much fog." I asked her, "Do you think we should turn around?"

"You *can't* turn around. You barely have room for the car."

"Right. I'm sure it widens up ahead."

"I'm sure it doesn't." She added, "Kill the headlights. The parking lights should be better."

I switched to the parking lights, which didn't reflect as much off the fog.

We pushed on. I was becoming disoriented by the fog, but at least the road remained fairly straight.

Kate called out, "John! Stop!"

I hit the brakes and the car lurched to a halt. "What?"

She took a deep breath and said, "You're going off a cliff."

"Really? I don't see it."

She opened the door, got out, and walked ahead of the car, trying to find the road, I guess. I could see her, but just barely, looking very spectral in the fog and parking lights. She walked off into the fog and disappeared, then came back and got into the car. She said, "Keep bearing left, then the road makes a hairpin turn to the right."

"Thanks." I continued on, and caught a glimpse of where the right edge of the blacktop ended and a very steep drop began. I said to Kate, "You have good night vision."

The fog actually got a little thinner as we climbed up the mountain, which was good because the road got a lot worse. I put the headlights back on. The road started to make hairpin turns, but I could see about ten feet in front of me now, and if I kept the speed down, I had time to react. Zig, zag, zig, zag. This really sucked. A city boy shouldn't be out here. I asked her, "Are there wild animals around here?"

"Besides you?"

"Yeah, besides me."

"Maybe bears. I don't know. I never came this far north." She added, "I think there may be mountain lions up here."

"Wow. This place *really* sucks. Why would the leader of the Free World want to be here?" I answered my own question and said, "Actually, it's better than Washington."

"Concentrate on the road, please."

"What road?"

"There's a road. Stay on it."

"Doing my best."

After another fifteen minutes, Kate said, "You know, I don't think they're going to send us back. They can't send us back. We'll never make it."

"Exactly."

Her cell phone rang, and she answered it, "Mayfield." She listened and said, "He can't come to the phone, Tom. He has both hands on the wheel and his nose against the windshield." She listened again and said, "That's correct. We're heading for the ranch. Okay. Yes, we'll be careful. See you in the morning. Thanks."

She hung up and said to me, "Tom says you're a lunatic."

"We've already established that. What's up?"

"Well, your special rapport with Mr. Khalil has opened the gates for us. Tom says that the Secret Service will let us into the ranch." She added, "They assumed you would drive up at dawn, but Tom will call and tell them we're on the way."

"See that? Present them with a fait accompli, and they find a way to give you permission for something you've already done. But ask for permission, and they'll find a reason to say no."

"Is this in your new manual?"

"It will be."

After another ten minutes, she asked me, "If we'd been turned back, what would you have done? What's Plan B?"

"Plan B would have been to dismount and find this ranch on foot."

"I figured. And then we'd be shot on sight."

"You can't *see* anyone. Not even with starlight scopes in this fog. I'm good at land navigation. You just walk uphill. Moss grows on the north side of the trees. Water runs downhill. We'd be at the ranch in no time. Over the fence and into the barn or something. No problem."

"What's the point? What do you want to accomplish?"

"I just need to *be* here. Here is where it's at, and here is where I need to be. It's not that complicated."

"Right. Like at Kennedy Airport."

"Exactly."

"Someday, you're going to be in the wrong place at the wrong time."

"Someday I will. But not today."

She didn't reply, but looked out the side window at a rise in the land that towered over the car. She said, "I see what Lisa meant about ambush heaven. No one on this road would stand a chance."

"Hey, even without an ambush, no one on this road would stand a chance."

She rubbed her face with her hands, yawned and said, "Is this what life is going to be like with you?"

"No. There'll be some rough moments."

She laughed, or cried, or something. I thought maybe I should ask her for her gun.

The road straightened out and the incline leveled off. I had the feeling we were near the end of our journey.

A few minutes later, I noticed that up ahead the land flattened and the vegetation thinned. Then I saw a road going off to the right, but I remembered that the motel clerk had said to go to the left. Before I got to the Y in the road, a guy stepped out of the fog and put his hand up. I stopped and put my hand on my Glock, as did Kate.

The guy walked toward us, and I could see he was wearing the standard dark windbreaker with a shield pinned to it, and a baseball cap that said SECRET SERVICE. I lowered my window, and he came up to the driver's side and said, "Please step out of the car, and keep your hands where I can see them."

This was usually my line, and I knew the drill.

Kate and I got out of the car, and the guy said, "I guess I know who you are, but I need to see some identification. Slowly, please." He added, "We are covered."

I showed him my ID, which he examined with a flashlight, then looked at Kate's, then shined the light on the license plate.

Satisfied that we fit the description of a man and a woman in a blue Ford whose names were the same as two Federal agents who were on the way to this location on the most fucked-up road this side of the Himalayas, he said, "Good evening. I'm Fred Potter, Secret Service."

Kate replied in the brief second before I could think of something sarcastic. She said, "Good evening. I assume you're expecting us."

"Well," said Fred, "I was expecting you'd be at the bottom of a ravine by now with your wheels spinning. But you made it."

Again, Kate, in a pre-emptive bid to keep my mouth shut, said, "It wasn't that bad. But I wouldn't want to try it downhill tonight."

"No, you wouldn't. And you don't have to. I have orders to escort you to the ranch."

I said, "You mean there's more of this road?"

"Not much more. You want me to drive?"

"No," I replied. "This is an FBI-only car."

"I'll get in the front."

We all got into the car, Kate in the back, Fred in the front. Fred said, "Bear left."

"*Bear?* Where?"

"I mean...*go* left. Over there."

So, my silliness indulged, I went to the left, noticing two more guys, with rifles, standing near the road. We were indeed covered.

Fred said, "Keep it about thirty. The road is straight, and we need to go another couple hundred yards up Pennsylvania Avenue before we come to a gate."

"Pennsylvania Avenue? I really got lost."

Fred didn't laugh. He said, "This part of Refugio Road is called Pennsylvania Avenue. Renamed in eighty-one."

"That's neat. So, how are Ron and Nancy?"

"We don't discuss that," Fred informed me.

Fred, I sensed, was not a fun guy.

Within a minute or so, we approached a set of stone pillars between which was a closed iron gate no more than chest high. From either side of the pillars ran a low wire fence. Two men, dressed as Fred was dressed, and carrying rifles, stood behind the pillars. Fred said, "Stop here."

I stopped, and Fred got out and closed his door. He walked up to the pillars, spoke to the men, and one of them swung open the little gate. Fred waved me on, and I drove up to the pillars and stopped, mostly because the three guys were in my way.

One of them came around to the passenger side, got in, and closed the door. He said, "Proceed."

So, I proceeded up Pennsylvania Avenue. The guy didn't say anything, which was okay with me. I mean, I thought the FBI were tightly wound, but this bunch made the FBI look like Comedy Central.

On the other hand, this had to be one of the worst and most stressful jobs on the planet. I wouldn't want it.

There were trees on both sides of the road, and the fog lay there like snowdrifts. My passenger said, "Slow down. We're going to turn left."

I slowed down and saw a split-rail fence, then two tall wooden posts across which was a wooden sign that said RANCHO DEL CIELO. He said, "Turn here."

I turned and passed through the entranceway. In front of me was this huge, fog-shrouded field, like an Alpine meadow, ringed with rising slopes, so that the meadow was like the bottom of a bowl. The fog hung in a layer just above the ground, and I could see under it and over it. Spooky. I mean, was this an *X-Files* moment or what?

I could see a white adobe house ahead with a single light on. I was fairly sure this was the Reagan house, and I was anxious to meet them, knowing, of course, that they'd be up and waiting to thank me for my efforts to protect them. My passenger, however, directed me to make a left on an intersecting road. "Slow," he said.

As we drove slowly, I could make out a few other structures here and there through the clumps of trees that dotted the fields.

Within a minute, the guy next to me said, "Stop."

I stopped.

He said, "Please turn off the car and come with me."

I shut off the engine and the lights, and we all got out of the car. Kate and I followed the guy up a rising path through some trees.

It was very cool here, not to mention damp. My three bullet wounds were aching, I could barely think straight, I was tired, hungry, thirsty, cold, and I had to take a leak. Other than that, I was fine.

The last time I'd noticed the dashboard clock, it was five-fifteen, meaning eight-fifteen in New York and Washington where I was supposed to be.

Anyway, we approached this big, tacky-looking plywood-sided building that had Government Structure written all over it. Not literally, but I've seen enough of them to know what they mean by the contract going to the lowest bidder.

So, in we go and the place looked really run-down and smelled musty. My *X-Files* guide showed us into a big sort of rec room with old furniture, a refrigerator, a kitchen counter, TV set, and all that. He said, "Have a seat," and disappeared through a doorway.

I remained standing and looked around for a men's room.

Kate said, "Well, here we are."

"Here we are," I agreed. "Where are we?"

"I think this must be the old Secret Service facility."

I said to her, "Those guys are grim."

"They don't mess around. Don't bug them."

"I wouldn't think of it. Hey, do you remember that episode—"

"If you say X-Files, I swear to God I'll pull my gun."

"I think you're getting a little cranky."

"*Cranky?* I am falling asleep on my feet, I just had a car ride from hell, I'm tired of your—"

A guy entered the room. He was wearing jeans, a gray sweatshirt, a blue windbreaker, and black running shoes. He was about mid-fifties, ruddy-faced and white-haired. And he was actually smiling. He said, "Welcome to Rancho del Cielo. I'm Gene Barlet, head of the protective detail here."

We all shook hands, and he said, "So, what brings you out on a night like this?"

The guy seemed human, so I said, "We've been chasing Asad Khalil since Saturday, and we think he's here."

He could relate to that bloodhound instinct and nodded. "Well, I was briefed about this individual, and the possibility that he has a rifle, and I might agree with you." He said, "Help yourself to coffee."

We informed him that we had to use the facilities, which we did. In the men's room, I splashed cold water on my face, gargled, slapped myself around, and straightened my tie.

Back in the big common room, I made myself a coffee, and Kate joined me at the counter. I noticed she'd reapplied some lip gloss and tried to paint over the dark rings around her eyes.

We sat on some chairs at a round kitchen table, and Gene said to me, "I understand that you've established a rapport with this man Khalil."

I replied, "Well, we're not exactly buddies, but I've established a dialogue with him." To earn my room and board here, I gave him a nice briefing, and he listened attentively. When I finished, I asked Gene, "Hey, where is everyone?"

He didn't reply immediately, but then said, "They're at strategic locations."

"In other words, you've got an understaffing problem here."

He replied, "The ranch house is secure, and so is the road."

Kate said, "But anyone could enter the property on foot."

"Probably."

Kate asked, "Do you have motion detectors? Listening devices?"

He didn't reply to that, but looked around the big room. He informed us, "The President used to come in here Sundays to watch football with the off-duty people."

I didn't reply.

Gene reminisced a bit, then said, "He got shot once. That's one time too many."

"I know the feeling."

"You get shot?"

"Three times. But all on the same day, so it wasn't too bad."

Gene smiled.

Kate pressed her question and asked again, "Do you have electronic devices here?"

Gene stood and said, "Follow me."

We stood and followed him into a room at the end of the structure. It was a room as wide as the building, and the three outside walls were mostly picture windows looking down the slope, I noticed, at the ranch house. There was a nice pond behind the house that I hadn't seen when we approached, plus a big barn and a sort of guest house.

Gene said, "This was the nerve center here, where we monitored all the security devices, tracked Rawhide—that's the President—when he went riding, and where we had communications with the entire world. The nuclear football was also kept here."

I looked around at the forlorn room and noticed a lot of dangling wires, and a terrain map still mounted on the wall, along with lists of code words, radio call signs, and other faded notes. I was reminded of the Cabinet War Rooms that I had seen in London, the place where Churchill had run the war, frozen in time, a little musty and manned by an army of ghosts whose voices you could hear, if you listened closely.

Gene said, "There's no electronic security left. In fact, this whole ranch is now owned by a group called the Young America's Foundation. They bought the ranch from the Reagans and are turning it into a sort of museum and conference center."

Neither Kate nor I replied.

Gene Barlet went on, "Even when this was the Western White House, it was a security nightmare. But the old man loved the place, and when he wanted to come here, we came here with him and roughed it."

I said, "You had about a hundred people then."

"Right. Plus all the electronics and the helicopters, and state-of-the-art everything. But I'll tell you, the damned motion and listening sensors picked up every jackrabbit and chipmunk that came on the property." He laughed, then said, "We had false alarms every night. But we had to respond." He reminisced again and said, "I remember one night—it was a foggy night like this, and next morning the sun came up and burned the fog off, and we see a pup tent pitched in the meadow, not a hundred yards from the ranch house. We go over to investigate and find this young guy asleep. A hiker. We wake him, inform him that he's on private property, and point him toward a hiking trail. We never told him where he was." Gene smiled.

I smiled, too, but the story had a serious point.

Gene said, "So, can we guarantee one hundred percent security? Obviously not. Not then, not now. But now at least we can limit the movements of Rawhide and Rainbow—that's Mrs. Reagan."

Rainbow?

Kate said, "In other words, they'll stay inside the ranch house until you can get them out."

"That's right. Brimstone—that's the ranch house—has thick adobe walls, the drapes and blinds are shut, and there are three agents in the house and two right outside. Tomorrow, we'll figure out a way to get the Reagans out of here. Probably we'll need a Stagecoach—that's an armored limo. Plus a Tracker and a Tracer. That's a lead and trail vehicle. Can't use a Holly—that's a helicopter." He motioned toward the surrounding rims of rising terrain and said, "A good sniper with a scope could take out a helicopter with no problem."

I said to Gene, "Sounds like you guys need a Hail Mary."

He laughed, then replied, "Just need a little night prayer. At sunrise, we're getting some reinforcements, including choppers with counter-sniper teams equipped with body-heat sensors and other detection devices. If this Khalil is in the area, we stand a good chance of finding him."

Kate said, "I hope so. He's killed enough people."

"But understand that our primary mission and concern is protecting Mr. and Mrs. Reagan, and moving them to a safe location."

I replied, "I understand. Most locations will be safe if you kill or apprehend Asad Khalil."

"First things first. We're in a static mode until the sun rises, and this fog burns off. You want to bunk down?"

"No," I replied. "I want to put on a pair of jeans and a cowboy hat, and ride out on a horse and see if I can draw this bastard's fire."

"Are you serious?"

"Actually, no. But I am thinking about taking a look around. I mean, do you have to go check the guard posts or anything?"

"I can do that by radio."

I said, "Nothing like the real thing. The troops appreciate seeing the boss."

"Sure. Why not? You want to take a ride?"

"I thought you'd never ask."

Kate, of course, said, "I'll come with you."

I had no intention of being protective, so I said, "If it's okay with Gene, it's okay with me."

Gene said, "Sure. Are you two wearing vests?"

I said, "Mine's in the laundry. You have some extras?"

"No. And you can't borrow mine."

Well, who needs bulletproof vests anyway?

We left the Secret Service building and went outside where an open Jeep Wrangler sat. I noticed that the Jeep had the new California license plates that said RONALD REAGAN LIBRARY, with a photo of the Gipper on the plate. I need one of those for a souvenir.

Gene climbed behind the wheel, and Kate sat beside him. I got into the back. Gene started it up, turned on the yellow fog lights, and off we went.

Gene said, "I know this ranch like the back of my hand. There are probably a hundred miles of horse trails, and the President used to ride all of them. We still have stone markers at strategic locations, with numbers actually drilled into them so that no one could mess around and change them. The Secret Service detail would ride with the President and radio in to the control center at each marker, and we'd plot the location." He added, "Rawhide wouldn't wear a vest, and it was a nightmare. I held my breath every afternoon until he got back."

Gene sounded like he had some real affection for Rawhide, so to be a good guest, I said, "I was once on an NYPD presidential protection detail back in April eighty-two, when he spoke at the Sixty-ninth Regiment Armory in Manhattan."

"I remember that. I was there."

"How about that. Small world."

We drove off into the boondocks, along horse trails obscured by fog and choked with brush. With the yellow fog lights on, the visibility wasn't too bad. I could hear night birds singing in the trees.

Gene said to me, "There's an M-14 rifle in that gun case. Why don't you pull it out?"

"Great idea."

I saw the gun case now, leaning against the driver's seat. I opened the case and pulled out a heavy M-14 rifle with a scope.

Gene asked me, "You know how to use a starlight scope?"

"Hey, starlight scope is my middle name." I couldn't find the On switch, however, and Gene talked me through it.

In a minute or so, I was sighting down this really nifty night scope that made everything look green. There were a few breaks in the ground fog, and I was amazed at how this high-tech toy illuminated and magnified everything. I adjusted the focus and scanned three hundred sixty degrees while kneeling on the back seat. Everything looked eerie, especially the green-tinted fog and these weird Martian-like rock formations. It occurred to me that if I could see the surrounding terrain, then Asad Khalil could certainly see a Jeep with fog lights moving around.

We rode around awhile, and I mentioned to Mr. Barlet, "I don't see any of your people out here, Gene."

He didn't reply.

Kate said, "This must be beautiful in the sun."

Gene replied, "It's God's country. We're about twenty-five hundred feet above sea level, and from parts of the ranch, you can look down and see the Pacific Ocean on one side and the Santa Inez Valley on the other."

Anyway, we rolled along, and to be honest, I didn't know what the hell I was doing there. If Asad Khalil was out there, and he had the same night scope I did, he could put a bullet between my eyes at two hundred yards. And if he also had a silencer on his rifle—and I was sure he did—I'd fall silently out of the Jeep while Gene and Kate went on chattering. It occurred to me that there was no upside to this ride, and it was a long trip back to the ranch house.

The bush suddenly ended, and the trail opened up onto a stretch of open, rocky ground. I could see we were approaching a precipice, and I was going to mention this, but Gene, who knew the terrain like the back of his hand, stopped. He said, "We're facing west and if it was a clear day, you could see the ocean."

I looked, but all I could see was fog, fog, fog. I couldn't believe I had actually come up that way from the coast.

Gene turned toward the left and drove too close to the edge of eternity for my comfort. Horses at least know not to walk off cliffs, but Jeep Wranglers don't.

After a few long minutes, the Jeep stopped, and a man appeared out of the fog. The guy was wearing black, had black stuff on his face, and was carrying a rifle with a scope. Gene said, "That's Hercules One— that means a counter-sniper response person."

Hercules One and Gene exchanged greetings, and the guy, whose real name was Burt, was introduced to us. Gene said to Burt, "Mr. Corey is trying to draw sniper fire."

Hercules said, "Good. That's what I'm waiting for."

I thought I should clarify this and said, "Actually, I'm not. I'm just getting the lay of the land."

Burt, who looked like Darth Vader all in black, checked me out, but said nothing.

I felt a little out of place in my suit and tie out here in God's country among real men. Guys with code names.

Gene and Burt chatted a minute, then off we went.

I commented, "The posts seem spaced a little far apart, Gene."

Again, Gene didn't reply. His radio crackled, and he put it to his ear. He listened, but I couldn't hear what the caller was saying. Finally, Gene said, "Okay. I'll take them there."

Take who where?

Gene said to us, "Someone wants to meet you."

"Who?"

"Don't know."

"Don't you even have a code name for him?"

"Nope. Got one for you though—Nuts."

Kate laughed.

I said, "I don't want to meet anyone without a code name."

"I don't think you have a lot of choice in the matter, John. It was a high-level call."

"From whom?"

"I don't know."

Kate glanced back at me, and we sort of shrugged.

So, off we went into the fog to meet someone in the middle of nowhere.

We drove another ten minutes or so across this sort of windswept high plateau, covered with rocks and wildflowers. There was no trail, but we didn't need one because the terrain was flat and open. We seemed to be on the highest point in the area.

Through the swirling fog, I could see something white ahead, and I picked up the rifle and focused in on it. The white thing was green-tinted now through this weird lens, and I saw that it was a concrete building about the size of a big house. The building sat at the base of a huge, man-made embankment of earth and stone. Beyond the building, at the top of the embankment, was a tall, strange-looking structure, like an upside-down funnel.

As we came within a hundred yards of these fog-shrouded, intergalactic-looking structures at the top of the world, Kate turned to me and said, "Okay—*this* is an *X-Files* moment."

Gene laughed. He said, "That's a VORTAC installation."

"Well," I said, "that clears that up."

Gene explained, "It's an aircraft navigation beacon. You understand?"

"What kind of aircraft? From what planet?"

"Any planet. It sends out omni signals—you know, three-hundred-and-sixty degree radio signals for civilian and military aircraft to navigate. This will be replaced by the satellite Global Positioning System someday, but for now, it's still in operation." He added, "Russian nuclear submarines off the coast also use it. No charge."

The Jeep continued toward this VORTAC station, so I assumed that's where we were going. I said, "That looks like crap duty."

Gene replied, "These things are unmanned. It's all automatic, and it's monitored by Air Traffic Control in L.A. But people come up here and do routine maintenance. It has its own power source."

"Right. That would be a long extension cord back to the ranch house."

Gene sort of chuckled. He said, "We're on Federal land now."

"I feel better already. Is this where we're meeting someone?"

"Yup."

"Who?"

"Don't know." He went on with his tour and said, "Right here, where we're driving, used to be Playground Three—the presidential helipad. Concrete and lighted. It was stupid to take it out."

He stopped the Jeep about twenty yards from the VORTAC site and said, "Well, see you later."

"Excuse me? You want us to get out?"

"If you don't mind."

I said, "There's no one here, Gene."

"You're here. Somebody else is here waiting for you."

I was getting nowhere with this guy, so I said to Kate, "Okay, let's play the game." I jumped out of the open Jeep, and Kate got out, too.

She said to Gene, "Are you leaving?"

"Yup."

Gene didn't seem to be in a talkative mood any longer, but I asked him, "Can I borrow that rifle?"

"Nope."

I said, "Okay, thanks for the tour, Gene. Hey, if you're ever in New York, I'll take you to Central Park at night."

"See you later."

"Right."

Gene put the Jeep in gear and rode off into the fog.

Kate and I stood there on the open plateau, mist swirling around, not a light to be seen anywhere, except one, coming from the extraterrestrial structure sitting all by itself. I half expected a death ray to come out of that weird tower and turn me into protoplasm or something.

But, my curiosity was piqued, so off I went toward the VORTAC, Kate beside me.

Kate was looking at the structure as we walked and said, "I see some antennas. Don't see any vehicles. Maybe this is the wrong VORTAC." She laughed.

She was pretty calm, I thought, given the situation. I mean, there was a crazed assassin out there somewhere, we were armed only with pistols, we had no body armor, no transportation, and we were meeting someone who I wasn't even sure was from this planet.

When we got to the concrete building, I looked inside through the one small window, which revealed this big electronics room with blinking lights and some other weird high-tech stuff. I tapped on the window. "Hello! We come in peace! Take me to your leader!"

"John, stop being an idiot. This isn't funny."

I thought *she* had made a joke a minute before. But she was right—this wasn't funny.

We walked along the base of the forty-foot-high pile of dirt and rocks, on top of which was the white upside-down funnel, rising about eighty more feet into the air.

We came around to the far side of the mound, and as we turned a corner, I saw a man dressed in dark clothing, sitting on a huge flat rock at the base of the embankment. He was about thirty feet away, and even in the dark and fog, I could see that he was peering through a set of what must have been night vision binoculars.

Kate saw him, too, and we both put our hands on our pistols.

The man heard or sensed our presence because he put down the binoculars and turned toward us. I saw now that he had a long object lying across his knees, and it wasn't a fishing pole.

So, we all stared at each other for a few long seconds, then the man said, "Your journey has ended."

Kate said, in a barely audible voice, "Ted."

Chapter 55

Well, I'll be a horned-toed hoot owl. It was Ted Nash. Why was I not completely surprised?

He didn't bother to stand and greet us, so we walked over to him and stopped at this Martian-red flat rock where Ted sat with his legs hanging over the edge.

He gave a sort of half wave, as if this was an office encounter. He said, "I'm glad you could make it."

Oh, fuck you, Ted. How cool can you get? I refused to play his silly game and said nothing.

Kate, however, said, "You could have told us it was you we were meeting." She added, "You're not cool, Ted."

This seemed to deflate him a bit, and he looked annoyed.

Kate also informed him, "We could have killed you. By mistake."

He'd obviously rehearsed this moment, but Kate wasn't reading from his script.

Anyway, old Ted had charcoal on his face, a black bandanna around his head, and was wearing black pants, a black shirt, black running shoes, and a heavy flak jacket. I said to him, "A little early for Halloween, isn't it?"

He didn't reply, but shifted the rifle on his lap. The rifle was an M-I4 with a starlight scope, just like the one Gene wouldn't let me borrow.

I said to him, "Okay, talk to me, Teddy. What's up?"

He didn't answer me, probably a little put off by the Teddy thing. He reached behind him and produced a thermos bottle. "Coffee?"

I had zero patience for Mr. Cloak and Dagger. I said, "Ted, I know it's important for you to be smooth and polished, but I'm just a New York cop, and I'm really not in the mood for this shit. Say your piece, then get us a fucking vehicle, and get us out of here."

He said, "All right. First, let me congratulate you both on figuring it out."

I replied, "You knew all about this, didn't you?"

He nodded. "I knew some of it, but not all of it."

"Right. And by the way, I won ten bucks from you."

"I'll put it in as a reimbursable expense." He looked at Kate and me and informed us, "You've caused us a lot of trouble."

"Who is us?"

He didn't reply, but picked up his night vision binoculars and scanned a distant treeline. As he scanned, he said, "I'm fairly sure Khalil is out there. Do you agree?"

I said, "I agree. You should stand and wave."

"And you spoke to him."

"I did. I gave him your home address."

He laughed. He surprised me by saying, "You may not believe this, but I like you."

"And I like you, Ted. I truly do. I just don't like it when you don't *share*."

Kate chimed in and said, "If you *knew* what was happening, why didn't you *say* something? People have been killed, Ted."

He put down the binoculars and looked at Kate. He said, "All right, here's the story. There is a man named Boris, an ex-KGB agent, who is working for Libyan Intelligence. Fortunately, he likes money, and he also works for us." Ted considered this a moment, then said, "Actually, he *likes* us. And not *them*. Anyway, some years ago, Boris contacted us and told us about this young man named Asad Khalil, whose family was killed in the nineteen eighty-six raid—"

"Whoa. Whoa," I interrupted. "You knew about Khalil *years* ago?"

"Yes. And we followed his progress carefully. It was apparent that Asad Khalil was an exceptional operative—brave, bright, dedicated, and motivated. And you know, of course, what motivated him."

Neither Kate nor I replied.

Ted said to us, "Should I go on? You may not want to hear all of this."

I assured Ted, "Oh, but we do. And what would you like in return?"

"Nothing. Just your word that you'll keep this to yourselves."

"Try again."

"Okay. If Asad Khalil is captured, the FBI will take charge of him. We don't want that. We need to take charge of him. I need you two to assist me in any way you can, including amnesia during official testimony, to get Khalil turned over to us."

I replied, "This may come as a surprise to you, but my influence with the FBI and the government is somewhat limited."

"You'd be surprised. The FBI and the country are very legalistic. You saw that with the World Trade Center defendants. They went to trial for murder and conspiracy and firearms violations. Not terrorism. There is no law against terrorism in America. So, as in any trial, the government needs credible witnesses."

"Ted, the government has a dozen witnesses against Asad Khalil and a ton of forensic evidence."

"Right. But I think we can work out a deal in the interests of national security whereby Asad Khalil is released and sent back to Libya in a diplomatic arrangement. What I don't want is either of you interfering with that by getting on your moral high horses."

I assured him, "My moral high horse is low to the ground, but really, Ted, Asad Khalil murdered a lot of innocent people."

"So? What are we going to do about that? Put him in prison for life? What good does that do the dead? Wouldn't it be better if we used Khalil for something more important? Something that can put a real dent in international terrorism?"

I knew where this was going, but I didn't want to go there.

Ted, however, wanted Kate and me to understand, so he asked, "Don't you want to know why we want Asad Khalil released and sent back to Libya?"

I put my chin on my hand and said, "Let me think... to kill Moammar Gadhafi because Moammar fucked his mother and killed his father."

"Correct. Doesn't that sound like an excellent plan?"

"Hey, I'm just a cop. But I may be missing something here. Like, Asad Khalil. I think you need him in custody to make this work."

"Correct. Boris has told us how Khalil is getting out of the country, and we're certain we can apprehend him. I don't mean the CIA—we have no arrest powers. But the FBI or the local police, acting on information from the CIA, will apprehend him, then we step into the picture, and work out a deal."

Kate was staring at Ted. I knew what she was going to say, and she said it. "Are you crazy? Are you out of your fucking mind? That man murdered over three hundred people. And if you let him go, he'll murder more people, and not necessarily the people *you* want murdered." She added, "This man is *very* dangerous. He's evil. How can you *possibly* want him free? I can't believe this."

Ted didn't reply for a really long time, like he was wrestling with a moral issue, but a CIA guy wrestling with a moral issue is like professional wrestling; most of it is phony.

Anyway, there was a faint light on the eastern horizon and birds were singing their little hearts out, glad the night was coming to an end. I felt like joining them.

Finally, Ted said, "Believe me when I tell you we didn't know about Flight One-Seven-Five. Boris either didn't know, or couldn't get this information to us."

"Fire Boris," I suggested.

"Actually, he may be dead. We had an arrangement to get him out of Libya, but something may have gone wrong."

I said to Ted, "Remind me never to let you pack my parachute."

Ted ignored this, and went back to his binoculars. He said, "I hope they don't kill him. Khalil, I mean. If he can get out of this area, he'll head to a rendezvous point where he thinks he'll be met by compatriots who will get him out of the country. But that won't happen."

I didn't expect an answer, but I asked, "And where is that rendezvous?"

"I don't know. The information on this case is compartmentalized."

I asked him, "If you're not hunting for Khalil, why do you need that rifle and scope?"

He put down his binoculars and replied, "You never know what you're going to need and when you're going to need it." He asked Kate and me, "Are you wearing vests?"

This question coming from a colleague was perfectly normal, but I was a little shaky about Ted at that moment.

I didn't reply, and interestingly, neither did Kate. I mean, I didn't think old Ted was going to try to whack us, but the man was obviously under some stress, though he wasn't showing it. But if you thought about what he and his company were trying to pull off, you realized that a lot depended on the next few hours. This was, for them, an extremely risky, long-range plan to eliminate Moammar Gadhafi without leaving too many CIA fingerprints, and the plan had started to unravel a few hours before Trans-Continental Flight 175 even touched down. Also, the plan might actually be construed as illegal under current U.S. law. So, old Ted was stressed. But was he going to aim that rifle at Kate and me and blow us away if we added to his problems? You never know what people with guns and problems are going to do, especially if they think their agenda is more important than your life.

It was getting a little lighter by the minute, but the fog was still hanging around, which was fine because it played tricks with night scopes. I asked Ted, "Hey, how was Frankfurt and Paris?"

"Fine. Got a little business done." He added, "If you'd gone to Frankfurt as ordered, you wouldn't be in this position."

I didn't quite know what position I was in, but I know a veiled threat when I hear one. With that in mind, I didn't want to bring up any unpleasant subjects, but I had to ask, "Why did you let Asad Khalil kill those fighter pilots and those other people?"

He looked at me, and I could see he was prepared for the question, though not happy about it. He said, "The plan was simply to take him into custody at JFK, bring him to Federal Plaza, show him incontrovertible evidence, including taped testimony by defectors, of his mother's adultery, and who killed his father, then turn him back on his own people."

Kate said, "We understand that, Ted. What we don't understand is, after he got away, why did you let him complete his mission?"

Ted replied, "We really had no idea what his specific mission was."

"Excuse me," I said. "Bullshit. You knew he'd be here at the Reagan ranch, and you knew what he was going to do before he got here."

"Well, believe what you want. We were under the impression that he was being sent here to kill Ronald Reagan. We didn't know he had the names of the pilots on that flight. That's classified information. In any case, it didn't matter *what* his mission was because he was supposed to be taken into custody at Kennedy Airport. If that had happened, none of the other things would have happened."

"Ted, Mom may have told you that when you play with fire, you get burned."

Ted didn't want to be pushed into any gaping holes in his story, and if I left him alone, he'd dig a few more holes of his own.

Ted said to us, "Well, the plan went astray, but it's not off the tracks yet. It's important that we apprehend Khalil and tell him what we know about his mother and father, then let him loose in Libya. By the way, it was a family friend who killed Karim Khalil in Paris. A man named Habib Nadir, a fellow Army captain and friend of Captain Khalil. Nadir killed his friend on direct orders from Moammar Gadhafi."

This was a tough crowd in a tough neighborhood.

Ted, who was not stupid, said, "Of course, it's possible that Asad Khalil will get out of the country and back to Libya before we have an opportunity to speak to him. So, what I was wondering is if either of you thought to pass on what you knew about Gadhafi's treachery toward the Khalil family."

I replied, "Let me think...we talked about his grudges against America, about him wanting to kill me...what else...?"

"I understand from your colleagues at the Wiggins house that you mentioned these subjects briefly at the end of your conversation with Khalil."

"Right. That was after I called him a camel-fucker."

"No wonder he wants to kill you." Ted laughed, then asked me, "And did you expand on this in your subsequent conversation with Khalil?"

"You seem to know a lot about what goes on in the FBI."

"We're on the same team, John."

"I hope not."

"Oh, don't be holier-than-thou. The halo doesn't look good on you."

I let that one go and said to Kate, "Okay, ready?" I said to Ted, "Gotta go, Ted. See you at the Senate inquest."

"Just a moment. Please answer my question. Did you speak to Asad Khalil about Gadhafi's treachery?"

"What do you think?"

"I'll guess that you did. Partly because you seemed keen about that angle during our meetings in New York and Washington. Partly because you're very bright, and you know how to piss off people." He smiled.

I smiled, too. Ted was really an okay guy. Just a little devious. I said, "Yeah, I got him all worked up about that. You should have heard *that* conversation when I told him his mother was a whore, and his father was a cuckold. Not to mention Gadhafi having Pop whacked. Jeez, he was pissed. He said he was going to cut my tongue out and slit my throat. I mean, *I* didn't fuck his mother or kill his father. Why was he so pissed off at me?"

Ted seemed to be enjoying my levity, and he was also very happy to learn that I had done his job for him.

Ted asked me, "And it was your impression that he believed you?"

"How the hell do I know? He wanted to kill *me*. He didn't say anything about Uncle Moammar."

Ted pondered a moment, then said, "For the Arabs, this is a matter of personal honor. Family honor, which they call *ird*. Almost any family dishonor has to be redeemed in blood."

"That probably works better than Family Court."

Ted looked at me and said, "I think Khalil will kill Gadhafi, and if he learns the truth about Habib Nadir, he will kill him also, and maybe others in Libya. Then our plan, which you seem to find so distasteful, will be vindicated."

Kate, who has a better moral compass than I, said, "There's no justification to goad people into murdering *anyone*. We don't have to act like monsters to fight monsters." She added, "This is *wrong*."

Ted, wisely, did not go into a big justification of his pet plan to clip

Colonel Moammar Gadhafi. He said to Kate, "Believe me, we struggled with this question and put it before the ethics committee."

I almost laughed. "Are you on that committee? And by the way, what are the ethics of you joining up with the ATTF in order to advance your own game plan? And how the hell did I wind up working with you?"

"I requested it. I really admire your talents and your perseverance. In fact, you nearly stopped Khalil from escaping at the airport. I told you, if you want to work for us, there's a job available. You, too, Kate."

I replied, "We'll talk it over with our spiritual advisors. Okay, gotta go, Ted. Great meeting."

"Just one or two more things."

"Okay, shoot." Bad choice of words.

"I wanted to tell you I enjoyed that joke. The one you told at the meeting about the Attorney General. Edward passed that on to me. There's a lot of truth in jokes. The FBI *would* call a big press conference, as they're doing this afternoon in Washington. My company doesn't like press conferences."

"Hey, I'm with you."

"And the CIA *would* make the rabbit a double agent." He smiled. "That was funny. Also, very prescient in this case."

"I hear you. And don't forget what the cops would do, Ted. They'd beat the shit out of that bear until he confessed to being a rabbit. Right?"

"I'm sure they would. But that doesn't make the bear a rabbit."

"It's only important that the bear *says* he's a rabbit. And while we're at it, double agents work only for themselves. Are we through here?"

"Almost. I just want to remind you both that this conversation never took place." He looked at Kate and said, "It's very important that Asad Khalil go back to Libya."

Kate replied, "No, it's not. It's important that he stand trial for murder in the U.S."

Ted said to me, "I think *you* understand."

"Am I going to argue with a guy who's holding a high-powered rifle?"

Ted informed me, "I'm not threatening either of you. Don't be melodramatic."

"Sorry. It's this *X-Files* thing. TV is rotting my brain. It used to be Mission Impossible. Okay, that's *it*. See ya."

"I really wouldn't walk back to the ranch house now. Khalil is still out there, and you two are sitting ducks."

"Ted, if it's a choice between staying here with you, or dodging sniper bullets, guess what?"

"Don't say I didn't warn you."

I didn't reply, but turned and walked away, as did Kate.

Ted called out, "Oh, congratulations on your engagement. Invite me to the wedding."

My back was still to him, and I waved. Funny thing, I wouldn't mind inviting him to the wedding. The man was a monumental prick, but when all was said and done, he was *our* prick—he really wanted to do what was best for the country. Scary. But I understood, which was also scary.

We kept walking down this slope away from the VORTAC station. I didn't know if I was going to get a bullet in the back from Ted, or a bullet in the front from Khalil in the treeline at the foot of the slope.

We kept walking, and I could tell that Kate was tense. I said, "It's okay. Just whistle."

"My mouth is dry."

"Hum."

"I feel sick to my stomach."

Uh-oh. "Like morning—"

"John, stop with the jokes. This is just...sickening. Do you understand what he's done?"

"They play a rough and dangerous game, Kate. Judge not lest you be judged."

"People were *murdered*."

"I don't want to talk about it now. Okay?"

She shook her head.

We found a riding path, which cut through an expanse of red rocks and thick bush. I was hoping to run into a motorized patrol, or a stationary post, but there's never a Secret Service agent around when you need one.

The sky was much lighter now, and a soft breeze from the sea started to move the ground fog away. Not good.

We walked in the direction of where we thought the ranch house and Secret Service building were, but the trails seemed to twist and turn a lot, and I wasn't sure where the hell we were.

Kate said, "I think we're lost. My feet hurt. I'm tired and thirsty."

"Let's sit awhile."

We sat on a flat rock and rested. There was strange vegetation here, like probably sagebrush, tumbleweed, and all that cowboy stuff. The brush was thick, but not very tall and not tall enough to provide good concealment when we walked. It occurred to me that we might be better off staying put. I said to Kate, "Assuming Khalil is out there, then he's probably within two hundred yards of the ranch house. So maybe we don't want to get too close to the house or the Secret Service place."

"Good thought. We'll stay here so Khalil can kill us without disturbing anyone else."

"I'm just trying to outthink this guy."

"Well, think about this—maybe he's not going to kill us. Maybe he's going to put a few rounds through our legs, then walk over to us, and cut your tongue out, then slit your throat."

"I see you've given this some thought. Thank you for sharing that."

"Sorry." She yawned. "Anyway, we have our pistols, and I won't let him take you alive." She laughed, but it was sort of an emotionally and physically exhausted kind of laugh.

"Get some rest."

About ten minutes later, I heard this vaguely familiar sound and recognized it as helicopter blades beating the air.

I stood on the rock on which I'd been sitting and hopped onto a nearby four-foot-high boulder and faced the sound. I said, "The cavalry has arrived. Air cavalry. Wow. Look at that."

"What?" She stood, but I put my hand on her shoulder and pressed her down. "Just sit. I'll tell you what's going on."

"I can see for myself." She stood on the rock on which she'd been sitting, grabbed my arm, and pulled herself up beside me on the boulder. We both looked toward the helicopters. There were six Hueys circling a few hundred yards away, and I guessed they were circling over the ranch house, so we were close, and we knew what direction to walk.

I now noticed a huge twin-engine Chinook helicopter coming over the horizon, and slung under the Chinook was an automobile—a big, black Lincoln.

Kate said, "That must be an armored vehicle."

"Stagecoach," I reminded her. "Six Hollys with Hercules personnel, flying cover over Brimstone while Rawhide and Rainbow get into the Stagecoach. Tracker and Tracer on the ground. Donner, Blitzen, and Rudolph on the way."

She let out a sigh of relief, or maybe exasperation.

We watched for a few minutes as the operation unfolded, and though we couldn't see what was happening on the ground, it was obvious that Rawhide and Rainbow were now headed down Pennsylvania Avenue in an armored car, with escort vehicles and the choppers overhead. Mission accomplished.

Asad Khalil, if he was anywhere around, could see this, too, of course, and if he was still wearing his phony mustache, he was right now twirling the ends and saying, "Curses, foiled again!"

So, all's well that ends well. Right?

Not quite. I had the thought that Asad Khalil, having missed the big one, would now settle for the little one.

But before I did anything about that thought, like get off that boulder and into the bushes to wait for help, Asad Khalil switched targets.

Chapter 56

What happened next, happened like it was in slow motion, between the beats of a heart.

I told Kate to jump off the boulder. I jumped, but she was a half second behind me.

I never heard the crack of the silenced rifle, but I knew the shot came from the nearby treeline because I could hear the bullet, buzzing like a bee over my head—where I had stood on the boulder a half second before.

Kate seemed to stumble on the boulder and let out a soft cry of pain, as though she'd twisted her ankle. In an instant, I realized I'd gotten the sequence of events wrong—she'd cried out in pain *first*, then stumbled. Again, as if it was slow motion, I saw her fall off the side of the boulder near the trail.

I dove on top of her, wrapped my arms around her, and rolled away from the trail, down a shallow slope and into some thin bushes as another bullet slammed into a rock near our heads, sending splinters of stone and steel into my neck.

I rolled again, Kate still in my arms, but we were stopped by a thicket of brush. I held her tightly and said, "Don't move."

We were side by side, my back to the direction of the fire, and I craned my head over my shoulder to try to see what Khalil could see from the treeline, which was less than a hundred yards away.

There were some bushes and low rocks between us and Khalil's line of fire, but depending on where he was in those trees, he might still have a clear shot.

I was aware that my suit, dark though it was, did not blend well with the surroundings, and neither did Kate's bright red jacket, but since there was no more firing, I was fairly certain that Khalil had lost us for the time being. Either that, or he was savoring the moment until he fired again.

I turned and looked into Kate's eyes. They were squinting with pain, and she was starting to writhe in my arms. I said, "Don't move. Kate—talk to me."

She was breathing hard now, and I couldn't tell where or how badly she'd been hit, but I could feel warm blood now, seeping through my shirt and onto my cold skin. *Damn it.* "Kate. Talk to me. Talk to me."

"Oh…I'm…I'm hit…"

"Okay…take it easy. Stay still. Let me check it out…" I moved my right arm between us and felt around under her blouse, my fingers probing for the entry wound, which I couldn't find, though there was blood all over. *Oh, God…*

I tilted my head back and looked at her face. There was no blood coming from her mouth or nose, which was hopeful, and her eyes looked clear.

"Oh…John…damn it…it hurts…"

Finally, I found the entry wound, a hole just below the bottom of her left rib cage. I quickly ran my hand around the back and found the exit wound just above her buttocks. It seemed to be no more than a deep flesh wound, and there was no spurting blood, but I worried about internal bleeding. I said to her, as you're supposed to do with injured people, "Kate, it's okay. You'll be fine."

"Are you sure?"

"Yes."

She took a deep breath and moved her own hand to the wound, exploring the entry and exit wounds.

I got a handkerchief out of my pocket and pushed it in her hand. "Hold it there."

We lay motionless again, side by side, and waited.

That bullet had been meant for me, of course, but fate, ballistics, trajectories, and timing are what make the difference between a wound that you can show off and a wound that the undertaker has to fill with putty. I said again, "You're okay…it's just a little scratch…"

Kate put her mouth to my ear, and I could feel her breath on my skin. She said, "John..."

"Yes?"

"You're a fucking idiot."

"Huh...?"

"But I love you anyway. Now let's get the hell out of here."

"No. Just stay still. He can't see us, and he can't hit what he can't see."

I spoke too soon because all of a sudden dirt and rocks started erupting around us, and branches snapped over our heads. I knew Khalil had a general idea of where we were, and he was firing the rest of the fourteen-round magazine at our suspected location. *Jesus H.* I thought the firing was never going to stop. It's worse when they use a silencer, and all you can hear are the rounds hitting without hearing the crack of the rifle.

On what must have been his last round, I felt a sharp pain on my hip, and my hand flew back to where I'd been hit. I'd caught a grazing wound across my pelvis, and I could sense that it was deep enough to have chipped the pelvic bone. "Damn it!"

"John, are you all right?"

"Yeah."

"We have to get out of here."

"Okay, I'll count to three, and we'll run in a crouch through these bushes, but not for more than three seconds, then we dive and roll. Okay?"

"Okay."

"One, two——"

"Hold on! Why don't we go back to that boulder we were standing on?"

I turned my head and looked back at the boulder. It was less than four feet high, and not even that wide. The rocks around it where we'd been sitting were no more than large stones. But if we could crouch behind the boulder, we'd be safe from direct fire coming from the treeline. I said, "Okay, but it's a little tight behind there."

"Let's go before he fires again. One, two, three——"

We sprang up into a crouch and ran toward the boulder—which was also toward Khalil.

About halfway there, I heard that familiar buzzing over my head, but Khalil had to fire above the boulder we were running for, and he wasn't sitting high enough in the tree to get a steep enough angle to pick us off.

Kate and I hit the rock, spun around, and sat side by side very close together, our knees up to our chests. She pressed the bloody handkerchief to her left side.

We sat there a second and caught our breath. I didn't hear any buzzing overhead, and I wondered if the bastard had the balls to leave the cover of the trees and was coming toward us. I pulled my Glock, took a deep breath, poked my head around the rock, and scanned the open space very quickly before pulling my head back in, just in time to avoid having it blown off by a well-placed shot that chipped the side of the boulder. "This guy knows how to shoot."

"What the *fuck* are you doing? Just *sit* here."

"Where did you learn to swear like that?"

"I have *never* sworn so much in my life till I met you."

"Really?"

"Sit and shut up."

"Okay."

So, we sat there, oozing blood, but not enough to attract sharks, or whatever they had around there. Asad Khalil was strangely quiet, and I was getting nervous about what he was up to. I mean, the asshole could be twenty feet away, slithering through the bush.

I said, "I'm going to fire a few shots in the air to attract attention and to keep Khalil away."

"No. If you attract some Secret Service people here, Khalil will pick them off. I don't want that on my conscience. We're not in any danger. Just sit."

I wasn't sure that we weren't in any danger, but the rest of it made sense. So, John Corey, man of action, just sat. After a minute, I said, "Maybe I can attract Ted's attention, then he and Khalil can have a shooting contest."

"Sit and be quiet. Listen for any sounds in the bush."

"Good idea."

Kate shimmied out of her red jacket, which was nearly the same color as the blood that soaked it. She tied the sleeves around her waist, fashioning a pressure tourniquet over the wounds.

Kate reached into one of her jacket pockets and said, "I'll call the Sea Scape Motel and advise them of our situation so they can alert the Secret Service here and…"

She kept searching through her pockets, then said, "I can't find my cell phone."

Uh-oh.

We both felt around on the ground. Kate reached too far to her left side, and the ground exploded inches from her hand. She pulled her hand in, like she'd touched a hot stove, and stared at the back of it. She said, "My, God, I *felt* that round brush my knuckles…but…I'm not actually hit…I felt the heat or something…"

"The man can *shoot*. Meanwhile, where's the cell phone?"

She rummaged around her jacket and pants pockets again and announced, "It must have fallen out of my pocket when we were rolling. Damn it."

We both stared out at the brush-covered slope in front of us, but there was no way to know where the phone was, and for sure neither of us was going to go searching for it.

So, we sat there, listening for the sound of someone moving toward us. In a way, I hoped the bastard *was* coming for us because I knew he'd have to come around the boulder or over the top of it, and we'd hear him. I wanted at least one shot at him. But if he circled wide, we wouldn't see or hear him, and he had the rifle with the scope. I suddenly felt less safe on this side of the boulder, knowing that Khalil could be circling around into the bushes we'd just come from.

She said, "Sorry about the phone."

"Not your fault. I guess I should get a cell phone."

"Not a bad idea. I'll buy one for you."

A helicopter flew by, about a quarter mile away, but he didn't see us, or sense us—or Khalil—with whatever sensing device he had. Neither did Khalil fire at him, which would have been an easy shot. This led me to believe that Asad Khalil was gone—or, Mr. Khalil was holding his fire because he really wanted *me*. Now there's an upsetting thought.

Anyway, I'd had enough of this bullshit. I got out of my jacket, and before Kate could stop me, I stood quickly and waved the jacket to my side, like a matador messing around with the bull's horns. Unlike a matador, however, I got rid of the jacket real quick as I ducked behind the boulder, just in time to hear the little buzz that ventilated the jacket and snapped some branches off to our side.

Before Kate could yell at me, I said, "I think he's still in the treeline."

"And how do you know that?"

"The shot came from that direction. I could tell by the buzzing and the impact, and there was a half-second delay, like he was still a hundred yards away."

"Are you making this up?"

"Sort of."

Well, back to the game of nerves. Just when I thought Khalil was winning, Mr. Steely Assassin became frustrated and started shooting again. The prick was amusing himself by firing chip shots across the top of the boulder and shards of stone were spraying into the air, and falling down on us.

He fired a full magazine, then reloaded and began firing on either side of the boulder so that the strike of the rounds was just inches from our tucked-up legs. I watched, fascinated, as the pebbly earth exploded into little craters.

I said to Kate, "This guy is an asshole."

She didn't reply, mesmerized by the flying dirt around us.

Khalil then shifted his aim closer to the sides of the boulder, and the guy was good, just skimming the sides inches from our shoulders. The boulder was getting a little smaller. I said to Kate, "Where'd he learn to shoot like that?"

She replied, "If I had a rifle, I'd show *him* how to shoot." She added, "If I'd had a vest, I wouldn't be bleeding."

"Remember that for next time." I took her hand and squeezed it. "How you doing?"

"Okay...it's hurting like hell now."

"Hang in there. He'll get tired of playing with his gun."

She asked me, "How are *you?*"

"I have a new wound to show the girls."

"How'd you like another one?"

I squeezed her hand again and said, stupidly, "His and her wounds."

"That's not even funny. This fucking thing is throbbing."

I untied her jacket, put my hand around her back, and gently felt the exit wound.

She let out a cry of pain.

I said, "It's starting to clot. Try not to move and break the clot. Keep holding the entry wound with the handkerchief."

"I know, I know, I know. God, this hurts."

"I know." Been there, done that. I retied the jacket around her waist.

Khalil had another idea and started firing at the smaller rocks around us, causing ricochets, like a pool player trying to make a shot from behind the eight ball. The rocks were sandstone, and most of them shattered, but now and then Khalil got his ricochet, and one of the rounds actually struck the boulder above my head. I said to Kate, "Tuck your head and face between your legs." I added, "Persistent little bastard, isn't he?"

She tucked her head between her knees and said, "He really doesn't like you, John. You've inspired him to new levels of creativity."

"I do that to people."

All of a sudden, I felt a sharp pain in my right thigh, and I realized he'd gotten me with a ricochet. "Damn!"

"What's the matter?"

I felt where the hot round had hit me and discovered a tear in my pants and a rip in my flesh. I felt around the ground near my thigh and found the still-warm distorted bullet, which I held up. "Seven point six-two millimeter, steel jacketed, military round, probably from an M-14 modified as a sniper rifle with interchangeable night and day scopes, plus silencer and flash suppressor. Just like the one Gene had."

"Who gives a shit?"

"Just making conversation." I added, "Also, just like the one Ted had."

We let that sit awhile, putting some silly thoughts out of our minds. I added, "Of course, the M-14 is a fairly common Army surplus rifle, and I didn't mean to suggest anything by mentioning that Ted happened to have one."

Finally, Kate said, "He could have killed us at the VORTAC station."

To continue the paranoid moment, I pointed out, "He wouldn't whack us so close to where Gene dropped us off to meet him."

She didn't reply.

Of course, I didn't really think it was Ted who was trying to kill us. Ted wouldn't do that. Ted wanted to come to our wedding. Right? But you never know. I put the spent bullet in my pocket.

We sat there for a quiet five minutes, and I figured—whoever he was—he was gone, but I had no intention of finding out for sure.

I could hear helicopters circling in the distance and hoped that eventually one of them would see us.

Despite the pain in my pelvis, I was starting to drift off. I was totally exhausted and also dehydrated, so I thought I was getting delirious when I heard a phone ring. I opened my eyes. "What the hell...?"

Kate and I stared down the slope to where the phone was ringing. I still couldn't see it, but I had a general idea of where it was. I could tell now that it wasn't more than twenty feet away. It was actually directly in front of us, and if I ran out to it, I'd be blocked from Khalil's line of sight by the boulder. Maybe.

Before I could decide if I wanted to risk it, the phone stopped ringing. I said, "If we can get that phone, we can call for help."

Kate replied, "If we go out to get that phone, we won't need any help. We'll be dead."

"Right."

We kept staring at the spot where the phone had been ringing. It began ringing again.

It's a fact that a sniper can't continually stare through a telescopic lens without getting eye and arm fatigue, so he has to take short breaks. Maybe Khalil was on a break. In fact, maybe Khalil was calling us. He can't shoot and talk at the same time. Right?

Before I thought about it too much longer, I sprang forward in a crouch, covered the twenty feet in two seconds, located the ringing phone, scooped it up, spun around, and charged back toward the boulder, keeping the boulder between me and Khalil's line of fire. Before I reached the boulder, I pitched the ringing phone to Kate, who caught it.

I hit the boulder, spun, and fell into a sitting position, wondering why I was still alive. I took a few deep breaths.

Kate had the phone to her ear and was listening. She said into the phone, "Fuck you." She listened again and said, "Don't tell me how a woman should talk. Fuck you."

I had the feeling that wasn't Jack Koenig.

She put the phone to her chest and said to me, "Are you very brave, or very stupid? How could you do that without consulting me? Would you rather be dead than married? Is that it?"

"Excuse me, who's on the phone?"

Kate handed the phone to me. "Khalil wants to say good-bye."

We looked at each other, embarrassed, I think, by our brief suspicions that it was Ted Nash, our compatriot, who had been trying to kill us. I had to get out of this business.

I said to her, "You ought to get your number changed." I put the phone to my ear and said, "Corey."

Asad Khalil said to me, "You're a very lucky man."

"God is looking after me."

"He must be. I don't often miss."

"We all have off days, Asad. Go home and practice."

"I admire your courage and your good humor in the face of death."

"Thanks so much. Hey, why don't you get out of that tree, put down your rifle, and come across that field with your hands up? I'll see that you get treated fairly by the authorities."

He laughed and said, "I am not in the tree. I am on my way home. I just wanted to say good-bye and to remind you that I will be back."

"Looking forward to a rematch."

"Fuck you."

"A religious man shouldn't talk like that."

"Fuck you."

"No, fuck *you*, Asad, and fuck the camel you rode up on."

"I will kill you and kill that whore you are with, if it takes me all of my life."

I'd obviously gotten him angry again, so to direct his anger toward more constructive goals, I reminded him, "Don't forget to first get things straightened out with Uncle Moammar. Also, it was a guy named Habib Nadir who killed your father in Paris, on orders of Moammar. You know this guy?"

There was no reply, and neither did I expect one. The phone went dead, and I handed it back to Kate. "He and Ted would like each other."

So, we sat there, not quite trusting Khalil to be hotfooting it through the mountains, especially after that last conversation. Maybe I needed to take a Dale Carnegie course.

Kate called the Sea Scape Motel and got Kim Rhee on the phone. She explained our situation and present position sitting behind a boulder, and Kim said she'd get some Secret Service people to us. Kate added, "Tell them to be careful. I'm not sure if Khalil is actually gone."

She signed off and said to me, "You think he's gone?"

"I think so. The Lion knows when to run and when to attack."

"Right."

To lighten the moment, I asked her, "What's the difference between an Arab terrorist and a woman with PMS?"

"Tell me."

"You can reason with an Arab terrorist."

"That's not funny."

"Okay, then what's the definition of a moderate Arab?"

"What?"

"A guy who ran out of ammunition."

"*That's* funny."

The sun got warm and burned off the remaining fog. We held hands, waiting for a chopper to get to us, or a vehicle or foot patrol to come by.

Kate said, as if to herself, "This was a taste of things to come."

Indeed it was. And Asad Khalil, or the next guy like him, would be back with some new grudge, and we'd send a cruise missile into somebody's house in retaliation, and round and round it goes. I said to Kate, "You want to get out of this business?"

"No. Do you?"

"Only if you do."

"I like it," she said.

"Whatever you like, I like."

"I like California."

"I like New York."

"How about Minnesota?"

"Is that a city or a state?"

Eventually, a helicopter spotted us, and after determining that we weren't crazed Arab terrorists, it landed, and we were carried on board.

Chapter 57

They flew us to a helipad at the Santa Barbara County Hospital, and we were given adjoining rooms with not much of a view.

A lot of our new friends from the Ventura FBI office stopped by to say hello: Cindy, Chuck, Kim, Tom, Scott, Edie, Roger, and Juan. Everyone told us how well we looked. I figure if I keep getting shot once a year, I'll look terrific by the time I'm fifty.

My phone rang constantly, as you can imagine—Jack Koenig, Captain Stein, my ex-partner, Dom Fanelli, my ex-wife, Robin, family, friends, past and present colleagues, and on and on. Everyone seemed very concerned about my condition, of course, and always asked first how I was doing, and waited patiently while I said I was fine, before they got into the important stuff about what happened.

Hospital patients get away with a lot of crap, as I recalled from my last stay. Therefore, depending on who was calling, I had five standard lines: I'm on painkillers and can't concentrate; It's time for my sponge bath; This line is not secure; I have a thermometer up my ass; My mental health worker doesn't want me to dwell on the incident.

Obviously, you have to use the appropriate line for different people. Telling Jack Koenig, for instance, that I had a thermometer up my ass... well, point made.

On Day Two, Beth Penrose called. I didn't think any of the standard lines were appropriate for that conversation, so we had The Talk. End of story. She wished me well, and she meant it. I wished her well, and I meant it.

A few people from the Los Angeles office also stopped in to see how Kate was doing, and a few of them even looked in on me, including Douglas Pindick, who turned off my intravenous. Just kidding.

Another visitor was Gene Barlet of the Secret Service. He invited Kate and me back to the Reagan ranch for a tour when we were up to it. He said, "I'll show you the place where you were shot. You can have chips from the rock. Take a few photographs."

I assured him I had no interest in memorializing the event, but Kate accepted his invitation.

Anyway, I learned from various and sundry people that Asad Khalil seemed to have disappeared, which did not surprise me. There were two possibilities regarding Mr. Khalil's disappearance—one, he'd made it back to Tripoli, two, the CIA had him and were turning him around, trying to convince the Lion that certain Libyans tasted better than Americans.

On that subject, I still didn't know if Ted and company actually let Asad Khalil go through with his mission of killing those pilots in order to make Khalil feel more fulfilled, and therefore happy and more receptive to the idea of whacking Uncle Moammar and friends. Also, I really wondered where the Libyans had *gotten* the names of those pilots. I mean, that's *really* an *X-Files* conspiracy theory, and it was so far out, I didn't waste too much time on it, or lose too much sleep over it. Still, it bothered me.

As for Ted, I wondered why he hadn't come to pay us a visit, but I figured he had his hands full juggling lies, juking and jiving through the halls of Langley.

On Day Three of our hospital stay, four gentlemen arrived from Washington, representatives they said of the Federal Bureau of Investigation, though one of the guys smelled like CIA. Kate and I were well enough to meet them in a private visitors room. They took statements from us, of course, because that's what they do. They love to take statements, but rarely make any statements of their own.

They did say, however, that Asad Khalil was still not in FBI custody, which may have been technically true. I mentioned to these gentlemen that Mr. Khalil swore to kill Kate and me if it took the rest of his life.

They told Kate and me not to be overly concerned, don't talk to strangers, and be home before the streetlights came on, or something like that. We made a tentative appointment to meet in Washington when we felt up to it. Happily, no one mentioned a press conference.

Related to that subject, we were reminded that we'd signed various oaths, pledges, and so forth, limiting our rights to make public statements, and swearing to safeguard all information that related to national security. In other words, don't speak to the press or we'll chew your asses up so bad, those bullet wounds on your butts will look like little zits by comparison.

This wasn't exactly a threat because the government does not threaten its citizens, but it was a fair warning.

I reminded my colleagues that Kate and I were heroes, but no one seemed to know anything about that. I then announced to the four gentlemen that it was time for my enema, and they left.

On the subject of the press again, the attempted assassination of Ronald Reagan was reported in all the news media, but it was played down, and the official statement from Washington was, "The former President's life was never in danger." No mention was made of Asad Khalil—the lone individual involved was unknown—and no one seemed to get the connection between the dead pilots and the assassination attempt. That would change, of course, but as Alan Parker would say, "A third today, a third tomorrow, and the rest when reporters start squeezing our nuts."

On Day Four of our stay in Santa Barbara County Hospital, Mr. Edward Harris, CIA colleague of Ted Nash, showed up all by himself, and we received him in the private visitors room. He, too, reminded us not to speak to the press, and suggested that we'd had a bad shock, loss of blood, and all that, and therefore our memories weren't to be trusted.

Kate and I had previously discussed this, and we assured Mr. Harris that we couldn't even remember what we had for lunch. I also said to him, "I don't even know why I'm in the hospital. The last thing I remember is driving to Kennedy Airport to pick up a defector."

Edward looked a bit skeptical, and he said, "Don't overdo it."

I informed Mr. Harris, "I won that twenty-dollar bet from you. And ten from Ted."

He gave me a sort of funny look, which seemed inappropriate. I think it had to do with the mention of Ted's name.

I should say at this point that nearly everyone who visited us acted as though they had some information that we didn't have, but that we could have it if we asked. So I asked Edward, "Where's Ted?"

Edward let a few seconds pass, then informed us, "Ted Nash is dead."

I wasn't totally surprised, but I was shocked nonetheless.

Kate was stunned, too, and asked, "How?"

Edward replied, "He was discovered, after you were found, on the Reagan ranch. He had a bullet wound through his forehead and died instantly." Edward added, "We recovered the bullet and ballistics prove conclusively that it was from the same rifle that Asad Khalil used to fire at you."

Kate and I sat there, not knowing what to say.

I did feel badly, but if Ted were in the room, I'd tell him the obvious—When you play with fire, you get burned. When you play with lions, you get eaten.

Kate and I passed on our condolences, me wondering why Ted's death had not yet made the news.

Edward suggested, as Ted had done, that we might be happy working for the Central Intelligence Agency.

I didn't think this kind of happiness was at all possible, but when you're dealing with slick, you have to be slicker. I said to Edward, "We can talk. Ted would have liked that."

Again, I detected a bit of skepticism from Edward, but he said, "The pay is better. You can pick any foreign duty station and be guaranteed a five-year posting. Together. Paris, London, Rome, your pick."

This sounded a little like a bribe, which is a whole lot better than a threat. Point was, we knew too much, and they knew we knew too much. I told Edward, "I've always wanted to live in Lithuania. Kate and I will talk it over."

Edward wasn't used to being jerked around, and he got real cool and left.

Kate reminded me, "You shouldn't smart-ass those people."

"I don't often get the opportunity."

She sat silently a moment, then said, "Poor Ted."

I wondered if he was really dead, so I couldn't work through the grieving process with any enthusiasm. I said to Kate, "Invite him to the wedding anyway. You never know."

By Day Five in the hospital, I figured if I stayed there any longer, I'd never recover physically or mentally, so I checked myself out, which made my government health insurance rep happy. In fact, I could have left after Day Two, considering my fairly minor hip and thigh wounds, but the Feds had wanted me to stay, and so did Kate, whose injury needed more time to heal.

I said to Kate, "Ventura Inn Beach Resort. See you there." And off I went, with a bottle of antibiotics and some really neat painkillers.

Someone had actually sent my clothes out for cleaning, and the suit had come back cleaned and pressed, with the two bullet holes sort of mended or crocheted or something. The bloodstains were still faintly visible on the suit, and on my blue shirt and tie, though my shorts and socks were nice and fresh. A hospital van took me to Ventura.

I felt like a vagrant, checking into the Ventura Inn, without luggage, not to mention stained clothes, and spaced out on painkillers. But Mr. American Express soon put things right, and I got California duds, swam in the ocean, watched *X-Files* reruns, and spoke to Kate twice a day on the phone.

Kate joined me a few days later, and we took some medical leave at the Ventura Inn, and I worked on my tan and learned to eat avocados.

Anyway, Kate had this teensy bikini, and she soon realized that scars don't tan. Guys think scars are badges of honor. Women don't. But I kissed the boo-boo every night, and she became less self-conscious. In fact, she started showing off the entry and exit wounds to some cabana boys, who thought a bullet wound was really cool.

Kate, between cabana boys and war stories, tried to teach me how to surf, but I think you have to have capped teeth and bleached hair to do it right.

So, we got to know each other better in the two-week trial honeymoon that we spent in Ventura, and by silent mutual consent, we realized we were made for one another. For instance, Kate assured me she loved watching football games on TV, liked sleeping with the window open in the winter, preferred Irish pubs instead of fancy restaurants, hated expensive clothes and jewelry, and would never change her hairstyle. I believed every word, of course. I promised to stay the same. That was easy.

All good things must come to an end, and in mid-May, we returned to New York and our jobs at 26 Federal Plaza.

There was a little office party for us, as is the custom, and dopey speeches were made, toasts were proposed to our dedication to the job, to our full recovery, and, of course, to our engagement and long, happy lives together. Everyone loves a love story. It was the longest night of my life.

To make the evening more fun, Jack pulled me aside and said, "I used your thirty bucks, and also Ted's and Edward's bets toward the caterer's bill. I knew you wouldn't mind."

Right. And Ted would have wanted it that way.

All things considered, I'd rather be back in Homicide North, but that wasn't going to happen. Captain Stein and Jack Koenig assured me that I had a brilliant future ahead of me on the Anti-Terrorist Task Force, despite a stack of formal complaints lodged against me by various individuals and organizations.

Upon our return to duty, Kate announced that she was rethinking things—not about the marriage, but about the engagement ring. She put me to work on something called The Invitation List. Also, I found Minnesota on a map. It's a whole state. I faxed copies of the map to my buds on the NYPD to show them.

A few days after our return, we made the mandatory trip to the J. Edgar Hoover Building and spent three days with these nice people from Counterterrorism, who listened to our whole story, then repeated it to us, in a slightly different form. We all got our stories straight, and Kate and I signed affidavits, statements, transcripts, and stuff until everyone was happy.

I suppose we caved in a little, but we got a major promise from them that might put things right some day.

On the fourth day of our Washington trip, we were taken to CIA

Headquarters at Langley, Virginia, where we met Edward Harris and others. It wasn't a long visit, and we were in the company of four FBI people, who did most of the talking for us. I wish these people could just learn to get along.

The only interesting thing about this Langley visit was our meeting with an extraordinary man. He was an ex-KGB guy, and his name was Boris, the same Boris that Ted had mentioned to us at the VORTAC.

There seemed to be no purpose to the meeting, other than the fact that Boris wanted to meet us. But in the hour that we spoke, I got the feeling that this guy had seen and done more in his life than all of us in that room combined.

Boris was a big dude, chain-smoked Marlboros, and was overly nice to my fiancée.

He talked a little about his KGB days, then gave us a few tidbits about his second career with Libyan Intelligence. He mentioned that he'd given Khalil a few tips about his trip to America. Boris was curious about how we got on to Asad Khalil and all that.

I'm not in the habit of spilling a lot of information to foreign intelligence officers, but the guy played one-for-one with us, and if Kate or I answered his question, he'd answer ours. I could have spoken to this guy for days, but we had other people in the room, and once in a while, they'd tell one of us not to reply, or to change the subject. What happened to freedom of speech?

Anyway, we all had a little nip of vodka together, and inhaled secondhand smoke.

One of the CIA boys announced that it was time to leave, and we all stood. I said to Boris, "We should meet again."

He shrugged and made a motion toward his CIA friends.

We shook hands, and Boris said to Kate and me, "That man is a perfect killing machine, and what he doesn't kill today, he will kill tomorrow."

"He's just a man," I replied.

"Sometimes I wonder." He added, "In any case, I congratulate you both on your survival. Don't waste any of your days."

I was sure this was just another Russian expression and had nothing to do with the subject of Asad Khalil. Right?

Kate and I returned to New York, and neither of us mentioned Boris again. But I'd really like to have a whole bottle of vodka with that guy some day. Maybe I'd issue him a subpoena. Maybe that wasn't a good idea.

The weeks passed, and still no word from Asad Khalil, and no happy news out of Libya concerning Mr. Gadhafi's sudden demise.

Kate never got her cell phone number changed, and I still have the same direct dial at 26 Federal Plaza, and we're waiting for a call from Mr. Khalil.

Better than that, Stein and Koenig—as part of our deal with the folks in Washington—instructed us to form a special team consisting of me, Kate, Gabe, George Foster, and a few other people whose sole mission is to find and apprehend Mr. Asad Khalil. I also put in a request to the NYPD to transfer my old partner, Dom Fanelli, to the ATTF. He's fighting it, but I'm an important person now, and I'll have Dom in my clutches soon. I mean, he's responsible for me being in the ATTF, and one good screwing deserves another. It'll be like old times.

There will be no CIA people on this new team, which improves our odds a lot.

This special team is probably the only thing that kept me on this screwed-up job. I mean, I take that guy's threat seriously, and it's a very simple matter of kill or be killed. None of us on the team intend to take Asad Khalil alive, and Asad Khalil himself does not intend to be taken alive, so it works out well for everyone.

I called Robin, my ex, and informed her of my upcoming marriage.

She wished me well and advised me, "Now you can change your stupid answering machine message."

"Good idea."

She also said, "If you catch this guy Khalil someday, throw the case my way."

I'd been through this little game with her regarding the perps who plugged me on West 102nd Street, so I said, "Okay, but I want ten percent of the fee."

"You got it. And I'll blow the case, and he goes up for life."

"It's a deal."

So, that out of the way, I thought I should call former lady friends and tell them I had a full-time roommate, soon to be my wife. But I didn't want to make those phone calls, so I sent e-mails, cards, and faxes instead. I actually got a few replies, mostly condolences for the bride-to-be. I didn't share any of these with Kate.

The Big Day approached, and I wasn't nervous. I'd already been married, and I'd faced death many times. I don't mean there are any actual similarities between getting married and getting shot at, but... there may be.

Kate was pretty cool about the whole thing, though she'd never walked The Last Mile down the aisle before. She seemed really on top of the situation and knew what had to be done, and when it had to be done, and who had to do what, and all that. I think this knowledge is not learned, but it has something to do with the X chromosome.

All kidding aside, I was happy, contented, and more in love than I'd ever been. Kate Mayfield was a remarkable woman, and I knew we'd live happily ever after. I think what I liked about her was that she accepted me for what I was, which is actually not too difficult, considering how nearly perfect I am.

Also, we'd shared an experience that was as profound and defining as any two people can share, and we'd done it well. Kate Mayfield was brave, loyal, and resourceful, and unlike myself, she was not yet cynical or world-weary. She was, in fact, a patriot, and I can't say the same for myself. I may have been once, but too much has happened to me and to the country in my lifetime. Yet, I do the job.

My biggest regret regarding this whole mess—aside from my obvious regret over the loss of life—is that I don't think we learned anything from any of this.

Like me, the country has always been lucky and has always managed to dodge the fatal bullet. But luck, as I've learned on the streets and at the gambling tables, and in love, runs out. And if it's not too late, you face facts and reality, and come up with a plan of survival that does not include any luck.

Speaking of which, it rained on our wedding day, which I discovered is supposed to mean good luck. I think it means you get wet.

Nearly all of my friends and family had made the trek to this small town in Minnesota, and most of them behaved better than they had at my first wedding. Of course, there were a few incidents with my unmarried NYPD buds being outrageous with these blond-haired, blue-eyed Wendys—including the incident of Dom Fanelli with the maid of honor, which I will not get into—but that's to be expected.

Kate's family were real WASPs, the minister was a Methodist, and a stand-up comedian. He made me promise to love, honor, and never again mention the *X-Files.*

It was a double ring ceremony; one ring for Kate's finger, one ring through my nose. I guess that's enough marriage jokes. In fact, I've been told that's enough.

Midwestern WASPs come in two varieties—wet and dry. These people were into the sauce, so we got along really well. Pop was an okay guy, Mom was a looker, and so was Sis. My mother and father told them lots of stories about me, which they thought were funny as opposed to abnormal. This was going to be all right.

In any case, Kate and I did a week in Atlantic City, then a week along the California coast. We'd arranged to meet Gene Barlet at Rancho del Cielo, and the drive up into the mountains was a lot nicer than the last time. So was the ranch, looking better in the sunlight, sans sniper.

We went back to the boulder, which looked much smaller than I remembered it. Gene took photos, including an R-rated shot of Kate's wound, and we gathered up some stone chips at Gene's insistence.

Gene pointed to the distant treeline and said, "We found fifty-two shell casings on the ground. I've never heard of so many shots being fired by a sniper at two people. That guy really wanted what he couldn't have."

I think he was telling us that the game wasn't over.

The treeline was making me a little nervous, so we moved on. Gene showed us where Ted Nash had been found on a riding trail, less than a hundred meters from the VORTAC, with a single round through his forehead. I have no idea where Ted was going, or what he was doing there in the first place, and we'd never know.

Considering we were on our honeymoon, I suggested we'd seen

enough, and we went back to the ranch house, had a Coke, ate a few jelly beans, and moved on to points north.

We had left Kate's cell phone back in New York, not wanting any calls from friends or assassins on our honeymoon. But just as a precaution, we both brought our guns along.

You never know.

Acknowledgments

Because of the nature of the material in this novel, some of the individuals whom I would like to thank here have asked to remain anonymous. I respect that request, and acknowledge their contributions with gratitude.

I would like to thank, first of all, Thomas Block, childhood friend, US Airways captain, *Flying* magazine contributing editor, co-author of *Mayday*, and author of six other novels, for his invaluable assistance with "airplane stuff" and other stuff. As always, Tom came through when I was up in the air without a propeller.

Thanks, too, to Sharon Block, former Braniff International and US Airways flight attendant, for reading the manuscript and taking my side in editorial arguments with her husband.

Special thanks to Joint Terrorist Task Force members, who wish to remain anonymous.

Very special thanks to a good friend, and former Port Authority cop, and Guns and Hoses guy, Frank Madonna, for sharing his expertise, and for his patience. Thanks, too, to Guns and Hoses men and women, and all the men and women I met at John F. Kennedy International Airport, who took the time to show me around and answer dumb questions.

The section of this novel concerning the American air raid on Libya could not have been written without the help of Norm Gandia, captain, United States Navy (ret.). Norm is a Vietnam combat veteran, a former Blue Angel, a good friend, and a light drinker. Thanks, too, to Al Krish, lieutenant colonel, United States Air Force (ret.), for putting me in the cockpit of the F-III.

I'm grateful to the staff of the Young America's Foundation for taking the time to give me a private tour of the Ronald Reagan ranch. Special thanks to Ron Robinson, president of the foundation, Marc Short, executive director of the Ronald Reagan ranch, and Kristen Short, director of development of the ranch. Many thanks, too, to John Barletta, former head of the Presidential Secret Service detail. John's professionalism and dedication are too rare in to-day's world.

Once again, thanks to librarians Laura Flanagan and Martin Bowe, who did wonderful research and helped me with pesky details that only a librarian could have the patience and knowledge to ferret out.

Thanks, too, to Daniel Starer, Research for Writers. This is the fifth novel that Dan has helped me with and by now he knows what I need before I know I need it.

This novel could truly not have been written without the help, dedication, and infinite patience of my assistant, Dianne Francis. It's not easy working with a writer on a daily basis, but Dianne makes my life easier. Thanks.

Once again, as with *Plum Island*, a million thanks to Lieutenant John Kennedy, Nassau County Police Department. As a cop and a lawyer, John keeps my fictitious cops honest, and keeps the author honest as well. With JK on the case, the truth triumphs.

The Long Island Cradle of Aviation Museum is a world-class facility, honoring the men and women who have made, and continue to make, America first in flight, and best in aeronautical and space science. I'd like to thank Edward J. Smits (planning coordinator), Gary Monti (deputy planning coordinator), Joshua Stoff (curator), and Gerald S. Kessler (president, Friends for Long Island's Heritage), for taking the time to show me the facility, and sharing with me their vision.

Facts, procedures, advice, and details that were given to me may at times have been misconstrued, forgotten, or ignored, and therefore all the errors of omission and commission are mine alone.

John Corey is back and in the middle of a
new Cold War with a clock-ticking plot that
has Manhattan in its crosshairs.

Please turn this page for a preview of

Radiant Angel

I f I wanted to see assholes all day, I would have become a proctologist. Instead, I watch assholes for my country.

I was parked in a black Chevy Blazer down the street from the Russian Federation Mission to the United Nations on East 67th Street in Manhattan, waiting for an asshole named Vasily Petrov to appear. Petrov is a colonel in the Russian Foreign Intelligence Service—the SVR in Russian—which is the equivalent to our CIA, and the successors to the Soviet KGB. Vasily—whom we have affectionately code-named Vaseline—has diplomatic status as Deputy Representative to the UN for Human Rights Issues—which is a joke—but his real job is SVR Legal Resident in New York—the equivalent of a CIA Station Chief. I have had Colonel Petrov under the eye on previous occasions, and though I've never met him he's reported to be a very dangerous man, and thus an asshole.

I'm John Corey, by the way, former NYPD homicide detective, now working for the federal government as a contract agent. My NYPD career was cut short by three bullets that left me seventy-five percent disabled (twenty-five percent per bullet?) for retirement pay purposes. In fact, there's nothing wrong with me physically, though the mental health exam for this job was a bit of a challenge.

Anyway, sitting next to me behind the wheel was a young lady I'd worked with before, Tess Faraday. Tess was maybe early thirties, auburn hair, tall, trim, and attractive. Also in the SUV, looking over my shoulder, was my wife, Kate Mayfield, who was actually in Washington, but I could feel her presence. If you know what I mean.

Tess asked me, "Do I have time to go to the john, John?" She thought that was funny.

"You have a bladder problem?"

"I shouldn't have had that coffee."

"You had two." Guys on surveillance pee in the container and throw it out the window. I said, "Okay, but be quick."

She exited the vehicle and double-timed it to a Starbucks around the corner on Third Avenue.

Meanwhile, Vasily Petrov could come out of the Mission at any time, get into his chauffeur-driven Mercedes S550, and off he goes.

But I've got three other mobile units, plus four agents on legs, so Vasily is covered while I, the team leader, am sitting here while Ms. Faraday is sitting on the potty.

And what do we think Colonel Petrov is up to? We have no idea. But he's up to *something*. That's why he's here. And that's why I'm here.

In fact, Petrov arrived only about four months ago, and it's the recent arrivals who are sometimes sent on the field with a new game play, and these guys need more watching than the SVR agents who've been stationed here awhile and who are engaged in routine espionage. Watch the new guys.

The Russian UN Mission occupies a thirteen-story brick building with a wrought-iron fence in front of it, conveniently located across the street from the 19th Precinct, whose surveillance cameras keep an eye on the Russians 24/7. The Russians don't mind being watched by the NYPD because they're also protected from pissed-off demonstrators and people who'd like to plant a bomb outside their front door. FYI, I live five blocks north of here on East 72nd, so I don't have far to walk when I get off duty at four. I could almost taste the Buds in my fridge.

So I sat there, waiting for Vasily Petrov and Tess Faraday. It was a nice day in early September: one of those beautiful, dry and sunny days you get after the dog days of August. It was a Sunday, a little after 10 A.M., so the streets and sidewalks of New York were relatively quiet. I volunteered for Sunday duty because Mrs. Corey (my wife, not my mother) was in Washington for a weekend conference, returning tonight or tomorrow morning, and I'd rather be working than trying to find something to do on a Sunday.

Also, today was September 11, a day I usually go to at least one memorial service with Kate, but it seemed more appropriate for me to mark this day by doing what I do.

There is a heightened alert every September 11 since 2001, but this year we hadn't picked up any specific intel that Abdul was up to something. And it being a Sunday, there weren't enough residents or office workers in the city for Abdul to murder. September 11, however, is September 11, and there were a lot of people working today to make sure that this was just another quiet Sunday.

Kate was in D.C. because she's an FBI special agent with the Anti-Terrorist Task Force, headquartered downtown at 26 Federal Plaza. Special Agent Mayfield was recently promoted to Supervisory Special Agent, and her new duties take her to Washington a lot. She sometimes goes with her boss, Special-Agent-in-Charge Tom Walsh, who used to be my ATTF boss, too, but I don't work for him or the ATTF any longer. And that's a good thing for both of us. We were not compatible. Walsh, however, likes Kate, and I think the feeling is mutual. I wasn't sure Walsh was with Kate on this trip because I never ask, and she rarely volunteers the information.

On a less annoying subject, I now work for the Diplomatic Surveillance Group—the DSG. The group is also headquartered at 26 Fed, but with this new job I don't need to be at headquarters much, if at all.

My years in the Mideast section of the Anti-Terrorist Task Force were interesting, but stressful. And according to Kate, I was the cause of much of that stress. Wives see things husbands don't see. Bottom line, I had some issues and run-ins with the Muslim community (and my FBI bosses) that led directly or indirectly to my being asked by my superiors if I'd like to find other employment. Walsh suggested the Diplomatic Surveillance Group, which would keep me (a) out of his sight, (b) out of his office, and (c) out of trouble.

Sounded good. Kate thought so, too. In fact, she got the promotion after I left.

Coincidence?

My Nextel phone is also a two-way radio, and it blinged. Tess's voice said, "John, do you want a doughnut or something?"

"Did you wash your hands?"

Tess laughed. She thinks I'm funny. "What do you want?"

"A chocolate chip cookie."

"Coffee?"

"No." I signed off.

Tess's career goal is to become an FBI special agent, and to do that she has to qualify for appointment under one of five entry programs— accounting, computer science, language, law, or what's called "diversified experience." Tess is an attorney and thus qualifies. Most failed lawyers become judges or politicians, but Tess tells me she wants to do something meaningful, whatever that means. Meanwhile, she's working with the Diplomatic Surveillance Group.

Most of the DSG men and women are second-career people, twenty-year retirees from various law enforcement agencies, so we have mostly experienced agents and ex-cops mixed with inexperienced young attorneys like Tess Faraday who see the Diplomatic Surveillance Group as a stepping-stone where they can get some street creds that look good on their FBI app.

Tess got back in the SUV and handed me an oversized cookie. "My treat."

She had another cup of coffee. Some people never learn.

She was wearing khaki cargo pants, a blue polo shirt, and running shoes, which are necessary if the target goes off on foot. Her pants and shirt were loose enough to hide a gun, but Tess is not authorized to carry a gun.

In fact, Diplomatic Surveillance Group agents are theoretically not authorized to carry guns. But we're not as stupid as the people who make the rules, so almost all the ex-cops carry. In situations like this, where I bend the rules, my personal motto is *Better to face twelve jurors than to be carried by six pallbearers*. Therefore, I had my 9mm Glock in a pancake holster in the small of my back, beneath my loose-fitting polo shirt.

So we waited for Vasily to show.

Colonel Petrov lives in a big high-rise in the upscale Riverdale section of the Bronx. This building, which we call the 'plex—short for complex—is owned and wholly occupied by the Russians who work at the UN, and it is a nest of spies. The building itself, located on a high hill, sprouts more antennas than a garbage can full of cockroaches.

The National Security Agency, of course, has a facility nearby where they listen to the Russians who are listening to us, and we all have fun trying to block each other's signals. And round it goes. The only thing that has changed since the days of the Cold War is the encryption codes.

On a less technological level, the game is still played on the ground as it has been forever. Follow that spy. The Diplomatic Surveillance Group also has a confidential off-site facility—what we call the Bat Cave—near the Russian apartment complex, and the DSG team who was watching the 'plex this morning reported that Vasily Petrov had left, and they followed him here to the Mission, where my team picked up the surveillance.

The Russians don't usually work in the office on Sundays, so my guess was that Vasily was in transit to someplace else—or that he was going back to the 'plex—and that he'd be coming out shortly and getting into his chauffeur-driven Benz.

Colonel Petrov, according to the intel, is married, but his wife and children have remained in Moscow. This in itself is suspicious because the families of the Russian UN delegation love to live in New York on the government ruble. Or maybe there's an innocent explanation for the husband-wife separation. Like they hate each other.

Tess informed me, "I have two tickets to the Mets doubleheader today." She further informed me, "I'd like to catch at least the last game."

"You can listen to them lose both games on the radio."

"I'll pretend you didn't say that." She reminded me, "We're supposed to be relieved at four."

"You can relieve yourself anytime you want."

She didn't reply.

A word about Tess Faraday. Did I say she was tall, slim, and attractive? She also swims and plays paddleball, whatever that is. She's fairly sharp, and intermittently enthusiastic, and I guess she's idealistic, which is why she left her Wall Street law firm to apply for the FBI, where the money is not as good.

But money is probably not an issue with Ms. Faraday. She mentioned to me that she was born and raised in Lattingtown, an upscale community on the North Shore of Long Island, also known as the Gold Coast. And by her accent and mannerisms I can deduce that she came from some money and good social standing. People like that who want to serve their country usually go to the State Department or into intelligence work, not the FBI. But I give her credit for what she's doing and I wish her luck.

Also, needless to say, Tess Faraday and John Corey have little in common, though we get along during these days and hours of forced intimacy.

One thing we do have in common is that we're both married. His name is Grant, and he's some kind of international finance guy, and he travels a lot for his work. I've never met Grant, and I probably never will, but he likes to text and call his wife a lot. I deduce, by Tess's end of the conversation, that Grant is the jealous type, and Tess seems a bit impatient with him. At least when I'm in earshot of the conversation.

Tess inquired, "If Petrov goes mobile, do we stay with him, or do we hand him over to another team?"

"Depends."

"On what?"

"No, I mean you should wear Depends."

One of us thought that was funny.

But to answer Tess's question, if Vasily went mobile, most probably my team would stay with him. He wasn't supposed to travel farther than a twenty-five-mile radius from Columbus Circle without State Department permission, and according to my briefing he hadn't applied for a weekend travel permit. The Russians rarely did, and when they did they would apply on a Friday afternoon so that no one at State had time to approve or disapprove their travel plans. And off they'd go, in their cars or by train or bus to someplace outside their allowed radius. Usually the women were just going shopping at some discount mall in Jersey, and the men were screwing around in Atlantic City. But sometimes the SVR or the Military Intelligence guys—the GRU—were meeting people, or looking at things that they shouldn't be looking at, like nuclear reactors.

That's why we follow them. But we almost never bust them. The FBI, of which the DSG is a part, is famous—or infamous—for watching people and collecting evidence for years. Cops act on evidence. The FBI waits until the suspect dies of old age.

I said to Tess, "Let me know now if you can't stay past four. I'll call for a replacement."

She replied, "I'm yours."

"Wonderful."

"But if we get off at four, I have an extra ticket."

I considered my reply, then said, perhaps unwisely, "I take it Mr. Faraday is out of town."

"He is."

"Why have we not heard from Grant this morning?"

"I told him I was on a very discreet—and quiet—surveillance."

"You're learning."

"I don't need to learn what I already know."

"Right." Escape and evasion. Perhaps Grant had reason to be jealous. *You think?*

Regarding the nature of our surveillance of Colonel Vasily Petrov, this was actually a nondiscreet surveillance—what we call a bumper lock, meaning we were going to be up Vaseline's ass all day. They always spotted a bumper-lock surveillance, and sometimes they acknowledged the DSG agents with a hard stare—or if they were pricks they gave you the Italian salute.

Vasily was particularly unfriendly, probably because he was an intel officer, a big wheel in the Motherland, and he found it galling to be on the receiving end of a surveillance. Well, fuck him. Everybody's got a job to do.

Vasily sometimes plays games with the surveillance team, and he's actually given us the slip twice in the last four months or so, which has earned him the name Vaseline. He's never given me the slip, but some other DSG teams lost him. And there's hell to pay when you lose the SVR resident. And that wasn't going to happen on my watch. I don't lose anyone. Well, I lost my wife once in Bloomingdale's. I can't figure out the logic of a woman's shopping habits. They don't think like us.

"So do you want to go to the game?"

Mrs. Faraday had already started the game. But okay, two colleagues going to a baseball game after work is innocent enough. Even when they're married and their spouses are out of town. No problem. Right? I said, "I'll take a rain check."

"Okay." She asked me, "You going to eat that cookie?"

I broke it in half and gave her the bigger half.

Surveillances can be boring, which is why some people try to make it not boring. Two guys together talk about women, and two women together probably talk about guys. A guy and a woman together either have nothing to talk about, or the long hours lead to whatever.

In the last six months, Tess Faraday has been assigned to me about a dozen times, which, with 150 DSG agents in New York, defies the odds. As the team leader, I could reassign her to another vehicle or to leg surveillance. But I haven't. Why? Because I think she's asking to work with me, and being a very sensitive man, I don't want to hurt her feelings. And why does she want to work with me? Because she wants to learn from a master. Or something else is going on.

And, by the way, I haven't mentioned Tess Faraday to Kate. Kate is not the jealous type and there's nothing to be jealous about. Also, like Kate, I keep my work problems and associations to myself. Kate doesn't talk about Tom Walsh, and I don't talk about Tess Faraday. Marital ignorance is bliss. Dumb is happy.

Meanwhile, Vasily has been inside the Mission for over an hour, but his Mercedes is still outside, so he's going someplace. Probably back to the Bronx. He sometimes runs in Central Park, which is a pain in the ass. Everyone on the team wears running shoes, of course, and I think we're all in good shape, but Vasily is in excellent shape. Older FBI agents have told me that the Soviet KGB guys were mostly lard-asses who smoked and drank too much. But these guys from the new Russia were into granola and health clubs. Their boss, bare-chested Putin, sort of set the new standard.

Vasily, being who he is, also has a girlfriend in town, a Russian lady named Svetlana who sings at a few of the Russian nightclubs in Brighton Beach. I caught a glimpse of her once, and she looks like she has good lungs.

I did a radio check with my team and everyone was awake.

A soft breeze fluttered the white, blue, and red Russian flag in front of the Mission. I remember when the Soviet hammer and sickle flew there. I kind of miss the Cold War. But I think it's back.

My team today consists of four leg agents and four vehicles—my Chevy Blazer, a Ford Explorer, and two Dodge minivans. We usually have one agent in each vehicle, but today we had two. Why? Because the Russians are particularly tricky, and sometimes they travel in groups and scatter like cockroaches, so recently we've been beefing up the surveillance teams. So today I had two DSG agents in the other three vehicles, all former NYPD. I had the only trainee, an FBI wannabe who probably thinks the DSG job sucks. Sometimes I think the same thing.

In the parlance of the FBI, the DSG is called a quiet end, which really means a dead end.

But I'm okay with this. No office, no adult supervision, and no bullshit. Just follow that asshole. And do not lose that asshole.

A quiet end. But in this business, there is no such thing.